A GOD'S PLEA

BOOK FOUR
OF
LEGEND OF TAL

J.D.L. ROSELL

RUNE & REQUIEM PRESS

Illustration © 2021 by René Aigner
Book design by J.D.L. Rosell
Maps © 2021 by Kaitlyn Clark and J.D.L. Rosell

ISBN 978-1-952868-27-6 (hardcover with dust jacket)
ISBN 979-8-846269-70-5 (hardcover case laminate)
ISBN 978-1-952868-26-9 (trade paperback)
ISBN 978-1-952868-12-2 (ebook)

Published by Rune & Requiem Press
runeandrequiempress.com

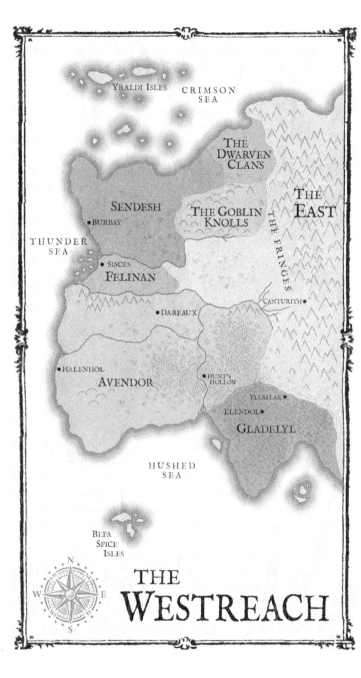

YRALDI ISLES

CRIMSON SEA

THE DWARVEN CLANS

THE EAST

SENDESH

• BURBAY

THE GOBLIN KNOLLS

THE FRINGES

THUNDER SEA

• SISCES

FELINAN

• DAREAUX

CANTURITH •

• HALENHOL

AVENDOR

• HUNT'S HOLLOW

YLLSALAR •

ELENDOL •

GLADELYL

HUSHED SEA

BEFA SPICE ISLES

N
W · E
S

THE WESTREACH

THE FAR DEPTHS
OF DU'ORLAM

THE RAINWOODS

HYALKASI RANGE

LEDFOLD

DREYGON

KAKSIS
WASTES

RAJEYA

VALE OF MISTS

VATHDA

NARUAH

HAUDDEN

ASPAR

VALANKESH
PASS

KAVAUGH

ISOCIL

REACH ROAD

VALANDUALI RANGE

IKVALDAR

FALANOR
GRASSLANDS

KYZAN

BAYAT

AGN OMMUL

KHWAM WOODS

VRORESH

GHAMIR NODH

HILLS OF
DAVAED

LEISLE
SEA

THE
EMPIRE OF THE
RISING SUN

N
NW · NE
W · E
SW · SE
S

A NOTE ON APPENDICES

You can find appendices on the characters, creatures, and world of Legend of Tal located near the end of the book.

PROLOGUE

THE LIES OF HEATHENS

To Your Supremacy, Father Hush—

You may already know what I divulge in this letter, for I understand you are a well-informed man. Yet I find it my obligation to ensure you understand the events transpiring here in Halenhol, and how they might distress the entirety of our order — nay, our very religion.

His Majesty, King Aldric Rexall the Fourth, has received a summons from the most unexpected of sources: the Sun Emperor himself, one "Zyrl Netherstar." Foolish as his name might be, his power is potent, and his reach far indeed. I fear he has significant resources that may gravely harm the Westreach should he be ignored.

Impossible as it seems, the traitor Tal Harrenfel is caught up in this confusion. Somehow surviving his flight into the East, he has gone to the capital of the Empire of the Rising Sun and allied himself with Netherstar. His companions are in the palace with him, those who survived — for it is said the warlock Kaleras the Impervious proved to be less than his name.

At any other moment, I would not fear our noble King receiving an invitation for a treaty from an enemy. But these are not ordinary times. For to His Majesty's hands I delivered a heretical tome, one duplicated by none other than Harrenfel himself.

I must confess, I have read the contents of these pages myself, though I found no pleasure in it. They are rife with lies and false prophecy, and its author speaks of things she should not. Yet something in them appealed to His Majesty, for he took a great interest in it. He questioned me at length as to my knowledge of its truth and meaning. I professed it — through quill and parchment, of course — to be lies and deception, as is everything Harrenfel touches. But somehow, I do not think His Majesty was satisfied with the answer.

I fear he may believe there to be some truth in these heathen words. I fear he means to answer Emperor Zyrl's call to arms.

But I leave further speculation to your hallowed head, Your Supremacy.

Your most humble and loyal servant,
Brother Causticus of our Order of Ataraxis

FATE'S EMBRACE

Deep in the land of the dawning sun, set in the heart of a shadowed empire, a man sparred in a courtyard.

Six men surrounded him, lashing with wooden staves, yet the man rebuffed all their attacks. He was like the wind as he turned and struck and parried: everywhere at once, yet never where his opponents retaliated.

He fought like a devil and a deity.

He fought like he struggled to survive.

His challengers continued as long as they could, but the sun had barely risen before they yielded. The man lowered his stave and breathed in the sorcery that sustained him. He could not ask more from them.

Yet it was not enough.

Soon, he would not fight men of flesh and blood. He would not stay his hand then, nor would his enemies show mercy. They would come for him with fire, tooth, and claw. They would seek to break him.

He could not allow that.

The man exhaled the fears and doubts that hounded him. Unburdened, he delved into a realm that no mortal should touch.

He descended into sorcery itself.

It was a place of light, warmth, and walls, all brimming with potential. It whispered promises from deep within the beating heart of its core.

It sought to draw the man into ruin.

He hovered there, beholding the light, flirting with the idea of entering it. He did not want to die. His friends and his beloved tethered him to the World above.

Yet he was tempted all the same.

The man faced oblivion for a time, then resurfaced. If he could defeat this flaw in himself, anything might be possible. The mad god that awaited him was distant, unknowable. This temptation was an enemy he understood and could fight.

Yet he had not smothered the desire. As he walked away from the courtyard, his shoulders sagged.

He went to the one who helped him press on, the one he most feared to lose, and found solace in forgetting.

In a garden both near and far, a youth listened to a song.

It was a song unlike any other, both terrible and wonderful. A song encompassing all life had to offer, all the vileness and beauty, the pain and the joy.

A song born of the World. The song of its creation.

For a time, the youth held the Worldsong in his mind, learning its ebbs and flows, its parts and its whole. He listened, then reached for it, like a child putting a hand in a river rapids.

The current swept him away.

It was a tempest, full of forging and fury. The youth tried to restrain it, but it was beyond him. He was flotsam floating through it; a passenger, not the captain.

But the youth would not be cowed.

He spoke sorcerous words, and they harnessed the Song, molding its furor. A killing power swept through the youth and into the garden surrounding him. It was meticulously managed, this refuge: topiaries trimmed, grasses shaved, flowers pruned. A thing of contrived beauty.

In one wave, the youth turned the green to brown.

Opening his eyes, he beheld what he had done and felt a cold hand press on his chest. The Song had lulled him into complacency, but he had to maintain his guard. The price of any lapse surrounded him. It was full of killing sounds, and he had touched one of them.

But life, too, lived in the Song. And so the youth closed his eyes, listened, and spoke different words.

Energy coursed through him and filled the shriveled plants. It was slower, this rebirth, but it soon took root. Leaves shivered and stems trembled as they turned yellow, then green, then became plump with vitality. The withered petals fell, and new ones blossomed in their wake, showing cheery faces once more.

The youth opened his eyes. As he saw what he had done, he smiled.

It was a hymn of happiness and sorrow, this Song. Their task would make him touch upon both, but he had accepted this. Fear had fled, and only the one who was once a devil remained.

He was strong. Resolved. He had accepted the price.

The youth closed his eyes, and with the quieting of his doubts, he listened again.

Tal gave a contented sigh as he slumped back onto the bed.

Ashelia nestled into the crook of his arm. They were quiet for a few moments, their breathing the only sound filling the dark bedchamber. He reveled in the warmth of her body pressed against his, the slight stickiness where their skin touched. How many times had he dreamed of this over the years?

A dream fulfilled. Silence knew he had few enough of those to treasure.

"Why are you smiling?" Ashelia levered herself up onto one elbow. Her springy hair had worked free of its braids during their activities and made a frizzy halo about her face as she stared down at him.

Tal brushed her hair back, to no avail. "At your prim appearance."

She raised an eyebrow. "Not much of a flatterer for being named Pearltongue."

"Fine words aren't the only reason for that name."

Ashelia rolled her eyes and Tal grinned like a boy. Without warning, she pushed him back down and kissed him. He regretted when she pulled away.

"Did you know?" she murmured.

"Know what?"

She traced a finger over his chest. His skin tingled after its passage as if she cast sorcery over him, though her glamour was no spell.

"How this would turn out," she continued. "Where we would end up. What you were... destined for."

"Destined?" He laughed as he captured her hand. "Fate is forged in my experience. If anyone should know that, it is I. But all I know of my future is that it's wound up with you, my mangrove bloom."

Her gray eyes were bright in the gloom. "You have me — at least until I must fetch Rolan from Falcon. But you know that's not what I mean."

His smile slipped away, and his eyes traveled to the curtained window. "I know."

Silence descended upon them, as swift as night in wintry mountains. Tal hoped she wouldn't break it. To speak of what must come brought that fate closer. He already felt the delay of each day during the months they'd spent in the Sun Emperor's palace. He needed nothing more to drag him to his purpose.

But Ashelia had sunk her teeth in now, and like a huntsman's hound, she rarely let go.

"Tal," she chided softly. "Don't bandy about life and death. Talk to me. This may be our only chance."

"What do you want me to say? That I knew I was different from the beginning? I did, but not in that way. All I knew was that I was a warlock's bastard. The son my father never wanted."

Tears surprised him, and he blinked rapidly as he glanced away.

"At least, he didn't want me then. I was different from the beginning. But of what flowed through my veins... I was never touched by power until after I'd left Hunt's Hollow. Adolescence or adversity brought it out during the years in the Avendoran army. Sometimes, when I needed to move quicker, or needed to heal from a beating in the training yard, I felt... something. Warmth. Relief. But always, I found an excuse. Only when my company was ambushed did my sorcery come on so strongly I could no longer deny it."

"What happened then?"

"Hard to say. Enemies surrounded us. My body seemed to burn from within, like I'd swallowed molten metal. Then my senses expanded. I heard and saw everything around me. I smelled the piss on the craven soldiers' trousers, and the shite on the dead ones. The wounds I had taken wove shut. There was no longer a barrier between what I wanted to do and my body's capabilities. Everything became possible."

Tal smiled bitterly toward the ceiling. "And what did I do with my newfound power? I cut down any who stood in my way and ran. I left my comrades to die. I betrayed the friends and mentors who ushered me into manhood. I became a damned deserter."

Ashelia's hand brushed over his brow, as if to smooth away

the lines there, then brushed over his hair. The white streak had faded during their time in the palace, his renewed sorcery slowly mending his old wounds. Yet even the force of his blood couldn't turn back time, and age had carved its mark upon him.

"So much guilt," she murmured. "When will you learn to put it down?"

He met her gaze and flashed a twisted smile. "When I fulfill my destiny."

To kill a god, he thought as she ran a hand through his hair. *Or be killed by him.*

"Some things are more important than duty." Ashelia whispered the words, as if afraid to speak them. "Not higher callings, maybe. But no less vital."

Tal looked away. He felt what she meant, wanted to speak the commitment she needed to hear. But she deserved more than a broken oath.

He said the only thing he could.

"If it's in my power to return to you, Ashelia Starkissed, I will. By the false gods, the dark Deep, and the uncertain heavens, I'll find my way back."

Her smile was more eloquent than any response, yet still, she gave one.

"You had better. Or I will drag you up from the hells myself."

Tal grinned, then abruptly rose and pinned her to the bed. Ashelia pretended to protest, her eyes betraying otherwise.

"You don't have to fetch Rolan yet, do you?" he breathed.

Her laughter was like birdsong, sweet and high, until he repressed it with a kiss.

CRADLE OF FIRE

GARIN WAS LISTENING TO THE WORLDSONG WHEN ILVUAN CAME to him.

He sat in his usual garden. With spring fully upon them, the flowers bloomed and filled the air with scents ranging from sweet to spicy. Though it was tame and cultured, the garden made for a welcome change from the stone, carpets, and finery elsewhere on the grounds.

Hunt's Hollow had none of those things. Its nicest rugs were those laid out for festivals and rolled up as soon as they were over. Only the forge was built with stone, the other buildings in town being made of timber and brick. But it hadn't lacked for greenery, and though the garden smelled far pleasanter than the East Marsh, for Garin, it was the closest reminder he could find of home.

So, he often sat on a marble bench before a fountain and, with the falling water providing a blanket of noise, he would close his eyes and listen.

He would seek the Song.

No longer did he think of it as belonging to the Night. Even if Ilvuan hadn't told an alternate story of the Night, declaring the mythical figure not to be the embodiment of evil, but the savior of humanity, Garin knew the Song that flowed through all things to be beyond morality. It simply was, just as the World was. The Worldsong contained all things: good and bad, peaceful and perilous. It could harm as well as heal, and what its power did was up to the listener. In the hands of a wise wielder, it could be harnessed for good.

Garin had learned how to do just that.

Even having experienced all that the Song was capable of, he disbelieved his own words when he reported on his progress each day. Of when he killed a wide swath of the garden, only to resurrect it again. Of breaking the marble bench on which he sat, then mending it. But it wasn't the effects he enacted that were most miraculous to him, but what he heard within that aria. Once odious to behold, it was now harmonious as it filled his mind. He'd touched upon the melodies woven through it and begun to understand how little he understood. But it was a foundation, a beginning.

And he knew enough to hear the Singers.

Their songs were small compared to the Worldsong, and it had been a great while since it had swallowed them. But as Garin spent long hours listening, he differentiated the dragon songs from the greater whole. They ran parallel to the Worldsong, but in their own distinct chorus. They were entities to themselves, apart from the material, above it.

Slowly, Garin realized the mastery that dragons possessed over sorcery. It only evoked more questions.

How could they fade from the World? How can Ilvuan lack a body? How could any mortal, be they Origin or elf, overcome their power?

He recalled the tale Ilvuan had told him. The *ava'duala* had sacrificed themselves in facing down the Three — the Whispering Gods, as the Singer had identified them. They'd restrained the Three's mighty power through the surrender of their own lives. And so dragons had disappeared from the face of the World for millennia.

Yet they hadn't died.

Garin heard them calling out to the World and commanding it. What their songs meant and what they forged by them, he didn't know. His grasp was rudimentary, his hearing keen enough only to comprehend his ignorance. Yet he'd seen Ilvuan enact his will upon the World, using Garin as a conduit. Though he was a spirit now, and a ghost of his former glory, he'd retained strength enough to challenge devils and save Garin on multiple occasions.

And dragons existed not only next to the Worldsong. Garin had found dragon essence in the black stone bracers that had restrained his and his companions' sorcery, as well as in the hearts of the Soulstealer Hashele's golems. They'd been fueled by the shadows of dragons, and had nearly killed them, until Garin set the dragon souls free.

He knew much more now than he had then. Months of listening had complicated and broadened his knowledge. But he was only one youth, just sixteen summers old. There were limits to what he could learn, even as he dedicated many of his waking hours toward that knowledge.

He craved the moments when his guide returned to him.

As he felt the welling up of Ilvuan's song in his mind, Garin eagerly turned his thoughts back inward. The dragon he'd once believed to be a devil, possessing him from a cursed necklace, was now a trusted companion. He thought he had the measure of his character, just as Ilvuan had grown to respect him.

Yet he could never fully predict the dragon's whimsies. He came and went as he pleased, and during Garin's stay at the Sun Palace, it had been infrequent that he visited. Garin knew only a little of why he stayed away, that it had something to do with a rift between the Singers, those who supported Yuldor and those, like Ilvuan, who opposed him. But regarding that conflict, the dragon remained close-lipped.

Still, Ilvuan was an ally, if not a friend. Garin extended feelings of greeting toward him before he noticed the dragon's mood.

It is time, Ilvuan announced with less sentiment. His song was full of gnashing teeth and beating wings and the roar of fire.

Garin guessed his meaning. *War?*

Impatience, like the lashing of a tail, filtered through the other sounds. *War has been with us for all the time I have lingered. No,* Jenduit. *It is your task, too long delayed, that must be completed.*

My task. The cold wave that poured through Garin came not from Ilvuan, but from himself. *You'll have to tell me what that is first.*

Amusement curled through his mind like a lazy hiss of smoke from nostrils. *You have always known what it is.*

Defeating Yuldor. It was the only thing Garin could imagine it could be.

That is only the second part, and not one you are likely to accomplish. Before the Pretender's defeat can matter, you must perform another duty first.

Don't leave me in suspense.

Ilvuan didn't immediately respond. His song recalled to mind a leisurely flight through the sky: the wind whistling past his ears, his flapping wings pushing aside the air, the feeling of nothing above or below him...

Sensations rushed over him and became real.

Garin stared with wide-eyed wonder at the land suddenly displayed below him. The wind pressed cold against his scales, but it couldn't touch his inner warmth. The air under his wings brought faint traces of prey to his nostrils: here a forest-rangy deer, there a pasture-fattened cow. Bright green land rolled over hills and forests and plains for miles in every direction.

He flew in a dragon dream.

Where are we? Garin asked.

Where the capital now sits. Ilvuan's rumbling response vibrated through the chest of his memory-body. *This is before Yuldor's dominion, when mortals were not the rulers of the lands, but were kept in their place.*

Garin sat with that realization. This was a glimpse of a long-past era, and he was perhaps the only living mortal to experience it. The thought was both terrifying and humbling.

Ilvuan apparently sensed his mixture of emotions, for his chest rumbled with the impression of amusement. He had no choice but to accept the dragon's derision.

Why are you showing me this?

Look, and you will see.

A blink, and the terrain shifted. Where there had been greenery, now golden sand dominated the view. The desert ended as abruptly as it began, and a shining blue sea asserted itself along the coast. Poking up from the water and sand were pillars of dark stone, like the grasping fingers of a giant buried just under the surface.

The sea?

We are nearly there.

Though curiosity gnawed at him, Garin held his thoughts in check until at last Ilvuan tilted downward. Looking through the dragon's eyes, which were far keener than his own, he saw the changes wrought over this section of the land. Black rock and sediment had replaced the sand. The pillars that had jutted up erratically were now a forest. Further inland, the sable stone mounded into hills and squat mountains. No vegetation seemed able to survive the desolation.

More riveting still was the orange river pouring into the sea. Garin stared at the lava, fascinated. Where the river of fire met the ocean, vast clouds of white steam rose up, and the flames died below the water's surface as the molten sludge turned to stone.

Ilvuan circled down slowly until the black land neared, then he alighted upon it near where the waves broke against the fingers. Garin watched through his eyes as he moved his massive bulk, swaying with each step, along the rock to a cave opening that barely looked as if it would fit him. The dragon had to fold in his wings and bend his grand head, but he managed to slither inside, like a snake entering its burrow.

A sharp reprimand stung Garin. *Not a snake,* Ilvuan reminded him with prickly pride.

But Garin's resentment only lasted a moment. Their dragon eyes lifted the depths of the darkness, though their surroundings were leeched of all color except hues of red that seemed to be strongest over living things and almost nonexistent over the stone. Not that there were many living things to see; even bugs seemed absent from the cavern. He wondered if the strange glyphs that glowed overhead were responsible for it.

Ilvuan sauntered down the tunnel until he reached a vast chamber large enough for him to spread his wings, then swept their gaze across it. Oval objects, each roughly the size of a human, were scattered about the cave, each possessing a red glow. There were hundreds of them, stretching back around the rocks and out of sight.

Garin had barely formed his query before Ilvuan answered it.

This is the Sha'aval, *the* ava'duala *hatching place. This is where our lives once began, and will begin once more.*

It took a moment for the revelation to sink in.

You were born here? And those things — they're eggs? Dragon eggs?

A somber assent filled Garin's being, and Ilvuan rumbled in their chest like distant thunder. *When we flew with the Night against the Three, we left behind this place full of our progeny, prepared to inhabit them upon our rebirths. But resurrection never came. Forced to stay to repress the rift in the World, lest it destroy all, our eggs remained behind, unoccupied. Yet a dragon's egg is not easily destroyed. Its shell is as hard as stone, and no natural beast can break it open.*

But someone did, Garin guessed.

The cave echoed with Ilvuan's anger. *Even without our essence, our eggs possess a measure of* ava'dual *might. When the Pretender learned of this place, he sent his followers here, and they butchered the eggs for their own purposes. From them, they formed bracelets such as his servants use to disguise their identities, and the bracers to repress your sorcery, and the hearts of the clay giants. They stole them, broke them apart, and have slowly whittled down our hopes of ever returning to this World. Mere dozens remain now. Only as long as our eggs exist may we retake our rightful place.*

Garin was silent as he absorbed the Singer's words. He hadn't thought about the origins of dragons, having been preoccupied with the mystery of their disappearance and how Ilvuan lingered on as a spirit despite their extinction. Now, he grasped after the intersection with his own life.

You wish me to go here, to this hatching place? This is the first part of my task?

Approval washed over him, scalding with its fervor.

Why? he queried, then quickly corrected himself. *Of course I will go, if I can reach it. But what do you wish me to do there?*

Ilvuan looked again around the cave, over the countless unhatched dragons that were long absent from the World. *Before, it was the Protectress who prepared a hatching. In her absence, you and I must do what we can.*

Garin tried to decide if it was anticipation or apprehension rising within him. *The dragons will return?*

Suddenly, Ilvuan raised his head and screamed at the roof of the cavern. It was deafening even tucked inside Ilvuan's dream-body, but full of more than just sound. Sorcery rent the air, splitting and tearing it apart. A dragon's sorrow was a hollowing fire, and Garin burned just to witness it.

When he'd finished, Ilvuan lowered his head to stare

sullenly at one egg. *We will return,* he told Garin with quiet conviction. *You will help us,* Jenduit. *This is what you were named for, Mender. This is why I chose you. You will repair the wounds wrongfully dealt to all the* ava'duala, *and to the World by consequence.*

Garin kept his reservations carefully tucked within himself, only allowing his agreement to radiate outward. Part of him did long for Ilvuan and his kin to return. For all the trouble the Singer had caused him, trust had grown between them. Reborn, he couldn't imagine that Ilvuan would do anything but uphold the same morality he'd shown thus far.

Yet dragons were forces unto themselves, if his Singer was any sign. Resurrecting the species would remake the World as thoroughly as Yuldor had. He couldn't do such a thing lightly.

If I have any choice in the matter.

Outwardly, he only expressed, *I'll do as you've asked, Ilvuan. But I have to know something.*

The dragon lowered his head to an egg and nudged it gently with his nose. The egg tilted in its stone cradle, but only minutely. *Ask, and I will answer.*

Why did you choose me? Was it an accident from taking the cursed pendant? Or had you always chosen me?

No. I never planned to bond with you, Jenduit, *nor did you have your name until we joined.*

A vast silence stretched between them. Garin waited.

It is because of Heartblood, the dragon answered at last. *You were close to him, and he has always been critical to the task. But I was only convinced when you showed your resolve by resisting me.*

In the Ruins of Erlodan? Before Soltor?

The dragon rumbled his assent. *You displayed a loyalty and strength worthy of a Listener. Our connection was established through the pendant, but it was only then that I claimed you as more than a temporary tool.*

Garin tried not to feel offense at the dragon's callousness. It

16

served as a potent reminder. As close as he and Ilvuan had grown, a gulf would always remain between them.

But that wouldn't do for a response. Garin tried to think of something to say.

Thank you for your... honesty.

With a disdainful huff, Ilvuan eyed the hatching grounds one last time, then turned his bulk and headed for the exit of the chamber. As he did, the dream started to fray, the darkness peeling back to reveal the brightness pressing against Garin's eyelids.

Do not delay, Jenduit, the Singer said, his voice fading with the dream. *The war has come, and time is short. Your task awaits.*

As abruptly as he'd come, Ilvuan departed.

It took Garin a moment to adjust to being back in his own body. Fluttering his eyelids open, he sucked in a deep breath, then exhaled. The Song, which had faded in the dream, again curled through his mind. With an ease attained through practice, he cut himself off from it and heard once more only the quietness of the gardens.

The war has come.

Garin stood and stretched with a yawn. If their time taking advantage of Emperor Zyrl's hospitality was ending, Garin had many things to be about.

Including deciding if he should loose dragons upon the World.

"Don't let a fly get in!"

Garin startled and spun toward the speaker, though he knew who it was even before he saw him.

"Sneaking about again, Tree Frog?"

Rolan grinned and bounded up to stand before him. "No — I'm helping! Wren wants to dance."

For a moment, he only stared at the boy. Then comprehension set in.

"Right — *that* dancing."

Garin mulled over it for a moment. They might not have

much more of a reprieve, and after what Ilvuan had revealed, a conversation with Aelyn in particular seemed prudent.

But he still had time, and considering there would be plenty of fighting ahead of them, scraping off some of the rust on his swordplay was just as necessary.

Garin placed a hand on Rolan's shoulder and turned him around. "Lead the way, then."

THE CALL TO ARMS

"I SHOULD SAY I COULD NEVER GROW USED TO THIS," FALCON murmured in Tal's ear, "but I think I rather have."

Tal flashed him a smile. "You're the Court Bard to the King of Avendor — or were, at any rate. If anyone has a right to be comfortable in a throne room, it's you."

"Ah, my storied friend, but what is a king's castle next to an emperor's estate?" Falcon raised his arms and gestured around the chamber. "Such wonders I could write of this palace!"

"About as wondrous as the wonders themselves," commented Helnor, who walked next to them.

Tal grinned wider as Falcon pretended offense at the tall elf's comment. Though the bard had grown thinner and more serious during their months of privation, he had recovered much of his old humor during their stay at the palace.

And his belly, besides.

Helnor, too, had gained back something of his former self. With months spent eating and training next to the palace guards along with Wren, he looked to have never suffered at the hands of the Ravagers. Yet there was a haunted look in his eyes that never seemed to fade, no matter how hard he laughed.

"Can anything be as miraculous as the sung word, my good Prime?" Falcon answered the Warder. "Surely even a fighting man like you can appreciate a stirring anthem!"

"I would appreciate some decorum, personally," broke in Ashelia, the last of their group. A twitch at the corner of her mouth betrayed her true feelings.

Tal took her in. She'd put care into her appearance for their meeting that day and wore an emerald dress nearly as resplendent as those from her old wardrobe in Elendol. Her hair was artfully plaited, and a necklace glittered above her low neckline. Yet it was none of these trappings that caught his eye, but a general glow that seemed to radiate out from her, like she swelled with vitality. She had suffered along with the others, yet Ashelia once more proved she was the toughest among them.

Let no one speak ill of healers and mothers, Tal thought with a smile.

Their banter had nearly carried them to the end of the throne room, its opulence largely ignored for all their talk of it. They'd spent enough afternoons arguing in the hall for the grandeur to lose its shine. Only as they reached their benefactor did Tal look up.

Sitting on the throne was the second most powerful man in the East, if not the whole of the continent. Zyrl Netherstar, the Sun Emperor of the Eastern Empire, twitched in his oversized chair as he grinned down at them. Tal had to admit the Emperor was nothing like he'd imagined him to be. First was his being a gnome, with the diminutive stature of his kind. Second, he was no puffed-up monarch like Aldric, nor dignified as Geminia had been, but was his own brand of sovereignty. He smiled often and cackled when the mood struck him. He never seemed to remain still, but moved like a bee in a flower garden. For all the richness of his robes, the seven-pointed sun painted upon his face, and the glistening crown atop his head, Tal could have easily imagined meeting the man in a tavern and sharing an ale with him — and what was more, enjoying their conversation.

As far as rulers went, Zyrl wasn't half-bad in Tal's book.

"My Westreach friends!" the Emperor greeted them, his short arms spreading wide, the voluminous sleeves of his robe flapping. "Welcome, welcome!"

Around Tal, his companions bowed to pay their respects to the Sun Emperor, but Tal refrained. To kneel before a man was to surrender one's equality with them, and that was something he valued above title and talent.

"You are just in time," the Emperor continued, his eyes alight with mischief. No doubt he noted Tal's lack of respect, as he did every time, but the good-natured ruler didn't point it out. "May I present to you my most loyal minotaur, Lady Rozana of Haudden."

Tal had noticed the others standing around the throne, including the minotaur, a rare sight even in the Eastern palace. But having grown used to a retinue attending the Emperor, he'd learned to ignore the numerous strangers. A rebellion they might be plotting, but the organization of an empire necessitated the spreading of secrets like wildfire. Scribes, marshals, and councilors abounded around Zyrl, and Tal and his companions had been forced to swallow the risks.

But at the minotaur's name, Tal stared at her in surprise. Rozana had changed since their time together in Low Elendol. Her spotted coat was marred with scars and burns beyond what she'd possessed before. Her dark eyes, always hard to read, drooped with deep-seated exhaustion. One of the twin horns curling from her skull looked to have been cut off, then filed smooth.

Yet for all her hardships, Rozana's fortunes seemed on the rise. She wore a silken shirt and trousers dyed bright red, with an orange sash tied about her middle. To Tal's eye, it was a garish way to dress, but most Imperial fashion struck him so.

"Rozana!" Tal strode up to her, hand extended. He ignored

21

the weary chastisement in Ashelia's gaze as he defied decorum and greeted the minotaur so boldly.

Rozana appeared unfazed, accepting his arm and grasping it. Had he not possessed the World's blood, he might have flinched at the strength in her thick fingers as they pressed into his forearm. Even still, he was glad when they released each other and stepped back.

"Ah yes, you know each other! Met in Elendol, is that right?" The Emperor flashed them a grin, then spoke even as Ashelia began to politely answer. "No need, no need, my good Peer — this Emperor knows it to be true."

"Not that I'm unhappy with the reunion, Zyrl," Tal said, "but what is she doing here?"

The Emperor leaned on the arm of his throne. "Well, my fair Fief Lady? How would you like to inform them yourself?"

Unlike Tal, the old Mire informant showed nothing but respect toward the old gnome, and she bowed before answering. "Thank you, Your Imperial Majesty. His Highness has invited me here to request my assistance in rallying the minotaurs of Haudden to your cause." Rozana shifted her great head around to glance at the Emperor. "Though what the cause is, I do not yet know."

"All will be unveiled momentarily, my lady. Peer Venaliel, perhaps you would like the honor of explaining?"

Ashelia bowed her head and stepped forward. "Lady Rozana, we seek to do what should have been done long ago: unseat Yuldor Soldarin from his bastion atop Ikvaldar."

Tal watched the minotaur, but her expression remained smooth. Others among the crowd, however, still winced. It was little wonder why.

Faith is the hardest thing to kill, he mused. *Even faith in idols.*

"And how do you mean to do this?" Rozana asked after a pause.

Ashelia didn't quail at the lack of affirmation, but carried smoothly on. "The plan is simple in design, difficult in execution. The first necessary action is to draw the Betrayer's eye from his citadel. That means gathering a force to challenge all the Nightkin across the East, and any of the fiefs that remain loyal to him."

"Then not all are aligned with the cause."

Ashelia's eyes flickered to Tal, and he shrugged. "Best she know now," he said, "than get a nasty surprise later."

A smile quirked at the corner of her lips before it smoothed away. Ashelia looked back to Rozana. "No, not all. We have not sent delegates to Rajeya or Vroresh, as medusals, sylvans, and orkans have always been the most loyal of Yuldor's followers. Agn Ommul declined to send soldiers, wishing to stay as neutral as they could, but consented to supplying artificery and weaponry such as gnomes are skilled in crafting. The others are allied with us, if your Ledfold so consents."

Again, Rozana did not indicate which way she leaned. "You said this is the first action. What is the second?"

"The second is to strike at the core of Yuldor's power, to take away that which allows him to act as a god." Ashelia darted a glance at Tal again before continuing. "A small party will wrest the Worldheart from him, and thus put an end to his reign."

The Peer's look hadn't gone unnoticed. Rozana turned to stare at Tal with her wide, placid eyes.

"Then you will lead this company," she said slowly, "that goes to the Worldheart."

Tal sighed. "I'm still disappointed myself."

Falcon and Helnor let out small chuckles, but the minotaur didn't laugh. Her expression was unshifting, though he knew her thoughts must be turning fast over these revelations. Up on his throne, Zyrl twitched and shifted, seeming unable to find a comfortable position. Tal stood motionless, waiting.

"I saw what you did," Rozana said at length. "In Elendol. You slew the one known as the Thorn. Struck down the fire devil Heyl."

Tal became conscious of his friends' eyes on him. "I had help," he hedged. "But yes, something like that."

"Can you do what you claim? Bring down the Peacebringer?"

Can I, indeed? It was a question he'd considered many times, and rarely with a favorable answer. He didn't want to give the honest response, but he'd long grown tired of lying.

"I don't know," he admitted. "But this is our best chance."

The minotaur stared at him a moment longer, then turned to the Emperor. "This is a great risk."

"So it is, my lady!" Zyrl piped. "Quite the gamble, and I must admit a weakness for dice."

Rozana bowed, though there seemed a stiffness to the gesture now. "Once, I united many of the peoples of our Empire and asked you to free us, Your Imperial Majesty. You refused me then and banished us on pain of death. Now, you invite me into your palace and ask for my aid in rebelling against a god."

Her words echoed throughout the throne room, and Tal had to admit, when spoken like that, the idea sounded fanciful. What could any of them do against a god? Yet Yuldor was no deity, immortal as he'd proven thus far.

He was mortal once. He can be made mortal again.

"He can be killed," Tal spoke aloud. "And he will be."

He didn't expect anyone else to back him up. None but he knew the true breadth of Yuldor's power, as the fell god had shown when speaking through the dying Hashele. Yet Falcon nodded his head enthusiastically, and Ashelia gave him a slight smile, and Helnor heaved a sigh, shook his head, and grinned. Zyrl nearly bounced in his seat at the notion, though his gaze was calm and calculating.

"So we must hope!" the Emperor said with a laugh. "Or this will be a fruitless rebellion from the start."

Rozana bowed her head again to Zyrl's declaration, but her eyes had settled again on Tal. She seemed to evaluate him, judging whether his words held any truth. Tal imagined she had a host of doubts, even knowing his accomplishments in Elendol.

But he was more now than he had been then. He was whole. In his wilder musings, he even wondered if he might be worthy of his legend, though the thought was always followed by a wry grin.

Rozana finally nodded and looked back to the Emperor. "Very well, Your Imperial Majesty. Ledfold will lend whatever aid it can. But I have one condition."

The Emperor scooted to the edge of his seat. "I know what you will ask, but speak anyway. I would not wish to steal your moment!"

The minotaur showed no sign of sharing in his amusement. "My fief must exist free of imperial strictures. It must be a nation unto itself."

"Ah, so this is what it all comes to." Zyrl's eyes had a mischievous gleam. "You wish to rule as I do? Queen Rozana! A fitting ring to it, do you not agree, my Westreach friends?"

Tal's companions were wise enough not to answer. The same couldn't be said of himself.

"It does sound rather nice." Tal smiled at both the minotaur and the gnome, as if the three of them shared a private joke. "Rozana certainly has my support in her move toward independence. After all, what is our plot about if not freeing the World of tyranny?"

As he was presently fomenting rebellion against the Prince of Devils, Zyrl couldn't appreciate any comparisons to him. Yet the Emperor proved as deft and devious as he'd been during the previous months. His lips never closed over his square teeth as he looked from Tal back to Rozana.

"A noble sentiment indeed, Tal Harrenfel, and one which I whole-heartedly affirm. But let us not confuse order with tyranny, for they are not the same — no, not in the least. The Empire provides stability, walls against the chaos ever encroaching upon our lands. Do you truly wish to forgo all we offer for — what, precisely, Lady Rozana? A title? An ideal? What is it that your independence gives you that I cannot?"

Rozana's response remained measured. "It is our right. I will not claim it will bring us great prosperity, but my people deserve to rule themselves. They deserve a chance."

"Yet another gambit! We are full of them here, are we not?" Zyrl grinned at Tal, but Tal found himself fresh out of humor. Rozana's brief affirmation had touched something in him.

People ruling themselves. Across the length of history, monarchs had imposed their rule over their subjects. Even for good sovereigns such as Geminia, it was the way things were. He couldn't imagine any other system of governance.

Yet, impossible as Rozana's dream seemed, he found it resonated within him.

Rozana wasn't finished. "Why do you seek rebellion, Your Imperial Majesty?"

Tal looked back at the Emperor. It had been one of the first questions he'd posed to Zyrl upon his proposal to Tal and his companions those long months ago. Fresh from fighting for their lives, having just encountered Yuldor through Hashele and still grieving for Kaleras, he'd been embittered and suspicious. Pim had lent his support for the Emperor, but the word of an Extinguished, even one who had provided Tal so much assistance, could only go so far. He'd believed it to be another trick of Yuldor's, the lure to draw Tal further into the East and the Night Puppeteer's clutches.

No answer could satisfy him, and Zyrl's certainly had not. He'd spoken of morality, of freeing the East and ridding the World of a deadly scourge. With monsters coming down from the surrounding mountains and preying on their own people, and magical mishaps occurring all across the continent, the Emperor had said he felt it his duty to protect them.

But the statement he made afterward finally swayed Tal to take a chance. *Suspicion is wise, Tal Harrenfel,* Zyrl had said. *I would never think my words could take it away from you, nor would I wish to. So all I will ask of you is this: Pretend with me. Pretend I am sincere in what I have told you. Pretend that we are allies in this war. See all that we could do together that you could not on your own. Do you know the challenges awaiting you atop Ikvaldar? Do you know the beasts you will face, the trials you must endure? You are ignorant, blissful as a babe, when it comes to facing the Peacebringer. And even as filled with sorcery as you are, it is nothing to what Yuldor wields.*

Tal had known Zyrl was right. That Yuldor could defy Tal's efforts at ending Hashele from hundreds of miles away and with seemingly little difficulty spoke of a power such as Tal could scarcely comprehend. The World's blood ran through Tal's veins, but its Heart was in Yuldor's hands.

He couldn't fight this war alone. And so he pretended the gnome and his Empire were allies until he believed it.

Mischief now danced in Zyrl's dark eyes. "It is our right, Lady Rozana. Just as you see Ledfold's independence as yours."

That, at least, was a belief the Emperor likely held true. Whatever else Zyrl Netherstar was, he was a monarch, and no sovereign liked to be beholden to a higher power.

The Emperor glanced at Tal, and he must have seen something in his eyes, for his smile finally thinned. He turned back to the minotaur.

"But if this is your price, Fief Lady of Ledfold, I'm afraid you leave me no choice. Your land will leave the Empire following our victory against the Peacebringer. Nofas! Be sure this is in the royal ledgers, would you?"

"It is done, Your Imperial Majesty." Nofas, the royal scribe, was an unflappable gnome who presided over the three lower scribes scribbling down the Emperor's words. She exhibited the same tyrannical control over the scribes as a cook in her kitchen.

"Good, good." Zyrl looked around the throne room, protracting the pause, as if to remind everyone that, though he'd made a concession, only one man reigned supreme in this chamber. Tal glanced at Ashelia and saw the same question in her spinning eyes. Why Zyrl had made such a deal when he could have negotiated a better compromise was beyond him. But he hadn't maintained an imperium through Yuldor's backing alone. The gnome was shrewd; some game was being played here of which Tal had only the vaguest impression.

"Now," the Emperor said, "we must bring our ally up to date regarding our campaign. Nofas! Recount those who have pledged to our war."

The royal scribe had apparently anticipated her lord liege's request, for she already held a scroll from which she began reading at once. "The following have sent word of their allegiance. The Honored Dithakar Chai'at of Bavay. Mater Izoalta Yoreseer of Naruah. Mayor Manee Kedmanee of Letmu..."

Tal swiftly lost interest and began examining the many tapestries lining the throne room. He'd attended countless meetings and knew well the present arrangement of their various allies. Their tenuous support provided an inauspicious beginning to their rebellion. But it was more aid than he'd ever expected, and Tal found himself contented by scraps.

His attention was brought back as the Emperor said, "But that is not all who have aligned with us! Peer Venaliel, if you would honor me by recounting our foreign allies."

Ashelia nodded respectfully, but with a pride and grace befitting her station. "We have conveyed Emperor Zyrl's summons to all the nations of the Westreach. Some have responded. Though Gladelyl does not come to our aid, the Warders have responded to Prime Helnor's commands. They ride even now to Kavaugh and are expected to arrive within the week.

"King Aldric of Avendor has also answered the call, promising a regiment of his finest knights. The Protector of Sendesh gave no response, nor did Queen Mysx Gemfang of Chychaxil'isk, commonly known in the Westreach as the

Goblin Knolls. The dwarven chiefs of Dhuulheim could not be reached, lacking any method by which magical conveyance can reach them.

"Last of all, the Magisters of Jalduaen's Circle are in consideration of our proposal. They have assured us it is of the utmost importance to them, though they gave no timeframe as to when we might receive a reply."

Her account complete, she nodded again to the Emperor and stepped back to rejoin Tal and the others.

"Thank you, Peer Venaliel, very much indeed. Lord Marshal! Outline for our new ally the specific strategies by which we hope to win this war. And briefly, if you please!"

The long-winded High Marshal Samup Dhardon, a grizzled human with a long, graying mustache and a bald pate, grimaced as he stepped forward.

"Yes, Your Imperial Majesty," he spoke in halting Reachtongue. "As Peer Venaliel said, the plans are simple, but difficult to, ah, accomplish..."

Tal again stopped listening. Though he'd spent some time serving a king, he'd never had much interest in the strategies of war, and even less so when it was explained by the High Marshal. Yet through sheer repetition, the scheme had soaked into his mind.

It was, as Dhardon said, simple. The past few months had been spent gathering and consolidating the soldiers, weapons, and other resources necessary for supplying an army on the move from the various fiefs that had pledged to their cause. Part of the difficulty lay in obscuring these movements. Though Tal doubted anyone truly believed Yuldor was ignorant of their uprising, they all operated as if they did. This meant that everything took twice as long to accomplish, and the machinery of war, already slow to function, proceeded with a slug's speed.

When and if the Imperial forces could ever gather, the strategy, too, would prove straightforward. Massing before

Kavaugh's walls, the soldiers would march for Ikvaldar, contending with any monsters Yuldor sent their way. There was only one approach to the mountain, and no amount of scheming had yielded a better prospect. Tal feared the Empire would suffer grievous losses when that day came.

But the army was only one part of the assault. While the High Marshal's forces drew the Enemy's eye, Tal and his companions would ascend Ikvaldar in secret. Then, with Yuldor unprotected — or as unprotected as a god could be — they would attack and overcome him.

It wasn't clever. It was riddled with holes and flaws and inflated by assumptions. But it was the best any of them had come up with, and Tal had stomached it along with the rest of them.

"That will be all, Lord Marshal." From Zyrl's tone, Tal guessed the Emperor had, once again, cut off the man's droning.

High Marshal Dhardon bowed, his frown a little more severe than before.

"So, Lady Rozana, there it is! Now, I must urge you to bring your people to our cause. Minotaurs are the strongest race found anywhere in the East or the Westreach, a fact that even our western friends cannot deny!" The Emperor beamed down at them. "You are mighty warriors, honed and blooded by your feuds. Free the Empire, and you free yourselves — let them hear that message!"

Rozana bowed. "I will convey it to them, Your Imperial Majesty, and hope it does not once more mean my exile."

"Exile? Oh no, my dear lady. If this ends poorly, it will not be banishment you have to fear, but death."

"How reassuring," Falcon muttered in Tal's ear.

Tal grinned. "But hardly surprising," he whispered back. "Death has always been the most likely outcome."

"Yet, as a bard, I cannot help but think that the way a thing is said can very much influence one's feelings on the matter."

Tal only shrugged as his eyes slid over to Ashelia. She'd put herself and her son at risk coming after him, and he knew it wasn't only to preserve Tal's life. She believed in this cause and would sacrifice everything for it.

But he'd be damned if he let anything harm her, be it a god, an emperor, or this war.

Then you'd best not lose, Tal Harrenfel, a part of him mocked, that voice of doubt that never silenced. *Stop clinging to your fears and press forward.*

Tal found the Emperor's eyes on him and realized he'd been addressed. "Yes, Zyrl?"

"I said we must be ready soon. None of us will delay in our duties, will we?"

As the gnome gave him a cutting smile, Tal found it hard to return. It took an effort not to look at Ashelia, especially as he felt her gaze upon him.

"No," he answered at length. "We'll do what we must."

AN INVITATION TO DANCE

No sooner had Garin entered the training yard than a long measure of wood flew toward him.

"*Jolsh heks!*" He instinctively spoke the spell as he threw up his hands, and sorcery swept away the short stave, sending it spinning across the packed dirt. The Song blared into his head, then subsided to a quiet chorus.

"Not exactly the reaction I had in mind," Wren noted wryly as she strode up to him. She wore her usual outfit for these past few months: a linen tunic and trousers, leather boots such as the palace guards wore, a belt with two tails trailing down her thigh, and a quilted gambeson to top it off. Her springy hair was cropped short, and the gold in her eyes spun with anticipation. Clutched in her hand was a stave identical to the one Garin had flung away.

"You could have just caught it," Rolan pointed out with a grin.

Once, when Garin and Wren first trained together back in the courtyards of the Coral Castle, Garin would have been mortified at flinching. Now, he smiled along and chased down the practice weapon.

"Been dueling with Aelyn and Tal too often," he said as he

returned. "Spells come more naturally than catching."

"Which is exactly why my loyal hound brought you here." Wren laughed at Rolan's outrage and waved a hand. "Scuttle along now! "

"See if I do you any more favors," Rolan muttered as he departed. He didn't go far, though, but grabbed a shorter stave from the nearby rack and gave it a few experimental swings. "You still have to teach me afterward!" he shouted at them.

Wren rolled her eyes. "As entitled as his father, isn't he?"

"Been a long time since I thought of Yinin."

"And good riddance! I don't even think Rolan misses him much... But don't sidetrack me." She pointed her stave at him. "Let's see if anything's stuck in that head of yours from your dancing lessons."

He didn't bother reminding her they'd fought in actual skirmishes several times in the intervening seasons. There was no arguing with Wren once she got an idea in her head. Raising his stave slightly, he settled into a ready but relaxed stance. *Like water,* Ulen Yulnaed, his deceased Dancing Master, would have called it.

"Is sorcery allowed?" he queried.

Wren snorted and began to circle him, her weight balanced with each step, as ready to attack as defend. "Is that what you need to be practicing?"

Repressing a sigh, Garin cut himself off from the Song, then noted their surroundings. Though set in the middle of the castle, the courtyard wasn't much to look at, little more than a long rectangle of packed dirt thirty paces wide. On the sides that didn't boast archways, doors opened into rooms that held practice equipment. They weren't entirely alone; a few guards sat around, half-heartedly polishing weapons and armor, though Garin saw their eyes flicker up as his and Wren's duel began.

He put them out of mind and focused on Wren. Garin wasn't dressed for a training bout, wearing the casual yet fine clothes Emperor Zyrl had provided their party. His emerald-green tunic alone likely cost a month's earnings for any of his brothers back in Hunt's Hollow. Instead of boots, he had on the slippers more suitable for walking about a castle.

Maybe she's right, he admitted as he waited for the first strike. *Maybe I have grown soft.* Days spent meditating and exploring sorcery and the Song would do little for him when it came to the hardships of the road. He could only hope he hadn't fallen too far.

Settling into the moment, Garin struck.

His weapon met only wind. A moment later, Wren's stave thwacked against his and sent it wide. Garin spun into the Form of Air, light on his feet and ready to parry, his stave held in both hands. Wren didn't advance, instead standing at ease, stave fallen by her side.

She's toying with me. With fresh determination, he shifted to the Form of Fire and charged.

His stave weaved through the air, unpredictable in its movement, until he lashed forward. Wren, a small smile perched on her lips, didn't react until the last moment, when she exploded into motion. Too late, Garin recognized her steady stance put her in the position to knock aside his stave, then use his momentum against him, tripping and throwing him to the ground as he passed.

The packed dirt of the yard was softer than stone, but not by much. Pain racketed up his knees and elbow as Garin rolled with the fall. He gained his feet with his stave up, but once more, Wren only stood waiting.

Belatedly, he registered where he'd gone wrong. "You used the Form of Stone. Since when do you know the dancing forms?"

Wren looked disinclined to answer, but Rolan, who had dragged out a stuffed dummy to whack at, shouted from his corner, "She's been training with *Momua* and Uncle Helnor, remember?"

It was obvious now that the boy pointed it out. He and Wren had sometimes talked of her training, but never in explicit detail. Yet he'd known both Ashelia and Helnor were pitching in to give her lessons, and even Tal on the rare occasion, when he wasn't busy whaling on the hapless guards. Of course she would know the elven dancing forms.

And that meant he was in even deeper trouble than he'd first thought.

He lowered his stave. "Alright. You're better than me. Happy now?"

Wren cocked her head. Though her body was relaxed, her eyes gave away her delight. "Oh, you're not getting off that easily. Raise your weapon. It's the last chance you'll get."

Garin was glad his back was to the guards who shared the yard. He would have hated to see their grins as Wren darted forward and showed him just how outmatched he was.

She flowed through the forms so rapidly he could barely note them, much less keep up. Air into Stone, Water into Fire, moving from offensive to defensive and back again with an ease that belied years of practice. He couldn't imagine how she'd so far outstripped him in a matter of months.

Finally, smarting from a dozen fresh bruises, Garin threw down his stave and held up his hands. "I yield! Silence, Solemnity, and Serenity have mercy, I yield. And I thought I was the one with a devil in me."

Wren grinned as she lowered her weapon. "Guess the training is paying off."

"You're like a Dancing Master already. Night's blood, how'd you do it?"

Ignoring him, she held out a hand toward his stave and sucked in a deep breath before speaking. "*Wuld droin.*" A gust whipped up against the dirt, and the wooden pole lifted from the ground to sail into Wren's hand. She looked breathless for a moment as the spell's cost took effect, but after a shaky inhale, the smile returned.

"Best two of three?"

"I feel like ground pulp. Maybe Rolan wants a turn at being your dummy."

Wren cocked an eyebrow back at the boy, who didn't employ any form Garin knew as he whacked at his uncaring opponent. "I wouldn't want to batter a defenseless boy," she said.

Garin crossed his arms, partly to cradle his aching ribs. "How about a nearly defenseless young man? Seriously, Wren. That was incredible."

Finally, the hint of a blush claimed her cheeks, and some of the facade fell away. "Think so?"

"I know so. So, are you going to tell me how you did it or not?"

She shrugged and raised both staves to her shoulders, a bit of her swagger returned. "Not much more to it than Rolan said. Having both Ashelia and Helnor as teachers has been key. They have different styles I can borrow from. I've also been practicing against the palace guards. They're not bad, but their training doesn't really hold a candle next to Gladelysh dancing."

"I'll say." Garin glanced back at the guards and wondered if he stood a chance against them. Both were bulkier by a large margin, though Garin was the tallest among them.

When he turned back, Wren had come closer, a coy smile perched on her lips. Anticipation prickled across his skin.

"What do you say we all try to take down Tal?"

As quickly as the heat rose in him, the words dashed it away. "You want to spar against him? Who, exactly — you, me, Helnor, and Ashelia?"

"And Aelyn, though I doubt he'll pry himself away from those dusty old tomes long enough to take part. But what do you say? Think the four of us can take down the 'Man of a Thousand Names'?"

Having practiced his spellcasting against the man and

witnessed the guards contending with him, Garin doubted it. As formidable as Wren had become, and as much as Garin had delved into the Song and its sorcery, Tal Harrenfel possessed an entirely different level of mastery. Not even Ashelia and Helnor, both deadly Warders in their own right, were likely to even those odds. But maybe one of the most potent mages in the Westreach might tip the scales.

"We need Aelyn," Garin asserted. "If I can get him, I'll take a few more bruises."

"Don't act like you can't just heal them." Flashing him a grin, Wren shouted over her shoulder, "Rolan! Want to see the rest of us beat Tal?"

Rolan had dropped his stave by the time she finished speaking. "How is that a question?"

"Go tell your mother, the nicer of your uncles, and Tal to meet us in the small courtyard tomorrow at noon. We'll meet you there with Aelyn."

The boy took off at a run.

Garin made to move after him, but as he passed Wren, she grabbed his arm and wrenched him toward her. Trying to hide a wince as his wounds protested, he took hold of her and met her in a long kiss.

When she pulled away, the golden tendrils in her eyes spun quickly. "That was fun."

"You enjoy beating me too much."

She tapped a finger against his nose. "Can't have too much of a good thing."

With that, she twisted free of his embrace and made to replace the staves. Garin looked after her a moment before following.

Playing with fire, he thought as he summoned to mind the words to a simple healing spell. *Sooner or later, she'll burn me.*

But he couldn't deny that their dance was the more thrilling for that.

LAMENT

TAL STARED OVER THE CITY AND RELISHED THE COOL BREEZE. The sunrise was brilliant that morning, a masterpiece painted in strokes of pink and peach. Light bled into the dun walls surrounding Kavaugh and limned the aqueducts in gold. The plains beyond glowed green with spring, and as the day was clear, he could just make out the hills beyond them.

Would that you could watch this with me, he thought to a man months gone from the World.

He'd often come to this spot to speak to Kaleras. As distant as they'd been in life, Tal felt closer to him now that he had passed. He imagined some part of his father's spirit lingered, though with as little faith as he had in the Creed, he suspected it was only his grief conspiring to trick him.

Still, people often took comfort in illusions, and Tal was no better than the next man.

He breathed in deeply, and a measure more of sorcery coursed in. It burned in his blood, day and night, both a comfort and an irritation. It was the power he would use to unseat his enemy, yet also a reminder of the fate that awaited him.

Still, Tal kept his connection open as often as he could. Even in an ally's palace, they were never far from peril.

Through his sorcerous sense, he felt the approach of a man and his retinue as they came up the wall stairs to stop next to him.

"You needn't chase me down to speak with me, Zyrl Netherstar," Tal said without turning. "Just lift your little finger and I'll come running."

The Sun Emperor chuckled between breaths. "The exercise... does me good. And how could I miss... this brilliant dawn! My empire is named for it... after all."

Tal finally glanced over. Sweat filmed the gnome's forehead, his short legs and advanced age making the wall's steps difficult to ascend. Yet his moist eyes were as lively as ever, and as his servants erected a simple wooden platform, he hopped up the stairs to stare through a crenel at the sunrise.

"Marvelous," Zyrl breathed. "Like a finely painted canvas, is it not?"

Tal nodded and watched the sun inch above the forests and hills. Nothing more needed to be said; the sight spoke for itself.

"As pleasant as it is to relieve my rear of the throne," the Emperor continued, "I will admit to an ulterior motive for seeking you."

Tal glanced over to find Zyrl gesturing to one of the many servants now crowding the stairs. The man, a bald Easterner human, bustled forward to present a wrapped object. Tal's eyebrows raised at the unmistakable shape and rose further still as the servant brought the bundle to him.

"Take it," the monarch urged. "A gift — or, if you prefer, a bribe."

Obediently, Tal grasped the silk-wrapped object and uncovered it. As suspected, a sword lay beneath, a weapon like no other he'd seen. The hilt was silver, and the pommel bore the aspect of a dragon. Along the winged quillons were carefully carved runes that flirted with his mind, yet defied his comprehension. Gold wire wrapped around a grip a hand and a half long.

Most striking of all was the blade. Dark was the steel, if it even was steel. Glyphs of the same strange script pulsed with golden light along its length with the regularity of a heartbeat. Every time they lit, the metal seemed to pull at Tal — or rather, at his sorcery.

Like a thirsty hound wishing to drink me dry.

"*Helshax* is its name," Zyrl said. "Lament, in your tongue."

"Lament," Tal murmured. Somehow, the name fit. Each time it plucked at his magic, he thought he heard an echo of a mournful cry. "How did it earn it?"

"The man who discovered it — in forbidden Origin ruins, no less — used the sword to slay a sorceress he loved, recompense for her betrayal." At Tal's glance, Zyrl waved a hand. "A maudlin tale, and one of little import. Needless to say, its past is less than pleasant."

"And so you give it to me. How fitting."

The gnome laughed. "It is for more than a jape. As you have no doubt felt, it has certain properties that you will find advantageous during your journey. For Lament, it is said, has the power to repress sorcery."

"Repress it? How, exactly?" Tal frowned down at the sword, then glanced at the dull gray ring on his left hand, just visible above his glovelets. He knew some artifacts had this capacity, but ones as potent as the Ring of Thalkuun were exceedingly rare.

"*Exactly*, I cannot say. It has been in my armory for quite some time and has yet to be properly tested. I trust you will find sufficient opportunities to do so."

Tal raised his gaze to meet the Emperor's. "I should thank you. Yet I feel this is a foreboding sign."

Zyrl's smile was sympathetic, but his eyes were hard. "I am sure the leisure of these months was enjoyed and needed, Tal

Harrenfel, and I was happy to supply it. But that time, I fear, is ending. There are whispers of those loyal to the Peacebringer moving in the shadows. Our enemies will soon make their move, and we must be ready."

Tal turned suddenly and made a few experimental swipes through the air, drawing gasps from the Emperor's protectors. He ignored them, feeling out the balance of the blade. Though the craftsmanship was superb, the pull of the dark metal was disconcerting, and it didn't flow for him as *Velori* had.

I've gotten used to worse. He ceased swinging the sword and turned back to the Emperor to find his guards had drawn their blades and stared at him with open hostility.

Zyrl laughed and motioned for the warriors to lower their arms. "He only does what I encouraged! And if Tal Harrenfel means me harm, none of you are likely to do me any good."

Tal gave them a tight smile as he let Lament fall to his side. "Thank you, Zyrl. Even if it is a thorny gift, I'm sure I'll appreciate it during the trials to come."

"I am sure you will," Zyrl said as he turned and descended his small platform. "To both of our regrets."

Tal took the offered scabbard and wished he didn't agree.

YULDOR'S SERVANT

It called to him.

Tal stood on the dirt of a training yard in the Sun Palace. Moments before, he'd been practicing with the sword the Emperor had gifted him the day before, moving through the multitude of sword forms he'd accumulated over the years.

Yet though Lament was a fascinating sword, his attention wavered. And as he had many times before, Tal's mind wandered from the material to the yawning, bright pit waiting deep in the World's core.

It called to him once more.

Expanding his sorcerous awareness, Tal saw every touch of magic upon the palace. The werelights illuminating the halls. The enchanted stones resisting age and mildew. The cursed traps and ensorcelled defenses warding against intruders. He saw those individuals with an affinity for magic, whether it was a torrent such as his own or the trickle that the Nightelf guards possessed.

He could identify every individual with greater potential. Aelyn, buried in the palace archives, as he so often was these days. Pim, walking the palace halls, as he went about some task only known to him. Ashelia, conferring with a conveyer as she tried to coordinate foreign alliances. The Emperor himself, his high station and compact frame not impinging on his potential.

But he hadn't strayed into this plane to spy on the others. Drawing back, Tal stared down into the molten stream leading away from him. It seemed a bright tunnel, a storm in a cavern leading deep into the World, full of latent energy.

But it was the sorcery's source that pulled him down.

He slipped into the stream even before he willed it, but he didn't resist. With freedom unknown to his body, he flung himself down the passage at an impossible speed. The other beings occupying this realm passed by, shades of gray in the white surroundings. Some were vast, perhaps as large as Zyrl's palace, though dimension and size had largely lost their meaning. None seemed to pay Tal much attention. To them, he was a frail and puny creature, unworthy of pursuit.

He continued down and down until he beheld the source of the call. He paused his foolhardy flight as the orb came into view. It was even brighter than the streams that led to the chamber that held it, so bright it was the only thing in the World that could be truly called white. Its name rang through his being like the toll of the palace belfry.

The *Doash.*

It was what Ilvuan had called it when he tried bringing him back after cleansing his *karkados*, the magical affliction that had ravaged his body and tainted his sorcery. Tal had later consulted Aelyn and his expanding knowledge of the palace archives on what "*Doash*" meant, but all he'd extracted was a translation from the Origintongue: "the Womb."

Tal understood what it meant. This was the birthing place of all sorcery, all life, all the World. It was the spring of creation, the font that would never cease to run. The Worldheart was little more than a breach in the planet next to this. The *Doash* was the World's true heart.

He yearned to join it.

The longing wasn't all his own devising; the *Doash* seemed to whisper to him. *Rest. Peace. Release.* All the things missing from his life, that he could never afford until he confronted the deified elf atop Ikvaldar. What peace could exist in a World ruled by the Prince of Devils? What unity could reign on the continent the Westreach and the Eastern Empire shared?

When could he ever rest?

He tantalized himself with the sensations, pretended to indulge them. But he was still yoked to the World above. As his corporeal senses tingled, urging him to return to his body, Tal reluctantly ascended.

Someday, he promised the bright orb. *I will return, perhaps someday soon.*

He rose with even greater speed until he surged back into himself and stood in the courtyard again. Tal blinked, adjusting back to the heaviness of his body and the smallness of his senses.

He wasn't alone. One swollen with sorcery stood next to him.

Pim regarded him with a smile as Tal met his gaze. The black threads in his green eyes were lively, writhing like eels over an ensnared fish. The Extinguished wore robes that brought out their color, a spring-leaf green lined with a deeper malachite and threaded with cobalt in whirling designs. As usual, a dark metal bracelet clung to his wrist, but he'd accented it with other jewelry, silver hanging from his neck and enwrapping his fingers. His illusory blonde hair was impeccably styled, a crown of braids encircling his head. In his disguise, he appeared a foppish elf at the height of Gladelysh fashion.

But Tal had long ago learned not to be deluded by appearances, and a Soulstealer's most of all.

"Welcome back to the World, Tal Harrenfel." Pim's smile seemed more for his own benefit than Tal's.

"Who was he?" Tal asked abruptly.

The Extinguished wasn't easily surprised, but for a moment, he only blinked. "Pardon?"

"The elf whose face you stole, whose soul is in that bracelet you wear. Who was he?"

Pim's borrowed features twisted, and his eyes spun faster. "Must we reawaken past injuries? It happened long ago. I regret it, but his body has long since been interred. There can be no correcting my crime."

"Then you consider it a crime."

"Of course!" Pim spread his arms wide. "How could it be anything else?"

Tal didn't reciprocate the gesture, but only watched the Extinguished with a wolf-eyed stare.

At length, his companion lowered his arms. "Have we not been allies long enough? Must I always prove my devotion to our cause? I have committed many errors in my lifespan — as countless as the stars, to be sure. But as a man with your history, I am certain you can forgive a few transgressions."

Tal still didn't answer. He wasn't sure why he was challenging Pim now. The Extinguished had been invaluable in exposing information about the Enemy, his monsters, and Ikvaldar where he awaited. He'd divulged the trials they would face ascending the mountain. He'd identified creatures Tal had never heard of before, nor could scarcely imagine even upon their description. And for each challenge, Pim had provided an answer or sought to. If they stood a chance against Yuldor, it was largely thanks to him.

If he's telling the truth.

Tal could never be entirely certain on that front. Though Pim had professed a desire to right the wrongs of the past, Tal suspected his ambition had never entirely dissipated. This was a man hungry enough for power to join the Prince of Devils in his immortality and shed all the trappings of life. Even centuries couldn't change a man that much.

Pim eyed him a moment longer, then his expression

shifted. With a control born of illusion, he went from suspicion to joviality and barked a laugh.

"Ah, Tal! How alive it makes me feel to be around you! Nothing like a contest of wills to ease one's age, do you not think?" Without waiting for an answer, Pim turned from Tal and paced the length of the courtyard. Conceding, Tal kept abreast of him.

Pim eyed him sidelong before speaking again. "I did not merely come to bandy words. At last, I have located our elusive alchemist."

Tal's suspicion lifted as his interest was piqued. "Did you?"

He'd been aware of Pim's stated mission these past months. After excusing himself from the war meetings, a prudent measure if Yuldor ever reclaimed him, the Extinguished had set to himself a different task: finding a way up Ikvaldar for Tal and his party. It wouldn't be as simple a matter as hiking up, nor battling through hordes of Nightkin — if that could be called simple. Rather, Pim's old master had put several safeguards in place, ones they would struggle to overcome without the proper preparation.

The first he'd read about in *A Fable of Song and Blood*, Hellexa Yoreseer's book. The Sentinel was reputed to be the gatekeeper for the mountain, watching over the only accessible route up. According to Pim, one had to answer the guardian's riddle and prove an immutable truth in order to pass. Tal had pressed him for more, but the Extinguished only threw up his hands.

"The riddle changes!" he would declare, then say no more.

The second trial held its own challenges. Paradise, the sorcerous jungle that claimed the high reaches of Ikvaldar, held a danger in the form of a mist Pim called "miasma." Its touch sapped the victim's will, eroding it until they were content to lie down and never move on.

It seemed a problem with no simple solution, yet Pim claimed to know of one who had solved it. This alchemist was somewhere in the East, and after months of searching, it seemed he'd found him.

"He is a medusal, our alchemist, if you can believe it," Pim said. "Never pinned their kind as particularly clever or interested in scholarly endeavors, but one can never assume. When I finally searched beyond the likely gnome, sylvan, and Nightelf candidates, my contacts found him with relative ease. A reminder of the frailty of assumptions!"

"Who is he, and where can we find him?"

"All duty today, are we?" Pim shook his head mournfully. "You were far more diverting when you were at my mercy back in the mountains. Can you imagine how amusing it was for me to watch you struggle just to walk?"

"More fun than our stroll right now."

"Far more!" Pim laughed again, a jolly fop by all appearances. "His name is Koax Mraaj, and he lives in the only city worth speaking of in the fief of Rajeya: Dreygoj."

"Dreygoj." Tal had spent time with Ashelia and Helnor poring over maps of the Empire during their planning, and the name evoked vague memories. "Off the coast of the Far Depths?"

"Indeed. It is a strange city, Dreygoj. The medusals and sylvans built it together, as they have always shared a symbiotic relationship in terms of their environment." Pim shrugged. "It will not be easy to pass through there disguised."

"Fortunately, we have a master illusionist on our side."

"Oh, no! I would not rely upon me. Never know when I will be whisked away, just like poor Hashele, if you recall?"

How could I not? The moment of contending with Yuldor's will and witnessing his shattered mind had haunted his dreams many nights in the months since.

"I assume you have another solution then?" Tal asked.

Pim cast him a coy smile as they completed one circuit of the courtyard and began a second. "Indeed, I do. My answer is to defer it to you and your talented companions. Surely, with all the sorcery, knowledge, and the Emperor's resources in your possession, you can come up with something."

Tal grimaced. This was a task for Aelyn, but supplicating the mage for even a small favor never boded well for his pride. "I suppose we can."

"I would also advise that you depart with all haste. My old master will not be long in discovering I have located Mraaj. When he does, your opportunity will evaporate."

"We'll leave as soon as we're able." In his mind, Tal started checking off the long list involved in implementing the Emperor's grand plan. "The High Marshal doesn't need us for organizing the armies, and we cannot help in rallying the fiefs. But Ashelia is still involved in coaxing over the Circle and the dwarves. Until she's finished—"

"Tal, Tal, Tal."

Tal glowered at the fell warlock. "What now?"

Pim wore a sympathetic smile that roused a prickle of heat from Tal's blood. "I understand your hesitancy in departing. Joy is never easy to abandon. But it is as I told you in Naruah — your relationships weigh you down. This would all be far easier if you followed my advice."

"If I'd followed your advice, I'd be dead." *Or as a good as.* He wasn't entirely sure what happened when one entered the *Doash*, but he doubted a continued existence was likely.

The Extinguished waved a hand dismissively. "It does not change the facts as they now stand. You are to be the sacrifice for the World. Do not let your fear — or love — get in the way."

Tal halted. Pim continued a few paces before stopping and turning back. For several long moments, they only stared at each other.

Tal lowered his gaze. "I'll do what I must," he murmured, then glanced up. "Not because of what you've said. It's for them; it's always been for them. They deserve a World emancipated from Yuldor's tyranny. A safe land. A free land."

His thoughts went further, back to Rozana's vision for her fief, but he couldn't articulate the dream. So he let it remain unsaid.

Pim's lips curled. "As you say, Stone in the Wheel, as you say. But in my long life, I have learned freedom is rarely what people desire. No; they desire power — over others, over the World, over themselves."

Tal burned a little hotter. "Is that what you desire, then? Power? Perhaps you wish to become greater than Yuldor. A god in your own right."

The Extinguished only smiled wider. "What is a god but the World's master? If you looked past your self-righteous blinders, you would understand how much more you could become. You could be a god, Tal Harrenfel, if you dared."

Something in his words echoed uncomfortably in Tal. *A sliver of truth, perhaps?*

Before he could think of a response, he noticed others approaching. He turned to find four of his companions stepping through a stone archway. Rolan walked in the lead, while Ashelia, Falcon, and Helnor came behind.

"Ah-ha!" Falcon looked over Tal and the courtyard with a raised eyebrow. "So this is what you've been up to when we all thought you were training."

The anger filling Tal eased, and a grin appeared on his lips. "Doesn't seem like I need more training. I wallop the guards anyway, don't I?"

"But that's why we're here!" Rolan piped up. "Or they are, anyway. We issue you a challenge!"

"A challenge?" Tal directed the query at Ashelia.

Her eyes flickered between Pim and Tal. Ever attuned to currents of relationships, she seemed to sense the tension between them. But though worry whirled in her eyes, she went along with the jovial mood.

"Wren had the idea of a sparring match," she said with a smile. "Between you and us."

"Us." Tal looked at Helnor, who crossed his arms and shook his head with a chuckle. "So, you two?"

"Don't be ridiculous — we know you can take them." Falcon waved a dismissive hand as he strolled to the edge of the yard.

"It's not such a certainty!" Helnor objected.

Ashelia put a hand on her brother's shoulder. "No need to boast, Tal — we know what you're capable of. Garin, Wren, and Aelyn should join us soon."

"Aelyn! I'll believe he'll leave the archives when I see it."

He was starting to feel more himself again. *If only Pim left,* he thought, *we might be as we were before him.*

"It would do him good." Ashelia sighed. "But we'll see."

Tal rolled his shoulders and swung his arms around to limber his body. "If I'm to take on the five of you, then I suppose I'd better be ready. Unless you want to join in, Pim?"

He addressed him reluctantly, knowing he couldn't drive a schism between them now. The Soulstealer only shook his head with another of his small sneers.

"I do not think so, Tal Harrenfel. We would not want to attract any undue attention, would we?"

Tal's smile slipped at the reminder. "A fair point. Well then, I suppose there's nothing for it but to wait."

But as he looked away from Pim's gaze, he wondered how much longer they could afford to delay.

THE LEGACY OF DRAGONS

GARIN AND WREN FOUND THEIR RECLUSIVE COMPANION JUST where they expected: locked away in the palace archives.

Recognized by the guards at the golden double doors, the two youths stepped inside the hall, and Garin breathed in. No other place smelled like the archives. Though its contents were preserved well, a hint of mildew snuck into the sprawling underground chambers. The air was dry and cool, courtesy of vast stone slabs that erupted from the floor, ceiling, and walls and glowed with glyphs, like the stones of the Ruins of Erlodan. Red werelights lit their way, the hue apparently the easiest for the archives' treasures to tolerate.

Bookcases towered around them, rising nearly as high as Kavaugh's walls. Innumerable tomes lined the shelves, time-frayed bindings facing outward in a muted, yet still colorful palette. Many had received treatment beyond the simple preservation tactics of human librarians such as Garin had encountered in the Coral Castle. Upon seeing how resilient the books were, he opened himself to the Song and heard a thousand trills sounding from the pages. A closer examination revealed the truth: they were enchanted, and thus in nearly the same condition as when they'd been recovered.

But books weren't the oldest artifacts within the Sun Palace's archives. Drawers held more ancient scrolls, and older still were the words etched into stone, petrified wood, and other natural surfaces. Though on hardier substances than paper, their age alone warranted the utmost care in handling them, and Garin had never dared the attempt.

As expected, he and Wren found Aelyn hunched over a table in this section. Before him was one of the stone scrolls that the Origins preferred. Enchanted in a way that even the mage had admitted he didn't understand, the gray rock bent just as paper would, though with a good deal more resistance, and would roll into itself as well. The runes on its surface were still as sharp and legible as if they'd been etched that day, though of course neither Garin nor Wren could read them. Even Aelyn, with his expansive knowledge of ancient lore, struggled to interpret the words of the elder race.

"Too many secrets…" the mage muttered as they approached, seeming to speak to himself, for he didn't look up at them. "Too many webs…"

Wren gave Garin a look, then put on a bracing smile. "There he is! Just the mage we were looking for."

Aelyn startled and glared up at them. "Ah. Of course you two would interrupt me now."

Garin grinned. "Bad timing?"

The elf only answered with a glower.

"Whatever has your thoughts in a tangle," Wren said, "you can unravel it later. Come with us — the others are waiting."

"Waiting?" For a moment, Aelyn seemed alarmed. "Have I forgotten something?"

Garin knew the mage was deep into his studies if he suspected he might be wrong about something.

"Nothing like that," he assured Aelyn. "We're sparring with Tal, remember? Rolan told you yesterday. Thought it might be good practice for all of us."

"And we're going now," Wren added. "Time to say goodbye to your relics and see daylight for a change."

A smirk twisted the mage's lips. "You expect me to leave off important research to further inflate that irksome man's self-importance?" He snorted a laugh and turned back to his artifact.

Garin nodded at Wren, indicating he'd take a turn. Crossing her arms, she shrugged as if to say, *Be my guest.*

He moved around the table and peered at the stone scroll. "Ikvaldar again?"

Aelyn looked up, but for a moment, he seemed to see through him. Then he blinked and his eyes narrowed.

"No!" he snapped. "Not Ikvaldar! The *ava'duala*!"

"Dragons?" Wren, unable to help herself, spoke up.

"What else has that name?" Aelyn shed his derision as he bent over the stone scroll once more. "This is an Origin treaty on the life cycle of a dragon. They seem to follow a similar pattern as ordinary reptiles, yet there are... irregularities."

"Such as?" Garin prompted, his interest piqued.

"They never possess young!" Aelyn seemed liable to strike the artifact from the furious spinning of his tendrils. "That is, they are born — yet they are born as they die."

"That doesn't make sense." Wren seemed curious as well, though by her twitching limbs, it was with the reluctance of a fly trapped in spider silk. "How can they never be young?"

Garin thought over the dream-memory Ilvuan had shared with him. "They at least come from eggs."

The other two stared at him.

"Since when did you become the dragon expert?" Wren snipped.

"Since one nested in my head."

"Oh." She winced. "Right."

Garin flashed her a grin. "Ilvuan showed me the cave where they kept them. Eggs remain there, ones that can hatch."

Aelyn stood so suddenly that Garin took a step back.

"There are viable eggs? And you are only just mentioning this?" With each utterance, the mage's voice became shriller.

Garin held up his hands. "Easy, Aelyn. He just showed me yesterday."

Aelyn continued to stare at Garin, but his gaze had gone distant again. "If there are eggs, and they are viable... This changes everything."

Garin felt fresh chills wash over him. He'd spent little time on his decision regarding Ilvuan's task, not knowing what he should do about it. But now, the implications became obvious to him once more.

Wren looked between the two of them. "What?" she demanded. "Are you saying the dragons could return?"

"Yes!" Aelyn snapped, eyes dancing with fiery light. "The *ava'duala* might once more soar through the skies!"

Garin pictured it through Ilvuan's memories. *Dragons.* The idea of it filled him equally with elation and trepidation. Ilvuan had saved his life on several occasions and lent him knowledge and power that had saved him countless other times. But though he trusted the Singer, goodwill could only extend so far. Ilvuan had always made it clear that his aid came with a price. From the time he'd first helped Garin defeat the Extinguished Soltor, he'd bound him with an inscrutable oath.

Bring balance to power. Return the Song to the Mother.

Often, he'd mentioned his task for Garin. And now he'd stated it explicitly.

Garin was going to bring dragons back into the World.

Silence greeted the mage's words as they each mulled over them. Wren was shaking her head. Aelyn practically trembled with ardor.

Garin roused from his thoughts first. "We'll think it through with the others later. For now, they're waiting."

Wren seized upon the reminder. "You're right. Aelyn, Garin will tell you more of his dragon's secrets if you come with us. We have to show Tal he's not invulnerable."

Not that he's ever boasted it. Garin had heard his former mentor make the opposite assertion plenty of times: *I've never claimed to be more than a man.*

When Aelyn hesitated, his gaze traveling back down to the stone scroll, Wren prodded him further. "You think that old thing will tell you more than an actual dragon could?"

The mage scowled and began carefully rolling the artifact back up. "Fine! But you will tell me everything you know following this folly, boy. Everything!"

"If I must." Garin wondered how Ilvuan would like him revealing his race's secrets. The Singer had never seemed fond of him sharing their conversations, but the dragon had been light in his reprimands of late. Almost, Garin could imagine they were growing fond of one another.

Almost.

BLOOD & SONG

"And just as Tal was about to run on stage and save the princess," Falcon said, "who else shows up but Kaleras the Impervious?"

Tal listened as the bard told the story to a wide-eyed Rolan, employing all the theatrics of a trouper before a crowd. He couldn't help but picture the late warlock. Kaleras' brown eyes, so similar to his own. His wry humor and sharp wit. The unrelenting stubbornness he'd passed on to his son. Tal wondered if, had he had a son of his own, he would have his grandfather's eyes as well.

Not liable to find out, he thought with a wry smile.

"So what did he do?" Rolan, ever the obliging audience, prompted the troubadour on.

Falcon spread his arms. "He ran, of course! Every trouper knows the escape routes from a venue, for you never know when a crowd will become unruly. Tal was every bit the stager in those days, and he was quick to find the exit. But Kaleras glimpsed him before he left, and so he pursued... Ah, but there they are!"

Tal looked up as the three companions they'd been waiting on entered the courtyard. His eyes locked with Garin's, and he nodded at the youth, to which Garin smiled. Over the past couple of months, something like reconciliation had finally come between them, time and proximity healing what no amount of words could. The youth had become more thoughtful of late, almost withdrawn, spending far more hours in the garden than Tal ever would have at his age. Yet he wasn't a misanthrope like Aelyn, but still as generous of spirit as Ashelia.

He couldn't claim any credit for the man Garin was becoming, but he took pride in it all the same.

"We finally dragged him away from his toys," Wren announced as they closed the distance. The gold in her eyes danced with anticipation, but it lessened as she glanced at Pim, who remained in the far corner of the courtyard. Garin also grimaced at the sight of the Extinguished, while Aelyn stared with a mixture of hostility and interest. Pim only smiled.

"Oh, do not mind me," the fell warlock told them. "I am an inquisitive bystander, nothing more."

Wren snorted a laugh, then ignored him. "Right. You found the practice blades?"

Helnor, who had fetched the weapons rack from its store-room, gestured to where it waited. "As you commanded, Your Grace."

As the young woman arched an eyebrow at him, Ashelia headed off any further remarks. "We shouldn't delay. There is still much work to be done, and I'm sure Aelyn would appreciate a swift contest."

While the mage scowled and looked over his shoulder as if to return to his work even then, Tal voiced the emotions broiling inside him. "Perhaps we shouldn't spar. As you say, there are many things to do, and our time here may be shorter than we hope."

His eyes slid over to Pim as he spoke, remembering his news and the words of the Emperor the day before. Despite the excuses Tal had made, he knew they couldn't delay in seeking this alchemist. But his resistance to action stood before him. Ashelia wore the bulky cloth gambeson that would guard against the sparring blades, and simple braids restrained her springy hair. Yet her eyes alighting on his was enough to set his pulse racing.

How can I yield even a moment? How can I give up what we've just rediscovered?

She'd never had Geminia's ability to perceive thoughts, yet Tal suspected Ashelia guessed his by the swirling in her eyes.

"Which is why we have to do this now," Wren pressed. "Rushing to Ikvaldar won't do us any good if we get killed there. We have to know what it's like to face someone of your power, Tal. And you need better sparring dummies than palace guards."

Tal glanced around and saw the argument had swayed the others. Even Ashelia gave him a slight shrug. He lowered his gaze and sighed.

"He's going to do it," Rolan confided in a stage whisper to Falcon.

Giving the lad a look of mock irritation, Tal spun on his heel and headed for the opposite side of the courtyard, setting Lament aside as he went.

"Fine. I'll make this quick."

By the nervous laughter of his companions, they knew how likely that possibility was.

After they'd equipped themselves, Garin gathered with the others inside Aelyn's orb of silence to plan.

"Here's what we'll do," Helnor said. "Wren, Ashelia, Garin, you three strike at him with me. We'll spread out so he can't hit us all in one sweep. Aelyn, you hit him with everything you have."

"Poignant instruction," the mage snipped in reply.

"Shouldn't more of us cast spells?" Wren queried. "He's a devil with a blade as well as sorcery."

"His first move will be to cut off our magic," Ashelia explained. "Blades will be more dependable."

Garin cleared his throat. "I think I'll still be able to cast."

His companions' gazes traveled over to him.

"Why?" Aelyn asked with eyes narrowed.

Garin shrugged. "I haven't tested it yet, but I know my sorcery works differently. Because of the Worldsong, or maybe from speaking the Darktongue."

Ashelia nodded. "We'll test it. Hang back until you know. If you can still touch sorcery, cover us. If you cannot, join in the assault."

Aelyn eyed Garin. "Don't make this a waste of my time," he warned.

"I'll try my best."

"Speaking of wasting time." Helnor nodded at Aelyn, and the mage let the orb of silence fall as they turned to face Tal at the other end of the courtyard.

Garin studied Tal as he positioned himself behind the three leading the charge. He'd never fought against his old mentor before. Now that Garin faced him, all his impossible deeds rushed through his head.

Red Reaver. Magebutcher. Devil Killer. Death's Hand.

The man wore a smile more often than not, but Tal was far from a gentle man. A warrior lived inside him, and they were about to glimpse it from the wrong side.

He clenched his jaw and steeled himself. He'd come through his own trials. *Draugars. Ravagers. Demons and Soulstealers.* Tal had his storied legend, but Garin heard the Song.

He opened himself to its strains as Helnor called their challenge across the courtyard.

"On my count!"

Tal still hadn't formed a plan as his companions broke from their huddle to face him.

He'd done little to prepare while they conferred in their orb of silence. Sorcery prickled his veins, itching like the sun's first touch upon shaded skin. He had no strategy.

But a different problem preoccupied him: how he would meet their charge and not harm them.

Tal knew he could match them. When sparring with the palace guards, he'd overcome any number of them, half a dozen as easily as a score. With sorcery flooding through him, he had access to boundless energy to fuel his movements and strengthen his blows. Should he cast spells as well, he didn't doubt even his formidable friends wouldn't withstand the onslaught. And hexes against him would be blocked by the Ring of Thalkuun on his finger.

But he hadn't sparred with them before for good reason. His power was the closest to matching a god's that he knew of. Since his canker's eradication, he'd gained finer control of the sorcery, but he couldn't guarantee their safety.

They've never been safe near me.

Tal sighed and hefted his stave, flourishing it to limber his wrist. He'd only just accepted the necessity of the bout when Helnor called across the training square.

"On my count! Three..."

Tal closed his eyes and inhaled. As he did, he opened himself to the torrent ever at the edge of his awareness. Sorcery blossomed within him. It felt like the birth of a forest fire, charging through him with blistering speed and touching every inch of his flesh. He felt his skin must burst into flames with the force of it.

"Two..."

With his connection to the World established, he saw with fresh eyes the web of sorcery connecting his friends. All of them were significant, though Aelyn's was easily the greatest of them. But it was Garin's that drew his attention.

Instead of streaming into him, the sorcery seemed to flow around and by him. Because of its movements, it was deceptive in how large it was. Almost, he thought it rivaled Aelyn's capacity.

"Now!"

Tal swept across their connection to sorcery, and not even Aelyn could withstand his severing. As the mage squawked, the foremost three charged at him. Helnor, Ashelia, and Wren had trained as hard as he had in the months they'd stayed at Zyrl's palace, and they swiftly closed the distance. Garin didn't join them, but advanced slowly along with Aelyn, though he kept his stave clutched in one hand.

Then they were upon him. Tal kept his sorcery tucked within him, using it for speed and strength. His weapon rebuffed their initial strikes, and soon he grew confident. If twice as many palace guards couldn't break his defenses, surely not even Helnor, Ashelia, and Wren could accomplish it.

But soon, he found himself hard-pressed to stay ahead. Wren flowed through the elven forms with nearly as much mastery as the two Warders. Tal barely had time to register a strike before he was forced to dodge or counter it. The three worked well together, timing their strikes so Tal couldn't meet them all at once. Yet with the sorcery incinerating his veins, he was faster than any of them, and he struck twice as hard. Helnor grunted as he took a hit to his buckler, which cracked down the middle and sent him staggering back. Tal twisted around to meet Ashelia's strike, then kicked her leg out from under her so she sprawled in the dirt. No time for guilt — Wren already pressed to take advantage, landing a light strike on his forearm.

Before he could punish her overextension, sorcery flourished from the far side of the courtyard.

Tal only just registered it coming from Garin before he threw up a wind shield against it. The Ring of Thalkuun could have weathered it for him, but instinct had seized him in the moment. The fire plume shot to either side, causing Rolan and Falcon to flee back toward the courtyard's entrance.

Garin wasn't dissuaded, but followed up his first attack with a second, a stone spell that uprooted the pavers at the courtyard's edge and threw them at Tal. Wisely, the youth was using an indirect spell, against which the artifact on Tal's finger wouldn't protect. Tal countered the hex, spawning a localized quake under the youth's feet to send him to his knees. How Garin got around the sorcerous blockade, Tal couldn't begin to guess, but he admired the youth for it.

Tal's lapse in concentration earned him a stinging blow to his back. Throwing himself into a forward roll, Tal faced Helnor, Ashelia, and Wren once again, all three recovered. Aelyn fought furiously against Tal's barricade and accessed a trickle of sorcery. Garin was shouting something in the Darktongue.

He only realized what as ice blossomed under his feet.

Tal went down on his knees as he threw sorcery against the packed dirt to thaw it. It was a vulnerable position, and his companions took full advantage. Ashelia kicked him in the chest, forcing him into an awkward roll. Helnor hit his arm with a blow that would have broken bones had his sorcery not bolstered him. Wren kept him too preoccupied to retaliate against either of the others, and Garin sent another spell down on him, a wash of rain that turned into deadly frozen daggers.

Despite himself, rage rose like a tide within him, fueled by pain and frustration. The sorcery bubbled in his veins, then boiled.

Tal rose, and a storm broke out around him.

Garin had only just summoned an ice storm against Tal when his old mentor changed the game.

Wind, so scathing it felt as if it would rip the skin from his face, billowed out from the man, driving Helnor, Ashelia, and Wren away and scattering Garin's falling ice. Garin immediately cut off the spell, fearful that an errant spike might find an unintended target, then cried out, "*Dord heks!*"

A slab of earth rose between him and the building tornado, but it only stood for moments before Tal's sorcery tore through it. The wind was so loud in his ears he could barely hear the Worldsong.

Aelyn gave a faint cry of triumph, then a glowing ray, like a beam of light made into fire, shot out from his hands. For a moment, it seemed it would land at Tal's feet, no doubt with the intention of throwing him, but nothing escaped the man. Tal didn't dodge, but threw up a hand, and with no apparent resistance, the lancing ray halted a few feet away from him, then shredded. The mage cried out in frustration, but a moment later he set into another incantation.

Garin knew then they didn't have a hope of matching Tal. Even with spells powerful enough to kill, they couldn't overcome his power, nor penetrate the protection of the Ring of Thalkuun. His sorcery was a flood as he threw it against them. Though Garin still accessed his own magic despite Tal's best efforts, it was far from enough.

He wondered if anything could stop him.

But this was why they were sparring. To challenge and improve one another. He couldn't surrender at the first sign of adversity. He had to be clever.

How to kill an enemy who's stronger, swifter, and more experienced?

An idea occurred to him, and he seized upon it.

Garin drew on the Song and let its sorcery sweep through his body, then directed it toward Tal. Like he'd seen his old mentor do, he tried to form it first into a knife, and when that failed, into a sharp gust. It was likely a vain hope, but he intended to do to Tal what he had done to them.

He would cut him off from the power that made him what he was.

With sorcery inhabiting him, Tal pulsed with his own song, just as the stone hearts of the golems and the black bracers had. But his mentor's was much louder and crashed as if with drums and horns. Garin aimed his sorcery for the heart of it, seeing if he could silence it.

Almost as soon as he made the attempt, he knew it was futile. Tal's song was too loud and furious. All he could hope to do was distract him.

Disappointed, Garin drew back in time for a wave of wind to send him sprawling to the ground.

The impact sent the air whooshing from his lungs. For a moment, he couldn't inhale; then his chest loosened and he sucked in a ragged breath. His head spun, but he fought his way to his knees and tried to think of another spell.

A shriek cut through the air, and the ground trembled.

Garin startled and whirled around. At first, he couldn't make sense of the sight. Pim, normally so smug and self-possessed, had fallen to his knees. His back was arched, his head thrown back. From his mouth eked out pained gasps. Garin watched in horror as the illusion of the golden elf fell away and left behind the crystal-pocked countenance with pit-dark eyes.

Tal's storm died at once, and the man raced past the others to fall to his knees next to the Extinguished. Only then did Garin realize what was happening.

At long last, Yuldor had come for his treacherous servant.

Ignoring his companions' cries, Tal crossed the courtyard at a sprint and fell before the possessed Extinguished.

"Pim! *Pim!* Damn you, man, stay with me!"

He didn't know what drove him to desperation. He'd been

suspicious of the Soulstealer ever since he learned his true identity. Inanis, as he'd called himself before, had manipulated Tal into killing innocents and provoking war between the dwarven clans. Yet Pim had also saved his life and brought him closer to his ultimate goal. He'd been a friend of sorts.

And now he suffered at the hands of the Enemy.

Before he could think better of it, Tal seized Pim's rigid hands. At once, the maelstrom that gripped the Extinguished spread to him.

Tal nearly lost himself in it. His power eclipsed anyone he knew, but the torrent that poured through Pim now was far vaster than he could hope to match. He felt like a pebble tossed in river rapids, unable to help being swept up.

Then the voices spoke.

"*Why do you delay?*" The mocking voice came first, and though it used Pim's tongue, Tal recognized it as the same one that had spoken through Hashele. "*We are waiting for you, Skaldurak!*"

The Soulstealer's neck twisted to one side so a normal man's spine would have snapped. Then his face came back around with a vague smile.

"*There is no need to strive as you have. Do you not flirt with death? We will give its comfort to you. All you must do is come...*"

Tal tried to seize these entities that inhabited Pim, but he barely had the strength to avoid succumbing to them. His resolution almost broke as a third being boomed through Pim.

"*Challenge us, Skaldurak! If you believe you can take the Heart for your own, then make the attempt! But if you refuse, we will hunt you to the ends of this World. You will not escape us to your dying day!*"

Pim sagged, and the sorcery that had seized him and Tal thinned. Before the last of the stream faded, one final voice spoke.

"*Peace... bring me peace...*"

Then Pim's eyes met Tal's, and the Extinguished collapsed into ashes.

Tal barely oriented back to his own body before his companions were shaking him. "Tal!" Ashelia spoke hoarsely in his ear. "Tal, are you alright?" She held him tightly, as if she feared he was dead.

Before he could respond, one horn sounded from a distance. Another joined it a moment later, then a horn came from the palace walls.

"What's that mean?" Wren asked, voice shrill. "Why do they call?"

"An attack." Helnor stared back toward where the horns had first called. "The Named has tired of waiting."

Tal grasped after his sorcery, seeing if he could sense more, when Aelyn hissed and pointed upward. "*Kolsk!* He sent cock-atrices!"

An attack. Tal met Ashelia's eyes, and only at her expression did he accept the truth.

Their respite had ended. The war had begun.

FAEFIRE

GARIN COULD ONLY STARE AT THE ABOMINATIONS AS THEY descended from the clouds.

Their bright hues shone in stark contrast to the gray sky. With feathers of lichen green and river-froth white, their broad wings stretched twice the length of their bodies as they dove toward them. Tails, thick and serpentine, curled against their backs, and massive talons bunched close to their feathery bellies. Their heads were like roosters, but malformed into horrific proportions. The comb and wattle were blue, and the yellow raptor eyes, innocent enough in a farmyard cockerel, promised swift deaths.

As they neared, Garin turned to Tal and caught his eye, then flashed him a manic smile. "It would be bloody chickens, wouldn't it?"

The one-time chicken farmer stared for a moment, then slowly returned the grin. "Yes. I suppose it would."

"Get inside, now!" Helnor spurred them into action, seizing Garin and Wren by the shoulder and hustling them toward the archway.

"We won't make it!" Wren retorted as she shrugged off the Prime's hand. Ignoring his shouts, she ran toward the racks of weapons. Garin ran after her, desperate not to let her stray too far.

"What are you doing?" he asked, even as he saw the unstrung bow in her hand.

"What's it look like?"

Unhooking a string from the rack, Wren straddled the bow, then used her leg to bend it back and slip the string over the tip. Hefting it, she slung a quiver over her chest, then drew and notched an arrow before staring at him.

"Are you going to grab one or what?"

Garin hesitated, then shook his head. "I'm better off with spells."

Wren grimaced and moved after the others. "Your grave."

The cockatrices were nearly upon the courtyard, buffeting out their wings as they slowed. An overpowering stench of reptile and bird feces blew over them. Soon, they would be within range to seize them with pitiless talons.

Helnor had followed Wren's lead and strung a bow of his own. Aelyn and Tal, who had hustled after him, appeared content with sorcery, while Ashelia had taken her son in hand and had her other on Falcon's back in a protective gesture. Rolan bared his teeth, desperately trying to be brave, while the bard made no secret of his trembling.

"In the middle of it every damn time," Garin heard Falcon mutter. "How am I to compose if I'm fleeing for my life?"

There was no more time for conversation. Focusing on the Worldsong flowing through him, Garin called upon its sorcery as three of the cockatrices dove for them.

"*Keld thasht!*"

Garin's spell joined the rest of the barrage against the Nightkin beasts. As his column of flames found one, Wren and Helnor's arrows shot into the breast of another, while Aelyn caught the third with a volley of stone spires. None were killing blows, however, and the cockatrices continued to hurtle toward them.

Shouts sounded all around him, and Garin threw up his hands. "*Jolsh heks!*"

But as a gust billowed out from his hands, skin-scathing winds rushed farther overhead to throw the Nightkin beasts across the courtyard. He knew where they came from even before he looked.

The winds swirled around Tal, pressing his tunic and trousers flat as he raised his hands up to contend with their next assailants. His hair whipped free of its tail, but he barely seemed to notice, his lips pulled back in a snarl.

And we believed we could match him.

But the next round of cockatrices was diving, and this time half a dozen came at once. Garin threw a rapid series of spells, fire and stone injuring two more of the beasts. Aelyn switched tactics, using ice to weigh down the beasts' wings to their squawking protests. When Helnor and Wren's arrows proved ineffective amid Tal's storm, they moved after Ashelia, Falcon, and Rolan, yelling for Garin and the others to follow.

As Tal threw the cockatrices again across the courtyard, the first three adapted to his tactics. Screaming, they didn't launch back into the air, but scurried across the broken stones and bore down on them. Garin saw now just how large they were, each stretching twice his height and with talons that could crush his head.

"Yuldor's prick — *Dord asht kild! Vuudisk rayn fend!*"

Garin ran after the others, throwing spells behind to cover their escape. At his words, ice spread across the packed dirt of the yard, sending the Nightkin beasts sprawling, followed by earthen spires erupting to impale two of the cockatrices. The Worldsong blared through his head with all the sorcery flowing through him, painful in its sharpness. He wondered if, at last, he pressed against his limits.

Aelyn hurried after him, his hands diving into his robes for spell implements, then using them in rapid succession. Lightning flared from a short measure of wood, though it seemed to shock the mage as well, judging by his spluttering curses. A golden disc shone brightly before light erupted outward, filling the air above the cockatrices with countless floating sparks, like dust motes in bands of light. As the sparks descended on the grounded Nightkin, they ignited on their feathers, and a rancid stench filled the air along with screeches of pain.

Garin caught Aelyn as the mage staggered through the archway to the next courtyard and ignored the elf's protests. Turning, he saw not all of their party had followed.

"Tal!" Garin called back. "Come on!"

The man was nearly lost from sight amid the swirling dirt and wind, which twisted about him like the dust devils Garin had heard frequented the deserts to the east. He battered away cockatrices above even as he stretched a hand toward the burning beasts before him. For a moment, Garin couldn't tell what he was doing; then he saw the stone walls surrounding the courtyard cracking and crumbling.

Tal meant to bury them all.

But before the walls could fall, a cockatrice, still struggling despite his wings being aflame, lunged for Tal, its talons stretched forward. Garin's mouth opened to yell a warning, though he knew it would come too late.

Aelyn lurched away from Garin and threw out a hand. Something bright burst from whatever he held and knocked into the Nightkin. The mage's casting packed a powerful punch, for the cockatrice went careening off its path to crash into the wall next to Tal.

The near miss still failed to rouse Tal. He closed a fist and pressed it down, and the walls cracked, then tumbled down. Finally, the man turned and ran toward them. The cockatrice who had tried to kill him stood drunkenly and gave a halting pursuit until a chunk of stone sent it back to the ground.

"He's coming!" Garin yelled to Aelyn as he hauled the mage away from the battle. There were two more courtyards before they could enter back into the palace interior. At the doors, their companions waited. Helnor and Wren had their bows notched. They yelled something, but between the racket of the cockatrices and the Song filling his head, Garin couldn't hear a word.

They stumbled through a second courtyard before Tal caught up. But no sooner had they reached the archway than the man stopped and threw his head back to stare at the sky. Garin stuttered to a halt with him, the mage he supported barely keeping his feet.

"Tal!" Garin yelled. "Keep going!"

But Tal was already flaring with his song again, sorcery flowing through his veins. "Go!" his old mentor shouted without looking around, the word reverberating with power.

Garin looked up and saw it. In any other circumstance, he would have thought the creature beautiful. Its plumage was red and gold, and as the wind blew through it, the feathers shimmered. Its body was an eagle's, but it was even larger than a cockatrice. Its eyes were like twin coals set in its bright head, and its talons boasted black curved ends.

But it was the infernal song that billowed from it that set Garin's hairs on end.

"*Go!*" Tal commanded again. This time, Garin obeyed, dragging Aelyn as quickly as he could behind him, and hoping Tal hadn't finally met his match.

When he'd learned of phoenixes under the tutelage of old Magister Elis, Tal had been fascinated by the single feather his master had claimed from one.

"Must be large," he'd observed as he saw how the feather stretched the length of his arm.

"Quite large," Elis had agreed with a smile. "But it is not

their size that should worry one pursued by a phoenix, but their sorcery."

Tal, then an arrogant youth, only snorted. "What can it do?"

Elis had shaken his head. "It is an inferno given flesh, Tal. With its faefire, it can set a city ablaze, melt stone to metal. What is more, it will be reborn from the ashes. You cannot kill a phoenix. You can only flee."

"And this?" Tal held up the brilliant feather. "How did you claim this?"

"Serendipity." The Magister, prone to suffering the occasional bout of mischief, smiled mysteriously. "Suffice to say that as a youth, I was sometimes as foolish as you are now."

Tal had brushed the feather under his nose and breathed in the sulfurous scent imbued in it before he grinned. "I doubt that."

The memory raced through his head as Tal stared up at the phoenix. It had been a happy moment, but echoes of alarm came with it. *An inferno given flesh*, Elis had said. *It can set a city ablaze.*

He couldn't run from this Nightkin, not without the risk that it would kill all of them as soon as they set foot within the palace. There was more than his companions to think of. A hundred thousand citizens lived within these walls. Would he doom them to fiery death as well?

You were never this foolish, Elis, Tal thought as he sucked as much sorcery into himself as he could bear.

The phoenix descended until it hovered a score of feet above him. With each beat of its massive wings, power flowed from it, pressing against his sorcerous sense. Tal saw a torrent of sorcery pouring into it from the World's core. At the sight of it, he believed the old Magister's claims. He couldn't say if his or the Nightkin's strength was greater.

It didn't matter; he would match it. He had no other choice.

Tal's first thought was to cut off its sorcery, then kill it before it could spread its faefire. But as he looked closer at its connection to sorcery, he knew it wouldn't work. Just as with Garin's power, the magic seemed not to enter the beast, but flow past and around it before reentering the ground. There was no one connection he could sever, and to cut through them all would likely be beyond him.

The great eagle grew brighter. Tal's heart hammered against his ribcage as panic set in. He had to contain it. Pulling on the reservoir boiling within him, he began weaving a sorcerous web around the phoenix, sealing it tighter with each pass.

The Nightkin's incandescent feathers shimmered as if already aflame. The phoenix threw back its head, and its call was as beautiful as its appearance. It seemed impossible that it could mean him or anyone harm. He longed to stop what he was doing and merely watch...

The Ring of Thalkuun burned cold on his finger, bringing Tal back to himself and shielding him from the creature's glamour. He clenched his jaw and kept weaving.

The heat radiating from the giant bird had become blistering, and it took all his will to remain where he was. There were too many gaps in his work, and it was too tenuous. He'd never done what he strove to do now. He didn't know if it was even possible.

As two needles of sorcery dove into the phoenix's chest, however, he realized he wasn't alone.

Glancing toward the doors, he saw Wren and Helnor notching second arrows to their bows, then each yell out a word of the Worldtongue to freeze the ends of their arrows. Aiming, they released them. Though they flashed with fire as they neared the phoenix, the ice negated the heat enough to allow the steel heads to pierce the majestic bird.

The phoenix cried, and Tal nearly fell to his knees from the sorrow in it. Wren and Helnor must have felt it as well, for their efforts faltered and their arms fell as if their bows had become too heavy to hold. But another stepped out between them and threw his head back to stare at the phoenix. His face was set in a desperate grimace, and his hands were clenched at his sides.

Tal tried to cry out to Garin, to tell him to flee with the others, but he couldn't get a word out.

The end was nearing. The phoenix was too bright to look at directly, its light like lancing knives in his eyes. His orb around it seemed so feeble and thin.

He couldn't contain it.

He wanted to scream, to rage, to strike at it. But all he could do was keep trying. Sorcery overflowed in him and burned away his other senses. There was only him and the phoenix. Kaleras' ring wouldn't protect him from what was coming. Only one of them would prevail.

The Nightkin eagle called again — then its final spell burst outward.

———

Garin could barely think through the noise.

The Song had faded as his use of spells eased, though it continued to caterwaul inside his skull. Far louder was the discordant strain thundering from the phoenix. Its song was enough to split his head open.

Yet all the same, he listened.

There was an allure to it, but misery was its melody. It was a song commemorating its coming demise and all the killing it would cause. A final requiem. It burned even to listen to, burned almost his sense of self away.

He couldn't merely listen.

Garin reached forth as he had with the dragon songs in the bracers, the same way he had into the golems' stone hearts. He tried convincing the phoenix to join the great Worldsong flowing around them, but this Nightkin was no passive remnant of a dead dragon. It was alive and full of vitality and purpose. It wouldn't willingly yield.

Garin gave up the attempt and retreated. His head felt as if an axe had cleaved it in two, but he refused to relent. He moved to his next desperate thought: to strike at its very sorcery. Forming the magic into a razor-thin edge, he tried carving into the phoenix's core. But it was like ramming a dull knife against a stone wall; though he threw all he had into it, it gave little ground.

The spell was coming to a climax. The death song rose and tried to swallow him down.

He swam above it, clinging to the Worldsong as he tried to come up with some plan that would save them. But he was out of ideas. He'd failed.

They were all going to die.

Garin retreated, but he didn't go far. Tal's song radiated strongly from him still as he wrapped sorcery around the phoenix. Garin moved toward him; why, he didn't know. Perhaps he craved comfort in these last moments. Perhaps it was mere instinct for the weak to go to the strong.

Garin let himself be swept up in his song. He pulled the Worldsong with him, and as it swelled around them, it amplified and intertwined with Tal's sorcerous sound.

With a final cry, the phoenix's song climaxed, and death rushed to claim them.

ASHES

TAL KNEW HOW THIS WOULD END.

He was insufficient. His sorcery, potent as it was, couldn't hope to contain the phoenix.

Then another joined him.

He couldn't say how they were connected. The presence spread through every fiber of his being. It felt like his belly did after swallowing a glass of whiskey, only the presence touched not only his body, but inundated his sorcery as well. The orb he'd made, thin and frail on its own, became hard and rigid, his efforts suddenly doubled.

Until that moment, he'd known the phoenix's faefire would kill them all. But after the joining, he could only hold to his web and hope.

The phoenix gave a final haunting cry. The light emanating from it drove claws into his skull. The heat became unbearable, searing flesh with its touch, then grew hotter still.

Sorcery erupted outward.

Agony split him apart, yet Tal clung to his weaving. Vaguely, he was aware he'd fallen to his knees, his fingers scrabbling against the stone, his forehead pressing against the dust, his lips whispering meaningless sounds. Fire lanced through him, body and soul. Within, he was ashes, a hollowed out vessel. Soon, his skin would burn away, leaving nothing behind but bones.

But as abruptly as it began, the assault ceased.

Tal clung to his spellwork still, not daring to believe what his senses told him. The faefire had stretched on as if for an eternity, yet as it ended, he became aware it had only lasted a few moments. His heart beat out the seconds that passed. He counted a dozen, then two. His body buzzed as his over-wrought senses reasserted themselves.

Only as the ghost lifted from his mind did he realize he had still been there.

Safe, the phantom whispered, like a murmur on a breeze. Then, as if it were nothing more than the wind, it lifted and faded away.

Tal felt the emptiness left behind with its passage. It felt lonely to be by himself in his skin. But he couldn't remain forever separate from the World.

Slowly, he refocused on his surroundings.

His eyes fluttered open to blurry faces above him. He'd expected a gray sky, but golden light on a distant ceiling greeted him instead. As he attenuated to his sense of touch, he felt carpet beneath his back through his shirt.

"Tal! Mother be blessed, you're alive, you're alive..."

Lips pressed against his forehead. As they pulled away, he squinted and recognized Ashelia. Her hair had sprung loose of its bindings, and her eyes were puffy around the spinning gray. Her hands cradled his head.

"How?" he croaked.

"We thought you could tell us." Aelyn's irritated voice sounded from above.

Tal smiled, the expression feeling foreign. "'Fraid I have to disappoint."

"We'll discuss this later," Helnor said, sounding more like the Prime Warder of old. "Garin, can you stand?"

"I'll help him," Wren spoke from farther down the hall.

"Ashelia and I can assist Tal," Falcon said from above Tal's head. "If you'll sit up, old friend…"

Knowing they were still in danger, Tal complied, or tried to. Every muscle protested and rebelled, trying to throw him back to the carpeted stone. He gritted his teeth and sucked at the sorcery waiting just at the edge of his awareness. It hurt to touch, yet a thin stream of it bolstered his strength enough to walk.

Falcon rose under one arm, while Ashelia appeared under the other and held to his belt. *Helshax* hung there again, though he'd removed it before their friendly bout.

"Let's move," his beloved said to the others, her voice phlegmy from tears. "We have to get somewhere safe."

"No." Tal's objection came out in a rasp. "Zyrl. We have to protect the Emperor."

Ashelia frowned at him. "Tal, you're barely standing. You cannot protect anyone."

"Much as I hate to admit it, Harrenfel is right." Aelyn's mouth twisted in a sour pucker. "Emperor Zyrl is central to our scheme. Should he die, we will fail."

Helnor clapped Tal on the shoulder. "He'll be fine! Won't you, Tal?"

Tal winced. "Fine as I can be," he said through gritted teeth.

Falcon let loose a small, mirthless laugh.

Ashelia peered at him a moment longer, then sighed. "Fine. Stay close, Rolan."

Tal hoped they'd encountered the last of the dangers facing them. But from the shouts and clashing steel echoing down the hall ahead, he suspected it was a vain hope.

"What in Yuldor's black name happened back there?" Wren muttered as she hauled Garin after the others.

He could only shrug. It was an honest response. Whatever he'd done had obviously worked, but the results were still a jumble in his head.

As he and Wren limped down the hall, he tried to remember. The phoenix had been just about to reach its song's climax. In what he'd thought were his last moments, Garin had reached for Tal. But he hadn't only reached for him — he'd intermingled with his old mentor. His song had joined with Tal's.

And he'd brought the Worldsong with him.

What had come after was hazy. He'd lost all sense of his body, but found his thoughts scrambled and confused. Only now did he realize why: not all the thoughts in his mind had been his own.

Garin sat with that realization for a long moment before he spoke.

"We merged," he whispered. "For a moment, Tal and I became one. Like… like Ilvuan did when he took control of my body."

But even as he made the comparison, he knew it wasn't quite right. When Ilvuan controlled him, it was a contest, not cooperation. Yet they had bonded before in a similar way. In the dragon dreams, Garin felt as Ilvuan did, and the Singer easily perceived his thoughts when Garin wasn't careful. He hadn't felt it as their songs interweaving then, but now, he wondered if that wasn't what had occurred.

Wren had been silent, but as the sounds of fighting neared, she finally spoke. "Pull yourself together, Garin. Don't go all Night-crazed on me now."

He silenced his protest before it left his lips. The experience he and Tal had shared was too intricate and vast to explain in a few minutes. Besides, they had more pressing concerns.

But instead of focusing on the fight ahead, Garin stared at Tal's back as he limped between Ashelia and Falcon. He wondered if he'd felt their merging the same as Garin had. If Tal knew he'd helped carry the burden.

Not now. With an effort, Garin repressed the circling questions and braced himself for whatever was coming next.

As they reached the double doors to the Emperor's throne room, Tal watched the last of the invaders fall.

His beloved and his friend still carried his weight. He thought he'd recovered enough to walk on his own, but pride wouldn't catch him if he stumbled. Besides, he'd thought he might need his strength for the fighting ahead. The bodies they passed, the blood they stepped through, and the black smudges from sorcerous fire on the walls pointed to one thing.

Ravagers stalked the halls of the Sun Palace.

But Zyrl's guards had taken care of the invaders already, and the gnome's diminutive form was apparent next to his guards. As they approached, the Emperor's protectors turned with weapons raised, the hands of mages ready to direct spells.

Zyrl halted them. "Wait! My eyes are not poor enough to mistake Tal Harrenfel, even in his sorry state."

Tal might have bowed at the relief of seeing the monarch alive, but he doubted he could have risen again. As they moved between the guards, the others gave small overtures of respect, though the occasion called for little formality.

"Your Majesty," Ashelia said with her usual courtesy, though it came out strained. "Are you well?"

"Well?" The gnome laughed as he crawled back into his throne, hopping from the stepping stool placed before it onto the cushioned stone. "Hardly been better, I dare say! It has been a long while since I cast a proper spell, but what finer occasion than this? To save my own life!"

"Glad to hear it." Tal extracted his arms from Falcon and Ashelia as he spoke, returning the Peer's look of concern with a smile. "I won't make for much of a bodyguard at the moment, yet we would offer ourselves as protection, if you'll have us."

Zyrl laughed again. "Protection? Oh no, my fabled friend. You must leave this palace before you bring down worse than Venators and Nightkin on my poor city!"

"What could be worse?" Wren muttered at Tal's back.

The gnome had sharper ears than his age implied, for he peered around Tal at the young woman. "Plenty of things, my fierce young warrior, plenty of things. But there will be time for you to encounter them still, if you leave now."

Tal swayed. Fleeing Kavaugh seemed nearly as unlikely as fighting. *But what if there is another phoenix?* He couldn't contain a second eruption, and it would be far less likely to spread its faefire if they weren't around, as Zyrl had said.

He glanced at the others. Seeing the fire in their eyes, he said, "Fulfill your end of the bargain, Zyrl Netherstar, and we will uphold ours."

"Oh, I keep in mind very well all our gamble might cost me." With an irreverent smile, the Sun Emperor waved them away. "Watch for the signal fires along the Valanduali Range! When they are lit, my armies are on the march."

"We will."

Tal nodded to Zyrl, then indulged in his pride by walking on his own, leading his companions from the ravaged throne room.

The sounds of battle echoed from distant parts of the palace as Garin moved with the rest of his party to each of their rooms.

They swiftly gathered the necessities for travel. In case there was the need for a quick getaway, they'd packed satchels full of the essentials in advance and intermittently restocked them with perishables as the weeks passed. The precaution paid its worth now.

Garin burst into his room and claimed the rucksack from where he'd tucked it at the bottom of his wardrobe. Next to it leaned *Velori*, still entrusted to him by Tal and never accepted back, despite Garin's insistence. Unbuckling his belt, he slipped the worn scabbard through before tightening the belt back into place. With the World going to chaos, it was a reassuring weight.

A leather jerkin and a traveling cloak, unworn but solidly woven, joined the rest, then Garin turned for the door to rejoin the others. Before he made it, he paused and glanced back. His room at the palace had been spacious compared to what he was used to. It put him in mind of just a year before, when he'd dreamed on a straw-stuffed mattress of walking through such corridors as this palace boasted.

You've come a long way from Hunt's Hollow, Garin Dunford.

The nostalgia fled as quickly as it had come. Peril still haunted the Sun Palace's halls. With a last glance around, Garin hefted his pack, wriggled the straps into place over his shoulders, and stepped through the door.

When the others were clad in their own light armor and had weapons in hand, they left the palace through the servants' door they'd first entered several months before, then headed for the stables. There, they recovered the stors remaining to them as well as the newly gifted horses. Garin had become familiar with his gray gelding in the months since he'd been given him, calling him Tempest. He was a strong, young beast with an overeager manner that Garin had to constantly rein in.

Mounts secured, they traveled around the estate to the back gate, where shipments of food, clothes, and other commodities necessary to a monarch were admitted. The gate hung open and unguarded, the palace guards not having yet reclaimed it. A measure of guilt curled through Garin at the reminder of their abandonment of Emperor Zyrl.

He told us to go, he reminded himself as he coaxed Tempest to follow Wren and her stor, Lighthoof. *This is the best way to help anyone.*

It was a tough argument to believe as they looked over the eastern quarter of Kavaugh. The air was filled with the remote cries of cockatrices and the other Nightkin that had invaded the city. He could see the silhouettes of the beasts diving in among the buildings through a smoky haze. Garin even saw someone drop from their claws to splatter on the street below.

Cockatrices weren't the only threat. Gryphons perched on towers and called out their challenges to the defenders below. Tal had spoken of his time among the lion-eagle hybrids, but those creatures seemed a far cry from those before them now. These were under Yuldor's thrall, and they hungered for blood.

Interspersed among the larger Nightkin were slighter forms. *Gamayuni*, Aelyn named them with a twist of his mouth. What Garin saw of them struck horror through him. Gamayuni had a humanoid appearance, but with leathery skin and wings that carried their bat-like bodies in flocks over the rooftops. Their hands and feet ended in claws, and instead of hair atop their heads they sported a seething tangle of serpentine braids. He was glad when Tal and Helnor gave them a wide berth.

Not only Nightkin fought here; Ravagers, too, assaulted the Empire's capital. Garin had always known they were loyal first to the Prince of Devils, but it was a strange sight to see Imperials fighting one another. The Emperor's rebellion hadn't gone unnoticed, it seemed, and now his people paid the price.

Garin hoped he and his companions would make their sacrifice worth something.

They moved around knots of fighting where they could. Had Tal not been exhausted from containing the phoenix, Garin didn't doubt he would have performed his usual heroics. As things stood, he remained slumped in his saddle, even more drained from the experience than Garin.

When battle became necessary, Helnor and Ashelia led the

charge. Ravagers were in the middle of mounting a decapitated head on a spear when the elves drove their stors into their midst, cutting down any within reach. Garin drew *Velori* and followed suit, feeling a slight sense of vindication at felling an orkan.

But those instances were few, and soon the outer city wall rose before them. The eastern gate, called the Du'orlam Portal by Imperials, had been drawn up just enough that the invaders could ride their mounts under the portcullis to enter the city. Ravagers held the winches that drew up the metal gate, though the city watch fought to reclaim them.

Helnor raised a hand for a halt when they were still out of bow range. "We'll have to secure the winches so they don't close the gate on us," he called. "Aelyn, Garin, be ready with your sorcery."

Garin met the mage's gaze and was surprised when Aelyn gave him a nod devoid of mockery.

"It's already done," the elf responded for both of them.

Turning back and wishing he could feel as confident, Garin saw Helnor nod. "*Kolesa*, Wren, Tal — we'll clear the way to the gate and protect the others from retaliation. Now go!"

The Prime roared these last words as he spurred his stor into a charge. Tal was slower to follow, but his black-steel sword was bared, as were Ashelia and Wren's rapiers. Falcon, who bore Rolan on his mount, held the lad tight against him as he rode swiftly behind them. Aelyn sped up his stor until it galloped beside Tempest.

"I'll cover left!" the mage called above the wind and the approaching battle.

Garin nodded and declared with more confidence than he felt, "The right is mine!"

There was no more time for doubt. The Ravagers and guards swarmed the half-raised portcullis, reeling drunkenly as they traded killing blows. The bodies of the dead mounded around the gate. Both sides spared glances back as their party neared, but their own pitched battles occupied them too much to respond.

The situation was similar on the wall. As Garin watched, a man in the Imperial livery of gold and red fell screaming from atop it, the orkan that had shoved him leering down to watch him splatter against the ground.

Garin swallowed his revulsion and opened himself to the Song. The haunting music was reassuring amid the ghastly cries of killers and the dying. He focused on the place where the winch hid behind a short stone wall and pried off a hand from Tempest's reins to aim at it.

"*Dord uvthak!*"

Even as the Song's sorcery bolstered his spell, he felt the strain of casting at such a distance, the strength in his limbs momentarily lapsing. But as he clung to his surging horse's saddle, he saw he'd accomplished his aim. The wall around the winch crumbled inward, and the Ravagers guarding it cried out. A stone must have knocked the winch's lever, for the portcullis shuddered. Garin feared it would fall closed, but by some mercy, it remained open.

A glance left showed that Aelyn had accomplished his own task, and with more finesse. Instead of collapsing the wall onto the winch, he'd broken it outward and exposed the Ravagers behind it, whom he then picked off with a flash of lightning. The efforts cost him, however, for the mage sagged and barely seemed to hold on as he bounced with his stor's mighty strides. Garin winced and hoped he could keep in the saddle.

"Arrows!"

Ashelia's cry jerked him back to the present. Acting on practiced instinct, Garin threw up a hand.

"*Jolsh heks!*"

Wind blasted from him, leaving his lungs tight and airless, while his invisible shield caught the falling missiles and sent them dancing away. Garin struggled to breathe. Dark spots speckled his vision. Finally, as the gate drew within a score of strides, he wheezed in air.

"Duck!" Helnor bellowed.

Garin only just complied. As he passed below the portcullis, his shoulder caught one of the sharp tips, tearing a shallow wound through his skin and ripping his new cloak. He pulled free, and then Tempest was breaking past the wall as they followed the rest of their company.

When they'd safely bolted away and the sounds of battle had faded, Garin spared one last look back at Kavaugh. Fires across the city made the sky glow orange, and smoke joined the thick, gray clouds above. Barely visible through the haze was the golden palace that had so recently been their refuge. He was just glad no more phoenixes appeared to be joining the assault.

"Take care, Zyrl," he muttered under his breath. "And stay alive."

With that, Garin turned back to his company, wondering who had the more harrowing road ahead of them.

PASSAGE I

As I recline here in Paradise, my every whim appeased, my mind begins to wander. It travels to darker places, for only contrast captures the interest, and here, there is only light.

First, I mull over the nature of Yuldor's monsters, the so-called "Nightkin," though anyone with an ounce of knowledge knows that name to be a misnomer. The elder word kael'dros *is much more suitable, though its meaning, "conservators," may strike many as ironic, considering their present behavior.*

But it is their origins with which I preoccupy myself now. From whence do they come? Did the World itself miraculously spawn them? Did Yuldor create them? Or is some other progenitor behind their appearance?

The full truth, I fear, is lost. But I have some insights.

Yuldor — or at least a part of him — undoubtedly spawned some of these creatures. His mad mind, endlessly fascinating, has merged natural animals into beasts that have no right to exist. The chimera, for example: what need has it of four heads? Does it feed four stomachs as well? The gryphon is his, though I would consider it a more successful fusion. Cockatrices, quetzals, and syrens also result from his genius.

But there are others that came from further afield. Ghouls, witikos, and devils like Heyl are not born of this World, but are summoned from another plane. Each conjuring scars reality's weave, leaving it a little weaker than before. I tremble to think what might happen if the veil ever failed to mend. If any beings are evil, it is they, for they possess no peace in their hearts and only crave violence.

The last cradle of creation is the Deep. I have had the misfortune of close experience with the dwarves, whose homeland teeters on the edge of this subterranean hell. The heart of sorcery lies at the core of the World; hence, the closer one comes to it, the more chaotic the creatures that are bred. The most horrific of monsters dwell in these dark places. I have seen some myself and barely survived the encounters. These rival the strength of any being I have known. Even the dragons at the height of their power would have been hard-pressed to defeat them.

We are fortunate they remain in their caverns and tunnels. If they were to surface, the World might truly end.

- The Untold Lore of Yuldor Soldarin and His Servants, *by Inanis*

SOJOURN

"HERE," ASHELIA FINALLY SAID. "WE CAN MAKE CAMP HERE."

False gods be praised. Tal nearly fell off his horse as he dismounted. It was more than being unused to the saddle. Weariness infected every part of him: mind, muscles, and magic. He'd kept up a steady trickle of sorcery just to remain upright and clinging to the reins, but even with the poisonous canker eradicated, it came with a cost. Now, he paid the price twice-over.

His mount, a fine thoroughbred stallion gifted to him by Zyrl, nudged him. Lathered from the hard journey, he was insistent on his rightful reward of food and water. Tal raised a leaden arm and scratched behind one of his flickering ears.

"Never fear, Savior," he told the horse. "I'll settle you shortly."

Ashelia, who dismounted nearby, led her stor up next to him. "Why must you mock him? A majestic beast deserves a better name."

Tal flashed her a slack smile. "Why does Aelyn call me Magebutcher? Most folks believe themselves to be better than they are. I like names that keep us humble."

"You like him calling you Magebutcher then?"

89

He shrugged. "A man can grow used to anything, I suppose."

"A woman as well." She flashed a teasing smile before guiding her mount toward the copse where the others set up camp.

Tal only shook his head and followed. The place Ashelia had selected for their camp was over two dozen miles from Kavaugh's walls and a mile off the main road leading east. They had ridden over unending plains since fleeing the capital with barely a tree in sight, much less other shelter, unless they commandeered a farmhouse from a hapless peasant. This small grove had been one of the few they'd happened upon, and with the nearest domicile back at the road, Ashelia deemed it safe for the night. No Ravagers seemed to pursue, but Tal had seen enough of Yuldor's minions to take every precaution.

By the time Tal had tied up Savior, the others were already well into their chores. Had they been able to leave the palace with more leisure, they would have taken shelters from the palace stores. As it was, they had to make do with tying horse blankets to the trees and anchoring them to the ground with heavy stones. He didn't look forward to the times their bedrolls alone would have to suffice.

They lit no fire, but by benefit of sorcery and the moons' illumination, Tal could just make out his companions' faces. Even the elves looked tired, Aelyn most of all. The day's castings had drained the mage, so he bowed forward like a bough heavy with fruit. At another time, Tal would have seen it as the perfect opportunity to mock him, but he couldn't muster the energy for it. Of Garin, Wren, and Falcon, only the bard still had any pep, and this from jangling nerves, judging by the way his eyes darted to the dark spaces between the trees.

By unspoken agreement, their party had gathered within the circle of their shelters. Silence reigned for a long moment.

"So," Falcon said with false cheer, "where are we headed?"

Aelyn, whom Tal had thought asleep, let out a derisive snort, while Wren crossed her arms.

"Our destination hasn't changed," the young woman said. "It's still Ikvaldar, isn't it?"

Ashelia glanced at her House-brother before speaking. "We must wait for our allies to gather, to draw away any forces atop Ikvaldar. Even if we didn't have reason to delay, we cannot go there until we know we can surmount its trials. Last we had discussed, we were to seek an elixir to Paradise's miasma, but I don't know where we might find it."

Tal roused himself to speech. "As luck would have it, Pim informed me of an elixir's whereabouts shortly before his master made cinders of him."

"That *is* fortunate!" Falcon, desperate for any good news, leaned forward, the gold bright in his eyes.

"Perhaps too much so," Aelyn said without raising his head.

"You don't think it's why Yuldor struck?" Garin asked. "Because of what Pim revealed?"

Tal shook his head. "If the Prince of Devils could listen through Pim's ears, I think he would have retaliated long ago. Besides, the Nightkin and Ravagers were already positioned to attack. This was just an unhappy coincidence."

"Perhaps not entirely." Helnor's rich baritone cracked, the Prime Warder worn down by the trying day. "They might have known of Pim's betrayal ever since he located the elixir."

"Does it matter?" Wren folded her hands behind her head and leaned back against a tree.

"Wren is correct — we can discuss this later," Ashelia said. "What we need to decide now is our next step. Tal, what information did Pim give you?"

Tal shrugged. "Little enough. A medusal alchemist named Koax Mraaj has supposedly created an elixir. Pim believed he's in Dreygoj, the capital of Rajeya."

"Dreygoj," Helnor murmured. "That is... unfortunate."

"They're loyal to Yuldor, aren't they?" Wren queried.

Ashelia sighed. "They are. We will have to either convince this Koax that our cause is worthy—"

"—or we steal it," Garin finished.

"Ah! A heist, is it?" Falcon sat up straighter. "How lucky we are to have a man talented in this very capacity!"

Aelyn let out a soft moan and collapsed further onto the ground.

Tal flashed the party a tired grin. "My thieving days are long gone, old friend. But I suppose it's never too late to reestablish bad habits."

"Because it went so well with the Hoarseer Queen," Wren pointed out acidly.

"Tal won't be alone," Ashelia said firmly. "And he won't be facing any Extinguished this time. Pim was the last remaining one; the others have been destroyed."

Wren snorted a laugh. "For the moment, at least. But how long will that last?"

"Haven't you listened to my stories, Daughter?" Falcon gathered an expression Tal knew well: the storyteller's smirk. "Soulstealers require a decade to resurrect. Unless things have drastically changed from past occasions, we have a large window yet free from their corrupting influence."

Tal kept his own thoughts on the matter private. Only he had felt the power behind Yuldor when he spoke through Pim and Hashele. The Peacebringer's power shook the World to its core. What was bringing back four servants quicker than normal to a god? But until he had more solid evidence, he saw no need to worry the others.

"Nevertheless," Ashelia said, "we know what our next step must be. We must go to Dreygoj."

The others nodded into the gloom, though Wren shook her head.

"Seems the opposite direction that we should go," she muttered.

Tal took her meaning. The entire journey eastward, he'd

been focused on ascending the mountain, but none of them had known the challenges that lay ahead. If they prepared before they went, they stood a better chance of success.

Scant as it still is.

Helnor started to rise, but Garin spoke and arrested his movement.

"There's somewhere else we have to go after Dreygoj."

Tal stared at Garin, perplexed. "Where's that?" *Lad*, he almost called him, and barely held it back.

The youth hesitated as he looked around at their companions. His eyes finally settled on Tal.

"Ilvuan has always told me he has a task for me. Then, just yesterday morning, he shared a memory with me. I flew with him over the East, back before it was the Empire, and saw the World from above, soaring through the clouds..."

As Garin trailed off, lost in the memory, Tal imagined what it must have been like. *To soar...* Even with the World's blood in his veins, it was a something he was unlikely to experience. He'd never envied the youth his Singer, but part of him longed to know the feeling.

Everyone remained quiet until Garin continued. "I believe we flew east from above Kavaugh until we reached the coast, then Ilvuan turned north. We went to a place where the stones and sand were black, and pillars rose from the beaches. Ilvuan landed, then walked into a cave just large enough to admit a dragon."

"How big is a dragon?" Rolan asked in a hushed voice. Tal had thought he was asleep as he nestled into his mother's side, but saw now his eyes were wide with Garin's tale, his tendrils spinning.

Garin smiled at the boy. "I don't know. The dreams are from Ilvuan's eyes, so the World seems normal for how he's used to seeing it. But I would guess when he flew through the skies, he is as broad and tall as any floor of a kintree."

The boy looked up at his mother, perhaps to see if he was

being teased. When Ashelia only shrugged, he shook his head in wonder. Tal smiled, gladdened that wonder could exist even now, so soon after seeing a city razed.

"We entered the cave," Garin continued. "The main chamber was enormous, at least twice Ilvuan's height. The ceiling and walls were scratched, but it seemed intentional, and the scratches glowed like glyphs, only in red and violet. Ilvuan wanted me to see what lay on the floor. Tucked in hundreds of grooves were what looked like large, round boulders, the same black as the rest of the stone. Only, in Ilvuan's eyes, each glowed with the heat of life."

"Eggs." Aelyn's head rose. "He speaks of dragon eggs."

Garin nodded. "The cave was once the dragons' hatching grounds. In Ilvuan's memory, eggs were everywhere. But Yuldor has taken them over the years. The shells, I suppose we could call it, can be formed into magical artifacts, like the bracers that restrained our sorcery."

A shard of a dragon's shell. It was too foreign a thought for Tal to wrap his head around.

"What does this mean?" Ashelia asked softly. "If there are eggs, can dragons be reborn?"

"And if they're all harvested, are they extinct?" Helnor rumbled.

Garin nodded. "I think so. That's why this task is so urgent. Only a few dozen eggs are left, and I'm supposed to prepare the grounds for their rebirth. Somehow." His gaze slid over to Ashelia. "But yes. Dragons can return."

Tal stared at the youth as his thoughts whirled. *Dragons can be reborn.* Only sixteen summers old and he'd been entrusted with the continuation of an entire species. And not only a race, but dragons, the onetime overlords and caretakers of the World.

Faced with such a revelation, what else could he do but smile?

Garin noticed it, and he returned a helpless one of his own.

No doubt the unlikeliness of his task had occurred to him many times since Ilvuan had pressed it upon him.

Their company was silent for a long moment before Falcon spoke. "Now, I am not one to interfere with the makings of a fabulous fable. But... should we not question whether we *wish* for dragons to return?"

Tal wondered how the same thought hadn't occurred to him. Even the memory of the illusory dragon Soltor had conjured in the Ruins of Erlodan struck needles of fear through him. Its size, speed, strength, and fiery breath... If dragons were half as mighty in reality, he didn't relish the prospect of fighting one. A phoenix had been too much for him alone — how could he face down a dragon's wrath?

Garin stared hard at the bard. "Ilvuan has saved all of us. He helped find Tal and he's continuing to aid us in the fight against Yuldor. I have to do this. I have to do whatever I can for him."

Tal met Falcon's glance with a measure of reluctance. No doubt his friend wondered the same as he did: how much of Garin's thoughts were his own. But he couldn't start doubting the youth now. He'd gained much wisdom since leaving Hunt's Hollow and had endured experiences no other in the Westreach or East had ever known. He had to trust Garin knew what he was talking about.

Tal cleared his throat, bringing the party's attention to him. "If Garin says it must be done, then I'm inclined to believe him. Perhaps the resurrection of dragons isn't the most reassuring prospect, but Ilvuan has been essential to our cause. Just now, we need all the allies we can get. Though I doubt dragons hatch and grow within a season, if they are as potent as Ilvuan as phantoms, we would do well to bring them to our side."

Falcon eyed him skeptically, while Ashelia looked contemplative. He wondered if she thought of what he'd told her: of his experiences with phantoms in the black presence that had found him when he strayed too near the *Doash* back in the snowy mountains, and who had guided him earlier in Elendol. Part of him had always suspected it was a dragon, though its mind felt more familiar than he'd expected one of those great beings to be.

For Tal's words, gratitude was etched in Garin's face. It was enough to silence Tal's reservations.

Aelyn straightened for a moment before slumping again. "I would have the dragons return. It would be most interesting to see them resume their natural role in the World... Perhaps it will bring some balance."

"Or more powerful adversaries," Helnor countered, his brow drawn.

Wren glared at the Prime. "Garin knows what he's talking about. We should do what Ilvuan asks." Her hand held Garin's, and the youth gazed at her. His adoration would have been cloying between different people at a different time. Just then, it only made Tal smile.

Tal leaned forward and caught Rolan's eye. "Well, lad, what do you think? Shall we see if we can bring dragons back into the World?"

The boy glanced at the others, his eyes wide. "Do you think it will work?"

"A dragon says it will, so I don't see why not."

"Then yes!" At a touch from his mother, Rolan quieted down. "I want to see a dragon. Will we get to see a dragon?"

Tal laughed and tousled the boy's hair, ignoring his protests. "That's the idea. Well, I suppose that settles it. First to Dreygoj, then to the dragon hatching grounds."

Though Falcon loosed a dramatic sigh, he rose with the others and made no protests about collapsing in his bedroll. Nor did Tal; Ashelia had lain her blankets next to his, and Rolan curled up on her other side.

He shifted to hold Ashelia when a lump dug into his side.

Ordinarily, he would have ignored it and assumed it to be a rock, but it was oddly shaped for one. Frowning, Tal felt around his blanket until he discovered the culprit and held it up. By the scant light and his touch, he could tell what it was: a small, leather-bound book.

"What is that?" Ashelia had turned back toward him and stared at the booklet in his hand.

Tal folded it open, squinted at a page, then smiled. "Answers, I think."

She frowned, but he merely secured the book in his pack. Perhaps too tired to inquire further, Ashelia began to turn away when Tal spoke again.

"Ashel."

She peered back at him, the silver in her eyes quickening. "Tal."

Tal extended his hand and opened it so she could see what lay in his palm. "I know it's a poor marriage offering for a princess, but—"

"No, Tal. I'm not taking your father's ring."

They stared at each other, neither budging, the Ring of Thalkuun held between them.

"So you're rejecting my proposal?" he said with a small smile.

Ashelia arched an eyebrow. "If the ring is part of it, then yes. But we both know what this is truly about."

His smile slipped away. Tal lowered his hand, but only to sit up and take hers in his. Ashelia let him, but she remained stiff and wary. The stone ring lay cold between their palms.

"Beloved, please, listen to me. I don't need it; I can protect myself."

"Not back at the palace. That ring saved you."

Tal winced. "I wouldn't go that far, though perhaps it helped. But if any lessons can be drawn from that bungling, it's that I cannot always protect you. Knowing this was on your hand, that you would be safe from spells, at least... It would make this much easier."

"None of this is easy. And none of us are safe." Ashelia

turned back to glance at her son, who huddled in his bedroll at her back. "It won't fit Rolan?"

"I'd thought of that. No, it's too large, and being impervious to magic, I can't change its size."

She sighed, betraying the hope that had risen at the thought. "Then you know my answer."

Tal searched her eyes as if he might find the path forward in them. But he only saw the usual stubbornness in her stormy irises.

He withdrew his hands, the Ring of Thalkuun coming with them. "I'll keep it, for now. But when the road becomes too perilous—"

"No, Tal." Ashelia reached for his hand again, but only to close his fingers around the artifact. "If you want to do something for me, then wear it and stay alive. I'm not the one who has to challenge a god."

"I appreciate the reminder." He softened the words with a smile.

Ashelia returned it, though hers was small and frail. "You need every bit of armor you can find. More than our safety depends on our success: the Westreach and the Empire rise or fall based on what you do."

The fate of two lands in my hands. Tal knew she didn't put this burden on him lightly. Being in line for succession to Gladelyl's throne, she understood the pressure of responsibility.

He only wished it wouldn't cost all he feared.

Tal slipped the Ring of Thalkuun back onto his finger, repressing a shiver as the mystical veil settled over him, then looked up. "Is marriage off the table then?"

Ashelia let out a small laugh and touched a hand to his arm. "I think you know the answer to that."

For the moment, it was all he needed. They settled into their blankets, and Tal set down the weight of the World — for the night, at least.

WHAT IS YET TO COME

"YULDOR'S POCK-MARKED PRICK, WILL THESE PLAINS NEVER end?" Wren grumbled.

Garin squinted against the morning sun, still hanging low on the horizon ahead. "Can't see any sign of it yet."

She groaned, but made no further complaints. *For the moment, at least,* he thought with a smile.

It had been three days since their flight from Kavaugh. While they had the good luck of finding a copse of trees to shelter within the first day, the next two had proven less fortunate, and wind and rain hounded them the night through. Bedraggled and ill-rested, their party had pressed on all the same. With the possibility of Ravagers and Nightkin in pursuit, and pressing errands still before them, they had little other choice.

Their one consolation was that the endless plains and rolling hills held a certain beauty. Though summer was beginning to grip the land, the tall grass was still green from the spring storms, while the skies were becoming clearer with each passing day. For miles in every direction, Garin could see the terrain rolling out of sight, and from atop tall hills, he saw farther still. Almost, it put him in mind of what Ilvuan might have seen from above. He tried to picture it, but his imagination flailed before the challenge.

Ilvuan roused. These days, Garin no longer startled at his intrusions, nor really thought of them as intrusions at all. In some strange way, the dragon was a part of him. He wondered if that would change when dragonkind was reborn. He wondered if he wanted it to.

You are headed to complete your task. The Singer already seemed certain of the fact, though Garin hadn't felt him when they'd made the decision three nights prior.

Yes. We have to do one thing first, but we'll go there afterward.

Irritation spiked through his mind, but it lacked any real discomfort.

It would be better to do it sooner, Ilvuan noted, almost sullen.

I know, Garin answered hastily. *I would go there first if it were left to me. But Yuldor is probably aware of our other errand. He'll thwart us if he has the chance.*

Ilvuan rumbled, a sign that he was mulling over the matter. *Very well,* he expressed at length. *But do not delay long. This task must be done swiftly.*

I won't, Garin promised, and unveiled his mind so his intentions shone through to the dragon. *You have my word.*

With his usual lack of manners, the Singer slipped away.

"Ilvuan come calling?"

Garin startled and looked around to find Wren watching him. "How'd you know?"

She smirked. "You get this dopey look, like you're about to drool down your shirt."

He rolled his eyes. "Don't know why I bothered asking."

"Hey, we're honest with each other. That's why this works."

"This?"

Garin arched an eyebrow, knowing how speaking of their relationship seemed to make her uncomfortable. It was one of the few things he could reliably tease her about.

As predicted, Wren glared at him, then looked forward. "Push it, and you may find *this* no longer exists."

"Very well, my thorny flower." He leaned over to push her and yelped as she nearly pulled him from the saddle.

The day continued in a similar fashion: the moors rolling by, quips given and taken. The dark cloud of pursuit faded to a vague unease, one Garin could almost ignore. He breathed in the fresh scent of grass, reveled in the summer sun on his skin, not yet too warm, but just enough to lift the day's chill. He enjoyed the time with Wren and their other companions. He was almost content.

But each night, the fear snuck back in. When not on watch himself, Garin would wrap up his bedroll and shift from one uncomfortable position to another, listening for any signs of intruders. Each rustling breeze and curious creature became a Ravager, or a cockatrice, or another deadly Nightkin. Only by opening himself to the Song and listening to its strange, lulling strains could he drift to sleep.

That third night was spent out in the open once more. But midway through the fourth day's ride, Helnor called back from the front, "Ahead! Trees ahead!"

Garin startled at the call, then breathed a sigh of relief. From next to him, Wren muttered, "Night's flaming balls, it's about time."

A minute later, he detected the forest on the horizon. It stretched in either direction and was thick enough to cast a gloom beyond its edge. The trees in its midst grew tall and thick, and it promised a refuge for beasts who felt exposed on the grassy plains. Garin not only looked forward to shelter from the sky, from which he always feared the sudden appearance of Nightkin, but also the opportunity to hunt meat. Their supplies were meager, suitable for a week at most, and after a steady staple of rich palace foods, he quickly tired of the same fare. The realization brought a mocking smile to his lips.

Garin Dunford, too fine a dandy for hardtack and salted pork, he thought. *What will you do when emperors and queens no longer wish to host you?*

The thought startled him more than he expected. With all the perils of the present, he'd thought little of the future. Now, as they neared the forest, he let his mind wander over what it might bring, and found his lack of answers disconcerting.

"What will you do after all this is over?" he asked Wren.

"Over?" Wren narrowed her eyes at him. "Why think about it? Isn't it enough to just get through it?"

Garin shrugged. Wren had never been one for thinking of the future. She rarely doubted or regretted her decisions. He was formed differently. His imagination ran down different alleys.

And so he began to dream on his own.

Of children with Wren, and a homestead in Hunt's Hollow with fields and fences and livestock.

Of a lonely life on the road, doing small deeds as he moved from town to town, a growing set of stories his greatest possessions.

Of being a warlock of Jalduaen's Circle, placed within a court to serve and to command.

Yet none of the imagined paths seemed quite right. Each expanded on a part of him, but none encompassed the whole.

Maybe Wren's right. Maybe I should just concentrate on the present.

But though he pushed the notion to the back of his mind, it remained there, lodged like a pebble in a boot.

Reaching the forest provided a welcome distraction. Though there was still daylight left, Ashelia called for a halt just within the tree line so they would have plenty of time to hunt and smoke any meat brought back.

They decided to hunt in pairs, with Ashelia, Rolan, Falcon, and Aelyn hanging back at camp to guard their mounts and packs. Garin assumed he would go with Wren, but Tal approached him before he could ask her.

"Garin," his old mentor said with a small smile. Had he not known better, Garin might have almost thought it shy. "If I can pull you away from Wren for a bit..."

"Sure." Wondering what this was about, Garin waved to Wren, motioning her to Helnor. She frowned, then shrugged and moved toward the Prime Warder without protest.

Garin and Tal strung their bows and belted on their quivers in silence, then set off north. The cheery sounds of Rolan and Falcon's debauchery, Ashelia's laughter, and Aelyn's griping soon gave way to the quieter sounds of the woods. Garin expected Tal to strike up a conversation, wondering if this was the reason he had paired with him, but the storied man seemed content to walk in silence. There was a wariness to him now, a hunter's stalk. Tal placed every footfall with what seemed instinctual care. There was a slight hunch to his posture and an intensity in his eyes. His lips had a slight upward bend to them, as if he reveled in the activity.

As he kept his own watch for prey, Garin studied the surrounding trees. They were a variety foreign to the East Marsh, broad-leaved with a musty scent to them. Foliage was largely lacking underfoot, the canopy above too thick for light to penetrate, though the trees were wide enough apart for a horse and rider to travel comfortably between. The dirt was loamy and soft. Birds whose voices he didn't know sang among the branches, calling to one another across far distances. An owl hooted from deeper inside the woodland.

It was a picturesque scene, peaceful and innocent. Yet with Tal prowling beside him, Garin doubted it would remain so for long.

"Here," Tal said softly, breaking the silence. He kneeled between an opening in the trees and studied the dirt. Garin joined him, careful where he tramped on the earth. He knew how to identify a hare's trail, but Tal was a far better tracker than Garin ever reckoned he'd become.

"What do you see?" Garin asked at length.

"Tracks — big ones. Like a horse more than a deer. They're recent, no more than a day old, judging by the sharp edges."

A prickle started at the base of Garin's neck. He looked around them, almost expecting to see the horse and rider who had made the hoofprints watching them.

"Should we follow the trail?" he asked, his voice low.

"No." Tal stood again. "It won't lead us to food, and it may have just been an innocent traveler. Besides, a single rider shouldn't concern us. Let's move on."

Garin followed as Tal edged around the glade and continued north, but his unease stayed lockstep with him.

He expected to continue in silence, but only a little way down the trail, Tal sighed and looked at him sidelong. Garin reluctantly met his umber eyes, though he had a feeling he didn't look forward to what the man had to say. Then he thought of a way to head him off.

"You should take this back." Garin halted and set his bow down, then unbuckled his belt to slide off *Velori* in its scabbard and hold it out.

"Garin…" Tal began.

"We're not in the palace anymore, Tal. We can't avoid something just because it's uncomfortable. Besides, it's your sword. I know you have a new one from the Emperor, but it doesn't feel right carrying this when you could."

The man stared at him for a long moment. Without accepting *Velori*, he set down his bow and unbuckled his own belt. Garin watched, perplexed, as he slid off Zyrl's sword and hefted it.

"A sword for a sword, then," Tal said with a sly smile.

It wasn't the exchange Garin had in mind, but at a loss for what else to do, he accepted the sword and gave *Velori* back to its master. For a moment, he could only stare at the scabbard. It was leather dyed black, with gold inlay curling up and down its length. The metal tip was gold, as was the throat, and gold wire curled about the sword's grip.

"Don't just stare at it." Tal had already secured *Velori* onto his belt. "Give it a swing."

Tentatively, Garin tugged the sword free. As soon as he made contact with the wire grip, he felt its sorcery hum through his body. But as he bared the blade, he became distracted by the sight of it. The metal was black as a moonless night, while the glyphs carved into the flat side of the blade glowed like evening light. *Velori* had a certain aliveness to it, but this sword took it a long step further.

"*Helshax* is its name," Tal murmured. "Lament."

"A strange name." But it felt fitting, somehow. Garin gave it an experimental swing and marveled at how Lament seemed to flow through the air, perfectly balanced and as light as a branch.

"It suits you." Tal smiled. "May it serve you for many years to come."

If we survive that long. But Garin only nodded and sheathed the sword. There would be time enough to practice with it later when Wren could marvel over it with him.

As he looped it through his belt, Tal spoke again. "While we're bringing up uncomfortable topics, we never talked about what happened before. With the phoenix."

Garin suppressed a sigh. His diversion hadn't worked as well as he'd hoped. Of course, he'd thought of that moment many times during the ride from Kavaugh, but hadn't come to any conclusions as to what had occurred, much less how he felt about it.

Raising his head and meeting Tal's gaze, he could only shrug. "Maybe there's little to discuss."

"Maybe. But considering you joined your soul with mine, I somewhat doubt it."

Joined souls. Was that what they had done? He hadn't thought of it that way, but what else could it be called?

Garin struggled to find the right words, staring sightlessly into the gloom between the trees ahead. "When I open myself to the Worldsong, I can hear other songs now. Sorcery songs, like I heard from the hearts of the golems or the bracelets."

Dragon eggs, a part of him thought, but he pushed the notion away.

"Yours is the strongest. When you were struggling against the phoenix, I heard both of your songs. I tried to quell the phoenix's, but it was too strong. So I reached for yours and... well, I don't know how to say it. I added my song to yours and brought the Worldsong with."

Tal watched him, a smile growing on his lips. "So that's how we survived. You saved us, Garin — you and your ingenuity."

That startled a laugh out of him. "No one called me clever back in Hunt's Hollow."

"Nor me." Tal's smile slipped as his eyes grew serious. "We cannot afford to stand apart, Garin. We have to put our power together. Alone, I would have failed to quell the phoenix's faefire, and we would have all perished. Together, we succeeded. If we knew what we did and practiced it, how much stronger could we be?"

Garin knew the path down which his thoughts traveled, but he knew he couldn't follow it. *Not strong enough to challenge a god. Not strong enough to take the Worldheart from Yuldor.* But it would be cowardice to say such things aloud, and it didn't change that this was the best avenue they had.

Garin nodded slowly. "You're right. We have to try it again, hone it."

"The World's blood fused with the Worldsong." Tal had a far-off look. "I wonder if Hellexa Yoreseer ever conceived of this when writing her heretical tome. I wonder if Yuldor knows it's possible."

Garin could only shrug. "What do we really know of the Prince of Devils?"

"Not much," Tal admitted. "Though perhaps we can confirm that devils live within him."

"You mean the voices?"

Tal nodded. "Each time Yuldor has possessed his Extinguished, four distinct voices have spoken. One strong; one mocking; one seductive; one pleading."

"And you think they're devils."

"Perhaps..." Tal frowned off into the woods, his bow swinging back and forth with his stride. "Pim had a different theory, however."

"He did?"

"Yes. Once, he told me a story — of a war between the Origins and dragons, and the One against the Three."

Long-buried questions rose back from the recesses of Garin's mind. "Ilvuan mentioned a similar story. He claimed one called 'the Night' was the champion of dragons, and that three with the names of the Whispering Gods fought against them with a power they'd wrongfully seized."

Tal stopped and turned to face Garin, his eyes pinched. "He named them Silence, Serenity, and Solemnity? And their adversary the Night?"

"Yes. But Tal, how can that be? The Creed says the Whispering Gods saved the World when the Night sought to destroy it. Our entire religion is based on their conflict..."

Garin trailed off, thinking hard. How many times had his worldview been undermined throughout their journey? When had doctrine, whether it was the Creed or the Cult of Yuldor, ever been a reliable source of truth?

Tal wore a strained smile. "I know, Garin. It's difficult to challenge what we've always assumed to be true. But in this case, facing one considered a god by many, I'm afraid we must."

It was Garin who searched Tal's face now. There was something in his posture that spoke of a suspicion confirmed, and Garin meant to hear it.

"You're not telling me everything," he accused. "If you're going to blaspheme my beliefs, the least you can do is explain why."

His old mentor let out a low chuckle and motioned him forward. "We'd best keep looking for quarries while we do, or Aelyn won't let us hear the end of it."

Garin normally would have responded with a quip, but eager for the answers Tal promised, he held his tongue and resumed walking beside the man.

After several strides, Tal spoke again, his eyes scanning the area around them as he did. "I asked Pim about the stories he told me on our journey on several occasions in Zyrl's palace. Each time, he deflected the conversation with little explanation. 'There will be time later,' he said, though he must have known even then how precious little time any of us had. When Yuldor took him, I feared answers were lost forever.

"But that first night at camp after fleeing Kavaugh, I discovered something in my satchel. A little book, travel-stained yet enchanted to endure, was tucked in my bedroll. I opened it and discovered a journal of sorts, titled *The Untold Lore of Yuldor Soldarin and His Servants.* Its author called himself Inanis."

"Inanis." Garin looked over sharply. "That's one of Pim's names." That piece of information had been revealed in one of their party's many discussions over the prior months.

Tal nodded. "It's what he called himself when we first met, and perhaps was his name as far back as when he was a mortal elf."

When we first met. It reminded him of the story Falcon had told him back in Vathda, of when Pim had manipulated Tal into becoming "Death's Hand" to the dwarves. When he'd shaped Tal into an assassin.

Garin tried to focus back on the questions at hand, dismissing his sudden unease. *He's not that man,* he told himself. *Not anymore.*

"So what did it say?" he asked aloud.

Tal seemed to have noticed his disquiet. His eyes, shadowed just then, studied him before looking aside. Garin tried to quell his guilt. If anyone should feel guilty regarding the storied man's past, it was Tal himself, not Garin. Yet the thought didn't make the feeling go away.

Tal didn't acknowledge the moment, but only continued. "It corroborated what you've said, at least regarding the Whispering Gods. Pim claimed Yuldor has referred to himself by names that, in the Origintongue, mean Silence, Serenity, and Solemnity. He didn't know if it's a madness that has manifested in the Enemy due to seizing the Worldheart, or if they exist as separate entities within him."

Garin absorbed the news in shocked silence. Even after Ilvuan had told him the Whispering Gods had been the adversaries of the dragons, he'd never truly believed it to be fact. But Pim had confirmed it. Surely, that meant it was true.

Unless both were lying to them.

No. I can't doubt Ilvuan now. He'd shared far too much with the Singer. Complex as the dragon was in his motivations, he was an ally. If Garin questioned that, what could he truly believe?

"Garin?" Tal glanced at him, concern in his crinkled eyes.

Garin let out the breath he'd been holding. "Sorry. It's just… I never expected to hear that the Whispering Gods are real, much less that they might be stewing in Yuldor's mind."

"We don't know that they are."

"What *do* we know?" Garin tried to sort through his whirling thoughts, but he was having difficulty putting them in any coherent order.

"We'll start at the beginning," Tal said. "We know the Three, the Whispering Gods, seized a power leaking from the World for their own — assumedly, the Worldheart."

Garin picked up the thread. "When they did, the dragons challenged them, but they couldn't fight them alone. So they selected a champion — the One, or the Night."

His old mentor nodded. "A war occurred. The Night and the Whispering Gods slew one another — or at least quelled their power, if Silence, Serenity, and Solemnity live on in Yuldor."

"The dragons sacrificed themselves in the final battle, but some linger on as spirits." He thought of Ilvuan and wished once more to see the dragon in the flesh.

"The war ended with the Severing — the transformation of the Origins into the separate Bloodlines we have today. And the Worldheart lay dormant, unclaimed and no longer tainting the World with sorcery."

"Until Yuldor."

Tal smiled bitterly. "Until Yuldor."

They walked in silence for a stretch. Garin noticed the stray sunlight that filtered through the trees was growing golden. The evening was fading, and they had yet to catch even a rabbit or squirrel. Yet before such revelations, he found it hard to be concerned.

"Do you think they still exist?" Garin asked quietly. He didn't meet Tal's eyes, almost embarrassed by the question.

His old mentor didn't answer for some time.

"I believe some remnant of them must. But Pim would say it's largely irrelevant, and in a way, I'm inclined to agree. Whether they are a figment of a mad mind or present in Yuldor in actuality, all the same, we must defeat them and put them to rest for good."

A thought occurred to Garin. "And the Night. Do you think—?"

Tal gripped Garin's arm, his body tense. Garin stilled as he looked around for what had alerted the man. His blood pounded in his ears. Had they stumbled upon the horseman whose tracks they'd seen earlier?

A moment later, he saw what it was. Between the trunks ahead, a deer stood in a shallow pool, its head bent to drink. Garin exhaled in relief, laboring to keep quiet as his alarm ebbed.

Tal released his arm and, with a small motion, beckoned

him to slink forward. Garin drew an arrow and followed as the older man kept as many trees as possible between them and their quarry, disguising their movements. He couldn't see the beast's eyes and hoped that meant the deer couldn't see them either.

She was a doe, judging from her lack of antlers, and small enough they could haul her back to camp. Tal, reaching a sheltered tree some fifty feet behind the deer, glanced back at Garin and nodded toward their quarry. Garin took his meaning and positioned himself by a parallel tree. At Tal's nod, he drew his arrow, then slowly came around the trunk with the point leading. The doe was positioned rear-end toward them, so he took aim at what he could see of the chest, hoping to find her heart.

Tal's lips formed silent numbers. Garin readied to release at their end. *Three, two, one...*

Two arrows flew from thrumming bows toward the beast.

Every lad in the East Marsh, and indeed in Avendor, knew their way around a bow. His boyhood skill came to the rescue now, his arrow finding the doe's breast, while Tal's went straight through the eye, though it had seemed an impossible angle from Garin's perspective. The deer went down at once, splashing in the pool. Garin winced as he lowered his bow. As much death as he'd seen, and dealt for that matter, he'd never truly hardened to it.

They advanced on their kill. The older man seized the legs and dragged it free of the water, and Garin realized it wasn't anything like the deer of the East Marsh. Its coat wasn't entirely fur, but became hard and leathery on its underbelly. Its coloring had tinges of blue and green as if algae grew among the hair. Stranger still were the four slits along its neck and the fleshy whiskers hanging from its jaw.

"Are those gills?" Garin asked, not entirely sure he wanted to know.

"Suppose they are." Tal ran a gloved hand along them and

shrugged. "The East has produced stranger things. I'm sure it's fine to eat."

Garin had less confidence in that, but he took Tal's bow and quiver so the man could drape their kill across his shoulders. Hefting it easily, though it had to weigh at least seven stone, Tal nodded back the way they'd come. Garin led, keeping his bow out just in case they stumbled upon more prey.

Beyond a hare that fled a rushed shot, however, no more opportunities presented themselves. Garin and Tal conversed little on the way back. For his part, Garin was preoccupied by their earlier revelations. *The Whispering Gods as enemies.* It still seemed too strange an idea to be true. But then again, so was the notion that he and Tal could face down a god.

The World is full of impossibilities, he thought with a glance at the gilled doe. *Hopefully, our success is one more.*

They made it back to camp just after sunset. Helnor and Wren had already returned, having claimed a brace of hares and a squirrel that now roasted on the fire. Garin wondered if they differed from the Westreach varieties, but didn't dare ask. As Tal presented their prize, both Wren and Aelyn seemed fascinated. The mage studied each unusual part until Tal ignored his protests and began skinning the beast. Rolan stared open-mouthed throughout the process, though he swallowed several times as if sick. Ashelia came up next to her son and placed a hand on his shoulder, bending down to murmur assurances in his ear.

Soon, they were making a meal of the small game meat and roasting the innards of the deer while Helnor, Ashelia, and Tal carved the rest of the meat into strips for smoking and showed Rolan how it was done. Garin, Falcon, and Wren had earlier refilled their waterskins and sat around the fire. Though the nights on the Eastern plains never grew cold like winter in the mountains, Garin was glad for the merry flames all the same.

He stared into them and thought of all the things that had burned on their journey.

The draugars before the ruins. Elendol's kintrees. Vathda. Ourselves, nearly.

He smiled, though it wasn't a happy one. Perhaps he was grateful for his experiences, but he never wished to go through them again.

Just as he turned to tell Wren of his and Tal's earlier epiphanies, Tal jerked up from the deer's carcass and held his bloody hands up as he stared into the dark forest. Alert, Garin looked in the same direction, but he detected nothing to cause alarm. Helnor, Ashelia, and Aelyn all seemed to sense something, for the Warders wiped their hands and seized weapons, while the mage muttered to himself and shuffled through his pouches, no doubt searching for spell components.

Wren darted to her feet and drew her sword, and Garin followed a moment later. By habit, he opened himself to the Song and readied himself for quick spellcasting.

"What is it?" he whispered to her, his fingers dancing nervously.

"Hoofbeats," she hissed back, her gaze intensely on the forest. "Coming our way, and fast. Sounds like a big horse…"

Garin felt them then, his human senses dull compared to elven ones. The horses and stors, tied up for the night at the edge of their small clearing, shimmied to one side. Falcon positioned himself next to Rolan, adopting his usual role of protecting the boy. Rolan tried to show he needed no protection, brandishing a bloody carving knife and staring into the forest with teeth bared.

Moonbeams shone through the canopy, so Garin saw their visitor coming from dozens of feet away. It looked to be a horse and a rider, though larger than ordinary. As they came closer still, something seemed wrong about their shape, though he couldn't put his finger on what.

"Halt there!" Helnor called out. He had an arrow nocked

and drawn as the intruder neared their camp. "Declare yourself, stranger!"

The rider and their mount slowed to a walk, then emerged into the firelight. Garin's breath caught. It wasn't two separate beings, horse and man — it was the two together. And by its furrowed brow, the beastman was far from happy to see them.

"Murderers!" the creature bellowed. "Savagers! Who are you to come into my weald and slay my children?"

MASTER OF THE WEALD

TAL STUDIED THE WRATHFUL BEING.

He was large, rising half and again as tall as Helnor's generous height. Most of his massive bulk comprised an equine body, with stout legs ending in thick cuffs of brown hair and a long, black tail that swished back and forth with a furious tempo. Where a horse's head should have been, a man emerged, but even he wasn't entirely human. A shaggy, black mane blossomed down his chest, and a spotted coat extended over the rest of his body. His face was much larger than a human's, broader and with exaggerated features. His eyes were set farther apart so he almost had to turn his head to stare with one or the other. A tangle of hair spilled off his scalp and down his muscled shoulders in a series of thick braids like ropes smeared in pitch.

Most unusual to Tal was the sorcery that rushed into the horse-man hybrid in thick, corded rivers. While Tal's and most other magical creatures only had one course, he was connected by many. A formidable being, and though Tal doubted he was a match for him, a fight was the last thing any of them needed.

Ashelia, diplomatic as ever, was the first to respond.

Lowering her sword, she gave the beastman a polite bow. "Pardon us — we were startled by your visit in the night and are sorry if we gave offense."

"Offense!" The creature didn't seem placated by her words. "It is a deep wound to slaughter the beasts of my weald! Save your words and leave this place at once. I will not ask again, *chadi*."

Ashelia glanced back at Tal, bafflement edging into her calm demeanor. He took it as his cue, clearing his throat and sheathing his sword as he stepped forward.

"Apologies, but this is all a misunderstanding. Let's try again, shall we? You tell us your name, and we'll share ours."

"Names?" The beastman snorted, very much as a horse might. "It is your heads I desire!"

"Yet I'm afraid you must content yourself with names. Mine is Tal. The kind lady you just spoke to is Ashelia. And the tall elf over there is Helnor. Aelyn, Garin, Falcon, Wren, and Rolan." He gestured to each of his companions as he introduced them. "Now, may we know yours?"

He felt Aelyn's incredulous gaze on him. Helnor and Wren looked no less skeptical, and Garin and Ashelia barely less so. Falcon appeared enthralled, no doubt already composing the song for the moment.

Tal stood his ground as the beastman stepped closer to loom over him. He thought he had his measure. Though the creature resented their hunting the forest animals, if he'd truly meant to kill them, he would have charged into the camp to start.

I hope, Tal thought as he flashed the beastman his best smile.

For a long moment, the tall creature only examined him with his head tilted sideways, one wide, equine eye staring. Then he stamped one hoof, provoking a flinch from Tal, and smiled savagely with a mouth full of square teeth.

"I am Zichodächini. *Chadi* such as yourselves may call me Holt."

"Holt." Tal bowed his head in acknowledgement, though he suspected that word, *chadi*, translated to an insult. "Pleasure to meet you."

"I cannot say the same, man Tal. I have killed *chadi* for intruding upon my weald before. I do not see why I should not do that now."

"Then why haven't you?" Tal kept his tone casual, though he readied half a dozen spells should the beastman lash out.

Holt turned to stare at the others. With his eyes set as they were, he could almost keep track of all of them at once. His gaze finally fell back on Tal.

"You may yet atone for your transgression," he rumbled at length. "Many of you touch *thacha*. You, man Tal, touch it with both hands."

Tal gathered his meaning. "You're rather strong in sorcery yourself."

Holt smiled again, still without warmth. "This weald is my domain. All within it are at my mercy."

And if I burned it down? But Tal kept the thought to himself and wore a smile of his own.

"Then we very much appreciate that mercy and would be glad to repay it, as well as for our inadvertent sins. I assume there's some task our sorcery can help with?"

The beastman exhaled sharply, froth blossoming on his lips. "My weald-tree has sickened. It is dire, for not even the *thacha* I wield can heal it." His gaze sharpened. "Succeed in a cure, and your debts to this forest will be paid — so long as you do not incur any further."

"And if we fail?" Aelyn interjected.

Holt looked at the mage across the fire. "If you do not, elf Aelyn, you will pay the price that the hart did."

"I'm sure that won't be necessary." Tal thought it best to avoid unpleasant subjects like either of their deaths. "Frail beings such as us require rest, however. If you might take us to the tree in the morning…"

Holt's wide nostrils flared, and for a moment, Tal thought he would refuse. But the beastman only snorted again and turned his massive bulk away, then began clopping toward the gloomy forest.

"First light tomorrow!" he bellowed over his shoulder. "Do not make me wait, *chadi!*"

With that, Holt set into the woods at a gallop.

Only when the thundering hoofbeats faded into silence did anyone speak. Falcon was the first to edge in a word as he stepped toward the fire and threw his arms wide.

"Is this not marvelous? An offended man-creature with a mysterious errand! A challenge ending in compromise amongst an ominous forest! A bard could scarcely hope for finer material."

"It would be better if we didn't tarry at all," Aelyn pointed out acidly. "If you fail to recall, bard, we have our own 'marvelous' errand to be about. We should press on — tonight, if we can."

Ashelia spoke even as Tal shook his head. "We still need to smoke the meat, as we won't travel far without food. And it cannot harm to attempt a healing."

"I agree," Tal said. "Holt looks like he could catch us if we flee, and I'd rather not kill anyone I don't have to. A day's delay will make no difference."

Garin, who had always seemed queasy at killing anyhow, nodded along. Wren beheld her father's vigorous nodding before she shrugged. Aelyn scowled and crossed his arms, which seemed to sway Helnor in the opposite direction.

"Very well," the Prime Warder said. "We'll stay, Mother watch over us."

"Good!" Rolan propped his hands on his hips and stood as boldly as if he hadn't been cowering behind Falcon just minutes before. "I wish to ride upon Holt's back anyhow!"

Tal laughed along with the others, though the boy's mother frowned.

"I don't think that's a good idea, lad," Tal told Rolan hastily. "Best stick with stors and horses for now."

Rolan shrugged and turned away. "We'll see."

———

True to his word, Holt returned to their camp before the morning light had penetrated the forest.

Garin was already up, having taken the last watch of the night with Wren, and was dressed and armed by the time he heard hooves. Glancing at Wren, who stood similarly arrayed beside him, he called to the others still rousing, "He's coming back!"

Rolan, the last to rise, poked his head out of his bedroll. "Can I ride him now?"

"Don't ask him that," his mother admonished.

The elf boy only stewed, wearing a mutinous expression.

Holt emerged from the woods a moment later. He seemed calmer than the night before, his movements less brash and imposing, and his expression a fraction lighter than a thundercloud. Heavy, bark-brown hair shaded his eyes, hiding them in permanent hollows. His pupils, wide like a horse's, darted over the clearing as he took in their camp.

"Follow me, *chadi*," Holt commanded in his resonant voice. Without waiting for a response, he turned and headed back in the direction from which he'd come.

Garin hurried over to Tempest, whom he'd already saddled, and swung himself up. Wren mounted Lightfoot next to him, and the rest of their companions weren't far behind.

"I told you to rise," Ashelia chided Rolan as she helped him hop into his trousers, then practically threw him atop the stor they shared.

"Ach! My bladder!"

Garin grinned as the elf boy squirmed into position, then followed Tal as he led their party after the forest caretaker.

Holt wasn't far ahead, having set an easy walk until they caught up. He led them east, deeper into the forest. Here, the trees grew taller than any others they'd seen in the Faernor Grasslands, and the shade was thicker. The vegetation thinned to little more than vines and fungi. Garin only glanced around every once in a while, for his gaze was often on the beastman's back. He found it fascinating how he moved, the unlikely pairing of bodies somehow graceful and grotesque at once. He marveled at the strength Holt seemed to possess, and fervently hoped they wouldn't be forced to fight him.

Garin gave little thought to their task until the forest opened before them to reveal a tree that dwarfed all the others in the forest. It was larger than any of the giants that populated the Nightelf fief, almost rivaling a Gladelysh kintree. Ten times their party could wrap themselves around it and still not touch hands. Its roots extended under its widespread branches in a seething mass, making it impossible for any other vegetation or trees to grow near. Set down in a hollow, its tallest branches only reached a bit higher than the rest of the woods.

Impressive as it was, Garin immediately detected the illness in the giant. Its branches, lean and subtle like a willow's, bore brown and shriveled leaves, though they should have been lively from the spring rains and the summer warmth. The trunk twisted and leaned in the middle, like an aged man grown tired of standing. The roots underfoot were still large, yet they looked as shrunken as old tubers, devoid of moisture and vitality.

The noble tree was dying. Garin grew somber at the sight.

"The goldwood is the most glorious of all plants," their reluctant host rumbled. Almost, he seemed to talk to himself, for he only had eyes for the tree. "Its leaves are as bright and yellow as the full face of *Hyshada*, and when the wind blows, they shimmer like sunlight on water. It should be blooming

now with catkin blossoms, each as silver as your *chadi* metal."
At this, Holt seemed to remember his company, for he looked
around with a pronounced frown. "You can see it is not as it
should be."

Tal slid from his horse and, without asking Holt's permission, approached the trunk. Garin hesitated, watching Savior
eye the beastman for a moment, then followed Tal's lead, and
their companions did the same.

By the time Garin approached the trunk, Tal had both
hands pressed to the bark. It was ridged and rough, and there
was a grayish cast to it. Tal's head was bowed as he murmured
words to the roots.

"The corruption is in the sorcery that feeds it," he said as
Garin stopped next to him. "Something arises from the World.
I cannot see how we'll fix this."

Garin winced and flashed a look back at Holt, hoping he
hadn't heard. The last thing they needed was for the beastman
to attack while they were spread out and distracted. But Holt
had returned to gazing mournfully upon his tree. The sight of
the forest caretaker's distress spurred a realization.

*He loves this tree, these woods. They're his home. And something
is corrupting it.*

With fresh determination, he turned back to the goldwood.
Closing his eyes, Garin opened himself to the Worldsong.

As usual, the disparate sounds took a moment to resolve
into harmony. When he focused on the components, he heard
them for the random cacophony they were. The whistle of the
wind through an open door. The hiss of bread steaming in the
oven. The gurgle of a fish's bubbles breaking a pond's surface.

They were meaningless on their own, mere noise. Yet
somehow, when they came together, they possessed all the
enchantment the World had to offer.

Through his months of slowly becoming attuned to the
Worldsong, Garin found his sensitivity grew with his appreci-
ation for it. Now, not only could he pull out the individual

sounds, but he could also concentrate on those that came from just around him. He'd done so with the phoenix and Tal back in the palace, and he found that once more, this deeper skill came into play.

The goldwood's song emerged first. The creak of old wood too long standing. The buzzing of corruption, like termites hollowing out the inside. The mournful swishing of dead leaves on brittle branches. Its sounds told of its eroding condition, of futility and decay. It wasn't a promising sign.

Though Garin knew he should concentrate on the tree, he found his curiosity drawn by the other localized songs he detected. As in the palace, Tal's was the most apparent. From him emanated a slow pulse like a heartbeat that flowed through their surroundings. Other sounds were attached to the man — his easy laugh, the creak of a leather saddle, the hiss of swinging steel — but the pulsing sound dominated the rest.

Even Holt possessed his own song. The nervous pawing of hooves on the loamy ground. The wind as he ran through the trees and fled this corruption. The roar of deep-seated anger against those who disturbed his weald. Garin suspected the beastman accessed much more sorcery than he first suspected, more than any of them except for Tal.

He tried to puzzle out what their having songs meant. Ilvuan had once said only dragons had songs separate from the Worldsong, but Garin's senses told him otherwise. Could he be mistaken? But how could he be, when his hearing them enabled him to join souls, or whatever he and Tal had done, to withstand the phoenix's faefire?

"Garin."

Garin opened his eyes, blinking and drawing away from the Worldsong so it faded to the recesses of his mind. "Tal?"

His old mentor gave him a small smile. "Can you hear it, the goldwood?"

Surprised by the question, he nodded.

"I thought you might." Tal stared up at the far-off boughs,

hundreds of feet above them. "The tree suffers. I suspect I know who's behind it."

Garin gnawed his lip for a moment. "Yuldor?" he guessed. "Or the Whispering Gods?"

"One and the same now, apparently." Tal lowered his gaze to meet Garin's again. "I still don't know what we can do. But I thought you and I might accomplish something together that we cannot separately."

Garin looked away, finding a distraction in noting what the rest of their friends were up to. Helnor stood next to the forest's caretaker and seemed to question him about a variety of possible causes. Wren, meanwhile, stood by the Prime Warder and just seemed to undermine his inquiry.

"Any unusual beasts, then?" Helnor pressed, his body turned away from Wren.

Not to be shut out, she leaned around the large elf. "Or any evil sorcerers?"

Judging by Holt's expression, their attempts were proving futile.

Falcon wandered around the tree, his lips moving silently. *Composing his songs, no doubt.*

Aelyn was just beyond the bard, where he kneeled on the network of roots and leaned in close. Garin saw he had various implements out and seemed to be taking samples from the tree, then testing them against strange powders and liquids. Holt cast him a glance every few moments, his face lined with disapproval, but he didn't stop the mage.

Ashelia had taken a more conventional approach. Like Tal, she pressed her hands to the bark and leaned against it, murmuring words of the Worldtongue that slipped past Garin's comprehension. They were healing words, he felt, though he couldn't say how. It was something in the way the Worldsong moved. But if her spells had any effect, he couldn't detect it.

"Well? Should we attempt a meshing?"

Tal brought his attention back with the query. Garin shrugged.

"I suppose we need to practice it anyhow."

"Suppose we do." His old mentor smiled, though a tightness remained around his eyes. "Now, do whatever you did before. I'm not sure how else to start this."

Nodding, Garin closed his eyes and expanded his awareness of the Worldsong. Especially with him standing so close, Tal's song instantly came into clarity. He tried to recall how he'd interwoven their songs before, but blanched at the answer. Garin had thrown himself into Tal then, blatantly ignoring any consequences. At the time, it seemed the only thing he could do. Now, however, caution was a better approach.

Tentatively, he reached for Tal's song. With invisible hands, Garin put forth his own being.

As soon as he touched Tal, he was swept up in his wake.

It was as if the man possessed a current of his own, and Garin was a branch on the river. He felt himself swirling down it, in danger of becoming lost. Desperate, he threw himself away, stretching back for what he knew was dependable and familiar.

He seized the Worldsong.

At once, it leaped to him, and like a boat's line to a dock, it tethered him. Yet, in a way he only vaguely understood, it also joined with them in the current.

Garin listened and marveled at what he and Tal had created. Their songs were merging, the sounds of their souls aligning, and the Worldsong underlay it all. The potential of it swept through his body, and though it felt distant amid the experience, sorcery was just a word away.

Now, Tal, he pressed onto the man. *Heal it now.*

CORRUPTION

HE HAD STEELED HIMSELF FOR THE MESHING, BUT TAL STILL flinched as Garin's soul threaded through his.

It wasn't a painful experience. As before, when they had faced the phoenix, Tal felt his sorcery blossom in his veins as its power multiplied. And such power it was! He felt he could move mountains if he willed it. Quell an earthquake.

Perhaps even slay a god.

But having his soul intertwined with another's, and the Worldsong coming with it — there was plenty of discomfort as well. Tal felt that foreign intrusion like a splinter under his skin, and he longed to dig it out. He only just resisted the urge. If he indulged it, who knew what might happen to Garin.

Now, Tal. Heal it now.

Garin's thoughts echoed in his mind, and Tal focused on the task at hand. *He's right. I have to heal it.* In this pairing, as in their previous, Tal was the conduit for their combined sorcery. He was the one who had to stave the corruption.

Tal set his hands to the goldwood's trunk and reached into it.

With sorcery burning through him, he saw its connections down into the ground where all magic seeped up from. What he saw perplexed him. The disease that was killing the tree came from no natural source, but from the core of the World itself.

Experimenting, he stretched forth his will and tapped the corruption. If the sorcery was a river, this blight was an inky, dark stain spread throughout it, pervasive and integrated. But it wasn't inert. As he brushed against it, it reached back, sucking at him like a leech searching for blood.

Tal flinched away. He could see no way of fighting such a thing. If he tried to drown it in a flood of power, he feared it would only absorb the magic and hunt for more.

Instead, Tal turned his vision downward to where it came from. The river of sorcery leading to the goldwood was wide, and the blight didn't fully stretch across it. Hoping his idea wasn't mere foolishness, Tal seized upon it.

He dove into the deepest root of the tree.

The World lost its hold on him as Tal swam down. He felt Garin still with him, straining to maintain their contact, and hoped it wouldn't cost him too dearly. They would have to go deep indeed to find the source of this issue.

Down he went. Garin and the Worldsong were double blessings as Tal passed the monochrome, shapeless beings that occupied this plane. Not only did they grant him sufficient power to challenge the creatures should they take too much interest, but they also kept him fettered to the World above. Considering the *Doash's* seductive whispers, he very well might need such an anchor.

The rot continued alongside him, expanding in the gold-wood's root the deeper they went. Tal feared what it must mean. *Is the* Doash *itself corrupted? Is that even possible?* It was the source of all sorcery, from what he could tell. If it was infected by this inky blackness, what could possibly resist it?

Just as he thought he might not slip past the foreign presence, the stream opened up into a wide, bright chamber. Tal's senses were drawn away from the darkness and the shapes flitting about the white emptiness into the enchanting orb at the center of it all.

The *Doash* murmured its usual promises to him. But before he could listen overlong, another voice intervened.

Heal...

Garin's distant thought echoed through Tal, and the agony of maintaining their meshing rang with it. It was enough to shake Tal free of his stupor and spring him back into action.

Ignoring the *Doash*, he focused again on the corruption. He was relieved to see it was localized, only spreading down the smallest part of the streams around the goldwood. But this showed him a perspective from the World itself. What was small here might be widespread on the surface.

Drifting closer, he followed the inkiness to the place where it ran thickest. There, a significant stream, far greater than what Tal or any creature could call upon, poured out the miasma into the core, gushing like a stream after the winter melt. He regarded it with equal measures of fascination and horror, knowing now what it was.

Yuldor.

He was entranced by the god-like presence. The rot didn't seem conscious, but more like a malevolent force of nature that asserted itself across the World. He thought of what he'd experienced of the Prince of Devils, of the secrets in Pim's books, of Garin and his conclusions. This added a new layer of complexity.

Yuldor wasn't just an elven sorcerer who had ascended, nor four beings living in one mind. He was a plague, a contagion threatening to swallow the whole of the World.

But how can I stop a disease?

Experimenting, Tal tried reaching out and manipulating the boundaries around the streams of sorcery leading out from the World's core, but he couldn't manage it. Changing them was like trying to touch air: though he could feel them, he had no power over them.

He tried channeling his sorcery, but as had occurred before in this realm, it was beyond his grasp. Magic's pure essence was all around him, yet he could only use it in the World above.

The inevitable conclusion lay before him, and though he didn't want to accept it, he knew it was the only thing he could do.

Tal returned to his own stream of sorcery and rose. His awareness of Garin became stronger as he neared the surface, the agony of the strain tearing at him as well. Tal drove harder, trying to relieve his onetime apprentice as swiftly as he could.

He returned to his body and reeled as Garin pried loose of him.

Tal found himself on his hands and knees. His vision was dotted with sparks. His throat felt as raw as if he'd been shouting, and his tongue was overlarge and swollen.

Recognizing voices, he shook himself free of his stupor and looked over to where the youth had stood before. Garin lay across the goldwood's roots now, Wren cradling his head. Falcon kneeled at his feet, and Rolan hovered just behind. All watched him nervously.

"Tal?"

Ashelia's hand brushed his shoulder. He turned up toward her and gave her a weary smile.

"I'm here."

"The tree…" She looked at the dead branches waving above. "Did you heal it?"

Aware of Holt observing them from the edge of the goldwood's roots, Tal spoke softly. "No. This isn't a disease that can be healed. Not now, at least."

Helnor had been standing near enough to overhear, and he leaned in close. "It's Yuldor, isn't it? He reaches his hand over this land."

Tal nodded. The Prince of Devils had always been the obvious answer.

"So I have also concluded." Aelyn had joined their small circle and looked down at him with an imperious air. "It is like no illness I have studied in trees or plants, and thus must be sorcerous in origin."

Tal raised an amused eyebrow. "So you're a botanist now, are you? Thought that was the purview of the Emerald Tower."

"Not now," Ashelia cut off her House-brother as he opened his mouth, eyes ablaze. "We have another disagreement to settle before quarreling among ourselves."

Tal didn't have to follow her gaze to know what she meant. He sighed and, though his limbs felt as if he'd been sprinting for hours on end, he levered himself upright. "I'll explain. Be prepared should I fail."

He didn't need to say more. By his companions' hard looks, they knew the possible price of the failure.

The beastman watched warily as Tal and the rest of their party headed toward him. "Do not trick me, man Tal," he rumbled as they drew near. "I can sense you have not cured the weald-tree."

Tal stopped a dozen paces away, hoping the precaution wouldn't be necessary. In the years since he'd been in his right mind, he'd grown to hate unnecessary killing. Doubly so for an individual who didn't seem to harm others without cause, cared for his own, and only wished to be left alone.

"I won't try to deceive you, Holt. You're right; we failed. But it's a feat beyond any mortal."

Holt shook his head with a snort and stamped the ground. With sorcery still curling through his veins, Tal sensed one of his companions edging back a step — Falcon, he guessed it to be.

"Explain!" the beastman demanded.

Tal stood his ground and spoke calmly. "It isn't a disease that affects your tree — it's a god's sorcery. Yuldor chokes the life from these lands."

Holt's expression became ugly with rage. "Yuldor! Long

have *chadi* spoken this name, and long have I hated it! *Yuldor!* How do you know this, man Tal? How can a mortal know his god?"

Tal held his gaze. "He's my adversary, Holt, not my god, and the scourge of all mortalkind. I've encountered him twice before; I know him now. But I know, too, because no other being possesses such power. He has claimed this goldwood — I suspect because of the breadth of sorcery it wields."

At his explanation, he began wondering what else might be possible for Yuldor to touch. If he could corrupt the tree, could he possess any person with access to sorcery? Could he seize Tal? Or his companions? The thought struck icy fear through him.

He had to kill this false god, now more than ever.

Holt's anger seemed to pass as quickly as it had come. The beastman twitched as he stared hard at Tal with one eye, the other observing Tal's companions.

"Very well, man Tal," he said at length. "Your slaying of my children was honest, if cruel. Your failure here is honest as well. Death does not sire death. But you, all of you" — Holt cast a furrowed look across their party — "will leave this place and never return. This is my gift for your empty aid."

Tal hid his wince. Failure had found him so often in his life he'd hoped he was used to it, but its sting was no softer than before.

"Thank you, Holt. And we are sorry, truly."

The beastman only snorted and turned away, arms crossed over his muscled chest. Keeping a wary eye on the caretaker in case he changed his mind, Tal led the others back west into the forest.

Someday, he thought to Holt, *someday soon, we will remedy this.*

But he didn't say the words aloud. As much as he wished otherwise, he couldn't guarantee it wasn't yet another false promise.

OASIS

As they left Holt's forest, Garin shared a deep sense of disquiet with his companions. Though all remained silent, he knew the same question circled in their minds by the bowed heads, the frozen stares, the fidgeting hands.

If we cannot beat Yuldor here, so far from his fortress, how can we defeat him at all?

He couldn't find much reason for hope. He'd been with Tal as he beheld Yuldor's presence creeping through that sorcerous plane. He'd felt the futility of their combined power, of any amount of sorcery. The Prince of Devils was exactly as Tal claimed him to be: a ravaging disease stretching across the World, sucking the life from all it touched.

There was nothing they could do to stop him.

Yet he thought back to all that Tal and Kaleras, before his death, had shared of the tome written by the Nightelf sorceress, Hellexa Yoreseer. He recalled Pim's claims regarding his master.

Yuldor's power lies in the Worldheart. If we can take that from him, he will become only a man again.

But Garin was finding that harder and harder to believe.

131

He chewed it over as they traveled east through the forest. For one, there were the Whispering Gods to account for. From all the tales he'd heard, Garin's best guess was that they hadn't died as Pim had once claimed to Tal, but lain dormant within the Worldheart until Yuldor came and awoke them.

If Tal — or, Silence forbid, Garin — took the Worldheart for their own, would they not suffer the same fate as the ancient elven sorcerer? Would they lose their minds and become possessed by three long-departed Origins?

He clenched Tempest's reins. *We'll find a way*, he told himself. *We must.* They'd seen the stakes in Kavaugh and in Holt's goldwood. Yuldor wasn't content to spread peace and "Paradise" across the World. He brought only war and pestilence and death. He would choke the life from the land and drain sorcery down to its core if he could.

Perhaps only in death can he find peace, he thought bitterly.

But Garin didn't wish to stew in his thoughts. Circling endlessly around the issue would do nothing but make him miserable and their quest futile. He had to believe they would find a way — or, at the very least, that his task for Ilvuan might sway the outcome in their favor.

Seeking consolation, he opened himself to the Worldsong. But almost as soon as he began listening, he discovered even this last bastion hadn't remained untouched. There was something to the aria that was different, something aligning the parts. It should have made it more harmonious; instead, it only stained its strains.

He stretches forth his reach.

Garin hadn't noticed Ilvuan's arrival, so concentrated had he been on the Worldsong. Now, he felt his claws touching lightly on the peripheries of his mind.

Like a dragon perched to take flight.

The idle thought seemed to please the Singer, for he radiated his approval.

Garin smiled as he replied. *Even into the Song? But why now? Why didn't he long ago infect the World as he does now?*

Ilvuan rumbled an assent. *The Pretender is threatened — you and Heartblood imperil him. Endure,* Jenduit. *Our resistance is not futile, for you do not fly alone.*

The surety of the dragon pressed through him like the feeling of entering a warm house after a cold winter morning.

I'll keep going, he replied. *I'll do as you've asked.*

The Singer rumbled again, then released his grip and slipped back into the ether.

"What are you smiling about?"

Garin reoriented himself to the World and met Wren's questing gaze. Her thin lips were still set in a frown, her dark eyebrows knitted together. The gold in her eyes shone dully and spun sluggishly. Even her short, springy hair seemed to lie flatter.

"Ilvuan says it's still possible," he murmured. "We can still defeat Yuldor."

Wren snorted. "How? We couldn't even save a tree. I'm starting to think a god might be too much for even Tal Harrenfel to handle."

Garin didn't want to admit that Ilvuan hadn't provided much in the way of specifics. As usual, the dragon had pressed forth his expectations with brief explanation. But he had to say something.

"We have dragons on our side," he said with as much confidence as he could muster.

"*Dead* dragons."

"The dead don't talk, do they? They'll resurrect at the hatching grounds — just wait and see."

"Oh, good. Baby dragons are much better."

Garin sighed. "If you want to believe the worst, I can't stop you."

Wren grinned. "No, you can't."

He felt warmed by her teasing. It was a little sliver of normalcy that they both desperately needed.

The forest was broader than anticipated and the lack of a discernible path made the journey longer. The sun was already falling by the time the trees thinned and the edge of the weald came into view. Not wishing to provoke Holt's wrath again, Ashelia instructed that they keep pressing forward across the plains.

They were fortunate. After the sun had set and only blue dusk light guided their way, they came upon a small grove Garin judged unlikely to be guarded by beast, man, or anything in between. Among the trees, they pitched camp and started a fire around which they sat and ate salted deer. Garin tried not to think about the doe's gills as he chewed through another tough bite.

Aelyn interrupted the silence, which had only been broken by Rolan's occasional strums on his small lute. "So, Man of a Thousand Names. I assume you know our next steps?"

Tal looked up at Ashelia. "Your House-sister has always been sharper with details than I."

"And here I thought there was nothing you weren't talented at," the mage sneered.

"Peace, Aelyn," Ashelia said wearily. "We head into more foreboding lands now. The Kaksis Wastes await us before we reach the shores of the Far Depths. From what the Emperor's cartographers could tell me, it will take at least four days to cross, longer if we're forced to detour."

Helnor rumbled his dissent. "That poses a problem, *Kolesa*. We only have food for two more days."

"I know. But this desert is regularly crossed by Imperials, and they have outposts where we can resupply. The first, Trader Springs, should be two days from us now." Despite the answer, Ashelia still wore a black expression that Garin found far from reassuring.

"At least we'll always have water," Tal pointed out with a

tentative smile. To illustrate his point, he raised his hand and pulled at the air. Water droplets formed from nothing, then beaded on his skin before Tal dashed them in Rolan's face, to the boy's giggling protests. Garin couldn't help but smile whenever the two got up to their antics. Almost, they acted like uncle and nephew, or perhaps even father and son.

"As long as the air is not devoid of moisture," Aelyn noted snidely.

Tal raised an eyebrow at the elf. "Careful, mage. Unless you wish to gather your own water in the Kaksis Wastes?"

"Perhaps I will."

Wren stood and brushed herself off. "Amusing as your squabbles are, I think it's past time for sleep. Especially for that one." She nodded toward Rolan with a smirk.

"Hey!" the boy objected. "I've faced Ravagers and Nightkin the same as you!"

Falcon, who sat on Rolan's other side, placed his hand on his shoulder. "Rolan, my boy, boasts are best saved for great accomplishments, not squandered on humble ones. If it is worthy of a song, then sing it far and wide! Until then, praises for yourself only sound like a cow's mooing."

The boy flushed and crossed his arms over his lute as the rest of them chuckled, and Ashelia drew her son away to comfort him.

"You coming?"

Garin rose quickly at Wren's quiet summons, a smile coming to his lips. He had a feeling that more than sleep awaited him beneath the horse blanket that night.

Tal squinted into the forbidding landscape ahead. As Ashelia had predicted, the plains beyond Holt's weald grew steadily drier and sparser in vegetation. With the dry heat of summer holding thrall, wringing water from the air became a chore rather than a simple matter of wishing it.

The flatlands wrinkled into hills, and the dirt became sandy. In place of tall grass and crops of corn and barley, now squat shrubs with scraggly branches scratched their mounts' legs, and spiny cacti threatened to lame the riders at every dismount. The sun had grown hostile; there was barely a cloud to be seen and even Ashelia and Helnor burned under its gaze. Only Tal was protected thanks to the sorcery in his veins.

But as disagreeable as the journey proved to be, it was their rapidly dissipating food that had him most concerned. They'd eaten through all but a few strips of the smoked deer they'd poached and now relied upon their emergency stores. In this desolate landscape, it seemed unlikely they would stumble upon anything larger than the rodents that poked their heads up from their burrows, and even those were becoming scarce.

They needed to find the oasis, and soon.

Tal glanced at Ashelia and was glad Rolan had nodded off in her arms. "Should be close, wouldn't you think?"

Her look betrayed her thoughts. "We can hope," was all she said aloud.

Wishing to offer her some comfort — and himself as well — he drew on the sorcery and, with a murmur, extended his vision to gaze over the landscape. Hills and dunes stretched as far as he could see, which was now far indeed. Only as he gazed upon an area slightly to their right did he get the sense that something broke up the landscape.

Dismissing the spell, he blinked as his vision distorted, then slowly resolved back into ordinary sight. "There's a spot of green about two miles ahead."

Ashelia sat up straighter. Glancing back, she murmured, "Don't tell the others yet. No need to raise their hopes before we're certain."

"And if we find our greeting to be less than friendly?"

She cast him a sly smile. "I'm not afraid. Not when we have you."

That smile always brought out a grin of his own, but it quickly failed. Tal wished he could reply the same, but the truth was he'd never been more afraid. Not for his own safety — of that, he had little concern. It was the well-being of her, and her son, and all their companions that kept him awake at night.

He'd failed to protect them before. He was desperate to never let it happen again.

But no matter how fast your legend grows, Tal Harrenfel, the danger grows faster.

The glimpse of green turned out to be no mirage. After several more rises, the oasis appeared in a basin below them. As expected, they weren't the only visitors. Tal counted at least ten caravans of the strange, humped reptiles that were being used as beasts of burden. Dun of skin, they had ridges along their sides, and a crest of spines fell over the rounded crown. From beneath it, cold eyes peered out, devoid of human warmth. Their backs edged up in one or two humps, and their bellies nearly scraped the ground when they walked on their powerful, stocky legs. A dozen feet long each, Tal hoped they were as placid as they seemed, for he couldn't imagine them to be pleasant opponents.

Deeper in the oasis, a collection of sandstone buildings stood. They matched the bland landscape and were arranged in an arc around one side of the watering hole. Their entrances lacked doors, and people spilled in and out of the archways. Many were Easterner humans, but those armed were more often medusal. Though Ashelia had warned of the likelihood, Tal's blood tingled at the sight of them. All the medusals wore red, symbolizing their fealty to the fief of Rajeya, and thereby marking them as their enemies. He could only hope they wouldn't realize it.

Their party halted at the top of the rise and gazed down on the oasis. Aelyn broke the silence first.

"We won't resupply by staying up here," he noted tartly. "If we must fight, then let's be done with it."

"Hold on, my dear curmudgeon," Tal said as Aelyn headed forward, grinning at the mage's scowl. "We have to approach with a plan."

Aelyn arched an eyebrow. "And here I thought you had merely to walk into a place to own it."

"Peace, for the Mother's sake." Ashelia looked tired, and her reprimand came out sharper than usual. "There is a grave likelihood this will come to blood. We must stay close together and look after our own."

"You need not dance around the issue," Falcon remarked, not bothering to hide his wounded pride. "Rolan and I will cower amongst you, as usual."

"I can fight!" Rolan asserted angrily. "Stop saying I can't!"

"Those are soldiers, lad, trained and blooded," Tal told him gently. "No shame in recognizing things as they stand."

The boy scarcely seemed placated, but he settled for silent stewing. Tal looked back over his shoulder at Garin. The youth wore an amused smile, though it had a sickly twist to it. He was only fifteen summers himself — or was it sixteen now? Either way, he and Wren were young to be facing such opponents. Yet they'd proven themselves time and again.

And you won't let any harm come to them, he told himself. *This time, you'll protect them.*

Helnor led his stor in front of the others. "That's as best as we can plan for. Come — we don't want to draw suspicion by waiting up here."

Tal wondered if they'd already tarried too long, or if the soldiers gave every newcomer those hard stares. Then again, he had to admit their party was most unusual. With four Gladelysh elves, two half-elves, two humans, and stors for half their mounts, they would be easily identifiable if word of them spread. Perhaps it already had, if Ravagers had preceded them, or if Yuldor had sorcerous means of posting his bounties.

It cannot start here, Tal promised himself. *I won't let us be hunted. Not again.*

He'd kill every last soldier if that was what it took.

With hardened resolve, he flashed the soldiers a smile, knowing it looked about as friendly as the humped lizards. The soldiers didn't immediately challenge them, but talked among themselves. Tal and his companions took advantage of the reprieve to dismount and tie up their mounts next to the watering hole. Per their earlier agreement, no one strayed far, though Rolan looked tempted to go for a swim by his darting eyes.

Tal rested a hand on *Velori's* pommel and, approaching Ashelia, murmured, "I should negotiate for food."

Her eyes flashed with gray light. "Not yet. The soldiers will approach us soon. We should all remain here until then."

"I'm the safest one to stray," Tal pointed out. "And if I can broker a deal before they challenge us…"

Ashelia was already shaking her head. "It won't be soon enough. I know you wish to avoid violence, Tal, but you cannot talk your way out of every fight."

She'd cut to the heart of it. Except during his blackest and bloodiest years, Tal had preferred to avoid violence rather than fight. He'd deserted the Avendoran army. He'd fled before the Extinguished more than once. Whatever gods remained in the World had gifted him in sorcery and swordplay, but that didn't mean he wanted to indulge in them.

But this was less about his natural reticence and more about his fear. After all, violence beget violence, and he wanted none of it aimed at those few in the World he cared for, whom he'd dragged into his reckless quest.

Tal sighed. "I hope you're wrong. But I suspect, as usual, you're not."

Ashelia gave him a tight smile before shifting her stance

into one he recognized as the Form of Water from elven dancing. Sighing again, he settled into a relaxed and ready position of his own and waited.

The medusals poured out of the buildings, numbering far more than it seemed such a compound should host. Tal noted two dozen before he lost count. They carried scimitars, javelins, and spears, many of which were already bared and ready. Bronze scaled armor protected their chests and shoulders, and scaled faulds fell down over their upper thighs and their tails. Their helmets were formed to their long faces and the fins projecting around their heads, and yellow eyes gleamed out from beneath the helms. Though they were lithe, Tal knew they possessed a wiry strength that was not to be underestimated. If they inherited any sorcerous abilities from their Bloodline, he couldn't detect them.

Tal kept his wolf's smile on, his hand resting on his sword, and sucked in sorcery until it smoldered through his blood. He was content with Ashelia speaking for their company, preferring to remain on the lookout for any signs of attack.

One soldier walked ahead of the others. By the polish of her armor, the plumage in her helmet, and the aura of command about her, he judged her to be the captain of this outpost.

"What are you *kurag* doing here at Trader Springs?" The captain addressed them in the common Darktongue.

Ashelia bowed in a respectful, almost servile manner, suitable for Imperial culture. "Our apologies, Captain," she replied in common Darktongue. "We are refugees from Elendol after the civil war there left us homeless. We have been wandering your glorious Empire ever since, hoping to find a place to establish ourselves."

The captain eyed her, betraying no sign of whether or not she believed the explanation. "What are your occupations?"

"A variety of trades, sir." Ashelia must have thought through their ruse beforehand, for she didn't miss a beat in her reply.

"We are bards, fortunetellers, dousers. Two are men for hire." She gestured to Tal at that.

The captain looked over them, but her gaze lingered on Tal longest. No doubt she evaluated how capable a fighter he was. But she showed no fear, as expected. With a score of her warriors at her back, she likely thought there was no contention as to who would win a conflict.

Finally, she said, "Do you have papers from Lord Kraul Shraxl condoning your passage?"

Tal felt his smile waver. This had always been a weak point in their plan for infiltrating the fief. With the Empire divided in its loyalties, it had been assumed that fiefs would close their borders to any but their own citizens. Zyrl had provided papers with his seal of office but Tal doubted those would matter in this land.

Still, Ashelia made the attempt. "Captain, we have papers from His Imperial Eminence Zyrl Netherstar. I can present these to you."

"Do they bear Lord Kraul Shraxl's seal?" The captain was relentless.

Ashelia hesitated. "No, sir. They do not."

"Then you and your party have entered Rajeya unlawfully. You will come with us to be questioned, then suffer whatever consequences the fief lord sees as right and fair."

Tal longed to strike then and there while the soldiers were still preparing to meet any resistance. But as he heard muttering behind him and felt a thread of sorcery stretch forth from one of his companions, he hesitated, hoping Aelyn had something up his sleeve.

"Excuse us, sir." Even under such dire circumstances, the mage couldn't say the honorific without a sneer. "We have valid passage into fief Rajeya. Surely you will allow us to restock our supplies and let us be on our way."

He must have been employing a spell of influence, for Tal felt the inclination himself to believe the mage, even guarded against sorcery as he was. He kept his eyes on the captain, watching those yellow eyes for any sign of success.

The medusal held still for a long moment. Then, with a shudder that went through her entire body, she sprang back toward her soldiers and drew her scimitar.

"Sorcery!" she shrieked, pointing her blade at them. "Kill the mages and take the others!"

Tal bared his teeth, and as he drew his sword, he lashed forward with all the sorcery brewing inside him.

SUN-BLINDED FOOLS

GARIN HELD OUT HOPE THAT AELYN'S TRICKERY WOULD WORK.

He stood next to the mage as he rifled a hand through a pouch, muttering to himself all the while. Garin guessed his intent at once: to find a catalyst for a spell. Considering the threat before them, he wasn't sure what any charm could do to stop the bloodshed.

Though unable to understand much of the exchange, having never learned more than a few words in common Darktongue, Garin could tell by the tense stances that negotiations weren't faring well. At what seemed the critical moment, when the soldiers shifted forward at one of their captain's statements, Aelyn muttered words that seemed to echo in Garin's skull.

"*Onegin, dae jes ild...*"

Garin, already open to the Worldsong, felt the shift as his sorcery wormed through the air. For a moment, it seemed to take hold. The captain went utterly still. Garin dared to believe the mage's hasty efforts would pay off.

But as was often the case with hopes, he found them to be wholly unfounded.

As the Rajeyans attacked, Garin acted on instinct, calling

forth a wind shield and directing it to spread above his companions. As it buffeted before Tal and Ashelia, who stood at the front of their party, Garin's spell intercepted several javelins and tossed them aside.

He barely had time for a moment's satisfaction for the medusals were suddenly among them. Though he felt Tal's sorcery surge, Garin knew he couldn't catch all the enemies in his web. They were too fast, and judging by the captain's reaction to Aelyn's spell, they possessed an innate resistance to sorcery.

Garin barely had time to pull *Helshax* free before a soldier stabbed forth a spear. He knocked the point aside, but almost got Wren skewered on it, preoccupied as she was with two more Rajeyans. Her rapier was a blur and cantrips rattled off in flashes of fire and wind to keep her opponents on the tips of their clawed toes.

He had his own worries. As sand whipped up toward the bulk of the soldiers in a mighty summoning of Tal's, Garin used another windshield to knock aside the spearman's second attempt to skewer him, then countered with a shouted, "*Dord uvthak!*"

He didn't know how sand would respond to the spell, as it was meant to command rock. Yet stone must have been hiding beneath, as the ground spit forth a column that crashed into the soldier's hip and sent him spinning to the ground. As his adversary shrieked and struggled to stand, Garin brought his sword to bear, cleaving into the medusal's collarbone and silencing his pained screams.

Garin raised his head just in time to parry a slash from a scimitar-wielding Rajeyan. The medusal's sharp teeth were bared as she slashed back and forth, trying to cut him down. He recognized the tactic for what it was: an unskilled, brute force method of fighting. It was just the sort of style elven dancing had been crafted to counter.

Adopting the Form of Air, Garin avoided and blocked the

medusal's strikes, waiting for his opportunity. He'd never fought in a sandy environment before, and unlike the medusal, he lacked claws to find a more certain grip. At each step, his feet slid and shifted, and he found more than once a strike coming too near to cutting him.

But finally, his chance came. Garin once again knocked aside his opponent's blade when the soldier struck forth with her buckler. Such a move exposed the left flank, and Garin went for it, lunging around the attack and whipping *Helshax* across the scaled armor. The impact jarred up his arm as the runic sword cut through the metal. The medusal collapsed with unintelligible curses, clutching at the blood streaming down her armor.

But Garin didn't have a chance to finish her off. A panicked shout from Wren had him turning around to see several of the large humped lizards bearing down on them with a speed that defied their size.

He didn't even have time to curse before they barreled into him.

Tal's focus split in a dozen directions.

A torrent of sorcery whipped through him, enough to wipe away all their enemies in a single spell. Yet the circumstances hamstrung his power. With the enemy interspersed among his companions, he had to contend with one at a time.

Having dealt with the main part of the company at the start, Tal maintained a barrier of wind and sand around them as he turned his attention to the medusals who had slipped behind. One by one, he took care of them, thrusting spires of stone through soldier's chests and limbs. He burned medusals until they could no longer stand. He commanded the sand to stick their feet in place, allowing Helnor and Ashelia to cut down their opponents.

But when the sand drakes charged into Garin, he found his efforts still weren't enough.

"Garin!" Tal roared as he reached forward with his sorcery. Ancient words twisted through his mind as he manipulated air and earth around his onetime apprentice, trying to block the clawed, pounding feet of the lizards stomping over him. "*Garin!*"

He ran toward him, but he was too far away. Only his sorcery could protect the youth, and he couldn't tell if it was enough. Sand from his spells spilled into the air and obscured where Garin had fallen. As more sand drakes headed toward him, Tal diverted them with quick spellwork, summoning walls of stone to turn them aside and instead run into the remaining soldiers, who fared no better than Garin as the beasts of burden trampled them.

Tal moved around the others and ignored their shouts as he made for Garin. He dismissed his spells around the youth, though he kept the orb of sand and wind around their party, protecting from further incursions.

The lad was bloodied, writhing and moaning where he'd been flattened into the ground. Tal fell to his knees next to him and looked him over. He saw no mortal wounds, but under the force of such heavy creatures, he knew internal injuries could be just as severe.

Ashelia was beside him the next moment. "I'll handle this, Tal," she assured him. She'd gained a fresh cut across her forehead, and the blood leaked into her swirling eyes.

He didn't want to leave it to her. She had access to a fraction of the power he did. But though Tal had some innate mastery of the World, he'd healed no one beyond himself, and then it had been by instinct. Now wasn't the time to experiment on one of his dearest friends.

Besides, enemies remained to be slain.

As Tal rose, Garin coughed out a sentence. "Sorcery... inside." He raised a hand to point.

Tal wondered what the youth had felt. Was it something Ilvuan had told him, or did he hear it in the Worldsong? Either way, he sensed what Garin had a moment later. In the direction he'd indicated, a spell had been cast.

There was a sorcerer nearby.

"Save him," he told Ashelia, his voice rough from breathing in the dust. Then he leaped to his feet and sprinted toward his spell wall.

He burst through it to a startling sight. Half a dozen more medusals waited, an uncertain line formed as they stared at Tal's ward. At his appearance, most took a cautious step backward. Only one dared challenge him, his lipless mouth pulled back in a snarl.

Tal cut him down, first stiffening the air around the soldier, then whipping his blade forward to slice through his exposed neck.

The other medusals were quick learners. As they fled, Tal felt a pull in his chest. *Spare them. Let them go. What harm can they do?*

But survivors would alert the fief to their presence. As little as he wished to do this, he had to protect his own party first.

Tal drew on his sorcery. A wave of wind crashed down on the medusals from above, while spires of stone thrust through their prone bodies.

None survived for long.

His gut in knots, Tal glanced around to make sure no other enemies remained, then headed for the first building. He didn't relish the idea of entering the enclosed space, knowing it was riskier than doing battle out in the open. Trusting his instincts and sorcery, he summoned an orb of werelight and stepped cautiously within.

He was soon disappointed. The building only contained sleeping quarters. Cots littered the ground and possessions spilled out of bags. Tal tried not to linger on anything. Look too long, and he might picture all the lives he'd ended, all the people who would mourn their departures.

Exiting, Tal moved to the next domicile. This one proved more promising, being larger and with several chambers built into it. Once more, he entered warily, sword and magic held at the ready. No one ambushed him in the fore, and he gazed around. It appeared to be the front end of a storeroom; perhaps this was where his party would have haggled for supplies had they been allowed to. He proceeded behind the table to the curtain over the entrance behind it. Someone seemed to have entered it in haste, for the curtain hung slightly ajar rather than covering the entire portal. Tal led the way with the tip of his blade and the werelight.

Only his readiness saved him from the spear thrusting toward his face.

The medusal leaped into view, spittle spewing from between sharp teeth. He fought with the fury of a cornered beast, spear darting back and forth in an attempt to skewer Tal.

All his pity died at the attack. Summoning fire, Tal ignited the spear in the soldier's hands. The stubborn medusal clung on for another thrust, then dropped it as the pain became too great. As he shrieked, Tal grabbed hold of him with a fist of sorcerous wind.

The soldier's wide eyes gleamed as the werelight's illumination caught in them. The fear in them sickened Tal, but he didn't release him. He had to know everything this man did.

Tal looked around, then located a chair in the far corner of the room. With a second summoning of wind, he brought it close and sat back in it. The Rajeyan stared at him, shocked into silence.

"I think we got off on the wrong foot," Tal said, as pleasant as if they sat down for a shared ale. "Let's start again. I sensed sorcery in here, but I don't see a sorcerer."

The medusal only continued to stare at him.

Tal sighed, then swept an arm around him. "I didn't want to do any of this; your captain forced my hand. I don't want to kill you, either. So tell me where the sorcery came from, and we'll work out a deal."

The Rajeyan held out a little longer before the words hissed out like a boiling kettle.

"Not a sorcerer — a charm. We use it to alert other outposts. They know intruders have come here. So no need to kill me." This last bit, the soldier said with a glimmer of hope.

Tal gazed at him a moment longer, then sighed again and rose. The medusal started babbling as he advanced on him and struggled against his sorcerous bonds, but to no avail. Tal snapped *Velori* up and through his heart. A few moments later, the man went limp, and Tal released the spell to let the body thud to the ground.

For a moment, he could only stare at the dead Rajeyan. Much as he wished otherwise, he couldn't leave him alive. Even if he told the truth, there was too great a risk. He'd seen Tal's face and knew of his company.

He had to protect them, even if it damned himself.

Breathing through his mouth so as not to smell the body, Tal focused back on the task at hand. Bags of grain were stored on one side, while the other was occupied by barrels of what smelled like salted fish. He saw nothing suspicious until he quested with his sorcery. Then he felt it: a thin thread connecting to a small bell hanging from the opposite end. There was the telltale knot of an enchantment worked on the object. It didn't take any great powers of deduction to figure out how it worked.

He stared at it by the werelight's gleam for a long moment, a sense of dread filling him as he thought of all that bell might portend. Fief Rajeya was alerted to their presence. Even Yuldor and the devils in his head might know where they were now. Their movements were no longer anonymous, but all too predictable.

But he couldn't worry about that now. Other Rajeyan soldiers could be hiding in Trader Springs, and Ashelia might need help in healing Garin. He had to protect his friends any way he still could.

Tal broke the enchantment on the bell, then turned and left the storeroom, feeling very much like the sun-blinded fool he'd always suspected he was.

FROM SAND TO SEA

"So," Aelyn remarked with false cheer, "not only did you fail to protect your apprentice, but you also alerted the entire fief to our incursion."

Garin winced, and not only from his healing wounds. Tal, at whom the mage's insults were leveled, didn't seem to be handling the aftermath of the battle at Trader Springs well. His shoulders were bowed, and he stared down at his hands as if they'd betrayed him. His old mentor had always accepted more blame than he had a right to, and Aelyn knew it.

"Aelyn," Ashelia said, a warning in her voice. "Now isn't the time."

The mage only smiled. "When is the time, then? When our heads sit on spears?"

"Yuldor's bloody prick, Aelyn!" Wren threw up her hands. "Shut up for one damned moment, would you?"

That shocked him into silence. Aelyn brooded and promised revenge with his stare at Wren, and she glared right back, her eyes making her own violent vows.

Garin heaved in a breath and winced again. He sat with the others at the camp they'd set up at the edge of the now-abandoned oasis. It didn't seem as idyllic as when they'd first arrived. The sand was stained brown with spilled blood. Many of the palm trees had splintered or been uprooted on the near-side of the watering hole, the one he leaned against one of the exceptions. The stench of the burning bodies curled inside Garin's nostrils. The other travelers had fled as soon as the violence began, and the abandoned buildings had almost as much of a haunted feel to them as the Ruins of Erlodan had.

The others had been busy while Garin recovered. Their food stores were replenished with the soldiers' stocks, and they'd gathered additional water bladders, insurance against the arid climate. Working through the heat of the day had exhausted them, and though evening brought bearable temperatures, tempers were still running hot.

Aelyn finally ignored Wren's remark and went back to easier prey. "I would have preferred if you had left the artifact intact, Harrenfel. I could have ascertained if it performed the function you claim it did."

Tal shrugged. "You're right. I acted rashly."

Garin found his shift in attitude unnerving. Tal was the crux of their plans, the foundation of their resolve. If their man of legend was having doubts, he feared they stood even less chance against Yuldor than he'd thought.

Ashelia, however, seemed to read differently into it. "There was nothing else you could have done. This was the way it had to be."

"Dozens of soldiers dead, and for what?" A bitter smile twisted Tal's lips. "For standing in our way. Doesn't strike me as any better than Yuldor might have done."

Garin pursed his lips. He didn't like to think they shared any moral ground with the Prince of Devils.

But it's always been a fight for survival, hasn't it? You'd do anything to preserve your life and the lives of those you love.

Moral or not, he'd found it to be true for him. He couldn't truly regret anything he had done to keep his companions alive.

Falcon cleared his throat and adopted an uncertain smile. "Our cause is just, my friend; do not doubt it now. It comes at a cost, 'tis true, but every great deed does."

Tal shifted his gaze over to the bard, smile never slipping. "And I suppose great deeds deserve great songs, don't they? Will you write an epic of today? Of the massacre of the medusals?"

"Enough, Tal." Ashelia's voice was low but firm. "If we must discuss this, we'll do it later. For tonight, let's press on for the shore."

Helnor heaved a sigh and rose. "I'll ready our mounts, then. Rolan, come help me."

As the others moved to make the final preparations, Wren kneeled by Garin's side. "You alright to travel?"

His insides felt like kneaded dough, but he gave her a weak smile. "I'll be fine."

She raised an eyebrow, then extended a hand. "Just don't rupture anything. Wouldn't want a mess to clean up."

He groaned as she hauled him to his feet, but didn't object to the swift peck she planted on his cheek. Thorny as Wren usually was, she had a softness to her. Though he moved like Kaleras had just before his death, worn down by the journey and his wounds, Garin found he still smiled.

Guess you can get used to anything, he thought as the smoke from the burning corpses stained the air above.

Once more, Ashelia's predictions proved correct, for it was three days of plodding over the dunes before they finally ended.

The Laksis Wastes were endlessly uninteresting. Garin stared with sun-dazzled eyes at the sinuous horizon, hoping to see something that would break up the monotony. Except on the rare occasion, when he imagined a mirage from the phantom heat, nothing emerged.

The only exceptions were the dust devils. Manifesting in small twisters of sand and wind, they appeared from nowhere and would harass their party until Tal or Aelyn banished them. Neither of the men could tell Garin whether they were sentient Nightkin or mere manifestations of the elements. If they were just a weather pattern, they had a strange proclivity for mischief, and Garin's eyes often stung with sand when the sun wasn't knifing them with reflected light.

Their nightly camps were less than cheery. Sand grains found their way into his bedroll and every garment Garin owned. Wren suffered the same issue he gathered from her incessant complaints. Even Falcon's cheer deflated, and he only continued Rolan's lessons on the lute at the boy's insistence.

Most everyone's skin had reddened to the point of peeling. Worse effects, such as "sun toxin," as Ashelia called it, were kept at bay by the Peer's evening anointments. Garin was glad to have her with them, for the wounds he'd taken at Trader Springs had all but healed, the scripts around them working to close the flesh with sorcerous haste.

Still, it came as a relief to all when, in the late afternoon of the third day, the sand merged with a bright, blue sea.

Garin stared at the Far Depths of Du'orlam with an awe that lifted the malaise of the days before. He'd looked upon it often during his time in the Coral Castle, but it had been a year since then, and he had seen many things in the intervening stretch. Now, he beheld it with fresh eyes. Water reached toward the horizon, entirely unlike the suffocating desert. It was a promise of more to come.

He shared a smile with Wren and eagerly followed the others to the beach, still some miles distant.

Garin smelled the salt on the wind first. The moisture it brought was a relief to his blistered skin and cracked lips. The land leveled out as they reached the shore, the tide having worn the sand smooth. The incessant roar of the water felt like the underpinning to the Worldsong he'd been missing.

They made camp near the beach, just beyond the reach of high tide. Though they still lacked wood for a fire, they sat around summoned werelights and stared off toward the misty edge of the World. Garin wondered what lay beyond it, if there were other lands like theirs suffering their own problems. He wondered how far water stretched before it fell into the black nothing that filled the night sky. Once, he had believed that was the Night coming to lay claim to the lands, but he knew better than to think that now. Still, his old curiosity awoke as he stared at the moons, both nearly full that night, and the stars. He longed to know their secrets. By habit, he traced the constellations with his eyes, pausing as he came to the one signifying the man sitting across from him.

It was seven points, and it was supposed to depict Tal challenging Heyl in Elendol. Garin glanced over at the man and wondered if he was more or less like the hero in that constellation now. Tal had been quiet in the days since the oasis, almost brooding. His smile, whenever it was present, was more often filled with mockery than joy.

Perhaps, Garin mused, *earning your stars isn't all it once seemed.*

He startled at a pressure on his hand, expecting it to be one of the crabs that frequented this beach. But as he looked over, he found Wren staring at him, her gold tendrils agleam. She leaned in close and spoke in his ear.

"Want to take a walk with me?"

There was only one answer to that. Trying not to worry about what the others would think, he nodded, then they made their excuses and stole away.

"Don't wander far," Ashelia called after them. Falcon's eyes seemed to bore into Garin's back, though he wondered if it was just his imagination. The bard had never been very disapproving before, but he was still Wren's father.

Werelights held before them, they walked the length of the dark beach. Shells crunched under their feet, the tide having pulled back out and exposed the sea's treasures. Wren wore a small smile and glanced over at him often. Garin's heart raced from more than wandering off through a dark, foreign land. The shiver that rushed over him was from more than the incessant sea breeze.

At last, when the werelights from their camp grew muted, Wren tugged him off his feet. Garin went down with a yelp, then let out a surprised laugh as Wren placed herself on top of him.

"Don't worry," she said as she began pulling off his shirt, then moved her hands down to untie his belt and trousers. "I'll be gentle."

"Not too gentle." He matched her grin as he twisted her around and won a surprised squeal from her.

After he'd slipped off her shirt and their skin pressed warm against each other, she touched a hand to his chest. He opened his eyes and met her gaze. By the werelights, he saw her pupils had grown wide, and her tendrils swam swiftly.

"If I have to fight against gods and demons," Wren murmured, "I'm glad it's with you."

He cupped her cheek gently before kissing her. "With you as company, I would have expected to do nothing less."

She laughed until his lips stole away her mirth.

THE HIDDEN ALLY

You could be a god, Tal Harrenfel, if you dared.

Pim's final words circled through Tal's mind during the days they wandered up the Far Depths shoreline. Sometimes, they seemed mocking, as the Extinguished often had been in life. More often, he reached for them with yearning.

He wanted them to be true. If they were, all their pain and heartbreak might have meaning. Kaleras, the father he'd never fully known, wouldn't have died in vain. All those he killed and were slain in this rebellion against Yuldor — at Kavaugh, at Naruah, at Vathda, in the Westreach — they would be martyrs, not casualties.

But he suspected a different truth. He couldn't be a god; no mortal could. Neither Yuldor nor the Whispering Gods had truly ascended. Judging by his few glimpses of the elven sorcerer, Yuldor lived in fear and agony, his mind split, its parts vying for supremacy.

There are no gods — just fools pretending.

"A ditty for your dilemmas?"

Tal glanced over with a tolerant smile as Falcon came abreast of him on his stor. The Gladelysh mount was stately in its size and crown, but Savior was larger and stronger still, so he had the pleasure of looking down on his friend.

"Oh, they're not worth the trouble," Tal replied with a look over his shoulder, making certain the others trailed far enough behind not to eavesdrop over the crash of the waves. "Just worrying that I'm going to get you all killed for nothing."

"I'd rather that not happen." His friend's face creased in a wide smile, but Tal saw his own anxieties reflected in his eyes. "The reasons are many. First, if I die, I'm not likely to complete your legend, am I? And second, if it ends in failure, then what in Silence's name am I writing it for? This is an epic, my noble protagonist, not a tragedy!"

Tal sighed. "I'm afraid, my friend, that remains to be seen."

He turned forward again. They'd already traveled two days up the shoreline. Provided that Zyrl's cartographers continued to be accurate, it would be five more until Dreygoj came near.

Then we'll see what awaits us. He sighed at the prospect.

Feeling Falcon's gaze still upon him, he glanced back. The bard had his head cocked and his lips pursed.

"Even now, Tal, you do not bear the sky's weight alone. You know that, don't you? Your friends are beside you until the end, be it bitter or merry."

Tal tried for a smile. "That's one of my worries, Falcon. In some ways, I'd rather you'd never found me."

The troubadour snorted a laugh. "Dismiss that counterfactual! You never would have gotten this far without us."

That finally provoked some genuine mirth from him, and for the first time in a long span of days, Tal chuckled.

"I'm sure you're right," he admitted. "But promise you won't die on my account?"

"That, my good Tal, is an oath I'll gladly swear."

That night, Tal drifted deep into the World.

It happened by accident. One moment, he was dozing at Ashelia's side, Rolan snoring lightly on the other end of the shelter; the next, the stark lines of sorcery surrounded him. Tal looked around with as little surprise as if it actually were a dream.

But he knew he'd descended on purpose. Part of him had longed to return here since departing the blighted goldwood.

Though he knew he should swim upward and return to the World above, he descended instead, following the branches of magic as they widened and converged. The amorphous beings of this World, in all their varied shades of gray, flitted by him. Their interest in him seemed to wane with each fresh visit. Tal had little idea what they were, or if they might ever mean him harm.

Still, he was drawn downward.

Eventually, it appeared before him, an orb brighter than any sun, moon, or star. The *Doash*. A shiver went through the part of him that occupied this realm.

He drifted closer, then closer still. The whispers, incessant since entering the *Doash's* chamber, grew louder and more insistent.

Rest. Peace. Comfort. Sleep.

I should be asleep, he thought. *I shouldn't be here.*

But Tal descended further. There was a part of him that caused him to throw himself into the thick of the fighting, to seek dangers best avoided. That part propelled him forward.

The *Telthaen*. The Rapture. A longing for his own destruction.

But I don't want to fade. I want my life, my friends. I want to truly live.

Yet if that was true, why did he always seek death?

Thalkunaras.

He startled and drew away from the *Doash* as he noticed one being had drawn near and addressed him with their voice-less speech. Even more surprising was that he recognized it.

This was the same pitch-black being that had spoken to him after the attack at Vathda. The same as had visited him in Elendol and led him to the truth of his blunted sorcery. An ally he'd never been certain he could trust, and who had never revealed their true face.

You, he thought in return.

Something in its watery shape spoke of amusement, though it had no expression. *You should not be here*, Thalkunaras. *You belong in the World above.*

I know.

They hovered there for a long moment, only the *Doash's* whispers breaking the silence.

You must remember, Thalkunaras. *Remember the wisdom passed to you. Remember who you are.*

The dark shape floated closer. It resembled the creeping blackness of Yuldor and his parasites, but Tal didn't feel threatened by it. He didn't pull away even as part of the being reached forward and touched him.

His strange surroundings disappeared, replaced by familiar ones. The smell of unwashed men and old urine filled his nose, along with the other stenches inherent to life spent in a large camp. Brown was all around him: brown tents, brown mud, brown trees. As if not even the World dared appear cheery here.

A figure, murky at first, but becoming clearer with each moment, stepped before him.

"Straight, I said! You call that straight, Tal? That's about as straight as a tomato vine!"

Tal, already standing as tall as he could, tried tugging his spine longer and thrusting his head up higher. He nearly trembled from the strain as his commander scrutinized him.

Maelor Yew was a grizzled veteran, one of the few men who had survived the Avendoran army to become one of its leaders. Like most old soldiers, he was missing a limb — a leg, in his case. In its place, a wooden peg had been secured, and it was on this that he stumped back and forth between his men. The ends of his thick, gray mustache drifted down past his chin. His eyes squinted beneath bushy eyebrows, dark and attentive. Few details escaped the commander's attention.

Despite his infirmaries, Yew stood as straight as he insisted his men do. And Tal had witnessed firsthand that a one-legged man could outfight many with all their limbs attached.

The commander eyed him for a moment longer, then snorted a laugh. "Don't strain a muscle there, kid," he muttered. "It's full attention, not a stretch on the rack."

Tal repressed a smile. He'd swiftly learned the commander didn't appreciate smiles as much as his comrades did.

Yew hobbled on and swept his gaze over the rest of the company. "You're a sorry lot on the eyes, and no mistake! But if I stop looking at each of your individual uglinesses, I see something else."

The commander halted at the end of the line. Tal, still at full attention, didn't turn to see whom he'd stopped in front of, but he was glad to be spared as Yew leaned forward and shouted in the man's face.

"No soldier stands alone! That sink in yet, Nudd? When you stand alone, you're about as useful to me as a bear on a bucket. Together — that's the only way to do war!"

The commander had mercy on Nudd and began making his way between the ranks of men. "The smart soldier stands with his fellows. Why's that smart? You run, you get a turn on a gibbet. You try to be a hero, you get cut down quick — 'the tallest grass is threshed first' and all that. We stand and fall together, men. Even if you hate the bastard next to you, make damn sure to stab the other bastard that tries to kill him."

There were several in the company that Tal would have liked nothing better than to have an enemy stab them through; Lyn, for one, who often tormented Tal at night with childish pranks. But he tried to take his commander's words to heart.

Stand and fall together.

At the words, the memory seemed almost to ripple. Tal felt a moment's separation, and clarity seeped back in.

This isn't real. This is a memory.

"Do you remember now, *Thalkunaras?*"

Tal turned and saw the man standing beside him had spoken. Nudd, a squat fellow with a squashed face and an unusually slow wit, now stared at him with sharp intelligence. As the realization of the memory-dream settled in, he recognized the dark being from the World's core.

"I remember," he answered softly, his voice coming out as a boy's, for he still wore his youthful form. "I remember disregarding that advice. I remember abandoning the men I called my brothers. I remember doing anything I could to stay alive, and it cost their lives."

Nudd's expression twisted into a look like he'd swallowed a lemon. "You cannot rewrite the past, but you can compose the future. You do not stand alone now, *Thalkunaras.* In the battles to come, you must rely on those by your side to survive."

Tal let out a small laugh, though the part of him that remained in the dream felt wary of the commander, who paced the lines behind them.

"None of us are enough, my mysterious guide," he continued. "Garin and I together couldn't touch the Enemy. I believed Founts might challenge Yuldor for the Worldheart, but I fear that I'm once again wrong. I'm a fool hunting for fool's gold."

Nudd shook his head. "Not in this. You and the youth must come to us atop Ikvaldar. You must challenge Yuldor for the Worldheart. And together, we will take it back and free the World of tyranny at last."

"Us?" He clenched his fists by his sides, though in his thirteen-year-old body, they felt small and weak. "Who are you? You come with advice and promises, but you've never revealed your identity, not even a name."

Nudd's face scrunched further. "Do you not know me?

After all I have shown you, all you have learned — still, you do not know?"

"That's not an answer!" Whether it was his own frustration or the anger of his youth that made him shout, he found it gratifying.

The possessed soldier stared at him a moment longer. Then the scene peeled apart, like a trouper's backdrop ripped to shreds.

Tal floated in the World's sorcerous core once more, the *Doash's* murmurs washing over him. The dark presence hovered before him, seeming an even darker shade than before. A sense of foreboding curled through him. He wondered if, in his frustration, he'd committed a grave error.

Yet, as the being's thoughts found him, he felt no offense.

I am an ally, Thalkunaras, *to you and all mortalkind. I was mortal myself, once, and wish I could have remained so. Do you not think I dream of drifting into the* Doash? *On many occasions through the unending centuries, I have almost done so. But each time, I remember who I am and who I must be. I remember that life must persist, and without my resistance, it will fail.*

A suspicion, too impossible to consider, claimed Tal. He had to know the truth.

Who are you? he asked again.

My name was once Maral Batomar. My people and soldiers called me Ava'thal, *the Dragonheart. But the mortals of this era only know me as the Night.*

The Night. He could scarcely believe it. All this time, the being the Creed claimed to be the source of all evil had been assisting his quest.

The Night had helped him discover what crippled his sorcery back in Elendol. She had warded him away from the *Doash* when he suffered through the canker's effects. For most of his life, when he'd spared any thought for the antagonist of the Whispering Gods, it was only to think of her as a vague threat behind Yuldor, the World's true Enemy.

Now, he saw her for what she was: the World's savior.

You must return, Thalkunaras. *Return to your companions and keep heart. When you bring the fight to Yuldor, I will be waiting.*

Thank you...

He'd barely expressed the thought before the realm of sorcery faded like a dream.

Tal sat up, breathing hard. His heart thumped like the Avendoran army drums when a battle was at hand. But a small smile curled his lips.

They weren't alone in the fight, his companions and him. The Night fought too, as did Ilvuan and the dragons allied with him. Together, they had stayed the full power of the Worldheart for countless eons. Perhaps, with Tal and Garin joining them, they might be enough to win the war.

He didn't sleep again for a long time, his mind spinning over the notion. But when dawn peeked across the ocean's horizon, he felt more alive than he had since leaving the palace.

Once more, he had reason to hope, and he clung to it with all his will.

THE SMUGGLER'S FAITH

As THEY CONTINUED THEIR TRAVELS UP THE COAST, GARIN EYED Tal with more than a moderate helping of suspicion.

Overnight, the man had transformed. Where before he'd been silent and brooding, now he japed and teased like he was once more Brannen Cairn of Hunt's Hollow, a humble and inadequate chicken farmer. There seemed no reason for it that Garin could detect, though he had a theory.

"Perhaps he and Ashelia found their own time apart from the company," he muttered to Wren, provoking a ringing laugh from her.

Whatever the cause, he was glad to have the old Tal back. Their journey, and the towering tasks throughout it, seemed much less foreboding with the Man of a Thousand Names at the helm.

They traveled for six days after reaching the coast. After the first day, vegetation reclaimed the land. Palm trees, heavy with coconuts, provided welcome shade from the blistering sun. At the mage's insistence, they all tried the milky liquid inside the hairy shells. Garin was surprised to find he didn't mind the lightly nutty taste, and actually enjoyed the hint of sweetness from the strips of white "meat" that they roasted over a fire.

By evening of the sixth day, they reached the mouth of a river. Mangroves grew there, resembling the kintrees but on a vastly smaller scale. The sight of them brought out a smile. A glance at the Gladelysh members of their party showed that they took heart as well.

As clouds advanced from the sea and choked out the light, they decided to make camp at the edge of the foliage. Garin and Wren took Rolan to go hunt up branches and wood for the campfire.

"I could carry a log if I had to," the boy bragged as he bent over to add to his bundle of kindling. "Just because you always make me gather twigs doesn't mean I can't!"

"Best save your clever fingers," Wren advised. "You'll need them for that lute of yours."

"Don't want to end up like Falcon with one hand," Garin added with a mischievous grin.

Rolan seemed to consider that. "A sword took off his hand. So shouldn't I just stay away from Tal?"

Not bad advice either, Garin thought. But he only gave the boy a bracing smile.

Wren, wandering by the bank of the sluggish river, kicked at a fallen limb experimentally, then shrugged. "Should be loose enough. Garin, help me with this."

He eyed the large branch. "Looks stuck to me. How about I cut it loose?"

Wren rolled her eyes. "You just want an excuse to play with your sword."

Flashing her a grin, Garin drew *Helshax* and admired the weapon for a moment. The runes etched into its length glowed a gentle gold in the dimness of the woods, a stark contrast to the black metal. He wondered how such a fine blade had been forged and how its smith would feel about it being used as a hatchet. But Tal had told him that, like *Velori*, it was supposed to never lose its edge.

He stalked around the branch, looking for the best way to loosen it from the underbrush that entangled it. As he raised the sword for his first swing, though, Wren hissed, "Garin!"

Halting, he looked in the direction she pointed and opened himself to the Worldsong. As the general sound of it faded, he detected through its strains smaller ones. With each day spent traveling, he practiced honing in on the little songs produced by the World's inhabitants. Plants, insects, and nonliving things still defied his detection, but larger beings could usually come into focus.

Now, he heard the faint song of a something that seemed human echoing from among the trees.

"Rolan," Garin said quietly. "Go back to camp and fetch the others."

The boy nodded and scampered off at once. Though he was usually as noisy as a rooster at dawn, he was as silent as a deer now. Rolan, it seemed, had been listening to Helnor's lessons for surviving in the wilderness.

Wren had drawn her rapier as well, slowly and with a hand clamped over her scabbard to muffle any noise. Garin edged closer to her, his eyes still set on the area from which the mortal-song emanated.

"Can you see what it is?" he muttered.

"No. You?"

"I only hear it."

By implicit agreement, they pressed forward. Garin knew it would be more prudent to wait for the others in case it was a threat. Most likely, it would only be an animal. Although he couldn't quite banish the notion that something about its song didn't quite fit...

Wren used her blade to part the foliage before them and brought their quarry into sight.

Garin blinked at the sight. A figure, bent and gray, hobbled through the open door of a dingy cabin. She looked female as well as human, judging by the roundness of her ears and the hue of her skin. He could detect no more than that, however, for the aged woman closed the door behind her. A moment later, light appeared through the smoky glass of the windows.

He exchanged an incredulous look with Wren, the same question in her eyes. What an old hermit would be doing out here was beyond him. Part of him longed to demand answers that very moment, and Wren practically twitched with her own eagerness. But they both waited until Aelyn, Tal, and Falcon joined them.

"What is it?" the mage asked mockingly, though he had the sense to speak softly. "Did a squirrel startle you?"

Garin ignored him and met Tal's questioning gaze. "A human woman; old, by the look of her."

Tal nodded. "Alone?"

"As far as we know."

"Where are Ashelia and Helnor?" Wren questioned.

"Keeping an eye on Rolan and the camp," Falcon answered. "They tried to make me stay, too."

She grinned at her father. "Perhaps you should have, old man."

Tal raised his hand for quiet. "Aelyn and I will go first. The rest of you follow on my signal."

Without waiting for a reply, Tal slunk forward through the brush. Aelyn looked annoyed, yet he followed, albeit with less grace. Elf and traveler he might be, but the mage had never been much of a woodsman.

Garin watched with his breath held as Tal circled the shack once, ducking under the windows to avoid being seen. When he'd completed a circuit, he peered through a window, then straightened and approached the door.

"He thinks it's safe," Garin murmured.

Wren snorted lightly. "Why wouldn't he? It's only one old woman."

"Never underestimate the elderly," Falcon warned her. "The Extinguished are hundreds of years old, and my guess is that Holt the Horse-man wasn't young either. Many beings live in this World under many guises."

Wren looked as if she had more to say, but Tal's knock on the door cut the conversation short. A few moments passed, then the door opened. Garin braced himself for an attack, but none came. A brief exchange later, which he couldn't quite make out, Tal and Aelyn entered the hut, and the door closed behind.

"Guess we wait here," Wren grumbled as she sat and laid her rapier across her lap.

Garin continued to stand, though he rested the point of *Helshax* on the ground. Though he detected nothing beyond a few scattered animals in the woods, he had a feeling they were missing something about this hermit.

But for now, all he could do was wait.

Tal smiled pleasantly as the aged woman invited them to sit.

She lived in a modest hovel, almost as modest as his home back in Hunt's Hollow. The seat that Aelyn and he shared was actually a trunk, well-made but weathered and scratched with age. The walls, composed of planks and cob plaster, showed their years, but seemed maintained and devoid of drafts. The floor even had boards rather than mere dirt and was elevated slightly from the marshy ground. A hearth was packed with hot coals ready to be reignited, and before it hung a black iron kettle. A table and a rocking chair occupied the rest of the room. Hanging from the ceiling were bunches of herbs, slowly drying out.

A humble home, Tal thought. *But not a poor one.*

The woman, who had invited them in with suspiciously little prompting, shuffled across the room as she gathered from the drying herbs to make her offered tea. She said little as she worked, grinding the leaves with a wooden mortar and pestle. Tal offered to assist, but the woman declined his offer.

When she turned her back on them to pour water in the kettle, Aelyn leaned in close and hissed, "The mantle."

Tal looked around and tensed. On the wooden mantle above the fireplace sat a series of carefully arranged objects atop a fresh palm frond. One was a stone that resembled a mountain, its peak painted green. Next to it sat a meticulously carved and painted wooden bust of an unfamiliar man. The man had mesmerizing gold eyes and silver hair, and his expression could only be described as enlightened. A spattering of smaller objects encircled these others: a cat with a woman's face; a sword intersecting a wheel's tines; even a small stone dragon. Next to all these was tucked an oft-read book, judging by the creasing in its leather binding.

He knew little of the Cult of Yuldor, but he had a suspicion these were exactly the sort of items a devout follower might gather.

Before he could reply to Aelyn, the old woman finished pouring the water and lighting the fire and, with a small groan, rose to face them. She smiled and her face became as wrinkled as a winter apple.

"There, that should do it," she said in the common Darktongue. "I am sorry to keep you waiting, but I had only just returned."

Tal struggled for a moment to find the words in the language, his grasp on it already rusty after weeks of scarcely using it. "Thank you, ah…"

"Sawat," she supplied with another smile.

"Sawat. We appreciate your, ah—"

"Hospitality, I believe my companion means," Aelyn finished for him. His grasp of common Darktongue had always exceeded Tal's, and he was more than happy to show it.

"But though I agree with him, I must confess: we did not expect to find anyone out here."

"Did you not?" The woman's smile faded. That set Tal's mind to spinning.

She thought we sought her out. Which means people seek her out for a reason.

"We are still grateful," Tal spoke, mangling the pronunciations in his haste to head off Aelyn. "But why would people, ah, meet with you?" It was a more direct line of inquiry than he would normally take, but he couldn't think of more eloquent phrasing in the harsh speech.

Aelyn cast him a derisive glance, but didn't contradict his question.

Sawat eyed them with a masked expression now. Her eyes flitted over their persons, no doubt making note of every oddity in their garbs and the weapons they carried. Still, she showed no fear. He wondered if she'd lived too long to be precious about her remaining years, or if she had another form of security waiting to be called upon. Sorcery tingled in his blood, yet he sensed no connection to magic from the woman.

Still, something wasn't right here, and he meant to uncover what.

Finally, Sawat spoke again. "Do you believe in Paradise? Do you trust in the Peacebringer?"

To that, Tal had no hesitation in answering. "Of course!"

"Why else would Reachfolk be in the Empire?" Aelyn added with a sharp smile.

Sawat answered with a smile of her own. "It gladdens my heart to hear it. Might you further bolster my spirits with a litany from his Message?"

Tal tried not to let his dismay show. How to answer such a request? He knew only the most basic things about the Cult of Yuldor. Before such a devout follower, he was unlikely to invent anything that would convince her.

Part of him wondered why he cared so much to deceive

her. After all, what could one old woman do to hinder their quest? Yet he had an inkling there was more to Sawat than met the eye. The mystery of her hermitage and well-kept house tantalized his curiosity. He had to at least try.

Tal opened his mouth, hoping his moniker as "Pearltongue" would come to the rescue. But before any words could emerge, Aelyn spoke in a low, even rhythm that resembled a chant.

"From His hands, the lands unfold
The mountains bend, the cattle low
Father World is His to sow
Seeds of life, calm, and gold

Peacebringer, Our Savior and Lord
We bow before your wisdom bold
Bless our crops, bless our folds
Prosperity rains where you soar."

Aelyn completed the litany with a twist of his lips, unable to completely hide his disdain.

Sawat stared at them, her parched lips pursed. "I did not know such devout believers existed in the Pagan Lands." A slow smile claimed her face, blossoming into happy creases. "But I am glad to discover it. Welcome, brothers, to the lands our Lord and Savior has preserved for his Paradise. May his peace ever find you."

"And his path be below your feet," Aelyn responded — wryly, to Tal's ear.

Tal smiled amicably, hoping she wouldn't notice his own lack of contribution.

Sawat's gaze lingered upon them for a moment before she rose with a small groan and shuffled over to the kettle of water. As she bent over it, she called to them, "Now, brothers, what are your names, and how do you find yourself on my stoop?"

Tal cast Aelyn a look, to which the mage only smirked, so he pressed on.

"I am Tal, sister, and this is Aelyn. We are refugees from Elendol since… its collapse." He couldn't think of a better way to describe the elven civil war that didn't condemn the Cult of Yuldor for its part in it.

"Ah, has it been emancipated at last? News is slow in spreading to this part of the World, and there are many miles between here and the Western elves. But it gladdens my heart. The Message spreads across all the lands and takes root."

"Bless his name," Aelyn added with a gleam to his eyes.

Tal continued in a more genuine tone. "We are making for Dreygoj, but fear it may be hostile to our kind — being Reach-folk, that is."

Sawat rose, the kettle steaming as she poured it into two painted ceramic cups — another unexpected luxury. "Wise you are to believe that, Brother Tal. For you shall find it exactly so."

"Is there no way to gain entrance?" Tal accepted the tea Sawat offered him with a grateful nod. "We hope to establish ourselves there, having heard such wonderful things about it." Truth be told, he knew little of the city beyond the races that occupied it, and he hoped there was at least something of note within.

Having given Aelyn his tea as well, the aged woman returned to her chair with a satisfied sigh. "Our Lord guides your path, brothers. For you have come to the precise place where you might find such admittance."

Tal breathed in the tea, searching for a hint of poison or some other debilitating herb. It smelled pleasant enough: chicory root, with honey and lilacs mixed in. He didn't yet risk a sip, nor did Aelyn or their hostess.

"How is that? Sister," Aelyn added belatedly, though he undermined the attempt at civility with a smirk.

If Sawat noticed the irony, she didn't show it. "I am not always alone in this cabin. People come visiting often… my niece, Jira, most often among them."

"How good to pass the time with family." Tal wondered what the woman was getting at.

Sawat smiled, but there was an edge to it now. "Indeed, it is. But she and I do not merely discuss weather and gossip. We have… connections, long established and secure."

Tal perked up. This was more like what they could use. *Smugglers*, he realized. *She and her niece are part of a chain of smugglers.*

"These connections," Tal said slowly. "They can help us enter Dreygoj?"

The aged woman nodded, her eyes firmly on his. "They can. Discreetly, as you wish. But all services, even between believers, must come with a tithe."

So long as the price was short of exorbitant, Tal was confident they could meet it. Zyrl had been generous in providing them coin, and they'd used none of it on the journey thus far.

He smiled widely, putting on whatever vestiges of charm remained to him, and answered, "We would be happy to, ah, contribute to our common cause, Sister Sawat. Bless his name."

Sawat sipped at her tea, then returned the smile as she lowered it. "Bless his name. Jira is due to visit tomorrow evening. Have your companions and yourselves prepared to depart then."

Tal nodded, even as he wondered how this aged woman had known about the others.

A devout smuggler. Even having traveled the World over, it seemed he still had many sights to see.

PASSAGE II

*THE OSTENSIBLE NIGHT PUPPETEER BECAME A PUPPET AS SOON AS HE
ascended to divinity.*

*My comrades and I did not notice it in the beginning. If our
master suddenly seemed far more knowledgeable in matters the
libraries of Elendol could not illuminate — well, he was Yuldor
Soldarin. No one knew more of the occult and forgotten secrets of
those who came before the Severing. It seemed only natural that he
had held back some insights from his disciples.*

*But slowly, the changes his madness wrought upon him became
apparent. Others would speak with his mouth, but name themselves
differently from him. Rothaen, Haimei, and Sachiel — they were
words unknown to us and therefore without meaning. Only when I
completed my endeavors in translating the Origintongue did I realize
what they meant.*

Silence. Solemnity. Serenity.

*To this day, I do not know if they are inventions of an over-
wrought mind or the Creed's divinities in actuality. But it is irrelevant, an intellectual exercise, for the results are the same.*

*Yuldor Soldarin cannot be treated with. He cannot be saved.
There is only one path left to those who wish the World to be
preserved, for long ago we exhausted all others.*

But I will not inscribe my schemes to ink and paper. My thoughts may already be enough to damn me.

- The Untold Lore of Yuldor Soldarin and His Servants, *by Inanis*

THE WATERY WAY

Garin had often heard of the travails of being seasick from his companions, Falcon complaining of it loudest of all in his countless stories. But he never knew how miserable it could be until he huddled below the deck of the *Star Prince*, the World swaying around him, trying not to spew his guts all over his companions.

He'd been skeptical from the outset of this venture, if for different reasons. When Tal and Aelyn had emerged from the old woman's hut, they'd borne with them news almost too incredible to believe: that they had stumbled upon a smuggler, and she was willing to sneak them into the very place they wished to go. It was only after Falcon puzzled it out that the coincidence began to make sense.

"We cannot be the only ones to travel up this way," the bard noted around their campfire that night. The fire caught on the thinning planes of his face, the privations of the journey finally taking their toll on his ample flesh. "Especially for those who wish to go unnoticed, this may act as a distinctive waypoint. There are only a few paths across the Laksis Wastes, and many of them would land sojourners here."

Helnor hummed assent as he stared into the fire. "I must admit, bard, that it makes a certain sense."

Falcon smiled at him. Garin noticed that though the two men rarely sought out each other's company, they had grown much fonder of each other than in the days when the Prime casually insulted him by calling him *kolfash*. Now, he rarely commented on Falcon's mixed blood, and never on Wren's, in whom he'd found a kindred spirit.

"And there's the matter of the river," Falcon continued. "No doubt goods go up and down its length, seeking ports both at Dreygoj and afar. It's an ideal location when one thinks about it a moment."

Garin conceded the point, but upon sharing a look with Wren, he found he wasn't the only skeptical one. Yet the older members of their party seemed resigned to trusting the dubious confederate, with Tal and Aelyn deeming her trust-worthy enough, though Garin saw little to trust in one devoted to worshipping Yuldor.

Still, he'd gone along with it. He had waited with the others on the shore the next evening as a ship sailed into the bay that formed around the nameless river's mouth. When a boat came ashore, he stiffly greeted the young Easterner woman who hopped off of it. Jira, her name appeared to be. Though he couldn't understand a word she said, he sensed a confidence about the young smuggler. She wasn't hard on the eyes either, with a pretty face and an infectious smile, and the unflattering vestments of a sailor — baggy pantaloons and a sweat-stained tunic — failed to disguise her ample hips and bosom. Garin took care not to look too closely, conscious of Wren's watchful gaze, an eyebrow cocked whenever Jira wandered by them.

Sawat came out to greet the young smuggler, who was apparently also her niece — or great-niece, rather, judging by their difference in age. The two women seemed close and smiled and laughed often with each other. As much as Garin tried to cling to his suspicion, he found it melting before the obvious affection the smugglers held for each other.

Wren didn't share the sentiment, but watched their interactions with narrowed eyes. When Garin challenged her on it, she retorted, "And what about all that Tal's smiles hide? I say you should trust smiles least, and find honest scowls pleasing."

Garin only shrugged and let it go.

They departed to their separate camps, then met again the next morning in time for a second boat manned by yet more Easterners to row ashore. With their journey set for that day, Garin and his party loaded themselves onto the boats. Convincing their mounts the trip was a good idea proved most difficult of all.

"You have more sense than us," Garin muttered to Tempest as he dragged the gelding onto the boat, then joined him in its belly.

He learned quickly he didn't have the fabled "sea legs" that stories about sailors always spoke of. His balance pitched with every wave, and he sat hunched, afraid of standing lest he fall overboard. Even Tempest seemed better adjusted to the passage than he. Over the water, the thick aroma of saltwater was everywhere, overridden only by the sweat of the men who labored at the oars.

Garin was already feeling woozy and unbalanced by the time they neared the ship, yet he forced himself to focus on it. He knew nothing of seacraft but was still impressed by what he saw. It was large enough to fit them all, horses and stors included. Its name was painted in silver paint on the side, though stains from seawater and seaweed had dulled its shine. Sails, huge and off-white, flapped in the constant breeze atop tall masts.

Once they'd filed up the gangplank, they met the *Star Prince's* crew. The captain had skin like tanned cowhide and more rings through his ears than a noble wore on their fingers. Black tattoos webbed around his eyes and across his cheeks and forehead, making him fearsome and otherworldly. Yet for all that, he clasped their arms readily and stared Garin in the eye with a gap-toothed smile.

The crew sported even more outlandish folks. Every Bloodline stood among them, even a minotaur, though Garin judged his hooves must be as uncertain on the damp planks of the deck as the horses and stors proved to be. The sylvans were much more nimble, and the medusals' claws made them difficult to dislodge. In the crow's nest, as Tal called the top of the center mast, a gnome held a spotting glass to her eye and piped down what she saw to her crewmates below.

But Easterners weren't the strangest ones to walk among them. One man looked more like an elf than a human, yet he lacked pointed ears. Though lithe, he was nearly as tall as Ox from the Dancing Feathers, and his skin was as dark and rich as the Befa islander's. His eyes, in contrast, were the palest blue Garin had ever seen, and were as alive as any elf's. Like the other sailors, he wore his tunic open at the collar, showing a circle of small, yellow glyphs inked into the hollow of his neck.

Curious, Garin opened himself to the Worldsong and found the man reverberated with magic. His tempo rivaled even Aelyn's, though it remained dwarfed by Tal's song. All signs pointed to the strange man possessing sorcery, yet he used no spells to assist in his tasks as he loped across the deck.

Garin didn't watch the man for long. No sooner had they come aboard than the captain directed them belowdecks. Already sick from the incessant rocking of the ship, Garin didn't look forward to the prospect of cramming inside its belly. But Jira, who had returned aboard the ship with them, insisted that it was the only way. They couldn't risk passing ships spotting them atop their deck and reporting them.

And so Garin found himself in a place that came closest to his imaginings of Yuldor's hells.

Before they summoned werelights, he couldn't have seen more than a hand's width in front of him. The hull and deck of the ship were closely sealed to keep out seawater. The wooden planks they crouched on smelled of papaya long ago rotten. Sweat and despair were fragrant in the dark space, mixed in with a healthy dose of urine and night soil. Almost, Garin could imagine they were Yraldi prisoners, drawing from the terrifying stories told around bonfires on Year's End Eve each winter.

The thought made him ache in a different way. *Mad gods,* he thought, *I hope I live to see Hunt's Hollow again.* At that moment, however, the prospect seemed unlikely.

"Shouldn't take more than half a day 'til we reach Dreygoj's port," Tal said to their party. He spoke softly, though they had no need yet to be quiet. By the werelights' illumination, Garin saw Tal glance his way and give him a bracing smile.

"Just have to grin and bear it," his old mentor advised.

Garin's stomach bucked, and he chose that moment to spill his dinner into the bucket Jira had wisely provided them up on deck. His contribution to the ship's perfume didn't improve their conditions, and it wasn't long before Falcon followed his lead.

The journey dragged on across the sluggish day. Garin eventually sprawled over the planks, such as the packed cargo and his companions allowed, disregarding the filth that must layer them from scores of trips. Yet when the untold hours had finally passed, and the shouts above gained an edge of urgency, Garin wasn't sure he looked forward to its ending anymore.

"What are they saying?" Wren asked. "Are we in Dreygoj?"

Tal had a look of concentration that spoke to his use of sorcery. A long moment later, he let out his breath in a sigh. "I think so. They're speaking of docking and unloading and finding 'Chaiya.' I assume that's their usual portwarden."

Through Aelyn's translation, Jira had explained the smuggling process. When they pulled into port, the inspections officers with whom they had a long-standing agreement would come aboard and claim to inspect all the cargo. In truth, they wouldn't even come belowdecks. Once they had given their approval, the crew would unpack all the rest of the cargo, while Garin and the others would wait to exit under the cover of darkness.

Garin had hoped that docking would prove to stabilize the ship's pitch. But as feet stomped above and men and women yelled at each other across the hours, he found his hopes, once again, were unfounded.

At last, long after the point that Garin felt he could take no more of his salty cell, the hatch swung open, admitting the gray light of a coastal evening. Dismissing his werelight, Garin leaned toward it, gulping in fresh air and hoping it would banish the shakiness of his limbs.

Jira poked her head below. Upside down, she grinned at them and said something in a cheery voice, then disappeared from view. Blessedly, the hatch remained open. Garin optimistically began scooting toward it.

"Not quite." Tal flashed a sympathetic smile. "Still have to wait for dark. But it's time that they unload the cargo down here."

Garin groaned and couldn't even muster the energy to respond to Wren's chortle at his expense.

They moved to one side of the ship's belly as sailors descended the ladder and shifted the crates. More than one laughed in Garin's face and spoke comments he could easily guess the line of. He turned his head aside and tried to drift off to sleep. It was to no avail; the World just continued to swim behind his eyelids.

When Wren finally shook him and murmured, "It's time," Garin felt such a surge of anticipation he thought he might faint from it. He was second up the ladder. His limbs felt stuffed with straw and his head liable to roll off his shoulders, yet he made it onto the deck, where he braced himself against the mast.

Through swimming vision, he took in his first look of Dreygoj.

It was a city like no other he'd seen. Even in a seasick haze, Garin found himself awed by the port. Around them, the docks connected tall ships to the city like threads on a loom. Between the planked walkways rose sandstone columns, their edges rounded smooth by sea and rain. Greater versions of these pillars ascended from the land, and some even appeared to be occupied, riddled with holes that glowed with interior lights.

Even more fascinating were the houses closer at hand. At first, he assumed the shore must extend as far as the buildings, yet as he peered closer, he discovered they weren't built on land, but suspended over the sea on wooden stilts. Hundreds of homes, shops, warehouses, and other buildings stretched into the nighttime gloom. He wondered how such a city could survive the fury of the ocean, both the rise and fall of the tides and its storms.

A glance behind illuminated part of the mystery. Dreygoj was built into a bay, with stone encircling it and acting as a breakwall. Barely more than a ripple, limned with moonlight, remained of the ocean's currents. It explained why the ship had quit pitching so violently, though still not as much as he preferred.

Turning back to the city, he saw the ocean-grown district was only part of it. Behind the homes on stilts and the sandstone towers rose a cliff, and from the top gleamed more lights, a sign of homes set atop it. The slope leading up to it showed evidence of more houses built along its side.

A shake from Wren interrupted Garin's reverie. "Don't pass out just yet. We still have to get off this damned boat and to the warehouse."

He blinked and tried to right his mind. The smugglers had a warehouse that acted as a base for those they snuck into the city. They could only stay there one night, but with any luck, that was all they would need.

But how will we leave? He felt sick all over again just imagining another sea voyage.

Wren thrust his heavy saddlebags into his arms, and he somehow remained upright and strapped them to Tempest. "Bet you don't like the ocean either, eh?" he said to the horse as he worked. "Not looking forward to the return journey either, are you?"

The gelding only continued to shake his head and paw at the ground. Garin brushed his mane with a hand while they waited to depart.

At last, the sign to disembark came. Helnor went first after Jira, but Garin was right on their heels. The docks were a little more certain underfoot, even though they had their own pitch, the salt-bitten planks creaking and shifting with their passage. He swallowed hard to keep the little he'd eaten that day down and followed the Prime Warder and smuggler along the dock and past the gazes of the few sailors and other workers lingering in the port. Most lost their curiosity quickly; their work carried them late into the night, and they no doubt wished to be done with it soon. Garin, however, couldn't banish the feeling that someone watched them. No matter how he looked around, however, he glimpsed no watchers.

At length, Jira stopped in front of two double doors and gestured inside with a bracing smile. The day's activities, and perhaps the danger they presently faced, had finally worn on even her resilient mood. Garin could commiserate, barely summoning the energy for a grateful nod before turning inside the dark warehouse.

Helnor illuminated it with a murmured, "*Fuln*," and let the werelight drift above his head. The place had a powerful stench of fish to it, provoking fresh nausea in Garin. Barrels and crates lined the walls in neat rows and stacks. For all their rough appearance, the smugglers kept a tidy business.

Jira spoke in her language and gestured toward a back corner to further illustrate her point. Helnor, also fluent in the Easterner speech, responded with a smile and followed her directions. Garin led the others after him. At last, it seemed, their smuggling was at an end, and their hunt for the alchemist would begin.

The easy part, he thought with a sardonic smile.

CITY OF STILTS

"KOAX MRAAJ?" JIRA COCKED HER HEAD TO ONE SIDE. "AN alchemist, you say?"

"Yes. Do you know him?"

Though Tal plastered on a smile, he didn't intend to rely much on the smuggler. From her tone, she'd never heard of the supposed inventor of the Paradise elixir. Not for the first time, he wished the Extinguished hadn't been destroyed. His counsel might have been useful during their journey, now most of all.

Just as Tal was about to dismiss the question, Jira straightened and gave him a brighter smile than she had all that night. "Ah! Yes, I know of this alchemist. He lives in Sra'ka — the district with the great tidepool. Involved in a fire that spread across water this past season, yet escaped with a mere fine by doing the watch captain a private favor." She leaned in close and whispered loudly, "Took care of boils on his privates, you see."

Tal chuckled. Jira spoke more like a sailor than the devotee she presented herself as in front of her great-aunt. He thought she might have gotten along well with him and his companions had they met under different circumstances.

"What was that district name again?" he asked.

"Sra'ka. You do not know it? Perhaps your pointy-eared friend might say its meaning."

Aelyn scowled at Jira's barb, and all the more when she bared her teeth at him and laughed.

"It means, 'Stilts,'" the mage snapped. "I would think that's rather straightforward even for you, Harren—"

He broke off the sentence with a cough as Tal, Ashelia, and Helnor all glared at him. They'd given their first names, but if Jira heard Tal's full name, even on this far side of the Empire, she could likely put the pieces of his identity together.

As it was, the smuggler tilted her head again, then shrugged and sauntered past. "Anyway, good luck finding him. You will find Sra'ka south of here. And remember, you will only be here one day. Any longer, and the Venators will find you. Neither of us would want that."

Chills ran up his spine. "Venators are here?"

Jira smiled sharply. "Of course; they are everywhere across the Empire, for they enact the Peacebringer's will. Stray too close to their fortress among the sandstone pillars and you will discover how unpleasant that can be."

"No need; we will remember." Tal paused, then added, "Thank you, Jira."

She gave a last, dismissive wave, then leisurely exited the warehouse.

When she'd disappeared through the doors, Tal rounded on Aelyn. "I know we've rarely gotten along, but I never thought you hated me so much as to spill my name in the middle of an enemy city, and with Ravagers close by."

The mage's jaw clenched and unclenched as he met Tal's stare. "I didn't say all of it, *Harrenfel*." He emphasized his name, as if to illustrate a point.

"You said enough."

Ashelia stepped between them. "That's enough. It was an accident, Tal. Let it go so we can think of more pressing matters."

More pressing than our heads on pikes? he wanted to say. Instead, he breathed out in a noisy exhale. His objections didn't matter now, not unless he meant to go after Jira and tie her up until they left. They would just have to hope she proved loyal, or better yet ignorant.

Though she raised an eyebrow, Ashelia spoke along a different line of thought. "Now, we need to find our way to this district Sra'ka — Stilts. We should avoid any guards along the way and leave as soon as we can."

Helnor rumbled in consideration. "Though I prefer the cover of darkness, I fear we'll attract too much attention. Few residents remain outdoors, and whoever does would be suspicious."

"I agree," Ashelia said. "We'll rest until dawn, then find this Koax."

"If I may, *who* will be going?" This came from Falcon, who had crowded forward at their discussion. He already seemed to have recovered from the trip aboard the ship.

"You're not leaving me behind," Wren said at once.

"Nor me." Garin spoke with less conviction, his seasickness lingering longer than the bard's.

"I want to go!" Rolan, who had often had to be shushed during the voyage, now brimmed with energy.

Ashelia looked at each of them, frowning slightly. "No, Rolan. You and I must guard our mounts. Anyone else who wishes to stay can. The others may go."

When no one volunteered to stay behind, Tal met her gaze. "Will you two be alright by yourselves?"

"We'll be fine." She gave him a wan smile. "Just don't be long."

He nodded and reached out to press her hand.

Aelyn rolled his eyes and pushed between them to return to his stor. "I, for one, must prepare for any eventualities we might encounter. Not something I would expect of you, Harrenfel."

Tal dredged up one of his old smiles. "I'm always prepared, mage."

Dawn slunk upon the city like a fox on an unwary warren.

Tal watched the glow brighten through the cracks in the warehouse's walls. His fingers spun the Ring of Thalkuun around and around on his finger, the same finger he'd worn it on before Soltor cut it off, then he'd regrown. He occupied his impatient mind with thoughts of Kaleras, inventing impossible pasts and imagining how his life might have turned out differently if the warlock had raised him as his son.

Perhaps I never would have become a soldier and a deserter. Perhaps I never would have earned my names: Magebutcher, Red Reaver, Death's Hand — hells, even Tal Harrenfel. Perhaps...

A smile twisted his lips. He'd spent enough time in idle dreams to recognize them for what they were. Even if his circumstances had been different, Tal knew he would have been the same. Stubborn. Rebellious. Yearning for something new.

Besides, Kaleras never led a quiet life.

Still, they were happy thoughts, of doing ordinary things with his wayward father. Walking through the woods. Kaleras leaning over him as Tal painstakingly bent his head to a book. Laughing together with his mother.

It had been a long time since Tal had been close to blood kin. And though the companions slumbering around him were as good as family, the loss of his father was an ache he doubted would soon depart.

Tal stretched and yawned. He'd barely slept that night, volunteering to keep watch while the others snatched a few precious hours of sleep. Though Ashelia had awoken in the dark and offered to stand guard in his stead, he gently refused her.

"My sorcery will sustain me," he reminded her. "Can you say the same?"

Reluctantly, she'd returned to sleep, though it didn't appear to come easily to any of their party. They had curled into their bedrolls, yet the brisk ocean air seeped up through the planks of the warehouse, and many of them shivered. Tal felt almost guilty at his tolerance. A life spent on the road had made him used to discomfort, and the trace of sorcery in his blood warded away the chill. The pain of sitting on hard planks was whisked away by his World's blood. Being a god's heir came with its perks.

And its share of peril.

When the light was bright enough, Tal roused the others, and they drowsily began readying for the day. Their mounts snorted and whinnied in another corner of the warehouse, protesting their own lack of amenities. He wrinkled his nose at the stench of their nighttime deposits and hoped he and his companions might avoid the unpleasant duty of disposing of them.

He had just set to a brief, cold meal when the first of the warehouse laborers entered. The initial bunch was all sylvans, and Tal had a difficult time not staring at them. Their hair was cropped short, but came in as varied of colors and textures as he'd seen in Elendol.

The sylvans watched them with piercing gazes. Though they were two heads shorter than Tal, they didn't seem intimidated by the size of their company. Each carried a knife on their belt, though they otherwise didn't seem warlike. He wondered if it was their sorcery that gave them such confidence. Judging it best to be polite, Tal greeted them with a friendly smile, but they only looked aside, their expressions stoic.

Considering they would be forced to leave their mounts and possessions in the care of these sylvans, Tal took it as a less than encouraging sign. He hated to abandon Ashelia and Rolan among these strangers. But as things stood, hope was all he could rely upon.

As his companions gathered around their makeshift camp again, they looked at Tal. He grinned back.

"Well, my friends. Are you prepared for a tour of the city?"

Aelyn's mouth twisted. "You'd do well to be prepared for more than that."

Wren patted the rapier buckled at her hip. "I, for one, always am."

Tal met Garin's eyes and gave the lad a nod, which he promptly returned. They two, at least, possessed weapons that weren't easily taken away. Garin, however, looked apprehensive of the endeavor, his eyes darting back toward the warehouse workers.

"We'll be fine," Tal tried to assure them, and wondered if his words had the opposite effect from the exchanged glances.

Aelyn was moving among them, pressing something into their hands. Tal watched, curious and bemused as the mage passed by him without offering the same.

"What are you up to now, my sly friend?" he finally asked.

Aelyn looked over with a smirk, while Helnor held up the object he'd been handed. "A leaf in amber?" he said quizzically. "I'm not sure this is the right time for nostalgia, little brother."

"It's not a memento!" Aelyn snapped. "Call it a charm if you must, but I, for one, do not rely on luck."

Tal had a suspicion then, including why he'd been passed over. "It's an aid in a spell. An illusion?"

Aelyn's copper eyes spun as he looked back at him. "Precisely. You'll have to make do for yourself, Harrenfel."

He shrugged. "As long as the rest of you are safe."

The matter settled, Tal led their company past the increasing press of sylvans and medusals and into the golden daylight. As he stepped out into the street, already thronging with the daily crowd, he admired the city at dawn. Dreygoj had already seemed a fascinating place under the cover of darkness; now, he found it doubly so. The buildings on stilts, set over sludgy ocean water. The sandstone columns riddled with holes and habitations. The cliff, along which houses were attached like barnacles to a ship's hull. It was the sort of place his younger self might have found plenty of trouble in, and plenty of wonder as well.

He lowered his eyes. He had friends to protect and a task to accomplish. Danger waited around every corner. No matter his words to provoke Aelyn, now was no time for idle sightseeing.

Tal turned south, and the others followed.

As they left the seaport and headed toward Stilts, the streets became clogged with passersby of all varieties. Most were medusal or sylvan, and they looked upon their party with undisguised disgust and intrigue.

But those standing behind shop stalls only saw potential customers. They shouted their wares at them, and a hundred varieties of food greeted Tal's eyes. Fish and rice spilling out of a seaweed wrapper. Shrimps, seared and skewered. Mussels and clams fresh from the Far Depths.

Food wasn't the only thing peddled. Baubles of sea glass and bright stones hung as door ornaments and pendants. Clothes, with fish-scale patterns and iridescent colors, were hung up so they shimmered in the light. Tal wondered what material they were made of, for they shone like metal, but had the flexibility of cloth.

Tal looked down with a grimace as his thoughts turned to his shabby state of dress. His trousers were threadbare around the knees and stained with blood, despite having scrubbed them after the battle at Trader Springs. His belt was cracked and dry, as were his boots. His overtunic was in little better condition, and the shirt under it was long past white. His dark cloak did little to hide the defects of the rest, being patched and threadbare itself.

In short, they looked like vagrants. *And I suppose we are*, he thought with a spare smile.

A tug came at his sleeve, followed by a hissed, "Tal!"

He jerked around to find Falcon at his side, staring wide-eyed ahead of them. It didn't take long for Tal to make out what had caused the bard's alarm. Pressing through the crowd was a knot of medusals and sylvans, their heads gleaming dully with bronze helms. Their spears, enhanced with a hook accompanying the sharp point, stabbed at the air as they marched.

A pit formed in Tal's gut. They were foreigners and appeared to be penniless wanderers as well. There was little chance they would be ignored. He had to do something, and soon, or they would have the entire city on their scent.

Tal had spent little time on subtle sorcery since he'd pried the piece of Heartstone from his side and overcome the canker that ravaged his body. It had barely occurred to him to do so, and when it did, it was easily ignored. Illusion and influence wouldn't help against Yuldor and his monsters when he ascended Ikvaldar for their final confrontation. It had made little sense before to concentrate on anything other than battle spells.

Now, he regretted his oversight. No amount of sorcery would triumph over all the garrisons in Dreygoj. And even if he could, how many innocents would be injured or killed along the way?

Tal couldn't bear more unnecessary blood being spilled. Not when he could avoid it. Their mission required a gentler approach than charging in and slaughtering every man or woman in their way. Unless he could divert the attention of these guards, they would fail before they'd even begun.

But just as he swelled his blood with sorcery and prepared for a working he had no idea how to accomplish, he heard a low muttering behind him. Though he couldn't make out the words, he knew what they were accomplishing at once.

Aelyn's illusion.

The sorcery summoned by the Worldtongue words whispered in Tal's mind as it settled upon him. But even as he registered the mage's incantation, he remembered it wouldn't help him. The Ring of Thalkuun pulsed on his finger, defying the magic.

He was on his own.

As the guards neared, just a dozen feet away, and the surrounding crowd thinned, Tal seized upon inspiration. Reaching out with an invisible grasp, he took hold of the sorcery that had failed to settle upon him and made it his own. It felt like donning a man's clothes after he'd spent all day wearing them, oily and repulsive, but Tal pushed the soiled feeling aside and used his own power to stretch and mold the spell to himself. It was of the same power as filled his veins, but with permutations, like the variations between gemstones.

He only hoped the spell would work better now than it had on the oasis' captain.

The city watch at last came abreast of their position, and the foremost medusal looked right at Tal. Recognizably male by his mane of fins, his yellow slitted eyes flickered up and down, and his tongue flitted out from his lipless mouth. His green-scaled hand tightened over the shaft of his spear.

"Out of the way, *gadik!*" the medusal snapped.

Tal obeyed and saw out of the corners of his vision that his companions did the same. All he could do was watch as the patrol pushed roughly past them before continuing down the street. None of them spared a backward glance.

Perplexed, Tal glanced at the rest of his party and startled. For a moment, he thought they'd all disappeared. A moment later, however, as he looked down at himself, he understood the truth.

Aelyn's spell had made them appear as Nightelves. Their features were largely the same, only shifted to match the Eastern race. It was especially odd to see Garin with the tapered ears of an elf, the bluish skin tones disconcerting as well. Their clothes, too, hadn't drastically changed, but had gathered minor improvements, becoming clean and mended where they'd been ripped and stained. The illusion lacked the sophistication of a Soulstealer's disguise, yet was impressive for the speed and reach it had at a moment's notice.

"You saved our skins," Tal admitted to the mage. "Again."

Aelyn smirked, the expression much the same in his Nightelf appearance. "A little invocation I learned in the Emperor's archives."

"Glad all your time wasn't wasted down there."

As the mage began to snap back, Helnor spoke, restraining his deep baritone to a low rumble. "Much as I love to tease my little brother, we must press on. People are staring."

Tal glanced around and saw the Prime Warder was right. Their abrupt transformation hadn't gone unnoticed, nor should they have ever expected it to, with a portion of Dreygoj's population constantly staring at them. Now, they stared with even wider eyes and whispered to each other, and the attention only seemed to be spreading.

Tal turned back to Aelyn. "Can you maintain the spell a little longer?"

He hesitated. "I will try. But as we move, it will become more difficult."

"Hold it for as long as you can. We need to get away."

Tal pressed south. Though the medusals and sylvans didn't look away, they parted before them, all reluctant to touch these sorcerous strangers. That was all the better; no doubt jostling elbows and shoulders would make Aelyn's job more difficult than it already was.

Walking with a brisk pace, Tal led them away, hoping rumors didn't fly fast in Dreygoj.

THE SORCEROUS SCIENCE

At last, the Stilts district came into view.

After their narrow escape from the city patrol, the illusion had lasted a few minutes longer before fading. The wary looks had returned, but Garin and the others had no choice now but to press on. They took to alleys whenever they could, but sidetracking only made the walk longer.

Eventually, they found their destination. The buildings were the first indication, shifting from sandstone back to wood and daub such as they'd been around the docks. As they neared, the shore of the pool, over which the district was positioned, became apparent. The stone was a striking salmon hue before it descended into murky brown water, the stink of nightsoil indicating how it gained its color.

As they'd been informed, Stilts stood over the largest tidepool Garin had yet seen. The structures limited his view, but the tidepool seemed to extend for a mile ahead. Promenades on their namesake stilts connected the domiciles in a wooden web above the boggy water. The homes here seemed shabbier than in other parts of the city, and Garin wondered if their medusal alchemist had boasted beyond his abilities. After all, if he could invent an elixir that defied Yuldor's sorcery, why would he live in such squalor?

He silenced his reservations and continued after Tal as he led them onto the walkways.

"Think we'll find this Koax here?" Wren wrinkled her nose against the district's stench.

"So Jira said."

"And we're trusting the word of a smuggler." She shook her head. "Let's just hope the alchemist doesn't use the water here. Can't imagine any concoction with this bilge would be drinkable."

"You may be surprised, my daughter." Falcon flashed a smile over his shoulder. "The marsh whiskey of Hunt's Hollow is made with scarce sanitation, yet I found it quite palatable on our journey through. And you nursed on it, didn't you, Garin?"

He grinned at the bard. "I know some who did."

"There you have it! All will be well."

Wren scowled at both of them. "Drink what you want. I swallow enough crap talking with you two."

Garin and Falcon laughed at that, and even Wren allowed a grin.

Their levity fled as Tal halted them by a group of medusal women who had gathered to wash their clothes. Though the task initially seemed pointless considering the state of the tidepool, Garin saw there was a separate pool within the larger one that boasted marginally cleaner water. Medusals' expressions were hard to read, but Garin judged by the sagging of their shoulders and the droop in their tails that their lives weren't to be envied.

Tal started speaking to them in the Darktongue before Aelyn took over. Even not understanding the words, Garin heard the waspishness in his tone and winced. The dull coins that Tal passed over to the women proved a sufficient balm for any wounds the mage's tongue inflicted, however, for it wasn't long before the women were all babbling at once and directing them deeper into the district. Garin gave them a polite smile as he followed the others forward, but none of the washerwomen returned it.

It wasn't much farther before Tal brought their company to a halt in the middle of a long stretch between houses. Through the gap to the east, Garin saw the sun sparkling over the ocean, while to the west stony hills rose from the edges of the large tidepool.

"Koax Mraaj should be at the end of this lane." Tal spoke in a low voice, as if afraid of being overheard, though no one lingered nearby. "Those women knew something they wouldn't share. Be prepared for anything."

"Such sage advice," Aelyn noted wryly as he turned away. "Less fretting, Harrenfel, and more doing."

Tal's jaw tightened momentarily as he looked after the mage, then the tension released with a shrug. Sharing a knowing look with Garin, the man turned after the mage, and Garin followed with the rest.

He saw the alchemist's home from a distance. It was a similar size as the others, only two tiny rooms within, and the roof was of terra-cotta tiles. A wind vane emerged from the middle of the roof. As they neared, Garin saw it wasn't an arrow or the typical rooster as could be found on many a Hunt's Hollow wind vane, but the flying beast they had so recently faced down: a cockatrice. The wind vane had long stopped serving its function, stiff and brown with rust, only laggardly turning in the Far Depths wind. A sandstone chimney came off the side of the house, but a smaller pipe emerged from the tiles as well, this made of copper, with green patina spreading over its mouth.

As Tal led them to the door, more oddities presented themselves. Garin stared at a string of glass baubles hanging from the edge of the roof. Within them, a substance of several bright colors, from incandescent orange to green to blue, moved of its own will, slowly churning like mud in water.

His attention was drawn back to the task at hand when Tal kneeled before the door. A moment later, Wren, who stood at the back of their group, spoke up, interrupting the murmuring among those at the front.

"Either knock or tell us what you found," she said irritably.

Helnor, who bent to look as well, turned back with his brow furrowed. "Something has stained the planks in front of the door. Dark streaks…"

Garin took his meaning at once. "Blood."

"Afraid so," the Prime said with a grimace.

Tal stood and looked behind their company, then at the door. Garin glanced around as well and found no one in sight. When he turned back, he saw Tal slowly pry open the door, which hung loose on its hinges, then enter inside with a flare of sorcerous light.

Drawing in a breath, Garin followed the others in, then tugged the door back into place behind him.

The alchemist's house was plainly a laboratory, judging by the scent alone, a caustic odor that bit at the inside of his nostrils. Something smelled as if it were burning, though he saw no flicker of flames. The dim interior was illuminated by more than their werelights; orbs of various sizes shone with the alchemical solutions they contained. Most appeared to have the same gelatinous liquid as the baubles outside, all moving in mesmerizing patterns.

By the sparse light, he saw more dire signs of Koax Mraaj's fate. Flasks and decanters were shattered across the tables that lined the walls and sparkled on the floorboards. Drawers had been left open and cabinet doors hung ajar. Whoever had invaded the alchemist's home had been searching for something. Garin hoped they hadn't found it.

As Helnor crouched in the middle of the floor, Garin saw at once what he stared at. More dark stains had soaked into the wood, undiluted by seawater or rain as the entrance had been outside. Blood — Koax's blood — had been spilled.

Garin stared at the bloodstains and tried to hold back a rising tide of despair. Had they come all the way to Dreygoj for nothing? What would they do to ward off Paradise's miasma now? If Pim had spoken truthfully, and Garin had to hope he had, they wouldn't even be able to reach Yuldor if they couldn't get this elixir.

Wren stood over the Prime Warder and placed her hands on her hips. "Ravagers did this. Had to be."

"Yes," Tal answered as he reentered the main room. "My guess as well. Though it remains possible that our concerns are unconnected, Ravagers seem the most likely culprits."

Aelyn remained silent, for he was bent over one workstation. As Garin watched, the mage pried a book off a shelf and began leafing through it. Part of him longed to tell him to stop, for the act felt like a desecration of the dead. But Garin knew that if the alchemist was lost to them, as it appeared he was, they needed to learn all they could of the elusive Paradise elixir.

Tal frowned at Aelyn as well, but he only said, "I suppose our next step is to see if Koax is alive. If Ravagers took him, they might not kill him, not outright. Even if they knew he'd discovered an elixir to counteract Paradise's miasma, they might wish to know its formula, who he had shared it with, and other details of his research."

He fell silent. Garin guessed the direction of his thoughts: the means by which they would extract such information from him. His breath came quick imagining it.

"It's gibberish!" Aelyn suddenly spoke. "These must be his records, but he has written them in code."

Tal sighed. "No chance we have the key to it?"

The mage glared back at him. "If he took the time to disguise his notes, I doubt he would be so careless as to leave the cipher lying around. Doubtless, this is why whoever attacked him left behind these books."

"Or perhaps they mean to return for them later," Helnor countered softly.

At that, Garin had an urge to look toward the door. All too easily could he imagine the savage warriors sneaking up on them, trapping them inside... He shook his head and grimaced, trying to banish the paranoia.

"Sounds like we're back to finding the alchemist," Wren said, her habitual impatience rising. "So what — we find the Ravager fortress, then politely ask them to let us in?"

"I'm sorry, Wren — not even in my tales would that work," Falcon said softly from beside another work table.

Tal sounded reluctant as he spoke. "We'll find their hideout, wait for darkness, then enter however we can. Preferably quiet, but if not..." He shrugged.

Garin felt sick at the thought. He could handle himself in a fight now, but the anticipation of one had never quite settled with him.

"What's this?" Falcon muttered. As Garin turned with the others, the bard held up something. Garin had to draw near to see what it was, for it seemed to suck in the light. When he did finally make it out, he saw it was only a black rock, rough on its surface. Small veins ran through it, glimmering scarlet where they caught the light.

A sudden suspicion struck Garin. He stared mutely at the stone, wondering if it could be true.

Wren asked a question, but Garin was no longer listening. Peeling off the veil around his mind, he let the Worldsong in.

After a moment, the initial rush of sound faded. Garin listened closer and heard melodies spiraling in song, a dozen of them scattered throughout the room. As he looked around the dim interior, it seemed he could almost see the sources of these smaller songs. The loudest one came from Falcon's hand.

"Dragonstone," Garin murmured. "Koax mined the eggs."

His companions were speaking, but Garin couldn't draw his

attention away from the dragon songs. As with his prior encounters with them, the songs in these stones were somber and mournful. A dragon had fragmented when the stone egg that supplied these shards had been excavated. It had died before it was even born, and yet some part of it was forced to live on.

He swallowed hard, his eyes stinging.

Part of him longed to free the dragon spirits interred in the stones, but considering what they faced, he knew he couldn't act rashly. Measure by measure, Garin wove his barrier back in place and sealed himself off from the Worldsong and dragon songs alike. When all he heard were his companions again, he sucked in a trembling breath, then let it out in a rush.

"Are you finally listening?" Wren asked drily.

He nodded. "They're pieces of dragonstone. Just like in the bracers and in the golems."

"I thought as much," Tal murmured. "There is nothing else like Heartstone. This matches Hellexa Yoreseer's description of the substance that makes up the Worldheart." He extended his hand toward Falcon, and the bard placed the stone, roughly the size of his palm, into his grip. Garin's old mentor looked surprised for a moment, then gathered a slight crease to his brow. "It sucks at my sorcery, like it wishes to drink it in."

"That only makes sense," Falcon pointed out. "After all, the sliver of Heartstone in your side long repressed your power, did it not?"

Aelyn stared at the stone, his eyes spinning, a fiery light flickering within them. Though he was usually the first to want to study and understand something, he didn't reach for the dragonstone.

"Why would the alchemist possess Heartstone?" the mage muttered as if to himself.

Garin desperately wanted to know the same thing. But they weren't likely to find answers where they were.

"We have to find the alchemist," Garin said, "and hope Koax Mraaj is still alive."

He wondered if the answers the alchemist gave would be ones he wanted to hear. If Koax had taken part in the butchery of dragons, how could he work with him in good conscience?

As the others nodded, Tal flashed him a lopsided smile that contained anything but mirth. "So we do, lad. So we do."

OATH

Tal sighed with relief as they entered the smugglers' warehouse.

Their party had more luck evading the city guard on their journey back from Stilts. Aelyn had prepared his illusion spell before leaving the alchemist's ransacked laboratory, but they were fortunate enough not to have to use it. Still, it was a nerve-racking walk, and Tal's skin crawled with all the eyes watching as they passed through.

But it wasn't only leaving behind prying eyes that made the return welcome. Entering the open doors of the warehouse, they sidled around disgruntled laborers who muttered unfamiliar words he didn't doubt were profanities. Tal looked past them to the far corner where Ashelia and Rolan waited.

He moved swiftly toward them, dodging around crates and barrels being lifted into carts. As they'd agreed, Ashelia and her son had only left the warehouse briefly to restock their supplies, yet she looked haggard and worn, her hand affixed to the pommel of her rapier. Her son was curled up on a barrel next to her, sleeping like a cat. At Tal and the others' approach, Rolan sat up and yawned, his eyes puffy.

"Took you long enough," the boy said as they came within earshot.

"Sorry, lad — got delayed." Tal ruffled his hair and grinned as Rolan swatted his hand away. He looked at the boy's mother and his smile slipped. "Don't have good news, I'm afraid."

Ashelia's expression tightened. "Tell me."

He recounted what they'd discovered of Koax's fate while the others grabbed a hasty meal and long drinks of water, having gone most of the day without both. Garin handed Tal some strips of meat and hardtack, and he smiled his thanks at the youth. *We've come far since Hunt's Hollow, you and I,* he thought as Garin turned away to lash back at Wren as she mocked him for serving Tal.

When Tal had finished his account, Ashelia leaned forward, elbows resting on her knees.

"We must confirm the Ravagers have him," she said at length.

Tal shrugged. "Of course. But how else can we except by seeing for ourselves? We spoke with some washerwomen who seemed to know more than they let on, but they looked afraid of admitting so. Whoever is behind Koax's disappearance likely has most people scared."

"Then we ask someone who doesn't flinch from consequences."

Tal nodded, realizing Ashelia's line of thought. "Jira."

"You are assuming we can trust anything the smuggler says," Aelyn said pointedly.

His House-sister inclined her head. "I am. But we trusted her to get us into the city. Given enough coin, I think we can be reasonably certain in this as well."

"So we ask this smuggler," Helnor said. "Let's assume we're right and she says Koax is captured by Ravagers. What then?"

Tal smiled grimly. "Then we go get him."

"What?" Aelyn's eyes widened. "Invade a Venator fortress? Even for you, Tal, that is a foolish gambit."

He rounded on the mage. "What choice do we have? We have one night here in the warehouse, and I can't see us finding shelter anywhere else, can you?"

Aelyn only sneered. "Given a little time, I am sure I will think of something better."

"And I'm sure you won't," Helnor rumbled. "We should plan as if we will invade. A Warder always accounts for the worst scenario."

"And that is the worst," Falcon murmured.

"Someone will have to stay to watch over Rolan again." Ashelia worried her lip before noticing her son watched her.

"I can come with!" The boy stood before his mother, arms crossed, face scrunched with determination. "I fought at the mountain pass, didn't I? And in the dwarven village? I can help!"

"You were taken hostage at the Pass of Argothe," Tal reminded him gently. "We're all safer if you're back here, lad."

Rolan turned his scowl on Tal, but only huffed.

Tal looked at Ashelia. "I thought you would stay with him again."

She shook her head. "Judging by our experiences with Venators, I expect I'll need to heal Koax Mraaj before we can speak with him."

Tal suspected she was right, though he scarcely wanted to admit it. A sigh escaped him.

"Fine. Then perhaps one of his uncles could stay."

He glanced at Helnor and Aelyn while the brothers glared at each other, a challenge in their eyes. Tal doubted it was courage alone that had them clamoring to enter the fortress.

"I'm the most skilled in alchemy among us," Aelyn said with a pronounced sneer. "Unless you've been studying behind my back?"

Helnor's brow furrowed. "It'll be close-quarters fighting in those sandstone halls, perhaps too close for spells. We need every sword at hand."

"We'll have enough." Ashelia's gray eyes swirled as she stared at the Prime Warder. "Please, *Belosi*. Stay for your nephew's sake."

"I could just go," Rolan pointed out again, though he muttered the words.

Helnor's shoulders sagged, but his voice was firm. "Fine. I'll stay. But you had best play me a tune or two while we wait, eh, Little Tree Frog?"

Rolan brightened at the prospect. "Never thought you would ask! Falcon has been teaching me all kinds of things."

"Speaking of which…" Tal turned to Falcon. "You should stay as well."

The bard was shaking his head before Tal finished speaking. "Not this time, my dear friend. You cannot leave me behind at every chance of danger. How else can I gather material if I'm absent from the most perilous parts of our journey?"

"How can you hope to finish my legend if you're dead?" Tal countered.

"Father," Wren interjected, "don't do this. Just stay safe for once."

Falcon smiled down at where she sprawled on the planks beside him. "I'm sorry, dearest daughter. I wish I could. But this is my calling. Besides, what kind of father would I be if I let you wander into danger I won't risk myself?"

"A sensible one!"

"No." The bard emphasized the denial with a shake of his head. "I'm going. The only way you can stop me is if you tie me up and sink me into the ocean. Not that I'm recommending that course," he added hastily, as Tal exchanged a mischievous look with Garin. The youth grinned back, though tension remained in his eyes.

Still, Tal had faced defeat enough times to know when it was before him. "Fine, Falcon, fine. But if you perish, I'm requisitioning Wren to complete my songs."

The bard looked scandalized. "Not even you would be that cruel, my old friend."

"Excuse me?" Wren stood, but she spoiled her affront with a groan. "Yuldor's balls, but I'm still stiff from hiding on that ship. I'd rather invade a dozen fortresses than be smuggled in again — or out, for that matter."

"Don't think you have much choice in that." Garin also stood, the youth's movements showing he was sore as well. "We'll be lucky if we have the chance to be smuggled out."

Tal winced. *As if we didn't already need a god's heap of luck.*

Garin was almost relieved when nighttime arrived.

They had spent the rest of the afternoon and evening in preparation, proceeding under the assumption that raiding the Ravager fortress would be necessary. Tal and Helnor had ventured out into the city to discover where the Ravager citadel lay, the Prime Warder going even though he wouldn't be in the invasion party. Still, Helnor knew the Darktongue well, and he was skilled at tracking down evasive prey. Garin suspected he also wanted to know where the rest of his companions would be risking their lives out of some guilty urge.

While the two men were away, Aelyn became occupied with organizing and preparing the catalysts and components for various spells. His assortment of items, from ground seashell to *yinshi* to a pile of brown, dried leaves he refused to identify, were arrayed over two crates. The mage often bent over them, moving ingredients from piles to small pouches he hung from his belt, muttering to himself all the while.

Garin and the others busied themselves with securing their belongings for a swift escape. When they checked their saddle-bags, satchels, and mounts for a third time, Garin finally begged free of the duty and retreated to a corner of the warehouse. He took with him a package, which he only revealed as he perched atop a stack of two crates, above where any laborers could easily see what he held.

Unfolding the cloth in his lap, Garin stared down at the red-veined black rocks.

He studied them with his eyes for a long while, then reached out with his hands. They felt like stone, yet even without his mind open to the Worldsong, he felt *something* pressing at his fingertips. As if the dragon fragments sought to escape their rocky prisons.

He winced and set the stone back down, wishing Ilvuan could guide him. No sooner had he formed the hope than the Singer swept into his mind like a cool breeze.

Garin pressed his welcome upon the dragon. *I didn't know if you could come again.*

I am here, Jenduit. *You have discovered something.*

Yes. Look through my eyes.

He was never sure how much information Ilvuan could harvest from his mind. Sometimes, it seemed the Singer could hear his exact thoughts, while in other moments he remained completely oblivious. Sensory details, at least, appeared readily available to him, as the dragon proved with his words a moment later.

Another egg harvested. Wrath, ancient and deeply burning, simmered through Garin's mind. *This must be stopped,* Jenduit. *You must go to the* Sha'aval *with all haste.*

We will, I swear, very soon. There's just one thing we must do here in Dreygoj first.

Ilvuan's displeasure curled through his mind, burning like the acidic air in the alchemist's house. Garin winced and hurried on.

But I wanted to ask you about these. He gingerly tapped at one of the black rocks resting on his legs. *Dragon shells have been used in many things. The bracers we wore as prisoners. The golem cores.*

The dragon's anger burned brighter. *Yes.*

Garin swallowed, the warring feelings within him making his palms clammy and his stomach churn. *Could they be used in an elixir? What is it about dragon shells that makes them useful in these... devices?*

Ilvuan's emotions tamped down. Almost, Garin thought he'd departed again, for his presence dimmed to the back of his mind, barely noticeable, until he spoke.

We ava'duala *were born masters of this World. Sorcery is instinctual, innate, even in our eggs. These properties translate to the abominations mortals have formed from their pieces.*

Grief poured forth from the dragon, and Garin had to swim hard against it to keep afloat.

Sorcery often fails against the promise of our flesh, Ilvuan continued. *Even Heartblood could not contend with a fragment of an* ava'dual *in his side.*

He thought about their bracers and the runes carved into them and wondered at their function. Maybe the glyphs hadn't dampened their sorcery, but the stone itself.

Garin kept the notion to himself and pressed forth a different question. *Could they be used to turn aside Yuldor's miasma in Paradise?*

The Singer rumbled softly. *Perhaps. But it is a desecration to use them so.*

A thrill ran through Garin, though he tried to hide it from Ilvuan.

It's only to put an end to all of this, he explained hastily. *To free and resurrect dragonkind.*

Ilvuan rumbled again, but it had a note of resignation to it now.

This is war, the dragon stated. *In war, we must do what is necessary. But in the time after, there will be a reckoning. Those who have wronged the* ava'duala *will fear our return.*

Garin winced at the oath. Once more, he hid his doubts regarding the part he meant to play in the return of dragons. His fears of what he might unleash upon the World.

Too late to doubt, he told himself. *Too late to turn back.*

Even if he'd wanted to, with Ilvuan's claws set in his mind, he wondered if he had any choice in the matter.

Do not delay, Jenduit. *I will visit you next in the place where I was born.*

With that, the dragon slipped away. Garin wrapped his arms around himself, trying not to shiver.

He was drawn from introspection as a familiar figure entered the warehouse. Garin stared at Jira as she strode through the rough workers with a confident, almost cocky smile perched on her lips. She wore the same plain trousers as before, but her silken shirt was red and clean now. Yet something other than her clothes seemed different.

The smuggler's eyes brushed over Garin, and she raised her eyebrows at him. He couldn't help a slight flush at being acknowledged by the beautiful woman, and he hastily checked that Wren hadn't seen. Relieved that she seemed preoccupied, he folded up the dragonstones, then clambered off the crates to rejoin the others.

Jira spoke loudly in the common Darktongue as she approached, stopping short of their bundled supplies. Her stance was wide and her arms crossed, every part of her declaring who was in charge here. Ashelia stood opposite her in a similar position, and Garin guessed she didn't much care for the smuggler's attitude.

She is a Peer of Gladelyl, after all.

He stood clutching his package of stones while the women spoke back and forth in what sounded like an argument. After a last word, Jira turned and flashed a smile. Her eyes lingered on Garin once again, and he tried to keep his expression smooth as she passed mere inches away before exiting the warehouse. She didn't smell of perfume or flowers, but an earthy, sweet scent that stirred his blood.

Garin swallowed and walked over to his companions. As far as he could tell, Wren hadn't noticed the silent exchange between him and the smuggler, for she demanded of Ashelia, "So? What did she say?"

Ashelia was as rigid as the boards they stood on. "She threatened us."

Wren stared after Jira, the golden tendrils in her eyes spinning fast. "Maybe we should take care of the problem now."

"Wren!" Falcon sounded scandalized by his daughter's suggestion.

Garin stepped into Wren's line of sight, uncomfortable as well. Jira might be a smuggler, but it didn't mean she deserved to die. She'd helped them enter the city, after all.

"What exactly did she say, Ashelia?" he asked.

The Peer's eyes also spun, though slowly, like a river with a powerful current just beneath the surface. "She asked where Tal was. I said I didn't know. That answer did not please her. Then she said that we must leave the warehouse this night or she would expel us."

"We can't leave yet!" Rolan scowled after the smuggler in a flattery of Wren's expression. "We still have to get that alchemist!"

"Patience, Rolan." Ashelia settled a hand on her son's shoulder. "Nothing will come of it. Perhaps we will have to pay further bribes, but the smugglers don't want trouble if they can avoid it. It is a show, an act, like you and Falcon practice."

"Then she is an adept player," Falcon muttered, his words audible to the party.

Ashelia cast him a long-suffering look as Rolan stared quizzically up at the bard. Garin shook his head. *Leave it to Falcon to sow seeds of doubt.*

"I'm guessing she didn't say if the Ravagers had Koax?" Wren asked wryly.

The Peer shook her head. "Something has changed for the worse."

Aelyn turned from his spell ingredients, to which he'd attended during the entire exchange, to face the rest of them. "Then we had best depart soon. If only our brother and that self-important man would return..."

Garin met Wren's gaze and saw they agreed. The raid couldn't come soon enough.

BLOOD & SAND

Tal led his companions across the dark shore. The stench of saltwater and seaweed hung rank in the crisp air. The sun had set hours before, and even the blue of dusk was fading. They were silhouettes as they hopped from stone to sand to stone again, making their way below the cliff looming to their left.

The ocean waves crashed against the rocky beach below, filling their ears and masking their movements, just as he and Helnor had intended. It wasn't Tal's first time entering a place uninvited, after all.

Their destination lay a few hundred strides out from the shore. The Ravagers' citadel was one of the largest sandstone columns in the city, and also the most formidable. Torches told of patrols along the pathway that led up to the tower, and more lights shone from the numerous holes riddling it four stories high. Its position on the outskirts of Dreygoj was both to the benefit and detriment of Tal's party. On the one hand, the ocean and the distance would obscure signs of attack, helping them avoid the notice of the city watch. On the other hand, it meant there was little place to hide in their approach and no innocent reason for their presence.

If they were caught, blood would spill.

But they'd known to prepare for violence. All were armed, even Falcon, though Tal had noticed the bard's hand trembling on his long knife as they set out. He still wished the bard hadn't come, but knew there would be no talking him out of it.

Once he sees the corpses fall, maybe he'll know better next time.

The reminder of all he had to lose made Tal summon yet more sorcery to his blood. It already filled his veins and burned down his limbs, but still he yearned for greater power. Sorcery could protect his friends. Sorcery could save them.

If I wield it well.

He had already employed some of it in a clumsy illusion spell that would hide them from view until they came within the pools of light or a patrol drew too near. Another spell he maintained to sharpen his hearing, and a third to make his eyes sensitive enough that he could see through the darkness. Crabs that thought themselves hidden scuttled off before Tal's footsteps, and he heard them all.

But it wasn't enough, could never be enough, for him to feel secure while Ashelia was at risk.

He turned to glance at her. She moved with the same Warder's grace she'd shown when he reunited with her on the road to Elendol, unabated by the miles they'd traveled into Imperial lands. Her rapier was bared and in hand, her other hand ready for quick spellwork. Wren and Garin had adopted the same technique, their sorcery as deadly as their blades. Aelyn and Falcon took up the rear, the mage nearly as nimble as his House-sister on the rocks, the bard decidedly less so.

Tal turned back, wishing he could feel heartened by the sight of his friends. When he'd first entered the East, he had longed for their companionship. Now, their presence only filled him with fear.

I am enough, he told himself as the sandstone tower drew nearer. *I have to be.*

The time had come to prove it.

Torchlight stretched across the sand and stones. The patrol came around the boulder that had obscured them from view. There were three of them: one minotaur, one Nightelf, one human. They were merry comrades, telling crude jokes and laughing and slapping each other on their backs. A sour taste filmed Tal's mouth as he held up a hand to the others to halt and watch them pass.

He could let them go by unharmed. They could keep laughing. Though they were Ravagers, how could he know of what crimes they were guilty?

But to leave any alive now would run the risk of encountering them later. And that was a chance Tal couldn't afford to take.

Wuld.

Holding the word in his mind, he pulled on his sorcery and reached forward with a spell. A gust twisted around the Ravagers, and they jerked about, their mirth replaced by alarm.

None had the chance to retaliate. He drew out the air from their lungs and held it from coming back in. All three of the Ravagers collapsed to their knees, mouths working like fish pulled on land. Weapons and torches fell to the sand as they clutched at their throats.

Tal clenched his jaw and tightened his fist. He held onto the spell as they began to spasm. He held on as they grew still.

Only then did he release it and suck in a ragged breath.

Ashelia's hand gripped his shoulder. Her voice trembled as she whispered in his ear. "You did what you had to."

He nodded, unable to meet her eyes. "We should keep moving."

She released him as he stood and walked over to the bodies, his orb of obscurance following them and, with luck, continuing to hide them from view. A few moments of rifling through the Ravager's clothes turned up five keys. Tal was confident he could open most locks, but it paid to be prepared against enchantments and wards. Entrusting the keys to Ashelia, he stood up and, looking askance at his companions, motioned them toward the next patrol.

He suffocated the next group as well, though his insides twisted into fresh knots. Glad they wouldn't have to loot these corpses, Tal pressed his party closer to the sandstone tower. Nearing their destination came with little relief.

There, blood would spill.

He huddled with the others behind a boulder, then peered around it. At the lowest level of the tower, there only appeared to be one entrance, a portal covered with a round wooden door that poorly fit the tunnel entrance. Six Ravagers stood guard there, crossbows cradled in their arms. They wouldn't pose much of a challenge, though they numbered just enough to make his casting tricky.

More worrisome were the warriors positioned on higher landings with a view of the door. Nearly a dozen in number, they also held crossbows, while two manned mounted ballistae with bolts large enough to take down a horse.

All it would take was one shot to endanger his friends. Tal would have to be swift and unyielding to keep them safe.

Do not doubt, he told himself as he steeled his nerve. *Do not fail.*

They hadn't been noticed yet, but as Tal motioned to follow him across the final stretch to the door, a Ravager atop a landing shouted and pointed out across the beach. Glancing back, Tal saw they had seen one of the fallen patrols. Either their lack of movement or the abandoned torches had finally alerted them to the danger.

He gritted his teeth, debating what to do. There was only one way in and one way out of the tower. If subtlety had ever been an option, he'd already blown it.

Only one thing to do now.

Tal looked back at his companions and met their gazes. Their eyes were wide with fear, though Wren seemed equally full of excitement.

217

"I'll draw their attention," he whispered, using a trace of sorcery to bring the words to Falcon and Aelyn, who kneeled farthest from him. "You make for the door. Once you're inside, I'll follow."

Ashelia glanced in the tower's direction, though stone blocked the way. "Take care of the ballistae first," she murmured.

He was grateful she didn't object to the plan. *At least she believes in you*, a part of him mocked.

He nodded to her words and donned a slight smile."Ready?" he asked, as the shouts of the Ravagers spread.

His party nodded back.

Drawing in a deep breath, Tal absorbed sorcery until he thought he would catch fire. Then he rose from behind the stone.

"Here I am!" he called up to the Ravagers as they turned their weapons on him. A wild smile spread wider across his face. "Come kill me, if you can!"

They took him up on his offer. Quarrels loosed. Machines roared. Spells rained down in fire and stone.

Tal would perish before the Ravagers' attack — Garin saw no other outcome.

As Garin cowered behind the last boulder between them and the citadel, Tal had stood. "Come kill me, if you can!" his challenge rang out. With Garin's mind open to the Worldsong, his old mentor sang even louder with the strength of his sorcery.

Yet as potent as it was, how could Tal withstand the onslaught of all the Ravagers at once?

The quarrels found the man first. As they ripped through the air, Tal's song flared, and magic broke out from him in a storm. Garin winced as the wind whipped across his face, so sharp it almost cut. The dun sand swirled around Tal, billowing up half as high as the Ravagers' tower. In the half-light of the night, it seemed a vast nest of hornets had awoken with buzzing fury.

The crossbow's bolts met the sandstorm, and it was like they hit a stone wall as they ricocheted into the darkness.

Wren wrenched Garin's arm and yelled something in his ear, but he could only continue to watch as the ballistae's shafts cracked toward Tal. A scream ripped from his throat, as if he could warn him.

"*Tal!*"

The winds couldn't deflect these heavier missiles, each nearly the size of tree trunks. They pierced through. Garin's only consolation was that the sandstorm didn't die. He could only hope that, somehow, Tal still survived.

Wren pulled on him again, and this time he budged, following her and the rest of their party as they bolted from behind the boulder and ran for the citadel. Tal's winds made their gaits uneven, and Garin stumbled drunkenly across the beach. The door seemed far away, an insurmountable distance, yet they'd gone too far to turn back. He tried not to tangle *Helshax* between his legs as he struggled forward. The World-song howled in his ears, louder even than the storm.

Then the winds buffeted forward, falling against the citadel in a wave, and nearly blasted Garin off his feet.

"*Sard keid!*" He couldn't hear his own words, but the magic obeyed them, securing his footing on the uncertain sand as it twisted up over his ankles and hardened. He felt his knees must shatter from the beating they took.

A moment later, the winds ceased. Garin, wheezing, couldn't help but turn back.

His heart leaped as he saw Tal still stood. The two bolts of the ballistae were split in half and lay around him, as if Tal had broken them apart just before they could run him through. An angry yellow glow surrounded the man, looking like a thousand tiny flames flared to life. A terrible smile split his lips as he stared defiantly up at the Ravagers.

The Ravagers' spells rained down. Globules of fire. Boulders and slabs of stone. Ice sharpened like arrows. Light burned Garin's eyes as it blazed. There were many sorcerers among their enemies, and all aimed their power at Tal.

Garin didn't see what happened next, for Wren once more pulled on his arm. Releasing the spell that had held his feet in place, he staggered forward, raising his head to see what awaited them.

The door hung open off its hinges, but it was still guarded. Four out of the six Ravagers remained, and they roared as they charged at Garin and the others.

Ashelia met the assault. With all the speed and deadliness of a viper, she ducked a minotaur's wild stroke and sliced at his legs. As the Ravager bellowed and collapsed, she spun past and sent him sprawling with a blast of wind. Never ceasing to move, the Peer parried the attack of another Ravager, then battered back the other two.

Aelyn struck next. "*Jask bruin!*" he cried, loudly enough that Garin could just make out the words over the tumult of battle. He threw up his hands as he spoke, and a fine dust shimmered in the torchlight before erupting into sparks. Before Garin could close his eyes, violet lightning thundered forward, enveloping two of the Ravagers. The Nightelf and medusal spasmed as they fell, skin burned with purple lines.

Wren darted forward to finish off the last Ravager facing Ashelia, a human who had despair written in every line of his face even before the two rapiers stabbed into him. Wren snarled as she kicked him loose of her blade and sent his body tumbling down the stone walkway to splash into the water below.

Wondering if he was needed after all, Garin bolted after his companions as they headed inside.

Within, the sounds of battle were strangely muted, but the

Worldsong marched triumphantly through his mind. After all that had happened outside, Garin felt strangely disconnected from his body, dizzy and air-deprived. There was nothing for it but to shake his head and press on.

Ashelia and Wren waited for the rest to enter, then shouted back before running up the stairs. Ahead of Garin, Falcon had an arm wrapped around Aelyn, the mage's strength depleted from his spell. Garin's lungs burned for air as he pounded up stairs worn smooth from wear.

No sooner had they reached the top than shouts, ringing steel, and flares of sorcery arose again. Garin pushed past Falcon and Aelyn to join the fight and only just ducked a spout of flames.

The hallway was too narrow for more than two to fight at a time, and Ashelia and Wren had already taken the fore. But there were more ways to fight than with steel. Garin threw forward his free hand and shouted, "*Dord uvthak!*"

The Worldsong soared as sorcery flowed through him, then out into the walls. Stone burst inward, crashing into the Ravagers behind the frontline to crush and stun them. Wren and Ashelia finished off their opponents, then pressed forward to take care of the rest.

Garin made to follow, but Aelyn seized his arm and held him with a surprisingly strong grip.

"You damned fool!" the mage shouted, pointing.

Garin followed his gaze, and his stomach clenched. Cracks spider-webbed throughout the ceiling. They were thin, but spread further with every passing moment.

"No more stone spells!" the mage shouted before shoving Garin forward.

Curses running through his head, Garin followed the women, stumbling on rubble and stepping over bodies. The Worldsong had turned frantic, and he couldn't tell if it was from the danger or his increasing anxiety. He'd compromised the entire tower with his idiotic idea.

He just hoped it wouldn't kill them all.

Ashelia and Wren had taken care of two sorcerers at the end of the hall. Wren's hair was singed at the ends, and a black smudge on the wall spoke of where a fire plume had nearly taken off her head, yet she grinned back at Garin before jerking her head forward and leading them on.

If I don't get us killed, he thought, *she'll do it herself.*

CRUMBLING FOUNDATIONS

Tal couldn't tell if his tears were from dust, rage, or sorrow as he broke the last stone balcony and sent its occupant screaming into the sea below.

He swayed for a moment where he stood. Destruction surrounded him. The beach had been rent apart by sorcery. The missiles the Ravagers had shot at him were scattered like needles under a giant pine tree. Rubble was strewn down the sides of the sandstone citadel. He was halfway surprised it still stood after all he'd thrown against it.

Tal wiped his eyes with a filthy sleeve, shook his head, and tottered forward. As usual, a smile found his lips, this time to be a mask. He hated the killing, but his friends dying was worse.

Ashelia. Falcon. Garin and Wren. Even Aelyn.

He had the strength to keep them alive, so long as he didn't let his conscience catch up to him.

Tal wondered why it bothered him now as he loped across the beach, past the bloody walkway, then up the stairs within. He'd killed countless foes in his lifetime, many of them Ravagers. Why question the necessity of their deaths now? Why rediscover guilt when he least wanted it?

He didn't have answers, nor could he give the question any more thought as he entered the hallway. Dust and smoke hung in the air, making the dim corridor hazy. Faintly, he heard fighting echoing down the hall.

But what caught his eyes were the cracks spreading above him. They appeared recently made, and they traveled halfway down the hall and claimed the walls as well. A sense of foreboding filled him.

Pushing away all doubt and guilt, Tal embraced his fear and let it fuel him.

He raced down the hallway and up another staircase. Signs of his companions' passage were everywhere: the blood, the bodies, the charred stone. When he reached out with his sorcery, he could feel them above, and he breathed a sigh of relief that all remained alive.

But with the tower crumbling around them, he knew that might soon change.

Up one stairway, down another hall, more stairs, yet another corridor. The place was a warren, its passages twisting this way and that, none level or straight. Though he felt the people he sought, he couldn't find a direct path to them. He wished he could just force apart the stone and climb his way up, but even he wasn't that rash.

He ran, sorcery burning through his limbs, and hoped he wouldn't arrive too late.

"Try here," Ashelia croaked, her voice almost gone from the dust choking the air.

Garin nodded with the others as the Peer stepped away from the door, allowing Aelyn to approach it. The mage was unsteady on his feet, yet knowing time was short and the elf was stubborn, Garin gritted his teeth and let him cast the lockbreak spell.

A moment later, the metal shattered, and Aelyn stood with a pained grimace. As he swayed, Falcon was there to steady him. The bard had long since sheathed his knife to better support the mage. It spoke to the depths of Aelyn's weariness that he allowed it.

Wren kicked the door open and went in first, werelight illuminating the way. Garin hoped that, at last, this would be the chamber that held their quarry.

As they stared around at walls strewn with beds, they were once more disappointed.

They'd checked every door as they fought their way through the Ravager citadel, yet though they'd reached the highest floor, they hadn't found the alchemist. Instead, storerooms and bunks and mess halls greeted their eyes. Garin hadn't needed more reminders of the massacre they committed, yet found they surrounded him. Perhaps these Easterners had been misaligned and served Yuldor, but they were still people living their lives. They hadn't sought their party and attacked them.

And yet Garin and the others had come here and butchered them all.

Stop. Don't think about that now.

He lurched out of the way as Wren came out, her expression furious. "Not there either," she rasped as she stalked down the hall. "Next one…"

Garin followed on her heels, making sure to arrive at the subsequent door before Aelyn could. Bending over it, he set his hand next to the lock and stood to the side. Motioning the others back with his head, he muttered the word Ilvuan had taught him back in Elendol and braced himself.

"*Uvthak.*"

Garin flinched as the metal shattered. Ignoring the splinters that shot into his hand, he straightened and, leading with *Helshax*, pressed open the door.

Fetid air wafted out. Garin scanned the room as his

companions pressed in after him. Like most of the citadel's chambers, the walls and ceilings were rough-hewn, hardly smoothed after their excavation. The floor was uneven, ridged with the strikes of the pickaxes that had carved it. Little occupied the dozen paces that the room stretched.

Only in its center was there an object: a chair, and a figure slumped in it.

Even as Garin edged closer, the figure didn't move. He swallowed as his werelight caught on the dark pools beneath the chair. Its occupant was clearly medusal, his reptilian tail lying slack in the drying blood.

Garin slowly raised his gaze. Restraints kept the medusal in place, ropes darkened with blood as well. The crest around his head identified him as male. His skin, a light lavender, was splotchy with wounds. The feathers projecting from his crown were thinned and pale, a stark contrast to the brilliant colors Garin had seen on other medusals.

He looked all but dead. Only the rise of his shoulders with each labored breath told otherwise.

"Is that him?" Wren asked from behind. "Koax Mraaj?"

At the name, the medusal shuddered and coughed. He barely seemed to have the energy to spit. The alchemist, as Garin assumed him to be, made a sound almost like speech. At first, Garin assumed it would be in common Darktongue; then he recognized the word through the Rajeyan's thick accent.

"Reachmen..."

Garin kneeled next to him, ignoring the blood soaking through his trousers. "Koax Mraaj. Can you speak? We came to rescue you."

At his low angle, he saw a glint of the medusal's yellow eyes between his swollen eyelids. The alchemist turned his head toward him as much as he could, his lipless mouth parted. A sickening rattle came out before recognizable words did.

"You... who are you?"

Garin was at a loss for how to explain. He glanced at his companions to find Ashelia kneeling on Koax's other side.

"I'm a Peer of Gladelyl, Master Mraaj," she said, her voice hoarse but certain. "I'm also a healer. With your permission, I would help you."

"Must we do this now?" Aelyn sniped from by the door. He leaned against the wall now, seeming to prefer it to the bard's help. Falcon stood at the portal, his head turning this way and that as he watched for approaching enemies. Garin wondered if they'd killed them all or if more lay in wait.

"We cannot move him without killing him," Ashelia said matter-of-factly.

Gently but firmly, she pressed Koax against the back of the chair and motioned for Garin to hold him there. He didn't want to touch the injured medusal, fearing to hurt him, yet he obeyed, gripping the alchemist by the shoulders and wincing as Koax groaned.

"We don't have time," Aelyn grated. "Listen! Our damned Founts have undermined the stone's integrity. The foundations are giving way!"

Garin winced again, but he listened and heard it was as the mage said. If not for Aelyn's insistence, he might have thought the rumbling and shifting were part of the Worldsong.

Marsh-headed fool, he thought to himself, hoping his mistake wouldn't cost them all their lives.

"A moment, Aelyn." Ashelia's words were strained, but she didn't cease to work. Her knife cut away the alchemist's filthy clothes, and Garin glimpsed bloody lacerations beneath. Koax hadn't been treated kindly by his captors. Garin had to look away, swallowing down his rising nausea.

Koax wheezed again as he tried to speak. Overcoming his revulsion, Garin leaned close to catch the words, fearing they would get too few from the alchemist.

"Why?" the medusal whispered. "Why are you... here?"

Garin glanced at Ashelia, but she was preoccupied with the

healing, now withdrawing a small brush and an ink bottle from a pouch at her hip. They were used to paint on runes, he knew, such as she had for Garin's wounds after Trader Springs.

"We need your elixir," he replied, speaking slowly so the medusal could understand him. "The elixir to safely navigate Paradise. On Ikvaldar, that is…"

Only as he made the request did he realize how strange it sounded. Why would a medusal, hundreds of miles from Yuldor's mountain, know anything about the god's secrets? And if he'd learned something, how had he done it?

They'd blindly trusted Pim to lead them true. But what if he had been a loyal servant to Yuldor all along? What if this was a delay so that the Prince of Devils could prepare for their arrival, perhaps even ensnaring them before they could ascend the mountain?

Garin tried to listen through his swirling thoughts as Koax coughed, then replied.

"Journals, my journals… The key is in three, backward then forward… The stones are the solution… Do not let it die, Reachman… I wish for eternity."

Garin committed the words to memory, repeating them in his mind, though he hadn't the faintest clue what they meant. Before he could ask, Falcon squawked from the entrance of the room. Garin jerked away, scrambling to grab *Helshax* from where he'd lain the sword on the floor. His sudden movement elicited moans from Koax.

"Garin!" Ashelia snapped.

Before he could respond, Falcon called, "Tal!" Garin let the blade fall back at his side, relief flooding through him.

Tal was here, not more Ravagers. They were safe.

The stone shuddered around him, and thunder welled up from below.

Safe. Garin couldn't decide if he wanted to laugh or cry more.

Tal was in the room a moment later. Grime layered him, and he swept back his loose dirty hair as he looked at each of them. A small smile appeared on his lips, though something remained haunted about his shadowed eyes.

"The tower's collapsing," he told them. "We have to leave."

"Astute observations, as usual," Aelyn said snidely as he edged toward the door.

"We cannot leave him, Tal." Ashelia still kneeled next to Koax, desperation lining her face. "He'll die if he moves."

Emotion spasmed across Tal's face. Garin could imagine his thoughts. *All this for nothing.* Or near enough. He doubted the words the alchemist had muttered to him had any real meaning. *Just the ravings of a dying man.*

The stone trembled again. Dust fell in a cloud from the ceiling.

"And we will die if we stay!" Aelyn called from the hallway outside.

"I'll carry him." Tal moved to the chair, and Garin felt him use sorcery to slice through the rope binding the medusal's arms and legs. The man bent and lifted Koax onto his shoulders. The medusal roused, wailing for an instant before it petered out in a series of wet coughs. Garin felt sick, remembering the wounds on his chest and imagining how it must feel to have them pushed on and twisted.

Ashelia had packed away her things, but she looked as ill as Garin felt. "Go then," was all she said.

Garin was the last to exit. He hurried after the others, eager to escape the unstable citadel. The Worldsong was a swarm of hornets in his head, buzzing with urgency. He tried to recall how they'd ascended the sandstone tower, but the place was a maze, and he couldn't keep the directions straight in his head.

The ground shuddered harder than before. Garin bit his lip. Terror made him tremble. He hadn't expected to survive their journey, but this wasn't the way he thought he'd go.

Don't let us die, don't let us die, he chanted in his mind as they ran down corridors and stairwells. He slipped on a rounded stair and barely caught himself, but only kept moving forward. *Don't let us die, don't let us die, don't let us—*

The stone above them cracked.

Garin stopped with the others, all staring up at it. They knew what it meant. They were still too high up. They'd never make it down in time.

Garin watched as the ceiling caved in, and great fragments of stone fell upon them.

ANY COST

A SCREAM RIPPED FREE OF TAL AS HE THRUST EVERY DROP OF sorcery in him against the falling stone.

He was barely aware of his body as he wove his spells. Veins of sorcery spread through everything in the World, living and not. Now, he exploited them, working his way into the stone and holding it in place.

Hold! he commanded it, and the sorcery burned as it exerted its influence. *Hold!* he told the ceiling, the walls, the floor.

Hold!

The strain was almost too much. He felt like a beetle trying to keep a giant boot from pressing down on him. The weight of the sky seemed to rest on his shoulders. Perhaps another pained scream escaped him — he couldn't tell any longer. All that was within him, he thrust into the stone.

It held.

Tal sensed by sorcery that his friends were alive, that the stones stayed where he commanded. Yet all around them, the tower was still collapsing.

He'd saved them, but only for a moment.

Hands touched his chest and back, then pressed in a direction. He tried to obey and not lapse in concentration, stumbling forward on feet he could barely feel. Whether he carried Koax or had dropped him, he didn't know. Carrying the medusal was the least of his burdens now.

They moved to the edge of the tower, but not quickly enough. He couldn't hold it; it was too much, too heavy. He was breaking. His legs gave way, his burden falling from his shoulders. *Koax*, a part of him realized, though it hardly seemed to matter. The stones shifted as his grip on them began to fail.

Hold, he ordered them again, but it was a feeble command. They continued reverting to their natural course.

Then a second presence twisted through him, and his grip on the stone firmed.

I'm here. The words echoed through him, almost too faint to notice. But Tal knew him still.

Garin had meshed with him.

The sharing of the burden lifted the pressure just enough for his senses to return. Pebbles fell around them. Dust choked the air. Ahead, open air loomed. They'd made it to a balcony, but the ground was still far below.

Yet at the bottom, beneath the water's surface, he saw a glimmer of the purest white light. It gave him the answer for what they had to do.

"Jump. We have to jump." He tried to speak the sentence aloud, hoped he had, but his mouth felt clumsy and foreign. He staggered forward and felt arms encircling him, holding him back from the edge. He turned toward them and through blurry vision made out Ashelia's terrified face.

He lifted a hand to touch her cheek. *"Jump,"* he told her.

Then, wrapping an arm around her waist, he pulled his beloved off the ledge and into the open air.

"*Jump.*"

The command echoed through Garin's every facet, yet he couldn't obey. Intertwined with Tal's power, he'd lost command of his body. Even if he still had it, he couldn't have obeyed.

To leap would spell their deaths.

But through their connection, he felt Tal already following his own direction. With growing horror, Garin sensed as Tal fell to the ocean below.

He'd be dashed upon the stones and the water. He'd be killed.

Garin would feel it all.

Yet death never came. Tal's sorcery flared in a different direction. *Wind*, Garin recognized by their connection, as the power of the Worldsong flooded through him to support the casting. Tal had cushioned his fall. He was held aloft by his sorcery.

But to do it, Tal had to release his grip on the sandstone tower.

Realizing the danger, Garin ripped free of the man and emerged back into his body just as Wren wrapped her arms around him. She was shouting something, but the roar of the collapsing stone drowned her out. Garin hoped she knew what they had to do as he wrapped his arm through hers, then wrenched her forward.

They fell toward the dark waters below.

Garin closed his eyes, bracing for impact. The moments stretched to breaking. The frigid wind howled past his ears. His body was unanchored from the World. It seemed he would drift through the air forever, unmoored, a ghost with no body—

It wasn't water or stone that caught him, but wind.

The wind wasn't a gentle savior. It tore at his skin as it surged upward to slow his fall. Gusts pummeled him, bruising and drawing blood as his head knocked against Wren's. But the speed of their fall slowed, enough that he dared to hope.

Water swallowed them, too cold and wet to be friendly, yet Garin found himself pathetically relieved to feel it.

He released Wren and kicked to the surface. His ears were clogged with water; his nose burned with it. Salt was all he could taste. A steady rumble coursed through his body, reminding him of the danger they were still in. He strained to see through the darkness, hoping to find his companions alive.

"Swim!" someone called. "Swim for shore!"

Something splashed in the water next to him, sending a wave over his head, choking and blinding him. Garin needed no second prompting.

Following the direction of the voice, he swam.

Tal dragged himself onto the sand and looked back.

Back at the harvest of his arrogance.

The sandstone tower lay in ruin. The apex had collapsed in on itself, and a great crack ran down the middle and into the water. Great boulders scattered around its feet.

But that was the least of his failings. Along the shore, his bedraggled companions clawed from the water to sprawl on the beach and gasp for breath. He counted them once more, reassuring himself they'd all made it out alive.

Falcon, Aelyn, Garin, Wren, Ashelia. All were there — battered, but alive.

Yet still, he had failed.

Koax Mraaj, the man they had gone to all this trouble for, lay dead among the rubble. He wouldn't have survived the fall even if Tal had dragged him out, his condition too fragile. And the alchemist's secrets died with him.

They had no elixir to Paradise's miasma and no other leads

for it. They would need a god's own luck to ascend Ikvaldar and face Yuldor.

Tal let his head fall back, reeling with exhaustion and despair. *Your last act means nothing now, Pim,* he thought to the departed Extinguished. *All our defiance is ash.* He wished he could sink down into the *Doash* and be cradled in the comfort it promised.

But such release was better than he deserved.

"Tal."

He lowered his chin to see Ashelia standing next to him. Her hair hung in loose, wet curls about her face, slowly dripping into the sand. The water had washed away some of the grime, but he could still see the many cuts and bruises their foray had earned her. His blood flared with heat, and he didn't know if it was self-hatred or sorcery that caused it.

Ashelia touched his arm. "We have to go, Tal. The watch will be coming. We must be gone before they arrive."

He nodded, though part of him wondered why he bothered. The futility of all they did had settled within him. Only a last glimmer of purpose remained. It was enough for him to stand and collect the others.

If all I can do is keep them alive, he thought as he moved toward Garin, still struggling to his feet, *then I'll do it. No matter what it takes. No matter the cost.*

"Here, Garin." He offered his hand. "Best that we're off."

The youth raised his head and stared through his damp locks, grown long from their journey. He didn't accept Tal's hand.

"Sorry," he murmured. "I… I let you down."

Tal let his hand fall, baffled. "You did nothing wrong. What happened here was my fault."

Garin shook his head. "I used a stone spell. I caused the tower to collapse."

For a moment, Tal could only stare. Then a smile spread across his face.

"I throw hell and brimstone at that citadel," he said, "and you think you did this?"

The youth stared at him for a long moment. Slowly, Garin smiled as well.

"Guess you're right. We did it together."

Tal only shook his head. *The blame lies heavier with one of us*, he thought. *Much heavier.*

Helping Garin to his feet, Tal clapped him lightly on the back, then they joined the others.

"Let's go," Tal said. "First the warehouse, then we leave the city."

"How?" Falcon sounded as disheartened as Tal felt.

Tal had always found mirth in failure. A grin blossomed from it now.

"One step at a time, bard. One step at a time."

Tal turned from his friend's mutterings and led them up the shore back to the glimmering city.

Garin sagged with exhaustion by the time they reached the edge of Dreygoj.

Sorry as he felt for himself, they had no time for weakness. No sooner had they reached the planked platform that led back to the docks than the distant pounding of feet sounded from ahead. Garin, who already had a foot up, dragged himself off and looked back to his companions, too tired to think for himself. Ashelia was already waving them toward the cliff.

"Behind the boulders," she called softly, then ushered them to the hiding place.

Garin sagged against the stone and leaned his head back. It was a hard resting place and ill-formed to his body, yet it took an effort to remain wary. He wondered if he'd ever felt so tired.

It's not everyday you break apart a tower, he reminded himself, *then help hold it together.*

The guards soon passed by. The light from their torches danced across the rocks as they jogged past, shouting in their tongue. He heard the rattle of weapons and armor and wondered who they suspected was behind the attack.

Surely not Tal Harrenfel — if they even know his name here. He hoped they did not. Better for all of them if the man's legend remained as much as it could in the Westreach.

It must have been a great number of watchmen, for they took a long while to pass. When the noise faded, Wren peeked her head out, then hissed, "They're gone!"

Hauling himself to his feet, Garin stumbled on.

The city held little charm for him now as they bustled down its pathways. He resented the creaking wood and the vibrations in the promenade from his companions' running, threatening to upset his balance. Garin wanted nothing more than to curl into their corner of the warehouse and sleep. *Helshax,* which he'd kept drawn, weighed like a cart of bricks in his hand.

"That's odd," Wren muttered from behind.

He looked up. The smuggler's refuge lay ahead of them. At first, he didn't see what Wren had; then he noticed the doors hung ajar. Despair clawed at him, but this time, it lent him strength and quickened his step.

Tal and Ashelia reached the doors first. With a glance around, the pair entered. Wren went in next, and Garin followed, Falcon and Aelyn coming behind.

They nearly crashed into Garin as he came to a sudden stop.

Helnor and Rolan weren't alone. Surrounding them were over a dozen humans, medusals, and orkans. Several held torches, and all had steel bared. They wore clothes similar to sailors.

Then he recognized the woman standing farthest back and knew this was no random attack.

Jira glanced back at their entrance, her lips curled. She called across the warehouse two words even Garin could understand, her accent turning them singsong and mocking.

"Tal Harrenfel!"

The night's trials, Garin feared, were far from ended.

HONOR AMONG THIEVES

IN TAL'S EXPERIENCE, LITTLE GOOD CAME OF OTHERS CALLING out his full name.

King Aldric had named him so, as had Queen Geminia, before they swept him into their schemes. Clan Chief Dathal and Hashele had as well before they condemned him.

His name was as much a curse as it was a legend. It came with hidden depths he didn't care to plumb.

And here it arose to cause him trouble again.

As Jira called that name at him, Tal bared his teeth in a smile and swept wide his arms. *Perhaps this time,* he thought, *I might charm my way out of trouble.*

Yet he'd never had as little faith in being called Pearltongue as he had just then.

"So you found me out!" He gave a short laugh, as if this were all a jape. "I wondered if my friend's slip-up would clue you in."

"Not only that." The smuggler returned his smile, as well-practiced in its nuances as he. "There is a hefty price on your head, Tal Harrenfel. Many people would like to cut it from your shoulders."

Tal let his arms fall, never halting his slow stalk forward.

"Ah, Jira. If you believe you can claim my bounty, you have not been listening closely to the stories."

Her eyes narrowed, though she kept up her grin. "That is all they are — *stories*. I have seen you crawl into Yae Sawat's stores with the fish and stolen goods. You are nothing to fear."

Sorcery burned in his veins, begging to be unleashed, but Tal only shrugged.

"You are right to be mistrustful, but wrong to cross us. Let us leave, Jira. I have killed too many tonight to wish for more deaths on my conscience."

Her lips curled. "We outnumber you two-to-one. If there are to be deaths here, it will be yours and your companions' — unless you submit."

At the sight of Rolan's wide-eyed terror, surrounded by those who would do him harm, Tal felt a familiar feeling work its way through him, and he resigned himself to it.

Tal sighed. His shoulders sagged. He was the very picture of surrender.

"Very well, Jira. We will do it your way."

As her eyes widened, he summoned forth his sorcery and sent it burning forward.

First, he attended to Helnor and Rolan. *Wuld,* Tal thought, and a billowing torrent encircled his companions and buffeted back the smugglers. One went sprawling against the barrels behind him, knocking one over and freeing the fish inside to slide over the planks.

The other rogues rallied and charged at Tal. He didn't flinch as he wove his next spell. Flames, ignited from the very air itself, flared amongst them.

He spared none.

As the smugglers went down howling, cinders seared against Tal's skin, a faint echo of what the mass of men and women before him suffered. The sorcerous flames quickly caught on the damp wood, racing up the sides of the warehouse.

Jira, who had been standing apart from the others, was frozen in place as she stared at the spreading fire, her narrow eyes wide. Tal could understand her stupor. She'd been a woman in control of her destiny all her life, a woman who always kept an edge over every adversary.

But she'd never met a legend before, he thought sardonically.

Cutting off the wind barrier around Rolan and Helnor, Tal watched the others in his party rejoin them. Ashelia wrapped her son in a tight embrace. Garin and Wren sheathed their weapons and went to their mounts. He watched them, feeling as little unable to move as the smuggler opposite him.

The screams of their attackers had died as the flames ate them away, yet they still echoed in his head. He'd massacred the Ravagers. He'd slaughtered these smugglers. Once, he'd thought the killer in him had been tamed, even laid to rest.

All a delusion.

Death's Hand. Red Reaver. Magebutcher. He pushed each name at himself like needles into a pincushion. *You've always been a monster. You always will be. Tonight was your reminder.*

Tal stared at Jira as the flames edged ever closer to her.

He barely noticed Ashelia until she gripped his arm. "Tal, we have to go. The watch might be distracted, but there are guards on the docks. It won't take long for someone to come looking. Tal?"

When he didn't respond, Ashelia followed his gaze. From the corner of his eye, he saw her face harden.

"Leave her," she said. "She made her choice."

Tal looked at her, the woman he loved, and wondered. Ashelia had always possessed more resolve and certainty than he could ever hope for. All it took was a threat toward her son or friends and her doubts vanished. She was like a mother gryphon, ready to tear apart any who threatened her nest.

He sighed and murmured, "*Kald uunae.*"

The flames retreated, then disappeared in a wash of smoke. The planks still glowed from where the fire had touched them.

Through the smoke, Tal met Jira's dark eyes. Then he turned away.

Ashelia followed him. "She deserved death," she muttered, anger still smoldering in her words.

"Maybe. But I didn't deserve to give it to her."

She didn't answer as Tal led their party from the warehouse.

———

It only took a few moments of deliberation before they settled on an escape by sea.

The *Star Prince* lay ahead, moored in the docks. A light burned on deck, telling of more conflicts awaiting when they boarded. Weariness piled up within Tal like snowdrifts on a winter slope. As they approached, each step felt heavy and plodding.

He was sick of violence. He only wanted to close his eyes to the World and drift down into oblivion.

Down...

He shook his head, rousing himself. For a moment, he remembered seeing the *Doash* in the ocean below the Ravagers' tower, the glowing core of sorcery that shone brighter than the sun. It had been a desire for its release as much as the need to escape that had made him jump. Only Ashelia in his arms and his companions falling behind them had reminded him to summon the gale that saved them.

He couldn't submit to the desire. Couldn't release his guilt. He had to embrace it. He had to become the man the Westreach and the Empire needed him to be.

Even if it was a man he hated.

The gangplank was raised and the ship was a dozen feet from the dock, giving no ready way to board. Tal glanced at Helnor and nodded up at the ship. The Prime Warder shrugged, and Tal knew he would follow his lead.

"*Wuld*," he murmured, then leaped as wind lifted him over the ship's railing.

Tal landed on the deck with an audible thunk. A Nightelf sailor had been sitting with his back to the center mast, dozing. At the sound, he jerked upright and raised his cutlass, then stared wide-eyed at Tal.

"Hello," Tal greeted him as his blood burned. With a thought, a forceful wind billowed up. Before the sailor could utter a word, he was knocked against the railing so hard the wood cracked. Tal hoped his skull hadn't done the same.

More of the sailors roused now, and they came roaring on deck with weapons in hand. The captain was absent, apparently remaining on shore this night. Tal only watched as the men and women surrounded him, seven of them in total.

"I don't suppose you'll surrender your ship peacefully?" he ventured.

"He's one of the cargo rats!" an orkan snarled, his tusks damp with spittle. "Lagahk's shadows, why are you back?"

"Didn't I make my intentions clear?" Tal gave a staged sigh. "Very well. I can be plainer."

He targeted the two crossbowmen first. "*Kald*," he murmured, and fire flashed before their eyes, dazzling and surprising them.

As he ducked to dodge any wild shots, he followed it up quickly with "*Wuld*." Sorcery spiraled out around him, then pressed down like the hand of a giant. Tal raised his head to see the unrelenting gust slam the smugglers to the deck, their limbs crumpled beneath them. None could so much as move.

He went to the orkan who had spoken. He tried to toe the axe away from his grip, but when the Imperial clung to it, Tal ground his heel into the man's hands until he was forced to release. With the sailor disarmed, Tal kneeled and dismissed the spell on him.

"Now," he shouted over the roar of his summoned storm, "how about you give me this ship?"

The orkan met his eyes with his beady, dark ones. His lips, gray and scabbed, pulled back, baring his yellowed tusks further. Tal raised an eyebrow and gestured, reminding him of his dilemma.

With a final growl, the orkan scrambled to his feet, bolted for the railing, and leaped overboard.

"I might have offered you a boat," Tal muttered as he moved to the next sailor.

He never reached him.

Tal's only warning of attack came from a glimmer of his sorcery unraveling. Whirling, Tal summoned a wind shield just in time to deflect the sailor's blow. By a flash of torchlight, he recognized him as the one from the strange Bloodline. Tal barely had time to register this before the sailor turned away and ran to the opposite side of the ship. Without a backward glance, he leaped over.

Tal stared after him, wondering how he'd escaped his spell, and without showing a glimmer of sorcery himself.

But he was gone, and the other smugglers remained. Dismissing the mystery, though keeping a wary eye out for the foreigner should he return, Tal moved to the next Imperial to repeat his offer.

A short while later, having loaded their horses and stors, Tal and his companions stood aboard the freed *Star Prince* and watched the last of the smugglers haul themselves up from the water and onto the docks.

"We could have made use of them," Falcon observed by his side. "Navigating unfamiliar waters and all that."

Tal shrugged. "Even thieves like us have honor. We stole their ship; let them have their freedom."

The bard chuckled. "You are ever full of wonders, my friend."

Tal thought of the odd sailor who had defied his sorcery. "Let's hope I have some left in me."

"What now?" The bard turned and stared up at the mast and the cloth lashed to it. "Do any of us know how to sail?"

"The only ships I've boarded were river vessels or Yraldi ones I burned." Tal stared over the incomprehensible rigging. "But how hard could it be?"

Falcon winced. "Let's hope the others have a better idea."

"I do," Aelyn countered from nearby. His face was pinched, the night having worn him down to the bones, yet he still strode doggedly about the deck as he went from this rope to that, tying and knotting them seemingly with purpose. "I have experienced far more than you could ever hope to, Tal Harrenfel."

Tal faced him without a smile. "And I hope you get to experience far more."

His lack of a quip seemed to give the mage pause, for he screwed up his spinning eyes. After a moment, Aelyn only snorted and continued on his way.

"And if the Ravagers or the fief lord send pursuit?" Falcon asked. "We've certainly left a trail to follow."

Tal glanced up at the sails slowly becoming unfurled. "They won't have the wind on their side, will they?"

"If they have sorcerers…"

He understood Falcon's worries, for he shared them. A dozen things could turn out poorly for their party. Perhaps his plan to summon a tailwind would be undermined by their lack of seafaring experience. Perhaps sparing Jira and the other smugglers had left too many witnesses. He could have done many more things to secure their safe flight, from burning down the docks to sinking all the boats in the harbor.

But he hadn't. Enough blood was on his hands this night.

Tal silenced the bard with a clap on his shoulder. "Sometimes, we must take a few risks, if only to ease our consciences."

THE CHARRED COAST

GARIN STARED AT THE SHORE HIDDEN BY SEA SPRAY AND wondered what gods he'd offended to wind up on a ship again.

"Let's see," he muttered to himself while fighting back the rising tide of nausea. "Could be Yuldor, or the Whispering Gods…"

The *Star Prince*, borne along by a sorcerous wind, rocked back and forth as waves knocked into its starboard side. One arm hanging over the thick railing, Garin racked his head for who he should pray to now for deliverance. All the gods he'd feared, both good and evil, had been exposed for charlatans.

Not that he'd ever been devout. His mother had forced him into prayer back home every restday, but as he'd kneeled before the Whispering Gods' altar, he fidgeted and thought of other things.

But there was something about the World being deprived of deities that made it feel… empty.

His gorge suddenly rose, and Garin had to swallow hard and concentrate on nothing but breathing for several long moments. *If there are no gods,* he reasoned as he tried to calm his stomach, *then there's no one to turn to — no one but the monarchs, and your friends, and yourself.*

The last notion scared him most of all. To have so much riding on his shoulders — had Garin ever wanted that?

"You set out from Hunt's Hollow to earn your stars," he murmured as a wave rushed by. "Here's what it looks like."

Had he seen what his journey would come to, he wondered if he would have had the courage to start it. Though, even as his guts threatened to turn themselves inside out, he couldn't say he would trade it for any other path.

"If we survive, I damn well deserve my constellation…"

"What are you muttering about? Finally gone mad, have you?"

Garin opened his eyes to Wren's merciless smile. "Just thinking of how much I admire you."

"Oh, really?" She spat into the ocean and watched the globule fly, while Garin watched her. Her sable hair, grown longer during their journey, now fluttered about her jaw and whipped into her eyes. Wren didn't seem to notice, her eyes spinning gold as she looked toward the shoreline.

She glanced over and arched an eyebrow. "You staring at me, Dunford?"

"Do you mind me staring?"

Wren smiled coyly. "Might cost you."

"I'll pay the price later then. At the moment, I'm giving all I have to the sea."

She laughed and turned back to the railing. "Think we'll get to your hatching grounds soon?"

"Maybe. I mostly saw it from the air in Ilvuan's memories, but I might recognize it. Or maybe Ilvuan will tell us."

Wren snorted derisively. "That doesn't exactly inspire confidence."

Garin shrugged. He still marveled at how everyone had agreed to their next step in the plan. When he thought about it, they had little evidence that it was a good idea. After all, it was only on the promises of Ilvuan that they would discover anything there, much less seed the way for the return of dragons.

And should we even want them to return?

Considering all his interactions with Ilvuan, he doubted dragons would make for good neighbors. Ilvuan was proud and impatient, selfish and haughty. Yet for all that, he looked out for Garin. Even if Garin was serving his purpose, he found it hard to believe Ilvuan cared nothing for him.

Yet it was all beside the point. As far as they knew, the Emperor was still marshaling his forces, their Reach allies traveling across the seemingly endless mountains of the East. Their own journey had taken months; an army would take longer. In a certain sense, they were merely waiting.

Not only waiting, but also avoiding. He'd seen the look in Tal's eyes whenever Ikvaldar or Yuldor or even the Whispering Gods were mentioned. Garin felt that same reluctance. Founts like them likely shared the same fate.

To ascend Ikvaldar would mean their deaths.

His thoughts disquieting, Garin broke the silence. "Do you think we should bring them back, dragons?"

He spoke quietly as if to escape Ilvuan's notice, though it would make no difference if the Singer appeared.

Wren glanced sidelong at him. "You're able to answer that better than I."

"Humor me."

Wren turned and braced her back against the railing. "If I were the goddess over all the lands, and knowing what I do of dragons... Yes. Yes, I would." She spread an arm before her. "After all, how much worse can the World get?"

Garin shrugged. Part of him agreed, but his doubts continued to clamor within him.

Tal stared over the bow of the ship and into the blue-gray expanse.

The weather was fair, a blessing for their day at sea. It made summoning a tailwind much easier when he didn't have to fight off a storm. Though it took an effort, he was glad for the distraction, for in spare moments, his thoughts returned to the same worn places.

My past. My flaws. My guilt.

He had picked at the scabs so many times that they'd opened into festering wounds. Yet he didn't know how he could do otherwise when he had yet to atone for any of them.

What have I done to protect anyone? What, but more slaughter?

Ravagers and smugglers weren't exactly innocent, but even so, he tired of blood staining his hands. He wanted to end it. And he knew the way he might, felt it tempting him whenever he relaxed his mind.

He was afraid of looking down, lest he glimpse the *Doash* and succumb to it.

"What're you smiling about?"

Tal startled and looked over. Rolan peered up at him, the boy's head cocked to one side. His eyes, stormy like his mother's, swirled with curiosity. His skin, mostly fair back in Elendol, had tanned during their travels, though not as deep a shade as Tal's own.

Tal arched an eyebrow. "At an amusing thought. Tell me: Do I look like a proper ship's captain?"

With aplomb, he propped one foot up on the railing and stared majestically over the *Star Prince's* bow.

Rolan chuckled before answering. "Not really. You don't have the right mustache."

"A mustache! And here I thought it was all in the pose." Grinning, he removed his foot from the railing and turned to the boy, hands resting in the loops of his belt. "Would you want to be the captain of a ship when you're older?"

Rolan's eyes screwed up, and he glanced off toward the sea.

"I like being a bard," he answered at length. "But I don't think I'd want to travel all the time like Falcon and the Dancing Feathers used to. I... I miss home." The boy winced at the admission.

"What do you miss?" Tal gently prompted.

Emboldened, Rolan looked back at him. "The kintrees. There's nothing else like them in the World — and I can say that now, as I've seen pretty much everywhere!"

Tal chuckled. "Pretty much."

"And the smells," the boy continued, his words picking up speed. "No place smells like Elendol. The leaves, the flowers, the moss, just the *air*..." Rolan sniffed then, as if he might detect a hint of his home on the salty sea wind.

"What else?"

"Oh — the shade! You can barely find sunlight in Gladelyl, but I think I've had enough of it. Squinting against it, baking under it — give me back my shade!"

Tal laughed, though the boy's words had infected him with his own sentimentality. "I miss home too, lad."

Only as he admitted it did the notion seem strange. What was home to him? *Where* was it? Hunt's Hollow? Elendol? Or simply an endless road?

No, he realized. *Home is not a place, but a feeling. Safety. Security. Rest. How long has it been since I felt at home anywhere?*

Only, he had felt that recently. Once more, he had the urge to look down, to seek the bright, vast orb at the World's center and dive into it.

Not yet, he told himself with a glance at the boy beside him. *Not yet.*

The coast slowly changed before Garin's eyes.

The tan sand, peppered with stone and kelp and seaweed, gathered darker strains. Black stone proliferated; it rose in nubs from the sea, ran like rivers through the beaches, dusted the hills that mounded against the land. To Garin's eye, the blackness was like a blight in a field, slowly infecting all the crops until it decimated the harvest. Soon, only rock would remain, if Ilvuan's memories held true.

His watch was interrupted by the approach of soft footsteps. Garin glanced over and was surprised to see Ashelia. He summoned a smile, and she returned it.

"How are you feeling?" she asked.

"Like an ogre has hugged me for the past day."

Her eyes spun faster. "Back in Elendol, I could have found you something to settle your stomach. But I didn't think we would need those herbs on our journey east."

Garin waved a hand. "I'll live."

They stood in silence for a long moment. Garin wondered why she'd approached him. Not that they didn't interact, but since Elendol, they had rarely sought one another's company.

Just as a suspicion settled in, she tipped her hand. "Have you noticed anything about Tal since Dreygoj? Has he been... different?"

"It's only been a day," Garin hedged. But he knew what she meant. The man still smiled, yet there seemed a haunted look behind his eyes now, the same as had appeared after the fight at Trader Springs. If he knew Tal — and after all they'd endured together, he thought he did — then guilt was eating him up on the inside.

Ashelia saw the truth in his eyes. A sigh escaped her as she leaned on the railing and looked out. "I cannot reach him, Garin. Not just now, with what happened in the citadel. He has been drawing away from me ever since our time in the palace. He holds me at a distance."

Garin worked his tongue around his mouth, as if the right words might hide in one of its corners. "It's because of Ikvaldar," he said at last.

She looked at him, and the intensity of her gaze reminded him that she was a Peer of Gladelyl.

"What do you mean, Ikvaldar?" she asked softly.

"He knows he has to go there and face Yuldor. And he knows it might not... well, turn out the way we want it to."

Ashelia furrowed her brow and opened her mouth, but it was a moment before words passed her lips. "We have always known where our path leads."

"True. But with every step we take down it, in a manner of speaking" — Garin gestured at the planks beneath him, to a quirk of the elf's lips — "it becomes more real, and the consequences as well. I've never asked him about it, but I'd guess he feels responsible for dragging you and Rolan into this, and that he should draw away before he hurts you more."

She was giving him a strange look. "Sometimes I forget you are only sixteen, Garin. You have grown wise for your short years. When I was your age, gowns and jewelry were my entire preoccupation."

"I find that hard to believe." He tried to imagine Ashelia being absorbed with her appearance. She seemed to be made for the journey they were on now, not for cosmetics and dances and dresses. Though, as he recalled the Winter Ball, she had seemed well-suited there as well.

Ashelia's lips curled, somewhere between amusement and disdain. "Adversity brings out the best in some. We are fortunate that it has held true for most of our party."

Garin wondered if they'd circled right back to where the conversation started. Not wishing to dwell on things they couldn't change, he said lightly, "You mean Aelyn, don't you? He is equally unhappy wherever he goes."

She laughed. "That's certainly true. I grew up with him, remember."

"I can only imagine the tantrums."

As silence stretched long, Ashelia turned somber once

more. One hand grazed across her stomach as if it pained her, then settled again on the railing.

"We cannot let him pull away, Garin. We must keep him with us. Even if we only have a little time left, then he should spend it with us. Especially if there is only little time."

"I know."

Garin wondered if anyone had ever corralled Tal to a purpose different from his own. The man had a strong inclination of moving in his own direction, no matter what others thought.

Ashelia touched his arm, then turned away with a smile. As Garin watched her leave, moving as gracefully across the ship's deck as if it were a tree bridge of Elendol, he knew that, for her sake, he had to try.

———

As was often the case, only the prospect of amusement could rouse Tal from his somber thoughts.

Turning from the ship's prow, where he'd continued to summon wind to propel them onward, he found Aelyn at the foot of the center mast atop a sea chest, hunched over a book and scrawling with an enchanted quill in a journal. His hat was pulled low over his face, and his long, black braid curled down to drape over his narrow chest.

Wearing a small smile, Tal made his way down the ladder to stand over the mage.

He could tell Aelyn was trying to ignore him, for his muttering grew louder as the moment stretched on. Tal felt Helnor's gaze on him, and they shared a grin. Nothing quite tickled either of them like harassing the Prime's Housebrother.

At last, the mage raised his head to glare at Tal with burning eyes. "Is there something I can help you with?" he asked pointedly.

"I don't think so." Tal crossed his arms, smiled, and waited.

One of Aelyn's eyes twitched as he continued to stare at him. "Perhaps *you* would like to translate the encrypted text, and *I* will distract you from it?"

"Sounds like tedious work."

The mage bared his teeth like an aggravated dog. "It is impossible work! I have tried every combination for the cipher, yet none have unlocked more than gibberish." He looked ready to slam the text shut and toss it away from him, but the elf's good sense prevailed.

"Hm. That is a puzzling proposition." Tal put a hand to his chin and pretended to contemplate the matter. Truth was, he had even less of a notion on how to proceed than Aelyn and was glad to have the mage take on the task. Between his determination and knowledge of the East accumulated over three months spent in the Emperor's archives, Aelyn stood the best chance of cracking the code.

"I can tell you are quite concerned," Aelyn noted drily.

Tal grinned. "Very."

"Are you talking about Koax's journals?"

He'd noticed Garin's approach by his sorcery, but Tal only glanced over when the youth spoke. They exchanged smiles, though at the sight of him, a measure of his amusement faded. Garin, through no fault of his own, was a reminder of many painful things both past and future. He knew that now more than ever, he should draw their strange bond tighter rather than pull away. But he'd often avoided doing what he should.

"What else?" Aelyn snapped.

Garin tactfully ignored the comment. "I hadn't thought of it before, as I've been busy heaving my guts over the side of the ship. But I might be able to help."

The mage's lips twisted. "Is that right? I suppose your *ava'-dual* whispered his secrets in your ears?"

"Not quite. Koax Mraaj did."

Tal perked up. "You spoke to him?"

Garin nodded. "Just a little, right before the citadel collapsed. I didn't expect him to speak the Reachtongue, but he must have heard us conversing in it. He said something that seemed like it could be important so I tried to memorize it. It went like... 'The key is three, backward and forward.' Then he said... 'The stones are the solution.' And finally, I think it was 'Don't let it die — I want eternity.'"

"The key is three..." Tal stared at the journal in Aelyn's hands and the scrawl across its yellowed pages. "It seems our alchemist loved riddles as well as secrets."

"Perhaps not." Aelyn seemed to have forgotten his ire as he scratched furiously in his journal. "'The key is three, backward and forward' — I think he told us the cipher as plainly as he could. 'Key' might have been the only Reachtongue word he had to identify it as a cipher — or perhaps he suspected Garin would not comprehend what a cipher was."

"Thanks for the confidence," the youth said tartly.

The mage only spoke over him. "If we take the first letter and move it backward three in the Imperial alphabet, then take the second letter and move it *forward* three... and apply it across the rest... Ah! Yes!" Aelyn held up what he'd written, beaming. "'Fortune'! A comprehensible word!"

"And an oddly relevant one," Tal noted, casting a roguish smile at Garin. "Well done, la— that is, Garin."

The youth returned the grin. "It's fine. I don't care if you call me 'lad' anymore."

Tal, finding himself tongue-tied with surprise, pivoted away from the topic. "Ah, good, good... But what of the rest of what Koax said? How did it go — 'The stones are the solution.'"

Garin's brow furrowed. "I think it might refer to the dragonstone fragments we found in his laboratory."

Tal glanced at Aelyn for another opinion, but the mage was lost to his deciphering. "It could be. But the solution to what? The elixir?"

The youth nodded, his hair falling in his eyes with the

movement. "Ilvuan made it clearer what pieces of dragon shells do. We've seen it ourselves: they absorb magic. Like the shard that was left in your side, it hampers or inhibits sorcery."

"So, if ingested with its other components, it might ward away sorcerous effects such as the miasma." Tal mulled over the implications. "But if my experience is any guide, that means it would also prevent our own sorcery."

Garin grimaced. "I suppose it would."

Tal thought about it a moment longer, then shook his head. "I'm sure the journals will tell us more. But the last part — 'Don't let it die — I want eternity.' It smacks of a man worried about his legacy, to my ears."

"Another man concerned with his legend," Aelyn pointed out snidely, proving he'd been purposefully ignoring them.

Tal halfway smiled. "A fair point. Garin?"

"That's the best I can think of."

Reaching out, Tal gripped the youth by the shoulder. "It's good enough. Thank you, Garin. You made our venture to Dreygoj worth it after all."

Worth it, was it? a part of him mocked. *Worth slaughtering men and women by the dozens?*

He tried to stifle the voice as Garin gripped his shoulder back. He had to hold tight to moments like these.

Silence knows too few of them remain.

"Mother above! Can that be it?" Aelyn raised his quill and frowned down at what he'd written in his journal.

"What is it?" Garin leaned down to peer closer. "Did you find something?"

"I believe so."

"For having made a breakthrough," Tal observed, "you seem awfully dour."

Garin gave Tal a look. "You know who you're talking to, don't you?"

As they shared another grin, Aelyn snapped, "Did you wish to know the answer to the riddle or not?"

Tal sobered at once. "Let's hear it, mage."

"The medusal said it plainly to the boy. 'The stones are the solution' — that was no riddle. He wrote it here at the end of his logs: 'These stones from the Glyph Cave have but to touch one's skin to confer their protective effects. While posing a problem for sorcerers, it is the surest way to defend against the effects of Paradise's miasma.'"

As Aelyn spoke, the others on deck gathered closer. Helnor laughed and shook his head.

"Then we have everything we need! Unless you lost those stones, Garin?"

"Of course not." The youth pressed a hand to a pouch on his belt, where Tal judged he must keep them.

"Disappointing as it must be to have such a short chase," Tal said to Aelyn, "at least you solved it."

The mage only muttered under his breath as he slammed the books shut. Without another audible word, he stood and stalked over to the captain's cabin, where he'd taken up residence, and slammed the door behind.

Tal met Garin and Helnor's eyes and shook his head. Only Aelyn could be disappointed by success.

Yet we have one less obstacle to surmount.

Despite his earlier thought, Tal was also less pleased by the discovery than he should have been. It meant he had one less excuse to delay ascending Ikvaldar, and one more thing pulling him toward his fate.

Let tomorrow fend for itself, he thought with a smile, *and I'll tend to this day.*

It was, after all, one of the few he had left.

SHA'AVAL

THEY NEARED THEIR DESTINATION.

Garin knew it from the increasing signs over the past few days. The rock pillars, black as East Marsh bogs, erupted from the coast with greater regularity, some rising as high or higher than the center mast of the *Star Prince*. A stench laced the salty aroma of the sea, one that reminded him of eggs gone to rot. The land was changing as well, basalt dominating the rocks and vegetation growing thinner. Hills grew higher and sharper, the terrain becoming hostile and foreboding.

Garin recognized what these marks meant from Ilvuan's shared memories. But only as the Singer clawed into his mind did he know they'd finally arrived.

Pain burst through him like a hit to the back of the head. Garin gasped and leaned against the railing, clutching it so he didn't pitch into the sea. He hadn't felt Ilvuan so strongly since Elendol, when he'd used Garin's body to fight against Heyl.

Ilvuan, he thought to him, teeth clenched. *Nice of you to make a soft landing.*

The dragon only greeted his words with disdain. Underneath, however, there buzzed an elation Garin had rarely felt from him. He knew what it meant even before the Singer put words to it.

The Sha'aval *is near,* Jenduit, *very near. You must make for the shore.*

Garin let his skepticism show. *Now or soon? Mortals don't walk as fast as dragons fly — I don't want to make landfall miles away.*

Ilvuan didn't even radiate annoyance at the refusal. *Soon, soon. But not too long. I will show you where.*

Garin grinned, the Singer's excitement infecting him. *The birthplace of dragons.* He marveled that such a place existed, much less that he, Garin Dunford of Hunt's Hollow, was going to see it.

I've come a long way, he thought as he stared ahead of them, searching for their destination. *A very long way.*

Within an hour, the air had turned almost noxious with the spoiled scent. Tal, always weaving the winds to propel their ship forward, had them push the surrounding air away. Garin cheered the man with his companions as Tal grinned. In that moment, the man almost seemed his former self.

With the increasing stench came a permeating haze, obscuring their vision ahead and hiding part of the coast. Garin wondered what spawned it until he detected an orange glow pulsating amid the rotten fog. He stared at it in wonder as they passed by, keeping at a safe distance. He knew of lava from stories, like the lava flows Markus Bredley had encountered in his journeys through the dwarven mines, but he'd never truly known what a "river of fire" meant until that moment. It moved like mud, yet from its fierce glow, he guessed it would consume him in moments if he had the misfortune of falling in it.

"Can you believe it?" Wren murmured from next to him. The others had joined him along the railing to watch the lava flow.

He shook his head. "Hardly."

"Falcon, how would you describe it?" Rolan piped up.

The bard frowned. "Art cannot be demanded, my young pupil. But if I must give an answer, I would have to say it is the closest thing to a veritable dragon I have ever witnessed."

"Or ever will, Mother willing." Helnor made a sign Garin recognized as honoring the elven deity.

Even Aelyn joined them at the railing. His lip curled as he said, "It is nothing like a dragon, bard. Perhaps like a dragon's breath. But it pales compared to the beasts."

"So you've seen one?" Tal smiled at the mage. "Illusions don't count."

Aelyn grimaced. "I've seen illustrations depicting them."

While I have one in my head. But Garin didn't voice the thought aloud, not liking to remind his companions of that fact.

Ilvuan chose that moment to assert himself in Garin's mind again. *Here,* Jenduit! *You must land here!*

He felt a moment's foreboding at that, but anticipation overcame it. "Ilvuan spoke to me," Garin said aloud. "He says we should land here. The hatching grounds are close."

"Here?" Wren's brow crinkled. "Not exactly an inviting place, is it?"

The Singer let his amusement curl through Garin's mind. He thought he detected a hint of pride as well. Having his home in a place that mortals could not easily navigate clearly pleased him.

"All the better for dragons," he pointed out. "This isn't exactly a place you want intruders."

Ashelia pursed her lips. "Very well. We'll drop anchor out here. Bring everything, our mounts included. Our journey will continue on land afterward."

Garin nodded with the others. They had earlier discussed that as the most likely plan. Not only might enemies from Rajeya be pursuing them up the coast, but Ikvaldar lay south-west of their position, and sailing along farther would only bring them marginally closer in any direction. Besides, Garin was sick of sailing and couldn't wait to have solid ground beneath his feet again — or beneath Tempest's hooves, at least.

"And how will we disembark?" Helnor turned to Tal.

The man only smiled. "Gather everything. I should be ready by then."

Garin wondered what the man had in mind. From his companions' expressions, he wasn't the only one. Yet everyone complied and went about the necessary tasks, collecting their bags and securing them to their mounts while Tal stood at the railing, staring at the water below.

When the ship was anchored and their few possessions readied, Garin regrouped with his companions around Tal. He heard crackling from below the ship and peered over the railing to find an unexpected sight.

In waters heated by lava floated a raft of ice.

Tal grinned at their expressions. "What do you think? Clever, wouldn't you say, Aelyn?"

"Only if it holds," the mage replied, unable to tear his eyes away from the raft.

"Now, my good Tal," Falcon spoke up, his eyes darting nervously over the magical concoction, "are you sure it will hold?"

"Quite sure! Would I ask you, my oldest and dearest friend, to board it otherwise?"

The bard only muttered under his breath, clearly unconvinced.

"You try it first, Harrenfel," Aelyn said with a sharp smile. "Call it an act of good faith."

Tal shrugged. "If that's what it takes."

Garin helped lower the gangplank to the ice, then watched as Tal nimbly walked down to set foot on the raft. After he danced a small jig to prove his point, even Aelyn had to admit it seemed solid. Along with Helnor, Garin ushered their skeptical mounts down the plank, pulling

Tempest down last. Even as he set foot on the ice raft, he remained none too certain of it. With the water steaming beneath them from the river of fire upcoast, it seemed the ice must soon melt. Even more than the boat, it bobbed with each wave.

Tal didn't leave them in misery for long. With another casting, he commanded the water to push them around the looming black columns and toward the shore. The movement proving too much for him, Garin crouched on the ice and ignored Wren's mocking grin.

We'll see who's laughing when she falls overboard.

Twisting his head around, Garin took one more look at the *Star Prince.* It would likely be the last they saw of the ship.

Garin spat in its direction and muttered, "Good riddance." His disdain didn't escape Helnor's notice, and the Prime grinned down at him.

At last, they reached the shore. As rocks scraped the bottom of their small iceberg, Tal murmured, "*Lisk,*" and a layer of ice grew out from their raft, slowly deepening and hardening. Tal crossed first with Savior, then waved for the others to follow.

"Certainly warmer over here!" he called.

Garin was one of the last to leave. "Come on, boy," he murmured to Tempest, then walked over the bridge, barely daring to breathe until his feet stood on stone. When he left the ice, he almost fell to his knees, weak with relief.

Land, blessed land, was beneath him once again.

We are close. Ilvuan, who had remained curled in the back of his mind, roused again. *Do not delay.*

I'm going, Garin thought back irritably. Straightening, he found that the others were staring at him.

"Well?" Aelyn said snidely. "Where to now, boy?"

Garin grimaced and turned inward again. *Can you guide me?*

Ilvuan answered with a tug such as he'd used when seeking Tal in the past. *There. You will soon find it.*

Blinking, Garin looked in the direction the Singer had indicated and nodded. "This way."

He led Tempest forward, and the rest of his party followed. Black rock extended before and above them. The ground looked like the surface of the ocean had frozen, waves rippling out toward the Far Depths. Spires erupted at irregular intervals as if they were the defiant talons of a drowned beast. After about a hundred paces of relatively flat stone, a sheer cliff towered overhead. Garin hoped the cave they sought wasn't up high. After all, since dragons had occupied it, the height would be no barrier to their entry. He could only continue walking along the shore as Ilvuan prompted him onward.

The rotten stench was even stronger now. A haze from the lava steam filmed the air. It wasn't long before Garin's eyes and throat itched. He took a swallow from his waterskin and tried to wash the sensation down.

"Not exactly a welcoming place," Wren noted from next to Garin.

"There are places worse in the Deep," Tal said from behind. "Caverns where the very air can kill you. Dark flows that can paralyze with a touch."

"And I suppose you survived them all," Aelyn snipped.

Garin could almost hear the smile in Tal's voice. "I'm here, am I not?"

The mage only huffed.

Garin was too nervous to laugh. He kept imagining what they'd find at the end of their path. *Will the air be too deadly to breathe?* It was a place meant for dragons, not mortalkind, after all.

Mortals have harvested our eggs. Ilvuan's fury flared as he answered. *You will survive.*

Garin bobbed his head, pressing his regret toward the dragon. *We'll save the others.*

A glimmer of approval came in reply, then another tug in the same direction as before.

Garin studied the cliff face they followed. It was made of the same black, rough stone as below their feet. The surface was riddled with holes as if thousands of worms had bored through it. Atop hummocks, a vibrant green moss proliferated, while in other places, a shiny, almost glass-like stone prevailed.

"Obsidian," Tal spoke at his look. "It's said it was used in past ages for tools and weapons, before iron and steel prevailed."

Garin cast him a grateful smile over his shoulder. The man had always shared his curiosity for the World. He hoped that, even with the trials before them, neither of them would lose that.

As he turned back, he stuttered to a stop. The cliff had opened up, the bottom of it falling away into a deeper blackness. He received confirmation of what they looked upon when Ilvuan radiated satisfaction.

At last, he rumbled in Garin's mind. *An ava'dual returns home.*

Garin stared at the *Sha'aval*, the birthplace of dragons. Now that he looked closer, he saw it wasn't just a cave. The opening was an even arch that stretched fifty strides wide and half as many high. Along it were timeworn carvings, so eroded that he couldn't tell what the mounds and lines had once depicted.

Regret rose in Garin as he thought of what wonders had been lost with the departure of the Singers.

Yet a touch of grandeur remained on the old archway. As they continued forward, Garin saw glimmers of light coming from the stone. Runes, they were, and of a kind he'd only witnessed in Ilvuan's memories. They didn't glow green like Nightglyphs, nor gold or blue like those along *Helshax* and *Velori*, but vacillated between crimson and violet. Their shapes were different as well, not the spidery Darktongue script nor flowing elegance of the Worldtongue, but rough and rudimentary, like scratches in the stone.

Scratches such as a dragon's claws might make, he realized. As he stared at the glyphs, they murmured to him as all others did, yet now it almost seemed strains of songs, and not pleasant ones.

They are warnings, Ilvuan told him. *Promises of death and pain to those who intrude uninvited.*

But Yuldor's people still invaded, Garin pointed out. *Did the wards fail?*

Both drowning sorrow and lacerating fury flared within his mind. *Yes. Even our magic has limits.*

As the conflicting emotions stirred through him, Garin almost regretted his questions. But he had to know all he could.

Soon, he promised the Singer. *Soon, all will be put right.*

Ilvuan lifted the onslaught of his grief, and Garin gasped in relief.

"Is he talking to you now? Ilvuan, that is?"

Garin glanced over at Wren and found her watching him, the golden tendrils in her eyes lively. She walked with her usual erect confidence, yet there was a slight slink to her step as she pulled Lighthoof after her and a tightness to her jaw.

He nodded. "We should be safe to enter. There were once wards, but they have failed over time."

"I should hope so." Wren eyed the glyphs distrustfully.

As they stopped before the archway, Tempest pulled harder at Garin's grip and whinnied. He looked back, wondering what had upset the horse now, when he caught a whiff of a new stench. It reminded him of Dreygoj and its medusals, yet was a muskier and heavier scent.

A reptilian smell. Even after countless years absent, the hatching grounds still reeked of its masters.

Ilvuan radiated amusement at the realization.

"Phew!" Rolan commented. "What's that stink?"

"It's an old dragon den," Wren shot over her shoulder. "What did you think it would smell like, mangrove blooms?"

"We should leave our mounts out here," Ashelia suggested,

her voice soft as if fearing to disturb a creature lying within. "This place is not for them."

They searched for a moment for a spot to hobble their beasts before Tal summoned a spire of stone from the ground, thin yet sturdy enough for the job. Garin gave Tempest a stroke down his long forehead before turning back to the cavern's entrance.

His companions were waiting. Wren drummed her fingers on her rapier's pommel. Aelyn and Helnor had their arms crossed, the first brother scowling while the second smiled grimly. Ashelia had a hand on Rolan's shoulder, while the boy stared with both trepidation and excitement into the darkness. Falcon touched at the cloth-wrapped nub where his hand had been as he stared at the ocean behind them, gaze distant. Tal watched Garin, the corners of his lips twisted up, his brown eyes calm and considering.

They waited for him to lead the way.

Ilvuan's presence swelled into his mind. *Enter*, Jenduit. *Enter, and complete my first task at long last.*

With a steadying breath, Garin nodded and entered the darkness.

THE CHOICE

"Fashk."

Garin held up his flaring werelight as the Worldsong murmured in his mind. The cavern proceeded into a tunnel, neither widening nor contracting. The ridged walls shimmered with fading glyphs, as did the pillars that were interspersed throughout the open space.

He eyed the runes as he carefully placed each step, mindful of the treacherous stone that might send him sprawling into an unseen ravine. As he looked down to watch his feet, he saw faded lines in the pitted rock, signs of others who had walked here before. He tried to imagine how it must have looked to see dragons travel through the passage, and for a moment, he could almost picture it: the grand creatures passing above, their majestic heads nearly scraping the top.

He shivered and wondered if it was in his imagination, or if Ilvuan's memories had leaked into him for a moment, like in the dragon dreams.

The others, almost reverently silent, waited behind him, so Garin continued forward. After a while longer, as the daylight faded from the entrance, the tunnel ended, and a chamber opened up. Garin brightened his werelight, yet its illumination couldn't reach the top. Only the faint gleam of dragon glyphs, like the twinkle of stars, showed where the ceiling began.

As he lowered his gaze, he found the ground had fallen away in places. A ridge twisted around pits that were pocketed with small cavities. Garin stared at them, and another memory filled in the empty spaces. For a moment, he saw smooth boulders nestled in the craters, large and black and shot through with red veins.

He blinked the mirage away. Dragon eggs had filled the entire cavern. Now, they were gone.

Stolen. Ilvuan's agony cut through him, deeper than any wound of the flesh. *All stolen.* Outrage followed a moment after, burning Garin's sense of self away. *They will know an* ava'dual's *wrath! What punishment awaits a thief of the World's Singers!*

"Garin?"

As Wren touched his arm, he realized he was clutching his head. Pushing away Ilvuan's overwrought emotions, he pulled away his hands and straightened.

"I'm fine," he murmured, loath to speak loudly, for the cave suddenly seemed a graveyard. "It's just… difficult for Ilvuan."

Wren, her features made strange by shadows, only nodded and released him.

Garin turned back to the empty hatching grounds. *You said eggs remain,* he thought to Ilvuan, trying to keep calm and not let the tide of the dragon's emotions overwhelm him. *Should I find them? Or what must we do for the preparations?*

Ilvuan still simmered with bitter rage, but his thoughts were calm as he conveyed them to Garin. *Yes. We will find them. Then a dragon must prepare them for birth.*

He frowned. Garin recalled Ilvuan saying only a dragon could ready the hatching grounds for birthing, and he'd always wondered how the Singer meant to circumvent the inconvenient fact that, though he might be present in spirit, no dragon was here in actuality. Figuring he would soon find out, he pressed forward along the ridged path, searching for eggs among the hollows.

They traveled deeper. With each empty cavity they passed, Garin's foreboding grew. *What if Ilvuan is wrong? What if no eggs remain?* He tried to keep the doubts small and private. The dragon brimmed with his own emotions, spilling them into Garin's mind. He needed no more burdens.

Then he saw them. As his werelight fell over the rim of the crater, the incandescent lines reflected its glow, and the oval shapes of the eggs resting in the basin became apparent.

Relief washed through him, too strong to repress. The Singer's eagerness eclipsed his own reaction.

It is time, Jenduit. *We must prepare the way.*

A sliver of unease worked back into Garin. *So you've said. What must we do?*

I have told you. Only an ava'dual *may prepare the* Sha'aval.

He tried keeping his irritation in check. It was understandable that Ilvuan was eager. They discussed the resurrection of his entire race, after all.

You'll have to be clearer, Ilvuan. I don't know what you mean.

The dragon seemed to collect himself for a moment. When his thoughts rumbled through Garin's mind once more, he sounded almost as calm and controlled as he always had.

This place, the birthing grounds of my kind, is as close as you and I may come to one another — except atop Ikvaldar. It is why we feel each other strongly here, with little effort: it is a connecting place in the World.

A connecting place. Garin had a glimmer of understanding of what that meant, though he couldn't put the epiphany into words.

Ilvuan continued. *Here, things are possible that were not before. Connections may form, or bind stronger.*

Garin swallowed. The Worldsong buzzed in his mind. He had a suspicion now where this was leading, and he didn't know whether to run or plant his feet firmer.

Connections, he echoed the dragon. *Connections like you possessing me?*

If the Singer felt any remorse for those early chapters in their relationship, he gave no sign of it. *More than that*, Jenduit. *I could join you in your flesh. I could inhabit you.*

Repulsion flared within Garin. *No! Why would you do that?* He shuddered, clutching his arms around himself. Having the Singer in his head was one thing. But for him to crawl beneath his skin...

No, he repeated, calm and firm. *You will not "inhabit" me.*

Distantly, he heard his companions speaking to him. Someone touched his arm, their hand hot against his skin. Garin ignored them, intent on Ilvuan's every movement now. He wondered if the dragon stalked him in his mind, waiting for his moment to pounce.

But the Singer still spoke in a reasonable tone. *We must join tighter*, Jenduit. *There is much you still do not understand.*

Then tell me!

In time. The foremost thing you must know is this: our binding is the only way to overcome the Pretender. Other allies will aid our insurrection, but it will not be enough if I am still bound to the Worldheart and within his power. I must be free, my Listener. Truly free!

An image of a dragon flaring its wings against a bright blue sky seared through Garin's mind. He pressed a hand to his head and gritted his teeth against the pain. Someone began shaking him. Still, he ignored them.

Only in you may I find escape, Ilvuan continued, his words softening. *Only if we share your flesh.*

He felt sick to his stomach. He'd guessed Ilvuan's task would be difficult and unpleasant. But this...

It was unnatural. Foul. Evil, almost.

And what if he's right? he asked himself. *What if this is the only way to fight Yuldor?*

But even as he tried on the argument, Garin shook his

head. Instincts of self-preservation rose within him, stifling the small notion.

I'm sorry, Ilvuan. I can't. His eyes burned, and Garin swallowed hard. *I can't let you share my body, or take over it, or whatever it is you wish. The price is too high...*

Ilvuan's temper was sharpening. The Singer had never enjoyed being defied. Garin hoped it wouldn't flare hot enough to burn his sense of self away.

Before the dragon could put thoughts to his emotions, Ilvuan jerked back. A resentful note undercut the Worldsong spiraling through Garin's head.

We are too late.

For a moment, he couldn't understand the dragon's reaction. Just as he thought to ask, however, a horrible sound echoed from the cave mouth.

The cries of dying animals.

"Tempest!" Garin's pained naming of his horse came out in a whisper, for prey instincts suddenly seized him. Something had slaughtered their mounts, and swiftly, by the quiet that now followed.

A foreign sound intruded upon his mind.

Garin held still and listened. Around and through the strains of the Worldsong wove other, smaller songs. Ilvuan's was one of those, Tal's another. Yuldor had claimed a part of the Worldsong itself.

But now there was another song, close and coming closer.

Garin stared toward the dim cavern entrance. The song was loud, challenging the volume of the Worldsong itself. Where it moved, it distorted it, twisted it, made it its own. It was a master of the Song and commanded it.

She comes. Ilvuan coiled tight in his mind. *You must decide, Jenduit. You will have no other chance, for she will slay us.*

Garin couldn't answer him. He could only stare as a looming shadow choked out the light.

THE QUEEN COMES

Even as Tal moved in front of his companions to shield them with his body, he sensed the futility in defiance.

He had only noticed the stranger's approach at the last moment. The hatching grounds were alive with magic, from the glyphs to the eggs to the very stone itself. The reek of sulfur, reptile, and hot stone was everywhere. And then there was Garin's odd behavior drawing his attention.

He'd let it all blind him to the hunter lingering just beyond the cave.

Tal stared at its silhouette. It was like nothing he'd encountered before. The cave rose several stories high, yet the Nightkin beast took up more than half the space, blocking out much of the daylight beyond. It stalked forward, slow and calm, a predator closing in on cornered prey. To his sorcery, it shone like a sun, blinding in its power. Magic rippled through its veins as surely as it did Tal's, and it far exceeded his.

He knew it saw them in the same way he saw it. With as much sorcery as it possessed, there was no way it could have missed the potency of his blood. Yet instinct forced him to douse his werelight and begged him to *hide, hide, hide*.

"Get Garin!" he hissed to the others as he thought of the

spell for darkvision. The cave came alive in shades of gray. He hardly dared look away from the oncoming monster lest it pounce.

"He won't budge!" Wren's voice was low and choked.

Tal risked a glance back, then began edging toward the youth. His companions shuffled out of the way, reeking of fear. He stifled all the apologies that longed to burst free of him.

Save them first, he told himself. *You can beg for forgiveness later.*

As he reached Garin, the youth spoke. "I'm here. I'm still here."

That came as a relief, if a small one. "Come on," Tal whispered, feeling behind him until he grabbed hold of Garin's arm. "We have to find a place to hide, or escape if we can."

The youth relented to Tal, but it felt as if he dragged a sack of grain. There was a lack of will behind Garin's movements.

"It's no use," Garin muttered. "She knows we're here. She already sees us."

"She?" Tal shook his head. "Never mind. Just stay close so you don't fall into one of these Night-damned pits. I'll lead you."

He herded his blind companions toward the wall. Aelyn, at least, seemed able to see, and the mage led from the front. They formed a chain of hands, Tal clasping Ashelia's, their palms slick with sweat.

"He'll survive," he murmured to her. "I swear to you, whatever else happens, Rolan will survive."

"Not now, Tal." But something in her voice told him she appreciated the hollow words.

He could hear the beast's movements now. They were slight for how massive it was, whispers of rough hide and scale brushing against stone, claws digging into it. He wondered what shape it took, if it was a creature Magister Elis had taught him about long ago, or some new abomination of Yuldor's.

Or perhaps some monster from the Deep, picking its way through the remaining dragon eggs.

His lips pulled back in a frantic grin as he searched for any way out and found none.

They reached a wall. A glance back toward the entrance showed no tunnels moving off of it, so Aelyn turned them toward the back part of the cavern. Tal scanned the other walls, but he saw no more likely candidates. A horrible suspicion crept through him.

They were trapped. There was only one way in and one way out.

The way the creature guarded.

Despair clawed up his chest and into his throat. *I cannot fail them*, Tal thought over and over. *I cannot let them die.* He had led them deep into hostile lands all while promising to protect them. He refused to break his oath now.

He wouldn't let them die as Kaleras had.

Tal breathed in sorcery until it seemed it must shine through his skin. Releasing Ashelia's hand, he put Garin's in her grasp and turned back to face the cavern's entrance.

Several hundred feet away, the Nightkin creature reached the hatching grounds and stopped. With his sensitive eyes, he could now make out its features. It took only moments for him to recognize what it was.

No. His mind went rigid. *It cannot be. They're dead. They're all dead.*

"I see you, little mortals. I know where you lurk."

Its voice was everywhere at once; not a sound, but a blade cutting straight into his mind. Tal rocked on his heels as each hammer-blow of a word fell upon him before he could brace himself against it.

But Tal knew the resistance was futile. It always had been, now that they faced a true, live dragon.

Garin stared toward the storm of a song and knew what hunted them.

A dragon. The word seemed flimsy compared to its reality. *She's a dragon.*

His body felt disconnected, numb. He'd shared his mind with a dragon for a year, yet with Ilvuan incorporeal, he'd never fully understood what he was.

A dragon. Powerful. Majestic. Deadly.

A hunter they couldn't hope to stop.

As Garin pressed against the cavern wall with his companions, he threw a desperate plea toward Ilvuan. *How can this be? How is it here? You said no dragons still lived!*

Though it seemed impossible, Ilvuan remained calm. *So it has been for many long ages. But she has allied herself with Yuldor and struck an accord. She alone resurrected and grew.*

She?

Yes — Yvärras. Queen of the Ava'duala. She Who Dances With Fire. Protectress of the World.

Chills blanketed Garin's skin even though the chamber was warm. His limbs trembled and threatened to spill him to the rough floor.

Dragons are supposed to be dead, he insisted, though contrary evidence loomed large before him. *We came here to rebirth you and your kin.*

Ilvuan's response was almost gentle. *Yuldor prevented us from continuing our cycles. All he needed to do was remove that obstruction for Yvärras to return.*

Yvärras. It was finally settling into his frozen mind all he knew of the great beast before them. It was a *she*, and she was probably like Ilvuan, both in mind and disposition. This dragon queen would be cunning and proud, especially judging from her titles. She would likely be cruel as well, judging from the early months of his and Ilvuan's relationship. She possessed sorcery to a degree that eclipsed even Tal's, and she had centuries of experience using it.

Yvärras could kill them all with a swipe of her claw or a single spell, if she wished it.

Before Garin could ask his next burning question, the terrible voice tore through his thoughts. *"Alärthoras! Or should I call you 'Ilvuan,' as the exile you have become? Do not think to hide from your Protectress! I have sensed your cowardice since I flew from Ikvaldar. It does not surprise me to find you on your belly among these worms. You were ever soft toward mortals!"*

Had he not been reeling from the dragon's speech, Garin would have laughed. If Ilvuan was soft, he couldn't imagine what an aggressive dragon was like.

You're about to find out, a small voice reminded him.

Though it seemed ill-advised to ignore Yvärras, Ilvuan's next words weren't directed at the dragon queen, but at Garin.

The time has come, Jenduit. *I named you Mender because I knew what destiny you would fulfill. This is your task. You must heal the rift that has riven the World. And to do that, you and I must bind our fates as one. What is your decision, my Listener? Will you open yourself fully to me? Will you allow me to inhabit your flesh?*

Garin stared at the dragon looming from the cave's entrance, listened to the howl of Yvärras's furious song. He glanced at his friends, thin shadows beside him, vulnerable and trapped. He looked at his hands, pale ghosts in the darkness.

He had often been afraid since leaving Hunt's Hollow. When he was chased by ghouls in the Coral Castle. When he fought against Ilvuan's possession while Heyl reached toward them. Countless other times, his life had balanced on a sword's edge, liable to end at the slightest misstep.

But never had he been more afraid than just then. Upon this moment hinged the rest of his life. With this one choice, he would doom himself to certain death or an uncertain torment.

She'll kill them. Yvärras will slay my friends. My family.

He couldn't see beyond an impression of their faces, but he

knew each one of them. He longed to reach out to Wren and hold her close. He wished Tal could grip his shoulder, call him lad again, and tell him everything would be alright.

But this wasn't their choice. It was his and his alone.

Only he could save them.

Swear to me. Garin's desperation put a sharp edge to the words. *Swear to me you'll protect them from Yvärras. Swear it!*

I swear it, Mender. I swear I will do everything I can.

It wasn't a certainty. But it was all he could hope for.

Do it. The thought was little more than a whisper.

It was enough.

Garin cried out. His mind was flayed open. He felt himself falling into a red sea.

He never reached the bottom.

***

Tal still hadn't dredged up the barest idea of how to keep his company alive when Garin fell.

Moving with sorcerous speed, he caught the youth and cradled him to the stone. The youth's eyelids fluttered, and the whites of his eyes showed beneath.

Tal clenched his jaw. Was Ilvuan behind it? Were the dragons working together against them?

He knew far too little. But he had to make a choice all the same.

Tal raised his head to the dragon as it continued its slow lumber forward. It had appeared larger initially than it looked now, though it was still plenty big. He guessed it to be three or four times as long as a man to the end of its sword-sharp tail. Its head, shaped like an arrowhead and erect atop a long, powerful neck, rose three men high. Color was absent in Tal's darkvision, but the glimmer of light from the entrance showed a scarlet sheen to its overlapping scales, except for the ones on its belly, which shone diamond bright even in the gloom. Four claws — three in front of each foot, one in back — extended menacingly, hooked and sharp. He could imagine how easily it might grip a stone perch with such claws.

Or crush the body of a mortal.

Its wings were folded, yet he could see it was a thin, fleshy membrane that extended between the bones, for it was a transparent gold with the light behind it. From atop its head, a crest extended in a striking shape, ending in three sharp spires. It appeared to be made of the same, hard plate as occupied most of its body, except around its legs and wings, where scaly flesh dominated. Gold, scarlet, and silver were patterned over the crest. Its jaw, shaped like a reptile's and no doubt able to unhinge like one, hung slightly open, so he could glimpse the forest of sharp teeth within its mouth.

Most mesmerizing of all were its eyes. They resembled an elf's in how they shifted, only exaggerated: a maelstrom of color and light, aubergine with lightning flashes of crimson and violet.

He had never been so awed and terrified at once.

Yet Tal clung to the small reasons for hope. The dragon hadn't immediately killed them. It taunted them, though he wasn't sure who exactly it addressed. Perhaps it was an idio-syncrasy of their kind, an inclination to toy with its prey before consuming it. But he had another suspicion.

This is their hatching grounds. Their kind's last eggs are here.

Perhaps, if this dragon was female, more could be laid. The race wasn't entirely extinct, as Ilvuan had led them to believe. Yet there was a chance, however small, that this dragon wouldn't wish any harm to come to the eggs.

Just then, he would grasp at any chance.

There was little doubt that it would harm them, however. The dragon's jaws dripped with a viscous liquid. Blood from their mounts, Tal guessed from the earlier whinnies. It had slaughtered them in moments.

How long will it take to kill us?

Laying Garin down as gently as he could on the hard stone, Tal stood and cleared his throat, then spoke with as much authority as he could muster. Sorcery swelled in his blood to augment his voice.

"We do not hide from you, dragon. Who are you? Do you mean us harm?"

As he spoke, he reached out with his sorcery, testing her defenses. The streams of magic flowing into and around it warned him of the futility of the gesture. Yet though it was strong, its magic didn't severely dwarf his own capacity.

Perhaps, with a chance...

The dragon rebuffed his prying as it sauntered forward a step and spread its wings. Air blasted over Tal's face, but he stood his ground.

"Mortals do not make demands of me. Cower, worms. Kneel before the World's Heiress. I am Yvärras, and though I have long been absent, each of you is my lesser and, therefore, servant."

Tal's lips pulled back in something between a grimace and a smile. With every word, the dragon assaulted his mind, wearing down his strength.

Ashelia clutched at his hand. "Tal," she hissed. "Do you know what you're doing?"

He squeezed her hand back as he gave her a helpless shrug. All he could do was continue down the treacherous path before them.

"Dragons are supposed to be dead, Yvärras," Tal called. "Your kind has been absent for thousands of years. How is it that you alone survive? Do you not still fight against Yuldor, who claimed the Worldheart for his own?"

The dragon tilted her head minutely, and her eyes swirled faster, as if he'd suddenly become interesting. *"You are him, then. The one with sorcery in his veins. The one the Pretender fears and desires. Skaldurak, he calls you — 'Stone in the Wheel.'"*

"Always glad not to make my own introductions."

A deep, threatening rumble filled the cavern from floor to

ceiling. Tal wondered if his usual irreverence might not be such a good idea now.

If it ever was.

"Yuldor wishes me to kill you, mortal. Your disrespect almost tempts me to it."

Tal forced out a laugh, though mirth came difficult just then. "You would serve him? You, Yvärras, the Queen of Dragons, would serve Yuldor? He is mortal as well, though the Worldheart hides it!"

It was a dangerous bid, but the only one he had. The creature seemed absurdly prideful, a flaw he hoped to make use of. But as disdain radiated through him, his frail hopes faltered.

"I serve no one, manling, mortal or immortal. None are a match for me in any realm."

"Is that so? Not all dragons agree with you."

Lying to a clever creature, as this Yvärras showed herself to be, was another gamble. But all he had were long odds. He'd never spoken with Ilvuan, but he could only hope that his pairing with Garin implied some sort of alliance.

Scathing amusement seared through his mind. *"You speak of Alärthoras, do you not? He is less than the ghost of an ava'dual now. His opinion is nothing, his aid even less. He cannot save you."*

Why delay? To what end could his taunting bring them? Tal was groping in the dark with every word, hoping to stumble upon the right statement that would allow them to escape. But the dragon remained at the entrance of the cavern, and as long as Garin was prone, they were stuck where they were.

Time for a different tactic.

"Let us say you are right, Marvelous Yvärras. Perhaps there is a different way to settle this matter. Perhaps there's something we can offer you, something you desire."

Her disdain and amusement twined together now. *"There is nothing worms might tempt a Protectress with."*

"No? What about the downfall of one who pretends to be as great as you, if not greater? You — Yvärras, Queen of Dragons,

Ruler of the World! Yuldor the Pretender places himself above you, Majestic One. He believes himself the god of these lands. And if he is a god, what must he think of you? A pet to do his bidding and kill his foes?"

As anger flooded through his mind, Tal dared to hope the tide had turned their way. But the dragon's next roaring words extinguished hope as quickly as it had ignited.

The Pretender will not fall to you, mortal! His time will come. But you — you are a mere notch upon the length of the World's history. You are barely worth my notice. And when you are dead, Skaldurak, *then my kind will live and spread once again.*

Tal could barely hear himself think through Yvärras's thundering voice. His breathing came quickly as she closed in, as slow and inevitable as death itself. He grasped for another avenue to dissuade her attack, though he knew he'd already failed.

He gripped Ashelia's hand in both of his as he leaned toward her. "Run," he breathed in her ear. "Take the others and run."

She whipped her head around to stare at him, eyes glowing with anxious light. "Tal…"

"Please. You must live. You must stay alive."

Ashelia glanced at the approaching dragon, then nodded. She peeled her hands off of his, and he ached as she pulled away.

All he hoped now was to survive long enough to let them escape.

Tal breathed in and swelled the sorcery inside him. He felt invulnerable, yet he'd never been less so.

"If you won't listen to reason," he said, his voice echoing in the large chamber, "then you leave me no other choice."

Without waiting for a response, he struck with all the power in him.

MORTALITY

GARIN FLEW.

The day was bright, the sun warm. The ground far below was green with spring. Clouds parted before his wings.

Wings...

The sky trembled. A sliver of awareness slipped in. Wings — he didn't have wings. Did he?

I'm dreaming.

But the realization didn't awaken him. Onward he soared, though where to, or even where he was, remained uncertain.

Who am I? What am I?

A sudden downdraft sent him into the cloud bank. His vision became obscured and the haze suffocating, his chest growing so tight it was hard to breathe. Sparks appeared before his eyes, dotting the gray fog.

Then he emerged beneath the clouds and hurtled toward the ground.

Garin tried flapping his wings, but he no longer possessed them. All he had were arms, frail and human. He was falling, falling to his death, and there was nothing he could do.

I am here, Listener.

And he was. Garin clung to the presence that formed

around his. The land still came on too fast, and the other being didn't lift him, but he was no longer afraid. He wouldn't face the end alone.

Ilvuan, he recognized him.

Alärthoras, the dragon gently corrected him. *But I am the same as before.*

You're here with me? Now and always?

Sorrow wound around him like vines on a tree trunk. *Now and always.*

The ground was near. Garin closed his eyes.

The impact rent him apart.

Tal struck at the dragon, but his sorcery faltered.

He blanched for a moment, then gathered back his wits. It seemed as if Yvärras had evaded the attack, yet she remained in the same place, blazing with power and stalking steadily forward.

Only then did he understand just how outmatched he was.

With his sorcery ablaze, Tal felt his companions fleeing behind him. Two of them — Helnor and Falcon, he thought — picked up Garin from where he'd fallen and pulled him away.

He couldn't win this fight. But he could give them a chance to escape.

Tal gathered himself, and with needlepoint focus, he lashed out again. This time, he felt the counter, but it came from an invisible force, like a phantom hand pushing aside an arrow.

"You possess power, manling, but you do not know how to wield it," Yvärras crooned as she came within thirty paces of him. *"You only touch the sorcery, not the strings that shape it. You do not see the World as it truly is."*

He didn't respond, having wasted enough time on words. Tal tried a different tactic, this time spreading his sorcery out in a wave, but forming it into the sharp edge of an axe. With a guttural cry, he slammed it into the dragon's connection to sorcery.

His titanic blow fell — then flowed around Yvärras's stream with no effect.

The strain of holding so much power, yet unable to spend it, took a swift toll. Tal sank to his knees, while the dragon stood over him. The Ring of Thalkuun might protect him from her spells, but it wouldn't stop a physical assault. All it would take was a quick dart of her head now to bite and swallow him down.

"How?" he asked through gritted teeth. "How are you doing this?"

Amusement burned in his mind. *I am the master of this World; so it once was, so it always will be. Mortals can know nothing of sorcery compared to the* ava'duala, *and I am foremost among them.*"

As expected, Yvärras couldn't resist taunting him. In those few moments her speech bought him, Tal abandoned his direct assaults and opted for a different approach.

His sorcery split three ways.

First came the wind. Tal whipped up a gale that both blew him away from the dragon and buffeted against his foe. Its lashing winds bruised and battered him even as it carried him from danger. He could spare his pain no more than a moment's notice.

Next came the flames. With warmth condensed from the air, he heated the space until sparks blossomed into fire. They flared before Yvärras's eyes, lashing against them, dazzling and hopefully blinding her.

Last came the stone. Tal pulled at the black rock beneath the dragon and threw every ounce of strength he had behind their rising. Sharp pillars, each a dozen feet wide, slammed upward with a force that would have impaled a ship's hull. A score he summoned, aiming for her vulnerable parts — the wings, the limbs, the scaled skin that ran in a narrow strip along the sides of her powerful body.

As he tumbled to a bone-breaking halt fifty feet away, Tal groaned and lifted his gaze. He hoped it would be enough. Perhaps, in her arrogance, the dragon had been unwary.

The Protectress screamed.

The sound was simultaneously a low rumble and a high-pitched shriek. It shook Tal down to his bones. He felt her fury claw into his mind and tear at him with abandon.

She stepped free of his spells. There was the barest evidence of wounds along her legs and along her long neck, but as Yvärras glared at him with lightning eyes, he saw he hadn't blinded her, but only inflamed her rage.

It was hopeless, yet Tal ground his teeth together, a smile on his lips, and pulled at yet more sorcery until it seared inside him. He felt his skin weaving together, his bones grinding back into place. He readied himself for a second assault.

It wasn't enough.

The dragon didn't approach with a slow stalk now, but pounced. Leaping forward, she flared her wings for a moment so she soared right to him. Tal summoned stones shards from the ground and flung them at the thin membrane of her wings, but the World twisted around the dragon as her own sorcery countered the spell, and the projectiles went spinning away.

Tal surged to his feet as the dragon landed before him, then launched himself back toward the entrance with a pummeling gust. He almost made it — then something tightened over his chest. Tal gasped for air as he felt the dragon's hot breath on the bare skin of his back, her teeth holding him by his shirt. Abruptly, he felt his spell countered and cut off.

He was at her mercy.

Yvärras shook him, a rag doll in a hound's jaws. The World spun about him. His limbs jarred. His neck snapped back and forth, nearly snapping.

Words of power echoed, and a spell burned through the

air. The dragon queen trumpeted in pain. Someone else had attacked; one of his companions had struck at the Protectress.

Tal had no time to fear for them, for suddenly he was flying, released from Yvärras' grip.

A chance!

Summoning wind, Tal knocked himself out of the way of snapping teeth and shot across the cave, barely able to orient himself as he hurtled toward stone. At the last moment, he summoned a wind shield, stopping just short of splattering across the cavern.

But he was spent. His sorcery, used so furiously, was thin as he tried to pull for more. His mind felt splintered, a makeshift raft pulling apart in a river rapids.

Tal desperately tried to rally himself. Had he bought enough time? Had his friends escaped? He didn't know; his senses were muddled and confused.

He didn't dare stop.

Through spinning vision, he saw the dragon closing in, lumbering across the cave toward him. She would kill him, be it by tooth or claw or clever sorcery. He had been a fool to think he could be her equal.

But I always was a fool.

Tal summoned his last defense when a thundering voice stopped him.

"Do not, Yvärras! Kill him and our kin will perish!"

Garin opened his eyes.

Someone carried him. As he roused, they set him down. Words were spoken, but they fell on deaf ears. Sounds of conflict echoed from afar, but they were quiet next to the Worldsong. It crashed with all the fury of a storm-ridden sea about his skull.

No, it wasn't the Worldsong — it was another being's song, wrapped around and through his.

He wasn't the only one looking out from his eyes.

Rise, Jenduit. *We will face her together.*

Garin's limbs moved without his willing them, and he called upon the Song without thought. As he watched, the World splintered into a web, one that reached into and across everything. His hands reached out to touch its strands. The web vibrated violently with the sorcery of those fighting before him, but his hands were steady as they pulled at the strings.

Then a voice blared out from his mind.

"Do not, Yvärras! Kill him and our kin will perish!"

Garin felt unmoored, adrift in a body that another commanded. Yet as he recognized the creature they faced across the cavern, he didn't reach for control.

Ilvuan was a dragon. He knew best how to contend with one.

Garin retreated. He watched. He waited.

Yvärras, who had been bearing down on one of his battered companions, turned her majestic head toward him. Her contempt was evident in every movement.

"Alärthoras," the dragon sneered. *"At last, you summon the courage to face me. But you cannot threaten me wearing that flimsy flesh, Brother. Nor with threats you will not keep."*

"But you are wrong, Sister." Ilvuan was calm as he replied, both in voice and mind. *"I do not threaten idly; I will make good on it. Do you not see my touch upon the Lattice? I hold our kin's fate in these mortal hands."*

Only at his words did Garin think to follow the threads that his hands held. They stretched across the room, past where Yvärras loomed over Tal, to the rear of the cavern. He tried to think of what Ilvuan could threaten that would give his fellow dragon pause. Then it came to him.

The eggs. He's threatening the eggs.

He felt a glimmer of a response from Ilvuan, of resolve and sorrow. Though it seemed impossible that the Singer would endanger his species, upon that wash of emotion, Garin didn't doubt he would do as he said.

Yvärras seemed to sense it as well, for anger now poured forth from her, blistering to behold.

"Your cage has turned your mind! Would you end your cycles forever?"

"I would." The words shook as Ilvuan spoke them, but grim determination was behind them.

"You cannot, Alärthoras! We are the rulers of this World and all others. We will never cease to exist!"

"And yet, I will bring about our end if you force me."

Enduring the dragon queen's frustration was like wallowing in a lava pool. Garin felt he must be burned away entirely from existence as she turned the brunt of it on him.

"You will allow us to leave this place, Yvärras," Ilvuan continued. *"You will allow Heartblood to walk away alive, as will all the mortals with us. In exchange, I will preserve our kin's cycles so they may continue forevermore."*

Had he been in control of his lungs, Garin would have held his breath. Everything hinged on this moment. Tal's life. His own. All his companions — Wren, Rolan, Ashelia, Helnor, Aelyn.

Yvärras abruptly radiated a different emotion. Disdain didn't sear like her anger, but eroded at Garin's resolve, like an alchemical solution that dissolved all it touched.

"You lie! You would not end our brethren. You have not devolved that much from your intimacy with mortals and jealousy of my position. I do not believe you, Alärthoras!"

A deep sadness almost drowned Garin. Fearfully, he wondered what Ilvuan had in mind and if the time had come to take control of his own fate. Before he could decide, however, Ilvuan spoke again.

"Then, Sister, I must make you believe."

Garin's hands moved, twitching along several of the strings he held. Where before there had only been the bright lines and air, now pure energy blazed into being.

Yvärras' outrage blasted over Garin. *"You will not—!"*

Ilvuan didn't give her a chance to finish. His spell rippled outward, arcing across the cavern and brightening the way as it traveled. It left a black afterimage on Garin's eyes, so he found it difficult to see its target. But as he heard the split and hiss, he knew.

He destroyed it. He destroyed an egg.

The grief pouring from his Singer nearly made Garin's knees buckle.

Yvärras threw back her head and shrieked. But Ilvuan had taken her measure. With Garin's arms, he motioned to the others, then began backing toward the cavern's entrance, as far away as it seemed. The others followed at once, eager to leave behind the volatile Protectress. Tal, streaked with his own blood, rose and trailed after them.

Hope warmed Garin's chest. Ilvuan kept a steady pace. As he neared the cavern walls, he reached up to touch the rough, black rock. Garin noticed his fingers found a glyph there, still faintly glowing. The sorcerous net came alive again for a moment, each thread singing, before Ilvuan plucked a few among them.

The glyphs in the cavern glowed brightly, then all went out.

Yvärras finally quieted, and her furious thoughts found Garin again.

"I knew you to be a fool, but you are a greater one than I thought. You have doomed yourself, Alärthoras. You will die within that flesh, die a mortal's death!"

Ilvuan gave no reply. He only continued backing them out of the dark cave until daylight pressed on them and they'd moved out of the dragon queen's shadow.

PASSAGE III

Though a mortal was pivotal in restraining the Origins who might have destroyed the World, it was the dragons whose sacrifice made it possible.

The ava'duala, as they name themselves, were once seen as nearly deities. Their physical dominance, which was a match for an entire mortal army, was still only secondary to their potent sorcery. Magic came as easily as breathing to them. With a thought, they could summon a storm on a cloudless day, breathe an inferno to match any erupting volcano.

How, then, did every last one fall to mortal hands?

In short, they did not. The dragons battled not the Origins who had seized the World's power for their own; they contended with the World itself. Only such an inundation of pure sorcery, which poisoned and malformed the lands and its creatures, could overcome their prowess.

The ava'duala preserved all of life, albeit in its present, decrepit forms. But the wise would not attribute much or any altruism to their actions. In what I have experienced of dragons, and drawing from the ancients' depictions of them, they keep the World as their inheritance, not out of love or care for mortalkind.

One day, dragons will return and reclaim the World, and mortals shall once more tremble at their shadows.

- The Untold Lore of Yuldor Soldarin and His Servants, *by Inanis*

FALLING SHADOW

TAL BACKED OUT OF THE CAVE.

It was a marvel that he was still alive. He'd battled a dragon, a Silence-damned *dragon*, and survived to tell the tale.

But he'd come out much the worse for it. Some of his ribs had broken, and deep cuts furrowed into his back. He felt as if he'd been pummeled by crashing waves against a stony shore for hours on end. There was a watery murmur as he breathed, and he occasionally coughed up blood.

Yet grievous as the wounds were, his sorcery would soon set things aright. That wasn't what bothered him most.

What in the red hells happened?

Tal hadn't understood half of what had occurred. There had been a standoff, a reckoning, an irrevocable decision. It had something to do with Garin and his Singer and their connection to the dragon queen.

But why Yvärras let them go free, he couldn't fully say.

He knew one thing: the dragon's wrath wouldn't be stayed for long. He'd sized up the Protectress while she tossed him about the cave and judged her to be quick to anger and slow to forgiveness. They had to flee as far as they could and hope that whatever Garin had said in the cavern would delay her long enough for them to escape. There was no time to rest and recuperate.

When is there ever?

Tal smiled grimly, the scrapes and bruises across his face pulling. With another rattling breath, he limped toward where the others had knotted together.

"Which way?" Ashelia's eyes spun fast as they stared at him. She, like the others, looked unharmed, though stricken by Tal's state.

Before Tal could answer, Garin spoke. His voice returned to normal, losing the unnatural resonance it had in the dragon hatching ground.

"She won't follow us; not immediately, at least. Ilvuan holds the eggs hostage, and he introduced a flaw to the defenses of the hatchery. Until the eggs are safe, she won't leave the cave."

"So we remain alive for a few days longer." Aelyn's narrow face was scrunched with fear and derision, his voice high-pitched with panic. "We cannot hope to run faster than a dragon flies! And we don't even have mounts!"

Tal winced, remembering their dying screams echoing up the cave's passage. He turned to where they'd left them tied up and saw none had been spared. Yvärras had torn open their flanks with tooth and claw, and their blood stained the sable stone. The stors' horns had shattered, the fragments scattered, tiny stars against the night sky of the rock.

"Calm, *Belosi*, calm. We will survive this."

Tal turned back to find Helnor squeezing his big hand over Aelyn's narrow shoulder. More surprising still was that the mage didn't cringe from his House-brother's touch, but seemed to take comfort in it, the furrows in his brows smoothing a touch.

Wren crossed her arms and stared back toward the cave. "Whatever we're doing, let's do it quick. I'd rather not risk Garin being wrong."

Ashelia nodded. "We leave anything we cannot carry and head into the hills on foot."

"We're not taking the boat?" Falcon sounded a bit hysterical himself. Tal once more wished he could have spared his friend this misery.

But wishing's as good as pissing, as the commander used to say.

Ashelia shook her head while Tal answered for her. "Too easy to follow. Not to mention it'll only get us a little closer to Ikvaldar and we cannot afford delays."

"We will take the straight path," Ashelia agreed, and she reached out and pressed his hand.

Their course decided, they descended upon the macabre pile of their mounts, holding their breaths and fighting back tears. Tal went to Savior, and even through his weariness, sorrow struck him at the majestic stallion being laid low.

"Rest easy, old boy," he muttered. "You deserved better."

He was glad to possess a strong stomach as he inhaled the stink of intestines and blood while sorting through their saddlebags. Only Garin and Rolan didn't take part in the search, and no one pressed them to. Every so often, they heard Yvärras moving within the cavern, the shifting of a restless, caged beast, and they went about the task faster still.

Soon, they'd separated the absolute necessities from the rest of the baggage, leaving behind additional food, changes of clothes, and other nonessentials. The abandonment of Rolan's lute was one of the more painful losses, and the boy's gaze lingered on it even as they turned away.

A groan escaped Tal as he straightened, his mending ribs screaming in protest. He ignored them and rejoined the others, a pack looped over one shoulder, his hunting bow and quiver over the other. His skin burned with the pressure, but it was just one more discomfort to put out of mind.

When all was ready, Tal spared a look at his companions. To a one, their eyes were wide with fear, resembling rabbits out in the open before a prowling wolf. *A metaphor not far from true*, he mused. But though they were stained with horse and stor blood and cringing with terror, he had pride in them.

Now, to keep them alive.

"Time to go," Tal said with a bracing smile, then started walking up the coast, looking for a way up into the hills.

A storm whorled within Garin.

He moved his limbs now, breathed with his lungs, commanded where his eyes turned. But no longer was he the sole master of his body.

A dragon lived inside him.

Though Ilvuan remained silent, concentrating on maintaining his threat to Yvärras, Garin always felt him. The mote of control he kept was like a splinter under his skin: irritating, infuriating, impossible to ignore. Even more, it was a reminder of what his life would be going forward, that his fate was intertwined with another's. With an ally he hadn't always trusted.

He didn't know if Ilvuan could sense all his thoughts and feelings now, but he suspected he knew most of them. He dared not delve into the Singer's soul, afraid of being swept up in the deep swell of his spirit. But their surface emotions were unavoidable, each fueling the others', like fire given fuel. Frigid fury and molten misery collided again and again, burning through Garin with each fresh collision.

It was all he could do to breathe through the tumult, grit his teeth, and keep marching after the others.

The hike wasn't easy, for the terrain was rugged. It took them the better part of an hour to find a passage around the cliff and onto the ridge above. In the end, they discovered a gully of broken stone that leveled off enough to scramble up.

Despite his own condition, Garin pitied Falcon then, for the going was precarious even with two hands. Rolan proved more nimble, trained by a childhood spent climbing along tree limbs while hunting for frogs and other creatures. Tal kept to the rear of the pack with Garin, though it didn't seem entirely as a ward against the dragon. He possessed sorcery to a degree no mortal man should, yet Yvärras had eclipsed him. That he'd survived as long as he had was a miracle.

But can he kill a god?

That Yuldor wasn't an actual deity was little comfort. Garin had witnessed the Enemy's power in the goldwood. He knew precisely what sort of being they sought to defy.

For once, however, that wasn't his most pressing concern. All the while they moved, Ilvuan kept a small part of Garin's mind in his control. Through his flesh, the dragon clutched tightly to filaments of sorcery with his invisible claws. If the terrible fire he'd summoned before was any sign, a slip up on his part could cause the extinction of his species.

Questions whirled in Garin's mind, black and blinding. Yet for the moment, there was nothing he could do except tear his way through them and keep climbing.

After many slips, scraped knees, and panting breaths, they reached the top. Garin staggered to his feet and stared over the desolate landscape before them. Following a gentle slope downward, the land leveled off into empty stretches of black and gray stone similar to the shore below. Occasionally, a conical mountain would interrupt the monotony, its top full of broken stone, like an eruption long ago had blasted its apex apart. The only color came from the moss that touched upon the black stone.

Garin felt his hopes sag. *Nowhere to hide.* As soon as Yvärras followed, she would spot them on the open land.

Tal lurched up next to Garin and exhaled. "Yuldor's flaming balls, broken ribs don't make this easy."

Garin flashed his old mentor a thin smile. "At least the walking will be easier."

"At least there's that." The older man wiped the sweat

filming his forehead back along the frizz of hair that had escaped his ponytail, then adjusted his bow and filthy knapsack. "Well, dragons wait for no man, eh? Best be on with it."

Garin only nodded.

For all the danger they were in, boredom soon joined his anxiety. Garin watched his feet so as not to trip as his mind traveled over his worries. How long could Ilvuan keep up his threat? Was Yvärras already repairing the damage he'd done? Would she even believe him?

She believes. Ilvuan's response seemed both closer than it had in the past, yet also distant. Garin could feel his focus remaining behind them, ready to pluck the strings he held.

Knowing he would receive no more answers from the Singer then, Garin stifled his thoughts and pushed his wooden legs faster.

"So, what's the plan?" Wren asked ahead of him, her words coming fast and sharp. "Or do we even have one now?"

Garin smiled slightly. She'd always tried to hide her fear behind irritation.

Ashelia remained as measured as usual as she shouted her answer from the front. "We'll travel as long and far as we can. There should be woods ten or so miles ahead. If we can make it to them, we might lose our pursuit."

"*Might.*" Wren barked a laugh. "Sure we will."

Ilvuan stirred, but gave no verbal response. Garin felt he had some idea of what they should do next, but he forcibly quieted his question regarding it. The dragon would make his thoughts known when he wished and no sooner, and Ilvuan needed no distractions just then.

Conversation died down for some time. Though a heavy weight pressed on his chest, Garin took some heart from their changing surroundings. Tufts of grass broke free from the tops of small ridges and hillocks. They were tough, fibrous plants, and he doubted they could be eaten, but any vegetation was a welcome change. His grumbling belly told him edible varieties would be even more welcome.

Shrubbery emerged next, tangled bushes that stretched in brown roots along the gray dirt with a spattering of leaves. Raising his eyes, Garin's chest leaped to see more green edging the distance. Somewhere ahead, the forest awaited.

And hopefully our escape.

Again, the Singer stirred but didn't speak.

Garin fueled every stride with fear and frustration. They didn't pause, and when Rolan complained of blisters, Helnor put him, pack and all, atop his shoulders for a mile, carrying him like a mule. The boy was so delighted by this that he laughed aloud, though he quieted at Aelyn's withering look.

Sunset glimmered on the horizon by the time they reached the forest, if it could be called one. The trees were sparse and short, many failing to surpass Garin's height, and the foliage was too thin to hide within. A dragon soaring above would quickly see them if the woods remained like this the entire way through.

"Not all we wished for," Tal admitted as he turned back to the others. He stood taller now, and though blood caked his clothes and skin, the bruises and wounds beneath seemed to have healed. "But it's cover nonetheless."

Ilvuan seemed about to respond, but again, he settled back into his task. Garin tried to blink away the shimmer of the web that trailed across his vision. In that moment, the World seemed like cracked porcelain.

Though everyone dragged from weariness, and Rolan was falling asleep on his feet, they pushed on past dusk. When Garin insisted Yvärras wouldn't yet be searching for them, they risked summoning werelights to see by. Garin peered into the gloom surrounding them and wondered what other creatures than dragons might roam this lonely wilderness. They hadn't seen a living thing larger than a rodent or bird all that day, yet he had the feeling it wasn't as deserted as it seemed.

He wished he could ask Ilvuan, but even now that the dragon had taken up residence in his body, he remained inaccessible.

They walked for several hours into the darkness before Garin surprised himself with a decision. "We should stop," he called ahead, causing the others to turn back.

"Are you sure?" Ashelia queried, her brow drawn.

"I am," Rolan groaned as he leaned into his mother's side.

"I would think you most of all would know better than to suggest that," Aelyn snipped. His mood had grown fouler as their discomforts mounted. "Or did you miss the dragon that nearly killed us?"

Garin ignored the mage and looked at Tal. "We have to flee across all the Faernor Grasslands still. We won't get far if we don't sleep."

His old mentor's lips twisted, but he nodded. "Garin's right. We have to rest; now especially, while Yvärras isn't giving chase."

"We can only hope," Falcon muttered.

Aelyn huffed out a breath. "I'm not inclined to agree with the bard, but I do. All we have to go by is the boy's word."

"She isn't pursuing," Tal said firmly. "Even if I couldn't sense it, I trust Garin. And considering how he just saved all our lives, you should, too."

I didn't save us, Garin wanted to say. *The devil in me did.*

He tried to stifle the thought as quickly as it came. Though the label "devil" had always amused Ilvuan before, he wasn't sure how their relationship might have changed now that they were bonded.

Garin startled as he realized all his companions had turned toward him. Though his pack had long ago become a heavy weight, he tried to stand up straighter and appear as someone they could rely on, though he wasn't entirely certain they should.

"I trust him," Wren said first.

Garin stared at her, awash with gratefulness. She gave him a thin smile in return.

"I as well," Helnor rumbled.

Ashelia sighed. "We'll take shelter then."

Tal drew Garin's eye with his stare and gave him a nod. Glad he'd been vindicated, Garin returned it. Only sixteen summers old, yet here he was making decisions for their party. A strange mixture of pride and fear flooded him, and he tried to ignore it as he set about the tasks of setting up camp.

When they finished, they sat around a fire, ate their sparse meal, and took account of their supplies. The situation looked poor. Without the additional rations stocked away in their saddlebags, they had four days of food, and only then if they took half-portions. Garin ate glumly, but Rolan looked saddest of all. The boy scarfed down his food and stared longingly at his mother's meal until she sighed and broke off a piece of her hardtack to hand him. Before he could eat it, however, Tal offered his.

"I can go without," he assured them at Ashelia's questioning look. "I have another source of sustenance."

Garin wondered if it really worked like that. Yet Rolan was more than happy to partake of his windfall.

Tal offered to take the first watch, and the others relented, though not without Helnor's warning that he would relieve him before dawn. Garin made for his own bedroll, but Tal halted him.

"Garin, come sit with me a moment." He spoke softly, no doubt to prevent from waking the already slumbering elf boy.

Garin paused, filled with a sense of foreboding. He had a feeling he knew what this conversation would be about, and he wasn't sure he was ready to have it.

No good in avoiding a thing that needs doing, he thought as he perched on the log beside his old mentor.

They stared into the red coals of the fire for a long moment before Tal spoke. "Are you alright, Garin?"

His chest tightened, but Garin tried to keep his voice steady. "Yes."

The man looked askance at him, orange light and shadows making a stranger of his features. "I know some of what occurred back in the cave, but I don't know why. I was hoping you could tell me."

Garin swallowed hard, aware anyone pretending to sleep could overhear them. Tilting his head back, he stared up at the stars dusting the sky. Once, he'd believed it to be the Night's mantle that swept over them, a malevolent entity waiting to strike anytime it could, and the stars were the heroes of the Whispering Gods keeping the adversarial force at bay. He'd hoped to be one of those heroes commemorated in a constellation — not to aid in a holy war, but to flatter his own pride. He'd wanted to matter. To make his mark upon the World.

Now, he knew what a burden it was to be significant.

Slowly, he met Tal's eyes. "I truly have a devil in me now, Tal."

Garin watched for the shift in his expression. Tal was talented at hiding his true thoughts when he wished to, but Garin knew him too well to believe his smile.

"What's that supposed to mean?" Tal asked lightly.

Garin shrugged. He knew the words he had to say. He just wasn't sure if he had the courage to say them.

"I had a choice back at the hatching grounds. A decision that could save us. So I made it. I did the only thing I could."

His throat surprised him by closing up. Garin stared at the coals, blinking fiercely, trying to hold back sudden tears. He felt Tal's scrutiny like the sun's pitiless glare.

Ilvuan roused, but his emotions remained muddled and unclear.

"Tell me what happened," Tal instructed, quiet but firm.

Garin sighed, and it almost came out as a sob. Anger blossomed from his frustration then, and he latched onto it. It was better than self-pity, and he needed strength just then.

"Ilvuan and I... we bonded together. I accepted him into my body; he shares my flesh. It's freed him, I suppose — freed him to challenge Yvärras in a way he never could have before. And he says he can help us against Yuldor now."

The Singer again stirred, and this time his feelings on the subject were clear. He didn't want Garin to speak of these things, to reveal secrets that were supposed to remain between them. But he didn't owe fealty to the dragon, no matter what they shared.

So he told himself.

More painful was Tal's reaction. Following the look of shock was a pitying wince Garin almost looked away from. Garin pitied himself, but he felt more miserable receiving it from Tal.

"That was... noble of you, Garin. You saved us — you know that, don't you? I wish it hadn't been necessary. I wish I could have..." His old mentor broke off with a shake of his head.

Garin only shrugged. He wished Tal could have been enough to challenge Yvärras as well, but he hadn't been. Acknowledging it aloud would help no one.

After several moments of silence, Tal murmured, "Is he listening now? Ilvuan, that is?"

Garin nodded even as the dragon's presence prickled throughout Garin's body. Then, to Garin's surprise, he found Ilvuan giving voice to his thoughts.

"Yes, Heartblood. I am here. I am always here."

Garin thought he'd spoken only to him, as had always been the case before, though now the words seemed to resonate. But when Tal startled, he asked tentatively, "You... did he speak to you?"

Tal recovered swiftly. "Yes. I heard him in my mind, just as I heard Yvärras before."

Amusement prickled throughout Garin's body, almost drawing out a laugh. It was disquieting, that another's mirth could stir up such a response. Somehow, it made Garin feel even lonelier than before.

You are never alone now, Jenduit. Ilvuan sounded as bitter as Garin felt. He thought he sensed the thought was private between them.

At least we share that, he thought back to the Singer.

Tal was watching him. "Can I speak to Ilvuan?" he asked, hesitant.

Garin smiled mirthlessly. "You're always talking to him now."

The man smiled back, though he'd never looked so uncertain. "Right. Well, Ilvuan... Thank you for saving us. And before in Naruah, for helping bring me back up from the depths."

The dragon's sense of approval radiated outward, and it didn't feel restricted only to Garin's body.

"It has ever been the calling of the ava'duala *to protect their mortals."*

Their mortals. Garin clenched his jaw. He wondered if Ilvuan thought of him that way now. Once, he'd been a mere vessel to the Singer. And despite his claims otherwise, having seen a dragon in the flesh now, he understood how they could never think of mortals as their equals.

That understanding made him no less resentful.

Tal combed a hand through his long, tangled hair, pulling more of it free from its tail. "Nevertheless, I'm grateful."

Ilvuan hummed his response, apparently gratified to hear it. *His proper due,* Garin thought with acid humor.

Garin found he was standing. "I'm going to bed," he announced, then moved over to his bedroll, which he'd laid out next to Wren. Tal didn't speak a word against it, though Garin felt his eyes on his back.

Once he'd settled down, Garin stared up at the sky. Wren shifted, drawing an arm out of the tucked blanket to stretch over him. He didn't know if she did it asleep or consciously, but he placed his hand over hers, grateful for the gesture.

But he couldn't sleep yet. He didn't have all the answers he needed.

Sometime during the conversation with Tal, the Singer had released his grip on the sorcerous threads he'd been holding. Garin wondered why he'd released them, forgetting for a moment that no thought of his was private.

Though he hadn't posed it as a query, the Singer answered him. *I cannot risk holding on too long lest my grip slip. They have grown too far away to safely threaten. But Yvärras will still be occupied. The* Sha'aval's *protections are complicated and difficult to mend. It will take days, as I have said.*

And then?

Instead of answering immediately, Ilvuan's presence curled around his mind. Garin imagined him as a dragon like Yvärras, but one confined to a space too small for it, so he had to curl his head over his tail.

If he found Garin's image insulting, the Singer didn't acknowledge it. *As I said before, Yvärras struck a deal with the Pretender. Over the past two years, he has helped her achieve the adolescent form she wears now.*

Adolescent. Garin wondered faintly what a full-grown dragon looked like. Could it even fit within the hatching grounds?

A dragon is never fully grown, Ilvuan answered his thought. *Only reaching the limits of our sorcery stunts our growth. As our Protectress, Yvärras has the potential to be the greatest among us. But even young in flesh, she is more than a match for any mortal.*

I know. I was there. Garin oriented his thoughts. *But there's something else I want to ask you, Ilvuan. Something I need to know.*

Ask, my Listener. I will answer.

Our bonding — is it permanent? And what did Yvärras mean when she said you'd doomed yourself?

The dragon was silent for a long stretch. Garin wondered if he would answer him at all when he finally roused again.

You were not the only one to make a sacrifice this day, Jenduit.

Garin's unease only grew. *What do you mean?*

Yvärras would not be swayed by words alone. Action was needed to show the depth of my conviction and intent. I had to make good on my threat. And so I destroyed an egg.

Garin inhaled sharply. Amid everything else, he'd forgotten that moment. *Does that mean you... killed a dragon?*

Emotions swirled through Garin, so intense he wasn't sure for a moment that they weren't his own.

In a sense, yes. The words were like the wind's whisper on his mind. *A dragon without their egg can never be reborn. Each of the* ava'duala *who remain has lived hundreds of lives, and always have we had eggs to call our own. But there are few eggs now, fewer even than remain to be reborn, and each egg has been claimed.*

So one dragon cannot be reborn.

But something needled at Garin, something Ilvuan was leaving unsaid. The Singer wasn't entirely devoid of empathy, yet he seemed interested in his own pursuits first and foremost. He didn't think such a deep sorrow could come of killing another dragon.

Then it came to him. *You destroyed your own egg.*

Garin tensed against the wash of feelings. It was like acid seeped through his skin to eat at his muscle and bone.

Yvärras had to see my conviction. Ilvuan sounded worn and thin, like a man at his wit's end. *She had to know that Yuldor will mean the extinction of our brethren if he is not stopped. There was only one way to show her I truly believed this: my own eradication.*

Garin felt sick to his stomach and wondered if this was what it would feel like to have a bellyful of dragonfire.

Will it convince her?

I do not know. I can only hope.

Hope. His lips curled. He was tiring of relying on such a flimsy thing.

But now you understand, Jenduit: *we are one, truly. For as long as we live, we are bound.*

As long as we live, Garin replied. *Or as short.*

The dragon shared in his tired irony, and though neither was much amused, there was a small comfort in it.

No matter what came next, no matter the hardships, the failures, the impossible odds, they would face them together.

BONDS REFORGED

Tal woke the others as the sun slunk across the empty sky.

Helnor had offered to take the second watch, but Tal never woke him. Even an elf's constitution couldn't match the sorcery bubbling through his veins. It contained the lull of liquor and the bite of winterleaf at the same time. With it, he could summon spells that invigorated and sustained him.

Though every casting came at a cost.

Still, with Yvärras promising pursuit, Tal had made the choice to let the others rest while they still could. As for himself... he doubted he would survive their next confrontation, anyway.

I can rest in my grave, as it's said.

With fatalist mirth, Tal greeted his companions. "Everyone sleep well?"

He received only mutters in return.

"I could use a bigger meal," Rolan grumbled.

Tal normally would have teased the boy, saying he already had a good portion of Tal's own meal the night before. Instead, he sauntered over and ruffled his hair.

"You could. Maybe soon we'll hunt something down for meat. What do you say?"

The boy, heartened by the prospect, grinned up at him and nodded. A moment later, however, his expression faltered.

"But... the dragon. Isn't she coming for us?"

Tal's eyes flickered up to meet Ashelia's. In her face, he saw all the worries of a mother for her child. No wound he'd taken the day before had pierced so deeply as that look.

"Possibly, lad," he said, looking back at the boy. "But I'll just fight her off again."

Rolan shrugged. "Wasn't it Garin who drove her off? Garin and his devil."

Everyone stiffened at that. Tal winced and glanced at the youth. Garin stood, his rolled blankets tucked under an arm, his head bowed and his eyes hidden behind his bangs.

"Better a devil on our side than theirs," Falcon endeavored.

Aelyn snorted. "They have plenty of devils."

"And we should act like they are chasing us," Ashelia intervened. "Pack up, quickly. We have many miles to travel."

They ate their sparse breakfast while they hiked. Tal again snuck his portion to Rolan, to the boy's grateful smile and his mother's conflicted glance. Yet though Ashelia disapproved of his privations, she uttered no reprimand.

For his part, the toll of the days was setting in. He'd burned through sorcery aplenty the day before, both in the battle against the dragon queen and in mending his body afterward.

It's the flight from Elendol all over again. Tal donned a resilient smile and brushed back a hair stuck to his forehead. He wouldn't suffer from *karkados* this time; he couldn't afford to. He had a god to kill and a dragon to evade, after all.

The emaciated forest in which they'd camped began to thicken around them, though never enough to obscure their passage. Tal kept one eye to the sky as they traveled, flinching at every shadow and silhouette. Each time, they were only ordinary animals: hawks, vultures, even the small birds for which Wren was named. Squirrels darted along their path, but they didn't stop to hunt them. Despite what he'd told Rolan, there would be no time for meat, not until they were sure they'd evaded their pursuit.

When they paused so Tal could wring water from the air to refill their waterskins, Garin spoke up for the first time that day. "Ilvuan says there's a place where we can take shelter ahead. It was a castle town eons ago, but is likely a ruin now. Still, it might provide cover."

Tal watched the beads of water he'd summoned coalesce into a ball the size of his palm, undulating slowly, before he willed it into a waterskin. "Will it hide us from all of Yvärras' senses? I'll wager she doesn't rely on sight alone."

Garin shook his head. "The town itself won't, but Ilvuan says he can take care of that."

A scoff came from one of the others. It took no stretch of the imagination to guess who.

"An objection, Aelyn?" Tal asked, eyes still on his task.

"We're trusting an awful amount of our safety to this *dragon*, are we not?" Aelyn made it clear he doubted Ilvuan qualified for such a label.

After seeing one in the flesh, Tal could hardly blame him. Still, his response was sharp. "Do we have a choice? None of us are experts in dragons. And Ilvuan saved us once, didn't he?"

He wondered why the dragon didn't speak to the mage himself. Hearing his voice and authority might be the convincing Aelyn and the others needed.

A firm hand — or a firm claw, as it were.

Aelyn started to respond, but his House-brother's deeper voice overrode him. "In this, I have faith in Garin. If he trusts the word of his dragon, then so do I."

Tal smiled, then looked around as he distributed the last of the water. Garin stared at the Prime Warder with a grateful look and Helnor gave him a firm nod.

"Is it out of our way, these ruins?" Ashelia asked, more reserved than her brother.

Garin shook his head as he accepted the flask Tal handed him. "Only a mile or two."

Tal glanced at those who hadn't voiced their opinions. Wren looked as if she was ready to fight anything just then, a hand clenched over her rapier's pommel, her eyes bright and whirling. He hoped she wouldn't have to, though he feared it had become a matter of when, not if, their enemies found them. Falcon only seemed miserable, his shoulders slumped, his remaining hand playing over his wrist stump. Either the dragon's appearance or the abandonment of Rolan's lute seemed to have crumpled his resilience, for he'd barely said more than a quip the entire flight westward.

At length, Tal looked back at Ashelia, whose eyes spun in contemplation. Finally, she nodded, as he'd guessed she would.

"We'll make for the ruins," Ashelia announced, "and pray to the Mother that your dragon is good for his word."

"I am, elf. As I always have been."

Ilvuan's voice rang in his head, and a shiver ran through Tal. Without meaning to, he stared at Garin, then quickly glanced away. The youth looked miserable, torn between helplessness and desperation.

I had a choice, Garin had said the night before. *I did the only thing I could.*

It cut Tal deeply that he'd been forced into that decision. That he hadn't been able to save Garin from it.

I wasn't enough then. But I must be now.

Silence had fallen in the wake of Ilvuan's words. Tal spoke into it, adding a cheery note to his voice that rang false in his own ears.

"No more daylight to burn. How close is it, Garin?"

"We should reach it tomorrow."

"Magnificent." Tal drew himself upright and plastered on a grin. "A walk in the woods is a fine thing, is it not?"

His exuberance was met with grumbles, then the crunching of marching feet.

Only a few minutes into the trek, Wren rounded on Garin.

"What in the red hells is going on with you?" she demanded, her words low and urgent.

He glanced over with a wry smile. She'd stayed quiet far longer than he'd expected. An outburst was overdue.

"What do you mean?" he asked, trying for teasing but falling short.

"Don't toy with me, Garin Dunford. Your devil, or dragon, or whatever it is — it's talking to us now. What changed? What changed with *you*?"

He couldn't repress his wince. He'd known this conversation had to happen, little as he wanted it to.

Glancing over his shoulder to make sure none of the others were near, Garin said, "Fine. I'll explain."

Then he told her all that had occurred back in the cave, holding nothing back. Whether she accepted or rejected him, he needed her to know the full truth.

Wren was quiet throughout the telling, but her expression spoke loudly enough. Garin tried not to look at her, but couldn't help his gaze returning to her face. Her pixie features were as hard and fierce as they'd ever been, and her eyes could have ignited a bonfire.

The reactions to his words weren't only from without. Now that Ilvuan had taken residence inside his body, he felt his presence with every movement, his emotions with every word. Many times, it seemed as if the Singer was slumbering, though he doubted that was the case. Occasionally, his vision would splinter into the sorcerous web the dragon used for his spells. Garin didn't ask what he did, trusting that it preserved their safety. Hoping it did, at least.

But throughout his explanation, Ilvuan was alert. Whenever Garin didn't explain a point to his satisfaction, the dragon made his displeasure known through an uncomfortable heat in his limbs. Garin could do nothing but grit his teeth and attempt another explanation while returning his own vexation to the Singer.

After he finished, they walked in silence for a time. Finally, Wren met his gaze. He wished he'd looked away; the anger in her face was hard to bear.

"So he lured you out there to bond with you? All this stuff about the eggs — that was a lie?"

Garin blinked, unsure how to respond. Ilvuan had become strangely complacent, especially considering the accusation. Panic rose that entirely belonged to Garin.

Is it true? he thought to the Singer. *Was it all a lie?*

"Garin?" Wren prompted him, her eyes narrowing.

He didn't know what to tell her, so he only waited for Ilvuan's response.

I did not lie. The dragon's words were soft but firm. *I did not know how advanced Yvärras' growth was. To develop her so quickly must have greatly taxed Yuldor's strength, and now seems a poor time for him to be weakened. I could not be sure she would ever be ready to prepare the hatching, or if the Pretender would make good on the promises he has made to her.*

Fury coursed through Garin.

But you always meant to inhabit me. It wasn't just to save us from Yvärras; you drew me to the hatching grounds to possess me!

Ilvuan's indignation grew to match his own. Their battling emotions, parallel yet opposing, wracked his body.

I never professed otherwise. Did I not tell you my intentions before my sister arrived? Did I not explain the necessity behind it? Do not accuse me of deceit, mortal! I have given what no ava'dual should!

Even as Garin fought to remain upright beneath the dragon's wrath, Wren's words lanced through him.

"Fine — ignore me like you always do. Hope your devil keeps you warm at night."

Garin fought his way through the mire of emotions as he looked after her. "Wren, wait!"

But she'd already turned away, going to the back of the group next to Ashelia and Rolan. Falcon eyed Garin with a mixture of fatherly hostility and male sympathy. Aelyn wore a mocking smile, while Helnor openly grinned.

"Lovers' quarrel?" the Prime ribbed.

Bristling, Garin only turned away, but he found Tal had materialized next to him. Unlike the other men, his old mentor's expression was devoid of judgment. Still, Tal looked as if he would talk, and that was the last thing Garin wanted just then.

Trying to make his wishes plain, Garin stared at the ground.

If Tal noticed his signals, he ignored them. "I know the look of a troubled man when I see one. If you need someone to talk to, Garin, I'm always here."

Even frustrated, Garin couldn't help but remember when he and Tal were in Hunt's Hollow, when he'd only known him as Bran. Back then, Garin had confided in him often while he lingered about the farm, avoiding chores and poking fun at Tal's methods for managing his hens. He'd told the older man his boyhood ambitions: the girls he would pursue; the achievements that would earn him his place among the stars. Garin told him that one day, he would join the Avendoran army like his father before him and become a captain, and he would hold all the Nightkin of the East at bay and keep his family safe — and Bran and Hunt's Hollow as well.

He hadn't known what the man's bitter smile meant then, how the injuries and guilt of the past dogged his days. He hadn't known how his words could cut with their innocent mentions of pretended heroics and forlorn loves and, most of all, his departed father. But Garin shared more in common with Tal now than he ever had in the five years he'd lingered about his farm. He understood what it was to have secret shames that no one else could comprehend.

Tal had inadvertently killed his father. But as Garin looked up at the man, still filthy with his own spilled blood, he couldn't help but see Tal as a second one.

But some things couldn't be spoken aloud. Garin lowered his gaze and only muttered, "Thanks."

They walked side by side through the wilderness, waiting for a dragon's shadow to sweep over them.

THE RUINS OF LETHYRANTH

AS ILVUAN PREDICTED, THEY REACHED THE CASTLE TOWN IN THE late afternoon of the next day.

Garin had been blessedly free of the Singer's intrusions the rest of the night and all that morning. Panic had fallen away, but his mood failed to improve. Always, the knowledge that Yvärras was right behind them dampened his spirits.

The night had been a chilly one, for Wren still refused to speak to him and had slept next to her father, to Falcon's delight. Garin had endured their whispers with simmering resentment until exhaustion finally pulled him into unconsciousness. He'd thought the morning after would bring forgiveness, but the hope proved too optimistic. Why Wren had to choose this moment to shun him, he didn't know, nor how he could patch things between them.

And you call me Mender, he thought derisively to Ilvuan.

The dragon's only response was a chilly silence.

It wasn't just Wren's behavior that grated on him; Ilvuan's treatment of him, too, was beginning to wear. If they couldn't cooperate while sharing a body, how could they continue to live together — for the rest of Garin's life, much less?

Not that he was likely to live for much longer.

Still, he worried about if they did survive. While facing Yvärras, time had been compressed, and just living until the next moment seemed a miracle. Now, however, Garin examined how the years would stretch out ahead of him. Could he endure living until his hair thinned and grayed with the dragon still in his head? How could he have a wife and children when he was as good as possessed?

Suddenly, he thought he understood what had made Wren upset. *She saw it before I did, saw how our lives would continue, if we live to see them.* It would no longer be just him and her, but Ilvuan as well. And the dragon would always share the closer intimacy with him, their very minds being intertwined.

Ilvuan rumbled with weary regret at his thoughts. Garin smiled bitterly. That, at least, was something they shared in common.

The dragon finally spoke as the burning rays of the sun lanced down from overhead. *It is near now. Ascend the hill and you shall find it.*

Garin looked to his right where a rise pushed the paltry forest upward. He saw no signs of ruins, but they had little choice but to trust that they would soon appear.

"This way," he called behind, having taken the lead. Without waiting for a response, Garin legged it up the incline.

How long have you been dead, anyway? He didn't temper his thoughts now, long grown tired of trying to placate the dragon. If Ilvuan wanted to get along, that was up to him.

Predictably, the Singer bristled. *I am not dead yet. Not while my spirit lingers.*

As you say, Garin retorted. *Now will you answer the question?*

The moment stretched, filled with Ilvuan's prideful anger. Garin thought he might receive a reprimand from the dragon such as he'd delivered in the past. He was in no mood to tolerate one and wondered if he could deliver one back, now that they shared one body.

To his surprise, Ilvuan's response was almost demure. *I do not know. A dragon's memory stretches long, but... It has been very long indeed since our cycles have renewed our* unae, *our spirits. Long enough that the past has begun to fade, and our mind erode.*

Garin felt a pang of regret that didn't wholly belong to the dragon.

I'm sorry, he offered.

Ilvuan seemed about to refuse the apology, then reluctantly exuded his acceptance.

Garin was hesitant to say more, but he had to press on. *I only ask because I want to know how likely we are to find shelter ahead. And can you truly hide us from Yvärras?*

For a time, yes. As for Lethyranth, I know it continued to thrive for some time after the Severing. It is possible something of it remains.

Lethyranth. He mulled over the name. *It was an Origin city, I suppose?*

Ilvuan rumbled in affirmation.

Garin imagined how it had been for the ancient people, living through the Severing. How had the Bloodlines been established? He knew what the Creed preached, yet he'd never thought of what the actual experience must have been like. Did they wake in their beds to find they'd changed? Was it painful? Origins were said to possess sorcery, which meant some must have lost it in the transition — including his ancestors, he supposed. It was strange to think that, at a point in the past, a man that would progenate his line had felt sorcery run through his veins, just as Tal did.

I wonder what they were like, Origins, he thought. *Were they so different from us?*

They were not and are not.

Garin perked up at that. *Are not?*

Scathing amusement cascaded from the Singer. *The Severing did not occur everywhere in the World, little Listener. Only across this land, the continent we ava'duala named Aolas, did the power of the Three extend. But on the far side of the oceans, Origins still reign.*

Garin marveled at that. For the first time in many days, he nearly forgot his aches and pangs. Curiosity awoke in him as it so often had in the days before his travels, when he was only a farmer's boy in a small, backwater town.

Could a ship sail to their land, then? he asked eagerly. *Could we one day meet Origins again?*

Ilvuan rumbled. *Perhaps. But it is a long way across the sea, Jenduit. So far that only a dragon could safely reach it.*

They lapsed into silence. Garin felt the shape of Ilvuan's thoughts clearly when he focused on them, so he knew the Singer remembered his own days of flight, and remembered, too, that he would never experience it again. To a dragon, flying was as natural as breathing, but filled with the pleasure of eating good food or coupling. There was nothing more a dragon was meant to do than fly.

Reluctantly, Garin released the last of his lingering resentment toward his mind's companion.

We've both lost something, he thought to him. *But maybe your loss is the greater.*

Ilvuan's rumble was gratitude enough.

Not long after, they reached a lane that led the way up the slope in switchbacks. Garin guessed it to be an old road even before Ilvuan told him.

Once, this was the path to Lethyranth, the Singer rumbled. *Mortals were like lines of ants, always streaming along it. Caravans laden with mortal goods would labor up the white stones to sell at the markets.*

Unbidden, images flashed before Garin's eyes, causing him to trip. For an instant, he'd seen the road as it had been. Individuals walked along it, humanoid yet unlike any known

Bloodline, tall and narrow-limbed and with eyes as odd as an elf's. Somehow, the Origins looked familiar, as if he had seen one before.

Probably just Ilvuan's knowledge seeping in, he told himself.

The unbroken road they traveled on was wide enough for two carts to pass by each other without touching. Everything — the shape of the pavers, the smoothness of the road, the dress of the Origins, the creatures that pulled the wagons, even the wagons themselves — was so foreign that it felt as if he glimpsed a different plane of existence. Yet at the same time, such a mundane scene could take place near Kavaugh, or Halenhol, or outside any town in the East Marsh.

The Origins had possessed sorcery and spawned all the known Bloodlines, but they were just people, likely with the same concerns and ambitions as those today.

Only, he mused, *their aims proved too great.*

Tal touched his arm. "Are you alright?"

Garin nodded. Unsure how to explain the vision, he said, "This used to be a road. An Origin road."

"Did it?" Tal frowned up it. "Could have left it in better shape, couldn't they?"

Garin managed a small smile.

They lapsed into silence only broken by the songs of small birds, the chatter of squirrels, and the crunch of their footsteps. As the quiet stretched on, the sense of doom crept back over Garin, stifling his excitement. He remembered what they fled from and why they sought the ruins at the end of the road. His hopes sank.

The wonders of the World's ancestors were forever lost. And soon, the few remaining in this era would be gone as well.

You can't give up, he told himself. *Don't admit defeat already.*

Ilvuan affirmed his thought with feverish resolve.

———

Garin was flooded with relief when the broken walls of Lethyranth emerged from among the twisted trees.

He saw signs of it being an Origin derelict at the first glance. The walls weren't like those of Halenhol or Kavaugh, which were bluff and thick, relying on their strength for impregnability. Lethyranth belied those principles. These were impossibly thin, just wide enough that a sentry could walk along the top. Their shape defied natural laws, curving outward from the base in a bulge. By Garin's limited understanding of military strategy, gained from overhearing talk of the battles to come in the Sun Palace, such a shape would make it difficult for an enemy to ascend by ladder or rope.

Whatever sorcery had formed the walls had faded over the eons, however, and the barriers had degraded with it. Thin as they were, they seemed like the base of a broken eggshell. Desiccated ivy crawled along the tawny stone. Towers had once been interspersed along the edge, but only disintegrating pillars remained.

They progressed through the opening where the gate had once stood, but had long ago been eaten away to rust. Catching his first glimpse of the town beyond, Garin was reminded of the Ruins of Erlodan. The blasted castle had captured his imagination, the setting fit for all the tales and legends he'd been weaned on throughout his childhood.

Lethyranth seemed another such place. No building remained wholly intact, and only a few kept their roofs. The hovels that remained resembled the city walls, their walls curving outward from the ground as elegantly as vases. Though fissures crawled through the rock, Garin detected traces of delicate carvings around where the walls met the eaves. These had been a people attuned to beauty, who sought to spread it through their domiciles, from all he could see.

Ahead, down a road that curled around a broken fountain and through the buildings like a drunken snake, rose the remains of the castle. It kept some of its height and dominance over the rest of the city, though its towers and halls hadn't weathered the ages any better. Its stone had a deep, scarlet hue to it that Garin imagined was once vibrant, but now was gray and dun. Hints of similar curvature as in the buildings below were evinced in the lean shape of the tower, the vaults, and the arched windows. Statues had adorned the stone, but most had been smoothed to lumps, obscuring the details painstakingly etched into them.

Garin looked around him, and everywhere his eyes fell, he saw ruin. Yet in the decay lay something mystical: a history untold, wonders unwound. He wished he could have seen them in their prime, but wasn't saddened by the loss, but awed.

If I wandered these places for the rest of my life, he thought, *I might be content.*

They were not always ruins. Ilvuan had remained as quiet as the rest of Garin's party during their entrance into Lethyranth. Now, he stirred, his presence filtering not just through Garin's mind, but throughout his body, even to the tips of his fingers and toes. Garin tried to stifle his discomfort, though he felt a moment's amusement at the dragon's dissatisfaction with the shape fate had forced him to adopt.

I know that, he thought back, with no small amount of sarcasm. *All ruins begin whole.*

The Singer only pulsed his presence. *See true — only then can you understand.*

Before he could return another biting reply, the World shifted before his eyes.

Garin stared around him, mouth agape. Through Ilvuan's memories, he saw the town as it once had been. Its buildings became intact, its streets bustling with Originfolk. The castle rose high above him, and the walls behind it. He turned and turned and still couldn't take it all in.

"Garin?" he heard Tal query, but he was too overcome to respond.

It was a silent procession; Ilvuan only lent his memories to

Garin's eyes. Still, there were sights enough to keep him occupied. The suggestions of designs he had seen in Lethyranth were alive. Curves and spirals and arches were everywhere, with a straight line hardly to be seen, even in the roads where they would have been practical. Gazing upon the Origins, he saw the same tastes reflected in their clothing. Many wore robes, the men included, all bright and colorful, though they ranged from flowing to tucked around them, as appeared to be the case for those of plainer garb. The hue of their skin ranged from alabaster to obsidian, all coolly toned, like precious stones. Inked into their features were runes, set in pale pastels of every color, so subtle that Garin wondered if they were tattoos or some strange hereditary trait.

And everywhere he looked, sorcery was alive. Glass orbs set atop bending poles glowed in colors that shifted every moment, lining the market streets and giving them a frivolous atmosphere conducive to commerce. The Origins themselves employed magic as easily as they walked. One woman, with a lined face and white hair, sat back on a chair that seemed too delicate and spindly to support her weight. As Garin watched, she summoned a flame to ignite a pipe, at which she happily puffed away. Elsewhere, a vendor used sorcery to raise a fruit with black, wrinkled skin, wind billowing under it. Glyphs were etched into doors and mantles and window glass, the last seeming to be a common luxury.

It was a glimpse into a realm lost, a land of plenty for all. And though he hadn't felt its absence before, with Ilvuan's regret in his body, Garin found it resonated with his own emotions.

A shadow fell over him, dark and broad. Fear struck like an arrow, and Garin cringed and cried out.

"Garin!"

Someone shook him, and the Lethyranth of old faded into vapor, then nothing at all. Garin blinked until he realized he stared into Tal's face, his eyes wrinkled in concern.

"I'm fine," Garin murmured. But his thoughts lingered on the last sight in the dream.

Was that a dragon? he asked Ilvuan. *Were you showing me an attack?*

Haughty mirth bubbled up. *Do you believe the* ava'duala *are so bloodthirsty? No,* Jenduit. *That was the natural order before the Three disrupted it. My kind and your ancestors lived in harmony.*

Garin tried to imagine a being such as Yvärras living among humans. Dragons were too proud and self-serving for peace with mortals, at least in his limited experience. That there had been an era where that hadn't been so baffled him more than all the other things he'd seen.

"You don't seem fine," Tal pressed. "Is it something about this place?"

He tried to focus on Tal's words and return fully to the World as it was. "No, it's not that. Ilvuan showed me something. He remembers Lethyranth from when Origins occupied it. And dragons as well."

Tal stared at him, a half-smile on his lips like he suspected Garin was pulling his leg. Their companions surrounded them. Aelyn and Wren seemed the most skeptical, while Falcon and Rolan were more captivated by the suggestion.

"Tell us about it," the bard prompted. "What was it like? What were Origins like? And *dragons*, you say? Leave out not a single detail!"

As Garin struggled to find a place to begin, Ashelia intervened. "We can discuss this later. For now, we must find shelter. Ilvuan said Yvärras is coming behind, did he not?"

The reminder of danger dashed away the last of the memory's hold. "Right," Garin muttered, then turned an inquiry inward. *Where should we go?*

Before Ilvuan could answer him, something shifted in the air.

At first, Garin thought another memory was seizing hold of him, but the World remained the same before his eyes. His gaze traveled to Tal, and seeing the older man's alertness, Garin understood what it meant.

"She comes," Ilvuan said, his voice calm and resonant through Garin's entire body as he spoke to the company.

Wren scowled at the Singer speaking, but even she was prudent enough not to pick at the scab just then.

"Yvärras?" Ashelia queried, though by her eyes searching the sky, she already knew the answer.

"Yes. And she is not alone."

Abruptly, Garin's senses changed. The strange network of bright lines segmented the World again, and the Worldsong filled his head. He tried to stifle his panic at the shift and wait for Ilvuan's guidance.

Look to the edges of the Lattice, the dragon commanded him. *Do you see?*

Garin turned his head, following the threads out into the distance. The individual lines faded into a white haze that obscured the buildings even a hundred paces away. But he saw something else amid the white, a purplish darkness slowly advancing upon them. A corruption such as he'd seen before.

"Yuldor," he breathed, blinking away the vision.

"Yvärras commands kael'dros *once more, the creatures you call Nightkin,"* Ilvuan said to the party at large. *"She seeks to drive us out of the ruins, or perhaps to trap us within."*

Tal drew his sword, *Velori* letting out a slight hum, then flashed their companions a wild grin. "Well, we wouldn't want to disappoint her."

Garin didn't feel his levity. His heart raced, and fresh sweat beaded his skin.

What do we do? he inquired of Ilvuan, hating how helpless he sounded, yet knowing the Singer was their best chance of survival.

"Follow me, mortals," the dragon replied to all, *"and we may yet survive."*

HUNTED TO HALLOWED HALLS

As they hustled through Lethyranth's streets, Tal stared at the matted hair on the back of Garin's head and clung to hope.

He trusted the youth deeply, trusted his loyalty and sound judgment. Garin had shown he was wise beyond his years and a good deal more prudent than Tal himself would ever be. So since the youth trusted this dragon, who had once masqueraded as a devil, he had to as well.

Or is he a devil pretending to be a dragon?

Tal wiped at the grime dripping from his face and blinked his stinging eyes clear. Now was not the time to harbor doubts. What other choice than Ilvuan did they have?

By the Singer's guidance, Garin led them deeper into Lethyranth with a specific place in mind: the town's temple. Tal had been as skeptical as Aelyn when the dragon announced their destination, particularly when looking at the surrounding buildings. Only the smallest had survived, all in varying states of degradation. That a grand temple, as the dragon made it out to be, had endured time's appetite stretched even Tal's ample imagination to breaking.

But when Garin set off, they followed. *"It may retain*

protections," Ilvuan had promised. *"For the Origins, sorcery was inseparable from religion, and their places of worship were the most heavily enchanted. Kael'dros plagued even them and were warded against. A Doashian temple is the safest place we can shelter."*

Kael'dros, Tal gathered, referred to what they knew as Nightkin, or close enough that the nuances hardly mattered. The protections would hold against them so long as they still persisted. He wondered about the other terms Ilvuan used, particularly the implications of "Doashian," but there was no time to inquire into it.

"And what about us?" Tal had inquired. "Will they lash out against descendants of Origins, or are we too changed to be recognizable?"

Almost, he'd seen the dragon in Garin's eyes as Ilvuan answered. *"We shall see."*

Now, they passed by collapsed walls and overgrown courtyards and statues worn to smoothness. Moving along the southeastern side of the city, they went around the derelict castle, which blocked the sun for the first part of their walk. Tal found the shadows unsettling, and his eyes flitted about as they grew longer with dusk's arrival.

But it was with his sorcery that he kept the closest watch. He felt the creatures that stalked them, the potency of their magic. They couldn't match him or Garin for power, their streams only as wide as Aelyn's or Ashelia's, yet there were five by his count. And Tal doubted they remained idle as they drew their net tight around them.

As they made their way around the castle, Garin slowed his jog and pointed, speaking between panting breaths. "There. That's the temple."

Relief washed through Tal as he saw the roof was intact. The temple was domed, following the same unlikely curvature as the other buildings of Lethyranth, but in a startling display of opulence, the dome was gilded with an opalescent sheen that remained even after the eons. He could only hope its defenses would prove half as impressive.

Tal worked a better grip on his sword, and it pulsed in his hand, an acknowledgment of the blood about to spill.

"Best hurry," he advised. "The first of our guests are near."

Garin's eyes met his briefly from beneath sweaty bangs, then he bobbed his head and turned, *Helshax* drawn and in hand. Tal hoped the blade would serve him well as he and the others followed.

They wound along the road, coming ever closer to the Doashian temple, until it finally loomed above them. Garin led them toward its rear, intending to enter from a back entrance, but they found themselves foiled by the collapse of the archway. The youth grimaced, then glanced back at Tal and the others. Tal knew it would be bad news before he spoke.

"We'll have to enter through the front." The youth ran a hand through his hair, slicking it back against his skull. "But we may have to fight to do it."

A wry smile perched on Tal's lips. Garin sensed the Nightkin creature around the other side of the temple as well, it seemed. It wasn't alone either, from what he could tell, though the sorcerous connections of the other beings weren't immediately identifiable.

"Are we sure we *want* to fight to get in there?" Wren demanded. "We'll be cornering ourselves." With her rapier drawn and the gold in her eyes swirling, she looked ready to run through the next person who crossed her.

Garin looked at her. "That's the idea," the youth admitted.

As Wren opened her mouth to argue, Ilvuan's voice broke into their minds. *"These creatures cannot be outrun. We must confront them from an advantageous position."*

Though Falcon's daughter seemed unsettled by the dragon's direct speech, her anger didn't dissipate. "It's not *advantageous* to get stuck somewhere Yvärras can easily burn us out of!"

"She will not directly intervene."

Tal exchanged a startled look with Ashelia. "Why not?" the Peer inquired.

Garin almost shook his head, as if Ilvuan were responding through him, but he masked the movement with a shudder.

"I have suspicions, but whether or not they are proven correct, our flight is the same. We must defend the temple as if it is your Sha'aval. *Our survival hinges upon this."*

A suspicion. Tal didn't like gambling the lives of those he cared for on a hunch. But as he met Garin's eyes, the youth nodded, and Tal nodded back.

Trust, he reminded himself.

"We'll do as you say," Tal said before Wren could protest again. He headed off objections from Aelyn and Helnor as well by saying, "Ilvuan knows Yvärras best. If we stand a chance of outplaying her, it is by relying on his insights."

Helnor nodded at once, the Prime Warder's mouth pulled back in a bracing smile. Aelyn only scowled deeper, but didn't speak against it.

"Fine," Wren said through clenched teeth, wrenching her head aside to watch for Nightkin.

Tal didn't have to look; he felt them nearby. They weren't hunting them, but lay in wait. As if anticipating where they'd go, the Nightkin had gathered in front of the Doashian temple.

"This way." Tal led now, *Velori* held low but ready, as he went around the corner of the temple to the alley that snaked next to it. His sorcery warned of what they would encounter ahead, the pulsing power as much an alarm as a wall horn. Yet as the creatures came into view, he halted in his tracks.

The foremost among them stood just under a hundred strides away, creatures he was all too familiar with. Their skin was as pale as rotting fish and peeled in strips. Even from the distance, he could smell the reek of their bodies, like the perfume of a day-old battlefield.

Tal's blood burned. A smile creased his lips. It had been too long since he'd faced down a horde of ghouls.

Silence, Solemnity, and Serenity, he thought, *thank you for finally giving me an opponent I know how to fight.*

But the ghouls weren't alone. Rising above them were Nightkin he knew of, but hadn't had the misfortune of facing before. Witikos, Magister Elis had called them long ago, when he'd forced Tal to study his dusty bestiaries. They were summoned creatures like ghouls, brought from whatever hellish plane such beings occupied.

In their own way, they were more terrifying than ghouls. Similarly skeletal, they were little more than flesh stretched across bones, yet with generous frames and hulking features. While their lower extremities were bare skin, their chests were covered in a thick, brown coat that transitioned into sharp spines. Their arms ended in clawed hands, and their heads were a blend of a wolf's and a moose's, sharp canines bared as they glowered at their party.

Even the witikos weren't the end of their enemies, for there remained the one burning with sorcery. Their summoner stood behind them, barely visible between the grotesque bodies. Yet seeing those arrayed before them, he knew its kind.

Nekrot.

The name alone made him want to spit. They were workers of magic, a form of Nightkin that could use glyphs to call or create ghouls and witikos. This ability allowed them to have armies at their beckoning, transforming a diminutive foe into one of the most dangerous they could face.

Behind him, Rolan stifled a whimper, and Tal glanced back at the boy. He was a pitiable sight, cringing against his mother's side, and seeing his state inflamed his blood. Tal met Ashelia's eyes and took her desperation as his own.

He turned back to the Nightkin. Steel settled into his smile.

"Hope you've kept your edge, old friend," he murmured as he advanced, and *Velori* hummed through his glove.

By his sorcery, he felt his friends coming behind, Garin the closest. Ahead, the ghouls and witikos, a score of them visible and more beyond, stalked forward; the ghouls on all fours, the witikos with a hunched, lumbering stride. Though Tal couldn't appear as much of a threat, he wondered if they had some attunement to sorcery and could see it burning molten hot inside him. It only made his smile widen, the anticipation in his chest gallop. He pressed forward faster.

His companions said something behind him, but the blood was pounding in his head, and his focus was wholly forward. *I'll kill you*, he promised the Nightkin. *I'll put down every last one of you.*

The ghouls leaped. The witikos lunged. The shadows writhed with sorcery.

Tal met and matched them all.

A DANCE WITH DARKNESS

The shadows struck first.

Snakes born of darkness rushed out, entwining Tal's arms, torso, and legs, and one finding his neck. Tal felt only a moment's panic before he retaliated. There were two nekrots hidden behind their army of deplorables. He cut them off from sorcery, and like ice suddenly melting, the shadows fell off of him and faded to dark mist.

By then, the ghouls had closed the distance and pounced. Tal dodged and whirled his sword as he summoned greater countermeasures. Those that hadn't leaped became rooted to the ground, the rubble at their feet churning downward, a greedy maw that swallowed any too slow to avoid its appetite. A dozen were consumed at once, decayed flesh and bone crushed into nothing.

Six others leaped at him, and these he met with steel. Their black eyes were wide with rage as they threw themselves forward, heedless of bodily harm.

Velori cut one straight through its chest, while another lost its legs and fell screaming to the stone. One latched onto Tal's back and sank sharp teeth into his sword shoulder. Shaking its head back and forth, it ripped at his flesh and whipped its seaweed-like hair against Tal's face.

He bellowed at the red-hot pain, then reached for another spell. Only after the dark strands shot out from the pooled shadows beneath the temple to enwrap his foe and drag it shrieking away did Tal recognize what he'd done: mirrored the nekrots' spells and made the darkness into matter.

A fresh smile broke over his face as he pushed healing energies into his burning shoulder. None of their weapons were beyond his reach.

His companions rushed forward to put down the remaining ghouls. Ashelia, her eyes whirling, shouted something, but the sorcery blazed too strongly within him to hear. Tal shrugged at her, then bolted forward, hoping to keep ahead of them.

His footing became uncertain where he'd told the earth to swallow the ghouls, but Tal danced across it to the waiting witikos. Six stood there, baleful gazes leveled at him. As one, they lashed forward with a speed that belied their size.

Tal retaliated.

The shadows churned behind them, black vines shooting out to wrap around his enemies and arrest their movements. Tal took full advantage of the moment, lopping off a hand here, a foot there. They were too big to get at anything more vital, but his attacks infuriated and maimed them.

He moved in for another strike when the shadows suddenly broke, and the dark coils writhed as they disappeared.

Yuldor's prick!

He threw himself back from a nest of claws. Lines burned along his legs, and he landed awkwardly, tumbling before regaining his feet. Tal staggered on the uneven ground, legs uncertain beneath him.

Others passed by him. *My companions.* And despite his resolution to keep them out of it, they engaged the enemy in his stead.

A broken yell erupted from Garin's throat as he charged into the monstrosities that had nearly torn Tal apart.

He didn't know their names, but Garin could discern their deadliness easily enough. The Worldsong howled with their corrupted spirits, the sounds falling into discord. Their grotesque features struck fear into him.

But Tal couldn't overcome them all alone.

Wren charged at the far left one next to him. Lament's golden runes shone brightly as he held it aloft to strike. The monstrosity faced them just as Wren jabbed at its leg. It struck with one spindly arm, and she was barely quick enough to dodge.

Garin struck then, and enchanted steel met Nightkin claws before *Helshax* rent the hand apart.

He went stiff with shock. Even with the spells bound to the blade, Garin shouldn't have been able to match the creature's strength, much less overcome it. Only in the moment afterward did he recognize he wasn't alone in the strike. Ilvuan was there, bolstering his will, the dragon potent even in spirit.

But the creature was striking again, and he was still within range.

"*Jolsh heks!*" Garin buffeted back the Nightkin with a hasty windshield as he stumbled away, the torn halves of its hand bending backwards with the spell. He fought down nausea as a second monster turned toward them. The first was far from defeated, and its eyes only seemed to burn all the darker for its pain.

The pair lumbered toward him.

Wren danced forward, drawing the attention of the injured

Nightkin. Garin threw out his hand to make use of the distraction.

"*Dord asht!*"

As the Worldsong swelled, a stone spire thrust free of the ground, impaling the hulking beast through the torso. A sound somewhere between a wolf's snarl and an elk's bugle loosed from its muzzle as it bent over the spire. Yet still, it wasn't finished. The Nightkin raised its horned head and leveled its baleful gaze at Garin.

Setting its massive claws to the ichor-slicked stone, it began to pull itself free.

Garin shot a glance at Wren, who was contending with the second witiko. Seeing she held her own for the moment, he set his mind to a different matter: how to defeat the horde. Injuries barely slowed them, and dire wounds weren't proving fatal.

Then it came to him: fire. They couldn't fight if he reduced them to ash.

Just as Garin resolved to try it, fresh shapes darted over the shoulders of the tall creatures. Though he should have felt more capable encountering an enemy he knew, panic seized his limbs as they darted with preternatural speed toward him and his party.

Ghouls.

He felt as if he were back in the halls of the Coral Castle, fleeing for his life, ghouls chasing after him. All his hard-won skill in swordplay and sorcery fled; he was helpless again, a scared farm boy who only saw the World in dreams.

But he wasn't that boy any longer. Though his mind remained frozen as the first ghoul leaped, Garin's body reacted, and *Helshax* sang a mournful song as it lopped off the head of a Nightkin.

Spinning out of the way, Garin felt he wasn't alone in his movements once more. Ilvuan was there, the dragon taking over when trauma had seized him. There was no time to protest; another ghoul charged, this one scuttling across the ground. With deadly cunning, it feinted left, then somersaulted right to lash at his sword arm.

By instinct or the Singer's guidance, Garin dodged and retaliated. Lament took the ghoul in the jaw, splitting open its mouth and spewing dark ichor over the stone. The creature spasmed for a moment, then went still.

Reprieve didn't last long. As Garin caught his breath, a dozen more ghouls crawled over and between the skeletal giants, several coming for him and Wren. His companions slaughtered them in droves, but they were too distracted to know their peril.

A spell! Garin thought desperately to Ilvuan as the Nightkin closed in. *Cast any spell!*

Instead of responding, he felt the dragon's presence well up inside him. A bloated sensation spread through his every facet. Garin could barely move for it, overwhelmed even as three more ghouls bore down on him.

The dragon roared.

The strange web Ilvuan called the Lattice flashed before Garin's eyes. In a moment, he felt an eternity of knowledge flood through him, and he understood. The violet on the lines that touched the Nightkin was contamination; it must be burned away.

The threads twisted around them. He felt the ripple of Ilvuan's power cascading outward, the World trembling where it passed.

As the wave of power crashed over the Nightkin, they spasmed, then crumbled into dust.

Garin stood on wobbling legs, Ilvuan's spell having taken a toll on his body. Yet their enemies were gone, reduced to motes, while his companions had been preserved. He didn't know what kind of spell the dragon had cast, but it seemed to affect the Nightkin alone.

There was no time to inquire further. Though the front

ranks had been vanquished, more ghouls and the horned giants were closing in from behind. Only for a moment would the passage to the temple be clear.

Tal was already running forward and shouting over his shoulder. "Follow closely!"

Glancing to make sure Wren was with him, Garin hurried after the man. The rest of their party had fared well, though Ashelia and Helnor sported several bloody scratches. Rolan seemed hardly to be breathing for fear, and Falcon carried the boy, though the bard looked only a measure more coherent. Garin fell in behind them, his breath coming quick as the monsters edged forward, slower than before, but implacable in their approach.

The temple stairs appeared to their right, and Garin took them two at a time as he sprinted after the others. The sanctuary rose above them, as whole as any building in Lethyranth.

Its portico shone with golden glyphs.

"Inside!" Tal roared, passing through the enchanted entranceway without a moment's hesitation.

Keenly aware of what was close behind, Garin pushed down his trepidation and followed the others.

The portico shadowed a tall archway where grand doors had once hung, but had long ago rotted away. Garin glanced at the glyphs glimmering on the stone two dozen feet above and gritted his teeth as he hustled after the others. Tal was nearly underneath.

Are you certain we won't trigger the defenses? he asked Ilvuan one last time.

But the dragon didn't answer before Tal ran across the threshold. Garin's breath caught, waiting for sorcerous fire to flash from nowhere and incinerate him. But nothing happened; his old mentor looked back, a relieved, weary smile stretching his lips. Either the traps no longer remained active, or they were sufficiently similar to Origins to pass through unharmed.

Hoping it was the latter, Garin pressed through. He tensed as he passed, convinced it would strike him even though it hadn't the others, but he, too, was spared. Letting out a held breath, Garin gasped for air.

But they weren't safe yet. With uncertainty remaining as to the temple's state, he had to be ready to fight again. He gripped *Helshax* tightly as he turned back to the temple entrance.

Wren stepped up next to him, weary but fiercely determined. "They'll work," she muttered, seeming to speak to herself as much as to Garin. "It has to work."

He wished he felt the same conviction.

Ghouls mounted the temple stairs. The traps still lay dormant. Garin was lightheaded with anticipation as he watched the Nightkin stalk slowly toward the archway.

One of the pale monsters moved ahead of the rest, then reached a clawed hand forward. Garin couldn't tell if it had crossed the threshold yet or not. He kept waiting for something to happen, and nothing did.

The doorway flashed.

Rolan cried out as their party was momentarily blinded. Garin blinked rapidly, and as his vision recovered, he squinted at the archway.

No ghoul had crossed into the temple interior. Only a pile of ashes remained where it had stood before.

"Well," Falcon said with a strained laugh. "At least we know the glyphs work."

"For now," Aelyn added snidely, though he lacked his usual bluster.

Despite the assurance, they all remained facing the doorway as they crowded closer together.

"Now what?" Wren demanded. "We're trapped in here with no way out. What good did that do us?"

Garin tore his eyes away from the ghouls prowling at the doorway to examine their surroundings. As the gloomy light from the doorway and through the yellow windowpanes was barely sufficient for them to see by, he summoned a werelight to brighten the area.

The nave hadn't entirely been spared from degradation. Mustiness hung in the air. Where wooden pews might have stood, there were only mounds of dust. At the back of the temple, the stone and its enchantments had given way and the building collapsed in on itself. Windows of cracked glass promised more potential ways in if the Nightkin were intelligent enough to find them. Cracks ran through the walls, further compromising the edifice's integrity.

Hardly the bastion we were hoping for.

Turning back to his companions, Garin found them staring at him. With a start, he realized why.

"I'll ask him," he said reluctantly.

But before he could form a query, Ilvuan answered their unspoken question for all to hear.

"We are not trapped here, but protected. We must allow Yvärras to muster all her forces and bring them to us. Only then might I turn them back."

"Turn them back?" Helnor frowned at the ghouls beyond, pressed tightly together like a nest of rats. "I don't think that's likely now."

Tal looked more certain. "You cast a spell back there that turned the Nightkin to dust. And back in the Ruins of Erlodan, you commanded the draugars to end themselves. I'm guessing you have more tricks up your sleeve, in a manner of speaking."

Thin amusement trickled from the dragon. *"Yes. It is a command that I am uncertain I may give more than once, given my vessel. It must wait for the last moment, when Yvärras is sure she has conquered and the odds we face appear hopeless. But we will prevail, mortals. I will preserve you."*

Something washed over Garin, a comforting sensation like shade extended on a hot summer day. *Or like being tucked under a dragon's wings,* he realized with a start. He wondered if the others felt the same thing, or if Ilvuan consoled him alone.

The archway flashed again.

Garin jerked around as fresh ashes spread across the nave's floor. A second ghoul had thrown itself at the barrier, and a third looked prepared to. He closed his eyes just in time for the spell to burst against his eyelids, even then blindingly bright.

They seek to break the wards, Ilvuan confirmed, his words once more for Garin alone. *They tremble under their attacks. After so long, there is only so much protection they can provide.*

How long until the wards fall?

Perhaps they will last the night. Likely, they will fail long before.

Garin's stomach clenched.

"We might have a few hours," he said to the others. "So we'd better rest while we can."

He followed his own advice, slumping to the ground and leaning against a nearby broken stone. Garin laid *Helshax* beside him and he watched the archway from the corner of his eye. Waiting for the moment when they must fight for their lives again.

THE OLD ONE

IT HAD BEEN A LONG TIME SINCE TAL FELT FRAIL.

He sat next to Ashelia, splayed over the stones at the rear of the temple, where the inner wall had fallen in a dusty heap. Rolan curled into his mother's side, trembling, silent tears trickling down his cheeks. Tal understood the boy's fear. They'd faced many perils in their journey, yet none looked as horrific as the half-rotted ghouls and the nightmarish witikos. No doubt the darkness that gathered with the sun's departure held worse terrors still.

But he could no more protect Rolan from his fears than he could defend the rest of the party from more tangible dangers.

The days of flight and incessant sorcery and a complete lack of sleep were finally taking their toll. He could barely keep awake now that they had a moment of reprieve. Every spell had its cost, and the price of his seemed to rise with each casting. He was parchment thin, his skin a shell that impossibly held his body together. He felt as insubstantial as a ghost. It wasn't like when *karkados* ravaged his body, but more like the erosion of a riverbed, its flooded waters spilling beyond its banks. He couldn't last much longer.

Yet Tal clung to the sorcery all the same.

Can't rest, he told his weary body and mind. *Not yet. Not while they're in danger.*

He doubted they'd ever be out of harm's way. Until his quest reached its end, Yuldor and his minions would threaten their lives and well-being. He couldn't stop the perils chasing them. He could barely keep himself alive.

He only hoped he'd last long enough.

Tal closed his eyes and leaned his head back. Sleep crept at the edge of his consciousness, lulling him toward its depths.

"Witikos," Ashelia murmured, interrupting his descent. "Helnor and I saw them once early in my training as a Warder. I had hoped never to see them again. How many more devils can be summoned from the hells of the Named?"

Tal shrugged.

"At least a dozen." Predictably, Aelyn put forth his opinion, though with less insistence than usual.

Tal didn't bother inquiring further. *We'll deal with them as they come.*

Their company fell silent. Only the sniffling from the elf boy and the distant noises of the Nightkin filled the empty nave. Awake again, Tal kept watch on their enemies through his sorcery. He mulled over if he could untangle all the glyphs binding the creatures to the World before they broke through, but it took only a few moments of investigation to dismiss it as futile. The effort and time required wouldn't be worth it, especially not when he felt the sorcery sucking at his bones already. No; there was nothing for it but to wait and hope.

His thoughts wandered away from their preservation and into idler territory.

"Doashian," he muttered under his breath.

"Did you say something?" Worry edged Ashelia's voice. He wondered if she thought he was fading, his strength giving out.

Would she be wrong if she was?

He mustered the energy to speak louder. "I said 'Doashian.' It's how Ilvuan labeled this temple."

"*Doash...*" Her apprehension filled the word. "Like the light you see at the World's center."

"Seems too close a match to be a coincidence."

Tal suspected the dragon was listening through Garin's ears. The youth had slumped onto the rubble nearby, drained from his own efforts of killing the Nightkin. Tal wondered at the spell that had finally cleared the way. He'd seen nothing like it before, and not even through his sorcerous perception could he fully understand what Garin had done. It felt as if he saw only the effects of it, like staring at a murky surface, while the true magic lay beneath. It had been the same feeling as when the blinding fire had burst from Garin's hand when the Singer first took full residence beneath Garin's skin. He wondered how, with as much mastery of sorcery as Tal had achieved, there could be so much he didn't know of it.

Dragon magic, he thought with a small shake of his head. *As if we needed another mystery.*

He hadn't expected Ilvuan to answer his implied query, and so Tal startled when the dragon's deep voice shoved between his thoughts.

"*The Origins held the* Doash *as the highest ideal, one toward which they aimed their lives.*" Ilvuan didn't bother hiding his bemusement. "*They knew it to be their source of sorcery, and believed it as well to be the Heart of the Old One, their highest authority.*"

"Their god, then?" Tal queried. His gaze alighted on Garin for a moment, then looked away, some part of him still unwilling to accept the dragon that lay within.

"*The Origins did not believe in deities as present mortals do. They accepted that the Old One, what you might know as simply "the World," possessed sentience, though in a way different from mortals. But as the source of sorcery and life, of good and evil, of mortalkind and the* kael'dros *both, they saw the Old One as deserving deference and respect, and the* Doash *within him was a sliver of divinity made material.*"

The highest ideal. Something about the phrasing bothered Tal. "How could the *Doash* be an ideal? It's a place, or a thing, at least. Things cannot be ideals."

"Yet it offers the same as the Pretender's promises. Peace. Comfort. Rest. You have heard these whispers, Heartblood. Do they not seem ideals to you?"

Tal felt Ashelia's eyes boring into him.

"They do," he muttered. "But that's the thing with ideals: they can never be reached."

Amusement bit into Tal's mind. *"Those of the* Doash *could if you yielded to them."*

Before Tal could respond, the temple's walls trembled.

He was on his feet, his sword in hand, before he detected the source of the disturbance. The temple portico had been steadily under assault since their sheltering within it. Now, it seemed the nekrots' plan was working. The stone was cracked, and the light from the glyphs shone with feverish brightness. Tal recognized the signs well: the last, desperate attempt of the sorcery to continue before it flared out of existence.

"Form up!" Tal shouted as he edged in front of his companions. "Rolan, Falcon, stay behind the others!"

"As if I'd dare be anywhere else," the bard muttered, his mutinous reply undermined by his voice cracking.

Ashelia stood to Tal's right, rapier drawn. Helnor took up his left. Tal sensed Aelyn behind him, ruffling around for spell components, judging by the sounds. Wren and Garin stood beyond Ashelia, similarly prepared.

They looked a ragged and worn bunch. He hoped they would be enough.

We have to be. I have to be.

He couldn't rely on Ilvuan's word alone for salvation. He'd do anything he must to secure their safety. Anything at all.

A silent snarl curling his lips, Tal breathed in sorcery until it burned.

More ghouls threw themselves at the barriers now, and

with increasing ferocity, yet each one still dissipated in a cloud of dust. They appeared endless. Tal wondered just how many nekrots there were to summon such an army of Nightkin. The standard conjuration was seven rounds of five, and he couldn't imagine any single nekrot managing more than two conjurations. And then there were the witikos to think of, the details behind their summoning murkier in his memory.

But in a way, it didn't matter. He'd still have to kill all that came before them, down to the last one, to keep his companions safe. Then he could take care of the nekrots.

As another pair of ghouls broke against the wards, the stone groaned again, and a chunk of the archway fell away. Tal ground his hand into *Velori's* leather grip. The waiting was worse in some ways.

Worse than your friends dying? a part of him mocked.

The glyphs flashed yet again, but this time, the flare lasted a full second.

Then, as one, their light faded to nothing.

The next ghoul to fling itself forward flew onto the rubble within. For a moment, it seemed confused by its averted fate.

Then it scrambled to its feet, turned its gaze upon them, and charged.

The other Nightkin were close behind it, shrieking in eldritch voices. Tal added a yell of his own to the din. The pale monsters streaked across the floor, rapidly closing the distance.

One leaped. Tal struck. A head rolled.

It would only be the first of many.

MASTER OF THE KAEL'DROS

THE ENEMY WAS EVERYWHERE.

Garin cast spell after spell against the horde. He thrust stone up from the floor, impaling and crushing bones. He called fire into being from thin air and incinerated rotten flesh. He summoned wind to push back the furious tide.

It wasn't enough.

As he cleaved a ghoul's collarbone with Lament's enchanted edge, Garin spared a glance for his companions. Wren stuck her rapier through a ghoul's eye even as she buffeted back a second with a fire hex. Ashelia was a whirlwind, spinning through the enemy near where Falcon stood in front of Rolan, the bard sheltering the boy with his body, a knife trembling in his hand. Helnor protected his House-brother, hacking off the hands of reaching witikos as Aelyn summoned a blaze nearly as mighty as Ilvuan had back in the hatching grounds. Where the blue-white fire burst, Nightkin went down in flames and did not rise again.

Then there was Tal.

His torrent of sorcery never ceased, nor did his blue-glyphed sword. Ghoul and witiko alike fell to his assault of steel and spell. The temple floor shook and swallowed foe after foe, while winds blasted at enemies so they struggled merely to reach them. The storied man lopped off heads and opened guts and tore through entire torsos.

And still, it wasn't enough.

They were slowing, all of them, but their adversaries kept coming. Where one was killed, three more replaced it. The nekrots, as Tal had named the Nightkin summoners, seemed to have an endless supply of minions. Despite the company's skill and determination, sheer numbers would inevitably drag them down. Garin's head pounded with the maddening beat of the Worldsong, and he felt stick-thin from all the sorcery he'd cast.

"*Keld thasht!*" Garin shouted, throwing out his hand to send forth a wide plume of flames. The seething mass of ghouls in front of him parted, but three were caught and fell shrieking to the stones.

Two more ghouls leaped forward, their lipless mouths parted to show their sharp teeth set in their rotten gums. He worked *Helshax* between the ribs of one, but the other rammed against his arm, wrenching his shoulder and throwing him back against the rubble.

Breathless from the fall, Garin struggled to eke out the words for another casting as he pushed back at his enemy. The ghoul's claws scratched along his arm, sending fiery pain up it and making his head pound harder still.

"*Jolsh heks!*"

The wind spell sucked the last of the air from his lungs, yet it pushed back the ghoul just enough for Garin to bring his arm around and ram the blade through the Nightkin's neck. Black blood streamed down the golden runes before he levered himself up and cleared the blade.

Staggering to his feet, he expected yet more ghouls to be leaping for him. Instead, he saw Tal had increased his wind spell's intensity so that their enemies could barely move forward. He turned his head toward the older man, wondering how he could keep up such a storm.

Garin looked just in time to see a witiko smash its clawed hand into Tal and send him flying into the wall.

Tal!

He stared for a long moment before realizing the winds Tal had summoned had died. Whirling, Garin saw four ghouls bearing down on him. Hopelessness choked him as he raised his sword once again. His arm, torn and bleeding, felt as if it would lose all its strength with the next blow.

He sent a plea inward. *Ilvuan! You can't wait any longer!*

The dragon echoed his anxiety, but resolve underlaid it. *Not yet, Listener. The nekrots approach. They sense the end is near. Only when they are close can I give my command.*

Garin didn't have time to argue, for the enemies were upon him. "*Jolsh forshald!*" he cried out, desperate for the wind bindings to hold back two of his opponents while he dealt with the other two. A brief glance showed that Wren, the closest of his companions, would be little help, for she was taking on two ghouls of her own.

He adopted the Form of Stone for its stability and strength as he hacked at the ghouls. Their numbers were enough to overwhelm the small party, and the nekrots drove them into a frenzy.

The first ghoul took his blow against extended hands, and *Helshax* sliced halfway up its arms. Yet even as it screamed with pain, the ghoul threw itself over the weapon, tangling it so Garin couldn't pull it free. The second ghoul leaped atop him, only stopped from ripping off his nose by Garin releasing the sword and punching it in the side of the head. He couldn't avoid its grasping claws, however, as they raked through his clothes and into his flesh.

Bellowing, the Worldsong clamoring in his head, Garin seized the ghoul's head in his hands, trying all the while to maintain the wind shield against the two other ghouls scrabbling to get at him. With its slimy hair between his fingers, he wrenched it around as hard as he could, trying to use their momentum to break its neck. The ghoul was too wily, however, and it twisted midair like a falling cat. Somehow, as they slammed to the floor, it ended up on top of him, and its legs rose, clawed feet ready to disembowel.

Before it could, its head jerked sideways, and its body slackened. Only as ichor dripped into his eyes did Garin see the blade that had pierced its skull.

Gasping, he threw off the Nightkin and gave Wren a grateful look. She barely had time to nod before spinning back to take on the two ghouls freed from Garin's spell. Others were held at bay for the moment, for Aelyn seemed to have ignited a wall of flames between them and most of the Nightkin.

Garin once more rose to his feet, mumbling "*keld*" to finish the ghoul still clinging to *Helshax*. The spell didn't even heat the blade as the golden glyphs shone brighter and absorbed the magic.

A high-pitched scream jerked his head around.

A witiko stood among his companions. In its great clawed hand, it clutched a terror-stricken Rolan.

Garin went cold. He couldn't move for fear of provoking the Nightkin into crushing the lad.

It was hopeless. He could do nothing to save the boy.

Ashelia stood before it, her back to Garin, desperation radiating from her. Helnor, Aelyn, and Wren were too far away to do anything, and Falcon, who rose bleeding from the rubble, was capable of even less.

The witiko's cruel features twisted. Its skeletal arm flexed. Its hand squeezed.

———

There was no time to lose.

Tal was battered and broken. He'd lost consciousness for a moment when he'd been unceremoniously tossed among the rest of the temple debris. But his sorcery wouldn't allow him to lie prone for long. With it burning undiluted in his body, he almost felt a phantom as he rose from the stones, a revenant returned to life for one final task.

That task became clear as he raised his head.

He saw the witiko. His stomach clenched at what it held.

Rolan.

Fury was all he needed. *Wind*, Tal thought, then threw himself forward as a gust carried him aloft. With as mighty of a swing as he'd ever taken, he chopped at the witiko's arm as he barreled toward it.

The Nightkin bugled as Tal flew by. With a rapid series of spells, he drew Rolan toward him, clutched the boy to his chest, then slowed their descent just enough to roll to a jarring stop on the floor.

Rolan clung to his tattered shirt, utterly lost to sobs. Tal held him and stood, *Velori* raised toward the witiko. His companions had promptly taken care of it, however, knocking it over. Ashelia's face was spattered with its dark lifeblood as she hacked its head apart, her rage plain through the gore.

With the threat repressed, Tal's injuries asserted themselves in full force. He crumpled as agony washed over him. Rolan tumbled to the ground next to him.

He wondered if his back was broken, and only sorcery enabled his movements. He wondered if he could continue fighting.

Some legend you are, a part of him goaded, trying to stir him back into action.

Tal raised his head to see Ashelia rushing toward them. Kneeling, she swept Rolan into her arms, cradling him and rocking him back and forth like he were a babe. The boy sobbed into her chest, black blood smearing his face.

Tal looked back toward the wall of flames and the Nightkin

just beyond it. Aelyn's spell wouldn't last much longer; already, he could see the sorcery that fueled it dying. He tried summoning the resolve to bolster it, but he was drained to the core. He had nothing left.

A voice thundered in his head, splitting it open.

"It is futile to resist, little mortals! You have fought well for your kind, but the kael'dros *will overwhelm you."*

By Yvärras's resounding words alone, Tal nearly came undone. She flew overhead, beyond the roof of the temple, the power radiating from her making her plainly visible to his sorcery. Perhaps she'd tired of her tests and had come to bring them to an end.

But another voice in his head rose in challenge.

"Ever have you underestimated me, Yvärras. Even in mortal flesh, I remain an ava'dual.*"*

Tal turned his head, as heavy as a boulder, toward Garin.

It's up to you now, lad.

The time had come.

Garin stared across the wall of flames and the heads of the Nightkin. In the shattered temple archway, a new enemy had appeared. It stood taller than the ghouls, but only barely. Its features were largely hidden by the dark armor layered over its body. The armor looked to have seen better days, and in many places, it was rent and twisted with old attacks repelled. In its metal glove, it clutched a wooden staff, atop which sat a glass orb filled with glittering iridescent gemstones. Sorcery sang from the being, and as it turned its helmed head, it seemed to stare over the melee with cold calculation.

A nekrot. Garin knew the overseers of the Nightkin had finally arrived.

Aelyn's fire barrier was dying, and ghouls leaped across its coals, heedless of seared flesh and singed hair. Even with Rolan saved and Tal alive, despair clutched at Garin's chest.

Yet he raised Lament and prepared to meet their charge. At the same time, he pleaded once more.

It's time, Ilvuan! The nekrots have arrived!

The dragon's presence surged back into his limbs. Garin felt his strength renewed, and even his many wounds seemed to hurt less.

They have, Ilvuan agreed. *And we will turn them away.*

Before the dragon could do anything, however, Yvärras spoke.

"It is futile to resist, little mortals. You have fought well for your kind, but the kael'dros *will soon overwhelm you."*

Her words trembled through his limbs. Only Ilvuan kept Garin upright before them.

"Ever have you underestimated me, Yvärras," Ilvuan responded, his voice lacking her power, yet still rising in challenge. *"Even in mortal flesh, I remain an* ava'dual.*"*

Yvärras' amusement seared Garin's mind.

"Show me then!" she mocked.

Garin felt the sorcery building within him, greater than ever before. The Worldsong expanded in proportion, swelling both higher and lower in pitch. All of reality became suspended between. His vision shattered, broken by the white filaments of dragon magic. *The Lattice.* He saw the complex web twisting around him, winding tighter and tighter, energy building to bursting.

Ilvuan released the tangle and sent his power rippling forward.

"FLEE. FLEE, KAEL'DROS, *BEFORE YOUR MASTER."*

It was like the eruption of a dozen volcanos, the breaking of a hundred tidal waves. Garin felt himself being shaken apart by the ferocity of the command, even as it issued from the being dwelling inside him. Sorcery cascaded out like an earthquake's aftershocks, traveling along the sorcerous web in sparks.

And wherever it touched Nightkin, they turned and fled.

They couldn't resist it. Mindless panic overcame them, twisting their ghastly faces. Every one of them scrambled for the temple's exit, trampling and clawing each other in their desperation to leave.

Garin swayed where he stood, sagging with exhaustion as the peril faded.

Yvärras spoke again. Her tone lacked some of the derision of before, though it wasn't devoid of it. *"So you are not entirely mortal yet. Very well,* Alärthoras. *I will allow you to live for now. We shall see how long you can cling to your power."*

With that, Garin felt her harsh song grow fainter as it faded into the sky. He stared at the ceiling and wondered why the World's Protectress had once again spared them.

Garin sank to his knees. So intense was his relief that he barely noticed the hard impact of the stone or the pungent stench of the dead Nightkin.

You made them leave, he marveled. *You repelled them all.*

Ilvuan seemed as weary as he, yet he radiated pride. *I did.*

How?

Garin didn't expect an answer and was surprised when he received one.

The ava'duala *are masters of the* kael'dros. *I command them, the same as Yvärras does in the Pretender's service.*

He only vaguely understood what had occurred, even having lived through it. Somehow, Ilvuan had manipulated the Lattice to make the Nightkin leave. He supposed that was all that mattered, but for one other thing.

Can you do it again? If Yvärras finds us?

It is not a question of "if," Jenduit. *She will find us, again and again. She may even come with the morning.*

Garin wanted nothing more than to sprawl over the

temple's stones. Even Wren shaking his shoulder couldn't make him lift his head.

Sleepily, he inquired, *Why didn't she finish us off instead of flying away?*

It serves neither her aim nor Yuldor's to kill us — at least, not to kill Heartblood. At worst, she weakens us so Heartblood cannot contest the Worldheart. At best, she tests us for her own purposes.

He wondered if he was missing something. His head felt stuffed full of wool, too much so to make heads or tails of the dragon's logic.

Why does she test us?

To discover if we are enough to accomplish our aims. To see if we can unseat the Pretender.

Garin shook his head. *If she wants us as allies, she has a funny way of showing it.*

I believe she is undecided in what she desires. Two routes lay before her: to side with Yuldor or to work against him. For now, testing us serves both purposes. If we can endure all she sends our way, she may consider us worthy of her aid. If not, she may either deliver Heartblood to Yuldor, or destroy him and deprive the Pretender of his prize.

Ilvuan paused, then continued in a softer rumble. *Whichever choice she makes will be irrevocable. This is why she tarries, for she judges what will be best for her aims and for all the* ava'duala *and the World, as the Protectress should.*

Garin smiled bitterly to himself. *You sound as if you admire her, yet you defy her.*

A swirl of emotions grazed over Garin's thoughts.

Yvärras is older and wiser than you can comprehend, Jenduit, the dragon stated. *Her mind may seem callous or contradictory, but I do not see her as either. As the Protectress and leader of our people, she weighs matters that will influence the lives of millions both living and still to be born. But yes, I defy her. Wise though she is, I believe I know which option she must choose, and we cannot afford to delay anymore.*

Garin sighed. *I don't know that I can take many more of her tests.*

The Singer radiated a stirring warmth that filtered through Garin's body. *Yet we must.*

Still, it seems a funny thing to weaken someone who you might want as an ally.

Impatience lashed through Garin, though Ilvuan's reprimand remained light. *Yes. But it is as I told you: weakening us now serves both her purposes. Uncertain of us as she is, she is unwilling to do anything that will appear as if she defies the Pretender. But when we endure, she will understand the time has come, and she will join our insurrection.*

Garin sighed, his head bent so low his chin nearly touched his chest, wondering if he dared hope for another uncertain ally.

FLEE

FOR THE FIRST TIME IN DAYS, TAL SLEPT.

He'd tried to avoid it, had insisted he could stay awake. But from Ashelia to Falcon to even Aelyn, he was argued down. Only Garin didn't urge him to rest, and that was because he'd fallen asleep himself.

Before anyone slumbered, however, there had been matters to attend to, the first of which was leaving the desecrated temple with all haste. Even as the bodies of the Nightkin fell to dust with the defeat of their summoners, the memories were too painful to remain there. Instead, they huddled between the ruined buildings of Lethyranth under the night sky, their bedrolls providing scant comfort against the lumpy rocks beneath.

Yet Tal fell unconscious like he were made of stone himself. And as he slept, he drifted down, down into the core of the World, to the same place he always went.

He only noticed what he did when he'd traveled most of the way to the *Doash*. By then, it seemed a shame not to continue. Tal descended, passing the multitude of gray, black, and white beings. He wondered, as he had before, who or what they were.

Spirits? Devils? Or some other creature not covered in Elis' bestiaries?

When he reached the bottom of the stream and entered the chamber where the *Doash* lay, the idle thoughts fled. For where the cavern had once been flooded with a brilliant white, now it was occluded by darkness.

Tal stared at the corruption. It didn't touch the *Doash* itself, but had spread far beyond the channel to the Worldheart. Yuldor was expanding his domain, both above and below. And he was doing so quickly.

Why? he asked of the World's Womb, though he knew he would receive no answer. *Why expand now?*

Because of you, Thalkunaras.

In his despair, he hadn't noticed the black form swimming up next to him. He recognized her presence at once, and though he knew he shouldn't trust so easily, relief flooded through him.

The Night, he greeted her.

She radiated her approval in a way beyond words. *So you have returned.*

I haven't slept.

No. There seemed a great sorrow behind the denial. *Slumber is a luxury for mortalkind.*

Am I not still mortal?

The amorphous dark shape before him lacked expressions, yet it seemed to cock its head. *Perhaps not entirely.*

Not knowing what to make of that, Tal turned back to the corruption and the blinding *Doash* beyond.

What can we do? Surely, he'll claim victory soon. When Yuldor takes the Womb...

They will not touch the Doash. *It is beyond their power to claim.*

That piqued Tal's interest. *They?*

If she noticed his implied question, the Night didn't answer it. *It is beyond any being's grasp. But that does not mean there is no danger. Sorcery can be dammed from the World. Life will perish.*

This is why you must awaken, Thalkunaras. You must come to Ikvaldar. And there, we will fight our enemies.

Tal felt himself rising, quicker and quicker. Abruptly, he sat up, caged in flesh once more.

Daylight had edged into the sky. His body ached, and not only from the night of sleeping on the hard ground. He turned his head to see most of his companions still restlessly sleeping. Only Helnor was on watch, slumped over his knees as he stared at the ruins.

For a moment, Tal turned his interaction with the Night over in his head, then shook free of it. He would tease answers from his mysterious ally when he next slept. For now, there were many more things to worry about.

Pulling on his boots, Tal picked his way over to the Prime Warder. They sat in silence for a long moment, listening to the surrounding stillness. Tal was glad to hear at least one bird had returned after the Nightkin had defiled the place, but was less pleased when a biting midge apparently had as well.

He studied Ashelia's brother from the corner of his eye. Though he was far from unused to adversity, Helnor Venaliel didn't seem suited to this life. He hadn't blossomed into his best self like Garin and Wren had. Even Ashelia and Rolan could keep a grip here in the East. But whether it was from duty or fear, the Prime hadn't been the same since leaving Elendol. He was somber instead of teasing, his eyes down-turned rather than filled with delight. Like Falcon, danger muted his natural jubilance.

Or perhaps he mourns.

None of them could forget the fate that had befallen Elendol. Split by civil war and treachery, it was now under Yuldor's sway, just as Avendor had once promised to be. Tal only hoped that with a reprieve from the Extinguished, the kingdoms might part ways with Yuldor. No sovereign truly wanted to be under the foot of another, even a god.

Ambition, after all, was ill-served by piety.

The silence stretched on too long, so Tal broke it. "Beautiful country, isn't it, the East?"

Helnor snorted a laugh. "The local beasts are my favorite part."

"Remember the time you took me hunting Nightkin? Back when I didn't have even a score of years put together?"

The Prime eyed him. "I remember."

"You told me then, 'Don't lose yourself to the hunt. There's always a way back.'"

Helnor's mirth faded like seeds in a strong wind. "Words to live by."

Tal gave him a small smile, clapped him on the shoulder, then levered himself to his feet. "And spoken by a wise man. Don't you forget them."

He walked away, leaving the Prime to his pondering.

Their own hunt was far from over.

It wasn't long before the others rose and were ready to leave. Falcon proved the slowest among them. Though the bard had done little fighting the night before, he was even less suited to the travails of the East than the others. The promise of a long flight while being harried all the while further deflated his spirits. Garin had informed them this would likely be the case, passing on Ilvuan's warning: that Yvärras was testing them, and it wouldn't be the last they'd seen of her and her minions.

"Leave me," the bard moaned as Tal helped him strap on his knapsack. "I have no lute, no songs, nor even two hands. What good am I to you?"

"You cheer us up," Tal countered drily, then gave his oldest friend a friendly slap on the back before moving to the front of the company.

He could almost hear his companions' rumbling bellies as

they set off from Lethyranth. Circumstances had forced them to reduce their portions by half, for their food wouldn't last long, especially as it seemed unlikely they'd be able to stop to hunt or forage. The forest grew thicker around them, and beasts occasionally made appearances, hares and squirrels and birds made curious by their passage. Tal resisted the urge to go after them, pulled at the straps of his pack, and marched on.

The quiet sounds and pleasant smells of the woods almost lulled him into complacency, but he kept a careful watch with his sorcery, probing the surrounding miles for any sign of enemies. None emerged that morning, nor during the afternoon. As evening bled into the sky, he dared to hope they might go the entire day without an attack. He wondered what that would mean. Was Yvärras allowing them to rest before attacking again, or lulling them into letting down their guard?

Or perhaps she's lost track of us. A smile curdled on his lips. Even one as adept as he at self-delusion couldn't believe that hope.

But it struck him as not the wildest notion to pursue. Tal fell back from the front of the company, responding to Ashelia's questioning look with only a nod back at the member of their party who walked farthest apart. She raised an eyebrow, as if to say, *Good luck.*

Tal matched his pace to Aelyn's. When the mage ignored him for several strides, he cleared his throat. At last, Aelyn glanced over, the colors in his eyes spinning faster.

"It's been too long since we chatted," Tal said lightly.

"Yet never long enough," the mage responded through clenched teeth.

"I have a question for you."

"It is my dearest desire to answer it, always."

Tal smiled and ignored his friend's vitriol. "Is there any possibility you can mask our movements? That is, do you know of spells to hide from a dragon?"

Aelyn's scowl deepened. "If I did, do you think I would not

have already done so? No, Harrenfel; I know nothing of drag-ons, and even if I did, I doubt my sorcery could outwit them."

Tal didn't needle him further, sensing how that fact rankled his pride. He needed results at the moment, not amusement. *Though Silence knows I could use both.*

Leaving the mage, he resumed his place at the front of the group, where Garin had ventured as well.

"Same question for you," he muttered to the youth. "Any chance Ilvuan has more tricks up his sleeve?"

Garin frowned, eyes filled with worry. "Not this time."

Tal sighed. "Too much to hope for, I suppose. Thanks anyway, to both of you. We'd be dead without you."

He clapped Garin on the shoulder, and the youth gave him a crooked smile back.

Tal hadn't yet released him when his blood prickled. Tal halted, feeling with all his senses for the disturbance. His gut clenched as he anticipated the only thing it could mean.

Yvärras's minions had come at last.

As he searched harder, he thought he felt what had alarmed him. But it made little sense. *Something* stirred, but in slow drips. Stranger still, the sorcery led into the trees surrounding them.

"What is it?" Ashelia had come up beside him and touched his elbow. "Nightkin?"

Before he could answer, movement blurred in the corner of his eye.

Tal grabbed Ashelia and pulled her to the ground even as he lashed out with a swift spell. He registered their assailant to be a tree branch a moment before his wall of wind crashed into it, snapping the smaller branches and cracking the bough so it hung askew from the tree.

Falcon gaped at the unruly tree. "Did that just—?"

The bard didn't have time to finish the question. Like a powerful storm swept through, all the trees were moving, limbs lashing and leaves shivering in the air. Tal felt sorcery flaring within them, but it didn't seem to have a source other than the trees themselves.

They can't be alive — can they?

There was no time to wonder. Trees leaned toward them, branches lashing out. Tal responded with spell after spell, buffeting back and breaking their strange assailants. In some ways, they weren't intimidating opponents, for they lacked mobility and flexibility. Yet each branch served as a club, and they had hundreds of them, all attempting to batter their company into pulp.

But even trees yielded to fire.

"*Kald!*" Tal called, and where he looked, trees burned. Soon, the surrounding area was aflame, and the writhing trees seemed almost to shriek with pain. Smoke choked the air, and Tal breathed into the crook of his elbow as he led the others forward.

Something edged into his awareness, a presence other than the trees. At once, he saw the connection it shared with them, the sorcerous rivulets running back to it. A wolf's smile appeared behind his arm.

"This way!" he shouted at his companions as he stumbled forward. Roots tried to trip and ensnare him, the trees unrelenting even as they perished. Tal evaded them where he could and burned himself free where he could not.

When he reached the edge of the flames, he turned off the path and into the woods, where he'd sensed the sorcerer.

As swiftly as it had appeared, their assailant fled.

But it was within Tal's range now. Calling upon the earth, he urged it to swallow the enemy magician and hold it in place. The gambit appeared to succeed. Tal ran forward, dodging around trees that hadn't been animated, and only glancing back once to ascertain the others followed.

He came around an oak, then laid eyes on their attacker.

At first, Tal thought he was mistaken, for an ugly hog was the only thing the ground had sucked down into it in swatches of hardened mud. But with the beast swollen with sorcery, he knew the truth. This strange beast was their attacker.

Kneeling before it, Tal kept a wary eye on its tusks. "Reveal yourself, creature."

As he brought his sorcery to bear, a spell fell shuddering over the creature, and the image of the hog dripped away. In its place remained a strange fey creature that took a moment for Tal to place. It was small, only four feet high and lithe of limb. It wore no clothes, and its skin resembled bark even more than a sylvan's. Its eyes were wide and ringed like a tree's core and of a striking amber hue. Its only hair to speak of was a crown of woven green branches.

"What is it?" Wren asked with equal measures of fascination and disgust.

Helnor answered first. "A leshi — a shapeshifter and forest mage. They like causing all manners of mischief. You can run into a few of them around the outer edges of Gladelyl."

"I wouldn't call what just happened 'mischief,'" Garin pointed out drily.

"No," Tal agreed, staring into the leshi's eyes. "That was a good deal more. Leshi! Can you understand me?"

It was unlikely it had ever spoken the tongue of any Bloodline. Yet Magister Elis had once informed him that some Nightkin had a natural affinity for language. He guessed that, through an attunement to the Worldtongue, a rudimentary grasp of language was often instinctually gained.

He wasn't surprised when the forest sprite slowly tilted its head in acknowledgment.

"I don't want to kill you," Tal continued. "If I free you, will you attempt to kill us again?"

As he asked, Tal shook his head, hoping to encourage the leshi in the proper direction. He was pleased when the fey creature followed suit, but didn't yet release it.

"Do you serve a dragon? Yvärras, Protectress of the *Ava'duala*?"

At this, the leshi trembled, like leaves in a stiff breeze. It was enough of an answer.

"You must run far, far away. She may be less kind than us if she finds you, for I fear she disapproves of failure. Do you understand?"

When the leshi tilted its head again, Tal released his casting and backed away. The others followed suit, widening their circle enough to allow the Nightkin to escape. The child-like creature darted its startling eyes around at each of them, then scampered off beside Tal and into the woods, running on all fours like the hog it had masqueraded as. Tal stared after it until it faded from sight, listening to the crackle of the flames until he extinguished them with a thought.

"Tal the Merciful, they'll call you next," Aelyn observed snidely.

"You know, that's not a bad idea." Falcon had a thoughtful expression. "You could use a counterweight to your martial image."

As the mage turned away with a huff, Tal only gave his companions a weary smile. "Come. That was only a minor test. I'm sure Yvärras won't let us off easy next time."

They continued their trek, and Tal's thoughts turned again and again to the matter. That the dragon did test them, he had little doubt now. The leshi had posed little danger to sorcerers such as themselves. She hadn't sought to test their power this time, but something else.

Was she looking for mercy?

He shook his head. It was impossible to guess her mind; only Ilvuan might illuminate her game further, and answers from the Singer didn't appear to be forthcoming.

Settling his pack more comfortably on his shoulders, Tal did the only thing he could. He continued on.

ENDLESS

THE NEXT SEVERAL DAYS BROUGHT ENDLESS TURMOIL.

Garin had never been afraid for so long. The encounter with the leshi in the forest had only been one of Yvärras' many trials. That night, as Garin slept next to his companions, an attack of the strangest kind awakened them. Memykes, Tal later called them. The name hardly fit the reality. They were as big as wolves, but shaped like beetles, with brown carapaces lined with spines and mandibles eager to rend flesh. Worse still, their exoskeletons were all but impervious to sorcery.

In the end, they dealt with all twenty creatures in the only way they could: entrapping them with spells of stone and wind, then dismembering them at the joints, the only vulnerable places on their bodies. Garin wasn't able to pack up camp quickly enough with their limbless bodies still wriggling in the surrounding forest.

But they found no relief afterwards. The next day, when they emerged from the trees into the vast Faernor Grasslands, another set of Nightkin stalked them: chimeras. Even Garin knew of these, for they were infamous for their occasional invasions of the East Marsh. Chimeras were as grotesque as they were deadly, a blend of lion, serpent, eagle — and, occasionally, dragon.

"They rarely travel in packs," Tal informed them as seven of the beasts surrounded them. "Can't see what would make them start now."

But the answer was obvious. Yvärras toyed with them yet again.

Garin was nearly breathless the entire battle, but in the end, they vanquished them as well. While Tal kept them back with a storm, Garin and the others took them out one by one. The three that had miniature dragon heads on various places on their bodies proved the most challenging, for their flaming attacks came close to penetrating Tal's barriers.

They received no rest after the battle, but pressed on. After another night of interrupted sleep and days balancing on the edge of death, Garin dragged with exhaustion. Only Ilvuan's presence gave him any measure of strength.

Now she tests our will to survive, the Singer told him. *We must show her we are capable.*

Why? Garin complained. *Why must she try to kill us?*

Ilvuan spread his reprimand throughout Garin's limbs in a prickling heat.

We do not have another choice. And remember the reward should we succeed. Yvärras would be a powerful ally.

Garin had his doubts about that and didn't bother hiding them. The dragon only let him stew, settling back into the recesses of his mind.

Early the next day, the hum of wings was the first sign that their brief reprieve was over. Fighting down despair, Garin craned back his neck to discover familiar creatures bearing down on them. Quetzals and cockatrices both descended from the sky. There were a hundred or more of the flying serpents, while the cockatrices numbered a dozen.

Once, when they were first leaving Hunt's Hollow, such a

host would have swiftly overwhelmed Garin. Now, with the Worldsong howling in his ears, he sent the quetzals plummeting to the earth with a wide ice casting, then buried them to suffocate beneath the dirt. Ilvuan's approval hummed through his limbs, a sensation that filled him with elation despite his best efforts otherwise.

Meanwhile, the others contended with the cockatrices. Tal sent them spinning and squawking with a twister. Helnor and Wren attacked them with bows and flaming arrows, while Aelyn and Ashelia wielded spurts of sorcery. Tal met any attempts to dive at them with wind walls or stone spires. In the end, only two remained to fly away.

Even after their victory, few smiles were shared. All bore wounds that Ashelia's nightly mendings couldn't entirely heal, and grime layered their clothes and skin. Worse still, Garin was feeling hollowed out from their regimen of spare rations.

But he clung on to their one hope for reprieve. Haudden lay ahead.

What aid they might find there, Tal didn't say. Yet Rozana had declared her allegiance to their cause, and she was widely held as the leader there now. Garin dared to hope it would be enough. He wondered if he should feel guilty, bringing Yvärras' wrath upon the minotaur town, but there seemed little other choice in the matter. Their fellowship needed food and rest if they were to make it all the way across the meadowlands to ascend Ikvaldar. And war would come soon enough to Haudden, if it hadn't already found it.

So he told himself to ease his guilt.

After the quetzal and cockatrice attack, they ate the last of their stale hardbread and tough, salted fish, the scraps sufficient to make Garin's stomach growl louder. Rolan cried over it, though he tried to muffle his sobs. Falcon, hunched over his knees, looking like he wanted to weep as well. Ashelia employed every trick she knew to ease their pains, but her materials were running low and she lacked the herbs that would have been most effective. Tal employed his sorcery to sustain them as well, casting spells of vitality such as they'd used on their mounts before. Though Garin appreciated the burst of energy, the man scarcely looked like he could spare it. His eyes were sunken, and through the gaps in his much-torn clothing, Garin thought he looked thinner as well.

Tal Harrenfel was fading before their eyes, just when they needed him strongest.

But they had no choice but to accept his aid and continue on the next morning. So long as they hadn't veered too far off track, Haudden lay just ahead.

Just a little farther, he coaxed himself. *A bit farther, then you can rest.*

Hours and miles passed. The sun glared down with increasing intensity. To their right, mountains loomed in the distance, the Valanduali Range they'd crossed to first enter the Empire. No fires burned that he could see; the Emperor's armies weren't yet ready. That blow, piled on top of the others, made Garin feel like a ghost, drifting through the World, forever lost. Only Ilvuan inside him kept him grounded and focused on their task.

We will survive, he told Garin. *We will prove Yvärras wrong.*

But another mountain rose above the rest, mocking the Singer's assurances as it reached impossibly high into the sky. *Ikvaldar*. Its rounded peak was green where snow should have spread. A curtain of clouds hid the bulk of it below, a permanent fog that seemed to come from the mountain itself.

So long as they could see Ikvaldar, there would be no forgetting what awaited them.

Hope became smaller in Garin's chest, threatening to go out like a candle in a strong gust. But finally, the monotony of the plains was interrupted. Garin squinted at the distant blots, hardly daring to believe it could be true, but Tal confirmed it a moment later.

"Haudden!" The older man burst out in a laugh. "Can you believe it? Haudden at last!"

The sight of the town put a spring in their steps, regardless of their blistered feet and worn muscles. If all turned out as expected, Haudden meant safety, even comfort. Haudden could give them an undisturbed night of rest. Garin almost felt faint at the thought of it, of releasing the strain required to endure their endless trials.

Just a little farther...

Ilvuan's amusement at his self-encouragement was like an itch under his skin. Doing his best to ignore it, he pressed on.

Soon, the town came close enough that Garin could make out its details. The town wall was made of stacked stone just taller than Garin, stone being more plentiful than wood on the Faernor Grasslands. Fields surrounded Haudden, the plants green and foreign to his eyes. The crops looked ripe enough for a harvest, violet vegetables plump with fresh growth. Garin breathed in. The aroma of fertilizing manure, healthy plants, and churned dirt — it almost made him feel back in Hunt's Hollow. All that was missing was the faint stench of the swamps that permeated the town.

Nostalgia made his eyes warm. Garin blinked rapidly and tried to ignore Ilvuan probing at his thoughts. Somehow, the dragon seemed intrigued by the sentimentality.

The gentle memories were banished as they reached the town's perimeter. Following the sharp-tipped wall, they found a gate facing the eastern side, where two minotaurs stood guard. Neither wore an identifiable uniform, nor much beyond trousers. Their broad, hairy chests were marred with scars. One had a black-and-gray coat and a horn lopped off. The other's coat was tan, and he sported an old wound through his snout that hadn't healed well. They glared at Garin and his party with beady, dark eyes as the company approached, big hands brushing over their weapons.

Garin wanted to weep with frustration. Even with all they'd suffered, their troubles went on.

The minotaur missing a horn grunted something in the common Darktongue, and Tal responded, his tone far more genial than the other's. By the Imperial's scowl, Garin sensed he wasn't amenable to his old mentor's supplication. The second sentry became involved in the discussion now, withdrawing a double-headed axe from his belt and clenching it in both hands.

Garin's gut tensed, and his hand settled on *Helshax's* scabbard, readying to pull the sword loose. He pushed away weakness and readied himself for violence, even though he didn't know the cause or reason. It was beyond his control.

Before it could come to blows, however, a piping voice intervened.

Garin stared in astonishment as a gnome waddled up to the gate and stood before the minotaurs, her chin lifted boldly. More astonishing still was the fact that he recognized her. His gaze slid over to meet Wren's.

Temmy? he mouthed to her, and she responded with an incredulous shrug.

He recognized her from their time down in Low Elendol together, though the gnome had changed for the better. Her clothes were just as loud as they'd been then, green and blue running in stripes down her dress, but it was her stance that struck him now. Even before two minotaurs that could tear her apart, limb for limb, she didn't quail, but spoke boldly and with an unshakable sense of authority.

Whatever she said had a distinct effect, for Cloven Nose reluctantly replaced the axe at his hip, and Missing Horn stepped back and jerked his head inward. Hopeful again, Garin followed the others after Temmy.

"What happened?" he asked Helnor.

The Prime wore a frown as he glanced back at the sentries.

"There seems to be some sort of power struggle here, and the gnome is on the opposite side as those two."

Garin's gut ached. *A power struggle.* It was the last thing he wanted to hear when they only sought shelter for the night. But given everything else they'd encountered in the Empire of the Rising Sun, he should have expected it.

CLASHING HORNS

Tal gazed around Haudden and was surprised to find he felt at home.

The town differed in many ways from Hunt's Hollow. Too few trees populated the streets, and the denizens were mostly minotaurs, so even normal activities like milking cattle seemed a strange sight. Yet the distinct feeling of town life swept over him so that he had to smile.

"Rozana welcomes you, friends!" Temmy piped up as soon as they were out of earshot of the gate. "She wondered if you would come through."

"Wouldn't want to disappoint." Tal lowered his gaze from the surrounding town to smile down at the gnome. "You look like you've kept well."

"As well as any can just now." But though her words were grim, her tone was light. Tal wondered if it was the place of authority she evidently occupied or the return to Imperial lands that had her so peppy. Either way, he was glad to see it. Temmy had been a hog out of mud in the Mire of Elendol. Here, she seemed as bright as a mangrove bloom.

"You saw earlier we are not all are unified," Temmy continued. "Rozana will explain when she visits you later. For now, you can rest in the inn."

Tal frowned. "The inn? As in, the only inn?"

The gnome's smile spoke volumes.

He sighed. *Nothing says "town" like a single inn.*

Haudden didn't stretch far, and they reached the nameless inn a short while later. Tal looked up at it apprehensively. It was like no inn he'd stayed in before, lacking evidence of separated rooms. Instead, it appeared to be one circular chamber, large and tall enough to boast a loft. A mocking smile claimed his lips.

Tal Harrenfel, born to dirt, now turns his nose up at a barn. How you've risen in the World.

He'd never been too good for lice-infested straw in the past; best not to begin now. Though, as his eyes slid over to Ashelia and the dismay in her swirling eyes, he wondered if all of them were so ready for further privation.

"In here!" Temmy called as she threw her weight into the door to push it open.

Tal stepped in after the gnome and looked around. As suspected, the building stretched out in one room, with a ceiling separating a loft that pressed low overhead. He wondered how minotaurs could traverse it without catching their horns on the rafters, for he himself felt a compulsion to duck, and he was hardly taller than most.

A firepit lined with stones occupied the center of the room, and a flume was built through the ceiling to funnel out the smoke. Yet a haze still filled the room, for it wasn't entirely unoccupied, and many of the minotaurs, gnomes, and humans who sat within puffed on sweet-smelling pipes. Tal was reminded of his days in the Avendoran army, where most every soldier had a vice or two, and for many, it was the pipe. No chairs spread out over the space; instead, visitors sat cross-legged on roughly woven rugs of erratic patterns.

Temmy led them to the fire, which burned low at the

moment. Tal saw a few pots simmering gently and smelled stew from at least one of them. His stomach rumbled mightily, and he smiled apologetically at their host.

She returned a nervous smile. "Hungry, perhaps?"

"Starving," Wren answered at once.

"Help yourself to whatever you see. All are welcome at our hearth."

"Thank you, Temmy." Ashelia inclined her head, her hands making the circular motions of respect among elves. "Perhaps there is some way we can pay back your kindness."

The gnome waved her hands before her. "Not with silver! Rozana welcomes our allies. Please, make yourselves comfortable. She will be by soon to explain all."

"And baths?" Aelyn spoke up, sounding annoyed that he had to ask.

"Perhaps you didn't smell that he needs one." Helnor gave his House-brother a sly look, which was returned with rancor.

Temmy flushed and gestured toward the far wall. "Of course! A tub is behind those curtains. And for clothes... I shall see what I can find." She eyed them skeptically, Tal most of all. He could hardly blame her. Though his sorcery had mostly healed his wounds, his clothes weren't so fortunate, stained with old blood and ichor and hanging off his frame in shreds.

"Thank you, Temmy," Tal said. "I'm sure you're up to the task."

The gnome looked less certain of that fact, but she only bobbed her head and departed.

They ate, then each bathed in the tub behind the curtain. The women went first, and Tal volunteered to go last, suspecting he would dirty the water the most. When he stripped off his clothes, wincing where they'd gummed onto sealed wounds, he gazed down at the brown water with twisted lips. An idea came to him.

"*Alm.*" With the cantrip, he guided the filth in the tub up to the surface, then into a bucket for scooping water next to the tub. He beamed down at the water, now almost clear. *Or close enough*, he mused as he stepped in.

The water didn't remain clean for long.

As promised, Temmy supplied them with clothes, and though the homespun tunic hung long and the trousers itched horribly, Tal was grateful for them all the same. He buckled *Velori* back on, then cinched his belt tight around the billowing tunic.

"Is Rozana on her way?" he queried when he was dressed. His companions were spread out beside the firepit, glancing at the other occupants of the inn. No doubt he wondered as they did just who they shared this chamber with and of the factions splintering the minotaurs. More pressing was the knowledge that Yvärras and her Nightkin still loomed beyond the squat stone walls. Even rival sentries deserved a warning of what horrors might come for them.

Temmy winced. "Rozana sends her apologies. Negotiations are difficult to get away from at the moment, but she will come soon."

Tal guessed from the light filtering in through cracks in the walls that daylight was fast disappearing. As they'd suffered no attacks that day, a sense of foreboding filled him. Surely, Yvärras wouldn't give them a full day's reprieve.

"Don't make it long," he said, then sat and accepted another bowl of stew from Ashelia.

He had worked his way through a third helping by the time the door to the inn opened to a familiar face. Tal wiped his mouth with the back of a hand and greeted the minotaur with a smile.

"Rozana!" he said genially. "It's been too long."

Their brief compatriot nodded solemnly in return. She had changed even in the weeks since they'd fled Kavaugh. Her brown-and-white spotted coat was ragged and her shoulders were bowed. Yet it seemed authority suited her as well as it did Temmy, for there was an aura of pride in her movements that had been missing in Elendol. Tal remembered her diatribe on freedom and a people's government, and he was even more glad she carried on.

The others chorused their greetings, all except Aelyn, who sat as stiff as a board. Falcon was especially enthusiastic in his salutation, no doubt feeling a special bond with the minotaur for having discovered her in the Mire. Tal wondered if he would compose songs in her name as well as his own.

Silence knows she's done enough to deserve one.

"Welcome to Haudden, all." Rozana nodded at the other patrons of the inn and received acknowledgments in return. One minotaur even raised his mug to her and drank to her health.

So she commands respect among her followers. It boded well, even if she struggled to impose her leadership.

When Rozana neared, she sat cross-legged on a rug and spoke in a low voice. "I am sorry you could not come at a more settled time. Temmy has told you the situation?"

"Only briefly," Tal replied. "But in days such as these, no time is more settled than another."

"This is truth." The minotaur scanned the group, bovine eyes wide and unblinking. "You arrived from the east, I am told. Does that mean you head west now?"

"And south." Tal let the direction speak for itself.

Rozana's expression remained as composed as ever. "You still mean to challenge him."

"There's no other way."

The minotaur didn't affirm if she shared his belief. "No fires light the Valanduali, nor have I reports that the armies have yet gathered. You must wait."

"There's no time, Rozana," Falcon spoke up. "We're being hunted!"

The bard's voice had risen with his words, perhaps overused to dramatic pronouncements. Tal winced and saw the other patrons glancing their way and muttering among themselves.

"Falcon, please." There was a reprimand in Ashelia's voice.

The bard flushed, but his eyes were ablaze with his golden tendrils. "It won't exactly be a secret when Yvärras flies over Haudden, will it? Better to know now!"

Rozana's expression darkened with each revelation.

"Flies?" she queried quietly.

Tal exchanged a glance with Ashelia, then sighed. "I suppose we have some explaining of our own to do."

In broad strokes, he informed her of the relevant parts of their journey: how a dragon had returned to the World, and how she commanded the Nightkin to hunt them. When he finished, he expected Rozana to question what they'd been doing up on the northern coast in the first place, but her concerns proved more practical.

"We cannot kill a dragon alone." Rozana glanced around the room, as if to be doubly certain no dragon slayers hid among their stock. "But neither can I turn you away."

"She may not attack herself," Tal offered. "Only on the first occasion did she directly intervene. Since then, she's let her minions soil their hands instead."

"Nevertheless. You saw at the gate that Haudden is divided." The words seemed to pain the minotaur, and she shifted as if hoping to find a more comfortable position.

"What happened?" Falcon asked, as hungry for stories as Rolan had been for food.

"It is not what has occurred, but what has been occurring. You may know that I overthrew the Emperor's original fief lord and established Ledfold as an independent state. When my followers and I were driven into exile, power-hungry bulls stepped in to rule as they saw fit. They carved up the plains into herds and established themselves so firmly as to resist when Emperor Zyrl placed a new nomarch in charge. I have been appointed by the people as the nomarch's replacement, but the bulls have yet to accept it."

Rozana turned her head aside, her placid expression like a cow staring at the moons. "I cannot fault them. I rejected the Empire's authority as well. But we cannot remain divided. Dialogue is the only way to plow a path forward." She looked back at Tal. "My people will be united. And I hope to accomplish this by the time the signal fires burn."

Tal mulled over Rozana's words. He knew little of her background: if she grew up poor or rich, or how she came to foster her ideas for an independent country. Yet it seemed impossible that conviction alone could be responsible for her leading a rebellion against Zyrl, much less Yuldor. Respect couldn't be a strong enough foundation by which to rule.

Then he remembered what she'd said back in the Sun Palace throne room. *Rule by the people.* Was this what she meant? It seemed such a feeble construct compared to the sacred lineage of kings and queens. Yet he couldn't help but hope she could make it real.

Their host rose, looking even wearier than before, yet no less determined.

"I must return to continue the negotiations. Rest here for the night. My people will keep watch."

Tal wondered how much strength could be behind that watch considering all the forces arrayed against them. But he smiled and nodded, hoping she didn't see his doubts in his eyes.

After Rozana left, Tal turned to face the others. "Best make use of what time we have. I'll go out and collect supplies. Anyone who wishes to accompany me is welcome."

"I'll stay," Helnor said. "Someone must watch over our packs. Garin, Wren, would you stay as well?"

Garin looked surprised, while Wren nodded. It spoke to all they'd endured that even she was too tired to explore.

Falcon, Rolan, and Aelyn also opted to stay, so Tal turned to Ashelia with a raised eyebrow.

"Just you and me then," she murmured.

He nodded, pleased by the happenstance. With more energy than he felt, Tal rose to his feet and offered his hand.

"May I escort you to the markets, Lady Peer?"

With a wry smile, Ashelia took his arm.

A TOAST AMONG FRIENDS

GARIN BARELY CAUGHT THE CLAY FLAGON THAT HELNOR THRUST into his hands.

"Drink up!" Helnor grinned as widely as if they were back in Elendol. "This might be our last opportunity!"

He, Helnor, and Wren sat down in the main chamber with the other patrons of the nameless inn. With Tal and Ashelia gone on their errands, their company had split off to make good on the sparse time for diversion. At the far end of the room, Falcon and Rolan were speaking together, the older man apparently wishing to confer some bardic knowledge upon the boy. Rolan seemed amenable to it, for he nodded with his eyes wide, the silver in them spinning. Aelyn had remained in the loft, sorting once more through his spells components and continuing to translate Koax Mraaj's journal, which he'd kept in case it held further revelations about Paradise.

Garin eyed the liquid in his cup. It was a foamy, white substance that didn't quite smell like spoiled milk, but certainly resembled it. He exchanged a glance with Wren, who had received a stoup of her own. She shrugged and sniffed experimentally at it, then made a face.

"What is it?" Garin ventured.

"*Kalmys!*" The Prime Warder laughed at their expressions. "Fermented donkey milk — at least, I think so."

With no reservations to his dubious knowledge, Helnor tilted back his cup and took a long swig. When he righted it, foam covered his upper lip.

"Ah, it's quite refreshing! Try it, try it — may as well squeeze one pleasant experience out of our travels!"

Dubious, Garin took a sip. It tasted much like it smelled: foamy, creamy, with a slightly sour taste and the bite of alcohol. He tried not to show his reaction, for the other patrons of the inn were watching them, no doubt amused by the foreigners sampling their local drink.

"Well?" Helnor prompted.

"I like it," Wren declared as she wiped her mouth. "And I like what it'll do to my head more."

The Prime clapped her on the shoulder, nearly spilling her drink. "That's more like it! Just keep your eyes on the reward."

Part of Garin questioned the wisdom of inebriation when a dragon and her horde of Nightkin were close behind. The greater part of him wanted to forget the entire business, and the dragon dormant inside him along with it.

He went in for another drink and sucked down half the mug.

"Ah, you two continue to impress me." Helnor looked fondly at them, silver tendrils spinning in his eyes. "Were you elves — or full-kin elves, I should say — I'd recruit you to be Warders."

Garin raised his eyebrows. "A human Warder would be a first."

"As would a *kolfash* one," Wren said bitingly. "I thought you didn't like half-breeds like me in Elendol, much less women as Warders."

Helnor held up his free hand as he took another swig before answering. "Even elves can change their opinions.

Gladelysh traditions are long-seeded, and I have adhered to them my entire life. Yet my sister began to uproot them, and you two have further done so."

Garin's astonishment grew into something else. "You weren't just joking, then? If we were back in Elendol, and peace reigned, you would take us on as Warders?"

The Prime nodded. Though a smile played on his lips, his eyes were solemn. "I would. You have everything it takes to be protectors of the queendom. Skill. Wisdom. Loyalty. Determination." He ticked off the qualities on his fingers, then waved them away. "Gladelyl would be lucky to have you."

Garin met Wren's gaze, and he found a desire blazing in her eyes that he hadn't expected to feel himself. *A Warder.* He'd given little more thought than before as to what might come after their journey's conclusion. But as Helnor dangled this vision before them, he yearned for it. Elendol had felt foreign at first, the customs of the elves strange. But before everything had gone wrong, he'd felt more at home there than he ever had in Halenhol, or even Hunt's Hollow, in some ways. He'd never imagined living there before.

But what if we did? Wren and I together?

Before he could follow the thread farther, Helnor spoke again. "I suppose it wasn't you two and Ashelia alone that changed my mind. There was a woman once, a half-kin with human blood, as most are wont to be. I met her in Low Elendol, when I was visiting a tavern there — always more entertaining than the establishments in the upper boughs, I tell you! I saw her there, drinking with her companions, and was struck dumb. Her hair was red as sunrise, and her skin was smooth, and her eyes were as brilliant as the sky. I shouldn't have been attracted to her, with her having mixed blood and being Lowkin — but the heart does not know bounds, eh?"

He gave the two of them a teasing smile, to which Wren only rolled her eyes.

Garin smiled and took another swallow of his *kalmys,*

wondering if Helnor had somehow snuck in a few flagons before theirs. He was speaking looser in front of them than he ever had before.

"I approached her that night," the Prime continued, "and in the weeks afterward, we had more than one dalliance..."

Garin grinned, while Wren made a face. "Why are you telling us this again?" she protested.

Helnor sighed, suddenly deflating. "Because, though we shared a passion for one another, I didn't allow it to continue. It was not worthy of a son of House Venaliel to be tramping about with a half-kin lowborn. Not that my mother, then Peer of our House, ever knew anything of it. Eiliyan — that was her name — did not take my ending it well. I suspect she avoided the places we had frequented from then on. I tried finding her once or twice, but never hard enough to succeed."

They were silent for a long moment before Helnor drank down the last of the liquor in his cup and sighed again.

"Ah, but I regret that now. Given the chance, I'd do things differently." He met Garin's gaze, and it took all of Garin's self-control not to look away. A mistiness had settled in the Prime Warder's eyes that was unsettling to see.

"You're doing right," Helnor told him, then looked at Wren. "Both of you are. That's the benefit of youth, isn't it? Correcting the mistakes of those gone before you."

Wren's mouth screwed up to one side. "Come, Helnor! You're not too old to fix your own mistakes — don't pass them off on us! We have enough of our own to handle." Her eyes flickered over to Garin, the gold tendrils spinning.

As he met her gaze, Garin's thoughts floated freely, his head already buzzing from the *kalmys*. He wondered if she would still want him now that he and Ilvuan were one. He wondered if, when this was all over, they would part ways or remain together.

He wondered if she loved him.

They hadn't said the words. He hadn't asked her to, and

she'd never seemed to need them. Given the chase from the hatching grounds, it had been too tender a conversation to have, to make no mention of Wren seeming to hate him half the time. While they stayed in the palace, though they often enjoyed each others' company, he'd been absorbed in exploring the Worldsong, while she'd trained with the palace guards to exhaustion most days.

But as she matched his look, his worries settled. He and Wren had never been ones to fret over what they meant to each other. They were a pair, and they had been since Halenhol. And there was something in her eyes that conveyed she felt the same way.

There were some things that were understood and couldn't be put to words, at least not words that didn't trample and destroy them. Like how a flower picked must eventually die.

Yet he knew what bloomed in that silence. He believed its roots went deep enough that, even if the shadow of death passed beyond them, it might persist. He saw it in her smile, in her gold-green eyes. He knew it from all they'd endured.

Perhaps it was only from the *kalmys*, but Garin found himself content.

Helnor rising startled him from his reverie. "Well, I've had enough of watching young lovers dote upon each other," he said with a teasing smile. "More *kalmys?*"

Garin shared another grin with Wren, then shrugged. "Best drink while we still can."

"Too true," the Prime Warder said as he turned away. "Too true."

SALVATION

Tal could scarcely keep from grinning as he walked next to Ashelia through Haudden.

It wasn't the sights arrayed ahead that cheered him. To look at it, the town was nothing special. The carts that thronged the streets sported rickety wheels and their shopkeepers were often hunched and sour-faced. The lane was made of packed dirt and uneven from the many hooves and feet pounding across it. Tal and Ashelia stopped at stall after stall, picking up foods that would last them the rest of the journey to Ikvaldar and reminding him of their inevitable destination.

He wasn't ready for this last leg of the quest. He was worn thin, a mere shell of a man from lack of sleep and incessant sorcery. Yet his exhaustion only made his elation fly higher.

No matter how much time he spent with Ashelia here at the end of days, it could never be enough.

"You're smiling to yourself again."

Tal met Ashelia's eyes. "Is that a problem, my fair Peer?"

She smiled as well, the storm in her eyes stirring. "No. I've always liked it."

"And I like your smile."

As soon as it had come, Ashelia's good humor slipped away. "There's not much to smile at these days."

His hand was quick to find hers, their fingers intertwining. "There's enough."

A pair of minotaurs almost bumped into them, and one snarled a curse. Tal only cocked an eyebrow and kept moving forward.

"Promise me you'll stay alive."

He had to work hard not to stiffen at her words. How he longed to swear it. How he wished to keep such an oath.

But he'd faced his enemies and knew their power. It wasn't an encounter he was likely to walk away from.

Ashelia was watching him, so he conjured another smile and squeezed her hand. "I promise I'll try."

She looked forward. "That's not enough."

"It may be all I can give."

Tal watched her, knives stabbing his gut as the woman he'd loved for two decades struggled hard not to crumple. He wished she hadn't brought up this discussion now, surrounded by a noisy, bustling marketplace. But time and leisure were something they had in short supply. If Yvärras intended to hound them all the way up the mountain, this could very well be their last reprieve.

He needed to take advantage of every minute.

Before he could offer false assurances, however, a commotion drew their attention. Ahead, the road spread into a dusty plaza filled with more sprawling markets. A gap had opened in the center near the great copper bell. There, two groups of minotaurs faced off with weapons drawn.

Tal's blood grew hot with anticipation. He knew that look in their eyes. Knew it well.

"Light-damned tyrants, you are!" one was bellowing. "Rozana never robbed a mother of food for her child! Can you say the same for Motarg?"

The opposing faction lowed with laughter. "Trust a heifer to care about mothers!" the centermost male said. "Motarg doesn't listen to cows and calves; he takes what he fucking pleases. You lot better be right with it, or we'll have a problem. You want a problem with me, cow?"

The minotaur who'd spoken first, a female with a white coat but for two black spots around her eyes, took a step forward, heavy axe clenched tight in her generous fists. "That's your call. All I'll say is Haudden would be better without you."

The other, a russet-coated bull, stepped forward as well, bringing them within striking distance. He held a mace that looked as heavy as an anvil and boasted a leather shield as well. "Think so? Want to find out?"

Their respective supporters edged forward, all suddenly shouting, drowning out any discernible words. Around Tal and Ashelia, the markets thickened with bodies. His blood burning hotter, Tal barely registered his decision before he was striding toward the would-be brawlers. He didn't stop at Ashelia's call, nor did he draw his sword.

Tal opened himself to sorcery until it seared through him.

"*Wuld,*" he murmured, and a gale whipped up from the still air, cutting between the factions with a strength that made all step back. Their eyes went wide as they turned toward the lone human walking toward them. Tal could read the disdain in their gazes, particularly those of Motarg's lackeys, but there was fear there as well.

He ceased the casting as quickly as he'd summoned it and stopped half a dozen strides away. Then he waited.

"And what does a fucking human want?" The russet bull snorted out phlegm.

Tal's smile only widened. "I'm glad you asked. I want you all to stop fighting."

Rozana's white-coated supporter eyed him. "Why's that?"

"Because we have greater enemies than each other, and I need you to be ready for them."

He could feel the force of all the eyes in the marketplace on him. In a strange way, it made his pulse race just as fast as in the middle of a battle. Contrary to expectations, he'd never been one for speeches. Falcon had helped him grow used to an audience through time on stage among the Dancing Feathers, but Tal had never possessed the same ease in a performance as the bard. Now, he'd landed himself on a different sort of stage.

Now would be a fine time to have the pearl tongue I'm claimed to.

The russet bull guffawed, provoking his companions to join with him. "The Nightlord will do as he likes! Not a light-blinded thing we can do."

"It's not your battle," the white cow noted. "You are from the Westreach."

Tal nodded. "I am. Which makes it all the more my fight. Yuldor has always threatened my homeland and all the lands beyond the mountains. His Nightkin kill our soldiers and harass our farmers. Wherever he extends his influence, he spreads conflict and suspicion. Yuldor is a plague. He must be eradicated."

Mutters sounded all around him. Tal wondered if he was inciting a mob, yet he stood his ground. Somehow, he felt this was something he'd long needed to say, and he didn't intend to leave until he finished.

Though, as Ashelia stepped up by his side, doubts crossed his mind.

The minotaurs exchanged looks. Some remained disdainful, but many were simply uncomfortable. Tal forged ahead.

Too deep now to do otherwise.

"The one your people have long named your Lord and Savior has deceived you. He longs not for salvation for the Empire, but enslavement. Have you not believed in his vision? Yet are you rich in health and home now?"

The mutters mounted. Tal pulled at his sorcery and projected his voice louder.

"Yuldor's greatest servant comes for Haudden. I don't know

when she'll strike or if she will. But if she and her minions come here, we must be united and ready to drive her back. For only together can we withstand the coming storm."

Minotaurs had always been difficult to read, and now their expressions were all but inscrutable. Tal doubted his words had any effect, for neither faction put away their weapons.

At least the crowd hasn't pulled us apart, limb for limb.

But it hadn't all been for naught. To his surprise, Tal's own resolve had strengthened. During their desperate flight before Yvärras, he'd lost sight of what this struggle was for. Only in expressing it aloud before others did it crystalize.

This wasn't only about protecting him and those he loved from an encroaching evil. It was about freedom — for the Westreach and the East, for all the Bloodlines. Brutality's shadow removed after centuries living under it.

Am I to be their salvation?

Tal turned his back on the minotaurs. He wouldn't force them not to fight. Experience had long ago taught him people could only change on their own terms, and minotaurs seemed a more stubborn lot than most. Ashelia walked beside him, her silence reproachful. He tried not to anticipate how the conversation afterward would go. He doubted it was something to look forward to.

The crowd parted before them, silent but for their muttering. Tal kept his sorcery burning hot just in case. Only after they left the plaza and the crowd long behind did Ashelia speak.

"I always knew you were a noble fool. But did you have to show everyone else?"

Tal grinned at her. He let the sorcery ease out of him and had to fight to keep his legs under him as weakness took its place. "Blame Falcon. He made me fond of monologues."

She shook her head, but took his hand again. "I want liberty as well, Tal. For my home. For us. But not at any price."

He drew her in close. "No. Not any."

But as they returned to Rozana's inn, he knew they meant different things, and suspected Ashelia knew it as well.

ABOVE

Tal's eyes drifted open.

As sleep relinquished its hold, he stared blearily at the woman next to him. Ashelia still lay in slumber. She was turned toward him, sleeping on her side as usual, her face smoothed of lines. A curl of hair had fallen across her nose.

Tal reached forward and brushed the tress from her face, causing her to stir. He smiled.

Lucky, he thought. *How lucky I am.*

No one else had yet awoken judging from the silence. They'd relinquished their watch for the night, considering it unnecessary while under Rozana's protection, and everyone had claimed some much-needed recuperation. Even the elves slept deep and long. Aelyn had stayed up long into the night translating in the far corner, and Helnor had imbibed too much of the local fermented milk to rise early.

Tal sat up slowly so as not to wake Ashelia further and stared about the inn's loft. Only then did he recognize something odd.

His blood burned.

Tal sprang to his feet and stared at the ceiling. With sorcery filling him, he sensed all beings that could touch magic. There were far more now around Haudden than the day before, far more than the town boasted. Minotaurs didn't inherit the inclination, and though Temmy wasn't the only gnome present, they couldn't account for all of the rivers he perceived rising from the World's core.

That was enough cause for alarm. But it was the being diving from above that struck terror through Tal.

"Yvärras!"

At his roar, the others threw off their covers and scrambled to their feet. They were all dressed, the precautions of the road not completely abandoned for one night of comfort, though they swayed with drowsiness.

"Where? *Here?"* Falcon's voice was shrill as he stumbled around, frantic.

"Above! We need to flee, *now!"*

But even as the others leaped to stuff their bedrolls and few scattered belongings into their packs, Tal remained where he was. He stared at the beams across the ceiling, seeing with a vision beyond his eyes as death descended from the sky. He summoned all the sorcery that he could hold. Weakness still pervaded his body. He had to hope it wouldn't claim him yet.

The only warning he had was a swelling of Yvärras' sorcery.

Tal threw up his arms and called upon every protection he knew. He cast wards to siphon away energy, such as Pim had once used on him, as well as heat. He summoned wind and ice in a furious blizzard that gilded the wood and straw in silver frost. He commanded the air itself to harden. He ordered all fire to be still.

An inferno burst through the ceiling.

Tal's knees buckled under the immense force behind the column of blue-white fire battering down his defenses. The ceiling was burned away in moments. He felt as if he stood in the middle of a volcano, the heat so intense his skin seemed to melt like wax on a candle. The Ring of Thalkuun was deathly cold on his finger, but he doubted even it could do much to protect against this. Flames ate at the walls, and between his sorcery and Yvärras' dragonfire, the ceiling beams were eaten away.

He couldn't hold for long.

"Run!" he yelled at his companions, but could barely hear himself over the din. He didn't know if it was even possible for him to run. His friends — Silence, his family — would die here with him.

His damnation was already sealed.

Yet amid the searing of his flesh, Tal felt hands touch his shoulders.

He didn't stand alone.

Garin clasped Tal's shoulders and dove into his song.

The Worldsong was a storm around him. Yvärras' sorcery beat down on them the same as her dragonfire. He heard its effects in the screams of the World — claws rending flesh, teeth gnashing stone, fire searing bones.

He threw himself into its midst all the same. At once, it tossed him about, a ship in a tempest. Though Garin swam against its swell, he was carried back and forth at its whim. Any moment could see him dashed to pieces.

Only the tether to his body kept him from being entirely swept away.

Fragile as his sorcery was, Garin didn't know what he could do to help. Yet as he'd done before, he wound what little strength he possessed around Tal's. Like vines growing over a tree, he interwove his soul with his old mentor's, and they stood stronger together.

But even then, it wasn't enough.

He felt Tal splintering beneath the assault, fractures creeping through him. Garin threw himself against them, trying to bolster the man where he grew weak, but it was like plastering a crumbling building. Tal was falling apart too quickly to patch.

No! Garin railed at him. *You cannot fail! Not now!*

To fail would mean their companions' deaths. They would be incinerated in seconds. He couldn't allow Rolan to die. He couldn't lose Wren.

Yet he, too, was coming apart. Fire burned his clothes, his skin. His hands no longer felt Tal's shoulders, if he still stood at all. He floated in a sea of flames. Garin sank down into its scalding depths, from which he knew he wouldn't reemerge.

Then another surged inside him.

Garin sprang back to awareness. He was kneeling, his hands touching Tal's legs. Blue flames filled his vision. But it was the feeling within that drew his attention. He'd fragmented, buckled in on himself, yet now he became whole again.

Ilvuan, he thought. *Alärthoras.*

The Singer acknowledged him with a pressing of his consciousness, but no more. Ilvuan was threading his way through every part of Garin and Tal. If Garin had been like vines, the dragon was like a new tree growing within the first. He mended Garin and bound Tal, then drew them all together in a new melding stronger than any they'd made before. They were like Holt's goldwood defying a storm, and no amount of wind or lightning could break them.

Yet Ilvuan didn't stop there. As Garin lifted his head, he saw the World splinter into the thin, white lines of the Lattice. Each filament hummed with a sound of its own, drowning out the roar of dragonfire.

But no — some of them *were* the blue flames. Threads wound through the inferno, pulsating with the power that spawned it. As if Yvärras didn't so much breathe the fire, but cast it like a spell.

Garin felt Ilvuan reach for the threads of the vast web that ran through the flames. With the speed and precision of a bard with his lute, the dragon manipulated the strings, too quick for Garin to follow. Whatever he did had an immediate effect; the fire receded from Tal's barrier, and the torrent of sorcery eased.

Ilvuan pressed further. Garin marveled as the dragon continued his work, ruthless and meticulous. He never faltered or slowed, attuned to the Lattice like a spider its web, and plying it with as much grace.

This was his realm. Here, he was master.

All at once, the flames disappeared. The departure of the heat felt like a huge hand released its grip on Garin, and breath wheezed into his lungs as he collapsed to the floor. It wasn't clean air, superheated and laced with smoke, but any air was welcome.

The smoke clued him in to what was happening. *The inn is burning,* Garin realized. *Burning down.*

Yet the greater threat still loomed above. With an effort that felt beyond him, Garin lifted his head. The ceiling had burned away, revealing the massive silhouette hovering above them. Each beat of Yvärras' wings blew a searing gust against his raw skin and forced his eyes nearly closed. Yet Garin gathered the Worldsong within him and clung to Ilvuan's strength as he readied for her next attack.

It didn't come. Instead, acid amusement splattered against his mind.

"Fly, manlings," the dragon queen taunted. *"Fly, if you can!"*

Ilvuan's fury rose, but before any of their party could reply, Yvärras trumpeted a cry that pierced both ear and mind, then surged into the sky and disappeared from sight.

Bewildered, Garin remained ready. He didn't see why the Protectress would relent now. They had barely weathered her attack and sagged from the effort, while she didn't seem the least wearied. Surely, she would return.

Yet with the Lattice still present in his vision, he felt

Yvärras moving away by the vibrations in the strings. The Worldsong that rose from them settled into a quieter volume, though many threads still sang with an anxiety not present before.

Lowering his gaze, Garin beheld the destruction left in the dragon queen's wake.

The loft had been decimated. Tal had extended a dome of protection around their party, even extending it to the walls of the inn to prevent the structure's collapse, yet he hadn't entirely insulated it from damage. The ceiling was gone, and the walls of the loft were little more than ashen teeth. A smog-filled sky spread above them. The floorboards were dusted with soot, as were all of them. The air stank of smoke.

Their companions gathered around. Something in their expressions gave Garin pause. He expected the fear and determination.

But the awe took him by surprise.

Garin was used to people looking at Tal that way. How could they not, after the miracles the man had performed — dispelling Heyl, tearing apart Hashele, challenging Yvärras alone at the hatching grounds.

But no one had looked at Garin like that before. There was no reason for them to. He'd done the least among the three of them. He didn't deserve their respect, not to this degree.

Yet it seems I have it.

Garin cleared his throat and mustered a coherent thought. "I think she's gone."

The words barely came out, the heat and smoke having tortured his throat. Though the surrounding flames had gone out, Garin hadn't yet recovered. He wasn't even sure anyone had heard him.

But Ilvuan read his thoughts. *She is for now. But you must listen with your ears,* Jenduit. *Yvärras is not the only peril we face.*

At the declaration, confusion and despair clawed through him. Garin tried to push them away as he strained to obey the

Singer. A ringing filled his ears, yet he could faintly detect beyond it harsh sounds.

Screaming filled the air.

His throat closed again. Listening closer, he made out further evidence that something had gone terribly wrong in Haudden beyond their inn. Metal crashing. Flames crackling. In his vision, the Lattice rippled with sorcery.

Another attack?

Ilvuan gave his reply to the party. *"We must flee now. Yvärras has issued her greatest challenge yet. Only by leaving this town may we assist its inhabitants. Do not delay!"*

The others reacted at once, shouting to one another and reaching for their packs and weapons. Garin, still kneeling at Tal's feet, knew he should do the same. But his limbs felt so heavy; he wasn't sure he could rise.

The dragon believed otherwise. Ilvuan pulled at Garin's body, coaxing him into motion. Claws prodded up and down Garin's skin. Gritting his teeth, he set one foot on the floorboards and strained to comply.

A hand extended before him. Reflexively, he took it.

"Best hurry, Garin," Tal rasped as he hauled Garin to his feet. The older man clapped him on the shoulder and flashed a spare smile. "I fear your dragon is right. All we can do is flee."

Garin nodded and began stumbling away, but Tal's grip on his shoulder tightened, holding him in place.

"And thank you. We all would have perished without you."

Garin attempted a smile. He placed his hand over Tal's and gave it a squeeze. "Thank me once we're out of here."

Nodding, Tal released him. Only with Ilvuan's support did Garin totter to his pack and follow the others down.

THE VAGARIES OF FATE

TAL STAGGERED INTO THE STREET OUTSIDE THE INN ONLY TO SEE a night terror come to life.

Haudden was in flames. Smoke rose in half a hundred pillars like black devils' tongues, searing his lungs with every breath. The scent of sulfur filled his nose; sorcery hung rank in the air and flared among their enemies and allies. The sheer number of spellcasters and Nightkin nearly knocked him flat.

Yvärras hadn't brought a mere raiding party. She'd mustered an army.

The battle could be seen on either end of the road on which they stood. Toward the central plaza, minotaurs and gnomes clashed with Imperials in dark armor. Orkans, he could just make them out to be, their skin in varying shades of monochrome, from ash white to obsidian black and all the grays in between. They weren't Ravagers; these fought as a unit, with ranks discernible even amid the chaos. Their armor was nearly uniform, much more so than the headhunters ever had been, and they were all of one Bloodline, something Tal had never seen among the Venators.

These were trained soldiers, likely come up from Vroresh, the fief home to the orkans. They couldn't have responded within a day or even weeks. This resulted from months of planning.

Further proof of just how far out of our depths we are.

There weren't only foot soldiers among the orkans. Scattered among their ranks stood those bearing feathered staffs instead of swords. The staffs appeared to be made of yellowed bone, though what creature had such long femurs, Tal didn't know. But he knew who they were: orkan shamans, those among the race capable of sorcery.

The shamans employed their magic with devastating effectiveness. When fighters from either side fell, the corpses would soon rise as draugars, swelling the enemy ranks. The dead weren't as effective of fighters, but through sheer numbers and the horror of facing one's slain comrades, they appeared to be swiftly overcoming the defenders.

The orkan regiment was only the beginning of those facing them. Nightkin prowled the streets. Chimeras hunted down their quarries. Memykes, shelled and impregnable against attacks both magical and material, launched coordinated assaults, swiftly overrunning even entrenched defenses.

Not all their enemies were on the ground. Above, the sky darkened with winged beasts. With Yvärras' departure, they swooped in like a thundercloud. Gamayuni, Tal saw them to be, the same humanoid bats as had invaded Kavaugh.

Hopelessness weighed heavy in his chest. So many invaders, and he was already so weary. It had taken everything he had to resist the dragonfire. Even with Ilvuan's support, he'd nearly broken a dozen times in minutes.

Now he was supposed to protect his companions against an entire army.

But a stronger emotion made him stand straight. Battle-rage burned as hot as sorcery in his veins. Yuldor had condemned these people to die — and for what? So his dragon servant could harass Tal and his party further?

It was cruel. Evil. He wouldn't let it stand.

In his anger, Tal almost forgot his weakness. But he knew how thin a wall hatred provided. Ilvuan's command to flee echoed in his mind.

He was pulled in too many directions. But only one path could he take, the one that made sense.

Flee.

Just as in Vathda, the best Tal could do for these people was draw the enemy away.

Someone tugged at his arm, and he turned to Ashelia, her brow knit with worry. Her hair, bound in braids tight against her head, was dusted with ash.

"The stables!" She shouted to be heard over the din. "We must take any mounts we find there!"

Tal nodded, knowing better than to object. They'd meant to purchase horses the previous night, but Rozana hadn't been able to secure any for them. And though they might rob others of their chance to escape, their absconding was Haudden's best chance for any to survive.

The criminal justifying his crimes, he thought grimly as he stumbled after Ashelia.

His rationalizations turned out to be for naught. No one occupied the stables behind the inn, neither beast nor stable-hand. Tal stared at the empty stalls for a moment, too weary to invent an alternate plan. Ashelia, however, kept her presence of mind.

"We'll flee on foot then." She remained cool and in command as she directed them back the other way. "The north entrance. The less of Haudden we see, the better."

That much, Tal could say for certain. He wasn't sure he could fight off a single enemy soldier just then, much less a battalion of them paired with their Nightkin pets. And Yvärras could return at any moment. But he had concerns enough without dwelling on that possibility.

Garin's cry jerked him back to full awareness. "Orkans!"

Tal spun toward the youth. A small company of soldiers

had been jogging down the side road past the inn when they pulled up short at the sight of their party. Below the visors of their helmets, sharp yellowed teeth bared in snarls as the orkans lowered their spears and charged.

Shrugging off his pack, Tal raised *Velori* and reached for his sorcery. It sparked painfully in his blood, causing him to flinch. Before he could call out a spell, he heard a cry behind him.

"*Kald veshk!*"

The orkans, a dozen paces away and closing fast, suddenly scattered with bellows of pain and fury. White-hot flames ate at them from the ground, Aelyn's spell producing a wall of fire five paces wide. As soon as it flared into existence, it disappeared, for maintaining such a spell would come at an incredible cost.

But even that moment was enough. Tal threw himself at the enemy. Though he felt like a fawn taking its first steps, he charged across the ash-flecked ground, *Velori* raised in one hand, his other ready for quick counterspells.

The orkans had been in two ranks, but Aelyn's spell had disrupted all organization. The foremost raised their spears against their party.

Tal was quicker. His sword swept forward and knocked aside a spear as he spun in close. His blade skittered across the plates of dark iron, scoring it but unable to penetrate. Abandoning his spear, the orkan punched at him with a gauntleted hand. Only a lucky dodge prevented Tal from suffering a crushing blow.

Having gained a bit of space, the orkan unhooked a short axe at his hip and spun it around to meet Tal's next strike. Tal backed away, slipping on the spear and nearly going down on one knee.

His body was betraying him. One night's rest was insufficient to recover from their harrowing journey, not when he'd been forced to turn aside Yvärras' attack. Even this opponent, who wouldn't threaten him ordinarily, might kill him through the slightest mishap.

He steeled his nerves and tried to ignore the orkan's grin as the soldier charged and swung.

Tal dodged back, countered, parried. The orkan's armor slowed him, but it protected all but his joints and face. They were narrow targets, much narrower than the entirety of Tal's body, and the Imperial knew to protect them.

Feinting left, Tal swung for the gap under the orkan's armpit on his right. The soldier pulled his arm tight against his side to deflect the blade with his pauldron even as he countered with a lateral swing. Tal ducked and twisted, narrowly avoiding a knee to his eye. Off-balance, he nearly went to the ground before he could recover.

Tal settled his feet under him as the orkan charged again. Stabbing forward with the spike on the axe's head, his enemy aimed for his gut. Tal turned it aside and saw his opening. Bringing *Velori* around from its swing, he stabbed into the gap beneath the helmet.

The orkan roared, stumbling and bringing a hand up to his gouged mouth. Tal didn't relent. He jabbed for the armpit of the raised arm, then spun around him and cut at the back of his knees. The heavy cloth draped there posed no barrier to *Velori's* sharp edge. Tendons severed, the soldier went screaming to the ground.

His cries ended a moment later, Tal's blade finding the gap at the front of his neck.

Tal heaved in a whooping breath and brushed back the hair from his brow. His companions were faring better than he, except for Garin. The youth looked to have been fighting an orkan that Wren had taken over for him. He now watched her, a vacant expression on his face.

He's as weary as I am. Tal grimaced. It didn't bode well for their party's prospects. He could only hope Ilvuan was still capable of his command over Nightkin. He had a feeling they might soon need it.

Aelyn cast another spell, this one of stone, battering the orkans with spires rising from the ground and upsetting their footing. But just as Tal thought them finished, he heard stampeding feet from the main street.

"More coming!" Helnor called as he whipped his sword across the throat of an orkan and turned to face the newcomers.

It was another dozen soldiers, and they didn't come alone. A shaman tramped behind them, eyes dark beneath a feathered helmet. Tal gritted his teeth. The last thing they needed was to face one of these warlocks.

Swelling the sorcery inside him until it hurt, Tal lashed out at the shaman's connection and severed it.

The shaman howled and stumbled to a halt. A few of the soldiers before it stuttered as well, babbling as they tried to divine the threat, while the others continued forward.

Tal and his party met them.

Flames and wind battered against the orkans. Tal evened the odds of his fight from the start, calling "*Kald!*" and blasting flames against the three soldiers before him. As they fell back, he chopped at their spears and battered his way forward.

But he'd been overconfident. One soldier raised a heavy foot and caught him with a crushing kick. Tal skittered backwards, pain blossoming in his ribs.

Broken, he realized. *You damn fool!*

He couldn't afford to slow. Gasping, Tal beat back a spear, then knocked another aside with a swift wind casting. But the orkans smelled blood. Though his fire had burned them, it had only inflamed their anger. They jabbed at him with spears, their reach keeping him too far away to retaliate. A glance back showed he was being corralled against the side of the decimated inn. Soon, he'd be cornered.

He couldn't allow that to happen.

Focusing on their feet, Tal called, "*Broldid ist!*" The ground erupted, capsizing the three and battering them as stone spires rose. Not even their heavy iron could withstand that without damage. Crying words Tal couldn't understand, they struggled to regain their feet and draw their weapons, for all three had dropped their spears.

Tal gave them no quarter. He leaped over the stone barrier and struck hard and fast. The first raised an arm, but his armor proved no match for a direct blow from *Velori's* enchanted edge. The blade split through the vambrace and lodged in the bone until Tal twisted it free.

As the orkan screamed and fell back, clutching his ragged arm to his chest, his comrades attacked. Tal buffeted one back with a blast of air as he met the second's assault. But though he locked his sword with the orkan's axe, he wasn't firm enough to push back as the soldier pressed forward. His feet slipped out from under him, and Tal fell to the ground, only just keeping ahold of his sword.

"Silence!" Tal hissed through gritted teeth as he raised both hands to *Velori's* hilt to hold the orkan at bay. But he was too weak and the orkan too heavy. Swiftly, his enemy's weight bore down on him, bringing the sharp edge of the axe toward his head.

The second orkan roared as he raised his axe to finish the job. Tal just managed a swift earth spell, making him stumble back and gaining a moment's reprieve, but it wasn't enough. If he didn't shove this orkan back, he was going to die. Cantrips of fire and wind sprang to mind, and in his muddled exhaustion, he summoned them together as one.

Velori's runes flared, then the sword burned with blue fire.

Tal and the orkan both stiffened in astonishment. The sword trembled with power in Tal's hands. As close as it was, the heat of its flames seared nearly as hot as the dragonfire had.

Tal recovered first. He pressed what little advantage he had with a wheezing roar, pushing *Velori* against the haft of the axe.

It sliced clean through, then continued to crash into the side of the orkan's head.

Tal jerked, trying to avoid the axe blade and only partially succeeding. Pain blinded him as the edge caught his skull, cutting his flesh and thudding on bone. Tal blinked his vision clear of the stars sparking through it as a body crashed heavily on top of him, sending fresh agony up from his ribs.

It took him a moment to see half of the orkan's head was gone.

Tal scrambled out from beneath the soldier and staggered to his feet. He fought down nausea from his wounds as he whipped his head around to find the last soldier facing him. The orkan stood a few paces away, but he didn't advance. He looked at Tal as if he were more monstrous than any of the Nightkin with which he'd arrived.

Tal wiped the blood from his eyes and grinned. Then he raised *Velori* toward the orkan.

The soldier turned and fled.

He let his arm fall as soon as his enemy's back was to him. He had a suspicion as to what had happened. But now was no time to dwell on it.

Holding tight to his anger, Tal turned to see how his companions fared. The second group of orkans had been taken care of. As he watched, Helnor cut down the last of them and staggered back, wiping his face of the blood that splattered it. The Prime Warder looked up to meet his eyes and gave Tal a weary grin. Tal returned it, though he hadn't even ironic mirth to pull on just then.

Helnor was still smiling as the arrow took him through the neck.

FURY'S FLAMES

THIS IS A DREAM.

Tal wanted to believe it. It was the only explanation he could accept.

How else could Helnor be falling?

Eyes lifeless. Body limp.

Gone.

He raced across the distance to his friend and fell to his knees, cradling Helnor's head and drinking deep of sorcery until it brimmed from his fingers. Tal knew only rudimentary spells of healing, but he spoke them all, willing the sorcery to do his bidding. Magic burned through him and into the Prime Warder, racing toward his wound. Before his eyes, the skin began knitting together.

Tal placed a hand to the shaft, then hesitated before lifting the elf slightly. The arrowhead was barbed, as he suspected it would be. He knew what he had to do.

Taking up *Velori*, he sliced off the end of the arrow, then set aside the blade again. Bracing himself, Tal thrust the arrow through.

His fingers brushed Helnor's spine as he pulled the last of it free.

Blood, so much blood. *An artery sliced*, an impassive part of him evaluated. The rest of his mind concentrated on the only thing he could do. Tal placed his hands over the wound on either side, coaxing the spells to work faster. He didn't allow himself to wonder if he was wasting the precious little strength he had left. He couldn't pause or doubt.

It would work. It had to work.

He couldn't let him die.

"Helnor! Mother below, *Helnor!*"

Ashelia collapsed beside them and cupped her brother's face in her hands. Tears streamed down her cheeks.

Do something! Tal wanted to shout. *You're a healer!* But he couldn't find the breath to say it. All he could do was keep pressing magic into his fallen friend.

Hands fell over his, prying them away.

"Stop." Ashelia's voice was choked. "Stop trying."

"No."

"Tal, please. He's gone. Look."

Tal opened his eyes, which he hadn't realized he'd squeezed shut. Where the arrow had entered, the wound had healed over, but Helnor still didn't move. His golden eyes stared sightlessly up at the sky.

Tal sank back on his arms, barely able to keep upright.

Helnor was gone. Truly gone.

Tal raised his gaze. "Ashelia…"

She was already wiping her nose and rising. "Not now. Your sword."

Slowly, he became aware of their surroundings again. Their companions ringed them. Aelyn, Wren, and Garin had wind shields up and were protecting them from the oncoming enemies and the arrows they loosed upon them. Beyond the blur of the wind, Tal could see all the invaders now closed in on them. Chimeras. Memykes. More orkan soldiers. Gamayuni.

They were surrounded. Trapped.

Tal climbed to his feet, *Velori* loose in his hand. Fury burned in him, but not as hot as it needed to be. He wasn't enough to face this, not by half. He was spent, thin, worn.

But he wouldn't allow anyone else to die. Not one.

Except myself.

Tal glanced at Garin. "Ilvuan. Can you send them away as you did before?"

The dragon answered with reverberating thoughts. "*I can, but only the* kael'dros. *The mortal soldiers will remain.*"

"I'll handle those."

He hoped it wasn't a mere boast. As Tal moved one leg forward, then the other, it felt more like one than he cared to admit.

Aelyn's head twisted back toward him. Only the tears tracking through the ash layering his face showed any sign of his witnessing his House-brother's death. "We should flee, Harrenfel. You are not fit to fight."

"Run, and they'll chase us down." Tal closed his eyes, wishing he could slip into forgetting darkness. Instead, he saw Helnor's face, waxen and still. He opened his eyes again.

"Tal."

Garin's tone drew his gaze. The youth had gained a dozen scrapes, bruises, and cuts from the battle, though none looked serious. A fierceness remained in his expression that would have made Tal proud had he not been so numb. But beyond it, fear and doubt ran rampant. The youth was at the end of his resolve.

Tal reached out and clasped Garin's shoulder. "You have your part. I have mine. Negate your shield."

"What are you doing?" Wren's voice was breathless from maintaining the spell. "Want an arrow in the neck as well?"

Her question provoked a fresh flame of fury, but Tal knew it wasn't for her.

"I want to kill them," he replied calmly, meeting her eyes.

His words had their desired effect. Wren silenced and

turned back to guarding her direction, chest heaving with labored breaths.

Tal turned back to Garin. "Now, Garin, Ilvuan."

He thought he glimpsed another intelligence behind the youth's eyes for a moment. Then Garin blinked, and he lifted the wind shield.

Tal walked out alone from the barrier. Only a moment passed before Ilvuan's deep voice burst through his mind, and sorcery poured forth from Garin.

"*FLEE*, KAEL'DROS!"

As before, the Nightkin obeyed at once. The memykes, the chimeras, the gamayuni — not a single one stood before the wave of power that spread from the youth and his dragon. The orkan soldiers had been preparing to charge, but now they stared after their fleeing allies, then looked at one another. Though the odds remained in their favor, they'd begun to have doubts.

Tal smiled and raised *Velori* in both hands.

"*Kald wuld!*"

As before, the blade blazed with azure flames. Tal pushed it further, imbuing it with so much sorcery that the hilt vibrated.

The orkans eyed the sword. Some raised their shields. Those with bows lowered them and drew.

Tal aimed for the archers first.

He slashed *Velori* through the air. An arc of white-hot energy burst from the blade, crackling as it sliced toward the enemy. Tal reeled as he reached the end of the swing. Screams told of its impact.

His vision spun as he regained his balance. He hadn't been entirely sure it would work until he'd tried it. Tal snapped his head back around, blinking furiously to see the results of the spell.

What he saw made him disbelieve his eyes.

The soldiers caught by the spell were dead to the last one. Some had continued standing upright and fallen in two halves.

Others had tried to duck out of the way and had their heads cut through. The orkans who still stood were backing away fast now, all except four shamans, who raised their hands and shouted words at him in the Darktongue.

Recovering, Tal bared his teeth and once again hissed, "*Kald wuld!*"

As *Velori* burned afresh, three shamans fled. The last held out a moment longer, his casting just coming to life before he turned after the others.

Tal swung, and all four were laid low.

Some of the orkan soldiers were also caught by the arc. Those who remained fled with fearful shouts. Tal wished he could pursue, but he sank to one knee. *Velori's* tip dug into the earth, the only thing allowing him to remain upright.

Sorcery fluttered within him, feeble as a fledgling bird. The spell cast through *Velori* hadn't cost him nearly what it should have, but it still drained the last of his reserves. Dark spots dotted his vision, yet he remained aware enough to notice his friends approaching.

Someone touched his arm, and Ashelia's voice spoke. "Tal, we must leave."

He shook his head. "Have to bring Helnor."

"We cannot." Emotion choked her for a moment. "We have no mounts."

"I can carry him."

Tal looked up at Aelyn as he spoke. The mage's mouth was set in a deeper frown than usual, and the coppery fire in his eyes had dampened. How the mage would do it, he didn't know, yet Tal nodded and endeavored to stand.

As he faltered, someone caught him by the arm. Tal turned his head and met Garin's gaze.

"Let me," the youth said quietly.

Tal sighed, then nodded. With Garin supporting him, Tal limped off with the others toward the north exit, the continuing battle echoing behind them.

PASSAGE IV

As the Night once contended with the Whispering Gods to a standstill, so will I be the World's savior.

This is my belief, the tenet which drives me toward the future. For mortalkind does not need Paradise to prosper; they already do so without it! The World should not be a place of contentment and plenty. It should have hardship and hard-won victories. All will attempt and most will flounder, but some few will discover their power, and all will have the opportunity to try.

Immortality is a disease, not a panacea. Only with a terminus does a venture possess meaning.

I speak this as one who has attained as much immortality as is presently possible. Only in the nearing destruction of all has urgency and vigor claimed hold of me again. Eight centuries I have doubted, and eight centuries I have tarried! I, most of all, know the truth of my belief, far better than any mortal could.

My dream differs from Yuldor's. It is viable. It is balanced. And it will not rent the World apart in a vain attempt to change it.

But while Yuldor and his gods exist, neither I, nor anyone else, may truly flourish.

- The Untold Lore of Yuldor Soldarin and His Servants, *by Inanis*

TO DIVINE SKIES

A COLUMN OF BLACK SMOKE MARKED HAUDDEN BEHIND THEM. Garin looked away from it, wiping the sweat from his forehead. His hand came away pink.

Blood. What isn't covered in blood?

His mind felt frosted over, a lake trapped in winter. The coppery tang of blood choked him along with the acrid smoke. A heaviness dragged him toward the ground, the grass seeming to whisper of rest and release with every gust across the plains. He wanted nothing more than to lie down and never rise again.

Yet he kept moving. Tal was relying on him; all in the Westreach and East were relying on him. Falter now, and what chance of peace would there be for anyone?

His foot chose that moment to trip him, and Garin went down to one knee. Tal collapsed against him with a grunt, and Garin gritted his teeth as he barely remained upright.

"Thank you, Garin," the older man murmured as he lifted himself off. "But you've done enough. I can carry myself."

Garin looked up at Tal, skepticism bleeding through the iron wall around his mind. The man swayed where he stood, his eyes drooping half-closed. But Garin was hardly in a state to object.

Nodding, Garin slowly stood. The rest of their party hefted their packs and kept moving.

At length, Garin glanced toward the rear of their miserable company. Aelyn, Ashelia, and Rolan made for an odd funeral procession with Helnor's body. The mage, having anticipated the need to move heavy cargo on their journey, had a spell handy that allowed him to levitate Helnor's body across the plains. It was an eerie sight, the big elf gliding over the ground, nothing beneath him but the grass that bent out of his way.

Garin could barely stand to look at the Prime Warder's face, at the stillness captured there. Though Ashelia had wiped away much of the blood from his wound, it was a pink film on his skin, making it seem as if his tanned face had gathered an unhealthy flush.

He looked away, knowing he would remember this sight for a long time.

If we survive.

Conversation was scarce, never going beyond practicalities. Even those who hadn't defied a dragon's breath were bowed from battle and grief. Garin had only kept up with the furious pace of the fight with Ilvuan's aid. When his focus faltered or his reactions slowed, the Singer had been there, reinforcing Garin's actions with his will. It was a strange feeling to have such help, though not an altogether unpleasant one.

Never thought I'd thank the stars for having a devil.

Ilvuan pulsed at that, echoing Garin's irony.

Even with the dragon's aid, his legs felt as if they'd fold at any moment. The straps of his pack dug deeper into his shoulders with each step. Yet before he knew it, the sun had fallen behind the mountains and Ashelia's voice rose above the plains' murmurs.

"Here. We'll do it here."

Garin continued walking three paces before his feet caught

up with his ears. Looking around, he blinked blearily at his companions.

Before he could form the words for a question, Wren asked, "Do what?"

Tal answered first. "Helnor's death rites."

Hunger and thirst assaulted Garin, his waterskin long since gone flat, but he didn't mention his gripes as he drifted closer to Helnor's body. Aelyn had released his incantation so that his late House-brother settled on the ground. Garin stared at the Prime Warder's face for several moments before tearing his eyes away. He couldn't seem to catch his breath.

He wasn't my brother or uncle, he told himself. *Best I don't intrude.*

Despite the thought, he wondered if it was his real reason for holding back. What was he afraid of finding if he lowered his guard? Sorrow? Rage at the unfairness of it all? Despair at their hopeless mission?

Once more, they'd lost one of their own. And the greatest trials still lay ahead.

Garin had admired Helnor, liked him, trusted him. The East had tried to bury the Prime Warder's spirits, yet he'd never let it. Garin remembered him as he'd been drinking the fermented milk in Haudden's inn: laughing, teasing, reminiscing.

May you be happy, Helnor, wherever you are now.

Impossible though it seemed, the thought awoke in Garin the smallest of smiles.

Tal barely remained standing against the current flowing through him.

He couldn't muster any emotion, much less a smile. He was numb, numb as ice itself.

Numb, because he couldn't bear to feel what lay beneath its surface.

He watched as the elves moved about their funeral rites. Aelyn, his face a rigid mask, bent to search his pack next to Helnor's body, drawing from it the journal of Koax Mraaj. His hands trembled as he moved to a page in the back of the manuscript and, with sudden savagery, ripped it free. The sound might have made Tal flinch had he had the energy to react.

Tossing the journal back in his pack, Aelyn withdrew his enchanted quill and set the nib to the page. The ink that oozed forth blotted the parchment as the mage stared at it, unseeing.

Ashelia, who kneeled next to their departed brother, watched Aelyn. "Just write," she coaxed him gently. "The words are not important. He knew."

Aelyn's tremors grew worse. With teeth bared, he scrawled across the parchment in a fury. His quill stabbed through twice, yet the mage didn't slow. His eyes, dull since Haudden, blazed with life again.

After several silent minutes, Aelyn finished his written diatribe and thrust the page across Helnor's body to Ashelia along with the quill.

She accepted it without comment. Tal gazed at her as she set to writing. A deep ache welled up in him. He knew her face better than any other, had looked at it long into the night after she'd fallen asleep. He'd traced its curves and lines, the dimples of her cheeks and the faint wrinkles in the corners of her eyes.

Grief furrowed into her every feature.

Ashelia's composition was shorter. When she'd finished, she wiped away silent tears, then beckoned her son to her side.

"What do I do?" Rolan whispered as he took the quill and paper from his mother.

Her hand rested on the back of his neck as she leaned in close. "Write as if you are speaking to him. Say what is in your deepest heart. How will you remember Uncle Helnor?"

His brow creased, the boy nodded and started writing. Tal watched as Rolan chewed his lip and carefully inked several lines onto the abused sheet. When the boy finished, he straightened and handed both the paper and quill back to his mother, relief clear on his face.

Ashelia turned and looked up at Tal, holding the rite's implements out in a silent invitation.

He shook his head. "I'm not his family, nor an elf."

Her tendrils spun faster. Light refracted in the unspilled tears gathered in the corners of her eyes. "You were his friend. He thought of you as a brother."

Tal turned his head aside. *Would his brother have allowed him to die?* But he didn't give voice to the unworthy thought. He wouldn't burden Helnor's passing with his own guilt and shame.

Ashelia didn't insist on it, but withdrew the paper and offered the quill back to Aelyn. Her House-brother took it and tossed it in his pack without taking his eyes from Helnor's face.

"Now what?" Rolan asked tentatively. He seemed averse to looking at Helnor, yet also as if his gaze couldn't help but be drawn to him.

His mother lifted the paper over her brother's body. "Now, we burn it."

The boy's eyes widened. "Why? How will he read it?"

A slight smile curved Ashelia's lips, and fresh pangs spread through Tal at the sight.

"Uncle Helnor cannot read now, Rolan. We burn them so the Mother might guide his spirit to our thoughts."

Rolan seemed to think it over, then nodded. "I want him to know we're thinking of him. So I'm going to write him a song, just as Falcon would."

Ashelia jerked, as if suddenly pained by her stomach. Tal turned his head aside, clenching his teeth and staring at the distant mountains. His mind had seemed the still surface of a dark pool, but now it rippled with the seething emotions beneath.

Falcon, sensing Ashelia's weakness, spoke into the silence. "A song is an excellent way to pay homage to your uncle, Rolan. I would be honored to assist you in it."

The boy flashed the bard a wan smile before turning back to his mother. "*Momua*, are you alright?"

It was the push she needed. Sucking in a ragged breath, Ashelia gave her son a broken smile and ran a hand through his ashy hair. "Yes. I will be."

She's strong. She's always been strong.

He'd always admired that in her. She put others first, no matter her needs. Even when becoming a leader and warrior, Ashelia never stopped being a healer and a mother. He wondered where it came from, that resolve, that coherence of self. He'd always felt fragmented into a dozen identities, the names anchoring him in the past weighing every step into the future.

She shook her head, curls winning free of her braids to bounce against her forehead. Her words were slightly choked, yet firm with resolve.

"We shouldn't delay. We must continue."

Her eyes flickered to Tal, then rose to Aelyn. Her House-brother still faced the tree, but at her look, he gestured for her to proceed.

Ashelia raised the page in both hands over Helnor's chest. "May the Mother usher our thoughts to you, *Belosi*," she said, a slight tremble in her voice and hands. She followed it up with a whispered "*kald*," and flames spread over the sheet of parchment, blackening the edges. It curled in on itself as Ashelia placed it on her brother's chest.

Tal watched with the others as the sorcerous fire ate at the page until nothing but smoking cinders remained. The smoke curled away from Helnor's body, and Tal wondered if what Ashelia had told Rolan could be true, if his spirit lingered somewhere in the World. As desperately as he wished it was real, he couldn't bring himself to believe. He'd known too many false gods to believe one watched out for them now.

"If we were in Elendol," Ashelia said to her son, "we would have performed this rite on the highest platform of our kintree, then processed his body down to the roots where he would be buried in the House mausoleum. But we cannot carry him all that way. So we will burn him, and each of his kin will carry his ashes to bury upon our return."

She glanced up at Tal again, and he held her gaze. *You will return*, he promised her silently. *No matter what it costs, you will.* He'd always intended it to be so, yet never had that resolution been so adamant. It grew amid his sorrow and fury like a firmly rooted tree amid a storm.

He noticed Garin staring at him and met his gaze with a shrug. His onetime protege tilted his head and returned him a small, sympathetic smile. Tal didn't deserve it. He didn't deserve any of his companions' loyalty.

This isn't about you, he reminded himself again, taming his racing thoughts.

Ashelia and Rolan were moving about the tree, collecting fallen branches and twigs to fuel the pyre. Garin, Wren, and Falcon moved to help them, leaving Tal with Aelyn and Helnor's body. He glanced at the mage, but Aelyn only remained glaring down at his House-brother as if he leveled accusations. Knowing Aelyn, Tal guessed that was precisely what he did.

There was little to gather, and soon the others were placing a spare weaving over Helnor. Ashelia positioned her House-brother as befit a Warder, his hands clasped over the hilt of his saber. Tal stared at the Prime's half-lidded, vacant eyes and wished he could see them light up once more with humor.

But the tendrils had faded and grown still. No life remained there.

When all was ready, Ashelia motioned Aelyn to Helnor's

side and took up the spot opposite him. With a shared glance, they held their hands over his body.

"*Kald,*" they spoke together, and flames spread over Helnor's body.

Only by magic could the Prime Warder's body be swiftly consumed. They remained around the pyre as he burned, trying to hide their distaste at the reek of seared flesh, though Rolan did so poorly, face wrinkled and small hands fidgeting. Tal breathed it in and accepted it as a sliver of the punishment he deserved.

He kept staring into the flames as they ate away Helnor's skin, then the tissue beneath. He watched one of his oldest friends return to the World.

Not for all his sorcery had he been able to save him.

The sight sickened him, made his stomach clench, yet he didn't look away. It fed a fervor that had simmered within him since Haudden, one that spread throughout his limbs and smoldered in his veins as surely as sorcery did.

He willed his weary body into motion and moved around the fire. The others watched him. Ashelia looked wary, her expression darkened by flickering firelight and the growing shadows of dusk.

Tal stood next to Aelyn.

The mage stiffened as Tal halted, but he didn't look up from the flames. Tal kept his gaze steady, willing him to meet his eyes. He knew how Aelyn hid from pain; he longed to hide the same way. But neither of them could afford to, not with what lay ahead.

Tal reached out and, gripping Aelyn's shoulders, he turned the mage toward him. Aelyn obliged, though not without a flash of his eyes. Tal ignored the warning and pulled Aelyn into a rough embrace.

The mage pushed at him, but his resistance didn't last. He shook in Tal's arms.

Tal didn't look if he wept, knowing it would only embarrass the elf. Instead, Tal put his mouth close to Aelyn's ear.

"We'll make her pay, my friend. You have my word: Yvärras will suffer for her part in his death."

Aelyn jerked away. For a moment, Tal thought he'd misjudged Aelyn's grief. He met the man's eyes and stared into the fiery orange pools, mirrors of the pyre behind him.

"You swear?" he whispered. "On everything you don't hold holy?"

Tal had a smile for every occasion. It was a black one that curled his lips then.

"I swear it, Aelyn. I swear."

A PROPOSAL

GARIN WATCHED HELNOR BURN.

Their party kept the vigil long into the night. The reek of burned hair and cooking meat clung in Garin's nose, choking and nauseating him. Yet he and his companions shared an obligation. They were the watchers who would usher their lost friend into whatever life lay after.

Then most keenly did Garin feel the loss of his religion. All his life, he'd believed the Creed as it had been passed down to him: that the Whispering Gods held the Night and its evils at bay, and they would be safest from its minions by remaining true to the teachings.

Yet the veil of myth had been torn down, and Garin found the hideous truth difficult to bear. He wanted to pray, to know something watched over him, cared for him. But none of his gods remained.

So he reached for the next best thing. He opened himself to the Worldsong.

Its strains were difficult to bear at first. Grating and grinding, they were at odds with the quiet death vigil, far louder than the whispering grass and the chorus of crickets. But after a moment, the discordant parts settled into the beauty of the whole.

Garin closed his eyes and listened. There was comfort in hearing the sounds of far-off places. The clink of crockery washed after a meal. Laughter, both harsh and melodious. The sigh of a laborer setting down a heavy load.

Life continues. It always does.

Thousands upon thousands of ordinary lives carried on, no matter the deaths those people faced. And so would it be for Garin.

Perhaps Helnor joined the Mother, goddess of the elves. Perhaps he only returned to the sky and earth. Garin liked to imagine some part of him melded with the song circling through his head, his voice joining the ceaseless refrain.

Someday, he hoped he would hear him once more.

Ilvuan had been quiet and almost invisible within Garin during the interment of the Prime Warder. Now he shifted, and Garin felt his presence curl around his bones.

A small smile curved his lips. Perhaps there were no gods, but at least he was never alone.

Some hours into the vigil, wariness returned to their fellowship, and they set aside their grief for more practical concerns. They made camp under the boughs of that lone tree opposite of Helnor's pyre. Aelyn and Ashelia insisted on keeping watch, and Garin didn't try arguing with them. He suspected sleep would have evaded them if they'd tried. He expected the same for himself. Instead, it claimed him moments after he lay down.

When dawn's thin light pressed against his eyelids, Garin was still heavy with weariness, yet some of his strength had returned. He gathered his sparse belongings, watching out of the corner of his eye as Ashelia beckoned Rolan to her by Helnor's pyre. Together with Aelyn, they bent and collected a handful of his ashes, then filled the pouches that used to hold their coins, the currency dispersed among Garin and the others. No one voiced any skepticism as to if they would need money again. Garin guessed he wasn't the only one to have the thought.

There was little reason to remain, yet they lingered until Tal approached Ashelia and whispered in her ear. She nodded, her gaze still on the remains of her brother. Garin had mostly avoided looking at the pyre, and he regretted doing so now. All that remained of the brave man were his blackened bones and his sword, the sorcerous flames having claimed the rest.

So quickly gone. Just like Kaleras. Just like any of us might be.

Ilvuan roused at that. *Such is a mortal's life. But you possess an immortal spirit,* Jenduit. *Never can this be forgotten.*

How the dragon intended his words, Garin didn't ask. He preferred believing Ilvuan was capable of kindness after a friend's death.

Soon after, they left Helnor behind and continued their never-ending march, always watching for pursuit. The mountains spread to their right, Ikvaldar high above them. The smoke from Haudden had thinned, but Garin could still glimpse it marking the town behind them. The day took on a dreary monotony, exacerbated by the reticence of their company. Every slight annoyance bothered him: chafing on his thighs, blisters on his feet, the filthiness of his skin.

Helnor died, and you're worried about how long it's been since you had a bath.

Yet for all his self-flagellation, his discomforts grew no less nagging.

After several hours, when the blinding sun added to Garin's list of grievances, his thoughts strayed down a more productive path. What had happened in Haudden was the last thing he wished to think of, yet there was a bright curiosity amid the pall.

Tal had manifested yet another miracle.

He lengthened his stride until he caught up to the older man, where he led the company along with Ashelia and Rolan. Tal glanced at Garin and seemed to sense his question.

"Something on your mind, Garin?"

"I suppose you could say that." They had spoken little since Helnor's death, nor had he interacted with Ashelia beyond a few words. Now, he flailed at finding the right ones to say.

Tal's eyebrows raised. "Don't start holding out on me. We've seen enough together to be honest and open, haven't we?"

Garin decided to take a risk. "It's nothing. Just wondering what in Yuldor's bloody name you did back there in Haudden with *Velori*."

His gamble only partially paid off. While Tal gave a small chuckle and Rolan came alive with interest, Ashelia only grew more somber. Garin winced, wondering if he should have brought this up after all. The last thing he wanted was to cause the Peer more pain.

But Tal was already answering. "The truth is I'm not exactly sure. But I have my suspicions."

"I thought we were being honest?"

Tal gave him a rueful smile, this one crinkling his eyes. "You know I've always been able to set *Velori* aflame with a cantrip. It isn't something that can be done to ordinary steel without concerted effort. I suppose I knew that; it's just been decades since I'd wielded another blade for any length of time. I'd grown used to the artifact's idiosyncrasies."

Garin's intuition leaped ahead. "So you're saying the enchantments on *Velori* allow it to... what? Sustain spells? Amplify magic?"

"Both, I think. I'd never attempted casting anything beyond

fire on the blade, and then only in a small amount. What use could stone or wind spells have on a sword? But now, I think I've been small-minded in my approach."

Tal fell quiet, his eyes dropping to his feet. Garin refrained from interrupting his thinking, though curiosity needled him.

"During the fight," the older man continued, "I was nearly overcome by one of the orkan soldiers. To remain alive, I tried casting both a wind and a fire cantrip at the same time. But my attention was also focused on *Velori* keeping his axe at bay. Instead of channeling the sorcery toward my enemy, I accidentally infused it into *Velori* instead. The result was… well, you saw it for yourself."

"How could we not?"

The conflagration that had blazed from the sword had been nearly blinding. Never had Garin imagined the sword he'd once carried held so much potential. He wondered if *Helshax* might be capable of similar things, and how he'd discover them. By channeling spells at it and hoping they didn't backfire?

Tal was speaking again. "I had only just discovered it when… well, it came too late. But when we were almost overrun, I imbued more power in it, and the results were further amplified."

Garin shook his head at the understatement. "You cut down entire ranks at once."

Though battles always became a blur afterward, Garin could still picture that scene vividly. The soldiers, clad in dark iron and screaming for blood. Tal, sweeping his sword before him. The arc of blue-white fire blasting forth, leaving a black afterimage on Garin's eyes and fatal wounds on their enemies.

A realization came to him. "It's like dragonfire."

Tal frowned. "How's that?"

"The color of the fire, the heat of it — it's like the flames Yvärras breathed."

Tal seemed to consider it, then shrugged. "I suppose so. Blue fire does burn hottest."

There was something more there, something Garin couldn't put his finger on. But before he could figure it out, Rolan piped up, eyes wide with eagerness.

"Does it work with any other spells?"

Tal smiled at the boy. "I wondered the same myself. Another time, I might experiment and discover which work and which don't. Would more complicated incantations take? Or is it restricted to cantrips?"

He grew somber as he looked forward again. "But I cannot waste time or energy on it now. Even if it yields useful results, staying alive is our first aim."

Garin held in a sigh as his eyes traveled down the mountain range to their destination. Ikvaldar was, as usual, lost halfway to clouds, yet it still surged above them, its verdant peak ever a startling sight. Staying alive would no doubt be difficult once they began their ascent.

If they survived long enough to reach it.

The days passed. Tal's burdens grew no lighter.

The absence of their enemies now seemed like an illusion. It had been nearly two weeks since Yvärras began to pursue them, and he could no longer remember how it felt to be at peace. There seemed no end to their trials, no way to set down the grief and hatred that weighed on each step.

Peace. Rest. No pain. No sorrow.

Whether it was the *Doash's* murmur or one born of his own mind, he could no longer tell. Only Ashelia by his side kept him rooted in the World above.

Tal glanced at her, subtle so she wouldn't notice. He needn't have bothered. Ashelia was absent behind her eyes. Her tendrils stirred sluggishly in her irises, like eels grown tired of swimming around their small cage. She had brushed aside his offer that morning of summoning water in which to wash her hair and skin clean of the battle. She carried the ashes of Haudden upon her the same as she carried her guilt.

Tal lowered his gaze to his feet again. *Though Silence knows the blame lies with me.*

But he didn't succumb to self-indulgent abuse this time. Instead, he raised his head and examined their surroundings while questing with his sorcery. Though he sensed no threats, he remained wary, every faculty open.

Their journey had given them many reasons to be cautious. Though they appeared free from pursuit for the moment, the rest of the Faernor Grasslands weren't so fortunate. Strife abounded with every mile. One town they passed within sight of was black with smoke. Many of the farmhouses they chanced upon were ransacked or abandoned. Once, they came to what appeared to be a battlefield no more than a few days old. The grass was trampled and burned, and the unburied bodies reeked like the memories of his soldiering days. Carrion birds layered over them like a blanket of black snow, seething and cawing whenever they neared. Tal was reminded how little he missed that old life as they went around the worst of the carnage.

For many miles, Kavaugh was visible in the distance. A haze of heat made its dun walls dance like flames. Tal often glanced at it, his mind delving back to their stay in the Empire's capital.

"It's strange," he murmured to Ashelia once, "but I miss our time there."

She took his hand, and though her face remained down-cast, her eyes whirled faster than they had in days. "We will share more like it. Afterward."

Tal had no response for that. His silence spoke loudly enough.

That night at camp, he sought her again. Both moons were

out and had waxed to a brightness that lifted the darkness. Their intermingled illumination cast a green glow across the ever-dancing grass. Ashelia held Rolan and quietly sang him a song in Gladelyshi that Tal didn't recognize. *An infant melody, perhaps.*

He approached on quiet feet. Though he was loath to interrupt, Tal cleared his throat. Ashelia looked up, the music dying on her lips. She didn't seem startled, but only weary.

"Rolan," she murmured to her son, "would you go ask Falcon what lullabies he knows from home?"

The boy's eyes had been drifting closed, yet he perked up at once as he glanced between them. Eyes narrowed, he did as his mother instructed, though not without muttering, "I'm too old for cradle songs…"

Ashelia looked up. Tal stared back. He listened as Rolan found Falcon. "Of course I know some!" the bard declared in boisterous fashion. Tal wondered if it was only to his ears that his bluster sounded pilled and worn.

At last, she broke the silence. "Speak your mind, Tal."

He kneeled before her. "Don't refuse."

"I will if I must."

Tal opened his hand and held it out to her. Ashelia only glanced at the object nestled in his palm before looking away.

"I already gave my answer," she said stiffly.

"Change it."

"You need it more than I."

He withdrew his hand, but didn't close it. The Ring of Thalkuun, dark and unremarkable but for the green glyphs upon it, seemed to taunt him.

"I need you to have it more," he muttered, his voice catching.

Ashelia's eyes held and trapped him, their silver light flashing.

"My brother knew the risks when he came with us. So did Kaleras, and so do I."

"Think of your son, Ashelia. He needs you alive."

It was a cheap shot, but with the prospect of what awaited them only days away, or what might find them at any moment, he would try any trick.

Ashelia only smiled, a sad and limp thing. "That ring didn't protect Kaleras from his fate, but it might assist in yours. I'm not the one challenging a god, Tal. Next to you, I'll be safe anywhere in the World, even if we stood before Yvärras herself."

Fire flared to life in him, the coals of hatred never dimmed in the days since Haudden. "I'd rather you not mention her."

"I must. Put the ring back on, and please, don't ask me to wear it again."

Tal sighed, his anger dampening. Reluctantly, he picked up the ring and slipped it over the middle finger of his left hand. His blood blushed as the enchantment settled over him, then swiftly calmed.

"Besides," Ashelia continued, her voice softer, "it belonged to Kaleras for many years. It's your father's last possession."

Habit made Tal glance around them to ensure nobody lingered nearby, though it was no longer any great secret. Gossip didn't take long to spread among such a small party. He clenched his hands into fists and stared at the shifting light of the ring's glyphs.

"Swear to me," he spoke without lifting his eyes. "Swear you will survive."

"No one can promise that."

"Swear you'll try."

Ashelia was quiet for a heartbeat, then two. Tal lowered his hand and lifted his gaze. The stormy tendrils swirled in her tired eyes.

"I'll try, Tal."

He lifted his hands to cup either side of her face, kissed her gently on the lips, then pulled her in close. Tal held his beloved, their bodies warm against each other, wishing his embrace could protect her, wishing he'd been strong enough to send her and the rest of his friends away when he'd had the chance.

You always were a selfish fool, he thought as he closed his eyes.

THE PATH TO IKVALDAR

TAL SENSED THE COMPANY BEFORE HE SAW THEM.

Raising a hand, he brought his companions to a halt and studied the strangers. They were miles distant, so all he knew of them was divined from their sorcery.

Yet that told him much. Their connections to magic were out-of-place for the East, but still familiar. He knew this Bloodline. Many of them stood nearby.

"Elves," he murmured. "Gladelysh elves."

Ashelia stared at him with eyes wide. "It cannot be. Are they truly here?"

A slow smile spread across Tal's face. "I think so."

Turning away, he called back to the others, "At least some of our allies have arrived! Warders await us a few miles ahead."

His companions were stunned into silence. Wren was the first to speak.

"Night's blood. They really came?"

"Did you expect otherwise?" Ashelia stood straighter than she had before, her chin tilted up. The sight brought out another smile from Tal.

She's proud. Proud of her fellow warriors. Proud of the men her brother led.

"It would be wiser not to approach." Aelyn, ever the pessimist, spoke with his brow furrowed. "You have been mistaken many times before, Harrenfel."

His House-sister answered before Tal could. "No, *Belosi*. The distraction of Yuldor's forces is an essential part of the plan. If the Emperor's armies are not coming, we must know so we can plan accordingly."

Aelyn frowned, but only huffed and turned away.

Tal looked forward, his smile undiminished. "Besides, there's always a chance I'm right."

"Slim though those odds may be," Aelyn muttered.

Despite Tal's outward nonchalance, as they headed for the camp, he remained wary. While he was fairly certain these strangers were indeed their allies, it was possible they were Nightelves unfriendly to their cause. Yet he'd spent months around the Eastern elves while staying in Zyrl's palace and thought he could tell the difference.

One of his old commander's sayings came to mind. *The wary soldier is rich in the only way that matters.* Tal pulled sorcery into his veins, loosened *Velori* in its scabbard, and kept their approach as stealthy as it could be.

Yet on the open plains, it didn't take long for the strangers to come into view, and Tal knew they would see them in turn. Soon after, he had confirmation of the assumption as riders came galloping toward them.

"Someone's coming," Garin said, the quaver in his voice betraying his nerves.

"A dozen someones," Wren affirmed.

Aelyn barked a harsh laugh. "We'll have our answer soon enough, then."

"Come." Ashelia corralled them up a nearby hill, making for a more defensible position. All kept their hands near their weapons. Tal had his sorcery ready, but soon, a farseeing spell made his smile grow wide.

"Turns out I was right after all, Aelyn. They're riding stors."

As his friends loosed laughs around him, Tal watched the company approach. Their mounts held their crowned heads high and the Warders' petrified bark armor gleamed. Though he was relieved, his smile began slipping away, remembering the news they would have to share.

Ashelia raised her hand toward her countrymen. Though elves were often reticent, the Warders shouted as they drew near. "Ashelia! Ashelia Starkissed! She's alive! Peer Venaliel lives!"

She smiled, but it faded as the Warders crossed the last of the distance. Tal grimaced. No doubt she, too, remembered the news she'd soon share. A pang went through him at the loss, and he thought of his oath to Aelyn.

She will pay. His eyes slid over to the mage. *Yvärras will pay for taking Helnor from us.*

Dismounting, the Warders came up the hill, making circling gestures of respect as they did. The foremost elf was a handsome man with a pale complexion for one who spent their time outdoors and blonde hair almost gone white. He seemed their leader, for he spoke for the rest of the Warders.

"You are the first welcome sight we have glimpsed since entering the Empire, Peer Venaliel." After speaking the greeting in Gladelyshi, the Warder switched to the Reach-tongue, no doubt for the benefit of the humans present. "But how have you come to be here? And where is Prime Helnor? I understood he traveled with you."

"I am glad to see you as well, Warder Elidyr. But my brother..."

Ashelia's jaw spasmed, striking a pang through Tal. He spoke up, seeing that emotion choked her words.

"I'm afraid Helnor fell. We've only just interred him." Tal struggled to speak himself for a moment, tears pricking his eyes. "He died defending us all."

Elidyr took the news with little more than a furrowed

brow. "This is sorrowful news. May the Mother guide his spirit."

Around him, the other Warders repeated the blessing in a murmur.

"I appreciate your words," Ashelia said, composed once more. "But I am afraid our errand is urgent and we cannot tarry long. Please, tell us: have the Emperor and his armies engaged the enemy forces?"

"Only skirmishes thus far, Peer. But the battle is soon to come. We Warders act as a vanguard to scout this field, as here is where we expect to meet the opposing armies and their monsters. Emperor Zyrl and his soldiers are but days behind."

Tal's companions exclaimed at this, Rolan even loosing a whoop of excitement. For the first time in days, Tal felt his chest loosen. *Zyrl's coming through, after all.* It seemed the first good news since their ill-fated trek began.

"Thank you, Warder." Ashelia's relief was clear in her voice. "It gladdens me to hear this. I know you will fight your best beside our new allies. Your part in this war is critical if my companions and I are to reach the Named."

"Of course, Peer Venaliel. Our sabers and spears will bleed the enemy dry."

The Warders behind Elidyr gave cheers of assent.

A slight smile creased Ashelia's lips. "I would expect nothing less. Now, with my brother's passing, a new Prime must be appointed. Until such a time as we may make an official decision, it would please me if you would inherit the position."

Elidyr circled his hands while bowing. "You honor me, my Peer. With the deepest gratitude, I accept."

Tal didn't entirely trust the Warder's attitude. He had an oiliness about him that attractive men were sometimes cursed with, and there was a falseness to his smile.

Though I'm hardly in a position to criticize.

Still, he seemed a loyal enough soldier, so Tal grinned along as the Warders congratulated their new Prime.

The Gladelysh elves lingered a few moments longer, and Elidyr attempted to press stors upon her, but he relented at Ashelia's refusal. Once they entered the miasma of Paradise, there were no certainties that they would stay with them, nor did they know if they could navigate the ascent up Ikvaldar, which lay not far ahead.

"You will need every steed," she told the new Prime, and Elidyr begrudgingly relented.

Tal watched the Warders ride back to their camp before his beloved beckoned them in the opposite direction. With the Warders rode the hope for the success of their mission, and as slim as that still was, he was glad it had grown.

If they had any remaining luck, the path to Ikvaldar would be clear, unguarded but for the Sentinel, Paradise, and the jungle's miasma.

And the dragon queen, if she's not done toying with us.

His mood sobered, and anger fanned back to flame. Though there was hope, it would be dearly bought, as it had been already.

Tal wondered how many more people would die for that hope before the end came.

Garin gnawed at his bottom lip as they drew near their final destination.

It was morning, and Ikvaldar was but a hazy shadow looming above them. The valley leading to it was hidden from sight, a strange fog having settled over the meadowlands and foothills of the Valanduali Range after they departed the Warders. Silence reigned, one respected by even the crickets and the birds.

Disquiet. It was the only word Garin had for it, this silence.

Back in Hunt's Hollow, he would have thought such a morning a magical experience and reveled in it. Now he knew what such silence could mean. If natural animals weren't near, something unnatural had likely driven them away.

Where is Yvärras? Her Nightkin? Her orkan minions?

He formed the questions, even as he knew Ilvuan, always listening, had no answers. He felt the dragon's keen awareness with every step they took toward the grand mountain. The Singer shared his suspicion of this silence.

It made Garin feel no easier as they marched forward, blind and vulnerable, toward the Enemy's stronghold.

His confusion only grew as the cliffs, gray smudges in the fog, rose high on either side. They traveled the road that bisected the valley, as defensible a position as could be hoped for, yet Garin neither saw nor sensed any signs of protectors. Ikvaldar was the center of Yuldor's power, and Garin had always assumed a garrison would guard it. Yet there was nothing.

Could we be wrong? Was this all a diversion? Or has the Emperor succeeded in drawing Yuldor's attention?

At this, Ilvuan roused enough to speak. *No,* Jenduit. *The Pretender waits above.*

Garin frowned. *Then why are you nervous?*

The dragon rumbled, a jumble of emotions filtering through Garin's thoughts. *Many streams interweave now, little Listener. I must attend to them all. Even the slightest divergence might sweep us away.*

It wasn't the rousing speech Garin had hoped for, but considering the circumstances, it would have to serve.

Then we'll keep watch, Garin asserted, and the dragon rumbled his assent.

"Eerie, isn't it? Almost inspires me to poetry."

Garin glanced over to find Falcon striding up next to him and Wren. It didn't speak well of Garin's wariness that he hadn't noticed.

"A fly drowning in tea would inspire you to poetry," Wren noted drily. She brushed a hand over her forehead and through her hair with a slight scowl. Her hair had grown longer than her preference, and she often complained of it falling in her eyes and making her skin itch. Garin was surprised she hadn't already taken a knife to it and sheared it off.

I guess even she has some vanity.

As he gazed at her, he was glad for it. Despite everything they'd suffered, no matter the scrapes and cuts and bruises she'd sustained, Wren maintained an allure Garin could never get enough of.

Wren glanced at him, and at his stare, flashed a mocking smile. He looked away, flushing.

"I'm not the only one moved to poetry, it seems," Falcon said. Tolerant as he usually was of Wren and Garin's relationship, there was too sharp an edge to his words to be teasing.

Garin cleared his throat and decided a change of subject was in order. "Ilvuan says to be wary. Considering what happened the last time we were lost in fog, I'm inclined to agree."

"Best keep an eye out, then," Wren muttered, following her own advice as she scanned their surroundings.

Falcon sighed and looked forlornly into the mist. "Sometimes I wonder if I'll finish my song. If I don't make it off of this mountain, promise me one of you will find another to write its end? Of my glorious last stand against an evil god?"

Wren pulled her father into a side hug. "Stop talking like that. You'll make it out, old man. Who else can be Court Bard to that choleric king of ours? And the Dancing Feathers need their conductor and composer."

"True," Falcon murmured. "I can only imagine how they suffer under Yelda's tyranny."

Wren rested her head on her father's shoulder, and he

grinned like a fool into the mist. Garin smiled, but fell behind them and avoided Wren's glance back.

At the end of their company came a lone, spare figure. His face was tilted down, and the wide-brimmed hat atop his head hid his expression. His narrow shoulders were bowed, and his long fingers wrapped about the straps of his heavy pack. His black braid swayed with every step along his chest.

Garin's smile dissipated by the time he fell in step next to Aelyn.

The mage darted a look at him, then as swiftly looked away. He seemed to ignore Garin, but the brightness of his tendrils, just visible beneath his hat, showed his awareness.

They'd barely spoken over the past several days. Garin, uncertain how to deal with grief, had taken to avoiding the mage as well as Ashelia. Only with Rolan did he remain comfortable discussing Helnor, the boy's disarming honesty making even such tricky conversations possible. Aelyn lent no such support. He had barely spoken a sentence inside Garin's hearing in their travels since Haudden.

But Garin couldn't avoid him any longer. It had gone past the point of grief into something more persistent and worrisome. They needed Aelyn at his best, now more than ever. And somehow, Garin needed the mage to be his old self. He was a balance to their company, never afraid to challenge the consensus or even sound reason. Through conflict, the mage forged a better path for them.

And, if he was honest, Garin missed his caustic remarks.

But as they walked side by side, he couldn't find the words to begin. Everything that came to mind was inane and contrived. But the silence, already oppressive around them, soon became unbearable.

"Maybe it won't help," Garin finally said. "But for what it's worth, I'm sorry about Helnor."

The mage jerked his head around, eyes aflame.

"Sorry, are you?" he sneered. "I'm sure that is quite comforting to my departed brother."

Garin tried pushing down his annoyance. He'd seen how Aelyn had nearly suffocated Tal for Queen Geminia's death at the Thorn's hands. Anger was how the mage dealt with grief.

Though it makes him no easier to be around.

Still, Garin made another attempt at reconciliation. "What do elves believe about death? Ashelia mentioned something about souls being guided by the Mother."

For a moment, Aelyn seemed about to supply another snippy reply. Instead, when he spoke, he sounded almost remorseful.

"They are old beliefs, unfounded in fact and endemic among our tradition-bound elders. But if you must know, the silver-hairs believe each elf possesses a soul, one born of the Mother and which must eventually return to her."

Aelyn pursed his lips. Despite all the skepticism he expressed, Garin sensed a small candle flame of hope held close to his chest.

The mage shook his head and adjusted his hat to sit more snugly on his head. "But it is a vain hope. We are bound to our bodies, and flesh must either burn or decay. Anything else we bring to death is naught but mere belief."

Garin nodded. He sensed a willing ear was what the man needed most just then. *And Silence knows I'm practiced at listening*, he thought to himself, to Ilvuan's weary groan.

But it became clear it wasn't just companionship Aelyn wanted, for he took his nod to mean more than Garin intended. "So you believe me insensitive, do you? Helnor is killed, and now I say he's forever gone in all forms! How cruel I must be to wish such a fate upon my… House-brother."

The mage's teeth clenched, and his jaw trembled. Garin mulled over the man's fumbling words. Suddenly, he saw one reason behind the man's mood. Though they'd rarely shared a kind word with each other, he found sympathy welling up in him.

"He was your brother, Aelyn. It doesn't matter what other words you use in Gladelyl. You two treated each other like brothers. You loved each other like brothers."

Aelyn darted a look from beneath his hat's brim. "What do you know of our relationship, boy?"

Garin ignored the slight. "I have three brothers of my own. I know what it's like. Believe me, you two were brothers in more than just name."

Again, the mage raised his head, and this time, Garin was surprised to find a shimmer in his eyes.

"He would have liked that." Aelyn's voice had gone grave. "Helnor always was soft, even for being the Prime Warder, as he so liked to remind us all."

Garin smiled. He remembered the last night he'd shared with Helnor, of the regret the jovial elf had expressed regarding the woman he'd loved and let slip away. He thought of all the other campfires before, all the times Helnor had made him laugh, or irritated him with his guidance, and how he'd felt safe in his company. For being a deadly warrior, Helnor had never been rough, but instead kind and considerate.

"He was," Garin replied softly.

Before either of them could say more, a call came from ahead. Garin squinted through the mist to see Tal, Ashelia, and Rolan, who walked at the fore, had stopped and turned back to them. Wondering what it meant, Garin hurried with Aelyn to meet them.

"What is it?" Wren was demanding by the time they reached the others.

Garin followed their gazes. Immediately around them, the fog had cleared, revealing a crumbled stone path beneath their feet and the sloped walls of the canyon veering toward it. The area they were in had a strange regularity to it, the stone carved into smooth bluffs. It appeared to have once boasted statues upon its faces, though any distinct features had long ago worn away. A staircase, twisting and formed of round-edged slabs of stone, led up to the base of Ikvaldar.

And midway up the stairs rose an archway.

"Arch" was perhaps a generous term in the sense, for it was little more than two enormous slabs of rock leaning together. The stone was flat and gray, the edges layered and weather-dulled, yet shimmering symbols lay all across its surface.

Glyphs, crimson and violet and somewhere in between, were scratched into the stone. *Dragon glyphs.*

Ilvuan stirred in recognition. *This is an ancient portal, one that marked the entrance to a hallowed place.*

Hallowed?

The dragon rumbled in his mind. *What you mortals might think of as holy. A place divine. A place blessed.*

From his impressions of Ilvuan's thoughts, Garin gathered his meaning. *A place of great power.*

Yes; power and peril.

As he conversed with Ilvuan, the others also discussed the archway.

"Is it safe to pass through?" Falcon asked. "We haven't precisely had the best luck with dragon runes."

Tal stared at the portal with his arms crossed. "It's the Sentinel's Gate. Only with its guardian's blessing may we pass through it."

"And how do we gain that?" The bard's voice had risen a pitch higher.

"Did your Extinguished friend mention anything of it?" Aelyn asked, his words dripping with sarcasm.

Tal glanced at the mage, wearing his usual smile. "Only that we must answer a riddle and be truthful."

Aelyn's lips curled. "How very helpful he was."

Garin stared at the ancient gateway. A thought occurred to him. Closing his eyes, he opened up to the Worldsong and pulled it into himself. It filled him to bursting, and even with Yuldor's taint upon it, Garin found his spirits lifting on its triumphant chorus.

But all thoughts of it dispersed as he heard a powerful song come near.

Garin stared through the gap in the portal. No sooner had he looked than the mist beyond it darkened with a shadow. It was as big as a chimera and also shaped like a great cat. Its body glimmered in the dim light, gold reflecting from part of it.

But it was its song that put Garin's nerves on edge. It wasn't mournful like the songs that filled the dragonstones, nor furious like the storms that rose from Tal and Yvärras. This was a dirge, a death song, the promise of demise and decay.

The Sentinel had come.

THE SENTINEL'S GATE

TAL GATHERED SORCERY IN A FLOOD AND STUDIED THE NEARING creature.

It had the body of a lion, or perhaps a tiger such as he'd seen in a Halenhol menagerie long ago. It moved with the same feline grace, its hackles raising with each measured step. Always, it was balanced and relaxed, yet also ready to pounce. Stripes of gold and bronze wound their way about its powerful body, including through the mane that framed its head. Its long hair was silken and shone with the scant light of the glyphs.

Though the rest of it spoke of a cat, its face was flat and featured like an owl's. Its eyes were wide and round, and behind them lay what seemed like a star-dusted darkness with a silver glow around the edges. Its beak was small compared to its large head, and its tail swayed from side to side, mesmerizing in its steady tempo.

With his sorcery, Tal sensed more. Not one thread wended into it, but four, twisted together like the trunks of the trees along Rajeya's coast. It wasn't near as powerful as Yvärras nor himself, but something about its sorcery made his skin crawl.

With a strange certainty, he knew the Sentinel might be the deadliest opponent he'd yet faced.

Tal itched to draw *Velori*, but he kept his hands at his sides. His thumb touched where the Ring of Thalkuun rested just above his glovelet. He wouldn't threaten this beast except in retaliation.

Still, he quailed at the thought of attempting to speak to it. Yet a glance at his companions showed none of the rest of them were inclined to.

You're supposed to be the godkiller, he mocked himself. *Past time you act like it.*

Clearing his throat, he broke the silence that had fallen over the mist-shrouded clearing.

"Are you the one who guards this mountain? The one called the Sentinel?"

The creature paused as soon as he spoke. The unnatural stillness of its body, with no sign even of breathing, made Tal even more unsettled than its movement had. His veins felt they would burst with all the sorcery he pressed through them.

A whispering voice, one stripped of gender and emotion, wove between his thoughts.

"Sentinel. Kef'thorex. Shänaeth fith Gaesh. I was. I am. I will be."

Tal ground his teeth together until he formed a smile. The way it spoke in his mind was both different and similar to how dragons had. Yvärras and Ilvuan's voices were distinct, almost heard in the way they projected their thoughts. But the Sentinel... its speech tried to meld with Tal's mind, hiding among his thoughts, scrambling and confusing. He hated it, yet he couldn't let the creature know lest it risk the negotiations.

If it hasn't already read it in my mind.

"We seek to ascend Ikvaldar," he declared. "To reach its peak."

The Sentinel still hadn't moved from beneath the archway. Tal wondered if it was truly alive, or instead a phantom that lingered through ancient sorcery, its source long lost from the World.

Its response came in the same probing, slithering way. *"You climb. You strive. You hunger."*

Tal had the strange urge to scrub his ears clean, as if it might banish the haunting voice from his head. More infuriating was how little its response told him how to respond.

He framed his next words carefully. "We don't wish to come into conflict with you, Sentinel. Will you oppose us when we proceed?"

There was the slightest movement in its eyes, then it stilled again. Tal kept a wary watch on its sorcery, but it only undulated as it poured into the creature, never pushing beyond the boundaries of its body.

"What do you carry?" it spoke again at length. *"Love or hate? Peace or war?"*

Tal wished he could consult with the others, but he wasn't even sure if they could hear the Sentinel's questions. This was down to him.

He knew of only one answer they could give. The honest one.

"We bring a hate born from protecting those we love. We bring war to establish a greater peace."

The Sentinel's head tilted, staring with the same unblinking consideration as an owl might give.

"Paradox," the guardian of the mountain whispered in his mind. *"Is this truth?"*

Tal swallowed, fumbling for an answer. "Every truth is the child of paradox."

Hissing filled Tal's mind, like steam escaping a tea kettle. It didn't seem malicious, yet his heart beat faster with each moment it continued.

Is it laughing? Is such a creature capable of laughter?

As suddenly as it began, the sound faded back to stillness, and the Sentinel's voice replaced it.

"*Paradox, you bring; paradox, you must resolve. An enemy who is an ally, and can never be.*"

Tal tried to unravel the strange syntax, to understand the riddle contained within it. But before he could, a sensation rattled through his mind.

His blood burned in warning.

Another approached, one familiar and powerful. He raised his head, teeth bared in a snarl, and watched the great being descend from the sky.

Tal could barely think, his reason lost to hate's flames. His sorcery begged to be unleashed, stoking the fire higher still.

The name squeezed free of his throat in a harsh whisper:

"Yvärras."

Garin felt her circle lower and lower, and though he couldn't yet see her, he knew her name.

Yvärras.

He shouldn't have been surprised. She had pursued them across the hills and plains, harrying them all the way. Ilvuan had said she could always find them; it only made sense that she'd appear here and now, before they could embark on their final step.

But her arrival doomed their plans. Though they'd turned aside her dragonfire before, they couldn't defy her for long. And the Sentinel's loyalties most likely aligned with hers, though he couldn't be entirely certain of the strange beast.

Yet even faced with the hopeless situation, Garin found an unexpected feeling smoldering within him. As he stared up after the blaring song descending from above, he remembered Helnor burning on his pyre. His lips pulled back to bare his teeth. He wanted to tear her apart, limb from limb.

It was a fool's fancy, and he knew it. But it didn't stop rage from suffusing him, body and soul.

Calm, Jenduit. *We must remain calm.*

Ilvuan spread his presence through Garin's body. Where the dragon touched, his blood cooled, and the flush faded from his skin. Garin tried to hold tight to his anger, fearing the Singer would steal that from him as well.

She killed Helnor!

As she was behind the deaths of many other mortals in Haudden. All the same, you must set aside your hate. The past is stone; only the future remains clay.

Garin didn't want to listen, to see the reason in his words. He felt a coward for even considering them. Yet a deeper part of him knew the truth.

Ilvuan seemed to sense him calming, for his presence retreated. *Many trials still await us. This is only the first. We must forge an alliance, here and now, for we will gain no more powerful ally than the Protectress.*

"If we can trust her not to kill us all," Garin muttered aloud. But his thoughts stumbled on a sudden connection. *An enemy who is an ally, and can never be.* In a rush, he felt he understood the Sentinel's game and the paradox before them. For both the battle to come and to get past the Sentinel's Gate, they needed to join with Yvärras.

His resolution folded in on itself, however, as her shadow loomed above.

Instinctual fear made him scurry for cover, as it did the rest of his companions. Yvärras was a storm unto herself, both in body and song. The wind from each flap of her wings tore at the air. Her song rippled through the sky like a boulder tossed in a lake. The reek of sulfur, hot stone, and reptile billowed over Garin, stinging his nostrils. He found himself on all fours, crawling behind a boulder half his height, wishing again and again for her not to see or notice him. Dust poured out in waves past his poor hiding spot, telling of her nearing the ground.

The dragon queen landed with a tremor, then loosed an ear-splitting screech.

"Mortals! I did not think you would come so far."

Garin's mind felt chopped in half. He doubted his legs would have held him if he tried to stand. His bladder strained. He'd withstood her inferno before, but he didn't know if he could do so again.

Before he found the courage to stand, another rose free of the sheltering rocks. The song cascading from him nearly seemed to match Yvärras'.

Garin watched with equal measures of fear and admiration as Tal faced the dragon queen alone.

"Yvärras!" Tal's voice, enhanced with sorcery, boomed in the clearing. "You killed our companion in Haudden. His blood is on your teeth and claws. And you will suffer for it!"

Scorn spattered like acid over Garin's mind.

"A lofty oath, Heartblood, even for you. But I am no sorcerer for you to overpower. I am ava'dual, and the greatest among them. You shall never prevail."

Garin felt Yvärras take a lumbering step forward. He dared to glance around the rock and saw her wings spread above her, making her terrifying size larger still. Her barbed tail flicked from side to side, and her eyes fragmented with molten gold. Dozens of long teeth peeked out from her powerful jaws.

Yet he could hear the rage in Tal's song, the tempo fast, the notes loud. Garin knew his response even before he spoke it.

"If you sought to test us, you pressed too far. We will never—"

"Wait!"

Garin was as surprised as the rest of his company to find he stood, his arms in the air, his tinny voice ringing through the clearing. His legs immediately shook, and his stomach seemed to drop out of his body.

Yvärras turned and studied him with blazing eyes.

"Alärthoras. You have protected this fragile flesh, then."

Though he'd intervened, Garin now found himself speechless. But he didn't stand alone. Ilvuan's presence inundated him, firming his limbs and banishing his terror. A strange serenity settled over his thoughts.

"Well?" the Protectress demanded. *"What does the parasite and his pet wish to say?"*

Ilvuan answered for him, his voice low and sonorous so it echoed in Garin's bones.

"You did not come here to taunt us, Yvärras, nor have you pursued and reaved us all this way for entertainment."

Contempt burned against Garin again.

"Would it not suffice?" Yvärras declared. *"Your struggles have been so diverting!"*

Ilvuan remained unswayed. *"No, it is not enough. You desire the same as I: the resurrection of our kind. The return of our rule. Separate, we will fail in this. Only together might we succeed."*

It wasn't a new assertion to Garin. Yet, faced with the prospect again, he doubted. *The return of our rule.* If all dragons were like Yvärras when in the flesh, he saw little reason to subject the World to their tyranny. After all, what they strove to do now was dethrone one despot, not raise many more in his place.

But as soon as he thought about it, Garin tried tucking the notion away. Though he trusted Ilvuan with his life, he didn't want him knowing his thoughts on this if he could help it.

He couldn't hide it in time. But Ilvuan didn't react as he expected. Instead of painful anger, a calming reassurance radiated out from the Singer, settling his jangling nerves once more.

Garin wondered if he could trust even this response. *But what choice do I have?*

Yvärras straightened her neck and stared down at him. Her words drove all other thoughts from his mind.

"I suppose you have fared well in my trials," she conceded. *"But*

it is not sufficient, Alärthoras. You lack the strength to defy the Pretender."

Denial, untainted by doubt, radiated from Ilvuan. *"With your help, we will have enough."*

Yvärras' head swayed, back and forth, back and forth. Garin couldn't decide if they were the movements of a snake about to strike, or the dragon queen considering the proposal.

Then another stepped in line with Garin and Tal.

"Yvärras." The Peer's voice held all the authority of her position, yet it remained a fly's buzzing compared to their adversary. *"Ava'dual.* You killed my brother—"

"*Our* brother!"

Aelyn approached to stand next to his House-sister, his slender frame trembling with wrath. Despair rose in Garin. The mage would prove even more intractable than Ashelia or even Tal. Yet he knew there was nothing to be done but wait for them to say their piece. Neither would be silenced until they had.

The siblings exchanged a look, then the Peer settled a hand on her House-brother's elbow and spoke again.

"His death was not your direct doing. Perhaps it was not even your intention. But whether it was from callousness or rancor, you remain responsible."

"Yes!" Aelyn's eyes shone with fervor. "And you will pay for that guilt a hundredfold!"

They're throwing it away. Garin tried to think of some way to fix this. But Yvärras didn't hide her feelings. Her anger was like facing the heat of flowing lava, and it grew more intense with each passing moment.

"Then what are your intentions, mortals? Do you mean to claim vengeance?" Disdain dripped from every word.

No! Garin wanted to cry out. But the word stuck in his throat.

He turned inward. *Do something!* he cried to Ilvuan. *They'll ruin it all!*

But once more, the dragon only radiated tranquility over him. It had the opposite effect now, infuriating him further.

Ashelia was already speaking. What she said brought all his spinning thoughts to a standstill.

"No, Yvärras. We do not."

The dragon queen's surprise washed over them in a chilling flood, extinguishing her fury to a simmer.

"What is this?" she demanded. *"What can you mean, elfling?"*

Ashelia took three steps forward, standing before all the others, before Tal closed in behind her, the arm that didn't carry *Velori* held out as if to protect her.

"It is a proposal, Queen of the *Ava'duala*. I offer an alliance as Alärthoras does. All prosper if the Named is defeated. Only he benefits when we fight among ourselves."

She took another step forward, then another. Half the distance she'd closed between them, now so near she wouldn't be able to avoid any sudden attack from the dragon queen. Garin's heart hammered in his throat.

"Ashelia..." Tal muttered, his voice just loud enough to be audible.

"Sister!" Aelyn all but shrieked. But he didn't draw any nearer to the dragon.

Ashelia ignored them both. Her head was tilted up as she held Yvärras' gaze.

"It is not flattery to say you are more powerful than Tal, even more than all of us combined, including Alärthoras. Yet there is something we possess that you need. So I ask you, Yvärras, Protectress of the World: Will you fight beside us? Will you defy Yuldor Soldarin, the enemy of the lands you claim to guard?"

Garin could barely draw a breath, his chest had grown so tight. He couldn't read Yvärras' emotions now. The Protectress had pulled them in tight about her, hidden beyond his reach.

Is she convinced? he thought. *Or preparing to destroy us all?*

But Yvärras hadn't given her response when Aelyn spoke up again, his words as shattered as a lightning-struck sea.

"Ashelia! How can you betray his memory? *This* is how you honor our brother? Blood must be repaid with blood!"

The red atmosphere returned to the air. Yvärras' anger grew once more. Garin swayed, his balance lost. For a moment, he thought he might lose consciousness.

Hands held him upright even as Ilvuan surged within him.

"Keep it together," Wren muttered in his ear. "We may have to fight soon." Her fingers clung to his sleeves, and he wondered if she was lending him strength or borrowing his.

Tal's voice boomed out, and by his words, he was either oblivious to the dragon queen's emotions or defying them.

"Ashelia, you know I'm not inclined to agree with Aelyn. Yet I must. Before Haudden, I might have forgiven Yvärras for what she put us through. But now... I cannot look aside. Helnor deserves more than to be forgotten."

A rumble, like the awakening of a volcano, shook the ground. Yet it was Ashelia who drew all their eyes as she whipped her head around to stare first at Tal, then her House-brother.

"You think I've forgotten him? I have not! Every bone in me screams to spill her blood! I yearn to claim justice for him!"

As suddenly as it had come, Ashelia's anger fled, leaving her shoulders slumped.

"But none of us can afford vengeance. I do not forget, nor do I forgive. I do not renounce my loathing for Yvärras the Callous. Yet that does not matter now; none of our feelings do. An alliance is the only path forward, the only way to defeat Yuldor. And victory is how we can truly honor Helnor's sacrifice — and Kaleras' as well."

At that, Tal sagged, like a puppet whose strings had been cut. Garin knew what it meant to mention Kaleras. Though they'd never spoken of it, he knew the Warlock of Canturith had been Tal's father. Even with as brief a time as Garin had known him, he found the thought of the aged man bringing fresh resolve.

For Helnor. For Kaleras. For all those who died in Haudden, and in Elendol, Kavaugh, and Vathda.

He didn't have a place of authority here. His opinions mattered the least. Yet Garin knew he had to speak all the same.

"We have to set the past aside," Garin said as loudly as his closed throat allowed. "We have to move on. Like with you and my father, Tal. And Aelyn, how Tal couldn't stop Queen Geminia's death — you forgave him, didn't you? We don't have to forget; we won't, and we can't. But like Ashelia said, we have to move forward."

His words seemed to land. Tal and Aelyn wavered; a curious smile played on Tal's lips, while Aelyn's frown deepened.

Before either could respond, Yvärras asserted her presence again, her emotions surging over them like water from a broken dam. Scathing amusement and haughty offense remained, but they were superseded by an unrelenting anger.

"Death approaches, mortals. I will not hurry it along, but neither shall I prevent it. Challenge the Pretender, if you believe you can prevail. But you fly on your own!"

Then followed words that carried power of their own — dragon words, Garin recognized. After several long moments of speaking them, Yvärras rose to her full height, her head towering dozens of feet above. Her mouth parted, and her forked tongue flickered out to taste the air.

The Protectress tilted back her head and rent the sky with her scream.

Garin came back to himself as the dragon's wings spread. Foul air rushed over him and battered him back, and only with Wren's support did he remain upright.

Yvärras bunched her legs, then leaped into the air. Her

wings snapped down again, carrying her aloft and into the fog above.

For a moment, he could only stare at where the dragon had disappeared. *Is that it?* he thought in a daze. *After all she put us through, that's how this ends?*

Ilvuan rumbled, and now he didn't exude calmness, but burned with buried emotion. *Ruined,* came his reply before he retreated deeper within Garin.

Unsettled, he wanted to inquire further, but at that moment, he remembered the Sentinel. Garin lowered his gaze to see the guardian remained under the stone arch, sitting on its hind legs and waiting for their notice. Its owlish face held equal measures of malice and sagacity.

"The third paradox is resolved," it said. *"Ascend the mountain. More questions there. Fewer answers. Will you fulfill? Or a vacancy remain?"*

Without waiting for a response, the Sentinel rose to its feet and sauntered back into the fog from which it had come. The glyphs on the stones flared once with violent light, then extinguished.

A moment of stillness passed. The fellowship gazed at one another.

"What in Yuldor's bloody name just happened?" Wren asked, the words strained.

Tal shook his head. He almost seemed overcome with mirth, though none of it touched his eyes. "We'll discuss it later. For now, it's best we don't wait until our gatekeeper returns. Through the gate we go."

Garin eyed the leaning slabs of stone skeptically. "Why don't we just walk around it?"

"The boy is right," Aelyn said, his voice hoarse from shouting. "Far safer to ascend by an alternate route."

Ashelia, stiff-backed, fetched Rolan from Falcon. Holding her son's hand, she trudged forward.

"It will take too long," she said, her voice chill and aloof. "Come. We must hurry before it returns."

Go, Ilvuan murmured in Garin's mind, seeming a measure calmer than before. *You will not come to harm here.*

It was all the confirmation he needed. Garin glanced at Wren, then nodded toward the archway. She raised her eyebrows, but only sighed.

They walked toward it together, and arm-in-arm, passed beneath the monolith.

When they'd crossed to the other side, Garin felt as if something had shifted. The sorcery had faded from the glyphs, yet he felt as if some enchantment had settled over him all the same. Shaking his head, he tried to dismiss the notion.

He followed his companions as they ascended the mountain, hoping against hope they hadn't thrown away their last chance.

PILGRIMAGE

Tal's footfalls were heavy as he and his companions labored up the mountain.

The fog had thickened, but he observed what he could of their surroundings. The landscape was gray and bleak. Boulders mounded around them in piles and slides, and pebbles slipped beneath their feet. A trail of crushed rock was their only markings of the way up the mountainside, though it was worn almost entirely away. Sporadic areas of purple flowers and the occasional gnarled tree broke the monotony. The sulfur of sorcery hung in the air, and his veins prickled with its heat.

Tal strained to perceive any sign of enemies, but only in the fog itself did he feel magic. As of yet, the Sentinel was Yuldor's only defense, and it hadn't proven difficult to circumvent.

Remembering Ikvaldar's guardian, however, reminded him of his latest failure.

He glanced up at Ashelia, who led their party, and stared at her back until he stumbled on an unseen stone. She had remained nearly silent since the encounter with Yvärras, but her anger was as palpable as any sorcerous aura. Though he was still furious at the dragon for her role in Helnor's death, he knew Ashelia's path had been the wiser one. Yet it had also failed in the end.

As usual, he mused, *you've proven the fool, Tal Harrenfel.*

How weary he was of his own name. It was too heavy a burden to hear. He longed to be Bran again, a man who was little more than a chicken farmer and the secret defender of lonely marshes. He longed for peace, and not only for himself, but for all those with whom he traveled.

But that's just it, isn't it? There can be no peace while Yuldor reigns.

Tal's spinning thoughts came to an abrupt halt as someone spoke at his elbow.

"Damned dragons," Aelyn muttered. "They claim to be the protectors of the World, but that *queen* has only tyrannized it!"

Tal noticed the mage didn't speak loudly enough that his House-sister could hear his complaints. He smiled wearily.

"True enough. All the same, Aelyn, we have to let it go. Our intentions may have been good, but we bungled a needed opportunity, and we both know it. Yvärras, bastardess though she is, would have been an invaluable ally."

The elf scoffed. "An ally who cannot be trusted is no ally at all. We'll do without her. Besides, who else do we need beyond you?"

Aelyn's smile mocked his words. Tal grimaced.

"I'm glad you don't change, Aelyn," he muttered. "I can always rely on your vitriol."

"Indeed, Harrenfel, you can. Until the very end."

Tal clapped Aelyn on the shoulder, and he found a moment's joy as the mage wriggled away from his touch.

Aelyn fell back, and soon after, Falcon stepped up in his place. The bard noticed Tal's gaze on Ashelia and cast him a sympathetic smile.

"Not your fault, my friend. Anyone would have been as angry in your place. And we don't know that Yvärras would have sided with us, anyhow."

Tal nodded at Ashelia's back. "She kept her head, and he was her brother."

"Ah, but she's an entirely different breed, isn't she? Not meant derogatorily, of course," the bard added hastily.

"A bard afraid to offend. Now I've seen all the World has to offer."

Falcon shook his head, his brow drawn. "I fear we haven't quite yet."

They fell silent, the sounds of stone crunching beneath their boots the only thing to be heard.

Falcon, as usual, didn't take long to speak up. "I'll bet you wish only syrens waited in the mist now."

"Nothing does, as far as I can tell. Nothing sorcerous, anyway."

"Pah! But it tastes funny, doesn't it? Like... an omelet of spoiled eggs."

Tal rolled his eyes. "You're getting rusty."

Falcon sighed. "Do I ever know it, my friend. A bard without music is like a lake without water."

"A pit?"

"I had 'nonexistent' more in mind."

Tal allowed himself a low chuckle.

After a moment, Falcon spoke again. "Did they tell of what lies ahead? Inanis, that is, and Hellexa."

He shrugged. "Some, but little enough."

"Ah. I see."

Tal put an arm around Falcon's shoulders and drew him close. "Don't worry, old friend. I'll protect you from whatever lies ahead."

Falcon patted his hand, like a grandmother might a child's. "Oh, I know you will, my legendary inspiration. But can you shield us from a god?"

Neither bothered to answer.

They pressed on until the glow of daylight faded from the fog, and a darker gloom settled in. Their party ascended with every step, yet the landscape scarcely shifted. Tal wished they could glimpse the World beyond to find out how high they were. From the labored breathing of the others, they'd risen thousands of feet above where they'd started, yet for all they could see, they were where they'd begun. All they could do was continue and hope some grand illusion wasn't being played on them.

Though Silence knows faith isn't my strong suit.

They set up camp in near silence. The fog seemed to dampen moods as well as sound, and it encroached like a jealous lover upon their camp.

Tal insisted on the first watch. His sorcery-enhanced senses were their best protection against any Nightkin prowling the mountainside, and everyone knew it. It wasn't long before his companions' breathing evened, exhaustion from the strenuous hike overcoming the discomfort of sleeping on stone.

As he sat there, Tal noticed a sensation pressing on the back of his mind. Now that it came to his attention, he realized it had been there for some time. It teased his sorcery, pulling at it and making his veins prickle. It was like hearing the far-off roar of a waterfall, its power projecting even from a distance. And this magic was powerful indeed.

The Worldheart.

He knew it must be the source, or the channel that fed up to the Worldheart, at least. He still had only the vaguest idea of what the elusive power was. A breach in the World, he'd heard from Pim. An enormous boulder shaped like beasts and formed of black, red-veined stone, he'd read in Hellexa's fable. Soltor had claimed it was what enabled Yuldor to become as near a deity as he had, and Pim had affirmed it.

Tal shook his head, trying to banish the distant sensation from it. Whatever awaited him up there, he would soon find out.

Sorcery rippled through the air before him.

His focus snapped back to the present, and his veins filled with fire as he squinted into the gloom. He shouldn't have been able to see far between the night and the thickness of the fog, yet as Tal stared at where the disturbance materialized, he saw humanoid figures emerging. Shining with internal light, their bodies appeared as insubstantial as the mist. Not knowing what to make of them, Tal hesitated, watching and waiting to see what would come next.

Details formed, their light cutting through the mist so he could see them clearly. They weren't clothed in any manner he recognized, but wore long robes with sashes draping over one shoulder. Sandals were lashed to their feet and up their ankles. Their hair was long though bound and braided in assorted fashions. Some of their features were of humans, while others were reminiscent of elves. They seemed to speak, their ghostly lips moving, but Tal only heard the wind above the rushing sound of the Worldheart.

His muscles tensed, his sorcery held at the ready, Tal watched as they passed, laboring up the same path Tal's party were traveling.

Behind him, he sensed one of his companions rising, both by their sorcery and the noise they made. Dread rose in him, suspecting what was coming, though he knew it was for the best. He didn't turn to greet Ashelia, but kept his eyes on the glowing phantoms. She stood silently at his shoulder until the ethereal company ascended the boulders above them and passed out of sight.

"What were those?" she asked, her voice hushed. Tal understood her reticence. He didn't want to risk attracting unwanted attention, either.

"I don't know," he admitted. "Apparitions, I suppose, but not of a malevolent kind."

At last, Tal turned around, though he kept his senses

strained for any warning of an attack. Ashelia's face was lined with weariness and grief. Her complexion was washed out, and not only from the pall of the mist. Her eyes matched the gray fog, and her tendrils were slow despite the potential danger.

Fresh pangs of guilt assaulted Tal. He wished he could take her in his arms and wash away her pain.

But you haven't helped, he lashed at himself. *You've only added to her misery.*

He opened his mouth to speak, but she beat him to it.

"I know, Tal. I know."

A small, rueful smile claimed his lips. "Let me say it, anyway."

Her shoulders sagged. "If you must."

"I lost sight of the greater goal, Ashelia. I let my emotions get the best of me. I thought I was doing right by you, but I was wrong. You had the way of it, what you said to Yvärras. The best path to honoring Helnor right now isn't vengeance or justice, but to make his sacrifice worth something. I should've seen it, and for that, I'm sorry."

He pressed his lips closed. He could prattle on, justifying why he'd done what he had, how none of this was the way he would have wished it. But Tal knew what wishing and whinging were worth. Ashelia deserved better, now most of all.

He forced himself to meet her eyes. He waited for condemnation.

At length, she smiled. Though it didn't extend beyond her mouth, Tal was relieved to see it all the same.

"I understand. And part of me is grateful. That you cared so much about him. That you would sacrifice so much for his memory."

Tal bowed his head. It was praise he didn't deserve. Praise that he craved.

"He would have done the same," he murmured.

When a third voice spoke, Tal didn't startle. He'd felt Aelyn approaching through the darkness.

"He would have done more, the damned fool. Likely would have thrown himself at the dragon and gotten himself killed."

Tal looked up at the mage. His face was set into hard lines, but the anger was as false a face as any the Extinguished had worn. His eyes burned with feverish light. Tal knew that pain, the anxious need to do something, anything, yet knowing nothing could relieve the guilt.

Ashelia looked over at her House-brother. "Perhaps. But that doesn't mean you have to. Let it go, *Belosi*. We cannot afford any luxury now, justice least of all."

Something in the mage seemed to break. His rigid posture bent, and he sagged under his own weight.

"Damned fool..." Tal could hear the mage muttering. "Damned noble fool..."

Ashelia took his hand and Aelyn allowed it. Tal turned back toward the fog and pretended not to hear them weep.

MIASMA'S TOUCH

GARIN SUCKED DOWN AIR, WISHING IT WOULD STOP THE BURNING in his lungs and the searing in his legs. But it couldn't; nothing could — nothing but an end to their ceaseless march.

Each breath seemed to stick in his throat, like the air were full of cotton. His legs, though well-adjusted to walking, felt as weak as they ever had. His shoulders ached from carrying his pack. Even his eyes felt strained from squinting into the gray mist as he searched for creeping enemies.

He didn't even have the Worldsong for comfort. The farther they went up Ikvaldar's winding path, the stranger it sounded. Many melodies seemed to wind through it, the notes conflicting and jarring, so it once more resembled little more than a riot of noise. Eventually, Garin had to close himself off from it, his head aching from echoes of discord.

What's wrong with it? he asked Ilvuan. *Why is it chaotic now?*

The dragon gave a noncommittal response, merely spreading his warming presence over his bones.

Garin tried a different tactic. *How much farther, then? We've been climbing a day and half, and there's still no sign of this Paradise.*

This finally evoked a response. *Can you not hear it? The* Doash'uunae *ails from its nearness.*

The news put energy into Garin's stride. Though the thought of Paradise's miasma still made his skin crawl, he was ready for a change from the monotony of their journey.

Well, perhaps not any change. No Nightkin had ambushed them yet, and he was happy for it to stay that way.

True to Ilvuan's word, the mist thinned soon thereafter. Garin's companions murmured at the change, but Garin only kept his eyes ahead and above, watching for the shift in the gray landscape.

It's near. The next leg of the ascent. He tried not to think of what the last leg held for them.

At last, it appeared: a wall of green looming from the fog. Tal, who led the party, slowed their pace, but didn't stop. Garin studied the tree line. After the sorry sights thus far, seeing such a verdant forest confounded him. The East Marsh had been thick with vegetation, as had the woods surrounding Elendol, but this was a true jungle. The canopy was so thick that the forest floor was entirely shaded. Vines, a startling red hue, curled around the great maple trunks and blossomed with broad leaves of their own. The noises of forest creatures — squirrels, birds, insects, and others he didn't know — increased in intensity with every step.

But what caught Garin's attention most of all was the mist oozing from between the trunks.

It was different in quality from the fog they'd traveled through thus far, more like smoke in the way it moved and cohered. Also strange was its coloring, a pale yellow that shimmered where sunlight caught on it. Garin was at once wary and fascinated. He could guess what it was.

Paradise's miasma.

Aelyn, walking at the back, shouted for a halt. "Now we shall test the results of Koax Mraaj's research."

Garin hid a smile as he turned with the others to throng

about the mage. Almost, Aelyn sounded as pompous as he had of old. It was the first definite improvement in his manner since Helnor's death. Melancholy threaded into Garin at the thought, but he quickly uprooted it. Now wasn't the time for sorrow.

Having gathered the party's attention, the mage gestured to Garin. "The Heartstones, boy."

Wondering why he'd missed the old Aelyn, Garin sighed and extracted the stones from the pouch at his waist. With his mind closed to the Worldsong, he couldn't hear the dragon songs as he cradled them in his palm, yet the memory of them echoed in his head.

As Aelyn beckoned again, Garin reluctantly placed the stones in the mage's hand. Ilvuan growled in the back of his mind, but though Garin's hand twitched, the dragon didn't stop the exchange.

"So how do they work?" Wren said, crossing her arms.

Aelyn smirked as he held up the stones. "Like with the shard that was in Tal's side, and the bracers that bound our magic, merely touching Heartstone appears to negate sorcery. Simple as it seems, all we must do to be protected from the miasma is hold one."

Wren plucked a stone from Aelyn's hand and held it up. At her cavalier handling of the black rock, Ilvuan rumbled again with displeasure. Garin tried to project conciliatory feelings in return, but the dragon wasn't easily appeased.

"There's a hole here," Wren announced after several moments' study. "Large enough to thread a string through. We could wear them as necklaces — or, better yet, bracelets. Have to maintain skin contact, don't we? Otherwise Garin couldn't have cast magic this whole time with them on his waist." She lowered the stone and raised an eyebrow at Garin.

"Clever, my daughter!" Falcon exclaimed. He reached out and shook her by the shoulder until she irritably brushed him off.

"We can use bandaging for thread," Ashelia said, pulling off her pack to rifle through it.

Aelyn watched the proceedings with his arms crossed, his displeasure just as radiant to Garin as Ilvuan's.

"I suppose we've decided then," he noted drily.

Tal chuckled as he kneeled to assist Ashelia. "That we did, my sulky friend. That we did."

They spent the next several minutes tearing the Peer's bandages into strips thin enough to pull through the holes in the stones, a trickier task than Garin expected. As he chewed his lip and made a fourth attempt at threading the hole, Aelyn spoke up again.

"There is another consideration: it is likely our own sorcery won't work while we touch Heartstone."

"A fair point, Aelyn," Tal responded. "Paradise should be safe from all I know of it. But if not, since I won't need one, I should still be able to protect you."

"And why's that?" Wren asked tartly.

His old mentor held up his gloved hand. With his fingers exposed, the dark ring with shimmering green glyphs was just visible.

"The Ring of Thalkuun," Garin murmured.

Tal nodded. "Does that ease your mind, Aelyn?"

The mage only huffed.

Soon thereafter, they finished making their bracelets and helped tie them on to each other. As soon as Wren finished knotting his, Garin flexed his wrist and tested it. The bracelet barely slipped, the cloth tight enough that the stone dug slightly into his skin. He didn't complain.

Better a bit of discomfort than chancing the miasma.

Ilvuan echoed his conclusion with a rumble.

By the time Garin thought to test the stone, Wren was already extending a hand and calling out softly, "*Kald!*"

Garin flinched, expecting a flash of fire. Instead, nothing happened. Wren lowered her arm and shrugged.

"The sorcery flowed through me, but nothing comes out. I suppose they work."

Tal turned back to the jungle. "Then there's no more reason to delay. Time to head up."

Trepidation filled Garin. Yet when his onetime mentor led the way up the mountain, he followed.

The sounds from the dense forest grew louder as they neared. Garin couldn't identify them all. There were things other than birds and insects back there, creatures he hadn't encountered before — or so he thought until Ashelia identified them.

"Do you hear that, Rolan?" she asked her son.

The boy nodded vigorously. "Monkeys!"

"That's right. And those birds — the ones with the colorful beaks. Do you know what they're called?"

Rolan shook his head as Garin squinted into the canopy. The bird's beak was half as big as its body, which wasn't much larger than his head, and displayed brilliant hues of red, blue, and yellow. Its plumage was black except for a white patch around its neck.

"Toucans," Wren identified them haughtily. "They have them in the Befa Isles. Ox hardly ever shut up about them."

Garin didn't know how he'd missed them before; now that he'd spotted one, many others were apparent in the canopy.

"Here it comes," Tal called back from the front, where he neared the tree line.

At the reminder, Garin looked down and startled. A tendril of the miasma wound over his ankles.

His skin tingled where it touched. The golden vapor seemed almost alive as it curled around his leg. Garin barely dared to breathe, wondering if the dragonstone's protection extended to his organs. More of the miasma joined the first seeking arm. Soon, he was entirely wrapped up in it, and he had no choice but to draw in a breath.

Without thought, he opened himself to the Worldsong and recoiled.

When he had accepted the Song into himself the first time, the din had become beautiful, but he still heard the chaotic individual components. Now, it was melodious in a way it never had been before, each note beautiful. Garin stood, mouth open, and listened. It filled him, lifted him as if he hovered on a yellow cloud. He remembered Ilvuan's dragon dreams of soaring above the World, only air below him—

Be wary, Jenduit. *Beauty often masks thorns.*

At Ilvuan's words, Garin roused. Though he didn't yet close himself to the Worldsong, the dragon's warning provided enough tether for him to distance himself from it. Still, he listened, trying to understand why it had suddenly changed.

The longer he observed it, the thinner the Song's charm seemed. Such perfect harmony needled. It was like eating something far too sweet, like scraping frosting from the tops of Coral Castle handcakes, as he and Wren sometimes had. It helped him comprehend what had happened.

He's corrupted the Song, Garin thought to the Singer. *Yuldor has made it his own here in Paradise.*

Yes, Ilvuan affirmed. *He sought to make the World harmonious in this place. But in peace there is senescence, for all life requires struggle.*

"Garin! Wake up!"

He startled out of his reverie as Wren grabbed and shook him by the arm. Uttering a wordless protest, he wrenched himself free.

"I'm fine, Wren, I'm fine!"

Her eyes spun madly. Somehow, her skin seemed more luminous than before, though they'd entered the shade of the jungle. Then he noticed the difference: the miasma clung to her like pollen to a flower.

"You look beautiful."

The words were out of his mouth before he could retract them. Wren looked caught off guard, then grinned.

"You *are* addled," she affirmed, then leaned in to peck him on the cheek. "Keep your head on straight, Dunford. We have a long way to go yet."

"Everyone well?" Tal called back. He stood deeper in the forest and had *Velori* drawn, the runes shining a brilliant blue.

When each had given affirmation, the man turned forward again. "Come on. The sooner we're through, the better."

Garin, remembering what lay atop Ikvaldar, somehow doubted that was true.

PARADISE

He hadn't believed all he'd learned of Paradise, hadn't thought it would be a wondrous place. How could it be, when all he had experienced of Yuldor was death and decay?

Yet, as Tal walked through the jungle, he couldn't deny it came as damn near to Heaven's Knoll as he could have imagined.

Everywhere he looked presented fresh wonders. The scarlet vines on the trees and rainbow-beaked toucans were only the start. The canopies were rife with creatures, each a delight to look upon. Monkeys, their coats orange and brown, bared their yellow teeth as they screeched at them from the boughs above. Deer skirted about their company, all with antlers and a shining opalescence. Creatures such as he'd never seen proliferated as well: some with fur, others with feathers, and a couple with both. Lizards and beetles scrambled up and down the trunks, and long, thick-bodied snakes hung from the branches.

The forest floor held its own charms. Stalk-like plants grew in a startling kaleidoscope. Tal wagered he could blow a dart from their tubular shafts, but he didn't dare touch them lest poison linger beneath their attractive veneer. Mushrooms came in every shape and size. Some had caps as wide as Aelyn's hat and rose to their knees, green spots decorating the top. Flowers, too, were more unusual than he'd thought possible. Some looked like bells, others like swords; some grew alone, others in neat rows like soldiers at attention. The air was redolent with their scent, sweet and soothing.

All his senses called for him to rest and relax, to embrace and indulge in the abundance surrounding him. Yet he kept up his guard and a tight grip on *Velori*.

Miasma layered the ground, a smoky film that swirled around their ankles and sparkled with a light of its own. He was glad his sorcery wasn't repressed like the others. Paradise reeked of magic, and its sulfur stank more than any flower could obscure.

And then there were the cats to consider. Each was as large as a man and black as obsidian. Wherever their party walked, the jungle cats stalked them from the shadows, eyes gleaming like crystals.

A good reminder, Tal thought as he stared back at them. He and his party were intruders upon this luscious oasis atop the mountain, and it boded well to remember it.

Paradise didn't belong to them.

His companions had been quiet as they absorbed the sights, but Rolan's piping voice broke the silence. "I'm hungry, *Momua*. Is it time to eat yet?"

Ashelia began to answer her son, then paused. Tal looked at where she stared and saw one of the deer approached. He guessed it to be a doe, for its horns were diminutive compared to the others. It stared at them with dark, unblinking eyes, as if waiting for something.

An inkling born of half-remembered passages sprang to mind. Tal shook his head with a smile. Now that he knew to look for it, he could feel the ripple of sorcery behind the occurrence.

"Paradise provides," he murmured.

"Tal?" Ashelia seemed wary, though the deer made no threatening overtures.

"Pim wrote of this. How none could go hungry in the jungle, for it provided for their needs." Tal gestured to the waiting doe. "Rolan proclaimed he was hungry, so Paradise sent meat for us to consume."

Ashelia's eyes whirled, as if the idea made her uncomfortable. The rest of their party seemed to share her reticence.

"They could have butchered it for us, too." Despite the comment, Wren's wry smile looked forced.

Before Tal could answer, monkeys came swinging toward them with startling screams. When they were positioned above the fellowship, they hung by their tails and threw objects cradled in their arms. For a moment, he thought they were under attack; then he realized that what was being thrown were nuts and fruits, though of varieties he'd never seen before.

He'd only just reconciled with this new marvel when toucans came flying in. Clutched in their colorful beaks were leafy greens and plants that looked like wild onions. These they deposited in a neat pile at their feet before launching back into the air with a cacophony of caws.

Tal looked around at his companions, and the astonishment writ across their expressions brought out a laugh. Yet no sooner had his mirth risen did it settle again. Staring beyond the nearest trees, he picked out the jungle cats among the shadows, the sorcery rippling across their hides and making them stand out clearly to his senses.

No matter how you lull me, he thought to the forest, *I won't be charmed.*

But it didn't stop him from kneeling with the others and partaking of the feast that had been gathered for them.

Garin looked at the two fruits he clasped in his hand. One was round and had a smooth, pink skin, which contrasted with the rough green leaves coming off its stem. The other was yellow and with a fibrous shell he judged should be removed before eating whatever lay inside.

He didn't reach for his belt knife, however, but raised his gaze to Wren. She kneeled beside him in front of the food piles, collecting a small pile of her own. Around the cornucopia, the others did the same — all except Tal, who kept watch on the trees.

"Think they're poisonous?" Garin muttered.

Wren shrugged, then spoke in a raised voice. "Anyone think these are toxic?"

"Doubtful." Tal didn't look around as he spoke, continuing to scan the woods. "From everything Pim told me and Hellexa wrote, Paradise was never intended to harm those who entered it."

"Then what did we guard against the miasma for?" Falcon exclaimed. "Why, we might have cut the time to get here tenfold, and we never would have…"

The bard trailed off. Garin's mind followed the trail Falcon had started them down, all they wouldn't have undergone had they gone to Ikvaldar directly. No massacre at the Ravager tower. No death hunt by Yvärras and her Nightkin. No slaughter at Haudden.

Helnor would still be alive.

Ilvuan roused. *But you and I would not be bonded,* Jenduit. *Remember: the past is stone.*

The future is clay, Garin finished wearily, though he couldn't help wondering how bad it would be if they never had joined together. He kept the thought as small as he could.

Tal sighed, signaling his thoughts had run down a similar line. "Not all poisons are unpleasant — just the opposite, in my experience. Pim described Paradise as conferring malaise and complacency. Had we entered without protection, I suspect we

473

would never leave, and be the happier for it. But you know it's more than that, Falcon. We were waiting for the Emperor and his armies to engage Yuldor's forces, to draw them away from us and clear the way for our ascent."

"'Tis true enough!" Falcon gave an exaggerated bow that seemed forced even for the bard. "I humbly retract my hypothetical."

Rolan brought their minds back to the matter at hand. "When can we cook all this, *Momua*? I don't want to eat onions raw!"

They all smiled at that.

"Nor do I, Little Tree Frog," Ashelia answered him. "If Tal says it is well to eat, then we shall."

But though Garin's stomach rumbled at the prospect of a fresh and bountiful meal, he couldn't shake the sense that more was off.

Something is wrong with this place, he thought to Ilvuan.

The dragon's presence spread through Garin's limbs. *It is.*

Is the miasma responsible?

Look, and you will see.

Garin hesitated, wondering what that meant, when the World exploded with light.

Lines fragmented the forest. Though Garin had seen the Lattice before, he found himself overwhelmed by the sight of it now. The threads shone more brilliantly than on previous occasions, so much so they were painful to look at. He closed his eyes, but their shadows remained imprinted on his eyelids.

It wasn't their brightness alone that felt wrong. Remembering how they'd looked before, Garin noticed they seemed thicker.

Swollen. It was the only way he could think of it.

Yes, Ilvuan affirmed, seeing the shape of his thoughts. *Yuldor has perverted this place. It is not the way the World should be.*

Garin breathed a sigh of relief as the sorcerous web disappeared. He wondered if Ilvuan had to endure seeing it all the time. But it wasn't his most pressing question.

Yuldor wished to spread this everywhere, this Paradise?

Once, perhaps. But no longer. Now, he only yearns for one thing.

Which is?

Death, Jenduit. *And death is what we shall give him.*

Part of him had suspected that was the meaning behind Yuldor's words spoken through Pim and Hashele. A god's plea for his own death. He wondered how the boy he'd been when leaving Hunt's Hollow would have wrapped his mind around that prospect. The man he was now could barely understand it.

Stranger still was the feeling bubbling up inside him. Not anger or resolve, as he should feel after all the evil the sorcerer had wrought.

Instead, he pitied him.

We will, Garin affirmed, hoping it was true.

THE MASTER OF TIME AND
MATERIAL

TAL WAS NO STRANGER TO SMILES. YET A SMILE HAD NEVER FELT so strange as he walked through the overgrown wilderness.

The doom lying ahead had grown no less foreboding; the Worldheart and its master still waited. Yet his belly was full, and of fresh fare such as they'd rarely had in the weeks they'd been traveling. Fruits and nuts and vegetables they had eaten, roasted as best they could over a small fire, made from fuel that the woodland creatures had gathered for them. They didn't partake of the doe, for Tal hadn't the heart to kill the beast before its companions, nor did any of them wish to take the time to prepare and cook the meat. Still, the meal had been delicious and wholesome, and all their moods lightened for it.

Then they'd pressed on, continuing to hike up the mountain. It was as laborious as before, and all his companions panted behind him. But in place of complaints or silence, Tal now heard levity. Wren teased Garin, and the youth did his best to rib her in return. Falcon had started up a chorus of song, and Rolan made stumbling attempts to sing with him, though he knew only a quarter of the words. Even Aelyn's occasional comments contained less acid. The pall of their sufferings had lifted, and they returned to the people Tal loved best.

But his smile felt odder for their behavior. *We ascend toward death and laugh all the way*, he mused. *But better to laugh at our fate than despair.*

He glanced at Ashelia and saw some of her lines had smoothed, the grief etched into her features since her brother's death lightening. She noticed his look, and her eyes flitted to his lips as she returned his smile. He yearned to call for a stop, for them to make camp early and steal a quiet moment together. After all, what was a day's delay, or even two? Yuldor would still be there, as he had been for long centuries. Nightkin didn't appear to come to Paradise, and even the jungle cats were seeming less threatening.

They were safe here, safer than anywhere else in the East or perhaps even the Westreach. They could stay...

Tal snapped back to his senses and glanced down at his feet. Golden mist swirled about them. *Miasma.* The Heartstone bracelets and the Ring of Thalkuun should have protected them from its influence — and they mostly had, if it was as powerful as his senses told him.

Yet they couldn't keep it entirely out. Their moods lifted because of its touch. Thoughts of repose and relaxation were born of its suggestion.

He hadn't truly understood what threat Paradise posed to invaders of Ikvaldar. Now, he thought he did. Paradise was a trap, seeking to ensnare them forever beneath the fertile boughs. If they hadn't come prepared, perhaps it would have succeeded.

But he couldn't submit to apathy.

Tal sought after his purpose, and the death and destruction that must come with it. He remembered his glimpses of Yuldor and embraced his terror. He edged his resolve so sharply it hurt. The only way to keep his wits was to bleed.

"Tal? Are you alright?"

He looked at Ashelia and smiled again. But now, it felt more familiar, like his wolf's smile of old.

"It touches our minds, the miasma. We must remain wary."

Though none of it was news, she startled at his words. "Wary," she repeated. The lines appeared again along her brow.

He was sorry to have brought them back. Slowing, Tal reached out and brushed a finger over her face, pretending to smooth the lines away.

"Never fear, Ashel," Tal murmured. "I'll remain vigilant. I'd rather you find what peace you can."

She took his hand and clasped it in both of hers. Yet the lines remained.

"Peace. Do you think it ever existed? And if it did, that we'll find it again?"

He wanted to assure her. Instead, he spoke the truth.

"I don't know. But you have my word, if it still lives, I'll find it and bring it down from this mountain."

Ashelia smiled, her stormy eyes spinning. "You always knew how to play the fool, Tal. But don't forget it's just an act, when we…"

"I won't," he spoke into the silence after she trailed off, wondering if the assertion rang hollow in her ears as well.

Garin collapsed to the ground, amazed once more at how soft the leaves and underbrush were here.

Then again, it is Paradise.

They had finally stopped to set up camp. Finding a spot was made simple by Falcon's spoken request to the forest. At once, one of the black jungle cats materialized to lead them to a clearing. Soon thereafter, the ideal spot for a camp appeared, complete with a supply of water from a gurgling brook.

Garin was only too glad to stop for the day. He was sore from foot to neck, and the hike had drained him further with every step. It seemed as if the very ground were sucking away his energy, though his mood and the rest of his party's had only lifted since entering Paradise. Now, he longed for sleep, but not before partaking of another meal.

"I'm hungry," he announced to the jungle, trying not to feel like a spoiled child as he did.

Wren, who unfurled her bedroll nearby, gave him a look, but the forest provided a distraction. Creatures skittered out from the foliage and swung down from trees to deposit their gifts in the center of their camp.

Despite himself, Garin grinned.

After they'd cooked the fresh harvest, Garin returned to his bedroll. The air was remarkably warm and moist for being as high up as they were, and along with the miasma, it made him sleepy. Part of him knew he should insist on taking a turn at watch, for Tal had kept it the entire night before, but sleep beckoned too strongly. His eyes had already drifted closed when Ashelia's hushed voice brought him back to awareness.

"They've returned."

"Or never left, I suspect." Tal spoke quietly as well.

Garin pried his eyes open and sat up. Tal perched on a fallen log, one leg brought close to his chest, the other hanging down. Ashelia stood by him, a hand on his shoulder. They were silhouetted by an eerie blue light, and Garin startled at its source.

Beyond the pair, shining figures walked.

Garin was on his feet in an instant, sheathed sword in hand and ready to draw. Tal and Ashelia glanced back, and Wren muttered curses into her cloak. He flushed, suddenly sheepish, for no one else seemed alarmed.

Still, he kept Lament in hand as he crossed their camp to stand at Tal's shoulder.

"What are they?" Garin whispered, staring at the ghostly procession.

"We don't know." Tal's dark eyes brightened as they caught

some of the phantom light. "We saw them last night walking up the path. They seem to be memories of this place, or wraiths doomed to retrace their steps for all time."

Garin studied them as they wended through the trees. Their features were indistinct, shifting like the glowing miasma at their feet, yet Garin detected signs they were humans and elves. Their clothes were foreign to him, though he knew he'd seen something like them somewhere before. It came to him a moment later when he thought to ask Ilvuan.

The Origins in Lethyranth.

In the dragon's memories, the ancient people had worn similar robes and sashes. Their feet, too, had been sandaled, though their hair hadn't been quite the same. These humans and elves had long hair, and it appeared braided in crowns about their foreheads.

"They're dressed like Origins," he spoke aloud.

Tal and Ashelia looked at him.

"Really?" Tal raised his eyebrows.

"How do you know this, Garin?" Ashelia queried.

"From my visions in Lethyranth."

He was grateful they both seemed to believe him.

A thoughtful look stole over Tal. "I wonder why. Did excursions take place before Yuldor's time? Or did they continue to wear such clothes even after his reign began?"

"Perhaps not," Ashelia interjected. "Perhaps they only wear the robes for pilgrimage."

Tal shrugged. "Damned inconvenient traveling clothes, if you ask me."

"Especially when trekking up a mountain," Garin pointed out.

Tal grinned. "Especially then."

Just then, one of the ghosts made a sudden movement, looking around until she faced Garin and his companions. Garin thought it must be a coincidence, for the specters had paid them no mind thus far.

The notion was swiftly banished as the rest of the woman's company looked toward them and began chattering.

Garin's hand fell to *Helshax's* hilt again, and he drew it an inch. Before he could unsheathe it, Tal settled a hand on his arm, guiding the blade back down.

"I don't think they mean us harm," the older man said. "They go unarmed. Best not to give threat before they do."

It went against his instincts, but Garin followed Tal's advice, letting the sword hang limp at his side.

Tal seemed to have the right of it. None of the phantoms came closer, nor did they make any menacing movements. They only continued to point and jabber in a tongue foreign to their ears, though something of it seemed familiar.

Ilvuan roused in him, heat spreading through Garin's limbs with his presence. *Long has it been since I heard this speech.*

What language is it?

An older variant of what you know as the common Darktongue. A mortal speech near to that spoken by the Origins. A language closer to my own.

Garin was surprised to detect a hint of nostalgia in the dragon's musings.

Then you can understand it? he urged. *What they're saying?*

Ilvuan hummed before responding. *They knew ghosts haunted the mountain. But you are odder to them than they expected.*

It took Garin several moments to reconcile what that was supposed to mean.

"We're ghosts to them," he marveled aloud.

Tal and Ashelia glanced at him, though their eyes drifted back to the spirits. "Is that so?" Tal asked with a quirk of his lips.

The dragon pressed affirmation through Garin, so he voiced it. "Ilvuan says so. But what does that mean?"

Tal pursed his lips, fingers drumming on his knee. "One of three things, I'd imagine. They might be a mere illusion, one of

Yuldor's tricks. Or perhaps they are real, echoes of their souls caught by the Worldheart's power, like flies in amber. Their spirits live in a delusion, and see the World as it is not — and thus imagine us to be the ghosts.

"But there's a third possibility. They might truly exist, but in the past, and yet have somehow glimpsed us here in their future."

That third explanation took even more for Garin to wrap his head around. From her expression, Ashelia shared his confusion.

"That's impossible." Garin wanted to exclaim his disbelief, but caution kept his voice soft. "Time flows in one direction. How could *they* see *us*?"

Tal smiled. "Once, while Soltor wore Falcon's face, he told me that the one who possessed the Worldheart became the Master of Time and Material. I assumed that alluded to the immortality Yuldor and the Extinguished had attained, but perhaps I was hasty in that conclusion. Perhaps he possesses more control over time than we ever suspected."

It was a sobering thought. They'd seen proof of Yuldor's mastery over time. Not only had he attained a measure of divinity, but he'd insulated this lush utopia on a mountain from the ravages of weather and season. And Yuldor had resurrected and grown Yvärras into an adult dragon in an impossible amount of time.

If our enemy commands time itself, what chance do we have?

Their only hope was that his power wasn't absolute. It had limitations. If there were none, after all, how could any of them ever resisted?

The spirits were fading into spiraling mist. Soon, their insubstantial bodies filtered away, and the glow of their presence dimmed.

Garin glanced at his two comrades, then silently turned and made for his bedroll. Only Ilvuan's warmth over his bones was any comfort as he tried to forget in a dreamless sleep.

STARKISSED

THEY CONTINUED THEIR CLIMB THE NEXT DAY, AND PARADISE amazed Garin with each fresh sight: the plants, the creatures, the smells. The air, thick with mist and miasma, cooled and calmed him with every breath. Part of him wished he could wander idly through it for the rest of his days, suspecting he'd never tire of its wonders.

But the greater part remembered the realizations from the night before. His chest ached as he wondered at the extent of Yuldor's power, and his legs never felt heavier.

Evidently, he wasn't alone in his lethargy. "When will it end?" Rolan complained from ahead. "I just want to fall down and sleep forever!"

Despite his low spirits, Garin shared a grin with Wren at that.

Ashelia hushed her son. "Don't make idle wishes, Rolan. This place may not fulfill what you ask for in the way you mean."

Her words stole Garin's smile as well as Rolan's, telling from the boy's slumped shoulders. He knew she was right. This place was a paradise in name, but there was something malevolent in the jungle's benevolence.

It bribes us to stay.

But they hadn't come all this way and endured all they had only to give up now. Garin set his teeth, braced his body, and pumped his legs all the harder.

Though they seemed to set a good pace, the wilderness didn't end by the time the thicker darkness of night settled in again. Only Tal's affirmation that he could feel the Worldheart nearing gave them any sense of progress. Garin tried not to think about what might await them tomorrow as he helped erect camp.

No sooner had he spread out his bedroll than he sensed someone approach from behind. Straightening, he turned to see Wren standing there, a peculiar lift to her lips.

"Want to gather some water?"

Garin glanced at his waterskin. They'd passed a stream not long before halting, and it still bulged with its contents. But by her expression, he guessed this wasn't really about water.

His throat went dry. Ilvuan roused to radiate amusement, furthering the flush crawling up Garin's neck.

"Sure, I could use some," he answered, attempting to be as casual as she was. Garin picked up his waterskin, and when he rose, Wren continued to stare at him, her golden tendrils stirring swifter.

"We'll be back," she called cheerily over her shoulder, then nodded toward the forest.

"Don't stray far," Ashelia cautioned from across the camp.

Wren only waved in response, then grabbed Garin's hand and pulled him after.

His heart thumped as hard as if they were laboring up the mountain again as he followed Wren through the trees. Leaves and vines brushed against his face, but he barely noticed. His thoughts had forged on ahead for what might await them. He felt as if this were their first time, back in his room in the Venaliel kintree.

He realized why a moment later. *I didn't expect her to want me anymore, now that another occupies my body.* Garin stared at the back of her head, at her matted black hair, but he scarcely saw it. She was as beautiful as she'd ever been to him.

As if repulsed by the thought, Ilvuan retreated to the furthest corner of his mind. Garin couldn't have been more grateful. If there was any time he wished to be alone in his body, it was now.

"Paradise," Wren spoke suddenly, "show us a pool, or a waterfall — or both, if you can." She cast a coy smile over her shoulder, making Garin grin.

They only waited a moment before a scuttling came from the brush to their left. A fox emerged, its russet coat shining and healthy. It gave them a brief glance, then pattered away into the jungle leading downhill.

"Don't lose it!" Wren cried as she yanked on Garin's arm. He tried desperately to keep his feet under him as they scrambled down the slope.

They only went a short way before Garin heard the rush of water. Anticipation made his weary body light as they hurried toward the sound. Wren loosed a laugh as she slipped, but she didn't slow their pace, still running full tilt after the woodland creature.

As the roar grew, the trees opened up into a grotto. Garin halted at its edge as the fox scurried away, its task complete. A waterfall loomed above them. It wasn't as full as the Ildinfor in Elendol, nor did it fall as far, but the sight of it made his breath catch. Moss grew up the cliffs angling in toward the falls. The pool below was a striking blue-green and flowed away into a series of rapids farther down.

Wren walked up to the edge of the pool and turned, hands on her hips. Her eyes captured and held him as they spun.

"How long has it been since we've had a proper bath?" She had to speak loudly to be heard over the falls. Without waiting for an answer, she nodded at the pool, her suggestion plain.

Garin couldn't have banished his grin if he'd tried. He

stepped close to her, closer than he'd dared to come since the dragon hatching grounds, and wrapped his arms around her. He forgot how lithe she was until he held her, her presence always greater than her appearance.

His thoughts quieted as he bent to kiss her.

Her lips brushed against his, then pressed harder. One hand curled around his neck, while the other touched the small of his back. His breath came quicker.

All too soon, Wren pulled her hands away and loosed his. But she didn't step back far, but looked up into his eyes, a promise in them.

"Let's get in," she suggested. Her lips remained parted, inviting.

Words were stolen from him. Garin could only nod.

Her hands brushed along his arms, his sides, down to his hips. She pulled at the hem of his shirt, lifting it, and he raised his arms so it could slip off. Garin repressed a shiver as cool mist touched his skin. By Wren's smile, it hadn't escaped her.

The rest of their clothes were swiftly stripped away. With each garment, Garin's anticipation grew. He worried how silly he must look as he hopped around while pulling off his boots. He thought he must sound like a panting dog as he unwound the wrappings from around Wren's chest. She had her arms raised as she spun in place, laughing all the while.

But it's Wren. At the thought, he relaxed once again.

Soon, only her dragonstone bracelet remained on. As the last of the wrappings pulled free, she scampered into the water, her pale body like a fish beneath its surface. Reemerging, Wren whipped back her wet hair and tilted her head, blinking against the water falling in her eyes. The droplets were bright as stars as they caught the golden shine of her tendrils.

"Coming?" she teased. "Might be our last chance."

He stood in only his smallclothes. "With or without these?"

Her eyes lingered over them, lips curling. "Without."

As quickly as he'd ever moved, Garin tore them off and darted into the water. Catching Wren in an embrace, they laughed softly with each other. The spray of the waterfall fell on their heads. Her body was warm pressed against his. Fire coursed through him wherever they touched.

He understood then how this place could be a paradise.

Sitting at camp, Tal stared off into the forest as he quested after Wren and Garin.

It was an arduous task this high on Ikvaldar. The Worldheart was a torrent, a column of fire always roaring against his senses. Sometimes, between Paradise and the Worldheart, he had to close himself off for a few moments' peace.

It wasn't only from the incessant force. Something about the pure sorcery called to him, beckoning him toward it the same as the *Doash* always had.

Even so, he swiftly found his young companions. As soon as he felt their sorceries intertwined, he pulled away with a grimace.

They're more than fine, I'd say.

"Tal?"

He looked up. Ashelia stood beside him, her face made strange by the flickering firelight. The corners of her lips were turned down, and her forehead was creased.

His heartbeat quickened. "Is something wrong?"

"No, nothing like that. I just want to talk. In private."

Her expression contradicted her words. Filled with foreboding, Tal stood and looked to the others scattered about the fire.

"Don't burn down the camp while we're gone," he said to Rolan.

The boy smiled, but it was fleeting. "Where are you going?"

"Tal and I just need to speak," Ashelia reassured him. "We won't stray far."

Tal had turned his back on the others when Falcon spoke up. "Ah, all the couples are sneaking off into the forest. What for, pray tell?"

"I can only suspect," Aelyn said snidely.

"They're going to talk," Rolan supplied, though he sounded less certain of it.

Shaking his head, Tal followed Ashelia between the trunks, the foliage soon hiding them from the firelight.

True to her word, she didn't lead them far, stopping at a rare opening in the canopy. Tal halted in the middle of it, where a tree had toppled to leave the gap, and stared up at the sky. He glimpsed the stars and the milky-white Night's Veil before a gust of fog blew overhead.

He lowered his gaze to find Ashelia sitting cross-legged on the ground, gold-flecked miasma streaming over her lap. She patted the fallen leaves next to her.

"Sit, please."

His unease grew with every gesture. As he complied, Tal felt as powerless as he had as a foot soldier. A strong suspicion stole over him.

She wouldn't, he thought. *Not now. Not when we're so close.* But he couldn't imagine what else would have her so grave.

As it often did, discomfort brought out his smile. "You're making me worried, Ashel. Is something wrong?"

Her eyes swirled, the brightest thing next to the miasma. The sign of a coming storm. "We'll soon reach the peak."

Tal lowered his gaze to the golden mist and ran his hands through it. His sorcery only prickled in his veins at the moment, yet he could still feel the Worldheart raging not far away.

"We will," he murmured.

"And then?"

Tal slowly met her eyes. They had rarely spoken of the fate

awaiting them atop Ikvaldar. He had thought it was understood. When challenging a god, it was unlikely for mortals to prevail.

Yet a fresh smile spread across his face. "You mean afterward?"

She startled. "After?"

"Of course! We cannot live atop this mountain, can we? Don't tell Yuldor, but I rather think calling this 'paradise' is an aggrandizement."

He'd always been able to make her laugh before. Now, she only grew more serious.

"Tal…"

She took his hand in both of hers. He gripped her fingers, pressing them gently. They'd never been smooth, roughened by her work as a healer, and their travels had calloused them further, yet her touch was as gentle as ever. He wondered if their checkered history was running through her head as it ran through his. The pleasant moments — their forest grotto, the nights he'd snuck into the Venaliel kintree, the time they'd shared in the Sun Palace. The sour ones — fighting upon their reunion in Elendol, Rolan threatened by Hashele. Losing Helnor.

He raised his gaze from their hands, and her eyes caught him for a moment, brighter than any star. She seemed poised to say something, a speech prepared, or perhaps a confession. Yet a moment later, she looked aside.

"We can still leave."

Tal went rigid. Of all she might have said, he'd feared those words most.

"Leave?" he croaked.

She nodded, still not meeting his eyes. Her body shook, and this more than anything raised his alarm.

"We don't have to reach the peak. We can turn back. There's still time, time we can claim for ourselves. For… family."

He was struck dumb. An incredulous smile spread across his face, but behind it, his blood pulsed in his veins.

Ashelia's eyes were wide, the tendrils spinning fast. Her chest rose with each quick breath.

"Why must you challenge Yuldor? He succumbs to his madness, does he not? He pleaded for release. This war, these omens — these are his dying throes. It may pass soon."

He didn't want to answer, didn't want to say what he knew he must. Yet he couldn't remain forever silent.

"And how many will die before it does? Ashelia, I..." Words failed him for a moment, but he struggled on and found ones that held. "You offer what I most desire in all the World. A quiet life, you and me and Rolan... Our friends alive and well..." His throat swelled closed, and he grinned against the heat pressing on his eyes.

All I want. All I cannot have.

Despair rose in a sea, threatening to drown him. He felt the pull on his limbs, its whispers in his ears to surrender. If he couldn't truly win, why did he continue to struggle?

But like a shining pearl at the bottom, a kernel of an idea came to him. He sniffed, wiped at his tears, and stared at the notion, wondering how it hadn't occurred to him before then.

Ashelia was growing yet more anxious. "Will you leave me alone again? Leave me to suffer believing you have died or lost yourself? You cannot do it again, Tal! I cannot bear it!"

Her voice rose with each word. Ashelia's resolve had cracked, the composure with which she surrounded herself evaporated. Tal looked upon the tender core of the woman he loved, the fears of failing those she tried so hard to protect. As tame as she often seemed, a wildness lay within her that was tearing free at the thought of losing him.

Tal nodded as if in agreement. Yet he felt his own determination returning as the idea blossomed within him. Iron seemed to flow through his veins, straightening his spine.

He tried to hide it by reaching out to her and drawing her

in close. She folded into his chest, quivering, though he didn't know if it was from anger or terror.

"I won't leave you alone," he spoke, and was glad it wasn't a lie.

Abruptly, she came upright and stared at him. Her eyes flickered back and forth between his, searching for the truth. Her breathing slowed.

"You won't ascend?" she asked, disbelieving. "We won't challenge Yuldor?"

He let his smile be his answer. "Let's give the others the night. We can tell them the news in the morning. I love you, Ashelia Starkissed, until the World's end and beyond."

The joy dancing in her eyes nearly broke him. She let out a small laugh. "You always had Falcon's flair for the dramatic."

Ashelia's hands encircled the nape of his neck, and she drew him to her lips for a long, passionate kiss. His cheek moistened as their tears intermingled.

He wished he could encase that moment in amber, preserve it for all time. He wished they might continue like this into eternity, phantoms embracing, to be viewed by all future and past travelers through this place.

But all too soon, she pulled away and stood, drawing him up with her. Hand-in-hand, they walked back to their camp.

Tal wiped his eyes and set on a false smile, readying for his last performance.

ALL THAT IS LOST

GARIN COULDN'T REPRESS HIS SMILE AS HE SNUCK BACK WITH Wren to their camp. Often, they broke into giggles and fell against each other, stealing one more kiss in the gold-limned darkness.

During their glorious time in the water, he'd forgotten all about their purpose there on Ikvaldar. Forgot what awaited them in the coming days. Forgot that none of them were likely to survive.

His head was full of her and her alone.

Yet when the camp came into sight, the glow faded and reality filtered back. Garin's smile slipped; his dread rose. He tried to cling to that sliver of happiness he and Wren had found, but it evaded him.

He pulled her to a halt among the trees. Her eyes spun as she leaned in close.

"We have to go back sometime," she whispered.

Garin smiled, but kept tight to his resolution. "Whatever happens, come out of it alive. Don't be stupid, alright?"

Her eyes widened. "You're one to talk, Garin Dunford. Don't *you* be stupid, and we'll be square."

He held her gaze, jaw set. But after a moment, he relaxed and pulled her taut body in for one last embrace.

"We'll both be smart," Garin murmured into her hair. "We'll survive."

He could only hope it wasn't a lie.

———

Long after Garin and Wren's breathing slowed, Tal opened his eyes and sat up.

The fire had burned down to coals, yet he could see by its light and that of the miasma who kept watch over their camp. A ghastly smile stole over him.

Apt, that you should be the one I last deceive.

He took a moment to center himself and prepare for the act. Once, Falcon had led Tal and the rest of his troupe through relaxation exercises before performances. Though he found it difficult to fully engage in them now, the memory calmed and focused him.

Tal rose and belted *Velori* on, then crept quietly toward the watcher, hoping to surprise him. At the last moment, his comrade's head snapped up, and bronze light spun in his eyes.

"Harrenfel," Aelyn muttered as Tal kneeled beside him. "I wondered when you would cease to feign slumber."

Tal grinned. "Can't fool you. Just couldn't sleep. Figured I may as well take a turn at the watch."

The mage stared into the orange coals. As the silence stretched on, Tal wondered if he'd somehow tipped his hand. If he was keeping watch, it only made sense to carry his sword. Yet perhaps it had been too presumptuous for his shrewd companion.

Just when he resolved to smooth things over, Aelyn spoke. "I didn't think it needed reminding, but perhaps it does. I lost a brother this past week, Harrenfel. Helnor and I did not always get along, but we... well, he was my brother all the same." He glanced up, his eyes catching Tal's, though he couldn't see more than the outline of his face. "Do not think you are the only one to have lost someone important to you."

"I remember."

Tal didn't outwardly acknowledge the hidden depths to his words. He'd never directly discussed his relationship to Kaleras with Aelyn, but he suspected the mage had guessed the truth long before.

We both lost family. Between them, the words didn't need to be spoken aloud. Silence had always served them better than speech.

Abruptly, Aelyn switched topics. "When we reach the peak, what, precisely, do you believe we'll face?"

Knowing the mage as well as he did, Tal heard what lay behind the question. He played up his smile. "Come now, Aelyn. We've faced down all the Extinguished and a Night-cursed dragon. What worse could Yuldor have in store for us?"

By the dim light, he saw his companion's lips curl. "Plenty. You're a fool, Tal Harrenfel, if you believe we've seen the worst the Named has to offer."

Tal shrugged. "If you insist. Whatever comes, we'll face it together. But you'd best get some rest so you don't stutter during an incantation."

Aelyn lingered a moment longer, then rose with a huff. "Be wary against midges. They're formidable here."

"Oh, I will be. Foul beasts, those."

The mage started to walk away. Tal knew he should let him go, yet words sprang to his tongue. If he was to say them ever, he had to speak them now.

"Thank you, Aelyn."

Aelyn turned as abruptly as if Tal had thrown a rock at his back. "Why?"

Tal smiled, wondering if it was the first genuine smile he'd ever given the mage.

"You, perhaps more than anyone, know me best. My flaws

and my failings, yes, but also my strengths and successes. Thank you for keeping me honest, my friend. You're just what a liar like me needs."

Aelyn's eyes narrowed, and Tal thought he detected his mouth tightening as well. After a moment, the mage looked aside.

"I suppose I have reasons to thank you as well," he said stiffly.

What those might be, he didn't enumerate. Instead, Aelyn turned on his heel and swiftly made for his bedroll, then wrapped himself in it.

Tal stared at his friend's back for a long time, smiling to himself. It was as good of a goodbye as he could have imagined between them.

Now, he thought as he settled onto the log Aelyn had used as a seat, *we wait.*

The night crept by.

Tal stared at his folded hands. A shiver of sorcery ran through him, just enough to keep tabs on anything that might sneak up on them. The winds of the Worldheart scalded his spirit. He tried to quiet his mind as it beguiled him with fears and doubts.

He'd made up his mind. There was no changing it now.

Aelyn fell unconscious eventually, but Ashelia awakened, wondering where Tal had gone. Though he reassured her, she had roused Rolan, who had a difficult time returning to sleep. Tal treasured every moment of delay, knowing they wouldn't last.

Finally, when the entirety of his party slept, he rose and crept toward them.

He went to Falcon first. Sliding his knife free so it wouldn't make a sound, he kneeled over his friend and sought the bard's wrist. His eyes lingered on his face for a moment, taking in the lines that creased it even in sleep. He didn't dare look long.

I'm sorry, my friend, he thought as he reached for his arm and drew it free of the blanket. *Sorry you won't see the end of your tale. Sorry you ever thought to finish it.*

The bard, ever a heavy slumberer, only muttered at his touch. Tal took advantage of the opportunity. Finding the thread that encircled his wrist, he worked the tip of his knife under it, then cut through. The bracelet fell away, the stone on it falling free.

Tal pulled sorcery into his blood until it burned. The Worldheart pressed in louder as well, but he ignored it, scooping up the bracelet and casting a spell on his friend.

Sleep.

It took only a sliver of power to enact, yet it would ensure that the bard remained unconscious while Tal dealt with the rest of his party.

Confident his plan would work now, Tal moved swifter to the next person. Aelyn was typically a light sleeper, yet he slept deeply now, and his wrist was already outside his bedroll. Tal cut the bracelet free and ensorcelled him just as he had Falcon.

Ashelia and Rolan also proved easy. He wondered, as he cut the bracelet free of the boy, if the miasma had something to do with it. It had affected them despite their precautions against it, relaxing them and depressing motivation. Perhaps now, its influence worked in his favor, putting them all in a deep enough slumber to continue his work in secret. He lingered by Ashelia, wishing to brush a curl from her forehead, but he didn't dare lest she wake.

Wren was snoring, and she continued to as he cut free her bracelet. Then only Garin remained. Tal descended upon him, eager to be done with the task. The youth slept on his side, his body curled around himself. The wrist with the bracelet was tucked under him, deep in the bedroll.

Tal clenched his jaw, debating whether it was worth the

risk of waking him. At length, he decided against it. If Garin woke, Ilvuan might make it difficult to put him back to sleep against his will. And though both the youth and his dragon had shown themselves to be helpful, Tal had made his decision.

Look after them, lad, he thought as he rose to his feet.

Tal placed the collection of bracelets in a small pile next to the coals, then moved to the edge of the quiet camp. There, he paused and looked over his resting companions. He thought of the things they'd endured together, the people they'd lost.

I cannot lose you, too.

He told himself he was making the right decision, the only one he could. He'd removed their protection from the miasma, but it wouldn't harm them. Its magic was a snare, not meant to kill, but to trap and hold. With Garin still protected, it wouldn't be long before he rescued the others.

No more. No more death.

He longed to stay, to look upon them until they woke. But the Worldheart burned behind him, beckoning him toward it. He could delay no longer.

Setting his smile, Tal turned and began his final ascent.

THE END IN THE BEGINNING

He walked alone up the verdant mountainside.

Even at night, Paradise was alive. Crickets and other insects sang an unceasing chorus. An owl hooted from somewhere to his left, and another from his right. Water babbled ahead. The leaves shifted as he passed, signaling he wasn't the only thing to prowl through the darkness.

Tal breathed in the jungle, knowing it might be the last slice of beauty he experienced.

As soon as the thought arose, he silenced it. There was seduction in regret. He wouldn't relent to it, not when he was so close. He would finish what Yuldor started long ago when he spread his influence into the Westreach and sent his monsters down from the hills. When his servants tricked and manipulated Tal and made him into their puppet.

No more. Never again.

The flame of his grievances warmed him through. He pulled sorcery into his veins and reveled in its power. He kept the Worldheart ahead of him, a storm without end, and squinted against the aura emanating from it.

The seed of doubt had long been growing within him, but Ashelia's plea had caused it to bloom. Tal knew the truth now, what their mission would come to. Even if Zyrl and their other allies succeeded in drawing away most the Nightkin, many other perils might await on Ikvaldar's peak.

There was no hope. Perhaps there never had been.

Then why go? a small voice whispered. *Why throw your life away?*

Part of him wanted to listen to it, to flee the mountain he and his companions had sacrificed so much to ascend. Tal imagined the life he could have with Ashelia and Rolan, all the somber times as well as the happy ones. The family they could become. He thought of Garin and Wren grown and coming into their own, both forces to be reckoned with. And Falcon and Aelyn, his greatest friend and his friendliest rival, would always be constant in their camaraderie.

But what of Helnor? Kaleras? What of all Yuldor has done, all he's stolen from you?

Tal shook his head and smiled. No — there was no turning back. He'd been a coward too often throughout his life to flee now. Besides, he couldn't outrun the Enemy forever.

It was time to protect those he loved. They were the reason he'd come, their safety why he'd abandoned them.

Even if he saved the World, what did he care if none of them survived?

I will do this. I will succeed or fail on my own.

This was why Tal had left Hunt's Hollow on this fool's errand. Yuldor stretched his hand over the World, and toward Tal in particular. That much had become plain when Soltor's deception was unveiled. Tal's past had always been bound to catch up to him. No one was safe by his side.

He wouldn't drag the others down with him.

Only with Garin did he wonder if he'd made a mistake. Tal hated to risk the youth as much as the rest, but Garin had proven that he could help. Together, they had withstood Yvärras' breath and a phoenix's faefire, while Tal would have failed alone. Ilvuan was a great boon as well, even if the dragon still seemed to withhold information.

But even together, we couldn't defy Yuldor at the goldwood. We weren't enough.

He didn't know the answer to this riddle, if there was a solution at all. Perhaps Yuldor truly was a god. Perhaps mortals would always falter before him. Maybe he would reign supreme and eventually claim the continent for his own.

And what of his plea and his parasites? What if Yuldor craves death as much as I often have?

Those small reasons for hope kept him moving up the slope. Those mysteries, if they fell the way he hoped, could be enough to turn the tide.

Slowly, Tal realized he didn't walk alone. He glanced to one side and saw a black jungle cat keeping pace with him two score feet away. Though they'd traveled in pairs or more before, this one loped through the shadows alone. It struck him as strange, but no more than anything else Paradise offered.

He faced forward and pressed on.

His sorcerous sense kept track of the creature, however. This one, unlike the others, didn't maintain its distance, but closed the gap between them. He wondered if they were the guardians of this place, though not to keep people from entering, but leaving. Tal coiled his power within him, readying to loose it on the beast at the first sign of aggression.

He came into a rare clearing and halted. The jungle cat sat on its haunches before him, staring at him. Waiting.

Tal stood motionless. He knew it wouldn't be long before Garin woke and roused the others. He had to engage Yuldor before his friends could pursue.

Yet the cat's behavior gave him pause. There was intelligence in its eyes beyond what an animal should possess.

He startled as a voice spoke in his mind.

"At last, you come."

He recognized it at once. "Maral Batomar," he acknowledged her aloud. "*Ava'thal.* The Dragonheart. The Night."

The beast maintained its gaze with unnatural steadiness. The voice that spoke in his head was more distinct than it had been before, and he could now identify it as feminine, if still deep-noted.

"I swore to be your ally. And so I shall be."

Tal gestured to the cat. "Have you been watching us here in Paradise?"

"You have not come to me. So I came to you."

It wasn't an answer. Yet under the circumstances, it was hardly the thing he was most concerned about.

A smile twisted his lips. "I suppose nothing's left but to make the attempt."

"There is one thing left still. Place your hand on the peuma's head."

Tal eyed the beast warily. "Is that its name? And why should I do this?" He had no doubt he could fight the beast if it became necessary. *Though I'd be hard-pressed to regrow a hand in time to fight Yuldor.*

"Trust me, Thalkunaras, as you have trusted me before. I will not lead you astray."

He blew air through his teeth and approached, a hand outstretched. "Good feline," he muttered under his breath. "That's a good cat."

The jungle cat didn't shift as he came within a few feet, then a few inches. His hand hovered over its crown, and he was ready to jerk back at the slightest movement. Too late, he realized it was the hand that bore the Ring of Thalkuun. There was no retracting it now.

His hand settled on its head. His eyes drifted closed.

When they opened, he stared at a door. The smell of fresh-baked rye bread lingered in his nostrils. He heard the sounds of someone moving about a house. *Mother.* He knew it was her intuitively, just as he'd always followed her movements with anxious attentiveness.

This was an ordinary day; no, it was better. Bread meant it wouldn't be a hungry day. Bread meant a happy day.

Yet he stared at the door, as if waiting for something.

A knock came.

He reached up for the bolt, the same height as his head. He was proud to have grown so tall already. Unlatching it, he hauled the door inward, then stared, blinking at the man who stood outside.

Kaleras smiled down at him. The corners of his brown eyes crinkled, the only furrows in his face. He stood straight and erect, and his shoulders were broad, though they didn't entirely fill out his linen shirt. His tawny red hair, bound back in a ponytail, bore only streaks of gray. His clothes were weather-stained, but appeared well-made. A cloak swept behind him as a gust passed through.

He stared up at him, mouth agape. "Father?" he ventured.

His father spoke, but it wasn't his words that came out.

"This is not a memory."

In a rush, reality came back to him. Tal blinked and oriented himself.

"No," he replied, his voice still high and boyish. "Only a dream."

Kaleras smiled again, but he saw the Night's presence behind the warlock's face now. "Come. There is more I must show you."

The one masquerading as his father turned and walked out into the bright day.

Tal hesitated, glancing behind him. His home was as he remembered it except for minor improvements. The table didn't lean on its short leg, but stood up straight. The floor was strewn with fresh straw that looked not a day old. His mother was nowhere to be seen, but he could hear her humming softly to herself out of sight, evidently in another room of the house that hadn't existed.

With a sad smile, he turned and followed Kaleras out.

As soon as he stepped outside, Tal found he didn't stand on anything, but floated. Disoriented, he took in his surroundings.

The light of the *Doash* pierced through him.

It burned like he'd leaped into the sun, yet there was relief in the agony. Whispers wound through him, promises of release.

Rest. Peace. Eternal sleep.

Part of him instinctively reached for it. What more, after all, had he ever sought? But the greater part of him recoiled. He hadn't come all this way just to sink into oblivion.

My friends deserve better. Ashelia deserves better. Silence, even I do.

Tal tore his gaze away and startled. Not all of this plane was as bright and shining as he was used to. Everywhere he looked, white sorcery was being eaten away by darkness. It moved through the streams like ink in water, only it writhed and shivered, showing the consciousness behind it. The great stream it spilled from was close to the one from which Tal emerged.

Yuldor's corruption, he recognized it.

Their hunger grows by the day, so they delve deeper into shadow. They are becoming desperate.

Tal focused on the figure hovering next to him. It was as dark as the corruption, but it didn't feast on sorcery as Yuldor did. That as much as what they'd experienced together told him to trust the Night, especially here at the end.

What can I do? I cannot contend with his — their — power. I cannot contain them.

His despair couldn't be locked behind a smile here, so it spilled forth in a ripple. His ally spoke not like Yuldor stood alone, but as if he contained many. Hope was scanter even than before.

The Night radiated assurance below the level of language. *Neither could I. Even fighting against them, the Worldheart's power remains theirs.*

The revelation came like a punch to the stomach. *Then there has never been hope.*

The Night's resolve banished his despair. *There is. There always is. You possess something they desire,* Thalkunaras. *Something they have long looked forward to claiming as their own.*

Tal trembled with the knowledge. *What? I have nothing they do not.*

There, you are wrong. Have you not wondered why Yuldor's servants ever sought to capture you, not kill you? Why you possess sorcery such as you do? Why you are a drovald, *a Fount of Blood?*

Even the *Doash's* seductive song could not match the temptation of these answers. He hadn't known he would have them before the end. Now, they dangled in front of him like a carrot before a horse.

I've never wanted to know anything more.

Then prepare yourself. The answer is far from pleasant.

He tried to do as she asked. But all he could do was yearn for it.

Very well, the Night relented. *You may know the young Listener,* Jenduit, *was made a* drovald *by the touch of one with whom I long shared the Worldheart. One of my truest allies.*

Tal's breath would have caught had he been breathing. *I suspected. Ilvuan was responsible then? He spawned magic in Garin?*

The Night's assent was like the touch of sunlight on skin. *The* ava'duala *command the World and have changed lesser beings to suit their needs. But that is not what happened to you.*

She must have sensed his thoughts traveling down that path. *If not a dragon, then what? Why am I a Fount?*

He should have worried at her reluctance. Instead, he longed to seize her and shake the answer from her.

Founts of Blood were created by the Three. Her words were

soft, yet conveyed with conviction. *Rothaen, Haimei, and Sachiel. The ones you know as the Whispering Gods.*

Tal froze. Sat with the knowledge.

I should have known.

Once, he'd believed the Creed's deities to be allies of good. Even now that he knew better, the truth knocked him like a hammer blow. Silence, Serenity, and Solemnity. Their names had always told the truth of their identities. The final silence was death, and they had brought little else to the World.

How? The question came out as quiet as a whisper. *How did they do this to me? And when?*

These answers I do not have. The Night hesitated. *To my regret. Even my knowledge has limits. But I assume that at some point in the past, you came close enough to sorcery and their influence that they could reach you.*

Tal felt the urge to laugh. *I suppose it doesn't matter now. What's done is done. More relevant is why they did this.*

It is wise of you to see it. For this question, I know more. The Three shape mortals into drovaldi *because they are necessary for their immortality. As parasites need hosts, so do the Three require Founts of Blood.*

Why do they need us? What purpose can we serve?

The Three require a renewal of their connection to the World, a conduit by which they lengthen their existence. They themselves are but specters; powerful, yes, but only sustained through the sorcery they feast upon. And they access this sorcery through drovaldi *such as you.*

Tal mulled over that, a warmth growing within his phantom body. *A flaw. This is their one flaw.*

Yes. And one we will exploit.

It seemed a slight weakness, in some ways; did it matter if a predator could starve if they always caught their next meal?

Yet these false gods needed Tal. It was enough to fan the coals of desperate hope into flame.

Yuldor was the last drovald *to come to them,* the Night continued, *but he has long grown thin.*

Yuldor was a Fount of Blood — yet another realization come belatedly. His talent, his compulsion to go atop Ikvaldar, all made sense to Tal now.

So the man I believed to be my enemy is a pawn, he thought. *A means to an end.*

In a way, the Night replied. *He came seeking power and found it. Though he believed he could master the Three, his will could not outlast them over the centuries. Little of him remains, yet he is still the source of the Three's sorcery. Even frail, he is potent and not to be ignored.*

Tal tucked the information away, though he scarcely knew how it could be useful.

And you? he asked. *How have you survived all this time?*

Her response came reluctantly, the words stuttering in his mind. *I am like the Three, except I am the leech of leeches. I prey upon their connection to Yuldor and thus persist. Long ago, they would have destroyed me if they could have. But like with the* ava'd-uala, *their influence is limited against other spirits.*

Tal wondered why this would be until he remembered Yvärras' power. With dragons as their counterweight, it was little wonder the Night had found a way to survive. Though her manner of doing so was more than a bit unsettling.

It is not for myself, never for myself, the Night supplied, as if she heard his doubts. *Long ago, I would have chosen to cease. But my fight is not yet won, the World not yet safe. The channel to the* Doash *remains open, and I cannot allow myself rest until it is sealed.*

He pondered her words for several moments before another question arose.

And this... corruption. They poison the sorcery with their presence, yet I don't understand how.

Her answer was long in coming. *That is difficult to fully explain. I can, at least, tell you the reason behind it. The Three are something new to our World. They have reached into planes of existence that would have been better left untouched. I believe this corruption they spread began in one of these other realities, and in their arrogance, they continue to allow more of it in.*

Tal flinched back from the inky blackness. *If we defeat the Three, will it cease? Will it stem the poison? Or will all sorcery be corrupted?*

It is another thing I do not know. But it does not change the task before us. The Three will only spread it if they are allowed to persist.

He felt as if the sorcerous plane surrounding them was spinning. Tal stared at the corrupting presence of his enemies and tried not to succumb to despair. More than ever, the *Doash's* song tempted him toward it. Only through continual vigilance did he remain where he was.

His thought came out as a whisper. *Why curse me with this burden? Hellexa Yoreseer spoke of other Founts created. Why am I the only one who has come?*

The Three have fostered many drovaldi *across Aolas through the centuries. Yet, as you say, you are the first in a long time to go to them.*

The Night drifted closer, her words growing softer. *It was not fate that brought you here,* Thalkunaras, *no more than it kept the other* drovaldi *away. You made this your destiny. You chose to fight rather than flee.*

There was still so much he still didn't understand. How could it take the Three so long to create a conduit they needed? Were they so limited in power and reach?

Yet the notion that Tal only had himself to blame for being here was somehow reassuring. It meant that he was still his own master. If only he hadn't been so much a fool, he could have chosen to live.

But there was no time for pity; a more pressing question demanded an answer.

Garin. Has he made his fate the same as mine? To be a sacrifice to these false gods?

No, the Night replied, *and yes. He is a conduit, but for dragonkind. I suspect their purpose has many folds, but once, they fought beside me. I believe they will be our allies again.*

Tal thought of Yvärras and her final decision, and his doubts abounded. Yet there was little point in undercutting hope further.

And if they break free, Tal asked, *they will be reborn to the World?*

Yes. Mortals will once more tremble at their passing.

After their experiences with Yvärras, it was a terrifying thought. Yet all he could do now was focus on the task at hand. The dragons wouldn't have Garin as their conduit; he'd done all he could to protect the youth. Now, he had to think forward to his own battle.

So the Three require me and my connection to sorcery. That doesn't tell me how I can fight them.

The Night seemed to hesitate before she answered. *Their salvation may be their doom. For as you are a vessel, so you are a cage.*

I don't understand.

But that wasn't entirely true. The shape of her plan formed in his mind and struck fear through him. He'd always known there could be no victory without sacrifice. Until then, he'd hoped against hope the sacrifice might not have to be his.

His ally radiated sympathy, yet she pressed on, voicing the unbearable truth. *You must give what they desire,* Thalkunaras. *You must submit yourself to them. Only then can we trap and defeat them. In that moment, however brief, the Three will be in your power.*

If I yield to them, will I not become their new host? Will they not possess me, control me, use me for their own purposes, as they have Yuldor?

Given time, they would. But at the merging, there is a moment where you can eclipse them. When all the sorcery they crave is in your power and not theirs.

But what good will it do? I can feel them! No amount of sorcery can harm what they've become!

He'd clung so long to the notion that he could fight against Yuldor. But now that Tal knew the truth behind his enemies, his resolve frayed. He longed to surrender. Every fiber in his being begged for it.

It is true that you cannot harm them, the Night conceded, *just as you cannot harm a contagion. But you can contain one. When plague comes to a city, the affected areas are quarantined. Once the infected are quelled, the entire area is burned. In just this way, you will cleanse the World of the Three by taking them to the one place no being can survive. You will drag them into the* Doash.

Tal stared at the blinding orb beneath them. He heard its whispers still, but for once, they'd lost their allure. Before, the *Doash* had been an escape from his troubles. Now it was their terrible answer.

But with the solution came the silencing of his inner conflicts. There was a chance of victory. A chance to put the Westreach and the East right. To save his friends, his beloved. To rid the World of an evil that had long since afflicted it.

And it would only cost his life.

He knew what he must do. All that remained was to do it.

The Night drifted closer, barely any space left between them. Her words were a whisper almost as soft as those coming from the World's Womb.

Do you understand?

Tal would have smiled if he could have. *I understand, Maral Batomar, all too well.*

HEART'S DRUM

Tal opened his eyes.

The black jungle cat remained under his hand, its yellow eyes staring at him. Slowly, he withdrew and backed away. He thought he saw the Night still behind its gaze, and he spoke in case she remained.

"I know you must go to prepare the way. I just have one last question."

Her response filtered into his head with the coolness of a cloud passing overhead. "*If it is necessary, ask.*"

"It's about Garin. I know he's not a Fount in the way I am, but I must know that he'll be safe afterward."

Silence filled his head, only broken by the incessant susurrus of Paradise.

"*He can never be safe,*" the Night responded at last. "*One of the* ava'duala *has made him a conduit. The dragons have grown as thin as the Three and require the same as they to influence the World. For what purpose, I cannot know, though they have ever struggled against our eternal enemies.*"

Tal shook his head. "It's not only that I worry about. They intend to return to the World in the flesh; Yvärras said as much."

"Yes. They have always sought resurrection. Yet if the World can endure a second coming of dragons, I am less sure."

At the pronouncement, he feared for Garin and all his friends should the dragons succeed in their aims. But the best thing he could do to protect them now was the same as before.

"I suppose that's all. Thank you, Maral Batomar. I daresay I'll see you soon.

"At the end." With that last glimmer of black humor, the Night departed from his mind.

The jungle cat's sudden break from stillness startled Tal, and he took a step back. But the peuma only crouched, clearly startled at where it found itself. Eyeing Tal, it seemed to judge him to be no threat, for it straightened a moment later and stalked from the clearing.

He breathed a sigh of relief and let out a laugh. "Off to challenge gods," he muttered, "and here I'm jumping at cats."

The mirth died as swiftly as it came. Only the wilderness had borne witness. It was time to leave his small concerns behind and face his fate.

He girded his resolve with a smile, then continued his hike up the mountain.

Dawn had begun to glow through the canopy. The miasma curled around his legs with each step. Tal wondered how much farther he had to walk. Soon after it came, the light was choked out again. In the few glimpses through the leaves, he saw heavy gray clouds hanging overhead, an omen of what was to come.

Let it be done with. I'm ready for the end.

As if Paradise answered his wish, his eyes caught on the emergence of gray ahead. Tal pumped his legs, sorcery fueling each step, air hissing in and out of his throat as he strode for the end of the trees. An ominous howling grew louder, wind shrieking as it lashed the branches.

He emerged from the jungle and beheld the end of his journey.

The landscape had morphed. Where it had blossomed with life behind, now it lay desolate. Nothing but broken gray stone spread around him. Sharp spires erupted from the mountain, angled in toward each other.

A pillar stood at their center, this formed of black rock instead of gray. Though it rose a hundred paces farther, the molten lines shot through it were still visible, their glow catching in Tal's eyes. Its surface was uneven, and though he suspected what beasts were entombed there, it took him several moments to detect their features. Statues of dragons crawled up and down the pillar.

At long last, he stood before the Worldheart.

If he hadn't known it by the sight, Tal knew it by the stench. Despite the furious winds, the reek of sulfur filled his nostrils and choked his throat. Sorcery hung so thickly in the air he was surprised he couldn't see it.

Yet he felt it. Even as the gusts clawed inside his flesh, the Worldheart pummeled his mind. He could feel no cold, his blood boiling with its nearness.

Blood knows its own.

His final destination lay before him, but as his eyes fell to the ground to find a path, he saw his trials were not yet ended. He stood on a wide ridge that dropped precipitously off on either side into deep furrows in the mountain before it rose again in spires. There was a path to the Worldheart, but something impeded his way.

Glyphs, thousands upon thousands of them, were carved into the stone, all pulsing with a ghastly green light.

He wondered who had conjured them, if it had been Yuldor himself, or his Extinguished, or perhaps even the Whispering Gods long, long ago. But in a way, it didn't matter. He had to cross to reach the Worldheart and the gods entombed within it. This was just another obstacle to overcome.

Questing forward, Tal felt the knots of their enchantments, sunk into the stone like anchors from boats. He'd thought he might untangle or sever them if they proved sufficiently simple, but a glimpse disabused him of the notion. None would be difficult on their own, but altogether, it would take far too long to do. He had too little time as things stood; not only to protect the companions that might soon come behind him, but to avoid any Nightkin the Three might summon if given long enough.

Tal withdrew his touch, closed his eyes, and breathed in deeply. The cold stung his throat, yet it was a relief with the inferno blazing inside him. He focused on the fire and stoked it hotter still, tending to it as a smith to his forge, readying for what was to come.

He opened his eyes and untied his cloak. Loosing it, he let the cloth whip free of his shoulders, the wind immediately sending it careening toward the edge. He loosed the waterskin from his hip, and it spilled open as it fell to the stone. He unlatched his belt and slid off *Velori's* scabbard, discarding it as he drew the blade. Its runes gleamed as brightly as they ever had, the artifact responding to the surrounding sorcery.

Tal sought deep within for a smile and found it. He was, at last, entirely unbound. Not even the hope for life restrained him, for he'd abandoned it as soon as he began this final ascent.

He would die, and so he was finally free.

Tal pulled at his power so he thought he must shine with sorcery. He stepped forward, raising his sword as he did. He set his eyes to his destination.

SHATTERED

TAL SWEPT *VELORI* DOWN. AN ARC OF BLUE FIRE BURST ACROSS the glyph-carved stone, and like a ship's prow cutting through water, the ground split open.

He'd expected an impact, but the resulting crash far exceeded his imagination. Where the fire fell, rock ripped upward, the line of glyphs activating others in an expanding cascade. Spires as sharp as the monoliths overhead sliced through the air. Tremors shook through Ikvaldar.

Stone rushed toward him in a rippling wave.

Tal threw up his free hand. "*Broldid!*" he thundered, and threw all his sorcery behind the command. The wave of stone split and poured like lava around him, like he were an island breaking the waves of a stormy sea.

It was all he could do to keep his small patch of rock together. Cliffs rose around him, closing off the stormy sky above. Magic boiled in the mountain; there seemed no end to it. This would be his cage, trapped in stone like his adversaries.

Then, at last, Ikvaldar stilled. The sorcery settled. Silence rang in his deafened ears.

Wuld, Tal thought, clearing the air in his chasm before sucking in a shaky breath.

He raised his head. The sky was gone, as was most of the light, little more than a far-off rectangle left of it hundreds of feet above. For the man he'd once been, it would have been an impossible distance.

But no matter how often he'd said otherwise, Tal was more than a man.

"*Broldid*," he murmured, and sorcery shot down into the rock beneath his feet. It responded at once, a hound eager to do his master's bidding. A grinding sounded, then he began to rise, the mountain lifting him like he rode upon a giant's hand. Tal kept his chin up and his head tilted back, watering eyes set on the patch of sky above. He was wary, ready for the final crushing impact that would bury him upon this peak.

It never came.

His head rose above the fragmented stone, and the biting winds found him at once. Squinting, he looked toward the Worldheart. A low cloud had blown over it, leaving it a specter in the mist. The raised peak brought him level with the base of the Worldheart now.

Tal stepped free of his temporary cage and onto the uneven stone. A powerful gust almost knocked him flat. "*Wuld*," he whispered, and sorcery curled about him like a cocoon. Where the wind tried to touch him, it was turned away. He stood strong once again.

It seemed impossible that any runes remained intact, yet a swift questing proved some had survived. As they lurked on the edges, he hoped they would stay inert.

But here, at the end, hope was too frail to believe in.

Unimpeded by stone or wind, Tal strode forth. Where the rocks jutted up in his path, he commanded them to smooth. He scanned either side, always aware that more obstacles and adversaries could be lying in wait. Yet Yuldor and his gods wished him to come. Surely, they wouldn't stop him now.

Abruptly, he halted, head raised to the sky. For a moment, he thought he'd seen something in the gloom, a shadow swooping overhead. He reached out with his sorcery, seeking the winged creature stalking him, but felt nothing. Tal frowned, but pressed forward. Perhaps whatever was up there could disguise itself as the Extinguished could. Perhaps it was a mere illusion.

It didn't matter. It didn't change how this day would end.

He was halfway across. The riven landscape around him grew still more oppressive. Sleet began to fall on his head and shoulders until a muttered "*alm*" made it curve around him instead. Lightning flashed atop one of the stone spires, followed by a head-splitting boom. Tal set his teeth in a grin and leaned in. His step quickened into a jog, then a run. A sound, feral and inhuman, welled up in his throat. He braced himself.

This wasn't the end, not yet. First, he had to battle the very World itself.

Tremors in the ground gave him a moment's warning. Tal sent roots of sorcery into the stone and braced himself as the peak rumbled again. More traps had triggered.

The sky grew dark as night, yet as lightning flashed again, he saw in his peripheries two dark, immense shapes to either side. Channeling fire and wind into *Velori,* he enhanced his vision so that the darkness lifted. What Tal saw brought him to a sliding halt.

Slabs of stone fell toward him, each as large as the foundation of a castle.

He shouted and whipped his sword down one way, then the other. The sorcerous fire blasted free, arcing with the motion and sizzling the sleet into mist. The spell slammed into the stone, and a crash louder even than the thunder rolled across the mountaintop.

The slabs split — yet they kept falling.

He fell to the ground and pressed his free hand against the rough rock, the Ring of Thalkuun scraping against it. Powerful as it was, the artifact couldn't preserve him from this. Tal deluged the stone with power, his unspoken commands riding with it. The tortured ground groaned in response, then writhed.

As the slabs neared, angled walls rose to break against them. Tal ducked his head, weaving pure sorcery around himself in a shell, hoping it would be enough, fearing it wouldn't be.

The World shattered.

He cried out, wordless and soundless in the din. Dust choked him, some seeping through his barriers. He felt as if he were Death's Hand in the Deep once more, fleeing the creature that had slain his comrades, filled with the same despair, the cringing terror of a mouse in a maelstrom.

Then it ceased. All grew still. A buzzing silence filled his head. For a moment, Tal wondered if he'd died, crushed beneath half a mountain.

But his heart still beat. Somehow, against all expectations, he'd survived.

Tal's sudden laughter broke off in a coughing fit. Wheezing, he opened his eyes and pierced the veil of darkness with a spell. Boulders mounded around him, entombing him even more thoroughly than before. He reached out and touched the rubble. It was warm, still buzzing from the glyphs. Withdrawing, he braced himself for the task. Tal drew in sorcery and wondered how much more he could take.

Enough, he told himself, then spoke his spell.

He felt the small mountain atop him with his sorcerous touch, then wrapped his intentions around it. The slightest shift could crush him before he had time to react. This excavation required precision, a precision he normally lacked.

But he hadn't come all this way to fail now.

Grunting, he tumbled the heap. Boulders rolled away at his command, one by one revealing the man trapped beneath their bulk. He whittled away at it, though it felt like trying to fell an oak with a knife. His every joint ached with the effort.

At last, a sliver of light broke through. Like a drowning man seeing the water's surface, he surged toward it, blasting aside the remaining rock that impinged his escape, then stumbling free to fall to his knees.

Undiluted power still poured through him, yet his body was growing weak. He shivered. It burned like poison in his veins. He couldn't hope to survive the flood coursing through him.

But then again, he'd never intended to.

Tal staggered to his feet and pressed forward. The World-heart was almost entirely obscured behind the fog, yet he knew it was there, its power pounding through his body and spirit. *Velori's* tip dragged along the ground, for he couldn't find the strength to lift it. Yet he knew he would endure.

I can. I must. I will.

His eyes fell to his feet. His sorcery pressed the uneven stone flat. Tal coughed hoarsely, wondering how he meant to challenge not one god, but four, when he could barely walk.

His head was in such a haze he had only a moment to register the amassing energy before it stormed down on him.

Tal reacted on instinct, throwing himself to the ground and whipping *Velori* above. He had no reason to believe it would protect him, yet it did. The lightning caught on the blade and curled about the enchanted steel, and the runes blazed with an angry violet light. The hilt burned against his hands, but it didn't break.

A second bolt smashed down.

The lightning found the sword again. This time, it proved too much.

The runes flashed. The steel fractured.

Tal roared as the shards cut into his face. A nauseating pain; there was an empty space in his vision. A sliver had found his eye.

A third flash.

Tal tried to ward it away with sorcery, but it came too

quickly. The energy crackled over his skin. Yet he didn't perish.

Instead, a circle burned cold on his finger.

Tal glanced down with his remaining eye at the Ring of Thalkuun and thought a silent prayer.

Thank you, Father.

But the glyphs carved into it glowed brightly. It wouldn't hold out much longer. He could afford no delay.

Defying his ruined body, Tal surged to his feet and ran.

Lightning flicked down at him as he went, laying him low each time it did. The stone band on his finger grew colder with each bolt. Each time, it seemed only one more would break it.

Yet it held.

The Worldheart was achingly near, looming above him. Tal's sorcery kept him pressing on, sustaining him past what he should have been able to survive. He scrambled over rock, scraped his knees and elbows bloody. His pierced eye trickled blood down his cheek as if he wept.

Only on that last, miserable stretch did he finally understand his enemies' intentions. These traps weren't meant to kill him, but to bring him to the brink of death. They were to waste his strength so that he had none left to fight.

But though he was broken, though he was only a mortal man, the World's blood ran through his veins. He transcended himself. The sorcery within him would be their match.

It must be.

Lightning blazed down yet again, and it proved the final straw. The Ring of Thalkuun broke, nearly severing Tal's finger as it did. But it had done enough.

Both of his eyes wept now, and his lungs squeezed flat. The Worldheart was just above, mere feet from his outstretched hand. It towered into the hazy heavens, lightning curling about its apex. His vision blurred, yet Tal plainly saw the petrified dragons upon it now, their mouths wide and roaring, their claws outstretched, their tails caught mid-lash, their wings spread. Violent red veins coursed through the stone.

But it was one of the figures at the base that caught and held his attention.

It was a small statue, a stone man. He faced the Worldheart, and both hands pressed against it. His features were dulled, his face turned away. Tal knew him all the same.

Yuldor.

He understood his fate then, but it scarcely made a difference. Tal lunged the final distance and brought his right hand around in a swing. In that hand, he still clutched *Velori's* hilt.

The broken edge of the blade crashed into Yuldor's stone fingers.

He threw every scrap of strength left to him into the blow. The digits splintered and fell away, and something emerged from beneath. It moved like smoke, but shone like the sun. Tal felt the crackling potential in its every movement.

Sorcery. Sorcery itself.

He knew it to be true, felt it in the failing capacity he possessed. His blood burned in recognition of its origins. Its mother. Its womb.

He reached for it, trembling — and came up short as lightning lashed him.

His body contorted. For a long, timeless moment, there was nothing but pain. Tal opened his remaining eye, but he could no longer see. The World had devolved into light and shadow. Stone pressed hard against his back. His limbs were slow to respond.

He was dying.

Not yet.

His sorcery roiled. It answered the call from the magic leaking above it. Only the thin cloud forming from the gap in the Worldheart could he see, for he sensed it in a way that went to the core of his being.

Tal rose. Blindly, he grasped for the stone. He lifted himself on tortured limbs, and inch by unseen inch, he dragged himself up. His head was craned back, face tilted toward the pure energy like a long-held prisoner feeling the sun's first touch.

It was there before him, within his reach. All he had to do was grasp it.

He thought about the people he had left behind. His friends; his family. *Be well,* he thought to them, his lips curling in a fatal smile.

He pressed his hands to the bright cloud and soared upon it.

AWAKENING

Garin was back under the waterfall, holding Wren. He smoothed her hair, smiling at how it always came back up, defiant as ever. She slapped his hand away, then drew his face down toward hers. He closed his eyes, reveling in the moment, wishing he could remain suspended there forever.

Ilvuan tore the dream open.

Wake, Jenduit, *WAKE!*

Garin jerked upright, heart pounding, clawing at the enemy smothering him — only to discover it was his blanket. Gasping for breath, he looked around for danger, but the camp appeared calm. It must have been dawn, for scant light peeked through the canopy above, though it seemed muted as if by storm clouds. Only the lack of a watch seemed out of the ordinary.

What is it? he shot back, nerves still on edge. *What's wrong?*

He is gone! Ilvuan seemed as close to panic as he'd ever felt him. *Heartblood has left us behind!*

Still groggy, it took Garin a moment to comprehend his words. *Tal left?*

He scanned the camp again. The rest of his companions

slumbered on, unaware of the crisis. But true to the Singer's words, Tal's bedroll lay empty.

Burn and blast you frail mortals! Ilvuan's rage seared away his anxiety. *You force me to sleep when I should have been wary!*

"Enough!" Garin hissed under his breath as he stumbled to his feet. His head was in a haze, spinning too fast to focus. *Plan. I need a plan.*

Pursue him! If we leave now, we might not be too late.

For a moment, Garin felt the dragon tug on his limbs, attempting to take control. He shoved Ilvuan back.

"Don't," he growled in warning. "Give me a moment. We have to wake the others."

Ilvuan seethed, but settled back as Garin set about the task. He kneeled next to Wren and shook her by the shoulder, rougher than he would have preferred, but his pulse raced too fast for him to slow.

"Wren," he whispered, then spoke louder, "Wren!"

She only moaned in response. Garin frowned. Even for her, this seemed a deep slumber.

Ilvuan understood first. *The egg shard — she no longer wears it.*

"What? Of course she does..."

He trailed off as he lifted her wrist, where the bracelet should have been, and found the dragonstone missing. Garin let her arm fall back to the ground, his fears rising higher with his every heartbeat. His gaze flew across the camp, not knowing what he hoped to find, only that he needed answers. His eyes caught on a small pile next to the ashes of the fire. He rose and moved toward it, knowing what he would see, yet not daring to believe it.

Five bracelets were collected together in an untidy heap. All the dragonstones except for Garin's.

He closed his eyes and kneaded them with his palms. *It doesn't make sense,* he thought to Ilvuan. *Why would Tal be gone and everyone's bracelets removed — all except mine?*

The answer came to him a moment before the dragon supplied it impatiently.

He wished to go alone, Jenduit. *To face his fate without us. But our destinies are intertwined — his, yours, and mine. We must go to him now, or all will be for naught.*

Garin knew he should obey, but he reeled with the revelation. *Tal abandoned us. Abandoned us... to save us.*

The man had always been stubborn and impulsive — his initial flight into the East had shown that much. He was also absurdly noble. If Garin wanted, he could let this run its course, allow Tal to pay the ultimate price to save the World. He and Wren could build a life and have nights such as the one they'd just shared for years to come.

Yet even as he flirted with the idea, Garin knew he couldn't embrace it. All their companions had known how this journey might end, Helnor and Kaleras included. Their sacrifices had to mean something.

And Tal had mentored him in a way his brothers couldn't have. Though he scarcely dared admit it, even to himself, he looked up to him. Almost as a father.

Besides, he thought, *someone has to save the fool man from himself.*

Ilvuan's lacerating approval spurred him into action. Kneeling, he swept up the bracelets and hurried around the camp. One by one, he retied them tightly to his companions' wrists. None of them stirred beyond groans and slight movements. He had to hope the miasma hadn't affected them too deeply in the hours since Tal had fled.

When he secured the last one to Rolan's wrist, Garin returned to his own pack and donned his gear. "Wake up!" he shouted as he worked. "Everyone, you have to wake!"

The response was laggardly and delayed. Falcon was the first to sit up, but he only stared at Garin, his gaze vague. Ashelia rose next, seeming to have to fight to stay awake.

"What... is it?" she asked, her speech slurred. "Something... wrong?"

Garin pulled his belt tight around his waist, Lament's scabbard knocking against his leg. "Tal's gone. He's gone to the peak alone. We have to go, and now."

The Peer stared at him in silence. Gradually, the silver tendrils in them spun, faster and faster, and her fists clenched.

"He left us?" she asked in a low voice. "Here? Now?"

"*Yes.*" He tried to remain patient, but urgency pressed too hard on him. "If we're going to follow him, we have to hurry."

The others began to stir. Aelyn wore a grimace and practically clawed at the ground as he struggled to gain control of himself. Wren moaned with every movement, but she was already on her feet and pulling her gear together. Even Rolan sat up, though the boy remained in a stupor.

But though Ashelia had come awake, she still seemed caught in disbelief. Her eyes stared at nothing. "He promised," she muttered, as if speaking to herself. "He promised to leave this place. And if he... then he'll never..."

Her hand rested briefly on her midriff, as if it pained her. The next moment, she seemed to come fully awake, and she rose with her usual lithe grace.

"We go," she said simply, and joined the others in readying.

Garin, having had a head start, was the first ready. While he shifted back and forth on his feet and debated relieving his bladder again, he mulled over what lay ahead.

Do you know? he asked Ilvuan. *What will we find at the peak? Will he still be alive?*

The dragon's answer was calm now that their company was moving.

I do not know, Jenduit. I reside within your body now. But when I dwelled within the Worldheart, there were runes protecting the path to it, traps laid over generations. If he overcame those, the Pretender may have assaulted him more directly. But...

525

The dragon's thoughts drifted into mist. Garin grasped after them, but he couldn't wrangle any reason from them.

But what? Don't hold out on us now!

They desire Heartblood. They have a purpose for him.

They? Fear cut deep inside him, an icy knife stabbing to his core. *You mean the Three actually exist, don't you?*

Yes. They exist through the Pretender, but they have wills and aims of their own. They have ever sought to extend their existence and strengthen their bond to the World. Heartblood is to be their sacrifice, his soul a tether by which to reign. That is what it is to be drovald.

Garin froze in place. He didn't want to ask the inevitable question, though he knew he must.

And me? Am I to meet the same fate up there?

No. You are Mender. I formed you, little Listener, let you hear the Womb's Song. You are not their tool. You are our deliverance.

Pride and purpose flooded through Garin, bolstering his flagging spirits.

I'll do what I can, he promised the dragon. *For the sake of the* ava'duala, *and for all the people of the World.*

An image flashed into his mind: a dragon, dark blue in hue, spread its wings and roared into the air. Garin's chest reverberated with the remembered sound. Almost, he threw back his own head to join his voice with it.

The moment passed, and he blinked. Only as he came back to himself did he recognize his companions were prepared and looking at him.

"Ilvuan?" Wren's expression was guarded as she posed the query.

He nodded. Almost, he smiled at their grave expressions, such was the elation that still filled him. He barely clung to reason.

"I'm back now."

"Good." Ashelia seemed in command of both herself and the party once again. "We move with all haste. Leave your packs here — the forest will guide us back to them when we return."

She hesitated, and Garin could guess her thoughts: *If we return.* But all of them were wise enough not to say it aloud.

Ashelia pressed on. "We are likely safe while we're among the trees, but be ready for anything."

"I always am," Aelyn replied drily, though he lacked his usual bite.

She nodded and turned, leading them up the hill. Garin gave one last lingering look at their camp, and their journey to that point came to him in flashes.

This is the end, he thought as he hurried after the others. *It's finally here.*

How strange it was that he was no longer afraid.

"I'm... scared... *Momua.*"

Garin grimaced and looked away from the panting boy stumbling up the mountain next to his mother. As his own lungs squeezed flat with the lack of air and his legs became as nimble as tree stumps. The fervor Ilvuan had filled him with had long burned away. All too well could he identify with the boy's fear, even having mastered his own.

He looked at Wren. She was breathing as heavily as he, yet her teeth were bared in determination, and her eyes blazed as brightly as they ever had. At his glance, her gaze turned on him, and her snarl transformed into a fierce smile.

He shook his head in wonder as he spoke between breaths. "How... do you... do it?"

"Do... what?"

Garin gestured vaguely up and down her length. "You."

A laugh broke free of her. "Trouper's... training."

"That's right... it is. Raised her right... didn't I?"

Falcon had come up next to his daughter. Like her, he

seemed to radiate resolve, though his was of a very different kind, like the desperate attempts of a drowning man to stay afloat. Yet something more glowed in his eyes, an eagerness that Garin hadn't glimpsed in the bard since their days in Elendol.

Wren shot her father a look, but didn't waste breath on a reply.

Garin had hoped the end of Paradise wouldn't be much farther from their camp. Yet the woods seemed to carry on and on, and the slope somehow grew steeper. Though the ascent proved easier without their packs, a heaviness still settled over his limbs and sapped his energy. Sheer willpower was all that pressed them forward.

Yet when the tree line ahead changed several hours later, it still seemed too soon.

Garin slowed as he stared at the ridge above. Between the trunks spread a slate sky. They'd reached the end of Paradise — and the beginning of Ikvaldar's final ascent.

Ashelia only increased her pace, as did the others, and Garin had to hurry to catch up. More than exertion made his breath come quick now, imagining what might be awaiting them just beyond the ridge.

As he had many times before, Ilvuan bolstered his spirit, exuding certainty in their purpose. Garin clung to it and hoped it would be enough.

Ashelia stopped at Paradise's boundary, staring forward. As the others lined up beside her, Garin beheld what awaited them.

He'd expected the peak to be barren, but the gray landscape was even more blighted than he'd imagined. Spires projected from the ground like spines from a dragon's back, bristling and threatening. The ground before them looked to have been ripped apart, and recently, judging by the sharp edges of the stone and the rubble and dust layering every surface. He remembered what Ilvuan had said of glyph traps and realized what must have happened.

Tal, he thought, almost a prayer sent after him. *What have you done?*

"He's already come." Ashelia sounded hollowed out.

"But where has he gone?" Wren voiced aloud the question plaguing them all.

A stirring through the entirety of his body was his only warning before Ilvuan spoke to the company at large.

"He has merged with the Worldheart."

Fear reared again, numbing Garin's mind. Around him, his companions stared at him, his confusion and horror reflected in their expressions.

Falcon's shoulders sagged. "Then we're too late."

"No!" Wren glared around their company. "We're not! We can't be!"

Garin couldn't find it in him to even hope she was right. If Tal had joined the Worldheart, he was already in their enemies' grasp. Either he'd succeeded and wrested power from Yuldor and the Three, or he'd failed — and considering he was nowhere to be seen, Garin feared he knew which it was.

Not yet, Jenduit. *Time is short, but we may yet shift the winds.*

He startled at Ilvuan's words, spoken only to him. *How?* he asked. *They have him.*

Time there does not fly as it does here. Days in the mortal plane may be mere moments there. Heartblood fights on — of this, I am sure.

Ilvuan could always sense Tal before. Garin had to hope he knew what he was talking about now.

"Tal still fights," he said aloud with more confidence than he felt. "I have to go help him."

Everyone turned to stare at him.

"Help him?" Aelyn sneered, but it failed to hide his true feelings. "He's beyond anyone's help now."

"Not mine. I — we — have to reach the Worldheart."

Understanding lit in his companions' eyes. They'd all witnessed their meshings often enough not to question it now.

"Fine," Wren relented, turning back to face the shattered peak. "But where is it?"

Ilvuan nudged Garin's legs forward, and he obliged in the movement, ignoring the protests from behind and trusting the Singer. Free of the sheltering trees, the wind cut at him with fresh abandon, freezing him to the bone. Understanding Ilvuan's intentions, he opened himself to the Worldsong.

He nearly fell to the ground, at once overcome by the storm that filled him. The Song had never been so strong, nor possessed such vivacity. It was like a thunderstorm wrapped in an eruption, and all of its power and fury poured through him.

He felt invincible. He felt he would shatter at the first touch.

But Ilvuan was there, wrapped around him, binding him together. The dragon guided his mind forward and into the heart of the storm. As they drew closer, Garin understood.

The Worldheart lay just beyond the ruined stones.

With the Singer's aid, he cut himself off again and turned to face the others. His mouth was open to speak before he noticed they were no longer looking at him, but beyond. Garin turned, but still in a daze, he didn't immediately understand what he saw.

A moment later, comprehension rushed in.

Four robed figures stood before the ruined rocks. They were two score strides away, yet their identities were unmistakable. He saw the unnatural texture of their skin, the fell glow in their eyes.

The Extinguished had resurrected.

SONG'S END

GARIN TOLD HIMSELF HE TREMBLED FROM THE COLD. BUT AS HE stared at the dread warlocks, he knew it to be a lie.

"Garin Dunford!" Soltor's high, mocking voice was just audible over the wind. "What amusements have you brought us today?"

Ilvuan's presence burned through him, firming his limbs and resolve. But he didn't direct his words at Garin.

"Move aside, slaves," he thundered, *"or I shall force you!"*

Soltor threw back his head and loosed an unfettered laugh.

Garin tried to reconcile with the sight before him. It was supposed to take Yuldor ten years to resurrect the Extinguished. Yet here they stood in all their stony flesh before them.

Maybe they're illusions. Or perhaps just shadows of themselves.

He had to believe their appearance came with a caveat. But whether or not his hopes proved accurate, he suspected he'd discover the truth soon.

As the shrill laughter faded, the Thorn spoke next in his grating voice.

"You are nothing, dragon, without our Master's power. Once, you might have stood against us, but no more."

The one Garin thought to be Hashele threw up an arm and splayed her hand upward. "Look to the sky, *ava'dual*," her cruel voice echoed over the landscape. "Witness all you have lost!"

Garin didn't want to look away from the devious sorcerers, yet movement among the clouds drew his eye. It was no more than a pool of shadow, like the vague impression of a fish underwater, yet enough to awaken suspicion. Something flew above the clouds, something massive. Something from which even Ilvuan recoiled.

A bellow, pitched both high and low, pierced the storm-riven sky.

Garin flinched, feeling like exposed prey before its predator. He didn't have to open himself to the Worldsong to know what stalked them.

"Dragon," he whispered, the word stolen by the wind as soon as it left his lips. Yvärras, it seemed, had finally decided upon her allegiance.

Then another cry came, and a third. The clouds seethed with silhouettes, flying just overhead, more than he could count at a glance.

All of them dragons.

It's all an illusion, he told himself. *Just like in the Ruins of Erlodan. Only one dragon exists in the flesh. There has to be only one.*

If these dragons were real and aligned with the Extinguished, he and his companions had lost the battle before it had begun.

He sought after Ilvuan — for comfort or confirmation, he didn't know. But he received neither from the Singer, for he issued forth a roar of his own.

"Corruptors! Defilers! What has your master done? This is not what was agreed! These are not true ava'duala! *You will suffer an eternity for this!"*

The Soulstealers didn't appear the least fazed by his threats.

"If you do not believe them to be true," Hashele taunted, "then test their fire!"

As if summoned, one shadow burst through the blanket of clouds and came screaming toward them.

It was recognizably a dragon, but only just so. Compared to Yvärras, it was a scrawny beast, too thin of body and limb and much smaller. Yet it still stretched three times Garin's length, and its teeth and claws were more than sufficient to tear his frail body apart.

Its maw hung slightly open, and behind the yellowed teeth, a brilliant light built. Dragonfire leaked between its incisors, ready to spill out through the air. Garin had seen the devastating impact that breath could have. He'd withstood it once, but only with Tal's help. He would die if he stayed.

But he was tired of running.

Ilvuan raged in his mind. *"Sister!"* he bellowed. *"See now what your bargain has bought! Come to our aid, or forever doom our race!"*

Garin knew with one look in those hateful eyes that Ilvuan's pleas would not touch this creature. It was as he said: a twisted thing that only sought to kill.

A greater trumpet than any of the previous blasted through the air, then something tore through the clouds, crashing into the corrupted dragon.

Even before he glimpsed the red scales, Garin recognized Yvärras by her song. Strong as it was, it cut through the tumult of the Worldsong and blasted over the landscape. It was a song lusting for death and destruction. It was a killing sound.

He'd never been so glad to hear it.

Yet more dragons descended from the clouds. Before them, all but one of the Extinguished were weaving spells. The last Soulstealer ran across the shattered ground, looking for all appearance as if he were fleeing.

"Coward!" Hashele shrieked. "Traitor!"

The figure reached the drop-off at the edge of the peak and

looked back. In that moment, Garin saw not the ravaged appearance from before, but the brilliant smile and countenance of a golden elf.

"Fight well!" Pim called, then leaped off the cliff.

Garin didn't have time to wonder about it. Glyphs, unseen to that point, flashed on the ground, and shapes grew from them, taking on substance and shape. The Worldsong was in a frenzy before the coming slaughter.

We strike now, Jenduit! Ilvuan roared, pulling at his limbs, filling him so entirely he felt he must burst.

He had no room left for fear.

A yell ripped free of him as Garin tore his sword from its scabbard and charged.

Blood roared in his ears. Song and sorcery flowed through his limbs. Garin pounded across the stone, sprinting as fast as he ever had. He knew his companions would follow without turning to look.

But creatures intervened before he could reach the Extinguished. Fully formed from the runes, ghouls loped toward him on all fours, snarling and slavering. Witikos rose above them, hollow eyes burning with malice under horned crowns. They closed in around, too many to contend with alone. Already, they numbered two dozen, and more joined them with every passing moment.

He didn't back down, but threw himself into the fray.

Lament danced forward, its golden glyphs blazing, as three ghouls sprang on him. Once, even a single one of their kind would have torn him apart.

But no more.

"*Keld thasht!*"

Fire ripped free of his hand, blasting back one and clipping another. The third's claws met *Helshax's* edge, and it fell back howling, skin smoking from the blade's enchantments.

Garin flowed with the Form of Water, pivoting as more enemies poured toward him. The Worldsong howled in his head, so loud it seemed it must lift him off his feet. It filled him with a swell of energy, seemingly boundless, even as it threatened to overwhelm him. Yet as he pulled at a second spell to break the stone beneath the Nightkin's feet, then a third to send wind to buffet them back, he was far from succumbing.

A witiko, too strong and stubborn to be deterred, lumbered toward him, huge claws reaching. Garin danced away and lashed at the grasping hands. Still, the monster came on, even when he shot more flames into its chest. With preternatural speed, it swiped at him, clipping Garin's shoulder and sending him spinning to the stone. The creature bugled its delight as it closed in for the kill.

Strike its legs! Ilvuan bellowed, and Garin felt the dragon's presence surge in his body.

He wasn't sure who guided the blow as he spun around and swung Lament at the witiko's legs. But he knew it was the Singer whose strength shattered first one femur, then the second, as the blade cut through the Nightkin.

The beast fell screaming to the stone, but Garin was already turning away. A second witiko stomped toward him, four ghouls flanking.

The Worldsong swelled, warning of a different danger. Garin spun toward the sound, his sword lifted, and registered the lightning flaring from Soltor's upraised hands a moment before the impact came.

Lament rattled in his hands. Heat spilled through his gloves as the black steel absorbed the spell.

He'd survived, but not unscathed. Garin's eyes were momentarily blinded, and pain lanced into his skull. He thought he cried out, but he could no longer hear himself through the ringing in his ears.

Something rammed into his side, and burning wounds tore down his chest.

Frenzied with pain, Garin lashed out at his assailant blindly, using the hilt as much as the blade. He knew it to be a ghoul by its stink alone. It fought like a wild beast, every part trying to rend him. Ilvuan roared, then bolstered Garin's strikes and fortified him against the agony.

At last, the claws fell away. Through his returning vision, he saw the ghoul lay on the stone, head bashed in, dark blood oozing.

There was no time to celebrate. Ilvuan roared a warning as another witiko — or perhaps the same as before — reached from nearby. With sparks still in his vision, Garin had to guess where to dodge and only narrowly avoided being skewered. He struck in retaliation, but only succeeded in clipping a nail.

Garin backed away, *Helshax* before him. Ghouls ringed him now, and yet another witiko prowled behind. He was surrounded and outnumbered.

I'm going to die.

The realization didn't make him afraid. As when he faced down Heyl's descending hand in Elendol, he found death held no fear for him. Now that it was a certainty, calmness filled him.

Ilvuan burned through him, pride and determination rising in equal measures. *We will not fall here, Jenduit!*

The Singer trumpeted a call, and power flowed out in a wave.

The Lattice blazed to life as the dragon's spell cascaded outward, the lines brightening and bulging. Garin watched ghouls fling themselves off the cliff's edge a dozen feet to his left. Witikos slammed into the stone wall behind the fell sorcerers, their horns breaking, their bodies impaled on spires. In moments, the mountaintop was cleared of Nightkin.

He risked a glance at his companions. Ashelia and Rolan remained back at the tree line, though the Peer had her rapier bared and seemed on the verge of rushing forward. Falcon was a few paces farther, a knife clutched in one hand, eyes wide as he looked for a way to help. Wren contended with Soltor, both moving with a speed that was difficult to follow. Beyond them,

Hashele was casting a spell, and by the glyphs appearing on the ground, it was to summon more Nightkin to the fight. Aelyn had his hands raised, his gaze fixed on some point beyond Garin, his lips moving in an incantation.

Garin turned to look at whom he aimed when the Worldsong cried out a warning.

Stone, moving like vines, whipped up from the ground and ensnared him. Desperately, Garin struck at them with Lament, but his arm was soon too hindered to be effective. In moments, they'd enwrapped him and squeezed the air from his lungs as they pulled tight on his chest.

His eyes caught on the Thorn's mocking smile as he stalked toward him.

"It will be a pleasure to kill you, dragon's pet," he spoke in a harsh whisper that curled inside Garin's ears. "Just as I enjoyed your master's death." A dragonstone knife was clutched in his hand, honed to deadly sharpness.

Garin tried to cry out in denial. *Save us, Ilvuan!* he begged of the Singer.

Before the dragon could respond, light flared from behind. Flames roared past Garin to envelop the Thorn.

Aelyn's scream rent the air even as his spell tore into the Extinguished. It burned with all the hate, the fear, the lost love for his people and his Queen, all butchered by the Thorn.

Trapped by the stone vines, Garin could only watch and hope the mage's might would be enough.

The flames ceased. Aelyn collapsed to his knees, but his eyes remained up. They both stared at the blackened form, still standing, waiting for it to fall.

The head lifted, and sickly yellow eyes stared out from the darkness.

"You cannot kill me, elf," the Thorn rasped. His voice was weaker than before, but still far from a dying man's last gasp. "You never could."

Garin writhed against his bonds. *Ilvuan, free us!*

Speak stone's name, and we shall! Ilvuan roared back.

So he tried. "*Dord! Dord uvthak!*"

But even now, the Soulstealer's spell held. It trapped Garin, leaving him unable to do anything but stare at his doomed friend.

Aelyn shivered badly and had collapsed on his hands and knees. His lips quivered as he spoke silent words. Did he utter a response to the Thorn's taunts? Or was he working a new incantation?

"You will die like your Queen," the Extinguished continued. "I butchered her like a calf on an altar. I will slay you just the same, gut you and summon a demon like—"

"*Broldid ist!*" Aelyn cried out, and stone erupted from the wall of rubble behind the Soulstealer.

One spire impaled the Thorn in the chest. The second took him in the shoulder.

The third burst through his head.

At once, the stone vines slackened around Garin, and he wriggled free, staring and waiting with bated breath.

He's dead. He's gone.

They'd felled one of the Extinguished.

Garin looked back to see Aelyn had collapsed. He wasn't alone. Another figure stood over him, one in tattered robes with a skull like scabbed charcoal.

Soltor.

Garin knew he should move past to pursue Tal, as he told the others he would. But he couldn't leave his friend to die.

He turned to Aelyn, wondering what had befallen Wren that she no longer fought the Soulstealer. Before he could take more than a few steps, however, he came to a halt.

Ilvuan asserted himself, fighting for control of his body.

No, Jenduit! the Singer demanded. *We cannot delay!*

He'll die! We can save him!

All here will die if we do not ascend!

He watched in horror as the Extinguished seized Aelyn's

hair and wrenched back his head. Garin tried to utter a spell, but he couldn't even manage that.

Once more, he was helplessly trapped.

A figure flashed in the corner of his vision. Wren limped and blood painted her clothes, but she sprinted with a wolf's speed as she charged at Soltor. Her blade darted forward and cut across the back of the Soulstealer's neck, and stony skin flew off in chunks.

Soltor released Aelyn and whirled around, very much still alive.

"I know you, girl!" the Extinguished sneered. "The bard's daughter. Still playing with steel, are you? Still upset about your father's hand?"

If Garin knew Wren at all, he suspected she burned with fury. Yet as she darted a look back at him, she seemed unsettlingly calm.

"I'll handle this!" she shouted. "Go, Garin! Tal needs you more!"

He was stricken, torn. The woman he loved fought for her life; all his friends did. How could he leave them?

If you do not, all will be for nothing, Ilvuan rumbled.

Garin knew it to be true. Finally, he accepted it.

He turned away from the fight and sprinted for the wall of rubble, then began to climb.

The sounds of the battle below echoed in his ears, the cries of pain and triumph, but he didn't look back. Look, and he might lose the will to continue. Now that their purpose was once more aligned, Ilvuan bolstered his flagging resolve.

This is the only way, the dragon told Garin as he strengthened their grip. *Ascend, or all the World will fall.*

Garin believed him; he always had. Even fighting against each other, he and Ilvuan were closer than ever before. Almost, he was forgetting the boundaries between them, the dragon's soul seeping into the seams of his own. It should have scared him, this closeness. But with death below, above, and all around, his only comfort was that he didn't strive alone.

The climb would have been difficult without sorcery. Even with it, the ascent took far longer than he liked. "*Dord,*" he spoke through numb lips, again and again. Relenting to his wishes, the rock smoothed where it was too sharp to touch, and handholds appeared as needed.

Ilvuan went further. Garin could feel him working in the back of his mind, weaving the Lattice as cleverly as the finest seamstress in Halenhol. He caught glimpses of the sorcerous yarns in the peripheries of his vision and felt as the dragon's spells took effect. The hounding wind faded to a breeze. The effort of hauling his body up dozens of feet faded. The way was smoothed, and Garin took full advantage.

He only hoped they weren't already too late.

Reaching the top of the cliff, Garin hauled himself up and took in their surroundings. He scarcely knew what he'd expected to see, but it wasn't the sight before him. Stones, uneven and sharp enough to skewer, lined their path. It would take an hour to cross, an hour they couldn't afford.

A scream tore through the tumult, and Garin couldn't help but look back. He froze.

Wren staggered upright, even more beaten and bloody than before. Her father, wrapped around Soltor, had his knife in the Soulstealer's eye. Unbelievable as it was, it looked as if he'd killed the Extinguished that had stolen so much from him and saved his daughter.

But a witiko loomed behind.

The Nightkin seized Falcon and lifted him. Its huge claws crushed into his chest. Garin couldn't think of a spell to help before the moment passed.

He knew the truth: the bard was gone.

Listener...

Ilvuan didn't fight him now; all that Garin felt poured

through the dragon as well. Yet their purpose also doubled as it filled both their minds.

He could do nothing to save Falcon. Nothing to save the others.

Nothing but press on.

Garin did the impossible. He turned away from his friends again, seeing how he'd doomed them.

This can't all be for nothing, he thought, as much to himself as Ilvuan. *It can't.*

The dragon only rumbled in reply.

As they turned, Garin felt another sensation scour his thoughts. The Worldsong emitted even more strongly here, mind-numbingly loud, coming from above the shattered rock field, where a dark pillar rose hazily amongst the mist.

The Worldheart.

Even stricken by grief, Garin felt his resolve harden at the sight. Their destination was before them. He and Ilvuan would reach it.

The dragon's approval coursed through him, propelling Garin forward, power flowing with each step. Garin kept tempo with a muttered spell.

"Dord firkist. Dord firkist. Dord firkist..."

Together, he and Ilvuan smoothed the way, their sorcery forming a road that cut through the desolation to the spire rising ahead. The Worldheart filled his head and his chest, bolstering his spell far beyond what he'd cast before. For a moment, Garin almost imagined they could succeed.

A bestial scream rent the sky.

Garin flinched and looked above until he found the source of the sound. The sight struck fresh despair through him.

Yvärras was falling.

Five of the malformed dragons attacked the Protectress, rending the tender flesh of her wings and impeding every flap. Yvärras shrieked in pain and rage, and the Worldsong boiled with her sorcery. Blue-white flames erupted from her mouth, carving through one of her assailants. It plummeted out of sight, blackened and trailing smoke.

But Garin didn't need to know Ilvuan's mind to understand their ally would soon lose. Once she fell, nothing would stand between the dragons and his friends, nor they themselves. Exposed as they were, heading toward the place the dragon guarded, they would likely be the first target.

Garin reeled, but the Singer steadied him. Ilvuan's fury was molten, his will as strong as a mountain's roots.

It is not too late, Jenduit! *We must join her! We must fight!*

Garin shared his conviction, but still, he despaired. *How can we fight them?*

Alone, we can do nothing. Together, we will fly.

Yvärras had managed to keep some altitude, but one wing had a long tear through it, and blood, dark red with a golden shimmer, streamed down her scarlet scales.

Trust me, my Listener. Ilvuan's presence enveloped him, a suit of armor, a wool blanket on a snowy night. *Trust me, as you have trusted me until now.*

He felt the dragon's intentions leaking into his essence. Boundaries eroded. All sense of his individual self faded.

They melded, and like steel being forged into a blade, they became something stronger.

He had no fear.

I trust you, Garin thought, and he opened himself up entirely.

A flash of scenes rushed through his mind, too fast and too many to comprehend. Knowledge, ancient and deep, seeded in him and grew.

Then their spirits were rising, Ilvuan pulling them up, away from the feeble flesh to become as they ought to be. Garin reveled in it and joined him.

They burst free, and together, they soared.

SOAR

IT WAS AGONY. IT WAS BLISS.

Sorcery flowed through him. Sorcery *was* him. It was everywhere — his eyes, his pores, his soul. It burned and battered, soothed and healed.

He'd always yearned to lose himself wholly in something. To meld with a greater purpose and leave behind his imperfect flesh.

This was what he had longed for. Unity. Belonging. An end to existence.

Then he sensed the others.

They circled above him like crows over carrion. But though they'd once had wings, they were no birds.

Ava'duala. Dragons.

Hungry and jealous, they watched him, waiting for their opportunity to seize him in their grasp. Too long had they been trapped, saving a World they no longer commanded. They resented his being alive while they were not.

The dragons weren't the only ones with him. He quested below and sensed a greater danger still. Their presence yawned like an abyss, the sort of oblivion in which there could be no rest. They were fourfold, yet one, melded as thoroughly together as the dragons were to their cage. In their bindings were divisions, flaws, yet their strength was nothing like he'd felt before, a force too overwhelming to be fought.

The insight served as his memory's catalyst. He couldn't lose himself, not yet. He needed to be whole one last time. He needed to be the man he once was.

He began to remember.

He grasped after the fragments of himself. He recovered his soul, piece by piece, like an angler fetching catches from the sea. As the parts came together, he recalled who he was. Why he was here.

Tal Harrenfel.

He spoke the name as if it were a binding spell. In a way, it was. It recalled the shards of the past, the sharp memories he'd bled from a thousand times over. In torment, he recovered his purpose.

Tal rallied his strength and met his foes as they rose from the World's depths.

Yuldor and the Three enveloped him. Pain lanced through Tal with their every touch. They ravaged his being as they explored it, their hands burning, their amusement mocking. Soon, his enemies gained voices, their thoughts given words.

So you came, one purred, feminine and inviting. Serenity, he remembered her. *All this way, you came to us. Across plain, mountain, and river, you sought us.*

As I said he would! another thundered, imperious and cold. *He is mine!* His words stretched the seams of Tal's spirit to breaking. Silence, Tal knew him to be; an irony for his disposition.

Ours! wheedled Solemnity. *We will possess him together, as we did the others. You cannot keep him for yourself, Rothaen!*

Peace... Give me peace... This last presence was weak, barely more than a whisper. By this, Tal knew him: Yuldor, or what remained of him.

Faced with the elven sorcerer's fate, Tal longed to strike against these beings invading his soul. He didn't want to end up an empty husk, hollowed out by immortal scavengers. Yet already, his will to resist was fading. In the gods' embrace, it was impossible even to maintain his sense of self, much less defy them.

You will have peace, Serenity assured Yuldor with soft disdain. *Peace everlasting, just as you endeavored to gift mortalkind.*

Enough! Silence boomed. *Victory at last! We seize* Skaldurak *now, together and without delay!*

Together, always together, Solemnity complained, but Tal sensed him closing in with the others.

Tal was a midge, trapped in a silken web and unable to do anything but watch the spiders crawl toward him. Terror shot through him, undermining his resolve, yet he desperately clung to it.

I'm the snare, not the prey, he told himself. *I'll destroy them all.*

Mirth boomed against him, nearly shaking him apart. *What harm can you pose us, Stone in the Wheel?* Silence mocked. *You will be used up and cast aside, the same as Yuldor Soldarin.*

No!

But Tal's denial rang false even to himself. He was a man striving against deities. He was a tool, a means to an end. Resistance was futile.

They came closer, closer — then, like a peuma, the first pounced.

The others were there a moment later, each seizing Tal's essence and trying to claim him for their own. He was torn and tumbled about. It was all he could do to keep himself together as the mad gods ravaged his soul.

One wrapped around him, enveloping him like a cocoon. *Peace!* Yuldor's desperate voice pleaded. *Please, please, give me peace!*

Tal tried to collect enough of himself to think of a reply. *I will give you peace. Help me, and I will give it to you.*

If his words meant anything to the withered elven sorcerer, he received no sign. The Whispering Gods raged at their fourth. Instead of battering at Tal, they turned their fury on Yuldor. The agony flooded into Tal, Yuldor unable to help but spill into his soul.

Scenes emerged before him.

Most sped by too quickly to comprehend, but some lingered. A young boy, elven judging by his eyes and ears, sobbed into his arms, hunched over in the corner of a room in a kintree. Tal felt his thoughts spread through, the promise to never again feel this way, to never be so powerless he couldn't bring justice to Elendol.

Memories. Yuldor's memories. He understood it as he absorbed and relived them.

Another scene swept him away. It was Yuldor again, but now as a youth barely older than Garin and Wren. He'd grown handsome, his features fine and strong, his eyes bright green with silver tendrils. Yet there was a hungry look to his face; his cheeks were too hollow, his eyes ringed with dark circles. He was clad in black robes and bent over a book, though his hands were spread before him. In the air suspended a rent in the World, a dark portal oozing darkness. From within, voices unknown whispered, summoning, beckoning.

That memory fled too, only to be replaced by another. Yuldor was a young man and a master of the Obsidian Tower in Elendol, evident by the elegance of his sable robes and the dark gem upon his pendant. He stood before four others his age, yet who lacked his station and authority. They bent their heads and pledged their allegiance. It gratified Yuldor, yet an emptiness lingered inside him, a void that all the power he'd attained had never sated. And in the void, whispers from unseen beings had emerged, growing louder with each passing day. During his explorations of the sorcerous streams, they first spoke to him, then stayed with him since. They promised him power such as he could never attain himself and justice for his fallen kin. They swore he could create the World he always yearned for. One with peace and prosperity for all.

The scene peeled away as if it were parchment ripped to strips, and behind it lay a fresh memory. Yuldor seemed little older, yet harsh experience had ravaged his appearance. He stood atop a mountain peak, snow heaped under his feet and mounding atop the surrounding stone spires. Before him, a black mound rose, the features of those petrified into it outlined in frost.

The Worldheart. This was Yuldor before his ascension.

His four disciples, those who would become the Extinguished, stood shivering behind. Yuldor didn't seem to feel the cold. His eyes blazed with unholy light as he raised his hands toward the column of black stone. The red veins shot through it seemed to glow brighter with anticipation. Whispers grew loud in his mind.

He cut into the stone, releasing a cloud of sorcery. Then he placed his hands on it and gold mist enveloped him.

Tal's mind burned white. A feeling like his veins were being pulled from his flesh erupted through him. A moment later, he felt his consciousness separating from Yuldor's, then he was once again in the clutches of the Three. Their attention wasn't entirely on him, however; the abuse of their fourth manifestation continued, punishing him with poison and pain.

Tal knew he should fight, yet he didn't know how. Just as within the goldwood, he had no weapons to employ against beings such as these. They were deities in some real sense. The most powerful entities in the World.

Despair made him long to sink into the *Doash* below. He could feel it like the sun's rays, but it was its whispers that touched him. *Rest. Peace. Release.* Like a honeysweet held just out of reach of a child, the Womb tantalized him with all he craved.

Some small measure of relief came, a coolness that defied the fury of the Three. A presence came with it, and words pressed into Tal.

I am here, Thalkunaras. *You do not fight alone.*

Night, he recognized her. *Maral Batomar.* He felt stretched and worn thin, a rag tugged between hounds, yet he tried to put the tattered remains of his thoughts back together. *You came.*

As I said I would. This is the final gambit, Thalkunaras. *Remember: you must admit the Three, but not yield to them.*

Admit them. He'd known the price. Only through sacrifice could they gain victory. But to let them in and not succumb — it was too impossible a task, one he couldn't hope to accomplish. The Whispering Gods stormed around him, indomitable as thunderheads high in the sky.

His ally seemed to read his thoughts. *I will assist. But the* ava'dual *and his Listener are needed as well.*

They're not coming.

Whether she read it in his mind or if there was no time to protest, he didn't know. The Night accepted the damning blow without hesitation.

Then we must hope we are enough. Keep yourself whole, Thalkunaras; *that is all you must do. I will handle the rest.*

Keep himself whole. When had he ever been whole? It was a task he'd failed at in life; could he expect more now?

But he didn't have a choice. He had to make up for his past failings or die in the attempt.

I'm ready.

All four gods turned their attention back to them, their own squabbles forgotten as they noticed the Night. His ally lifted her veil. Tal was vulnerable once more.

Silence, Solemnity, and Serenity seized him, and pain became all he knew.

They soared up from the mountain, defying the whipping winds and bellowing dragons. They left behind the ground and all the fragile beings crawling upon it. Once more, they took their rightful place in the sky, the domain from which they'd always ruled and would rule again. All around, the Worldsong rose in celebration, its adulation flowing through them, powering each flap of their wings.

Garin abandoned his body and joined the new one he and Ilvuan had forged.

They were a dragon, but of a kind he'd glimpsed in Elendol, when Ilvuan had briefly burst from him. Sorcery and spirit together formed their tendons and claws, their wings and spines. The Lattice, sundering the World into countless fragments, flowed into them like arteries. They were formed as Ilvuan remembered himself, larger than any of Yuldor's twisted creations, greater even than Yvärras herself.

They flew toward the dragon queen as the others burned and bit at her. Ilvuan opened their jaws, and Garin loosed a sky-splitting roar. The sound of it shuddered the threads of the Lattice, and the air vibrated with its power.

They picked up speed, fast nearing their opponents. Their intentions and movements merged, and they flowed in tandem, harmony and melody aligned.

The lesser dragons scattered from Yvärras to meet them. Of the initial score, a dozen remained, the Protectress having made quick work of them. Yet both Garin and Ilvuan knew numbers could overcome an unwary attacker. Even surging with the sorcery of the Song and the Worldheart, they had to be clever and quick and strike without hesitation.

Ilvuan burned with anticipation, and Garin burned with him.

Three of the dragons swept down from the clouds above, a bald attempt to take them by surprise. Garin felt the mindless intentions with which they acted, and Ilvuan disdained them.

They weren't true dragons, no more sentient than any beast, and they fought with the same lack of inventiveness. They were *kael'dros*, not *ava'duala*. They were blighted things, a scourge upon the World.

We will destroy them.

Together, they tucked their wings in and flipped over, their jaws snapping open. Power swelled in their belly, then shot up their throat.

Blue-white flames erupted, booming as they tore through the sky.

One enemy fell in smoke and ruin. They turned their great neck, the fire cutting a bright path through the clouds. The second dragon twisted out of the way, careening and screeching. The third was not so fortunate. The flames caught its head, and as it fell, only blackened bone remained.

Yvärras roared. *"So you remain an* ava'dual, Alärthoras*! Let us show them a dragon's might!"*

Their enemies didn't remain idle. Five more flew at Garin and Ilvuan from all directions. Yvärras threw herself at those remaining near her, her torn wing barely keeping her aloft. Yet all concern for the dragon queen left Garin's mind as he and Ilvuan met their own assault.

As the first came within striking range, Ilvuan tucked in their wings and spun them around, so swiftly the World blurred and Garin feared the Lattice's threads might tangle together. The barbs on their tail caught one dragon in the face, shattering its jaw and cutting a deep furrow in its neck. The second they met with raking claws and biting teeth. The beast matched their savagery, but Ilvuan proved the cleverer fighter. Moments later, the defiled dragon fell toward the ground, eyes gouged and entrails spilling from a grievous wound in its side.

But even as Garin righted them and spread their wings to break the freefall, the other three dragons caught up. Pain ripped through them as claws cut into the fragile material. Their aim accomplished, two of the attackers banked away, letting the sky's weight do their work for them. The last wasn't content with that, latching onto Garin and Ilvuan's spine, claws digging around the plate and into the softer scales along their sides.

But though Garin felt the pain of each wound, their body wasn't truly flesh. Ilvuan bellowed out their fury and radiated sorcery in a blistering wave. Their wings spread, and the thin membrane became whole once more. The sorcery hurt as it healed, battering their hanger-on, and it loosed its own pained roar.

Garin lashed with their tail, but it was nothing more than a glancing blow. Ilvuan twisted into another mid-air roll. Finally, the dragon's hold loosed. As it slipped free, it smacked into the jagged stone below and lay still.

Garin gave voice to their victory with a roar as he and Ilvuan regained altitude. Yvärras radiated her approval as she dispatched an enemy of her own and flew next to them. She wobbled, but stayed aloft.

"Well fought, Brother," she spoke. *"It was my honor to battle by your wing. But you have another front on which you must fight. Go — overcome the Three. May the sun ever shine upon your scales."*

"Thank you, my Protectress." Ilvuan turned them back down into a sharp dive, aiming for the body they'd left behind.

Garin wanted to pull up, to remain forever flying. He didn't want to return to his body. Here, they were powerful and free. Down there, they were trapped in earthbound flesh. Yet their power was quickly thinning, and he knew they had to save the rest of their strength for the battle to come.

They crashed into Garin's body.

Next he knew, Garin was on his hands and knees, blinking rapidly as he stared at the gray stone beneath him. Red trickled from his palms where he'd gouged them.

We must make haste, Jenduit, Ilvuan urged. *I cannot sense Heartblood any longer. I fear we are too late.*

The flight's elation faded. Garin heaved in a breath and

forced himself to his feet. Eyes set on the monolith looming from the mist, he moved them toward their final battle.

DIVINE

THE SHATTERED STONE FIELD STRETCHED ON. GARIN AND Ilvuan quickened their passage with sorcery, yet they still had to fight for every stride. The stone resisted their manipulation, and both their strength flagged. The dragon flight had instilled in Garin a weariness even the Worldsong couldn't lift.

A different weight also crushed him. Though they knew Yvärras prevailed against the dragons above, Garin didn't know his friends' fates. He'd left them outnumbered by Nightkin and Hashele still standing. Guilt tore through him deeper than any of the blighted dragons had managed.

Yet even those concerns were pushed aside as the World-heart rose above them.

Garin stuttered to a halt, staring up at the spire. It didn't rise as high as some of the surrounding stone towers, yet it alone drew his gaze. Power radiated from it like light from the sun. It was both a pain and a pleasure to behold. The World-song had kept an order and rhythm until then, but now there was only tumult and an insistent beat. It wasn't stone, but a heart, as it had always been claimed. Blood didn't flow here, but sorcery itself.

The figures melded into the column caught his eye. Ilvuan

growled in the back of Garin's mind, and Garin finally understood what this pillar truly was: not stone, but the piled corpses of dragons. They'd sacrificed themselves to stem the corrupting power bleeding into the World, to negate the influence of the gods who lingered beneath it. Ilvuan had been one of those sacrifices. Now and always, the Singer mourned the loss of his life and his people.

But Garin's attention was drawn to the base of the black tower. There, five humanoid figures stood in contrast to the dragons. Four of them were stone like the *ava'duala* above and weathered beyond recognition. He wondered who they were: the discarded bodies of the Three? Or those like Yuldor who had been lured into their trap?

Yet it was the last one that caught Garin's eye. This one wasn't stone, but wreathed in a brilliant gold cloud. It moved like Paradise's miasma, but was too pure to look at directly. The figure's hands were placed over the statue's, reaching around him as if he'd lunged to reach the spot.

Garin knew who it was. Who it had been.

Tal.

Though the Worldsong shook him with urgency and drowned out his heartbeat, he hesitated. Tal had been consumed by sorcery. Was that what would happen to Garin if he drew near, if he touched it?

He didn't want to die. He'd always known it was a possibility, had even thought he'd accepted it. But now, here at the end, his courage faltered.

I am here, Jenduit. *You are not alone in this.*

Ilvuan's voice was faint amid the Worldsong, but his presence was strong. He suffused Garin's limbs with purpose and strength.

You have already begun to mend this land. Now you must finish it. Touch Heartblood, and we will join him as we did before.

Garin wished he could be like Tal, to do what needed doing without hesitation. Instead, he asked a damning question.

Will we die if I do?

Ilvuan paused before responding.

Yes.

Garin closed his eyes and clenched his fists. The bones in his hands ground and popped. He was young, too young to leave everything behind. All his hopes and dreams, his friends and family. He'd only just begun to experience all life had to offer and discover what he could make of his.

And yet...

He opened his eyes and forced himself to look at Tal's blinding figure. Garin had left Hunt's Hollow to follow in the man's footsteps. Now, he had the chance to take his place among the stars. It didn't matter that no one would know what he did here, only that he did it.

A man did what was right, no matter the consequences.

At the turn in Garin's thoughts, Ilvuan roared within him. Garin smiled as he stepped forward and reached out, smiled like he imagined Tal would have. He grasped his mentor's shoulders.

The moment splintered.

His body burned.

The Lattice flared around him, brightening at his touch.

A cloud of sorcery enveloped his body. Swiftly, it became a chrysalis readying him for transformation.

He wasn't one individual soul wandering the World's surface, but every soul across it. He was both living and not. He was eternal and only lasting for this moment.

Then Ilvuan took him in his claws and pulled him through a blinding tunnel.

They emerged into a war.

Tal tried to remain whole as gods tore him apart.

Again and again, they grabbed for him, like children never

taught to share a toy. Each tried to take sole possession as if he could be a vessel only for one, each afraid of being shut out.

Only the Night kept him together. But even she couldn't keep him entirely whole.

Like threads torn apart, Tal sewed himself back together. Each time they broke him, his thoughts scattered, and he almost forgot who he was.

Yet a glimmer of his core remained, a part that wouldn't relent. Though he shattered countless times over, still he endured.

As he brought his being back together once more, Tal tried to grasp at any semblance of a plan, but his mind was too fragmented. There was nothing he could do, nothing but wait for one god to triumph over the others or a compromise to be struck.

Or death, come to relieve me at last.

It was like knives carved through him, dismembering and disemboweling, only so he could shove his organs back inside. Each time he was torn apart, he lost something. He was becoming like the Extinguished: less than human, his life a thin existence.

After all he'd strived and fought for, this was to be his fate. A fleeting amusement for beings that sucked the World dry of life.

At the thought, the river of sorcery pulsed as if in recognition.

He reached for that vague sensation like it were a piece of driftwood in a flood. But the Whispering Gods had returned, and all volition disappeared before their wills.

Tal fragmented once more.

I can't. Not again.

He was strained too far. He couldn't contain one god, much less three. He hadn't even Yuldor's strength to last centuries like this. He would perish here, his aim unaccomplished, the deaths of so many to no avail.

Yield. Rest. Sleep at last.

The *Doash* murmured promises into his being, constant in its offer. If he could have surrendered to it then, he would have. But he was caged in talons, and the Three wouldn't easily give him up.

Tal no longer had the choice to die.

Then, like glimpsing a coin at the bottom of a pool, he felt something stir. Another presence brushed past him, then grasped hold. He feared it was Yuldor, but it wasn't one being, but two, so closely intertwined as to almost be inseparable.

Tal! Tal Harrenfel! We're here — don't give in now!

Somewhere deep within him recognized them. *Garin and his dragon.* An image of the youth's face, crinkled in a smile, sprang to mind. He would have smiled had he possessed the faculties for it.

You came, he thought back. After all he had done to prevent it, Garin had come. To Tal's shame, he was glad for it.

Hold on, Tal! We'll fight them off together.

All of us, Ilvuan rumbled in his mind.

Alär, old friend. The Night spoke now, her voice as warm as sunshine through clouds. *It has been too long.*

Ilvuan roared in response. *Far too long, Maral Batomar! So we reunite here at the end.*

Tal, reprieved from the Whispering Gods' assault for a precious moment, regained enough presence of mind for a leap of intuition. *The war with the Three. You fought next to each other. You flew together.*

The Night and Ilvuan affirmed it, while Garin's shock buzzed through them all.

So we did, she said. *And as we once flew together...*

...now we shall fall, Ilvuan finished for her.

Garin pulsed with uncertainty and confusion, but there was no time to address it. The blessed respite was over, and Silence, Solemnity, and Serenity bludgeoned their way back to Tal.

But this time, he didn't break. Garin, Ilvuan, the Night — where Tal alone was insufficient, together, they held.

Yet it still wasn't enough. Tal knew it took all their strength just to attain that much. To do what they needed to do, to drag the Three into the *Doash*, they would need to do far more.

The gods' outrage at being thwarted redoubled their efforts. They battered at the shield his allies put around him until Tal felt their very souls fracture. A mortal cry burst through the surrounding torrent, and Tal didn't know if it was one of theirs or his own.

They would break. They had to.

They held.

Only as the battery eased did Tal comprehend how. They four had been joined by a fifth, one both strange and familiar to him. A man whose life he had just shared.

Yuldor, he acknowledged him, surprised and relieved in equal measures.

The husk of man could only answer with his repeated plea. *Peace. Bring me peace...*

I will, Tal told him. *However I can.*

Yet he didn't know how. Always, he'd wondered how to match the strength of gods. The Night had promised an answer, but it had always been a false hope. Even when possessing Tal for their conduit, the Three were too boundless to be restrained.

In the moment that the gods took to rally their strength, sorcery worked its way into Tal again. It was as inviting as the *Doash's* promises, and for a moment, he tried to push it away. Yet, as he focused on it, he noticed this was a different feeling. Not the seduction of cessation, but an ascension.

Something reared inside him.

He didn't turn away, but faced it. And as he beheld that desire within him, to unite with that all-consuming power, an epiphany struck.

For all their power and immortality, the Whispering Gods

had fallen short of divinity in one crucial aspect. Their arrogance and fear were enough that they sought to break the World to avoid it.

They had never unified with the World.

They hadn't embraced the heart of sorcery, but kept separate from it, their minds distinct. They kept themselves apart and leeched upon it instead of merging with that which sustained them.

As Tal welcomed the sorcery into himself, he realized it was as familiar to him as the blood that had flowed through his veins. It had been with him his whole life. The sorcery had always called to him whenever it was near, no matter what form it took. He'd thought this a happenstance, an innate protection.

It was neither. It had been a summons, a beckoning. A call home.

He belonged to the World. He *was* the World. That he'd ever been anything separate had been but a fantasy, one to which the false gods still clung. They, like their disciples, had always been too fond of illusion.

But he could no longer share in it. The sorcery was a key, set in the lock and ready to turn. It was the piece of divinity that had lain dormant in him, but was now awakened. He had but to reach for it and, at last, he could be what he always strived for.

He feared it. He yearned for it.

He had no other choice.

Tal pulled in more of the sorcery, then took the last step. He released the boundaries around himself and spilled into the stream.

He became nothing — then everything.

His soul split across a sky of stars. He was the emptiness between the pinpricks of light, the cold abyss. He was the light. Worlds flowed past and through him, debris on an unyielding current. A force moved behind reality, adhering to rules of its own making and in too complex a pattern to comprehend.

Sorcery.

It touched everywhere. It was the core of the World, the Womb, but not only contained there. Even the sky possessed a magic of its own. All living, all dying, all existence between — sorcery moved through and in and around.

It was the beginning. It was the end.

For a moment, he went to all those places and eons it touched. He was infinite, the Master of Time and Material.

Then he remembered.

I am.

Names flared into his mind, but detached from meaning. Tal Harrenfel. Brannen Cairn. Gerald Barrows. Ringthief, Devil Killer, Man of a Thousand Names.

None could contain him as he was now. He was beyond them; he always had been. They were mirror shards in which he glimpsed what he truly was. Fragments of the truth, each incomplete on their own.

I was.

Even before his birth, he had lived beyond this moment. He was as old as the stars themselves, the past that haunted him a blink in eternity, a chance history made meaningless by its capriciousness. He was not that man; he was every man that could have been, every man that was.

He'd lived a thousand lives and would live a thousand more.

I will be.

The future — it focused him back on this moment, this intersection. Fate was potential, clay to be molded, and his hands would shape it. Though he'd become vast, he narrowed himself to this insignificant planet, this tiny conflict, its inconsequential players.

To everything and everyone he cared for.

They struggled against him, but it was for naught. He had

all the power of the World and beyond. He was the sorcery, and it was him.

Not even gods could prevail.

Only the three minor deities did he seize, yet others came with. One of these, he knew couldn't be there. Like he once might have leaned down to inspect an insect, he focused his attention on this individual life and pressed his intentions on it.

On him.

Garin, watch over them. Ashelia, Aelyn; Wren, Rolan, Falcon. Protect them from the World. You are capable of it. You always were.

He paused. The small gods fought with all their strength, but they didn't move him. They possessed only the fractions of power they'd scraped together. They were like slivers poking at the hull of a ship.

He focused on the mote of life again, his message decided.

I'm proud of you, Garin. I always have been; I always will be. You're already a better man than I ever was. And you will become even more.

He withdrew, ignoring the youth's cries. He thought he'd extinguished the man he'd been, freed from his boundaries. But something of him remained.

He couldn't tolerate it. He had to belong entirely to the sorcery, or he would fail.

He cut off that remaining mortal part and freed himself, setting it adrift in the stream. Then he carried the little gods down.

Down to their end.

He would have screamed if he could have. As it was, Garin shouted into the World around him.

Tal! Tal, come back!

He felt as if some part within him had broken beyond

repair. Tal had spoken, his words like thunder, their meaning even more shattering.

I'm proud of you, Garin.

How long had he yearned to hear it? Yet never like this. They were spoken as a farewell, a dying man to his surviving friend. They carried a finality Garin couldn't accept.

Don't do this, Tal! There must be another way! Don't leave, don't go...

Despair cut off his cries. He felt a fraction of what Tal had become, and even that small portion was too vast to comprehend. He'd become like the Three, but more.

He had become the very World itself.

But now he carried them down toward its center. Garin was trapped with the others. Ilvuan, the Night, Yuldor — all of them too enmeshed with the Whispering Gods to win free of Tal's encompassing grasp now. Despite his words, Tal seemed unaware of the fate he thrust upon them.

Garin settled, resigned. He'd known he would die. That it came at Tal's hands made no difference.

Then, like a sword chopped him in half, he drifted loose.

For a lingering moment, he was blind with pain, then Garin came back to himself. Floating adrift in the sorcerous stream, he was tossed in the wake of the others as they went down to depths from which there was no return.

Yet the faintest touch of one remained with him. Garin knew who it was, long grown familiar with the dragon's soul. As Ilvuan's mind brushed his own, he felt himself break anew.

Do not grieve, little Listener. There was mirth in his words, but a sea of other emotions as well, many unfamiliar coming from the Singer: fear, nostalgia, regret. *I live on.*

Garin startled. *Will you be reborn? Like the other dragons?*

He hadn't realized how close he'd kept that hope until that moment. Before, when he thought of the resurrection of dragons, it had been an event he feared, but no longer.

Ilvuan sank his sudden hope.

Not in that way. Time is short, Jenduit. *Listen, as you have thus far, and listen well. I did not name you Mender idly. Remember what an* ava'dual *sacrificed for you. My people will be weak when they emerge, and feared. Be faithful to them. Mend this World and the rifts that will form.*

Despair almost drowned out any coherent response. But for Ilvuan, Garin pushed it down.

I will, Ilvuan. Always.

A glimmer of gratitude came through their connection, growing more tenuous by the moment.

May the wind ever find your wings...

Then he slipped away.

Garin didn't grasp after him, but neither did he depart. He remained there, floating, without a body or purpose. He felt the others draw near the Womb at the World's center. The Whispering Gods let out their last cries, rippling through sorcery without sound.

Then — nothing. In the end, they become nothing more than their names.

Silence reigned.

Garin couldn't feel Ilvuan, nor Tal, nor anyone else. They were gone, all gone. He alone remained.

Whispers sounded up from the depths. For a moment, it reawakened hope in him. Then he comprehended their meaning.

Sleep. Peace. Cease.

The offering tempted him. After all he'd endured, Garin wanted nothing more than to sleep and never wake.

But he couldn't. Those sacrificed, who had brought them to this moment — Kaleras, Helnor, Ilvuan, Tal — they bound him to his life on the World as thoroughly as the promises he'd given.

He wouldn't let their deaths be in vain.

Garin gathered the drifting pieces of himself together, then ascended to the World waiting above.

MORE THAN A MAN

GARIN RESURFACED ALONE.

He opened his eyes and jerked his hands away. He continued to stare even as the strength went out of his limbs, and he stumbled back into a boulder behind him.

Tal had turned to stone.

Garin fought back tears. He'd witnessed what had happened below the World's surface, yet until that moment, he'd clung to the hope that Tal had escaped in the end. Now, the dream faded.

He's gone. Really gone.

He clenched his fists, screwed his eyes shut. Tal had seemed eternal in his own way. No matter what obstacle his old mentor faced, he'd prevailed. Even coming against beings that were nearly gods, Garin had believed he could endure.

Now he saw it for what it was. He'd believed in his legend. He'd believed him to be more than a man.

But wasn't he, in the end?

Tal had succeeded in his calling. He'd defeated Yuldor and his devils, done what all the dragons, Origins, and centuries had failed to do. He'd merged with sorcery itself and become something Garin could scarcely comprehend.

Reaching forward, he gripped *Velori's* hilt over Tal's motionless hand. He'd miss the man more than he had the words to express. Yet that Tal's sacrifice had done so much filled him with a strange gladness.

Before he could think on it further, a rumbling started beneath his feet. Garin's eyes snapped open. The stone at his feet was cracking and crumbling, but it was the Worldheart that posed the greatest peril. The black rock splintered along its red veins, and great chunks of it fell off even as its base sank.

Garin reacted on instinct. Defying death, he wrenched the broken hilt of *Velori* free of Tal's stone hands, gaining gashes in his fingers for his hasty effort. Then he sprinted away, dodging debris and sheltering his head from the pelting pebbles.

Before he could leap clear, the ground beneath him dropped.

"Dord firkist!"

Only after the words left his mouth did he doubt. Ilvuan was gone as well. He had no dragon. What was a Listener without his Singer? It seemed impossible that he would still hear the Worldsong, that sorcery would pour through him.

Then the melodious discord filled his head. Somehow, he remained a Fount of Song.

The spell took effect, and the rock settled and smoothed. Casting it again and again, Garin clambered free of the sinking Worldheart. Only as the stone quieted into tremors did he look back.

The black pillar had before risen hundreds of feet into the air, yet it had already fallen to half its height. He watched as the mountain swallowed the rest and thought of those buried with it.

Rest well, Tal Harrenfel. Ilvuan — Alärthoras. The Night, Maral Batomar. Even you, Yuldor Soldarin.

He had nothing more to offer them than wishes, so he sent them into the air and hoped they were enough.

The Worldheart disappeared from sight, leaving behind only a pit of rubble and a cloud of dust. Garin turned and, coughing, made his way back to his friends.

Only then did he remember how he'd left them. Garin hurried, taking the path he and Ilvuan had carved across the stone field on their way there. His heart squeezed tight with fear. Falcon had died, crushed in a witiko's claws. He could scarcely believe it was true, even having witnessed it. Hashele had summoned more Nightkin than his companions seemed able to overcome. The Thorn and Soltor had fallen, and Pim had fled, but was it enough? That he might have failed them was too dire a prospect to entertain.

He reached the edge of the cliff and peered over.

Relief washed through him at the initial sight. Rolan was alive, and Aelyn as well; he spotted them at the periphery of the battle, closer to the edge of Paradise. He saw Wren and Ashelia next, and though they looked the worse for wear, his knees went weak to see they'd survived.

Yet as he saw whose body they kneeled next to, his chest tightened again. He hadn't imagined it.

Falcon Sunstring was gone.

Head spinning, Garin searched for a way down. He had to go to Wren, to comfort her, though he scarcely knew how. Before he could find a viable route, however, a shout came from below. He looked to his companions and found Wren's face upturned, eyes shining, relief clear even at the distance. Garin waved and shouted back her name, the word cracking in his tortured throat.

He found a way down, nearly slipping twice in his haste, then ran past the ashes that remained of ghouls and witikos to fall down next to Wren. She turned from her father's body to seize him, and he embraced her back. Only her sudden gasp made him release.

"Sorry! Are you hurt?"

A stupid question, but Wren didn't tease him for it, only

indicating her side. Now that she pointed it out, he noticed how she leaned over it and guessed she suffered from at least one broken rib. He winced, but didn't draw away.

The scent of blood and guts hit his nose then, and Garin slowly looked down at Falcon.

He wished he hadn't. The Court Bard of Avendor lay in ruin. Though he closed his eyes, Garin could still picture the red rivulets that led from his crushed skull, the torn flesh of his gut. He tried to remember Falcon as he lived and found the task beyond him.

"Wren," Ashelia said. From her tone, it wasn't the first time she'd spoken her name.

Wren sniffed loudly, fighting back a sob. "Fine. We'll burn him like an elf. He'd have liked the drama of it anyhow."

Garin rose with the others and made for the jungle, exchanging brief acknowledgments as they gathered fuel. The dragonstone bracelets, kept in pockets, were donned again to resist the miasma still layering the forest floor. Already, it seemed to thin, the sparkles in it less luminous. Paradise died with its maker.

Soon, they had gathered branches and kindling and arranged it in a pyre. Before they could move Falcon's body onto it, Ashelia drew near.

Garin reluctantly met her eyes. Twin storms spun within them. Cuts had scabbed on her face, yet the pain in her eyes was worse. He knew what she wondered, knew he had to tell her what neither of them wanted to hear. Yet now that the moment had come, it seemed like a boulder had lodged in his throat.

Garin drew out what remained of *Velori* from where he'd tucked it into his belt and, tentatively gripping the broken blade, he held the hilt out to her.

For a long moment, she only stared at it. Then, with a trembling hand, she took it. She turned it over twice, as if searching for something in the faded glyphs, then raised her head.

He nodded, fighting back fresh tears. By *Velori* alone, she knew the truth.

Ashelia said nothing. The hand holding the broken sword fell to her side, while the other brushed along her belly. Turning away, she limped back toward the waiting pyre.

Garin assisted Ashelia and Aelyn in moving Falcon's body onto the branches. Wren ignited it with a cantrip, then stepped back next to Garin as they all watched her father catch flame.

"Rest easy, old man," she murmured so softly the wind almost stole the words.

Aelyn, after a glance at his House-sister, spoke the elven benediction. As he concluded, he added, "No matter what I said to the contrary, you were a loyal friend, an amusing companion, and a damned fine trouper. Your stories will outlive you."

Garin hid his astonishment at the mage's candor. Even after all their time together, his friends could still surprise him.

"I'll finish your legend," Rolan blurted. His eyes were a storm of tears, and his bottom lip quivered, yet he stubbornly pressed on. "The Legend of Tal. You told me to remember our journey, and I have. It may take me a long time, maybe a year… but I'll do it."

The boy's gaze rose to meet Garin's. He smiled at Rolan and nodded, and the boy nodded back before his courage reached an end. Rolan drew close to his mother's side.

Ashelia, silent to that point, at last spoke. "Wren. May we also dedicate this to Tal?"

Wren nodded. No one seemed surprised by the Peer's query. Garin had seen the glances and whispers exchanged among their remaining companions after he'd shared the man's fate with Ashelia. They'd seen the broken blade, the Peer's posture. Perhaps they'd known as soon as Garin descended the cliff alone.

He fought to stay above his rising sorrow.

Despite her stated intention, Ashelia didn't speak for several minutes. Garin was glad for the wind, for it whisked away the stench of Falcon's burning body. He wondered if it would have been better or worse to have Tal's body as well.

At last, she spoke, but only to Garin.

"Did he do what he intended? Did he stop Yuldor for good?"

Garin thought back to those last moments and the quiet that had come after. "Yes. For good."

The Peer nodded, then tilted her head toward the sky. "I know you're here, somewhere. So you must know the truth. I'm sorry I hid it. I wanted to share it with you. But..." She swallowed, then continued with fresh tears trickling down her cheeks. "You had lived with guilt long enough. You can rest now. We'll be fine."

Again, a hand rested on her belly, and Garin stared at it, struck with an insight. He glanced at Wren, but she seemed oblivious to anything but her own misery. Aelyn, however, nodded at Garin's look, a small smile twisting his thin lips.

Garin shared a smile of his own. Somehow, the news was the balm he needed. Even after all the death they'd suffered, life continued.

We'll never forget, he promised his fallen friends. *Nor will the World.*

THE WAR BELOW

After Wren had gathered a pouchful of Falcon's ashes, they began their long descent.

The journey down was somber. Each bore their share of guilt and pain, heavier than their packs had ever weighed. Yet at moments, glimmers of happiness shone through. Garin would find himself smiling at Wren, and she would smile back.

The World had been remade. Against all odds, they had succeeded. Yuldor and the Three had been defeated.

And will the dragons be reborn?

He didn't know if Ilvuan had been correct in assuming Yuldor's defeat would bring about their rebirth. But though his dragon hadn't survived, one had. Garin's companions had reported that after Yvärras had defeated the last of the Nightkin dragons, she'd flown off with a final roar. Wounds had covered her from head to tail, yet Garin had seen enough to know the dragon queen was nigh on impossible to kill. She would bring back her kin.

And then Garin would see if their resurrection was a reason for pride or shame.

The descent proved swifter than the ascent, and they

reached the end of Paradise on the morning of the third day. The last stretch they completed that very evening, and the Sentinel's Gate loomed out of the dusky gloom. Garin, open to the Worldsong, quested after Ikvaldar's guardian, yet he sensed nothing of it. With Yuldor's departure, it seemed, the mystifying gatekeeper had moved on, and not even Silence knew where.

The next morning, they traveled through the valley leading away from the base of the mountain. Their guard was raised now, for Aelyn had opined that Nightkin likely remained even after their creator's destruction. Yet, if it was true, they were fortunate enough not to encounter any.

Garin had begun to believe they would escape further desolation when they emerged from the vale.

A battle had taken place in the shadow of Ikvaldar. Bodies of the Bloodlines and Nightkin alike mounded across the trampled and blood-stained field. The sparse trees that had dotted the plains had been reduced to blackened husks. A stench unlike any Garin had known accompanied the nightmarish scene. Flies and carrion birds layered the corpses and filled the air with a chorus of humming and squawking. Foxes and wolves joined the feast, and in the distance, Garin thought he detected still stranger scavengers. Gryphons, cockatrices, and quetzals tore at the bodies of both enemies and allies, showing few qualms about eating their fellow Nightkin. Though some glanced up at their party, none seemed interested in leaving their meals.

Aelyn tilted his head up and sniffed the air, then grimaced. "Sorcery," was all he said at Garin's inquiring look.

Ashelia brought their attention forward again. "The field is not abandoned. One army still camps here."

Garin followed her gaze and took her meaning. Columns of smoke rose from beyond a barrier of hills; campfires, the Peer seemed to assume. He gnawed his lip, wondering if they were their allies or Yuldor's adherents.

Wren seemed to share his thoughts. "Maybe we shouldn't find out which."

Ashelia shook her head. "There will be scouts. Likely they have already spotted us. If they are our enemies, we won't surrender willingly. But we must see all the same."

But when riders soon came toward them, they saw it was the Warders again, Prime Elidyr at their head. The Warder seemed incredulous at their pronouncement of victory, yet he remained loyal to the Peer, giving their ragged company stors to ride back to the camp. Garin's new mount thundered beneath him, bearing him swiftly through the gory battlefield. Even with the wind stealing some of the reek away, he could barely breathe.

Still, it wasn't long before they were past and reached the edge of the encampment. A few more Warders lingered there, but most of the camp's occupants were of other origins. Garin marveled at the host that had gathered. Minotaurs, gnomes, Nightelves, and Easterner humans walked among each other, even exchanging words with the Gladelysh elves on their periphery. And they weren't the only factions present. His eyes caught on the flag of Avendor, bearing the red and orange hawk and crown, waving in the wind above another group of tents.

Avendor came, he marveled, and was surprised that he swelled with pride. *Aldric heeded our summons.* He hadn't expected the King, conniving and self-serving as he was, to send troops to a war that could cripple the Empire. He wondered if Aldric had discovered some long-buried nobility in himself, but realized a moment later it was more of the same.

Now he can claim to have dethroned Yuldor. All this was to spread his own fame.

Garin shook his head and put the matter from his mind. Ashelia had dismounted her stor and was waving them in.

They were being summoned deeper into the camp — though by who, he had yet to see.

As they approached the grand tent at the camp's center and he saw a golden sun on its flag, the truth became clear.

With a hurrying of formalities, they were stripped of their packs and ushered inside. Though guards and Imperial sorcerers ringed the periphery, Garin found himself less nervous than the first time they'd come before the Sun Emperor. Zyrl Netherstar had a way of putting him at ease. Still, he wondered if they were truly allies. Now that their common enemy had been eradicated, what interests did they share?

Either way, the old gnome had survived. He looked frumpier than usual as he sat atop a makeshift throne, little more than an elevated chair. His robes were wrinkled and his jewelry dulled, yet a spark remained in his dark eyes that not even war could dim.

As they stopped a respectful distance before the Sun Emperor, Zyrl grinned and beckoned them closer. "My allies! My friends. And my saviors, I might say, if my suspicions are correct. Your quest found success, I trust?"

"It is good to see you as well, Your Majesty." Ashelia gave a small bow. "I feared you would not marshal your forces in time."

"Yet I did, and what is more, we prevailed — though you had the greater challenge, to be sure!" The monarch scanned their party as he spoke, eyes narrowing. "Though I see it was not without cost."

Ashelia stood with her chin high, yet Garin detected a tremor running through her body. Still, her voice was almost even as she answered.

"No. It was not."

The elderly gnome did something unprecedented in Garin's presence: he rose from his throne and descended to stand before Ashelia. Though each member of their party dwarfed him, his presence remained large. Zyrl reached up and clasped Ashelia's hand in his. A glance at the others made Garin feel as if he included them in his words.

"You have my deepest condolences, Peer Venaliel, truly. Tal Harrenfel was a man like no other — a fact confirmed by what he accomplished. He was as noble in sentiment as he was mighty in sorcery."

Ashelia bowed her head. "Thank you, Your Brilliance," she murmured.

The Sun Emperor smiled and released her, then clambered back onto his throne. "As I said, I believe your efforts saved my life and that of my entire army — and our allies from the Westreach as well, let us not forget."

Ashelia recovered her composure and gave another slight bow. "We are honored to serve, Your Majesty."

"For such a deed, I wish I had more to offer you as reward, yet alas, I cannot bestow more than scant hospitality. Another of those sun-forsaken phoenixes came after you departed and infiltrated the palace walls. No doubt our adversary wished to make an end of his disloyal subject." A wry smile twisted the gnome's painted lips. "Fortunately, I anticipated such a tactic and evacuated the place but for a skeleton crew to maintain the appearance of a functioning palace. Their deaths I regret, yet such is the cost of war."

Aelyn made a small sound that might have spoken of disgust. Garin bristled with a similar sentiment. *But those are rulers for you*, he thought, *just as Tal always said. Power makes you callous, or perhaps only the callous claim it.*

If the Sun Emperor noticed the mage's reaction, he ignored it. A thoughtful expression stole over his wrinkled features. "Without a seat to my power, I fear that for the Empire of the Rising Sun, the sun has set. Some of my subjects would not think that such a poor thing."

He turned to one corner of the large tent, and Garin followed his gaze to see someone he recognized: Rozana of

Haudden. She bowed her horned head at their glances, and Garin acknowledged her with the others. She looked strange in battle mail and had clearly suffered several wounds, yet with her usual placidity, she showed no sign of weariness or pain.

Much as he liked the little Emperor, Garin found himself glad at the prospect of a dissolved Empire. If he had learned one thing from Tal, it was that power shouldn't be too closely consolidated. The weaker the rulers of a land, the better for all.

"Nevertheless," Zyrl continued as he turned back, "we must endure. But let us talk of happier things! I hope I do not sound ungracious by asking if you will soon be on your way home?"

The word struck Garin like a falling stone. *Home.* He looked at Wren and found her eyes wide and spinning. He wondered if she was thinking the same as him.

Where is home now?

"Yes," Ashelia answered for them. One hand touched upon her midriff before falling away. "Soon, we will be home."

The Sun Emperor bobbed his head. "Very good, Peer Venaliel. The East is always open to you should you or your companions wish to return. But I trust other lands call to you."

Garin's chest ached, and his mind drifted as the formal farewell carried on. *Home.* He thought of his mother, Lenora, and his three quarrelsome brothers, and a smile found his lips. Yet, as good as it would be to see his family, was Hunt's Hollow his home any longer?

Soon, he would find out. Until then, all he could do was keep moving forward.

HOMEWARD

Only a few days after their descent from Ikvaldar, Garin and the others began the long journey home.

They set off atop horses gifted them by the Emperor while the military encampment continued to disband. With the war won, the troops from the various fiefs hurried home — for the wars ahead, if Aelyn's predictions were accurate. Though Garin little wished for them to come true, he had a feeling the mage would be proven correct before long.

Particularly if dragons take to the skies, he thought with a grimace.

Their small party didn't travel alone. The Warders of Gladelyl, two scores of whom survived, formed an honor guard at Prime Elidyr's insistence. No one knew what the roads back would be like: if Nightkin would prowl them, or the remaining Ravagers prey on hapless travelers. Garin was grateful for the protection, though the austere men and women didn't make for the finest conversationalists. They were nothing like Helnor had been.

Less welcome were the Avendoran soldiers who accompanied them. A young knight, one Sir Rhydian, had approached them soon after their arrival at the war camp, introducing himself and inquiring into their names. Garin hadn't wanted to yield his, suspicious of anyone with connections to King Aldric, yet knew there might be consequences for deception. The knight's eyes lit up with each name, and he declared they were the very people he'd sought in these wild lands.

"But where hides Tal Harrenfel?" Sir Rhydian pressed at the end. "And Kaleras of Canturith. I was informed that both traveled with your party."

"And Aldric's Court Bard," Wren replied acidly before anyone else could.

As the knight's face reddened at her lack of respect for the King, Ashelia hastened to smooth matters over, her voice only hitching a little on the declaration. "They have fallen, Sir Knight. Tal, and Kaleras, and Falcon, and my brother Helnor. They fought against the Named and his Soulstealers, and they won."

Though sorrow weighed down her words, pride lifted them higher. Garin drew up straight just hearing them. He still ached for the lack of Tal's smile and Falcon's laugh, and when the party made decisions, he looked for Kaleras' wisdom and Helnor's knowledge. But he was glad to be proud of them.

Sir Rhydian bowed his head, though by his eyes sliding toward Wren, her insult to his monarch hadn't gone unnoticed. "I am deeply aggrieved to hear it, Lady Peer. They were valiant men, I am sure."

"Sure you are," Wren muttered, though she at least looked chagrined when Garin shot her a warning glance.

As he looked back to the conversation at hand, he startled to see the knight's piercing gaze settled on him.

"Garin Dunford," he said. "His Majesty will be very keen to speak with you. Be certain to return with us to Halenhol. And the girl as well," he added, as if Wren was an afterthought.

Garin hastened to answer as Wren's face flushed, fearing her barbed tongue. "We are His Majesty's subjects."

He was relieved when Sir Rhydian nodded approvingly. It

was a sufficiently vague response that, when the time came, he might wriggle his way out of the arrangement.

Though Silence knows kings usually get their way in the end.

His thoughts caught on the reference to the fallen deity, and he smiled a smile devoid of mirth. What would befall this World empty of its gods? Would the Creed and its institutions continue? Would anyone heed the truth, or even care?

He pushed down the questions as the knight turned with his two accompanying soldiers and rode back to the Avendoran tents. There would be time enough to ruminate on religion in the months ahead.

So they set off surrounded by allies and those masquerading as them. With late summer still upon them, the passage through the mountains was fair, and they made swift progress. They traveled back through the forest of Fornkael, and Garin was glad for their honor guard then, for the patrolling Nightelves seemed not to have forgotten what he and his party had brought to their town on the way in.

Vathda they visited as well, and Garin saw evidence of dwarven industry first-hand. In the half-year since they'd witnessed its destruction, the town had been almost entirely rebuilt. The new great hall was grander than before, and more ancillary buildings had risen than when they'd first passed through. It made him smile to see it.

Even after all this, he thought, *life endures.*

The leaves had already begun to turn by the time they reached Gladelyl's borders. Ashelia's pregnancy was showing and riding atop her horse had long grown uncomfortable. Instead of pressing onto Elendol, where their last report from the Warders was of ongoing conflict with little resolution in sight, they made for a Venaliel estate in the south just off the coast of the Hushed Sea.

Garin marveled at the kintree and its surroundings upon their arrival. The mighty tree grew nearly as large as those found in Gladelyl's capital, and its branches stretched so far that they shadowed the sandy beaches hundreds of feet away. The sun sparkled over the wave's crests, and the salty scent of the ocean wafted in on the breeze.

He smiled and wondered if this place might become a home to him.

When Sir Rhydian insisted they press on, Garin stood tall, and with Wren by his side, informed him they would not be going to Halenhol after all. The knight's expression darkened, and took a threatening step closer.

"His Majesty does not take insults lightly. I would ask that you reconsider, Garin Dunford. Should you cross into Avendor again, you may find yourself less than welcome."

Garin smiled as he imagined Tal might have. Though the knight was broader, he was the taller and possessed power the man could only imagine.

"Perhaps the King has more to fear from me than I do from him," Garin said softly.

Sir Rhydian sneered. "You do not even know what you refuse. King Aldric would have honored you above all others! Would you make an enemy of him? And for what, pride?"

Garin glanced at Wren, and she rolled her eyes. They both saw this for what it was.

"The only reason I might have gone is pride. No, Sir Rhydian. Tal Harrenfel once accepted a deal from Aldric to have his name spread as a legend to amplify the King's own glory. I believe he always regretted that choice. I won't make the same mistake."

Sir Rhydian glared at them both for a moment longer, then turned on his heel and barked over his shoulder, "Beware where you travel!"

Garin had to repress a chuckle, especially as Wren stuck out her tongue at the knight's back.

The Avendoran convoy left soon after, and Garin was glad to see the hawk-and-crown flag flapping in the wind as they rode off into the forest.

Yet his wonder at the Venaliel estate soon faded, and somber thoughts pressed in on the idle days. His life had come to a standstill, waiting for a birth that seemed never to come. Elven pregnancies were lengthy affairs, taking months longer than humans. It made him no less impatient.

Snow layered the sand, and winter ushered them inside. Ashelia, in contrast with the weather, seemed to come back to her normal vigorous self as her child's birth grew nearer. She gathered their old companions together and began speaking of taking back Elendol from Peer Lathniel and her fellow usurpers.

All talk of revolution was put on hold with spring's arrival. The leaves and flowers weren't the only things to come alive. Ashelia at last gave birth to a second son. The name she gave him surprised Garin, yet it seemed fitting. He was sure Tal would have felt the same way.

The babe was barely a month old when Garin decided there was a trip he needed to make. He and Wren saddled up their steeds and went easier with Aelyn's assurances that he and the Warders would protect Ashelia and her child.

Before they departed, Ashelia called them to her private chamber. The babe slept in her arms as she spoke to them, thanking them for all they had done and assuring them they had a friend in her no matter where their futures took them.

Her implied question rang loud in Garin's ears, yet he remained silent, even when Wren averred to the Peer they would return as soon as they could. Ashelia's eyes lingered on Garin, swirling for a moment, before she looked back at her swaddled child.

He left with Wren and the messenger, his spirit disquieted. Though Gladelyl's plight called to a part of him, Garin couldn't make promises until he knew what lay in his future. The road ahead would clarify that for him, or so he hoped.

They moved swiftly, and it seemed only days before a familiar wooden archway appeared out of the trees. A smile claimed Garin's lips as he read the words etched into it. *Hunt's Hollow*.

At last, he was home.

As their horses trotted through town, Garin felt the eyes of the villagers follow their company and heard their whispers. He hid a smile and kept his eyes straight ahead, even as he noted each of those who came to witness his return. *Smith. Tanner Badan. Midwife Beca and her help, Gwyn.* He wondered if any recognized him. He'd been fifteen when he left, and was seventeen upon his return. He'd gained height and stood as tall as most elves, and his frame had filled out as well. Perhaps even more ostracizing were his clothes, the green Gladelysh garb etched with patterns of leaves and flowers. Upon his hip rested Lament, sheathed in its ornate scabbard from the Emperor.

I must look as much a stranger as Tal once did to me. To his surprise, the thought wasn't unpleasant.

When a few calls came to him, he returned them with greetings of his own, only further inflaming the talk. Garin didn't delay, however, but spurred his horse to a familiar door, where he all but leaped off.

His family, already waiting outside, rushed to greet him, and Garin met them with open arms.

With embraces shared and tears shed, Garin and Wren spent the night in his childhood home, catching up on all the developments in his family. He was shocked when not one, not two, but three of his siblings had found spouses and begun their lives. Honry and Naten even had their first children, a girl and a boy respectively, born within months of each other and young enough to wail through half of the reunion. Though he was delighted to discover himself an uncle and to meet his niece and nephew, Garin felt a strange nostalgia as he brushed a hand over their tender heads. It took him a long moment to figure out why.

Part of him had expected Hunt's Hollow to be just as he left it. Instead, it had moved on without him.

For his own part, he teased them with tales of his adventures, doling out choice fragments that aggrandized his own part in events — though often with only a little embellishment. Tal had been the nail, but Garin had wielded the hammer. Only together, and with the aid of their companions, were they able to accomplish what they had. Wren kept him honest at times, yet also invented lies of her own to perplex and amaze his family. He often had to hide a smile.

"Garin the Unburned? Garin Godkiller?" Corbun shook his head. "You're a legend in your own right, little brother!"

"If any of it was true, that is," Naten said with a wink.

Garin only grinned. His family would be the last people convinced of his fables. He wouldn't have it any other way.

Lenora was the exception. In a quiet moment, she pulled him aside and murmured, "Always told you there was a fire in you, didn't I? I'm glad you finally let it show."

There were no words he could offer to that but his thanks. Only for his sister's belief in him had he ever left Hunt's Hollow, and he would never forget it.

With regret and an edge of eagerness, he departed with Wren the next morning to return to the Venaliel estate. The visit had filled him in a way all the months in Gladelyl had not, yet it had also served as a reminder. His childhood would always belong to Hunt's Hollow, but no longer was it his home.

Where, then? He mulled over the question across the miles and still found no answer.

"Now what?"

At Wren's query, Garin brought his horse to halt and glanced over. They were only two hours departed from Hunt's Hollow, and the glow of seeing his family had yet to fade.

"What do you mean?" he asked.

She threw out an arm back down the muddy road. "We burned our bridges with King Aldric, no doubt. Yuldor's prick, we'll be lucky if he doesn't send men to hunt us down." Somehow, she looked excited at the prospect, her golden tendrils spinning. "But since you won't be Aldric's puppet, what are you going to do?"

Garin shrugged. "Thought you promised to help in Elendol."

"I did. But I noticed you didn't."

He winced. He hadn't been sure she'd made a note of it. But Wren had always been too sharp to let anything slip by her.

"True enough," he admitted.

The light in her eyes had faded, and a guarded expression stole over her. "What about staying here in Hunt's Hollow? You could marry and settle down like your siblings."

"As a farmer?" Garin laughed. "I don't think that life fits me anymore."

Wren smiled, but worry remained in her eyes. "Tal was a farmer once."

"And you should have seen how poorly he did it. No, Wren. Whatever awaits me, it's not a quiet life in a provincial town."

Finally, she seemed to relax. "Then you'll return to Gladelyl with me."

Garin held her gaze until she demanded, "What? Are you going to say something or just stare?"

"I'll go to Gladelyl — for now. Help Ashelia and Aelyn retake their home."

He urged his horse close enough to hers to take her hand. She laughed at how they had to stretch to make it work, but didn't pull away.

"But," he continued, "as Tal once told me, 'A traveler's home is the road.' Eventually, we'll move on and find something else."

"We?" One of her eyebrows quirked.

Garin grinned. "Don't make me regret saying it."

Wren laughed and pushed away his hand. "Fine, Garin Dunford. I suppose I can keep you around a little longer."

With a smile on his lips and a lightness in his chest, Garin followed her down the hoof-beaten path.

At last, he was home.

EPILOGUE

LEGACY

HIGH ABOVE THE ROOF OF THE WORLD, SHELTERED BESIDE A PILE of broken stone, sat a warlock, unfeeling of the biting winds, waiting for the event he knew must soon come.

He had long, golden hair and eyes that danced like forest shadows. His smile was a language all of its own, and his robes were the finest that coin could buy. A dark metal bracelet clung to his wrist, contrasting with snow-pale skin.

How long he had been waiting, he could not say, for he'd long lost track. Time was, in some respects, irrelevant to one such as him. He'd survived its throes for an eon and intended to see the next one through to its end.

As the warlock idled away the hours, he kept his eyes on the eastern horizon. There were many things he waited for now: some from self-interest, some out of mere curiosity. He'd always been more inquisitive than was good for him and yet found nothing else moved his silent heart more.

A shadow in the distance drew him from his musings. He narrowed his vision and lengthened it, closing the miles between him and his quarry, until it came into focus.

A beast, as large as a boat, veered and wheeled across the sky.

The warlock smiled. He'd known it was coming. The wheels of the next age had been set into motion years before. Now, they would turn, and the carriage, unimpeded, would roll down the road.

And his own plans would come to fruition as well.

His grin widened as the boulders behind him stirred. The warlock stood and swiftly approached. Had he possessed a heartbeat, he supposed it would have been racing.

A hand thrust up from the ground, grasping for purchase. A second followed it a moment after.

The warlock bent and hauled at the protruding wrists, drawing out the man to whom they belonged. He was human and naked, his tanned skin caked with dirt and scraped with shallow cuts. As the man collapsed, he wrapped his arms around himself and shivered, the mountain winds excruciating to his mortal flesh.

The warlock smiled, then went to his pack and rummaged inside it. When he returned, he bore clothes in his arms.

"I thought you might need these." Long had he awaited the moment, but he had not thought he would enjoy it so much.

The buried man raised his head. "P-Pim?" he said through chattering teeth.

"Dress," the warlock said. "Then we can talk."

The buried man pulled on the garments, moving stiffly as if his limbs were long disused. The warlock watched, a smile playing on his lips. He'd waited this long to speak. He could bear a few moments longer.

Yet he couldn't deny a flutter of expectation as the man sat on the boulder opposite of him, sighed, then raised his eyes to meet the warlock's gaze.

"An odd place for a reunion," the man said. "Even for us." His voice warbled, as if not entirely used to speech yet.

"Perhaps. But how fortunate for you that I am here."

"Yes. Fortunate." The man eyed his rescuer, lips twitching. If the warlock knew him as he thought he did, a smile was trying to work its way free of him. Even he had no answer for why he'd restrain it.

The warlock waited for the inevitable question, keeping his own in reserve. The best conversations were like hunts, and he meant to corner his quarry before drawing the arrow.

The man cleared his throat and spread his hands. "Fine. I'll bite. How'd you know?"

"Know you would resurrect, you mean?"

"If that's what we're calling it."

"What else could it be called? But as to your question, I will confess, I was not entirely certain you would return. Your demise, after all, appeared quite final."

"Yet you waited."

"I did." The warlock gestured to the rubble behind the buried man. "You see, I know a thing or two of resurrection. With your victory secured and the gods of this World vanquished, I hedged my odds as the gambler I sometimes am."

"How long?" The buried man looked around him, as if his surroundings would bear some clue to the answer. The warlock supposed they might. The jungle that had once flourished behind them was dead, green shriveled to brown, the verdant forest fading with the magic that had sustained it.

"Ten years, at my last count."

"Ten?" The buried man folded in on himself as if taking a blow to the gut. "A decade?"

"I am afraid so."

His head remained bent for a long moment. Long, unbound hair spilled over his face, hiding it from view. When he straightened, he combed it back, revealing a smile.

"Right on time, I guess. That's how long you Extinguished took before, though I don't suppose you'll tell me why."

The warlock cocked his head to one side, intrigued by the response. But he decided, with his prey on uncertain footing, now was his time to strike.

"Perhaps another time. The truth is I tarried here not only

to save you. There are questions I have after all this time. Questions only you, Tal Harrenfel, can answer."

To his surprise, the man laughed and wrapped his arms tighter about himself. "We'll see if I can. I'm not Tal Harrenfel, Pim. Not any longer."

The warlock had anticipated much that occurred thus far, but he hadn't foreseen this development. He narrowed his eyes and felt the dark tendrils in them turn.

"What can you mean? Did you not return... whole?"

The buried man shook his head. "In a way, I'm more whole than I've ever been. But of the sorcery that made me a legend... that didn't come with."

For a moment, the warlock could only stare. Then mirth took him, his lithe body shaking with laughter. After all the centuries he'd seen, he still found himself delighted at the surprises this one man conjured.

"Very well. If I cannot name you Tal, what shall I call you?"

The buried man paused. His gaze grew distant as he stared off across the clouds filming the land below.

"Bran," he answered at length. "Brannen Cairn. As I came into this World, so I mean to leave it. One day," he added with a wry smile. "Though hopefully not soon."

"Bran." The warlock tried out the name and found it wanting. His lips twisted; his eyes screwed up. "In every name lies a story. Beware the tales you tell yourself, Brannen Cairn. They might blind you to the truth."

The buried man shrugged. No tendrils stirred in his eyes, yet there seemed a light in them all the same.

"Perhaps," he answered. "But even a single stone can divert a river's flow."

The warlock laughed. "I believe your days of influence may be at an end. You are mortal, Bran; worse still, a human bereft of the sorcery that once filled you. I cannot understand why you refused a god's power. Perhaps what you claim is true, yet a part of me doubts all the same."

The buried man lifted his chin and sighed into the wind. "Pim, Pim. You know what happened to the last man who seized divinity. I never wanted to be more than a man." He lowered his gaze and spread his arms. "Now, that's all I am."

The warlock shook his head. "If I did not believe it before, I do now: some men are not made for immortality."

His companion lowered his arms to wrap them about himself again, hunching against the cold. "There are different kinds. If Falcon's legacy endures, I've attained all the immortality I could want."

It was a point on which they could never agree, the warlock saw then. But it was tangential to his true interest. He straightened his back, folded his hands, and manipulated his appearance to be entirely at his leisure. Even with his mastery over illusion, however, he suspected the buried man didn't need sorcery to pierce through it.

"You did not become a god," the warlock said slowly. "Yet you killed Yuldor in all his manifestations."

The buried man smiled. "I wouldn't say kill — especially not of Yuldor, for he was his own unraveling. As to how… you once said that even a mortal may touch divinity if he dares. In a way, you were right. A god's power lived within me, as it lives within all who touch sorcery. We may each become more than we ever knew."

The warlock had knowledge of most things, yet this was something he did not understand. He thought of a different approach.

"So you ascended," he asserted, hoping to provoke the man into revealing the truth.

The buried man shrugged. "You might say some of me did, the part that was attuned to the divine. It carried down our adversaries into the Womb at the center of the World and eradicated them. But to do it, the profane had to be cut away, the connection to the material plane." He shrugged. "Me."

The warlock was seeing the edges of revelation now. He

suspected there was much more there. However, as the buried man tottered to his feet, he had a feeling he would have to remain patient for some time longer to discover it.

"Much as I appreciate what you've done for me, Pim, I'm afraid I have to get going. If ten years have passed, I've left some people waiting for too long." He grimaced. "Far too long."

The warlock repressed a sigh and stood with far more agility. "I suspected as much. As luck would have it, I, too, have pressing matters requiring my attention. Though I treasure our time together, it appears this is where we part."

The buried man glanced at the pack sitting next to the warlock's boulder. "That's for me?"

"I never was one to neglect the details."

The man smiled. "Thank you, Pim, truly. We haven't always seen eye to eye in the past, but I hope we will moving forward." He paused, his smile souring and his eyes hardening, as if before a battle. "Just remember, Inanis, what happened to the last man who played at divinity. I hope you devote your mind to bettering the World, not carving off your own slice of it."

The warlock turned away, then paused. "I believe my ambitions are the least of your concerns. And would you deprive a spider of its web?"

The buried man seemed about to respond, but the warlock turned his back on him.

"Farewell, Brannen Cairn," he called over his shoulder. "I hope you are prepared to meet the World you wrought."

He took three steps, then brought a veil of invisibility over himself. To the man, he appeared gone.

Yet the warlock paused and turned back to the man he'd waited so long to rescue. He still stood and stared at the place where the warlock had seemed to vanish, but if it astonished him, he didn't show it. Instead, the buried man smiled and shook his head, bent for the pack, and heaved it onto his shoulders. Then he walked toward the shriveled trees below.

He followed until their paths branched, then went his own

way. It was past time the warlock was in charge of his own fate.

Many days and many miles later, after suffering discomforts and delays aplenty, Bran stopped and stared at an open gate.

Once, it had been closed to all the East, the last barrier to the Empire of the Rising Sun. It had been a wall to keep out those both feared and hated.

Now it hung open.

He smiled. That much, at least, was a piece of good to come from all that had occurred.

The mirth swiftly faded. Guards had taken his name and, with shared looks, had sent a runner ahead. He suspected his identity wasn't so unknown as it had been on his journey thus far. He braced himself. His palms sweat. His heart pattered. He couldn't tell if he was more excited or afraid.

She found him just as he reached the top of the rope bridge up to High Elendol.

Bran raised his head from the last plank and stopped mid-stride. There she stood, not a dozen feet away, exactly as he'd left her.

Ashelia.

A smile crept over his lips, a vain attempt to hide his nerves. She stiffened like a doe caught by a hunter. Only her eyes stirred, swirling with all the fury of a waterfall.

He opened his mouth, but she spoke first.

"Where have you been?"

Bran cleared his throat. "Oh, you know. Resurrection can take some time."

Ashelia didn't smile, nor did she close the distance between them. He racked his head for something, anything to break down the wall he felt building between them.

It's now or never, Pearltongue, he cajoled himself.

But if he'd ever been that man, he wasn't any longer. All he had now was the truth. He hoped it would be enough.

"I came as soon as I could, Ashel. Not even death could—"

She cut through his maudlin line with a razor-edged question. "How?"

A laugh bubbled out of him. "How did I survive, you mean? That's a story, and a lengthy one. I would tell it to you, if you'd give me the chance. The main thrust of it is that, miraculous as it is, I'm here."

The distance remaining between them was excruciating, but he knew better than to cross it. He'd left her to mourn him for ten years. He couldn't imagine the pain she'd endured by his death and absence.

She deserves to be angry. Deserves what answers I can give.

Hope fluttered back to life as Ashelia took a step closer. Her shoulders had been raised like the hackles of a spooked cat, but now they lowered.

"It is you," she whispered. "Truly you. Not a phantom, a ghost?"

Bran spread his arms. "Come and find out."

Then she was there, clinging to him, pressing tight into his chest. He held her, feeling as if he could never again let her go. Her presence filled him with a greater warmth than his sorcerous blood ever had. He lowered his nose to her springy hair and breathed in deeply, gratified that beneath her earthy scent, he detected a hint of white mangrove blooms.

Too soon, she pulled away. Where she'd touched him ached at her absence. He was glad she didn't back away far.

"Tal," she murmured, "there's someone you need to meet."

Ashelia turned back, and he saw all the people with whom she'd come, who had been all but invisible to him at first. One stood separate from the rest: a boy, perhaps nine or ten years old.

A shock ran through him.

It cannot be. He held still, afraid to awaken from the dream into which he'd stumbled. He didn't dare hope it could be real.

Ashelia reached toward the boy, and at her silent invitation, he came over and held her hand. Bran studied his every feature. He had much that was elven about him, but lacked the sharp definition of the Eldritch Bloodline. His ears were pointed, yet only a little longer than Bran's own. His eyes had silver tendrils like Ashelia's, but their light was muted by oak-brown irises. Though still a child, his features were already bluffer than other elven children.

Bran stared at him, barely able to attend to Ashelia's words as she spoke.

"Tal, this is Kaleras. Kaleras Helnor Venaliel."

Kaleras. The word seemed to stick in his throat as Bran smiled down at the half-elf boy.

Not any boy — his son. The son he never expected to have.

I have a son.

Attempting to hide his trembling and suspecting he failed, Bran kneeled before Kaleras. "Hello, lad," he said, then cleared his throat. "Kaleras."

"Leras." The boy spoke with High Elendol precision. "Call me Leras."

That broke a chuckle free of Bran. A glance at Ashelia's frown only furthered his mirth.

"Very well, then. Leras, I'm Bran."

"No, you're not. You're Tal Harrenfel."

Bran shrugged. "Once, I was. But I'm a different man than I was then. And you seem to understand that much can be made of a name."

Leras frowned, his silver tendrils swirling. He seemed a serious boy, so serious Bran wondered if his own blood had been squashed out by Ashelia's stubborn nature.

"Yes," the boy admitted at length. "I suppose."

Bran hesitated a moment before speaking again. "I suspect

you already know, Leras. I'm sure your mother has told you many lies about me in my absence." Bran flashed a smile at Ashelia, then continued. "But this, at least, is the truth. I'm your father."

He could have been sharing news of the rains for all Leras was affected by it. "I know," the boy replied stiffly.

Bran scrutinized Leras. He sensed something smoldering within that mind, something that pained and shamed him. It didn't take him long to understand what.

He let out a long sigh before speaking again. "You're right to be angry, Leras. All your life, you've grown up without a father. I'm sorry I haven't been around; you cannot know how sorry. But there's an oath I'll make to you now, a promise I'll never break so long as it's in my power to keep. Are you ready to hear it, Leras?"

The boy seemed to be holding on to his anger. His eyes showed his conflict. As Ashelia prompted him by clearing her throat, he finally relented. "Fine."

Bran smiled. "I'll be here from now on, lad. Never again will you be without a father. I'll hover so near you'll wish I was gone again. This, I swear to you, the World as my witness."

Leras' expression spasmed. He was as young as Rolan had been during their journey, yet already, his son showed signs of maturity that belied his age. He'd seen sorrow and pain and fear such as no child should experience. Bran wondered what his brief years had held.

Ashelia seemed about to speak, but Bran gave her a warning look. Several moments longer, and the response he'd been waiting for came.

Leras nodded. His voice had lost its edge as he whispered, "Alright."

Bran grinned. "Alright. And maybe we'll work on smiling every once in a while."

The boy scowled, and Bran laughed. Ashelia seemed to relax once again, and a smile found her lips, too.

Bran stood and gave her his arm. To Leras, he tentatively extended a hand. The boy seemed appalled at first, but after a glance at his mother, he took it.

Together, as a family, they went home.

AUTHOR'S NOTE

Thank you for reading *A God's Plea!* I hope you enjoyed this conclusion to the Legend of Tal.

Writing this series has been a true pleasure and joy, and it's bittersweet for it to end. It was particularly difficult to say farewell to a couple of characters who met their end, characters I hope you've grown to love as well.

But while this is one ending, this will not be *the end*.

I am presently in the initial stages of a sequel series to Legend of Tal. I won't say much about it here, but you'll likely be able to guess which characters it follows.

The best way to be sure you catch when it releases is to sign up for my newsletter, The Fellowship Broadcast. You can do that by visiting my website, jdlrosell.com.

While you wait for the new series to come out, it would be of great service to me if you helped Legend of Tal find more readers. One way to do that is by leaving reviews for the series. You can find the series page by looking up Legend of Tal on Amazon.

Another way is to spread the word by telling a friend or a family member about the books. Maybe they'll enjoy them, too!

Every journey must end. But with one story's ending, another begins. Thanks once again for reading the Legend of Tal. I hope you'll join me on the next adventure.

Josiah (J.D.L. Rosell)

APPENDIX A

THE CHARACTERS

THE WESTREACH

AVENDOR: HUNT'S HOLLOW

Brannen Cairn - A chicken farmer of dubious talent who recently moved to Hunt's Hollow.

Garin Dunford - A youth growing up on a local farm.

Nyssa Dunford - Garin's mother.

Lenora Dunford - Garin's sister.

Honry Dunford - Garin's oldest brother.

Naten Dunford - Garin's second oldest brother.

Corbun Dunford - Garin's third oldest brother.

Helan - Garin's aunt.

Badan - A local tanner.

Beca - A local midwife.

Gwyn - A midwife in training.

"Crazy" Ean - A local man with a reputation for eccentricity and a thirst for whiskey.

AVENDOR: HALENHOL

Tal Harrenfel - A recent folk hero. Attributed to him are many deeds both miraculous and horrific. Yet the man behind the legend is not always as his tales describe.

Aldric Rexall the Fourth - The King of Avendor. Reputed to be cunning and ruthless.

Kaleras Trethon - Also known as the Impervious and the Warlock of Canturith, he is a former Magister of Jalduaen's Circle and the only warlock outside of the organization.

Brother Causticus - A conniving and scholarly monk of the Order of Ataraxis. Has dedicated his life to the study of folklore, focusing especially on Tal Harrenfel.

Brother Nat - A monk assigned to assist Brother Causticus in his ventures. Also part of the Order of Ataraxis.

Father Hush - The head of the Order of Ataraxis.

Duke Vandon - A duke of dubious character and an unfortunate medical condition.

Nathiel Faldorn - A young knight and son of a count with a proclivity for liquor and bluster.

Krador - The half-dwarf Master-at-Arms of the Coral Castle.

Jad - A trainee under Master Krador.

Kendall - A trainee under Master Krador.

Petier - A trainee under Master Krador.

Haruld - A trainee under Master Krador.

Nalda Deliese - A marchioness who is a keen player of social politics.

Teline Deliese - A young girl who suffers a mysterious ailment.

Sir Rhydian - A loyal knight of Avendor.

Falcon Sunstring - The half-elf Court Bard to the King of Avendor and leader of the Dancing Feathers troupe.

Wren - The rebellious daughter of Falcon Sunstring. Also a member of the Dancing Feathers troupe.

Ox - A gentle Befa Spice Islander and a member of the Dancing Feathers troupe.

Jonn - A half-elf member of the Dancing Feathers troupe.

Mikael - A goblin member of the Dancing Feathers troupe.

Yelda - The lead actress in the Dancing Feathers troupe, the dwarf acts every bit the prima donna.

Bendor - A diminutive human member of the Dancing Feathers troupe.

GLADELYL: ELENDOL

Geminia the Third - The wise and calculating Queen of Gladelyl. Also known as the Gem of Elendol and the Elf Queen.

Aelyn Belnuure - An irritable elf with several titles and roles: Emissary to Avendor, Peer of Gladelyl, Master of the Onyx Tower, and itinerant mage. Adopted brother of Ashelia and Helnor Venaliel.

Ashelia Venaliel - A Peer of Gladelyl, the first female Warder, a healer of the Sapphire Tower, and also reputed to be the lover of yore to Tal Harrenfel. Sister to Aelyn Belnuure and Helnor Venaliel. Mother to Rolan Venaliel. Wife of Yinin Lathniel.

Rolan Venaliel - A young and precocious elf boy with an inclination for mischief, lutes, and frogs. Son of Ashelia Venaliel and Yinin Lathniel.

Helnor Venaliel - The jovial Prime Warder of Gladelyl. Brother to Aelyn Belnuure and Ashelia Venaliel.

Yinin Lathniel - A minister to the Queen, he is also the houselord of House Venaliel and a mage of the Emerald Tower. Husband to Ashelia Venaliel. Father to Rolan Venaliel.

Jondual Lathniel - Houselord of House Lathniel. Husband to Jondual Lathniel. Father to Yinin Lathniel.

Maone Lathniel - A Peer of Gladelyl and leader of the Sympathist faction. Wife of Jondual Lathniel. Mother of Yinin Lathniel.

Ulen Yulnaed - The foremost Dancing Master of Elendol.

Condur - The Ilthasi captain in Low Elendol.

Prendyn - The Ilthasi captain in High Elendol.

Balindi Aldinare - A Peer of Gladelyl. Also known to be a gossip and acts as an informant to the Royalists.

Melina - A human adolescent girl with a talent for acting.

Celica Heilinis - A Peer of Gladelyl and a part of the Sympathist faction. Sister to Fantir Heilinis.

Fantir Heilinis - A mage of the Ruby Tower and a master of Conveyance. Brother to Celica Heilinis.

Yeshil - A medusal informant in Low Elendol.

Pylas - A Nightelf informant in Low Elendol.

Uke Hesh - Pylas' sonku monkey. Translates to "Old Man."

Temmy - A gnome informant in Low Elendol and ally to Rozana of Haudden.

CHYCHAXIL'ISK (THE GOBLIN KNOLLS)

Mysx Gemfang - Known as the Hoarseer Queen. Leader of the Hoarseer goblin tribe.

HISTORICAL

Talania Cairn - Deceased mother of Brannen Cairn, a fletcher and launderer who died when her son was young.

Nevendal Elendola - Geminia's late husband and the Prince Consort. Died during the first attack on Elendol by the fire devil Heyl and the Thorn.

Yardin Hardrog - A former Clan Chief of the Hardrog dwarf clan.

Norir - A dwarf copper mine warden.

Henmor Craulton - A Hardrog dwarf elder.

Magister Elis - The warlock who mentored Tal Harrenfel.

Maelor Yew - Commander of Tal Harrenfel's company in the Avendoran army.

Nudd - A slow-minded soldier in Tal Harrenfel's company in the Avendoran army.

Lyn - A prankster soldier in Tal Harrenfel's company in the Avendoran army.

Eiliyan - A former flame of Helnor's from Low Elendol.

RELIGIOUS

The Whispering Gods - The three deities of the Creed: Silence, Solemnity, and Serenity.

The Night - The antagonist to the Whispering Gods.

OTHER

Ilvuan - A spirit that plagues Garin Dunford.

THE EAST
EMPIRE OF THE RISING SUN

CULT OF YULDOR

Yuldor Soldarin - The immortal elven sorcerer who reigns as a god from atop the mountain Ikvaldar.

Soltor - One of the four Extinguished. Said to be involved in the story that led to Tal Harrenfel being known as "the Magebutcher."

Thartol - Also known as "the Thorn." One of the four Extinguished. Known to have summoned the fire devil Heyl in the city of Elendol and killed the Prince Consort, Nevendal Elendola.

Inanis - One of the four Extinguished. Rumored to be behind the civil war between the dwarven clans of Dhuulheim.

Hashele - One of the four Extinguished. Acts as Yuldor's link to the Sun Emperor.

HYALKASI RANGE: VATHDA

Dathal Hardrog - Clan Chief of the Hardrog dwarf clan.

Kherdorn - An older dwarf of the Hardrog clan.

ASPAR: NARUAH

Captain Fexe - A Nightelf captain enforcing the laws of Naruah.

Izoalta Yoreseer - High Pellar of Aspar. Sister to Hellexa and Ysilda Yoreseer.

ISOCIL: KAVAUGH

Zyrl Netherstar - The Emperor of the Empire of the Rising Sun. Also known as the Emperor of Dawn and the Sun Emperor. A gnome as infamous for his size as his cunning.

Nofas - The royal scribe to Emperor Zyrl Netherstar.

Samup Dhardon - The High Marshal of the Empire of the Rising Sun.

ISOCIL: FAERNOR GRASSLANDS

Holt - Full name is Zichodächini. A centaur who is protective of his weald and distrustful of mortalkind.

RAJEYA: DREYGOJ

Koax Mraaj - A medusal alchemist reputed to have discovered an elixir that allows passage through Paradise by counteracting the effects of its miasma.

Kraul Shraxl - The Fief Lord of Rajeya.

Sawat Kangsorn - An old smuggler. Grand-aunt to Jira Phya.

Jira Phya - A young smuggler. Grandniece to Sawat Kangsorn.

Chaiya - A portwarden in Dreygoj.

LEDFOLD: HAUDDEN

Rozana of Haudden - A minotaur informant in Low Elendol and former leader of an Eastern rebellion.

Motarg - A bull minotaur who stands in opposition to Rozana.

HISTORICAL

Hellexa Yoreseer - The former Pyramidion of the Blue Moon Obelisk. Author of *A Fable of Song and Blood.* Sister to Ysilda and Izoalta Yoreseer.

Aqada the Conqueror - A rebel warlord that reshaped the East during his reign.

Sage Hester - A reputed healer from the Sun Obelisk.

Ysilda Yoreseer - Also known as Keeper. The watcher of the ruins of the Blue Moon Obelisk. Sister to Hellexa and Izoalta Yoreseer.

Maral Batomar - Also known as the *Ava'thal*, which translates to the Dragon-heart. A hero during the era of the Origins.

Rothaen, Haimei, and Sachiel - Three Origins who were recorded as living during the time of the Severing.

Yvärras - The queen of dragons. Also known as She Who Dances With Fire and the World's Protectress.

Alärthoras - A dragon who flew during the time of the Origins.

APPENDIX B

THE WORLD

Continent historically known as "Aolas."

THE WESTREACH
The western countries of Aolas. Considered by its inhabitants to be the "civilized" lands.

AVENDOR
The largest and most powerful nations of the Westreach. Its populace is mostly human, but it is populated by the various Bloodlines of the western lands.

Halenhol - Capital of Avendor. Home to the Coral Castle, from which King Aldric reigns.
Hunt's Hollow - A small, unremarkable town in the East Marsh.
Jakad - An annexed territory of Avendor. Renowned for their vineyards.
Dareaux - Former capital of Jakad. A major city in Avendor.
Ruins of Erlodan - A derelict castle ravaged by time, once belonging to the warlock Erlodan.
Canturith - An ancient fortress along the Fringes

GLADELYL
The elven queendom on the outskirts of the Westreach. Possesses significant clout, particularly because of their mastery of sorcery.

Elendol - Capital of Gladelyl. Home to the kintrees of the elven noble houses, including the royal kintree, from which Queen Geminia reigns.
Yllsalar - An ancient mountain fortress along the Fringes.

SENDESH
The second largest nation of the Westreach. Predominantly human. Has a history of conflict with Avendor and suffers raids from the Yraldi to the north.

Burbay - Capital of Sendesh. The Sendeshi Protector reigns from here.

FELINAN
The third and least of the human nations. A place where, though the martial prowess flounders, the arts flourish. Their reputation is further bolstered by boasting the home of the warlocks of the Westreach.

Sisces - Capital of Felinan.

Avolice - The citadel at the center of the Jalduaen's Circle, the order of human warlocks.

DHUULHEIM

Also known as "the Dwarven Clans." A subterranean nation of dwarves that is often forced to contend with monsters from the Deep. Long has conflict simmered between the clans, inflamed by enemies from without.

CHYCHAXIL'ISK

Also known as "the Goblin Knolls." The Hoarseer tribe, led by their queen Mysx Gemfang, currently rules, though dynasties usually last only as long as the ruler lives.

OTHER

The Fringes - The hilly lands separating the Westreach from the East. Home to Nightkin coming down from the mountains.

The Yraldi Isles - The unforgiving islands in the northern Crimson Sea. Home to sea raiders who regularly invade their southern neighbor, Sendesh.

The Befa Spice Isles - The verdant islands in the southern Hushed Sea. Renowned for exports of exotic fruits and colorful weavings.

THE EAST

Also known by its inhabitants as the Empire of the Rising Sun. Though large swaths of the land remain untamed, beyond the mountains flourish various fiefs united under the Sun Emperor and the god Yuldor above him.

ISOCIL

The largest of the fiefs. Primarily occupied by humans, but also boasts all the other Eastern races. Set amid fertile plains. Also home to the capital of the Empire and the seat of the Sun Emperor.

Kavaugh - Capital of Isocil and the Empire. The Sun Palace of the Emperor is also here.

Bavay - A town renowned for its carpets.

ASPAR

The fief of Nightelves. Set amid tall, gigantic trees.

Naruah - Capital of Aspar. Home to the High Pellar, the primary priestess of Yuldor among the Nightelves.

LEDFOLD
The fief of minotaurs. Set amid plains and hills.

Haudden - The primary town of Ledfold.
Lethyranth - The ruins of an ancient Origin city.

RAJEYA
The fief of medusals and sylvans. Deserts, ocean shores, hills, and fjords all exist here.

Dreygoj - Capital of Rajeya.
Trader Springs - An oasis town amid the Laksis Wastes.

VRORESH
The fief of orkans. Set on a rocky and forbidding peninsula.

Ghamir Nodh - Capital of Vroresh.

AGN OMMUL
The fief of gnomes. Set in the heart of the Valanduali mountains.

Kyzan - Capital of Agn Ommul.

OTHER
Ikvaldar - The tallest mountain in Aolas. Despite its height, its rounded peak is largely dominated by a magically preserved jungle known as Paradise. It is also known to be home to the immortal sorcerer Yuldor Soldarin.
Vathda - The new home of the exiled Hardrog dwarven clan.

APPENDIX C

BESTIARY

NOVEL ANIMALS

Gilled deer - A deer found in the forests of Isocil in the East. Judging by the texture of their skin and the gills on their necks, they are suspected of living on both land and in water.

Peuma - One of the large black cats that act as protectors of the jungle Paradise atop Ikvaldar.

Sand drake - Called *zuthka* in common Darktongue. It is a large lizard habituated to arid landscapes. Its kind is used as beasts of burden similarly to the Sendeshi's use of camels.

Sonku monkey - A silver-haired monkey native to the Rainwoods in the East. It is believed to possess a touch of sorcery, for when it expresses emotion, its thick mane can glow golden.

Stor - A deer-like mount used by Gladelysh elves. As large as horses, but with long, lean legs and antlers atop their heads.

ORIGIN CREATURES

Dragon - Call themselves *ava'dual* (pl. *ava'duala*). Though now extinct, dragons are thought to have been the foremost predators of the World. Formidable in size and physicality, their mastery of sorcery was even more deadly. Legend has it they perished around the time of the Severing.

Leshi - A forest shapeshifter with a talent for illusion sorcery. These ancient creatures are believed to have been common in the time of the Origins, but have either retreated into hiding or been killed off as the mortal races encroach upon their woods.

HUMANOIDS

Centaur - A blend between an Origin and a horse. Like the Bloodlines, centaurs are intelligent and every bit as capable of language and thought as any mortal. They also possess a strong affinity for sorcery. Their solitary nature and need to protect a territory, usually a forest they name their "weald," is believed to be the reason they never established societies like the other mortal races.

NIGHTKIN: CREATED

Chimera - A lion blended with a cobra as its tail, an additional goat's head, and sometimes a small dragon's head.

Cockatrice - A large flying monster with resemblances to a farmyard rooster, but with large functioning wings, green and white feathering, and serpentine tails.

Gamayun - A small flying monster that resembles an oversized bat with humanoid features and snake-like hair.

Gryphon - A blend between a lion and a large eagle.

Ijiraq - A monster with the torso of a humanoid and the body and antlers of a caribou. It possesses an instinctive touch for illusion, making its appearance to be like that of an ordinary caribou when it suits it.

Memyke - A beetle-like monster as large as a wolf with a brown carapace impervious to magic.

Phoenix - An eagle-like bird with gold-and-red plumage and larger than a cockatrice. It is one of the deadliest Nightkin due to its faefire explosion, which can level a small city. Even after this expulsion of sorcery, the phoenix will resurrect thereafter. It has not been observed how long it takes for a phoenix to resurrect. There are no known ways to permanently kill a phoenix.

Quetzal - A flying serpent with colorful feathery wings. Often travel in a flock and take down their prey by overwhelming numbers.

Syren - A mysterious monster found among misty vales and foggy seas. Partly because of its habitat and predatory nature, no one has seen a syren and survived. Syrens appear to live together in groups. Rumored to lure travelers and sailors to their deaths by mimicking the voices of loved ones in pain or in seduction. They are believed to consume their victims down to the bones.

NIGHTKIN: SUMMONED

Soulshade - A phantom creature formed of shadows. It is summoned by the sorcerer corrupting a piece of their own soul. The summoner can command it to carry out simple tasks, as a soulshade lacks intelligence of its own.

Draugar - Similar to a zombie. It is reanimated by the inhabitance of a summoned spirit in a cadaver. This spirit takes on the characteristics of its vessel when it was alive; hence, a draugar fights and dies similar to the mortal it once was.

Ghoul - A creature summoned by Nightglyphs. Its appearance is humanoid, but with pale rotting flesh, inhuman speed, and sharp teeth and nails.

Heyl - Also called "Yuldor's Fury." Heyl is a fire devil summoned through life sacrifice and is one of the deadliest creatures to walk the World. As tall as a tower, it has two tails, four legs, and eight arms. Anything it touches burns.

Nekrot - A summoned creature that can summon others through Nightglyphs. Bearing staffs to aid in their sorcery and wearing the armor of their victims, they are most dangerous because of their ability to command armies of ghouls and witikos. They are humanoid in appearance and about as short as a dwarf.

Witiko - A creature summoned by Nightglyphs. Giants that are as skeletal as ghouls, but with a thick brown coat over their bones and a head somewhere between a wolf and a moose.

CREATURES FROM THE DEEP

Brigkakor - A mountain troll that once conquered the fortress Canturith, which the warlock Kaleras later drove out.

Khaovex'das - Also called "The Darkness From the Water." A fell creature from the Deep under Dhuulheim. It is said to have killed a hundred dwarves in their copper mines before the warlock Kaleras vanquished it.

APPENDIX D

GLOSSARY

Many of the terms not referenced in the previous appendices can be found here.

Bloodlines - The various races of the Westreach. Said to be created by the Whispering Gods from an ancestral race, the Origins, during an event called the Severing.

Canker - Also known as *karkados*. A magical malady of mysterious origins, but it appears to be caused in part by an overindulgence in sorcery.

The Chromatic Towers - The six schools of magic founded in Elendol by the Gladelysh elves.

Conveyance - A sorcerous method of transferring messages to other sorcerers through paired artifacts.

The Creed - The predominant religion in the Westreach, dedicated to the worship of the Whispering Gods.

The Cult of Yuldor - The pejorative name given to the predominant religion of the East, dedicated to the worship of the ascended elven sorcerer Yuldor Soldarin.

Dancing Master - A master of elven swordplay. Often teaches the art to pupils.

The Darktongue - Though conflated in the Westreach, the Darktongue comes in two separate strands. First, there is "common" Darktongue, also called Imperial, which is the primary language of the East. Second, there is the Worldtongue variant Darktongue, which can be used for sorcery.

The Deep - The bowels of the World, from which terrifying monsters originate. Most typically, the Deep refers to the area under Dhuulheim, the realm of dwarves.

The *Doash* - Also known as "the World's Womb." Believed to be the source of all sorcery at the center of the World.

The Eternal Animus - The latent conflict which sometimes flares into war between the Westreach and the East.

The Extinguished - Also called "Soulstealers" and "the Nameless." The four servants of Yuldor Soldarin. Through their master's power, they have attained immortality, and though they can be killed, they are known to resurrect ten years later. Experts in illusion magic, the Extinguished have successfully manipulated politics across Aolas, both in the East and Westreach, to serve their master's needs.

Fount of Blood - One believed to possess the blood of the World in their veins. Sorcery comes naturally to these individuals, even if they are of a Bloodline or race that is not inherently sorcerous.

Fount of Song - One believed to hear the Worldsong. Sorcery is made possible to these individuals, even if they are of a Bloodline or race that is not inherently sorcerous. Also sometimes called "Listeners."

The Four Roots - The four principles required for sorcery, according to Gladelysh elves. The First Root is an affinity for magic. The Second Root is a spoken word of the Worldtongue. The Third Root is the transfer of energy or energy potential. The Fourth Root is proper concentration paired with imagination.

Gildoil - Also known as "pissleaf." A pain reliever; an analgesic.

Gladelysh - The elvish people of Gladelyl.

Gladelyshi - The language spoken by the elves of Gladelyl.

Glyphs - Also called "runes." Written versions of the Worldtongue, they can spawn magical effects of their own when imbued with sorcery. Unpowered glyphs are used to teach magic to pupils.

Glyph-seal - A small object that carries the sigil of a Highkin House of Gladelyl. Denotes the bearer to have the authority of the House in minor matters, such as accessing reasonable resources or gaining admittance to exclusive locations.

The Greatdark - The afterlife concept of hell to those following the Creed of the Whispering Gods.

Half-kin - The term used by the Gladelyshi to refer to a mixed-blood elf, or an individual with only one elven parent. *Kolfash* is the derogatory term that means the same.

Highkin - The upper-class elves of Gladelyl. They live in High Elendol, which is built into the upper boughs of the kintrees of the city.

Heaven's Knoll - The afterlife concept of heaven for those who follow the Creed of the Whispering Gods. Also called "the Quiet Havens."

Helshax - The Darktongue word for "Lament." A bastard sword with the ability to absorb sorcery. Rumored to originate from the time of the Origins.

Heyl's Fall - The kintree that the fire demon Heyl burned down, which remains as a monument to the event.

Highkin House - A noble family of Gladelysh elves.

Ikvaldar - The tallest mountain in Aolas. Dominant across the landscape, it is known as the fortress of Yuldor Soldarin. Atop it also grows Paradise, a verdant jungle that is claimed to be Yuldor's dream that he wishes to spread to the entire World.

The Ilthasi - The secretive agents of the Queen of Gladelyl. Responsible for covertly enforcing her will, especially in the capital city of Elendol.

The Ingress of Elendol - The event during which Easterners were admitted into Gladelyl.

Jalduaen's Circle - Also known as "the Warlocks' Circle." The order of warlocks who derive their power from the mysterious god of knowledge, Jalduaen. Based in Avolice, a citadel in Felinan.

Kael'dros - Translates to "monsters" from dragon speech. The dragon term for Nightkin.

Kintree - One of the gigantic trees resembling mangrove trees that dominate

Gladelyl and Elendol. The Highkin noble families make their homes within the kintrees, and their boughs form the upper part of the tree city known as High Elendol.

Lowkin - The lower-class elves of Gladelyl. In Elendol, these elves live in Low Elendol, also called "the Mire."

Medusals - The lizard-people of the East. Standing as tall as humans, they have colorful, feathery manes. They primarily live in the arid and coastal environments of the fief Rajeya.

The moons - The moons have many names. Among the names for the blue moon is "The Sorrowful Lady." Foremost among the yellow moon's names is "Cresselia."

Nightelves - The elves of the East. They live in the forest of Aspar, which is dominated by towering trees, and differ from Gladelysh elves by having cooler skin tones. Like their Westreach counterparts, Nightelves have an innate ability to use sorcery.

Nightkin - The monsters believed to be under the control of Yuldor, the immortal sorcerer who is the enemy of the Westreach. Most are said to be created by Yuldor as well.

The Nightsong - The noises that Garin hears after being possessed by what he believes to be a devil. Often accompanied by the use of sorcery.

The Obelisks - The Eastern equivalent of the Chromatic Towers of Elendol. Schools of sorcery scattered across the Empire of the Rising Sun, where mages are taught and delve into magical matters.

The Order of Ataraxis - One of the monastic orders of the Creed of the Whispering Gods.

Orkans - The hog-people of the East. Typically have skin in hues of gray and sport tusks jutting from their lips as well as other hog-like features. They primarily live in the fief Vroresh. Like humans, orkans do not have the innate ability to use sorcery, but can access it when acting as the conduit of a god. Whereas in the Westreach this takes the form of warlocks, among orkans, these magic-users are known as shamans.

The Origins - The ancestral race before the Severing of the Bloodlines. Believed to be departed from the World, they are thought to have shared features with all the races of the Westreach and the East.

Origintongue - The language of the Origins. Conflated to mean both a common speech and a sorcerous speech, though the two were likely separate.

Peer - The foremost nobility who leads an elven Highkin House.

Pellar - A priestly healer of the Nightelves.

Pyramidion - A leader of one of the Empire's Obelisks.

Quiet Havens - *See "Heaven's Knoll."*

Qorl - An elven game involving strategy to dominate one's opponent.

Ravagers - Officially called "Venators" in the East. The brutal headhunters who are said to directly serve Yuldor. Known to occasionally raid the Reach Realms.

Reachtongue - The common language of the Westreach. Assumed to have derived from a human language out of Avendor, as they have no other native tongue.

Ring of Thalkuun - A powerful artifact that makes its wearer immune to sorcery cast against them. Written on it are the words *Thalkuun Haeldar*, which translates to "The One Impervious to the Heart."

Runes - *See "glyphs."*

The Severing - The event during which it is said the Whispering Gods created the various Bloodlines in order to preserve mortalkind from the Night, who sought to destroy them.

Singer - A term by which dragons refer to themselves on account of how they perceive their use of their magic.

The *Sha'aval* - The hatching place of dragons.

Stonetongue - The common language of the dwarves of Dhuulheim.

Sylvans - The plant-people of the East. Shorter and slighter than humans, they often have appearances matching several geographies. Some have hair like wheat, others like vines, and still others resemble the coral found along the Eastern ocean shores. They have an innate sense of sorcery, though it appears to be limited.

The Worldheart - Said to be a stone of sorcery possessed by Yuldor Soldarin, which grants him access to great power and makes him the Master of Time and Material.

The Worldsong - The magical song that emanates from the World's core, only heard by dragons and those termed "Listeners."

The Worldtongue - The sorcerous language used by magic-users of the Westreach. Combined with the other principles of the Four Roots, speaking a word or combination of words of the Worldtongue will produce a spell.

Velori - The bastard sword wielded by Tal Harrenfel. Said to be forged and enchanted by goblin smiths from ages past. Its blade is etched with glyphs that glow a gentle blue. The full extent of its sorcery is not known, but it appears to keep its sharp edge and resist rust.

Yinshi - A dried red herb with a peppery scent. Often used as an aid for concentration by mages, as ingesting it produces an obsessive state of mind.

Yethkeld - Means "hellfire" in Gladelysh. A yellow combustive powder used as a catalyst for minor spells.

ACKNOWLEDGMENTS

There have been so many people who have helped Legend of Tal come to life. In particular, thank you to:

Kaitlyn, my wonderful wife as well as my first reader. If I stick the landing in this final book, it is thanks in large part to your insightful feedback. (And if it didn't land, I promise not to blame you.)

René Aigner, for once again delivering a captivating illustration.

Shawn Sharrah, for his fine proofreading and endless enthusiasm.

The Chapter, my early reader team, for catching any final errors and helping others take a chance on my stories through your poignant reviews.

My patrons on Patreon: Nick, Ben, Ruth & Tarris, Don, GhostCat, Debbie, and Arthur. Your support means more to me than I can say.

My family for cheering me on during the high points of my career and providing comfort during the low points.

And you, dear reader — thank you for spending your precious time journeying with Tal, Garin, and the rest. I hope you'll embark on more adventures with me in future books.

Josiah (J.D.L. Rosell)

BOOKS BY J.D.L. ROSELL

Sign up for future releases at jdlrosell.com.

LEGEND OF TAL

1. A King's Bargain

2. A Queen's Command

3. An Emperor's Gamble

4. A God's Plea

THE RUNEWAR SAGA

1. The Throne of Ice & Ash

2. The Crown of Fire & Fury

3. The Stone of Iron & Omen

RANGER OF THE TITAN WILDS

1. The Last Ranger

THE FAMINE CYCLE

1. Whispers of Ruin

2. Echoes of Chaos

3. Requiem of Silence

Secret Seller *(Prequel)*

The Phantom Heist *(Novella)*

GODSLAYER RISING

ABOUT THE AUTHOR

J.D.L. Rosell is the author of Legend of Tal, Ranger of the Titan Wilds, The Runewar Saga, The Famine Cycle, and Godslayer Rising. He has earned an MA in creative writing and has previously written as a ghostwriter.

Always drawn to the outdoors, he ventures out into nature whenever he can to indulge in his hobbies of hiking and photography. Most of the time, he can be found curled up with a good book at home with his wife and two cats, Zelda and Abenthy.

Follow along with his occasional author updates and serializations at jdlrosell.com or contact him at authorjdlrosell@gmail.com.

CPSIA information can be obtained
at www.ICGtesting.com
Printed in the USA
BVHW042213130922
646984BV00003B/24